**ON T
AND IN T**
**IT WAS WINNER TAKE ALL.**

*Briar McKenna*   Her brief marriage to a much older man gave her the happiest years in a life plagued by her search for her heritage. Now her dreams are about to come true—if the past doesn't destroy her.

*Stefan Yager*   One of the finest horse trainers in the world, his fierce attraction for Briar is all-consuming. But he has other reasons for staying at Caulfield Farms and other claims to stake. . . .

*Rupert Jaeger*   The cold, cruel, powerful tycoon had bested one Caulfield woman in the past, and by the time he was finished with Briar McKenna, the mortal blow would finish the Caulfield line for all time.

*Charlotte Jaeger*   Rupert's vindictive daughter, she secretly hired the private detective who located Briar to seek revenge against the father she hated—only to discover Rupert has been one step ahead of her. . . .

Also by Janis Flores
*Published by Fawcett Books:*

LOVING TIES
RUNNING IN PLACE
DIVIDED LOYALTIES
ABOVE REPROACH

# TOUCHED BY FIRE

## Janis Flores

FAWCETT GOLD MEDAL • NEW YORK

For Irma Ruth Walker . . . Ruth
Friend, confidante, mentor, surrogate mother.
With more thanks than I could ever say for all the advice,
encouragement and support (not to mention the chicken
salad sandwiches!) you've given me over the years
of our friendship.
I hope I'll be able to do the same for you one day. . . .

# AUTHOR'S NOTE

This book could not have been written without the help of some very special people who were so generous with time, counsel, and candor regarding racehorses and the sport of racing.

Many, many thanks to Dr. Karen Valko, stable veterinarian at Santa Anita and Hollywood Park racetracks for allowing me to share with her those touching, thrilling, bittersweet glimpses into racing, where it's truly run—on the "backside" of the track . . .

And to Tom and Kathy Bachman of beautiful Pegasus Ranch in Petaluma, who opened their home, offices, and barns to me so I could see what a real working ranch was like.

And finally, a tribute to my own Thoroughbred, Sea Cane, whose racing career was cut short by injury. She, and others like her, inspired me with the awe I always feel when I see racing Thoroughbreds doing what they were born to, and what they do best.

# CHAPTER ONE

Wearing a hat to cover her hair and sunglasses to shade her green eyes, Briar McKenna pulled into the lot behind her office in downtown San Francisco. It was late February, in 1980, and she had just turned thirty-five, but the last thing on her mind was celebrating her birthday. Her hope that she could pass unnoticed vanished when she saw the crowd of reporters standing by the building's rear door, and she had barely come to a stop before the throng spotted her and rushed over. With so many people surrounding the car, it was a struggle to get out of the low-slung Mercedes, and when microphones bristled in front of her face she wanted to reach out savagely and sweep them all away. *Why can't they just leave me alone?* she wondered angrily, and looked for the security guard.

"Miss McKenna, have you heard that—"

"Mrs. Lord, did you know—"

"Ms. McKenna, would you care to comment on—"

*Now what?* she thought, wishing they would all just . . . go away. But they wouldn't, of course. As the widow of Hayden Lord, of Lord Industries, she was news. Why that should be, when *Hay* had been the celebrity, was beyond her. Her husband's brief illness had been a nightmare with these people dogging her every step; Hay had been on a private floor, but some had bribed their way in to talk to the nurses and even, in one case, to catch a glimpse of her husband's medical chart. The funeral had been a further atrocity, reporters practically falling into the grave itself to get their pictures, and she'd been so distraught she wanted to sue them all—or at least have them arrested. But Spencer Reed, one of Hay's attorneys, had gently told her it was impossible. Hay had been a public figure; as distasteful and distressing as it was to have the media hounding his family, she had to put up with it.

*But not anymore*, Briar thought, ignoring the babble and

reaching back into the car for her briefcase. Hay was gone, out of her life forever, and these people had no more claim on her. She had endured enough, more than anyone should have to put up with. Didn't they understand that her *husband* had just died?

"No comment," she said brusquely, and turned away from the car toward her office building. One aggressive reporter stood in her path, his tape recorder thrust out, obviously prepared to block her way physically until she answered his questions. Since she had no intention—desire, but not intention—of shoving him aside, she just stared at him coldly, her face under the hat and glasses a pale mask of disdain and contempt, until he glanced uneasily around, dropped the recorder into his pocket, and stepped aside. That didn't stop the rest of the crowd, which followed her into the building, shouting questions as she strode directly to the elevator, her head high, looking neither right nor left. Mercifully a car was waiting, but just as she was about to enter, one last shrill shout rose above the other voices, demanding her attention.

"But surely you can give us *one* quote about your step-daughter, Fredrica Hudson, and her intention to contest her father's will, can't you, Mrs. Lord? I mean, you *did* know she filed this morning, didn't you? Are you going to fight her, or aren't you?"

*So that's what this is about*, Briar thought, and wondered how the press had gotten hold of it before she knew. Then she realized wearily that Fredrica had probably called the media herself. Her stepdaughter had made no secret how she felt about her father's will, which had established huge trusts for her and her brother, but which had left the bulk of the estate to Briar; in fact, Spence had barely concluded the reading before Fredrica had stormed out, announcing that she was going to contest. Briar was surprised that it had taken her this long; after all, she thought, the funeral had been two weeks ago.

"No comment," Briar said again curtly. She was not going to discuss family problems in public, and when a wail of collective protest arose, she reached for the button that would close the elevator doors.

"All right, people, that's enough," a new, authoritative voice said from the back of the crowd. "Come on, give Ms. McKenna a break."

Muttering, the throng parted, and Briar saw her executive assistant, Gabe Atwater, pushing his way through. He wasn't a tall man, barely two inches over her own slender five-foot-eight, but he seemed taller because he carried himself with almost as much confidence as she did. He'd been with her since she moved the office downtown six years ago, and she didn't know what she'd do without him. He seemed to read her mind at times, and he was grinning as he got into the elevator with her. Ignoring the renewed outburst from the reporters, he firmly punched the button for their floor. As the doors started to close, he said to those milling around, "We'll issue a statement later. That's all for now, folks."

Briar expelled an angry breath as the elevator began to rise smoothly upward. Taking off her sunglasses, she glanced at Gabe. "A statement? Was that really necessary? You know I don't like to comment on anything Fredrica does."

"Yes, well, I had to tell them something," he said, shrugging. "It was either that, or have them all get in here with us. You didn't want that, did you?"

"God forbid," she muttered. "Running the gauntlet in the parking lot was bad enough. How in the world did they ever find out?"

"You mean you didn't know?"

"I never know what Fredrica is doing. Furthermore, I really don't care."

"You should about this. She held her own little press conference this morning."

"I see," she said. "On the court house steps, I imagine."

"In front of God and everybody," he agreed. "I take it you're not surprised."

She took off her hat and shook her hair free. "Not particularly," she said. She really didn't want to talk about it.

Gabe heard her tone and took his cue. Casually changing the subject, he said, "By the way, what are you doing here? I thought you were going to take some time off."

She had planned to, but to what purpose? When she thought about it, she couldn't believe that it hadn't even been a month since the funeral; it seemed a lifetime—and no time at all. When would this horrible emptiness she felt inside ever subside? When would the pain go away? Would she ever stop turning to say something to a man who was no longer there? She couldn't bear staying home alone in that big, empty house, waiting to find out. "I was," she said, as the elevator doors opened. "I decided I didn't need it."

Gabe was wise enough not to pursue it. Holding the doors for her, he waited until she had stepped out and then followed. The offices of McKenna TimeSave, the executive time management company Briar owned, were right in front of them, the double glass doors inscribed with the company logo, a stylized sun that could have been rising or setting, shedding its rays over the 'M' of McKenna, which had been depicted as a mountain. Briar, who had designed the logo herself, had often been asked by clients whether she'd intended for the design to represent sunrise or sunset; she always answered that no matter where you were, the sun was always coming up or going down somewhere, and the important thing was what happened to the time in between. It had amused and pleased her to think that the logo, and her explanation of it, had generated more business over the years than a direct mail campaign. Now she took no pleasure in it; the only thing she could think of was how she was going to fill all those hours without Hay in her life.

Seeing her expression, Gabe tactfully left her at the door to go along to his own office, and as Briar headed to hers, her secretary, Patsy Summer, looked up in surprise. Half rising from her desk, she exclaimed, "I didn't expect you! What are you doing here?"

Briar was beginning to wonder that herself. What was the saying? No matter where you go, there you are. It had never seemed more true than now; she had left the house to escape memories, but they had just followed her here.

"I don't know," she said. "I just couldn't stay home any longer. Would you hold any calls for a while, please? I want some time to get my bearings."

"Well, sure," Patsy said, with the ease of long familiarity. She had been Briar's secretary for ten years, from the days when McKenna TimeSave had first opened its doors in that tiny office in San Jose. There had been two desks then, one for each of them, one phone line, and nothing else but Briar's fierce determination to succeed. They had come a long way, and Patsy looked at Briar with the eyes of a friend. "Are you sure you should be here? Are you all right?"

"I'm fine," Briar said, although she wasn't, and knew it. She tried a smile. "Just pretend I'm not in."

Patsy gave her a look. "Oh, sure. I knew it the instant you walked in the building. If I'd known you were coming, I would have warned you about those stupid reporters."

"If I'd known about those reporters, I wouldn't have come in."

"You want some coffee?"

"No, not just yet," Briar said, walking into her own office. Shutting the door behind her, she leaned against it for a moment, her eyes closed. She hadn't expected it to be so hard; she'd just arrived and already she was exhausted. How would she concentrate?

But anything was better than moping around at home, she knew, so she pushed away from the door and tossed her things on the sofa against the wall before going to the window. Her corner office had a beautiful view of the city, and as she stared out at the gray day, she absently twisted her wedding ring—a wide gold band with a raised setting for the perfect three-carat solitaire. The diamond flashed fire whenever it caught the light, and when she realized what she was doing, she glanced down sadly at her hand.

When Hay had died, she had debated about continuing to wear the ring. She thought she remembered reading somewhere that it was bad taste, or at least a social faux pas, for a widow to wear her wedding band, and she wondered if she should put it away. Surely Fredrica thought so; Hay's outspoken only daughter had already expressed her disapproval. But then, Fredrica, who was five years older than she was, had never approved of anything Briar did anyway. She had never figured out whether Fredrica's dislike stemmed from the fact that Briar was younger, or that such a nobody with no family, no background, and hardly a name to call her own, had snared a man like Hayden Lord.

Not that it mattered, Briar thought. At the time of her wedding to Hay, only five years before, he had already been married three times (twice divorced, once widowed) and had been thirty years older than she was. She had felt that a man of his age and experience knew what he wanted better than his spoiled, pampered adult daughter did, and she had finally become so exasperated with Fredrica's innuendoes and sly intimations that she'd told her so.

A mistake, she thought with a heavy sigh, but one of many she'd made with her stepdaughter, who had promptly proceeded to tell anyone who would listen that Briar had only married her father for money. Fredrica had conveniently overlooked the fact that her new stepmother owned her own lucrative company and was successful even before she met Hayden Lord—and that, in fact, Lord Industries had been Briar's client when she and Hay met, not the other way around. Recalling again that distasteful scene Fredrica had made at the reading of the will, Briar's mouth tightened. How little Fredrica knew her father.

Or me, she mused, and turned away from the window at the soft buzz from the intercom on her desk. Reaching out, she started to depress the speaker bar, but just then the diamond caught the light again, and at its fiery sparkle she closed her eyes against a new spasm of grief.

Would there come a time when she was able to think of Hay without this terrible sense of loss? she wondered. Would there be a day when she didn't see him in her mind's eye as he had been in that private room at Stanford Medical, hooked up to machines, tubes snaking away everywhere, while that incessant *beep-shoosh* sound of respirator and monitor filled the suite, robbing him of dignity and making her want to scream?

Sometimes she thought the image she would take to her own grave would be the sight of Hay's silver hair, mussed and untended, a strand or two falling across his pasty forehead as he lay against the pillow. He had always been so meticulous, so polished and fastidious and precise about everything, especially his appearance. He would have hated knowing how disheveled he looked, and there had been moments when she wondered if that thought had been uppermost in her mind the day she signed the papers terminating his life support. Those disordered strands of hair made him seem so fragile, so defenseless and vulnerable, and she knew he would have hated that most of all.

She had signed, despite Fredrica's insistence that she had no right to do so. Her stepdaughter's outburst of fury and outrage had filled the hospital corridor until Jarris, or Jaz, as the family called him, Fredrica's younger brother by ten years, had managed to haul his sister almost forcibly away.

But that had only been a continuation of her problems with Fredrica, Briar thought tiredly, and she pressed down the speaker bar to the intercom.

"Yes, what is it, Patsy?"

Her secretary answered in a cautious tone that meant she was going to ask Briar to take care of something she probably wasn't going to like. Formal as always in front of visitors,

Patsy said, "A Mr. Weitz is here, Ms. McKenna. He says he's from Appleby, Cromwell, Attorneys-at-Law, and he insists on seeing you. I told him he had to make an appointment, but he claims the matter is urgent."

Certain this had something to do with Fredrica's decision to contest her father's will, Briar felt herself tense. "What does he want?"

"I don't know," Patsy said disapprovingly. Briar could just see her eyeing the intruder with mistrust, ever the protective guardian of her valuable time, and she smiled involuntarily until her secretary added, "He won't tell me. He says the matter is private."

Patsy's tone indicated that Weitz, whoever he was, was probably prepared to camp outside the door until she agreed to let him in. Wondering if he'd been sent to intimidate her, Briar decided abruptly to see him. "All right," she said. "Send him in. Tell him he has five minutes—no more."

"Yes, Ms. McKenna," Patsy said demurely, and a few seconds later, she ushered the visitor into the office.

Briar took a seat behind her desk. She looked up coolly as the man came in. He seemed to be appraising her, and that irritated her.

Brusquely, she said, "Mr. Weitz, is it? I'm Briar McKenna. Please sit down and tell me what I can do for you."

Weitz, who was a big man with considerable bulk, gingerly sat down in the chair she had indicated before the desk, placing a somewhat-battered briefcase on his knee. Grinning broadly, he said, "It's not what you can do for me, but what I might be able to do for you."

She wasn't in the mood for sparring. "I'm afraid I don't understand."

"Oh, you will," he replied, and held up the briefcase, gesturing toward the desktop. "Do you mind?"

Thinking he had about thirty seconds to get to the point, she gave a curt nod. "Go ahead. But can we make it brief?"

"We can make it however you want," Weitz said, drawing out a folder. Taking a ballpoint from his pocket, he opened the folder and looked up at her. "Now, then, this is just for form's sake, but your name is Briar McKenna?"

"You know it is, I just told you that."

"Yes, yes, of course," he agreed, making a note on one of the papers. "But we have to go by the book."

"What book? Listen, Mr. Weitz, I don't know what your game is, but you told my secretary that you represented a legal firm. If you're—"

"No, I told her I *worked* for Appleby, Cromwell. I'm not an attorney; I'm an investigator for them."

Briar was really angry now; she stood. "In that case, you may leave right now. I don't appreciate your using under-handed tactics with my secretary to get to me. Good day, Mr. Weitz. Please show yourself out."

"Hey, wait—I really am legitimate," he protested. "Would you like to see some identification?"

"No, I'd like you to leave."

"Aren't you interested in what I'm investigating?"

She gave him a cold look. "Don't be coy, Mr. Weitz. Since you're here, I presume it has something to do with me. But unless I'm under some sort of criminal investigation, in which case you will have to contact my attorney, I am not in the least interested in whatever you might have to say."

"Not even if it involves your family?"

"The Lords—"

"No, I mean *your* people."

She stiffened. She had no people. "If this is some kind of cruel joke—"

"Oh, it's no joke, I assure you. Would you like me to continue?"

Without realizing it, she sat down again. She wasn't sure what to say. Hay's death had precipitated so much publicity; as his grief-stricken wife, and then his young widow, she had been at the center of much of the media storm. With all that coverage, maybe it wasn't surprising that someone had started to delve into the background she preferred to leave behind, and as she stared at Weitz, she wondered if he—or whoever was paying him—was trying to cash in by attempting a little black-mail. She really didn't have anything to hide, but neither did she care to have the facts of her bleak childhood existence become public knowledge.

Aware that she had allowed the silence to go on too long, she said abruptly, "What 'people' are you talking about?"

But instead of answering her, Weitz asked a question of his own. "Have you ever heard of a woman named Juliet Caulfield?"

The name was unfamiliar. "No, I haven't."

"How about a man named Duncan McKenna?"

She couldn't prevent an involuntary start. Her maiden name was McKenna; to Hay's amusement, she had kept it after they were married—and not only for business reasons. He had understood how important her name was to her; because she knew next to nothing about her background or family, or even if her parents had been married or not, she'd always felt that her name was the only thing she truly owned, and she wanted to keep it. Dear man that he had been, Hay had simply laughed and shrugged and told her she could call herself Godzilla if that made her happy—just as long as she agreed to be his wife.

But now she thought: *Duncan McKenna. Could he be . . . ?*

No! she told herself fiercely. She had been through this before, and she would not raise her hopes. Coolly, she said, "The name isn't familiar. Mr. Weitz, why—"

He held up a hand. "Patience, patience, please. I have to get the facts right."

She'd been patient long enough. "What facts? I'd appreciate it if you would tell me just why you're here!"

Her tone wiped the smile from Weitz's face. "I'm here about your inheritance, Ms. McKenna."

Thinking that Fredrica had sent him after all, her face froze. "What are you talking about?"

"If you're who I think you are, and we can prove it, then you've just become the heir to some property north of here near Sonoma. At one time, it was a horse breeding farm. But now, I'm afraid, it's just a rundown old ranch—" he grinned again despite himself "—on some of the of the most prime real estate in California."

Outwardly, she didn't change expression. But inside, she was seized by such a fierce hope that she felt almost physically weak. Could this be the answer she had been seeking all these years? Unconsciously, her hand clenched on the desk. The land itself, or the monetary value of it, was inconsequential to her at the moment; what was important—breathtakingly, achingly important—was the thought that maybe, by some miracle, she . . .

Ruthlessly, she controlled her runaway thoughts. She had been searching for years for even the slightest clue to her parents, her family, her roots, and she had learned nothing.

Was she really going to believe that this man could walk in out of nowhere and tell her that he had the answer she'd been seeking all this time?

"I see," she said, in command once more. She looked at Weitz. "And what makes you think *I* inherited this property?"

"If you're a descendant of Sloane and Marguerite Caulfield, you have."

"Then I'm afraid you'll have to continue your investigation, Mr. Weitz," she said. "You see, I have no family. I've been an orphan since birth."

But instead of looking surprised or dismayed, as she had expected, Weitz just smiled. "Everybody has a family, Ms. McKenna," he said.

"Well, I don't."

"You know who your mother was."

At the mention of her mother, she tensed again. "My mother died in childbirth."

"And her name was Ariana McKenna."

"So the orphanage records state," she said, unable to throw him out as she so desperately wanted to do. How had he known that? Did she really intend to let him go on with this? It seemed so, for she couldn't prevent herself from adding, "But since you seem to know so much about me, you're undoubtedly aware that even though efforts were made to trace her family, no one was ever able to find any evidence that that was actually her name."

"That's true," he said calmly. "There isn't any evidence— that we've been able to trace so far, that is—that Ariana McKenna was legally married. However, evidence *does* exist to prove that her given name was Ariana Caulfield."

Involuntarily, Briar drew in a sharp breath. Even she had never been able to find that out. She started to ask what proof he had, then she caught herself. She would not get her hopes up again. She had spent years of her time and thousands of dollars of her money trying to find a single clue that might lead her to someone in her family—to a relative, any relative, even a remote cousin. But despite hiring her own investigators—and despite even Hay's efforts on her behalf after they were married—nothing had ever turned up. Her eyes narrowed.

"Just what is your game, Mr. Weitz?" she asked coldly.

"No game, Ms. McKenna, honest. I was hired to find the last surviving heir to the Caulfield property, and—"

"And you don't want anything from me."

He looked injured. "I've already been paid, if that's what you mean."

"Well, unfortunately, evidence is not proof, Mr. Weitz," she said curtly.

"I agree that evidence is not proof, especially in a court of law," Weitz said. "However, we do have a statement—"

Briar looked at him sharply. "What kind of statement?"

"From someone who knew your mother."

Someone who knew her mother? Her pulse began to race even as she told herself that was impossible. She had dreamed of such a moment for years, she thought; as a child she had spent so much time imagining how it would feel to meet someone who had actually known her mother—who could tell her what Ariana had looked like, or what color her hair had been, or whether her eyes had been blue or green—that to hear it aloud now was like being told she wasn't going to die after all.

"Oh?" she said coolly. "And who is that?"

"I'm sorry, but I'm not at liberty to tell you."

Her expression set, she leaned back. "I see," she said. "How convenient for you."

He flushed at her tone, but she didn't care; she was holding herself under too tight a control as it was. She'd been right to deny that this man, this . . . stranger . . . held secrets to a past she had tried for many fruitless years to unlock; she'd been right not to get her hopes up again. Had she really believed she would ever know what her mother's laugh sounded like, or how tall she had been, or how clever or talented or kind? And had she really thought that she would ever learn anything about her father, who had always been even more an elusive shadow than her mother?

Involuntarily, she thought back to those lonely, cold years at the orphanage. No one had ever mentioned her father directly, but there had been times when she had heard herself referred to as "unfortunate," or, even more ominous, "misbegotten." She had been twelve years old before she'd gotten up the courage to sneak into the office one night to search for her file; she had used a flashlight to avoid detection, and she had never forgotten the icy pall that gripped her when the feeble beam of the light finally illuminated her record, and she saw, for the first time, the word *Unknown* written in the space where her father's name should have been. Choked with tears, not daring to cry for fear of being found out, she had crept back to her bed in the ward. Misery nearly overwhelmed her, but then, as she drew the chilly coarse sheet up to her chin, she became certain that someone had made a terrible mistake. She wasn't a bastard, she told herself, and her parents loved each other, and they had loved her. One day they would come and take her home with them, and all these sad years would be just a horrible dream.

It hadn't happened, of course, and as time went on, she finally abandoned her fantasy. But she never stopped believing that her parents *had* loved each other, and she was certain that if it had been possible, the three of them would have been together. Over the years, despite all lack of proof, that belief had become an absolute, unshakable conviction she had never shared with anyone, even Hay.

Looking at the investigator again, she said, "I'm sorry, but I don't believe you, Mr. Weitz. If you knew how much time and effort I've spent on my own trying to find one scrap of evidence, one inkling that what you just said is true . . ."

Weitz glanced appreciatively around her well-appointed office. "I can imagine," he murmured, and reached into his briefcase again. "But as I said, I have a statement—"

"From an anonymous source."

"Not anonymous," he corrected. "Someone who wishes to remain unknown. But I assure you, the statement is legal, authenticated, and binding."

Imperiously, she held out a hand. "Let me see it then."

"Not yet, I'm sorry."

She sat back disgustedly. "I see," she said again. "I suppose I'm to take all this on faith."

"You have my word it's true."

"And that's supposed to mean something to me?"

He handed across a card. "Call Appleby and Cromwell. The office will vouch for me."

Briar took the card with two fingers. "I might do that," she said. "Now, is there anything else?"

"As a matter of fact there is."

Briar withheld a sigh of exasperation. "What now?"

"According to my statement, Ariana Caulfield possessed a very distinctive piece of jewelry, a gold pendant with the initials "C.F." on it. The witness claims to have seen her with it many times. Would you have any knowledge of such a pendant?"

Just for an instant, Briar's formidable composure faltered. Without her knowledge, her hand stole to her throat, and as she stared at Weitz, her green eyes seemed enormous, the only color in her suddenly ashen face. "How did you—" she started to say, and then caught herself. Angry color suddenly flooded her cheeks again as she demanded, "Who put you up to this? How did you find out about the pendant?"

"Ah, so you do know about it," Weitz said. Apparently unfazed by her show of temper, he sat back. "If you have it, it will make things so much easier."

"For whom?" she demanded. She'd thought she had herself in hand, but the mention of the pendant had shaken her badly. No one but her husband knew about that pendant; it was her most prized possession, even more valuable to her than any of the gems Hay had given her. That pendant was the only thing, the *only* link to the mother she had never known, to the identity she would never have, to the roots she would never put down. Not trusting even the bank, she kept it in the vault at home.

"For the court," Weitz said, apparently answering her question. "We still have to prove that you're the heir to the Caulfield property, and that pendant, along with the statements I've gotten, will establish your identity beyond the shadow of a doubt." He suddenly looked anxious. "You *do* have it, don't you? The orphanage said they gave it to you when you left."

Briar didn't hear him. She was thinking of the pendant, tracing every intricate line and whorl of the markings on the gold face by memory. She had taken it out and looked at it so often that she could have drawn the engraving herself. She had never known what the letters "C.F." stood for; no one else seemed to, either. The locket had been the only thing of value in her mother's possessions, and it had been sent with Briar, the infant, to the orphanage.

She couldn't count the times she had daydreamed about those letters; growing up, she had made up stories about them, conjuring up tales about how the locket had come into being, and why her mother had it. At one time, she'd had a cold, empty, little room at the Y. She'd been about sixteen, seventeen, then, and worked at the diner across the street while she went to school at night. She hadn't money for a television, of course; she'd had barely enough for a little portable radio, so imagining stories about the locket had been her meager entertainment. Flinging herself down on that hard, narrow bed in her room, she'd made up names to go with those letters she thought stood for her father's initials: Charles Falstaff . . . Christopher Fairchild . . . Craig FitzGerald . . . Each one more dashing than the last.

"Ms. McKenna? You do have the pendant, don't you?"

Did she dare hope? She looked at her visitor. "If I do?"

"If you do, then we're going to prove you're the rightful heir to that land in Sonoma."

She still would not allow herself to give full rein to her feelings; she'd been disappointed so many times. "What's in this for you, Mr. Weitz?" she asked. "Beyond your finder's fee, I mean."

"Oh, the money's nice, of course," he said. Then he smiled. "But I'd say it's more a satisfaction, you know? I enjoy doing my job—putting people together with things they've lost—or that lost them." His smile broadened even more. "You see, I was adopted myself. I know what it is to wonder about roots—to feel . . . incomplete. Know what I mean?"

She stared at him for a moment, then, ashamed of herself, she dropped her eyes. "Indeed, I do."

"Well, it's all right then."

She made herself look up again. Standing, she held out her hand. "I'm sorry for my behavior, Mr. Weitz. It's just—"

He stood, too, enfolding her hand in his. "Pay it no mind," he said gently. "I'll be in touch."

She didn't go with him to the door, but as he reached for the doorknob, she said, "Mr. Weitz, there's just one thing."

He turned. "What's that?"

She was almost afraid to ask. She had thought about it, dreamed about it, imagined it for so long that she wondered if finding out at last would be a disappointment. But she couldn't let him leave without asking, so she said, "Those initials on the pendant . . . 'C.F.' Do you know what they stand for?"

Obviously embarrassed by his lapse, he slapped his forehead. "Didn't I tell you? Well, that's something, isn't it? They stand for the Caulfield Farm, Ms. McKenna. That old horse-breeding farm you inherited was once one of the premier racing farms in the country, it seems. People came from all over the world to buy those horses, as I understand it. Back in Sloane and Marguerite's time, the ranch was called the Caulfield Farm; it needed no other introduction than that." He grinned suddenly. "You like horses, Ms. McKenna?"

"Yes," she said faintly, thinking of the Thoroughbred jumper she kept at a nearby stable. "I . . . like horses."

Weitz winked. "Then maybe we'll be hearing about the Caulfield Farm again sometime soon, eh? Well, good-bye for now. As I said, I'll be in touch."

Briar hardly noticed him leave. As she sank into her chair again when the door closed, she was still reeling from hearing the names of people who might have been her forebears. *Sloane and Marguerite Caulfield. Juliet Caulfield . . . Ariana Caulfield.* It took her breath away.

Her hand shaking, she reached for the telephone and called her attorney.

———&———

# CHAPTER TWO

When the phone rang, Charlotte Jaeger was standing near one of the floor-to-ceiling windows in the living room of her family's landmark antebellum mansion in Sonoma, about an hour north of San Francisco, in the heart of the wine country. She was tall and spare, with a weathered, outdoors-woman complexion that made her look older than her fifty-two years. Her hair, which had turned prematurely gray when she was still in her thirties, added to her age; it had silvered over the years, and was cut in a no-nonsense style that was like a smooth cap over her narrow skull. In her youth, she had been considered "handsome" more than pretty, with large blue eyes her best feature. But those eyes had lost their glow long ago, and now she just looked severe and uncompromising, which she was. As the manager of the Mondragon Stud, one of California's best-known horse-racing and -breeding ranches, Charlotte Jaeger was in a tough business. But long before that, she had learned to be hard.

Charlotte had never married and had never discussed her reasons for not doing so, although she knew people speculated. Well, let them, she'd always thought. What was her business, was her business. They weren't entitled to an explanation, anymore than they were permitted to ask why she had never left this house, where she had been born, to establish one of her own. The reason why, of course, was the Stud. The ranch was Charlotte's husband, lover, family, and friend; she couldn't imagine being anywhere else.

She had been expecting a call all morning, pacing the vast living room, or stopping to stare out at the hills, green again at the end of February, dotted with oaks and thick shrubbery, the meadow grass beginning to turn . . . before beginning to pace again. She was just wondering if Weitz had misunderstood and decided to drive up from the city instead of calling, when the telephone shrilled. To her taut nerves, the noise sounded like a saw blade cutting the silence, and she jumped. Before one of the servants could answer, she quickly snatched up the receiver.

"Charlotte Jaeger here," she said, controlling her eagerness with an effort. It didn't have to be Weitz, she knew; people phoned all the time. There were constant queries from clients, calls from prospective horse buyers, invitations to various charities, pleas to participate in some function or other; the list seemed endless. It could be anyone, she thought, but to her relief, it was the man she had hired.

"Hello, Ms. Jaeger," the by-now familiar voice said. "It's Albert Weitz."

"Yes, I know," she said, and became aware that she was holding on to the receiver as if it were a lifeline. She tried to relax, but it seemed impossible. She had waited for this moment for years, she realized, and the thought that she might have succeeded at last was so heady that for a moment she felt almost dizzy. A high-backed Queen Anne chair, upholstered in rose brocade to match one of the colors in the magnificent Aubusson covering the living room floor, was placed by the phone stand; she sank down into it, still holding tightly to the phone.

"I . . . uh, I'm calling just like you told me to," Weitz said. "Sorry I'm late."

Charlotte had no need to look at the ornate grandfather clock in the corner. She'd agonized over every minute, wondering what had caused the delay. But now Weitz was on the line, and she took a deep breath. She felt calmer now, but even so, she was almost afraid to proceed. If something had gone wrong at this late date, and after so much searching, she didn't know what she would do.

"You were supposed to call an hour ago. What happened?"

Weitz sounded embarrassed, an unnatural state for a man whom she had discovered was blusteringly self-confident. Charlotte had despised that aspect of his rather abrasive personality when they'd first been introduced by her attorney, but it was finally that very quality that had convinced her to hire him. She had needed someone who was sure of himself, who wouldn't be afraid to dig deep; she had wanted a man who would ask questions others might not want asked, and who would find out things some might prefer be kept hidden. In the end, of course, her judgment had been vindicated.

"Nothing happened," Weitz said, answering her question. "It's just that when I couldn't get hold of her at the house, I had to wait until she came into town."

Charlotte didn't ask how he'd known that the woman would decide to go into the office today; that was his job. Tersely, she said, "Go on."

"Well, then there was a crowd of reporters here this morning that you wouldn't believe. I know I should have expected that, but still, I had to wait to follow her into the building. Then I had to get through her secretary—"

Charlotte closed her eyes, her free hand clenching in her lap. "I'm not interested in your problems, Mr. Weitz, only your results. I presume you have some?"

When there was a little silence, she realized she'd stolen his thunder. He'd obviously planned to make a dramatic announcement, but now she had ruined the moment. Well, that was too bad. She didn't have patience to indulge him; she wanted to know what he'd learned, and she wanted to know *now*.

His response was a little stiff. "As a matter of fact, I do," he said, and then added nastily, "Would you like it over the phone, or shall I write up a report and send out it?" He paused. "Maybe I should come in person. It would only take me an hour or two."

She didn't want him here. Her father was already home, and her brother, Carl, would be arriving shortly from the big company offices in San Jose. The last thing she wanted was for Albert Weitz to show up at the house; she had been so careful these past months to keep their relationship secret because she wanted everything in place before they found out. If she and

Weitz had to meet, as had happened several times, it was either in her attorney's office or away from home. She didn't want anything spoiling her big surprise.

"Don't be coy, Mr. Weitz," she said. "Just say what you have to say over the phone."

He knew her well enough not to push it. "Okay, here goes," he said resignedly. "When I went in, she was surprised, all right, but . . ."

As he told her about the interview with Briar McKenna, Charlotte listened carefully to every word, thinking that despite Weitz's disagreeable personality, she had to grant him one thing: he was thorough. By the time he finished, she not only knew the gist of the conversation, but could almost picture what Ms. McKenna's reactions had been as though she'd been there herself.

"I see," she said, when he had concluded.

Weitz was silent for a moment. Then he said, "You don't sound very thrilled."

Thrilled? She was elated, but, of course, she wasn't about to tell him that; she was a Jaeger, after all. "On the contrary, I'm very pleased, Mr. Weitz—"

To her annoyance, he interrupted. "Pleased? That's all you can say? Do you realize how many other investigators have failed to find this woman?"

"I'm well aware of the efforts that were made to locate Miss McKenna," she said coolly. "But then, they were not privy to the information you had, were they, Mr. Weitz? Information, I needn't remind you, that you received from me."

"Yeah, well, so you gave me a hint or two about where to find her. But that doesn't m—"

"I really don't intend to discuss this further, Mr. Weitz," Charlotte said. "Now, then, shall we move on?"

He was silent for a moment. Then, almost sullenly, he said, "Yeah, might as well, I guess. Go ahead. What do you want to know?"

For Charlotte, there was another question. "Are you certain she's the one?"

"Oh, she's the one, all right."

She had to be positive. "How can you be *sure*?"

"Remember those old pictures you showed me of . . . who was it? The great-grandmother, Marguerite? Well, those newspaper shots of Ms. McKenna sure don't do her justice; she and that Marguerite are the spitting image. They could be twins, I'm not kidding you. But for the clothes and the hairstyle, it was as if those old photos had come to life.''

"Yes, yes," she said impatiently. "But did she know about the pendant?''

He sounded smug. "She not only knew about it, she has it.''

Charlotte drew in a quick breath. "She described it?" she asked. And then, before Weitz could reply, she had a sudden, awful thought. "Did you ask *her* to describe it? You didn't give her any hints about what it looked like so she could guess, did you?''

Stung at this implication of professional negligence, Weitz sounded indignant. "No, she described it all right," he said, and then added meaningfully, "Without any help from me.''

She hardly noticed his tone. Feeling dazed, she said, almost to herself, "Then she really *is* the one.''

He was still miffed. "I'd stake my reputation on it.''

"You just did, Mr. Weitz," she said, eager now to get off the phone so she could consider the ramifications of this wonderful news. "Now, I'll take it from here. Please make your report to my attorney, as we agreed, and send your statement there as well.''

"Well, that's just great, lady," he said with an edge. "A simple thank you for the good job would have been nice, but it seems my bill will have to do.''

"Well, of course," she said, a little surprised. What else had he expected?

"Right then," he said, "Well, I'll be seeing you.''

Charlotte hung up, her thoughts in a whirl. As she replaced her receiver, she was surprised when it clattered in the cradle, and she looked at her trembling fingers with astonishment. Suddenly cold, she rubbed her hands together. Despite the growing overcast, it was still a mild day for March, but suddenly she felt as if she'd caught a chill.

*It's excitement*, she thought, getting up from the chair and going again to one of the front windows. As she pulled aside the heavy satin drapery, she felt a tremor run through her entire body. She had waited a long time for this day, she thought; she could still hardly believe it had finally come.

Restless, she left the window and went out to the long front porch. From this position, she could see the whole of the Sonoma Valley, a sight that never failed to calm her. The house, and the seventy-three acres upon which it sat were—had always been—known as the Mondragon Stud. Spread out to both sides of the main house and to the rear were the long pastures and the big barns and paddocks for the Thoroughbred racehorses the Jaeger family had bred and raised for nearly a hundred years, and she felt a thrill of satisfaction at the thought that the current crop of sleek, running horses was due solely to her. She had control of the Stud; only she, and had now for the past twenty-five years.

A slight breeze ruffled her hair as she stood there, and when she glanced out at the hills surrounding the ranch on three sides, she debated about saddling up one of the horses and taking a ride. Riding had always soothed her, too; she had grown up with horses, and she often took one of the youngsters up into the surrounding mountains to condition it before sending it off to the sales.

But it wasn't riding she wanted today, oh, no. What she wanted was to throw this into her father's face and watch his expression change. The great Rupert Jaeger, she thought with a twist of her lips. What was he going to say to this?

Her eyes gleaming with triumph, she looked in the direction of Caulfield Farm—or what had once been Caulfield Farm. It lay on the other side of the thickly wooded hills, one hundred and fourteen acres of the property hidden from view. But even though there were no fences, she knew the layout so well that she could have walked unerringly to the boundary marking the end of the Jaeger property and the beginning of the Caulfield land. She had gone there so often in the past, but she hadn't been there for years; the memories were too painful.

*And now?* she asked herself. *Now what will you do?*

Thoughtfully, she looked down at her hands, holding tightly to the porch rail. With an effort, she made herself relax her grip. She hadn't allowed herself to think what it would all mean until now; despite Weitz's high recommendation, she hadn't expected him to succeed any more than the others she knew of over the years who had failed. Now that he had, she wasn't sure of what she felt.

Slowly, she turned and looked in the direction of Caulfield Farm again. First her grandfather, Heinrich, and then her father, Rupert, and now her brother, Carl, had coveted that land. Over the years, it had become a bitter symbol, the only unattainable conquest for her family, the one looming defeat. And

now, just when the Jaeger men believed they would triumph at
last in their quest because old, crazy Juliet Caulfield had finally
died, she, Charlotte, was about to prove them wrong yet again.
Without warning, an exultation rose in her, and she wanted to
swing around and shout in triumph and do a victory dance
down the length of the porch. This moment had been so long
in coming, she thought; she could hardly wait to see their faces
when she announced that Juliet hadn't been the last Caulfield
after all.

Laughing aloud in sheer delight, she whirled around suddenly and went quickly inside. The family dressed for dinner,
and soon Carl would be home. They would all meet for cocktails before they went in to the dining room. Should she tell
them over highballs, or wait until dessert had been served? She
wasn't sure what she would do, she thought, as she went
swiftly up the stairs; she just knew that no matter how it turned
out, she was going to enjoy herself tonight. She had waited a
long time for this moment, and she planned to draw it out to the
fullest.


Both Rupert and Carl were in the living room when Charlotte came down again in time for dinner. She had prepared
carefully for this very special evening, and was wearing a long
gown made of a glittery silver material that shot sparks whenever she moved. Her father and brother looked at her in surprise as she entered; not expecting guests, they were both
wearing dark business suits, and Charlotte smiled sweetly at
them as the maid appeared with her usual aperitif.

"Good evening," she said, taking her white wine from the
tray.

Although he was now seventy-nine years old, white-haired
and slightly bowed, Rupert Jaeger was still in command of all
his senses, his family, and the business he had inherited from
his father and subsequently shaped into an empire. He had
never been a tall man—none of the Jaeger men were; the height
in the family had always belonged to the women—but he
seemed to tower because he carried himself with such supreme
self-confidence. Where his son Carl tended to bulk, Rupert was
lean and spare, and his mind was as razor sharp as it had ever
been; his blue eyes, while faded slightly, were just as cold.
Charlotte had never understood why women found her father
fascinating; that gaunt, ascetic face with the thin, cruel lips had

always sent shudders through her, and she couldn't imagine him excited about anything, even in bed. Several years before, Rupert had nominally handed over the reins of the family conglomerate to Carl, but there was still no question in anyone's mind about which of them truly commanded Mondragon Enterprises, the Jaeger corporate offices in San Jose.

Rupert had a small glass of Absolut Vodka straight up in his hand, and as he took a sip, he stared at her over the rim of the glass. Charlotte wasn't like her brother; one of the reasons she and her father had never gotten along was because she wasn't afraid to stand up to him. Although he wasn't in the least afraid of her, he was still alert to something in her expression tonight, and he said carefully, "Good evening, Charlotte. You're looking particularly well tonight. Is this an occasion I don't know about?"

Charlotte smiled into her white wine. "You might say that."

Carl, who had been helping himself to another drink from the wet bar in the corner, turned with glass in hand. At fifty, age hadn't yet stooped him as it had his father, although, Charlotte had often thought that if he kept up his heavy drinking, soon he would be as wide as he was tall. Already fleshy folds drooped beneath his reddened eyes, and the tire around his hefty middle was growing by leaps and bounds. To Charlotte he looked more like a used-car salesman than the president of a giant industrial company, and the fact that one of his conceits consisted of dyeing his hair a flat black only added to that unfortunate comparison. Possessed neither of the supercilious self-assurance of his father, nor the outward confidence of his sister, Carl seemed perpetually anxious and eager to please—a distracting facade for those who had to deal with him as the president of Mondragon Enterprises.

"Yes, Lottie," he said, using her detested nickname, which he knew she hated. "What's the occasion?"

Thinking contemptuously what a fool he was, Charlotte took her time to answer. She had never liked her brother, either, and as he stood there with the glass in his doughy hand, she knew he hadn't the least conception why the so-called Jaeger-Caulfield feud had been going on so long—nor did he care. Long ago he had joined in the vendetta against anyone named Caulfield to please his father, and he pretended to share the same hatred of the family that had caused the Jaegers such grief over the years, but Charlotte knew that he really didn't give a damn if an army of Caulfields showed up tomorrow, waving land grants to the entire Sonoma Valley. The only thing he'd be concerned about was how it might affect him.

"No occasion," she said sweetly. "I just felt like getting dressed up tonight, that's all."

Carl, who knew his sister very well, snorted. "That's never *all* with you, Lottie. You're up to something. I can tell."

"You're so suspicious, Carl," she chided mockingly. "Why don't you tell us about your day. Did you topple any companies, or raid any new corporations?"

Since they both knew that Carl never made any decisions, even about how much toilet paper to order for the executive washroom, without asking his father first, he flushed. "Very funny," he muttered, and turned to freshen his drink just as the maid appeared to announce dinner.

"You'd better bring that with you," Charlotte said, indicating the highball Carl had poured. "You might need it."

Rupert didn't care for games, unless they were of his own design. As he got to his feet, he said, "Coyness doesn't become you, Charlotte. If you have something to say, I would appreciate your just saying it."

She wasn't going to be rushed. Leading the way into the dining room, she said, "Oh, I just have a little news, Father, that's all. It's nothing important. I'm sure it can wait until dessert."

Bringing up the rear, Carl said, "I bet I know what it is. You sold a horse or something. That's it, isn't it, Lottie?"

She gave him a cool look as her father, ever the proper gentleman, seated her at the long, mahogany table, which was set, as always, with a heavy, starched damask cloth, candelabra, and bone china so fine her mother had once boasted that she could read a newspaper through it. As she glanced from her father, at the head of the table to her left, and then across the ornate flower arrangement to her brother just opposite, she said, "As a matter of fact, I bought a horse the other day—a new broodmare called Jewel of Orpheus." She paused, knowing what Carl's reaction would be. "She was a steal at only a million two."

Carl had just taken another sip of the whiskey he'd brought in from the living room. Choking, he banged the glass down, tried to look at her through the flower arrangement, then swept it furiously aside. "A *steal*? My God Charlotte, if you keep spending money like that on horses—"

"The stud farm is my business, Carl," she reminded him coolly. "What I spend on it is none of your affair."

"It will be when you go bankrupt! Who do you think will bail you out then—the company?"

"Why do you always say *The Company* as though the words should be inscribed in stone?" she asked, shaking out her napkin and putting it in her lap. "And besides, have I ever asked you for one cent for the farm?"

He glared at her again. "You keep going like this, and you will!"

"Don't hold your breath, little brother. I know you're waiting for me to fail. But it hasn't happened yet, has it?"

"It's only blind luck."

"On the contrary, luck has nothing to do with it."

"The hell it doesn't! You'd be nowhere without the Mondragon name to back you!"

For the first time, her control slipped. Her eyes flashing, she snapped back, "We could say the same about you!"

"Children, children," Rupert said mildly. "Must we quarrel at the dinner table?"

Charlotte turned impatiently in his direction, intending to tell him that she didn't appreciate being called a child, but she remembered in time that she had something much more important to discuss, and she didn't want to be diverted into an argument with him. Controlling herself, she made an abrupt gesture to the hovering maid to bring in the first course.

"You're absolutely right," she said, when the girl had eagerly disappeared into the kitchen. "It's a waste of time to continue this absurd conversation, especially when the ranch has posted a profit the past two years." She glanced disdainfully at Carl. "*Despite* an industry-wide decline, I might add, and not counting all the business generated for the company because of *my* horses!"

"The horses have nothing to do with that," Carl said sullenly. His father's remark had stung him, too.

"Oh, don't they?" Charlotte demanded. "Then why do you and Father attend the Keeneland sales every year? Because you appreciate good horseflesh—or because of the business contacts you make?"

"Oh, so now you want to take credit for that, too, is that it?"

"Credit where credit is due, little brother," she snapped back. "If it hadn't been for me, you never would have met Myles Davisson, the head of Optical Engineering. And that's only one example."

"Aren't we straying from the subject?" Rupert put in mildly. "I thought you were going to tell us about this new acquisition of yours, Charlotte. The Jewel of Orpheus, did you say?"

But Charlotte knew her father could have cared less about the broodmare she'd just bought. It was obvious that he suspected something was up, but she wasn't ready to discuss it yet, so she shrugged and reached for her spoon. Soup had just been served, and as she dipped into the excellent consommé, she said, "Oh, the mare will arrive the day after tomorrow; you can see her then if you're so inclined. I'm much more interested in the Caulfield property. Have you made any progress with your offer to buy, Father?"

Rupert had just tasted his own soup. Suddenly attentive, he carefully set his spoon down again. "As a matter of fact, I haven't. Why?"

Although Charlotte knew from bitter experience that it was impossible to make her father squirm, she knew one subject might agitate him, and that was the so-called Jaeger-Caulfield feud. Demurely, she said, "Well, it *is* of primary consideration around here, after all, Father. It's no secret that you've been trying to get your hands on that land for years now. I just wondered if you'd made any progress now that the last Caulfield heir has died."

His eyes hooded, Rupert stared at her. "And what," he asked softly, "makes you think that Juliet was the last Caulfield?"

Charlotte didn't know what to say. The thought raced through her mind that she hadn't been so clever after all, but then she told herself not to be so easily outfoxed. If Rupert had even *suspected* another heir existed, he would have moved heaven and earth to find him—or her, as the case happened to be—and buy her off. He would have used any weapon to force a sale; after coveting the property that had been a symbol of defeat for him all these years, he would not have rested until that land was his.

Now that she saw the ruse, Charlotte became even more determined to have her say. Taking a sip of water from the heavy Waterford goblet, she shrugged. "I think that's self-evident. This is a small community. Juliet lived alone on that place for years—"

"Fighting us every step of the way," Carl put in darkly from his side of the table. "I can't count the offers—and damned good ones, I might add—that we made for that property over the years." He finished his highball with a last hefty swallow, muttering as he reached for his wineglass, "Damned stubborn crazy old woman."

Charlotte gave him a dismissive glance before turning to her father again. "Yes, well, be that as it may, in all those years, *I* never heard of any relatives, and neither did anyone else, I'm sure. No one considered 'family' visited Juliet, at any rate, and certainly no one has come forward since the funeral. So it would *seem* that she was the last Caulfield, except . . ."

Rupert wiped his thin lips with the heavy napkin. "Except . . . ?"

This was her moment. Her heart was pounding so hard she felt almost sick with excitement. Oh, sweet revenge! she thought. She'd waited so long for this!

"Well, I'm sorry to have to be the bearer of bad news, Father, but it seems . . ." Charlotte paused, deliberately prolonging the moment. She had planned to play it to the hilt, but the excitement was too much for her, and before she could help herself, she blurted, "It seems that they've found another heir after all!"

"*What*!" Carl shouted, leaping up from his chair before Rupert could speak. "That's impossible! We conducted a search ourselves!"

"Obviously it wasn't a thorough one, then!" Charlotte said angrily. She didn't want to hear from Carl; she was staring at her father, expecting him to be shocked, furious, distraught. But when she saw that slight, condescending smile curving his narrow lips, she felt suddenly chilled. Had he been aware of this development all along?

"It was thorough!" Carl cried. "It was! I hired the best people I could find!"

Charlotte dragged her eyes away from her father's face. "Then they weren't good enough!" she snapped. She couldn't understand why her father wasn't reacting more strongly—why he didn't seem to be reacting at all. She *knew* how important the Caulfield land was to him; she had been steeped in the story of the Jaeger revenge against the Caulfields ever since she was old enough to understand what hate meant. Could even a man as cold and controlled as her father remain completely emotionless when faced with the news that his old enemy had somehow bested him yet again?

Rupert was silent, but Carl's reaction was forceful enough for both of them. Livid, he shouted, "There *is* no other heir! Juliet was the last one! You're just making it all up, Charlotte! I know you—you're lying!"

"Why would I lie?" she demanded harshly, her own nerves beginning to be stretched taut. This wasn't having the effect on her father that she had so lovingly imagined at all, and she couldn't understand why. "You don't seem surprised about this," she said to Rupert. "Did you already know?"

Calmly, Rupert took a sip of his wine. "I'd heard something, yes."

She stared at him. "Why didn't you say anything, then?" she demanded. She could hear the shrill note in her voice, but she couldn't help herself. "Why did you let me go on with this?"

Rupert smiled that cold, lipless smile. "Because you were having such a good time, my dear. I didn't want to spoil your moment."

Charlotte looked at him, hatred seething inside her. She couldn't believe this was happening. She had waited so long to ruin all her father's plans for that land; she had dreamed about it and fantasized about it and schemed for years, only to discover that he had already known what she was going to say before she said it? She wanted to yell or throw something, pick up one of these paper-thin, priceless plates and throw it as hard as she could against the wall. There he sat, smug and superior and supercilious as always, giving her that condescending look that made her feel so incompetent, such a fool no matter how old she got.

She didn't know how it had happened; she only knew that it had, and as she looked at him, her hatred boiled over, and she wanted to hurt him as he'd hurt her; she wanted to make him squirm and feel as foolish and stupid and inept as she did right now.

"Well, then," she said, between her teeth, "do you know that the heir's name is Briar McKenna, Father?" Her voice was rising again with every word, but she couldn't control it. "Briar

McKenna," she repeated. "She's Ariana's daughter, Father. You remember Ariana, don't you?"

Something flashed in those cold eyes, something so quickly gone that in her agitation Charlotte couldn't believe that she had seen it at all. "I remember Ariana," he said.

She wanted to take him and shake him, slap him right across the face. "And Duncan," she said, her voice becoming even more shrill. "You remember Duncan, too, don't you?"

He didn't even change expression. "Yes," he said calmly. "I remember Duncan."

She felt so overwhelmed with rage and bitter disappointment and the sudden, bleak knowledge that she would *never* best her father, that she hardly knew what she was saying. "Well, then, tell me this, Father. Did you know that Briar is their daughter? Yes, that's right," she went on harshly when he didn't answer, "Briar is the daughter of Ariana and Duncan McKenna. And I found her, Father. *I* found her!"

Carl, who had been quiet for a few minutes, jerked forward. "What do you mean, *you* found her?"

Swiftly, she turned to him. "Just what I said, brother. I hired an investigator—"

"An investigator?" he repeated. "An *investigator*?" His face darkened, and he banged his fist down so hard on the table that the cutlery jumped. "Jesus Christ, Charlotte! What in the hell were you thinking of? Are you crazy?"

She leaped up to face him. "No, I'm not crazy, *you* are! How else can you explain why you *hounded* Juliet all these years. Yes, hounded!" she cried, when Carl tried angrily to protest. "What else do you call it? You did everything you could to force that woman to abandon her property so you could get your hands on it! Well, now, you're just going to have to wait, aren't you? The infamous Jaeger-Caulfield feud is going to go on just a little longer. Because there was another heir in the wings, someone neither of you knew about. But I did! *I* did! And now she's going to take over Caulfield Farm and to hell with you!"

Carl couldn't have looked more shocked if she had taken an ax from under the table and attacked him with it. "I don't believe this," he said. "How could you do such a thing? How could you do it? What was Juliet to you? Why do you even give a good goddamn? I don't understand!"

"I do," Rupert said calmly.

Both his children looked at him.

"You do?" Carl said.

Rupert looked at Charlotte. "I do," he said, holding her eyes. "And it has nothing to do with Juliet, does it, my dear? Oh, yes, I understand why."

She stiffened. In the light from the chandelier over the table, her silver dress glittered, making her blue eyes seem cast in pewter as she stared down at him. An expression of sheer and utter contempt flashed across her face as she said, "No, you don't, Father. You could never understand my reasons, not in a million years."

And with that, she threw down her napkin and walked from the room. In the ringing silence she left behind, a sudden noise from the kitchen caused Carl to jump in tense surprise, but Rupert, sitting at the head of the table, never moved.

---

# CHAPTER THREE

"Well, now it's legal," Spencer Reed assured Briar a month after her visit from Albert Weitz, the investigator. He smiled across the desk at her. "Any questions?"

They were sitting in Spence's mahogany-paneled office, out near the marina. The office had a gorgeous view of San Francisco Bay, and normally Briar was entranced by the sight of sailboats skimming across the choppy water, looking tiny against the magnificent backdrop of the Golden Gate Bridge.

But today she was more interested in what Spence had to say. They had been going over seemingly endless documents all morning, in what had become only one of many meetings that had taken place these past weeks to establish her as the rightful heir to the property up north. A transaction like this was even more complicated than Briar had realized, necessitating numerous phone calls back and forth between her and

Spence, between him and the office that Albert Weitz had worked for, and then between them and several government agencies about procedure.

After that there had been court appearances, affidavits, documentation, and endless legal details before everyone seemed satisfied, but at long last, she was signing the final documents today. It seemed like another lifetime since Albert Weitz had appeared in her office and totally altered the course of her future, and she still felt dazed by it all as Spence handed across another complicated-looking testimonial.

"As soon as you sign this, you'll be the legal owner of those one hundred plus acres in Sonoma," he said, smiling again. "On the site once known as Caulfield Farm."

Caulfield Farm, Briar thought, marveling. It was hard to believe that her hand was steady as she signed her name yet again; she couldn't help feeling excited at such a momentous occasion. After all, it wasn't every day one acquired not only an inheritance, but a previously unknown family, and she had to convince herself that she wasn't dreaming after all.

"I feel like Alice in Wonderland and Snow White and Cinderella, all rolled up into one," she said, handing the document back. "Sometimes I wonder if it's all real."

"Oh, it's real, all right," he said, adding the most recent document to the big stack by his elbow. "If you doubt it, just remember your writer's cramp."

Laughing, she flexed her fingers. "Is that a segue into telling me I've got more things to sign?"

"No, you're all finished—for now," he said, looking at her fondly. "I admire you, Briar. Things have been in such an uproar since . . . well, since Hay passed on, but you're handling everything so well."

"That's what you think," she said, and abruptly got up to go to the window. As she stared out at the glittering water, she wondered if she would always feel that sense of loss whenever Hay was mentioned. It had been nearly two months now, and there were still times when it hurt to hear his name.

"Briar?"

Noting the concern in Spence's voice, she turned from the window with a slight smile. "I'm sorry," she said, trying to make light of it. "I guess it's all been a . . . little more than I was prepared to cope with."

They had been friends for a long while now, ever since she

first met Hay, and she had liked the attorney from the moment they were introduced. Spence was a big man, tall and broad, with thinning brown hair and kind brown eyes—unusual, she'd always thought, in a member of his profession. In her experience, lawyers had a cynical look, as though cleaving their way through the labyrinth of the law had given them a cutting edge and made them hard. Not so with Spencer Reed. He wasn't hard at all—just extremely competent, and tough, when he needed to be. Hay had trusted him to manage the estate, and so did she. She was glad now that he was handling things; her inheritance aside, she knew this business with Fredrica was going to be difficult—especially when she told Spence what she had in mind to soothe her stepdaughter's hurt feelings. To put it mildly, she thought, he was going to have a fit.

"It's no wonder you feel a little overwhelmed," Spence said. "First Hay, and now this. It's a lot for anyone to deal with."

She didn't want to talk about Hay, so she changed the subject. "That's true. It's certainly not every day that one gains and loses an entire family." Then she sighed. "I can't help but be struck by the irony, though. I've wondered all my life who my family was, where I came from, what name I could really claim as my own, and now that I have some clue, it's too late. Everybody's gone." She gave a quick shake of her head. "I've always despised people who whine about life not being fair, but this is one time I'm tempted to join in. Why couldn't I have found Juliet before she died? We were so close, only sixty miles apart. It just doesn't seem fair that I never even knew she was there."

"Yes, it does," said Spence. "Sometimes the older I get, the more I wonder about things. I'm beginning to think that fate has a warped sense of humor after all."

"Yes, well, I don't think it's funny."

"I don't, either. But look at it this way—at least you know that you had a great-aunt named Juliet—"

"*Crazy* Juliet, you mean," Briar corrected him, a little sardonically. "That sounds ominous for the rest of the family tree, don't you think?"

Spence smiled at her tone, and Briar smiled, too. Encouraged, he said, "But it's a start, anyway. And now you know your mother was a Caulfield instead of a McKenna—"

"Which makes me—"

"Just what you are—a beautiful, successful, lovely woman," Spencer said quickly. "And, I might add," he went on, "one who is going to be quite . . . comfortable financially. Hay aside, that property you inherited in Sonoma is worth a pretty penny."

"I know, if I were going to sell it."

"Is that what you're going to do?"

"I don't know. I haven't gone to see it yet."

He seemed surprised. "You haven't? I would have thought—"

"No, I didn't want to until I knew for sure that everything was settled."

He turned up a corner of his mouth. "Superstitious, eh?"

She looked uncomfortably away. "I guess you could call it that."

"Well, you can cast your doubts aside," he assured her, giving the thick stack of papers a pat. "As far as anyone's concerned now, the place is yours. And if you need a good real estate agent to handle the sale, I'll be glad to put you in touch with someone."

"That or a contractor."

He looked startled. "You're not thinking of *living* there, are you?"

She laughed. "Spoken like the true San Franciscan! There *are* other places to live, Spence," she teased. "And Sonoma is a beautiful area. Just ask all the tourists who come for wine tasting."

"Well, yes, but . . . but what would you do with the house in Pacifica?"

"That house belonged to Hay."

"But it's yours now."

"Legally, yes. But not if Fredrica has her way." She held up her hand at his instinctive protest. "It's all right, Spence. I don't want to fight her about it. It's filled with too many memories for me. I don't really want it."

He looked horrified. "You're not thinking of . . . of *giving* it to her, are you? That place is worth . . . well, God knows! Several million, at least. It's right on the beach, for God's sake!"

"I know. But if it means more to Fredrica than it does to me, why not let her have it?"

Abruptly, he became her attorney again. "Now, look here,

Briar, the only thing that place means to Fredrica is dollar signs. You know that the ink won't be dry on the deed before she's got it on the market!''

She really didn't want to discuss this now. If he became so upset at the thought of the house, what was he going to say when she told him her idea about sharing the estate with her stepchildren?

"Yes, I know," she said, feeling like a traitor to Hay's memory even for criticizing him to this mild extent, "but I never did think Hay was completely . . . fair setting up the estate the way he did. I mean, why should *I* get everything—"

"You didn't get *everything*, Briar," Spence said sternly. "Hay was more than generous to both Fredrica and Jaz. Those trust funds he set up will keep them comfortably for the rest of their lives."

"Still . . ."

"There's no 'still' about it," he declared. Then his expression changed, and he suddenly looked wary. "Briar, you're not thinking—"

Hastily, she stood. "I think it's time for me to go," she said. "Thank you so much, Spence. I don't know what I would have done without you."

He still looked suspicious as he accompanied her to the office door. But before he opened it, he paused to stare down at her. "I wish I knew what was going on behind those beautiful green eyes of yours," he muttered.

"Someday I'll tell you," she said lightly. "But until then . . ."

"Until then," he said, reaching for her hand, "be careful, Briar. That kind heart of yours is going to get you into trouble."

The compliment embarrassed her. "Only you would say such a thing," she said, trying to force a laugh. But then her smile faded. "You've been such a good friend," she said. "I don't know what I would have done without you."

Now he was embarrassed. "It's what I'm here for," he said with a smile. Then he, too, became serious. "Hay was a good friend, Briar," he said quietly. "There wasn't anything I wouldn't have done for him, and there's nothing I won't do for you now."

She knew he meant it, and she was more grateful than she could ever say. "Spence—"

He shook his head. "I know. Go on, now. We've both got a lot to do."

He was right, so she said good-bye and left. In the parking garage below, she handed her parking ticket to the attendant. But then, as the boy ran off to fetch her car, she thought about Hay again, and how he had inspired loyalty in everyone he knew.

*Oh, Hay,* she thought mournfully. *How I miss you so!*

Tears came to her eyes, but just then the squeal of tires rescued her. Wincing when she saw her car speeding up the ramp, she stepped back just as the attendant brought her fire-engine red Mercedes 450SL to a flourish of a stop.

"Nice car, lady!" he said with obvious appreciation.

"Thanks," she said wryly, getting in while he held the door. She handed him the parking fee plus his tip, but he continued to stare at her car.

"Uh . . . if you ever want to sell it, let me know," the boy said, and grinned. "I can't afford something like this myself, but I know somebody who could."

"Thank you, I'll keep that in mind," she said, thinking that she would never sell this car, which was the first symbol of success that she had ever allowed herself. It was more than ten years old now, and she'd bought it used, but she could still remember the thrill she'd felt when she had driven it out of the lot. When they married, Hay had wanted to buy her a new Rolls, or at least a new Mercedes, but she wouldn't hear of it. Long before then she had decided that she would replace everything on or in this car if she had to, but she was going to drive it until it wouldn't go anymore. Hay, amused at such irrational loyalty to what was, after all, only a machine, laughed and hadn't mentioned a new car purchase again.

That was only another thing she had loved about him, Briar thought, as she drove up the ramp and out onto the street. Maybe it had been his age, or his experience, or simply the fact that he'd loved her despite her idiosyncrasies and her fierce intensity about some things, but she had never felt she had to prove herself with him. Even during that first meeting, when she had come to his office to explain the services McKenna TimeSave offered, she had felt at ease with him. She couldn't explain it, and this morning, as she headed up the ramp to the 101 before changing over to 280, and then Highway 1 toward Pacifica, she thought about that meeting and smiled. She'd been so nervous before she went in. At that time, an account like Lord Industries was quite a plum.

It still was, she thought, and remembered just how she felt when she had been introduced to Hayden Lord that momentous day by his secretary, Mrs. Prin.

"Ms. McKenna, Mr. Lord," the secretary said, and quietly retreated, leaving her alone with a man who was already a legend.

Briar's first thought was that the photos she'd seen of him hadn't done him justice. He had been on the covers of *Newsweek* and *Time* and heaven knew what else more often than she could count, it seemed, and she had always thought him good-looking, in an ascetic sort of way. Silver-haired and lean of face, in his pictures he appeared distinguished, remote, cerebral.

Consequently, she was unprepared for the sparkle in his gray eyes and the quick grin that flashed across his face several times during their conversation, making him seem even younger than he looked, and not at all the intellectual industrialist she had imagined him to be. Later, over dinner that same night, he confessed that she wasn't what he had pictured, either.

"What did you expect?" she had asked curiously.

He had asked her out to dinner as she was leaving his office after their appointment, and—surprising herself—she had accepted. She couldn't understand it; she *never* mixed business with pleasure, and the *only* time she went out with a client was to some official function.

But, like everything about her relationship with Hay, that had been different, too. He had taken her to the Aerie, a new restaurant on the twentieth floor atop one of San Francisco's downtown skyscrapers, and as they were seated, the city sparkled far down and all around them. It had been one of those rare nights for San Francisco, clear with no fog, she remembered, lights twinkling as far as the eye could see. The sight of a jet taking off from San Francisco International caught her attention for a moment, and she wondered, as she sometimes did, if it was heading to some exotic locale, carrying people who were eager to begin the vacation of a lifetime with someone they loved. She had been twenty-eight years old at the time, but she had never experienced that feeling with anyone, and had given up expecting that she would. The life she had led, the way she had grown up, the necessity of taking care of herself from such a young age had all contributed to a mistrust of anyone but herself.

Of course, she'd had several affairs along the way; a woman didn't reach the age of nearly thirty without experiencing something of life. But that night, with Hayden Lord sitting across from her, so handsome and attentive and courteous and interested—and something stirring in her that she'd never thought to feel—she thought suddenly that she had never been really emotionally involved with any of her lovers. Her relationships hadn't been cold and calculating; she wasn't *that* much of an opportunist; they had just been . . . empty. On her part at least. Ashamed, she remembered how, when several of those men indicated they wanted to marry her, she had shut them out—of her life, her apartment, her heart. Alone all her life, dependent only on herself, she felt threatened by committing herself to another person; she hadn't been able to tolerate the idea of giving up her space or her independence, and so she had sent them away. It hadn't seemed strange, until now.

Hayden had been staring at her, and something in his eyes was making her increasingly nervous. It was a strange sensation for her; she rarely reacted to men in this way, and she'd asked quickly, "What did you expect?"

He had smiled. "Well, for one thing, I expected someone older," he said. "Your company came very highly recommended, and it seemed unlikely that someone so young could have come so far so fast."

"It doesn't seem far or fast to me," she said wryly, thinking of the struggles she'd had along the way. At that time, the concept of executive time management was a relatively new idea for the business sector, especially where executives were concerned. But to Briar, for whom time had always had such monumental importance, the idea of her working to save both people and companies those precious moments better spent in other pursuits seemed an ideal field. Her own time spent in all those minimum-wage positions while she worked to put herself through high school and then college had fueled her ambition. Not for her a low-level job; she wanted something more. And because she was organized and efficient and hated waste of any kind, she turned her talents in that direction. As she told him, thus was born the idea of McKenna TimeSave.

"It wasn't quite that easy, of course," she went on, after he had encouraged her. "I began by analyzing time wasters and their causes by using the simple method of observing people at work. At first it was difficult finding companies that would let me come in and survey work habits, but I discovered that by promising a free analysis of the problems I had observed, that opened other doors. Then, with experience, patterns began to emerge, and after I had reorganized several large companies, my reputation began to grow.''

"And now?'' Hayden asked.

She smiled, proud and suddenly shy at the same time. "Now, I've expanded from my first tiny office in San Jose to an entire floor of the Brenneman Building right here in downtown San Francisco.''

"And along with numerous others, you list among your clients two aerospace companies, three electronics corporations, a variety of industrial businesses, and a Fortune 500 computer company.''

She gave him a quick look. "You've done your homework, I see.''

He shrugged deprecatingly. "I like to know with whom I'm doing business.''

She accepted that, approved of it. "You mentioned that I came highly recommended, Mr. Lord,'' she said. "But from what I've seen so far, and from what you've told me, your company seems so well organized that I doubt you need my services. I'm not sure just how much I can do for you.''

"I'm interested in your executive burn-out concept,'' he'd said, and gave her a smile that stirred something inside her. "And please, call me Hayden. Or Hay, if you prefer. All my friends do.''

If any other prospective client had said that to her, she would have politely insisted on formality. She despised the current relaxed trend among business people, who seemed to believe a breezy attitude indicated their professional sophistication; to her, it seemed just the opposite. She'd always felt that people conducted business the way they presented themselves, and she didn't regard her work casually.

But then, she realized, Hayden Lord was even then much more than just another client. As she sat across from him in that elegant restaurant, with San Francisco spread out like a glittering carpet so far below them, she sensed their relationship had already changed. Even so, she surprised herself by saying, "If you wish . . . Hayden. And you must call me Briar.''

"Briar," he repeated slowly. "Such an unusual name. It's quite beautiful, I think."

She had been so astonished at herself for relaxing her number-one rule that she said something she wouldn't have dreamed of saying to anyone else. "Do you think so? I used to hate it. When I was a child, I was teased unmercifully for having a name no one had ever heard of before. Then, when someone found out that a briar was also a thornbush, well, you can imagine the nicknames that arose from that."

He seemed amused. "Now that you mention it, I can," he said, and paused. Then he said softly, "A pity no one thought to mention that a briar is also a rose."

She was taken back. "What a . . . lovely thing to say," she murmured, and knew she was blushing.

"You're a lovely woman," he replied, and then seemed to sense how embarrassed she was, for he became businesslike again. "Now, tell me about this executive burn-out concept of yours."

After his touching compliment, she had difficulty concentrating on what she wanted to say. Surely, she couldn't be attracted to a man who was old enough to be her father, she thought, especially when he hadn't indicated by even one word or gesture that there was anything sexual between them.

Then why did she feel there was?

Hastily, she forced her mind back to business. "Surveys from major companies indicate that the higher the position—barring the President, chairman or owner, who have different problems—the less time top executives take away from work," she said doggedly. "It's more than a refusal to delegate responsibility; it seems to be based on two completely opposite beliefs: one, that if they leave, even for a day or so, they'll be replaced; and two, that if they leave, everything will fall apart."

To her relief, he seemed to be listening intently. "That sounds like a catch-22."

Telling herself that as long as she stayed with business and didn't think of anything else—like how courtly he was, how polished, and sophisticated and good-looking—she'd be all right, she said, "Yes, it is. But the dilemma is real. If a man—or a woman—believes that if by taking some much-needed vacation time, even a few days off, their job won't be there when they get back . . . or worse, that things will have degenerated to such a degree that they'll be blamed for being gone, they won't take the time. This produces a 'ripple' effect.''

''What's that?''

''A series of widening disasters. The executive who won't take time suffers because he allows himself no rest. His family—if there is one, and there usually is—suffers because that person has so little time to spend with them. And in the end the company suffers—in decreased productivity, in mistakes or errors of judgment, or simply because, overloaded and exhausted, and feeling underappreciated and overused, the executive either quits, or, as in many cases, suffers a serious illness like a heart attack that necessitates his leaving the company, or being let go. The very thing he was afraid of in the first place.''

''So we've gone from a catch-22 to a no-win situation,'' Hayden said, shaking his head.

''Not exactly. It's true that no one wins when this happens, but it could be avoided so easily.''

''If you have any suggestions or solutions, I'm eager to hear them. I've experienced the same thing among several of my top people.''

''Every major company has, I think,'' Briar said. ''So after analyzing the causes and reasons for this phenomena, I've come up with some solutions. One is to mandate vacation time—''

''But I already do that. All my top executives are given a month or more vacation a year—''

''Given, not required to take,'' Briar pointed out. ''There's a difference.''

''But you can't force people to take vacation time.''

''Yes, you can,'' Briar said. ''If by not doing so, it's going to affect their productivity. And it doesn't have to be a month, all at once; I've found that it's the concept of *so much* time away at one time that seems so daunting, especially to someone who doesn't feel comfortable taking even an afternoon off. But a week, or even a long weekend to start, isn't quite so threatening, and if those times are scattered throughout the year, it's enough to regenerate interest and enthusiasm.''

Hayden thought about it a moment but still seemed doubtful. ''I don't know. I've forced executives to take some time off, and all they do is sit home anxiously by the phone waiting for something to happen so they can go into work.''

"Yes, I know, that can be a problem. But it's alleviated in some instances by the company providing vacation packages in exotic locales and offering to send the executive with his entire family. I've even suggested to some corporations that they invest in a boat—not necessarily a yacht, but something big enough for a family, or two families, and send people out sailing. If they can't manage on their own, the company provides a pilot, or a crew. There are all sorts of imaginative ways to convince employees to take needed time off," she finished, and then smiled teasingly. "The difficult part is to convince equally hard-working employers to take the initiative. For instance, how long has it been since *you've* taken a vacation?"

"Touché," he said, wincing, and then shook his head. "Who would have thought we'd have to hire someone to remind us to take time off?"

"Well, my job is not only saving time, but suggesting how to make better use of it," she said. "And I've found that the pressures and stresses that come with the top jobs sometimes make us lose sight of other equally important things. One of my functions is to point that out."

"You seem to do that very well," he commented. "But let me ask you something."

"What's that?"

"When was the last time *you* had any time off?"

She laughed, embarrassed. "I can't remember," she confessed, but added quickly, "But I don't need a vacation. I love my work."

"What's sauce for the goose is good for the gander, you know."

"Yes, I know, but we were talking about you."

"In fact, we were talking about my top executives," he reminded her with a twinkly smile. His gray eyes never left her face. "You said the problems faced by presidents or owners of corporations were different."

She couldn't look away from his glance. "That's true."

"So with both of us owning our own companies, what do you suggest we do?"

Without warning, the atmosphere between them changed again. She could feel her skin tingle, as though some kind of electric charge had passed through, and suddenly she felt a little breathless. She couldn't understand what was happening to her, or even if she liked it. "I . . . I don't know," she said. "I'll have to think about it."

Something changed in his lean, handsome face. He sat forward, gazing into her eyes. Softly, he said, "Can you think about it in Maui?"

She couldn't ingenuously pretend that she didn't know what he was talking about; they were adults, after all. But she still wasn't sure how she felt. Things were happening too fast! she thought in sudden panic . . . and knew that wasn't true. Dropping her eyes, she said, "Hayden, I—"

He reached across the table for her hand. It wasn't the self-conscious gesture between two people who had just met, and it wasn't the blatant sexual invitation of a man who was interested; it was so much more than that. His fingers closed over hers almost tenderly, but with assurance, and a courtliness that stirred something inside her again. She watched, completely bemused, as he drew her hand up to his lips.

"Would you go with me?" he asked softly.

She didn't know what came over her. She had never done anything like this; she didn't believe in being spontaneous—especially with a man she had just met and hardly knew. Yet she barely hesitated. Gazing into those calm gray eyes holding hers, she said, simply, "Yes."

That weekend in Maui was the beginning of an affair that Briar never wanted to end. She hadn't wanted to marry Hay, and not because he was thirty years older than she was; by the time he finally convinced her to accept his proposal, she would have been content just to live with him, something she had avoided with any other man because she so valued her independence.

But as she had sensed right from the first, Hay was different. And even though he *was* so much older than she, the age difference never seemed to matter. With her background, she had always felt old in spirit, and Hay was so young in heart that to her they seemed to balance.

In quiet, odd moments, she had occasionally wondered if their relationship had a father-daughter aspect to it. She supposed to someone on the outside looking in, it might seem so. It didn't to her. Hay never treated her as anything other than an equal either in business or in their private lives; he valued her opinion, he took her advice . . . sometimes, she thought with a private smile, when it suited him. Just as she did where he was concerned. He not only approved of her career; he encouraged her. He was interested in everything she did, just as she wanted to know all about him. They never lacked for anything to talk about, and she had always looked forward to their being together again at the end of the day.

As a bonus to all these things, Hay had been a wonderful lover, too. He was tender, experienced, considerate, passionate—a completely different man behind closed doors than he was in the office. He had surprised and delighted her that first weekend in Hawaii, and he continued to surprise her during their courtship, and then the five precious years of their marriage. They had been more than husband and wife; they had been friends, lovers, business partners, and confidantes. She had never felt a twinge when they were out together, not even when she happened to catch a sly look here and there, or perhaps overhear a certain kind of comment. On Hay's arm, or with his hand at her waist, she had never felt anything but proud. When he died, she knew she had not only lost a husband but her best friend. She didn't know which she mourned more.

*Oh, Hay*, she thought sadly as she drove, *why did you have to leave me so soon?* She still felt his loss so keenly at times; until he was gone, she hadn't realized how much she had come to depend upon his advice. He always seemed to know what to do or what approach to take to a problem, and as she left the freeway and took the street that led to the house, she thought of Spencer Reed and how glad she was that he was her friend as well as her attorney. As Hay had, she trusted Spence completely—a reassuring feeling, since the Sonoma inheritance wasn't the only thing they had to deal with. There was still the business pending with Hay's estate, and of course, Fredrica's suit to contest the will. She and Spence would have to meet to discuss strategy, to make plans, to appear in court. It sounded so overwhelming that she felt a surge of panic.

Well, she'd just have to deal with it somehow. She had learned early in life not to run away from problems but to tackle them head on.

But not right now, she thought, reaching for the button to open the big gates that led up to the house on the bluff. When she saw that they were already open, and caught a glimpse of the midnight blue Rolls Royce Corniche parked up ahead at the house, she muttered a curse. She recognized the car at once, of course, and as she pulled in behind it, she forgot all about her other difficulties. Right now she had a bigger problem to deal with, and her name was Fredrica. The last thing she wanted was another confrontation, but it seemed she had no choice. As she cut the ignition, her stepdaughter emerged from the open front door, carrying a big box.

Fredrica stopped when she saw Briar getting out of the car. "What are you doing here?"

"I live here," Briar said, and looked pointedly at the carton Fredrica was holding. "What are *you* doing here?"

As if she had forgotten she had it, Fredrica looked down at the box, too. With her tinted black hair cut straight in a chin-length Prince Valiant cut, and her pale skin and invariable red lipstick, she had always reminded Briar of a cross between Gloria Vanderbilt and Mary McFadden. Her enormous black eyes—an inheritance, Hay had told Briar, from her Castillian mother, Paloma, who had been Hay's first wife—would have been her best feature if they hadn't been outlined in kohl, and held such a hard, contemptuous expression. But that look, combined with that slash of red mouth, and her penchant for dressing in black from head to foot, made her look like something out of a vampire movie. Briar had never liked Fredrica, and she knew that despite her efforts to hide her feelings, they showed. It was just that she couldn't understand how Hay, so just and generous, could have produced such a daughter—just as she had always wondered how he could have sired the lazy, opportunistic Jaz, the son of another wife, the beautiful, blond socialite named Camilla Van Der Vere, who had tragically died in a car accident.

"If you must know," Fredrica said, immediately going in for the attack, "I came for a few of my father's things." She lifted her sharp chin. "Things I know he would want me to have."

"I see," Briar said, slamming her car door. She noticed only then the van parked to one side of the drive, and she raised an eyebrow, which irritated Fredrica even more.

"I brought some help," Fredrica said defensively, and then, before Briar could respond, added a nasty, "And don't worry, I'll only take what's mine."

Briar felt too weary to argue about it. She didn't care if Fredrica emptied the entire house if it was that important to her; as far as she was concerned, she had everything she needed to be reminded of Hay in her mind and in her heart.

"Take whatever you want," she said, starting up the steps.

Fredrica wouldn't move out of the way. As Briar came up to her, she said, "It's not as if I'm stealing anything."

Forced to stop or try to push Fredrica out of the way, Briar said, "I didn't say you were."

"He was *my* father, after all."

"That's true."

"And I have a right!"

"I didn't say you didn't."

"You haven't said anything!"

Briar sighed. "What do you want me to say?"

Her black eyes narrowing, Fredrica hissed, "I always *knew* you didn't really care about my father. And this proves it!"

Briar stiffened, but before she could reply, she was nearly knocked aside by a man in overalls who was carrying out the red leather captain's chair that Hay had used in his study.

"Sorry, lady," the man said, as Briar quickly stepped aside. She watched him go down the steps and put the chair in the van before she looked at Fredrica, who lifted her chin. Without another word, she turned and went inside.

Fredrica followed, still carrying the box. "You said I could have what I wanted," she said aggressively.

Briar didn't want to argue about it; she just wanted Fredrica to leave her alone. Things had happened so fast these past months that she was still trying to adjust to Hay's death, as well as to the idea that she actually had a family, even if they were all gone. Signing the papers today had made it more real than it had seemed before, and she needed to be alone to sort out her thoughts. It was all so overwhelming that she felt a little dazed, and without answering, she went on out to the deck. She would wait alone out there until Fredrica and her moving men had gone.

To her annoyance, Fredrica followed her outside. Briar was standing at the rail that enclosed the cantilevered redwood deck, staring out at the ocean when she heard the door open. She turned around with a sigh.

"What is it now?" she asked.

Fredrica came to the rail. "I just want to know one thing. How long are you going to keep up this pretense?"

"What pretense?"

"That you loved my father," Fredrica said. "That he loved you." She waved a hand, a gesture that encompassed the big house behind them, the deck they were standing on, the hot tub at the end of it, the pool beyond. Her eyes came back to Briar's face. "Enough to give you this."

Briar's first impulse was to brush this hateful woman aside; her second to slap Fredrica's harsh red mouth. But she had long ago learned a hard lesson about self-control, and as she stared at Fredrica now, no one would have guessed the struggle that churned inside her, the emotions she kept under tight rein. Not even Hayden, who had known her so well.

"I did love your father," she said. "And he loved me."

"That's a lie! You seduced him; you know it!"

"Seduced him?" Briar repeated, taking a step forward. Fredrica tried to hold her ground, but she had to take a step back. "How little you know your father, if you could say that," Briar said. "Hay was—"

Fredrica interrupted fiercely. "Don't call him that!" she cried. "No one called him by that ridiculous nickname! He was Hayden Jarris Lord, not some . . . some *hayseed* straight from the farm!"

Briar took another step forward. Her green eyes bored into Fredrica; she wouldn't allow the other woman to look away. "That's true," she said, her voice low. "Hay was a sophisticated man of the world. No one *ever* put anything over on him, least of all me."

Taking another step back, Fredrica clenched her fists. Her long, crimson fingernails dug into her palms. "You did, I know it! All you wanted was his name, his money—"

"I had my own name, my own money—"

Fredrica's lip curled. "If you mean your little time-management business—"

Briar took another step forward. "That little 'time-management business' you're referring to is one of the most successful in the country, Fredrica," she said, beginning to wonder why she was pursuing it. Hadn't she already learned the futility of trying to defend herself against Fredrica's irrational accusations? But she went on, anyway. "And, just in case you've 'forgotten,' Lord Industries was *my* client when I first met your father, not the other way around."

Fredrica tossed her head. Her blunt-cut black hair swayed with the motion, emphasizing her high cheekbones and giving a glimpse of sapphire earrings that shot out blue sparks in the sunlight. It was that sparkle that caught Briar's eye, but before she could do more than register the fact that those earrings had come from her own jewelry box, Fredrica was advancing, her eyes like black tar.

"You bitch!" Fredrica hissed. "You're a nobody, and everyone knows it! You married my father because you wanted a name, a place in society, prestige . . . a family! Well, you fooled him, but you didn't fool Jaz and me! We know you for what you are!"

Briar couldn't believe that even Fredrica could go so far. Controlling her anger, she said, "I think you've said enough, Fredrica. Now, I'd like you to get out of my house."

"*Your* house!" Fredrica exclaimed. Her pale face suffused with ugly color. "Well, not for long, if I have anything to say about it—and I do! I don't know how you did it, but you trapped my father into giving you everything, and I'm not going to stand by and get robbed by a . . . a *gold digger*. I'm going to fight for what's mine. By the time I've finished with you, dear stepmother, the only thing you'll have left is what you came with! Now, what do you think of that?"

Briar had gone very still during this outburst. For a moment or two, she didn't say anything at all. At last, she said, almost wonderingly, "Why do you hate me so much, Fredrica? What have I ever done to you?"

Fredrica looked as though she might explode. Her face crimson with rage, she cried, "You've got the *gall* to ask me that? It wasn't enough that you *tricked* my father into marrying you, oh, no! You had to *work* on him to change his will in your favor. Until *you* came along, everything was going to stay in the family, but now you—a nobody, an orphan, someone without even a name to call her own—you inherit everything. You made a fool of my father, Briar McKenna, and I'll never forgive you for that, never. If it takes to the end of my days, I'll see that you pay!"

Wondering how anyone could sustain such hatred, Briar waited until Fredrica was finished. "You know, Fredrica," she said quietly, "before today I was prepared to give you anything you wanted, even this house, if you desired. But now—"

Breaking off, she looked up at the house where she had shared such happiness—the only personal happiness she had ever really known—with Hay. The tall windows on this side glinted in the warming sun; the pool sparkled. She glanced at the hot tub, covered now, picturing the last time she and Hay had enjoyed it together. They'd made love right here on the deck that night, steam from the hot water rising from their skin, steam of another kind increasing their passion. Afterward, they had refreshed themselves with a dip in the pool and had gone upstairs to make love again. Hay had been such a wonderful lover, so tender and passionate. . . .

With an effort, she thrust away the poignant memories and looked at Fredrica again. "I was going to split the entire estate with you and Jaz," she said. "But not now. By your actions you've forfeited any right as far as I'm concerned to anything that Hay didn't give you himself. Furthermore, he wasn't incapacitated or incompetent or senile, and I won't allow you to claim that he was. So if it's a fight you want, Fredrica, that's what you're going to get. I'm not going to have his memory sullied by anyone, especially his daughter!"

"Oh, really?" Fredrica sneered. "Well, just wait until we get to court! I've got surprises you don't even know about!"

"Is that so?"

"Yes, it is! For one thing, I *know* you entered this farce of a marriage agreeing not to take anything out. How are you going to explain that?"

Briar was holding on to her control by a thread. When Hay had first told her about changing his will, she had been horrified at what he had done. She immediately pictured all the problems it would cause if she inherited everything but the two trusts for Fredrica and Jaz, and she had begged him to divide things three ways. He was adamant. His children would be well taken care of, he insisted; he wanted *her* to be secure.

Now, after what Fredrica had said, she realized that Hay had known his children better than she did, and the realization made her determined not to give up without a fight. To do any less would be to make a mockery of Hay's last request. He had shown his love for her by giving her everything he had; she couldn't just . . . give it back.

"I want you to think about this, Fredrica," she said. "I'd rather work it out without a court fight."

"You want," Fredrica mocked. "You'd rather. Well, you can want and rather all you want, right before the judge. Because Jaz and I are going to contest this, Briar, make no mistake. I'll do whatever I have to to break my father's will."

That was it. She had tried everything she could think of to get through to this woman, all to no avail. If Fredrica wanted war, Briar wasn't going to back away from the fight. Her loyalty was to Hay, now and always. "In that case, I'll break you, Fredrica," she said. "I'll make you sorry you ever thought about going to court."

Fredrica tried to meet Briar's fierce gaze, but she faltered. "You don't scare me," she muttered, but Briar saw that wasn't true. She was sure she had seen a flash of fear in those black eyes, and she wondered, suddenly, if Fredrica's determination to break her father's will stemmed from a reason that none of them yet knew.

They looked at each other for a long, tense moment. "We'll see," Briar said at last, and turned back to the rail to stare out at the sparkling sea.

---

# CHAPTER FOUR

Briar didn't allow the distasteful scene with Fredrica to ruin her plans for the following morning. Signing the papers in Spence's office made the fact of her inheritance real, and nothing was going to dim her pleasure at her first visit to her property. Up early the next morning, she climbed into the car and headed north on 101.

The trip took over an hour, plenty of time to come to grips with the idea that at last she was going to set foot on land that had been in her family—her family! she thought with a thrill—for almost a hundred years. As she crossed the Golden Gate Bridge and sped through Sausalito and then Marin and Novato, across 37 and up 121, she thought that the only thing that would have made the day better was being able to meet a relative, even a distant one. What a pity it was that her great-aunt had died before they'd been able to meet; if only she had known that Juliet was so near, nothing would have kept her away.

The only thing she'd been able to find out about her family so far—besides the fact that the house on the property was a falling-down wreck—was that her aunt had been a true recluse. Apparently she hadn't been adverse to slamming doors in visitors' faces or running them off the property because they were trespassing.

*Not too promising*, Briar thought humorously. But now that she legally owned the property and could prove her relationship to Juliet, perhaps she could find out more. She certainly intended to, anyway; things had happened so quickly these past few weeks that she hadn't had time to sort out all the details, but now that the dust was settling a little, she was determined to go ahead with her search.

The place to start, she thought, was finding out who had identified *her*. Albert Weitz swore he'd never been told, and Appleby and Cromwell, attorneys, had been adamant about no disclosure. The court had agreed with them. The information Weitz had uncovered, the documents subsequently produced, the affidavits from the orphanage where she'd been brought up, and her mother's pendant itself combined to provide sufficient evidence to identify her as the last heir to the Caulfield Farm. The judge had seen no need to abrogate the witness's claim to anonymity, and that was that.

"You should be grateful, Ms. McKenna," he said severely, "to have been found at this late date at all."

Well, she agreed with him on principle, but that didn't make her any less determined to find out everything she could. The person who had put Weitz on her trail had known her mother, perhaps her father, as well, and she wasn't simply going to shrug her shoulders and accept her good fortune—not when she had an opportunity to find out more about her parents.

But as eager as she was to get started, she supposed that would have to wait a bit until she got her bearings. Spying the sign that pointed the way to the town of Sonoma, she felt another little thrill. A map had been provided for her, but she didn't have to look at it; she had already memorized the directions, and soon she was taking one back road after another, leaving the historic old town behind as she climbed higher and higher into the hills.

Soon the road became narrower, finally thinning down to a point through which two vehicles couldn't pass. The blacktop was old and cracked, and when she hit a particularly nasty pocket and nearly cracked her head on the roof of the car, she wondered if she hadn't gotten lost after all.

Still, it was beautiful; sloping hills rose all around, some staked out in carefully tended vines, some studded with magnificent oaks. Every now and then she caught a glimpse of a hawk soaring high above in the china-blue sky, and the colors of the grass and puffy clouds and the trees were so vivid they almost hurt her eyes.

Usually she appreciated such natural splendor, but she was too preoccupied today. The more the road wound around, the more excited she felt. She knew she was getting close, and she could feel her heart begin to pound. When she noticed her white knuckles on the steering wheel, she uttered a short laugh and told herself to relax.

But how could she be calm? she wondered as she slowed for another turn. As rundown and decrepit as it might be, she was about to visit the ancestral home she had only been able to dream about for years.

Her fantasy about the house hadn't abandoned her even when she reached adulthood, and she could still see the place she had conjured so often in her mind: it would be painted white, made of wood, at least two stories, with gables and clerestory windows, all in green trim. The house would have a porch that ran the length of the front, with an old-fashioned swing at one end, and inside, all the floors would be pegged—except for the kitchen, which would have linoleum. A large kitchen table would sit right in the middle, and there would be a pantry with shelves. The house would have a formal dining room, of course, with a sideboard and an étagère, and a cherrywood table would seat at least ten. In her dream, the table had always been covered with a hand-crocheted lace cloth.

The fantasy spun on in her mind, all the details she had so often imagined in her childhood returning like old friends. The living room of the house would be dim and cool, she thought dreamily, with screens on the windows, and an India rug covering the floor. There would be a piano, perhaps, certainly an escritoire. Upstairs would be the bedrooms, reached by a staircase with two landings and a banister that shone, and in the bathroom would be a claw-foot tub, and windows that opened outward, to let the summer breeze in. Secret cupboards would have been built under the eaves for storage, commandeered in the past as playhouses by generations of children, and she would find all sorts of treasures there, toy soldiers and broken dolls and storybooks and discarded curtains to play dress up in.

Oh, she had imagined it so many times, lying awake in the dormitory-style room at the orphanage, where the cots had been lined up in a row, heads against the walls, feet toward the center of the aisle. She had always felt that the only privacy she really had was when the lights went out and she could pretend to be asleep. Away from the keen gaze of the nuns, she could dream awake with her eyes closed, thinking what she liked. There had been no partitions in that big room or anywhere else, not even in the showers, so she had to seize those precious moments when she could. The sisters were always on the look-out for daydreamers; from the instant the overhead lights snapped on in the morning, harshly announcing that it was time to get up, to the moment the same lights switched out at bedtime, everyone had a job to do. The sisters truly believed in the maxim about idle hands and minds; chores and school and homework and meals were planned to the minute.

But the nuns couldn't make her sleep if she didn't want to, Briar thought, bouncing over another big bump and coming back to earth with a thump. The road became even worse as she drove on, and only the Mercedes's suspension kept her head from banging against the roof time after time as the tires hit one bad rut after another. She had convinced herself that because her aunt had only died a short time ago, the house couldn't be a true derelict, but now she wondered if she had been too optimistic. From the condition of the road going in, heaven knew what she'd find at the end.

After hitting yet another pothole, she slowed to a crawl. She was so intent on not destroying the underside of the car that she nearly missed the sign. By accident she caught a glimpse of white through tree branches that had grown up around the post, and she quickly braked to a stop and peered out. Stone Mountain Road, she read. This was her last turnoff.

This road was even worse than the others she'd taken, and after a few hundred yards, she debated about turning back. Maybe she'd taken a wrong turn somewhere, she thought, and then exclaimed aloud as the tires found another rut and she banged her elbow against the door handle. Tall trees rose up around her, making it impossible to see anything other than vegetation; now she'd gone from cracked blacktop to plain dirt, and as she jounced around, she prayed that she wouldn't meet someone coming the other way. Cautiously, she rounded another corner and then slammed on the brakes.

Something was blocking the road. At first it just looked like some boards, but as she leaned out the window to look closer, she realized that the jumble was part of a fence that had fallen down.

"What in the world . . . ?" she muttered, and cut the ignition. Climbing out, she checked first to see if she'd done any damage to the car, then she went over to the tangle of boards and examined the problem. She couldn't drive around; if she wanted to continue, she was going to have to move the blockage.

"Damn it," she said. Beginning to wonder if this was worth it, she shaded her eyes with her hand and looked around. It was so quiet that she could hear the grasshoppers in the weeds and the gentle sighing of the wind through the trees. It was a warm day, and being so far inland, Sonoma was always much warmer than the coast. She hadn't thought to bring a hat, and the bright sun beat down on her unprotected head and shoulders as she stood there; even the air had a heavy, breathless quality. She was just starting back to the car when she had the strangest feeling that she wasn't alone. Despite herself, she stopped and looked around quickly.

All she could see were trees and bushes—and one gray squirrel staring down at her from a high branch. Feeling silly, she went to fetch a pair of gloves she kept in the car trunk and resignedly began moving the fallen boards to the side of the road. If this was part of the property she owned, she thought, it was obvious that she was going to have to put some money into maintenance. She had already noticed that the boards were part of the fence alongside the road, and when she gave it the once-over while she worked, she could see gapes and holes where other boards had fallen and not been replaced. Wondering if this were another omen, she finally finished her task and climbed back into the car.

This time she didn't have to drive far; ironically, the entrance to the property was just around the bend, and when she saw it, Briar rolled her eyes. If she'd known that, she would have left the car where it was and walked in.

As she drove up and saw the rusted gates, one leaning precariously toward the road, the other buried up to the bottom bracing in dirt and fallen leaves, she couldn't help grimacing. She'd thought she was prepared for anything, but this certainly wasn't what she had envisioned.

She couldn't turn back now, so she drove through the gates without looking. She was just thinking she'd have to make a list of things to fix when she almost ran afoul of a rock the size of a wheelbarrow near the side of the road. Where it had come from, Briar didn't know, but she detoured carefully around it, wondering what might be next. Would the house itself still be standing, or would it be in the same state of disrepair as the rest of the place? With the fences falling down, the gates rusted, and fallen trees and broken branches all around—not to mention giant rocks littering the road—her catalog of things to repair seemed to be growing by leaps and bounds.

But then, just as she was starting to feel disheartened despite herself, she looked up and saw the house. Without realizing it, she drew in a sharp breath and slammed on the brakes again. Was she really seeing what she thought she was seeing? She blinked to make sure. But when she opened her eyes again, it was still there.

Her hand shaking, she turned off the engine. Opening the door, she got out and leaned against it, her eyes bright with sudden tears.

The house—her house! she thought in wonder again—had been built at the end of a beautiful little vale. The gentle sloping hills rose up to the side and the back of the ranch like sentinels, protecting the house but not crowding so close as to cramp what had once been huge, grassy pastures. Clumps of green still struggled inside what fences remained, and as she blinked away tears, she could picture the land as it had been in its full glory, a lush backdrop for the jewel of the place, the house up the rise.

The house commanded attention even from here. As she had always imagined, it was two stories—dilapidated and unkempt now, but obviously once a showplace. Tall front windows, grimed and dirty, still glinted here and there in the sun, and the sagging roof supported no less than four chimneys. It was a huge house, far bigger than even she had envisioned, and it wasn't quite white, as she had pictured so many times, but a weathered sort of gray from neglect. What paint there had been had peeled off, probably too many years ago to count, but as she climbed back into the car again and drove the several hundred yards around the curving, overgrown drive that bordered what had once been pig paddocks, she could see by patches here and there that the house had once been white, and she shivered with delight.

How could she have imagined this place so clearly? she wondered, and then she told herself firmly that there was nothing mystical about it. She wasn't psychic, far from it. If she recalled her history, most farmhouses from this period of time had been painted white.

But with green trim? she asked herself as she parked the car by the sagging front porch and got out, and with a front porch that extended the length of the house with the swing at the left end, just as she had pictured it?

Once more, she felt that shiver down her spine, and to distract herself, looked at the front steps, wondering if they were safe to climb.

They didn't seem to be. There were four of them, and they sagged as badly as the roof did, but with the added peril of broken and cracked boards. Wondering if all this had happened during the few short months Juliet had been gone, she cautiously tested the bottom step. It creaked under her weight, and on impulse she decided just to forget the steps and jump right up onto the porch. The boards groaned alarmingly as she landed, but held, and she let out a breath. Spence had given her the key, and as she fished it out of her purse, she wasn't surprised to see her hand trembling. She felt shaky all over, but from excitement, she knew, not from any sense of danger.

Raising her head, she looked around.

An eerie feeling came over her. Not frightening, but . . . odd. Although she knew she couldn't possibly have been here before—even in her dreams—she couldn't rid herself of the sudden feeling that this was all familiar, that if she wanted to, she'd know where everything was—that the living room would be to the left when she opened the door, and the dining room to the right. That the stairs would be straight ahead, and beyond that, the kitchen. And down in front, the barn would be . . .

Where was the barn? she wondered suddenly. She hadn't seen one. But there had to have been a barn; this had once been a thriving horse ranch, and she knew it could not have been without a stable.

But where was it? She knew she hadn't passed it as she was driving in; a structure that big would definitely have caught her attention, even if it had fallen down.

Puzzled, she walked carefully down the length of the porch, ignoring the ominous squeaks and groans from the boards underfoot, and peered around the edge of the house. Apart from what had obviously been paddocks back here, now with only rusting watering tanks inside, and more sagging fences, there wasn't a barn behind the house, either.

There was another set of steps here (but she had known that, too) leading off the porch, and she went cautiously down, headed around toward the back. Here the land sloped up to the hills and she realized immediately what a good conditioning run the rise would make. She had some experience with horses herself—she kept a Thoroughbred at a stable near the house in Pacifica. Irish Coffee was his name, and she had bought him when he'd become too much for his previous owner to handle. Given the opportunity, she knew Irish would love to run up this hill.

*That would take some of the salt out of him*, she thought humorously, and then, just for a second, imagined she heard the sound of a delighted laugh somewhere behind her. She whirled around, her arm upraised, but no one was there. Slowly, she lowered her arm. She must have imagined that laugh . . . but it had seemed so real.

She listened intently again, but all she heard was the sigh of the breeze through the tall eucalyptus trees that bordered the property. It must have been the wind, she thought with a frown. It had to have been. But she wasn't convinced.

"Weird," she muttered, and decided to abandon the puzzle of the missing barn for the time being. It was getting late; she should inspect the house. Remembering that she still had the key in her hand, she tried it at the back door. It worked, but when she pushed it open with an eerie creak, she froze. What was wrong with her? If she kept this up, she'd be imagining all sorts of things. Maybe the next thing that would happen would be the appearance of the ghost of her aunt Juliet.

Thinking that if Juliet did appear, she should ask her what happened to the barn, Briar smiled at herself. Closing the door behind her, she peered ahead into the gloom.

As she had somehow known she would, she had entered a small service porch, empty and bare except for the cracked and stained linoleum she'd been sure would be here. Beyond was the kitchen, wrapped in shadows; ivy overgrowing the window added to the dimness by shutting out the sun.

Briar hardly noticed; she was staring at the big scarred

wooden table that stood in the center of the floor. How many times had she imagined that? she wondered, and without realizing it, she shivered. Jerking her glance away from the table, she looked around.

The rest of the kitchen was unremarkable, a few of the cupboard doors hanging open to reveal empty shelves lined with remnants of old paper, the countertops cracked here and there from neglect and long use. The white ceramic sink was stained with rust around the drain, and when she tried the faucet, nothing happened. Giving a last glance around, she left the kitchen through the swinging door and emerged into a short hallway.

Once again she was struck by that eerie sense of déjà vu. As she had pictured it so many times in her daydreams, the hallway led to the living room, now on her right, with the dining room, of course, to the left. Ahead of her were the stairs. She knew without a doubt that the bathroom upstairs would have a claw-foot tub, and there would be hidden cupboards built into the eaves in the bedrooms.

*This isn't happening*, she thought, wrapping her arms about herself. It was too odd. She had never believed in precognition or whatever this might be; she was too grounded in reality. She prided herself on her practicality, her common sense. But how had she imagined all these details so perfectly without having seen the house before? How had she *known* the back door would lead to a service porch or that there would be a wooden table in the center of the kitchen?

*Because all those things were usual in a house this age, that's why*, she told herself firmly. There was nothing paranormal about it. She probably could have chosen any old farmhouse at random and seen exactly the same thing; it was the silence that was getting to her, she thought. That, and the gloom. Without lights, dust motes danced in the few shafts of weak sun that fought their way through the grimy windows; it all added to the aura of helpless neglect.

Then why, despite her common sense, did she almost *feel* another presence here? It was ridiculous, but if she didn't leave soon, she was going to start imagining ominous creaking noises upstairs or hearing voices. Then she *would* begin to think this house held ghosts.

Shivering slightly again, but wondering at the same time why she really wasn't afraid, she forced herself to go down the hall toward the shadowy living room. Sheet-covered bulky shapes added to the ghostly appearance of the room, and when she looked down and saw the faded India rug covering the floor, she wasn't surprised. Thinking that at this point it would have been more of a surprise *not* to see the rug, she turned and looked toward the dining room.

Sure enough, there was the big oval table she had always pictured. But as she counted the chairs, she saw that she'd been wrong. Instead of the ten she had always imagined, there were only six—proof, she thought shakily, that her imagination wasn't infallible. But what was she was going to find upstairs?

Deciding that could wait for another time, she turned toward the front door, which was decorated with an ornate stained-glass panel set into the wood. She had just realized that the intricate curlicues and lines was the same design as that of the two letters on her pendant when a shadow appeared in front of the door. Caught off guard, she gasped. Just for an instant, her overwrought imagination conjured up the presence of the elusive laughing ghost, before she realized she might be in far more danger than the supernatural could supply. Abruptly, she became aware of how isolated this place was, and that only Patsy knew she was here. But Patsy wouldn't send anyone out, no matter how important it was.

The shadow moved again, and before she could think about it, Briar reached out. She had always believed it was better to seize the offensive, if she could, and when she jerked the door open, she was prepared for anything . . . but not for the man dressed in a suit and tie who was just raising his hand to knock.

Without giving him a chance to speak, she assumed an aggressive stance, demanding, "Who are you, and what do you want here?"

Startled, the man stepped back. Briar had time to inspect him now, and immediately saw that his suit was tailored, his tie imported silk, and his shoes handmade. His hair was expertly tinted to black—a mistake, she thought vaguely, because the color was much too harsh for his pale complexion and doughy face. But at least he didn't look like a vagrant or an escaped convict, and she relaxed slightly.

"I'm sorry, I didn't mean to startle you," he said, pulling out a monogrammed handkerchief and mopping his face with it.

He seemed more surprised than she was, although why that

should be, since her car was parked right out front, she wasn't sure. Still wary, she said, "Can I help you?"

He put away his handkerchief. "You're Briar McKenna, I assume?"

"Yes," she said, wondering how he had known her name.

"I'm Carl Jaeger."

The name meant nothing to her. "How can I help you?"

He tried a smile. "I called your office, and when they said you weren't in, I took a chance and came here."

"I can't imagine why," Briar said coolly. Then, "What is it that you want, Mr. Jagger?"

"I came to make you an offer."

"For what?"

He peered beyond her, into the gloomy interior of the house. "For this property," he said, and looked at her again. "You are the new owner, aren't you?"

She didn't see any point in denying it. "Yes, I am. But I really don't think that's anyone's business but mine."

"Perhaps I should explain."

She wasn't interested in his explanations. She wasn't interested in him. Remembering that she'd locked the back door when she came into the service porch, she came out and pulled the stained-glass door firmly shut behind her. "I'm sorry, Mr. Jaeger, was it? But I'm not really interested in what you have to say. I've just inherited this property, and I haven't decided what, if anything, I'm going to do with it. Now, if you'll excuse me. . . ."

She started down the steps, but he called after her. "I'm prepared to be more than generous."

She turned and looked up at him. "I said I'm not interested."

"Not even in twenty million dollars?"

She stopped. "I beg your pardon?"

"I'd hoped that would get your attention," he said, looking pleased with himself. He smiled, but Briar, who had experience in dealing with men like him, noted the fact that his smile didn't reach his eyes.

"My attention, perhaps, but unfortunately, not my interest," she said. "I'm afraid you'll have to look elsewhere for property, Mr. Jaeger."

"You don't understand," he said, following her as she

started down the steps again. "This isn't just a piece of property to me."

Suppressing a sigh, she turned and looked at him again as she dug her car keys out of her purse. "Don't tell me," she said. "You have a sentimental attachment to it."

He beamed. "You're right, we—that is, my family and I—do. You see, we own the property next door—"

That *did* catch her attention. "Then you knew the family who lived here!" she exclaimed, thinking she had found someone who could answer her questions about her family. . . . Juliet, at least, she amended, realizing that Jaeger was only in his fifties. But that was a start, she thought, and she suddenly decided that she wasn't in such a hurry to get rid of him.

"Oh, yes, indeed," he said eagerly, before he caught himself. "I mean, we weren't close, you understand—"

"But you knew Juliet Caulfield, didn't you?"

An expression of distaste flashed across his face. It was gone in an instant but lingered in his tone. "Yes. Well, I mean, I knew *of* her."

What did that mean? she wondered. If he had been Juliet's next-door neighbor, surely he would have known more than that—despite the certain distance between the two properties. "I see," she said, beginning to wonder if he had fabricated the entire tale.

Seeing her skeptical expression, he said hurriedly, "It was just that our families weren't . . . close. But that doesn't mean we can't do a deal, does it?"

Briar looked around. "I don't know," she said, thinking that it really was discouraging. In practical terms, renovating would require a big investment on her part, both in terms of time and money, and she had the business to run in San Francisco. She'd be rushing back and forth between the two trying to oversee everything, and even though she suspected in the end it would be worth it, she wondered if she wanted to commit herself to such a big project.

Too, she couldn't deny that Jaeger's offer, if it was genuine, was generous—more than generous, she thought, looking around again, seeing the condition of the fences, the curling shingles on the roof, the crumbling mortar barely holding the bricks together in the fireplaces. Weeds grew up everywhere, choking off what had once been lush green pastures; there wasn't any water, so perhaps the well had even gone dry and would have to be drilled again. And even if she repaired everything and restored the place to its former glory, what would she do with it then?

As though he sensed the direction of her thoughts, Jaeger insinuated himself again. "You can see the condition of the place," he said persuasively. "As it is now, it's more of a white elephant than anything. I doubt you'll receive an offer like mine anywhere."

"I'm sure you're right."

"Then you'll sell?" he said, not bothering to disguise his elation.

"I didn't say that, Mr. Jaeger," she said. As his face fell, she looked around again. "I need more time to think about it."

"How much time?" he asked anxiously.

She brought her glance back to his face. Why was he so eager? she wondered. "I don't know," she said. "As I said, I'm not sure at all that I want to sell."

"You won't get a better offer."

"So you've stated. But that isn't the only consideration."

He seemed dismayed. "It's not?"

"No, it's not," she said, thinking that money was the last thing on her mind. Infinitely more important was the question of whether she should give up her inheritance so willingly. This land was her only connection to her family, and after all this time of wishing and hoping, her dreams had finally been realized—albeit a bit more shabbily than she had expected—but realized all the same. This run-down old place was her single link to her roots, her past, her identity; how could she think of giving it up just when she'd found it?

"I don't understand."

"You don't have to," she said.

He became angry. "This offer isn't good indefinitely, you know."

She looked at him coolly. "Is that a threat, Mr. Jaeger?"

He flushed but persisted. "No, it's a statement of fact. As I've said, you won't get a better offer than this, and you know it."

"And as I've said, Mr. Jaeger, money isn't the only consideration."

He was having a difficult time holding on to his temper. Watching his struggle, Briar suspected that there wasn't much he wanted that he didn't get. He had a petulant, spoiled look. "All right, then," he said finally. "Will you at least think about it?"

"I will," she agreed.

"No, I mean it," he persisted.

"I said I would," she repeated, and looked at him again. "Tell me, Mr. Jaeger, why are you so anxious to buy this property? Is there something I don't know about?"

He laughed shortly. "You mean, does it have a lake of oil two feet under the surface? Or natural gas just begging to be pumped out of the hills? No, no, Ms. McKenna; it's nothing like that."

"Then what?"

"I told you. My family has wanted this property for years. We offered to buy it from Juliet Caulfield, but she turned us down. We wanted to take it off her hands, to help her, and ourselves, too. She wasn't . . . well. It was too much for her."

Briar tried not to smirk. She had already recognized that the last thing this man would feel was sentiment. No, that wasn't his reason, but she would like to know what was. "And now that Juliet is gone?"

"Juliet's . . . passing doesn't change anything. We still want the land."

"Well, if I decide to sell, you'll be the first to know," she said, opening her car door. "Beyond that, I can't promise."

Since she was obviously determined to end the conversation, he had no choice but to say good-bye. A big Lincoln Continental was parked near her little red car, and as he heaved his bulk inside it and started the engine, she knew by his angry expression that she had probably made an enemy. Wondering why, since all she had done was turn down his offer for her land, she waited until he had gone, and then left the ranch behind her. But as she drove slowly away, looking back now and then at the dilapidated old house and the sagging fences and rusting water tanks, she wondered why he had made such a high offer for the place. Land was valuable here, there was no doubt. But twenty million?

She was preoccupied all the way back to Pacifica. The conversation with Carl Jaeger had disturbed her more than she was willing to admit, and the more she thought about it, the more she wondered if she shouldn't look a little deeper into Jaeger's real reasons for wanting her land. By any standards, his offer to buy had been astounding, if not outrageous; there had to be something she wasn't aware of yet. But what could it be? she wondered, and suddenly thought of Albert Weitz.

As soon as she pictured the burly investigator, she knew she had found her answer. She'd been thinking of asking him to do some detective work for her—or, if he felt there was a conflict of interest—recommending someone else. Now this seemed the perfect opportunity to contact him and ask how he felt about working for her. When she got home, she went immediately to the phone. Because of all the legal activity the past few weeks, she had his number in her directory, and she dialed it, not even realizing what time it was. He answered on the fourth ring.

"Mr. Weitz? This is Briar McKenna," she said. "I hope I'm not calling at an inopportune time."

"Not at all. I was just going out to get some dinner, but since it was only McDonald's, it can wait. What can I do for you?"

Now that he'd asked, she wasn't quite sure what to tell him. Deciding it was best just to get to the point, she said, "Mr. Weitz, are you available to do some work for me?"

He sounded surprised. "You want to hire me?"

"You do free-lance, don't you? Or are you retained solely by Appleby, Cromwell?"

"No, no, I do outside work. It's just that you took me back a little. What do you want me to do for you?"

"Do you know a man by the name of Carl Jaeger?"

He hesitated. "I've heard of him, yes. I don't actually *know* him."

"What have you heard?"

"Well, he and his family run Mondragon Enterprises, a big industrial conglomerate based in San Jose, for one thing, and for another, they own the Thoroughbred ranch right near your property, called the Mondragon Stud. Beyond that . . ." He paused. "Why?"

"I met him today."

"You did? Where?"

"When I went out to inspect my property, he came by. He offered me . . . a substantial sum for the land, and I wondered why."

"Well, land's pretty valuable up that ways—"

"No, it wasn't that. I got the feeling there was something else."

"Something else? What?"

"That's what I'd like you to find out."

"Oh."

"Does that mean you'll take the job? You don't have any conflict of interest?"

"Conflict of interest? Why would you say that?" He seemed hesitant.

Alerted to his tone, she paused, "I don't know. Would there be?"

"No, no, 'course not. I mean . . . no, it's all right."

She frowned. "Are you sure?"

"Sure I'm sure," he said, sounding like himself again. "Anything else you want?"

Since he had agreed to work for her, she decided she might as well make full use of what she had already seen were considerable talents. "Yes, there is. I want you to find out as much as you can about my great-aunt, Juliet Caulfield."

"Oh, now . . ."

"Is there a problem?" she asked.

"No, no—at least, it's not what you think."

"What is it, then?"

He seemed reluctant to say. "Well, you know I had to do some research on your family background to find you. . . ."

"Yes, go on. You told me you hadn't found much."

"Well, now, that's true. It's just—"

He wasn't usually so evasive, and she said, a little sharply, "Just what?"

"You're not going to like it."

"Let me be the judge of that. What is it?"

Weitz sighed. "Do you know why they called her Crazy Juliet?"

He was right; she could tell by his tone that she wasn't going to like it. Sinking down on the little chair by the telephone stand, Briar took a firm grip on the receiver. "No, you never said. Why?"

"Oh, I know this is going to be a mistake," Weitz said mournfully, "but Juliet—your great-aunt Juliet—spent a lot of time under a psychiatrist's care. I don't know what the diagnosis was, but . . ." He hurried on when Briar was silent. "The only reason your great-aunt was allowed to stay on at that ranch as long as she did was because she'd run everybody off with a shotgun who tried to get near. I'm real sorry to have to tell you this, Ms. McKenna, but they didn't just call Juliet crazy. . . . She really was.''

———— *⁂* ————

# CHAPTER FIVE

Briar was still preoccupied when she went in to work the next morning. No matter how she tried, she couldn't get that conversation with Albert Weitz out of her mind. When all this business first started, and she had initially been told that her great-aunt had been called Crazy Juliet, she'd thought . . . what had she thought? That the woman was just old and crochety, certainly *harmless*. She hadn't *dreamed* Juliet was truly mad, and now she couldn't help but wonder about the rest of her family. She'd been so shaken that she'd told the investigator there had to be more to the story, and to find out everything he could. *Everything*.

Her morning at the office was demanding and chaotic, as always, and while she tended to numerous details, her concern about Juliet was pushed to the back of her mind. But she had a break in the afternoon, and when she read the same report three times, and still had no idea what it said, she decided to leave early for once. She couldn't concentrate when she kept thinking how ironic it was that she'd finally located a member of her family only to learn the person had been mentally ill. Would she next discover that there had been an ax murderer in the family tree? It didn't seem to bode well for any future discoveries, she thought, and she called Gabe in to ask if he'd take care of things the rest of the day.

Her assistant was surprised and showed it. "What's up?" he asked when he came into her office. Briar was already gathering her things, stuffing papers into her briefcase with the promise to herself that she would read them tonight or not sleep.

"I decided to leave early. You can take care of things, can't you?"

"Well, sure . . ." he said uncertainly. In the past, it was

rare that Briar left early; more often than not, she was the one who locked up after everyone else had long gone home. He hesitated. "Are you all right?"

"I'm fine," she said, smiling at him before she checked her purse for her keys. "I just can't seem to concentrate today."

He looked sympathetic. "I understand."

She knew he thought she was feeling depressed about Hay, and she felt like a heel for letting him continue to think it, but she just didn't feel she could talk about what was really bothering her. Not yet, anyway. Later, she would tell him and Patsy the whole story—when and if Albert Weitz found out what it was. For now . . . She smiled slightly. "Thanks, Gabe. I appreciate this."

"No problem," he said. "Hey, you deserve some time off. God knows you work harder than any six people around here. Don't worry; I'll take care of everything. You just go home and rest."

Thinking that's the last thing she needed, she thanked him again and went on to explain to Patsy, who was just as surprised and concerned about her early departure as her assistant had been.

"You sure we can't do anything for you, Briar?" Patsy said anxiously, her red hair a nimbus around her pointed face. Her eyes were already blue, but she had recently gotten new tinted contacts, and the azure effect with the red hair was striking. With her funky style, she looked more like a model for *Seventeen* than the almost-thirty woman she was. Today she was wearing a black knit dress that just touched her knees, and a purple, red, and orange knit cummerbund around her tiny waist. On anyone else, the outfit would have looked ridiculous, but it suited Patsy perfectly.

"No, I'm fine," Briar said, and became aware that Gabe was at the office door looking at her with concern, too. She turned to include him. "Really. Stop worrying, you two. I just need some . . . air."

"You're sure?" Patsy asked.

"I'm positive," Briar said firmly, and gave them both a meaningful look. "I'll be in early tomorrow morning, so be prepared. We've got a lot of work to do on the proposal for Kibbe Discount Stores, among other things."

Her mention of Kibbe Discount did the trick. She had been angling for that account for months now; Kibbe was a national discount clothing company that seemed to open another outlet in a new city nearly every week. Considered a "cushion" account here at the office because it would always need servicing, they had been eager to acquire it. Gabe especially. Briar had already told him he could handle most of the work if Kibbe signed, and she knew he was looking forward to all the travel. The discount company's motto was "Across the nation, a Kibbe in every town."

Gabe grinned. "I'll get all the data we've gathered so far together this afternoon."

"Anything you want me to do, Briar?" Patsy asked.

Briar considered. Despite Patsy's unconventional appearance, she was a compulsive, organizational nut. If she didn't have something to do every minute of the workday, she felt that she was wasting time, so Briar reeled off a long list of things that had been pending, and which she hadn't had the time—or energy—to get to yet. Patsy's eyes glowed, and she sat down eagerly, reaching for her pad and pencil.

"I'll get right on it," she said. "You want me to bring the letters out to the house tonight for your signature?"

Knowing Patsy would do just that, Briar said hastily, "No, no, I'll sign them tomorrow. You don't need to come all the way out to the beach."

"I don't mind."

"I know, but it's all right. You go home and take care of your menagerie."

Patsy had never married; she lived alone in a tiny apartment with her two Rottweilers, Daisy and Demi, and a lop-eared rabbit called Max that she took for walks on a leash. She was perfectly happy without a man, she always said; what more could she ask for than the company of two loyal dogs and a bunny?

Briar had sympathized, until she met Hay; then everything changed. Unlike Patsy, she had always traveled too much to have any small pets, but for the past eight years, she'd had her horse. Irish was eleven years old now, but just as much of a handful today as he'd been when he'd come off the racetrack. He had injured a tendon then, but with good vetting and her own endless care and patience, no one would know it now. A big, bold blood-bay, he stood nearly seventeen hands, had a habit of rolling his eyes and pinning his ears, and took five-foot fences with ease. Briar had won ribbons at jumping shows with him and could have gone on for serious contention if she hadn't had the business to run. She hadn't entered a show in a long time now; she just didn't have time for training. And she had never thought of adding to her stable of one, she thought in amusement; a single dose of Irish Coffee was more than enough for anyone.

Thinking that a ride was just what she needed today, she left the office in Gabe's capable hands, with Patsy happily typing away, and headed toward the stables down in Pacifica. Because she often went there after leaving work at night, she had all her riding clothes in the trunk of the car and didn't have to stop at the house.

With traffic light at this early hour, it wasn't long before she turned in at the gates of the Pacific Riding and Hunt Club. As the gate guard recognized her and waved her through, she shook her head sardonically. She'd always been amused at the pretentiousness of both the people here and the grounds themselves, but when she had been scouting locations to stable Irish after marrying Hay and moving to the beach, she had to admit that the riding club by far offered the best accommodations for her spoiled horse.

Remembering back now, she smiled a little sadly again when she recalled how Hay, darling man that he'd been, had offered to build her a barn and riding ring at the house—there was more than enough acreage—because he thought she should have her horse at home. She had appreciated the offer, but after thinking about it, finally had to refuse. Irish would have been lonely by himself, she thought, and when she and Hay were both away on business, they would have had to hire someone to come in to feed and exercise him. Because he so enjoyed giving her things, Hay had reluctantly agreed. But when she found the riding club, he had insisted on going out to inspect it himself. As a result, Irish had been assigned to the best stall, right in front, so that he could see all the comings and goings and have plenty of room to move around on those days when Briar couldn't get out to ride. The stall he was in had been a foaling stall when the stables had been primarily a breeding farm, and Briar couldn't deny that her pampered darling had plenty of room. Others stalls were the standard twelve-by-twelve, with a few in the fourteen-by range, but Irish grandly presided over a twenty-by-twenty corner stall with a window on one side and a half wall with a grill. The stall door had originally had a grill, too, but despite regulations Hay had insisted that it be removed. He'd thought Irish would feel less like a prisoner—albeit in a luxurious cell—if he could hang his head out the door.

Remembering those moments with Hay, Briar felt tears come into her eyes. He'd done so much for her, she thought, so many little things that she'd laughed about or thought were so silly at the time. Now those memories only served to make her loss all the more poignant.

*Oh, Hay*, she thought with a sigh, *I do miss you so*.

Fortunately once she left the front gates behind and started driving along the curving road toward the clubhouse and the stables, she didn't have much time to dwell on Hay. Horses and riders were all around, and she had to concentrate on her driving until she got to the clubhouse. Counting on Irish to lift her spirits, she parked the car in front and went inside to change her clothes.

The women's locker room was done in blue and white, a color scheme carried throughout the entire club. Briar's locker was at the far end of one row, and she had just changed into jodhpurs and was sitting down to pull on her Dehners, the custom-fitted, tall English riding boots that were hard enough to get *on*, and almost impossible to get *off* alone, when two other young women came in. She knew them both; they had all competed at one time or another at local shows, and she nodded at them as she inserted the hooks into the tabs inside her boots.

"Haven't seen you for a long time," one of the women commented. Her name was Amber, and she was typical California: tanned, blond, slender and with the tell-tale lines around her eyes that meant she'd already had too much sun and would soon be finding a plastic surgeon. As Briar recalled, she was barely thirty-one.

Her companion, a shorter, not so blond or tanned, woman named Gretchen, nudged her in the ribs. "What's the matter with you?" she said in a stage whisper. "Don't you remember that her husband just died?"

Amber groaned. "Oh, that's right. Sorry, Briar. I guess I forgot." She tried to look sympathetic. "How are you?"

Briar finished tugging on the second boot. She'd had them long enough so that the stiff leather had eased down at the ankles and the tops didn't rub at the backs of her knees when she walked, and she stood and wriggled her toes experimentally. She didn't want to talk about Hay, not to two self-involved women who wouldn't understand anyway. She said, "I'm fine. Anything new around here?"

As she had anticipated, they were instantly distracted. "Not unless you want to count the new man," Amber said, winking.

The last thing Briar was interested in was a man, but she couldn't just walk rudely away. Remembering that the resident instructor had given notice, she forced herself to ask, "Oh, did we get a new trainer?"

Gretchen giggled. "Let's hope so. Supposedly, he's here from England, but he has hardly *any* accent—"

"Who cares?" Amber interjected, with a broad grin. "Accent or not, this guy is to *die* for! He's got the best body of any man around, and the bluest eyes, and the sexiest mustache—"

Briar had never liked men with mustaches. "Yes," she said dryly, "but does he know how to ride?"

Amber rolled her eyes again. "*Does* he! You know the man from Snowy River? He makes him look like an amateur!"

"Oh, good. Just what we need around here—a cowboy."

"Hardly that," Gretchen said eagerly. "He used to manage a training stable in England—running horses, in fact." Her eyes widened. "He even trained some horses for the royal family, I hear."

Already tired of the subject and eager to go and find Irish, Briar grabbed her hard hat and crop. "If he was so successful there, what is he doing here?"

Amber looked as thoughtful as she ever could. "You know, that's the funny thing, Briar. We were just talking about that ourselves. Why do you think he came?"

Already disliking the man, even though she'd never met him and hadn't even heard of him until five minutes ago, Briar slammed her locker door shut. "Maybe he wasn't quite so successful as he wants everybody to think," she said, and went out to saddle up.

Fifteen minutes later, her horse prancing and dancing and seeming about ready to jump out of his skin in an excess of pent-up energy, Briar climbed into the saddle. She hadn't time to find the other iron before Irish bucked a little out of sheer exuberance. Gathering up her reins, she laughed. A less experienced rider would have been unseated, but Briar was used to her horse's antics. If he hadn't done his obligatory little hop and duck, she would have thought something was wrong with him.

But bad manners were permitted only so far, and she was ready the next time when he tried to whirl at some imaginary leaf that flew by as they started toward the warm-up ring. Checking him effortlessly, she kept the horse firmly between her legs and smiled as he tossed his head.

"Feeling good today, Irish?" she said. He answered by sidestepping at a minuscule piece of paper on the ground before settling down into a more mannerly little jog.

The warm-up ring was a hundred yards or so away, and as they trotted sedately along Briar lifted her face to the slight breeze that came off the ocean. Oh, it was good to be riding again after these past few weeks, she thought. Communicating with a creature as elemental as a horse had always helped her perspective, and it was during these precious times that she could put her problems and worries aside.

"Come on, Irish," she said, touching her heel lightly to his flank. He responded by breaking into a controlled canter—or as controlled as he could ever be at this initial stage. She knew he wanted to speed up into a gallop, and for a moment she debated between taking the path to the beach and riding along the shore, or going to the warm-up ring before taking him around the jumping course.

In the end, the jumps won, as they often did. She convinced herself it was because he hadn't been ridden for a while, and she didn't want Irish to overreach himself at the beach, but she knew her decision was more selfish. No matter how many times she tried it, she had never gotten over the exhilaration of jumping her horse. It was an endless thrill to set him at an obstacle, regulate his stride, feel him gathering strength and speed, and suddenly be lofted into the air. The sensation was like flying on a horse with wings, and she knew why Pegasus had always been such a potent symbol. That adrenaline rush was the best feeling in the world, a drug in itself, and sometimes she felt she could never get enough of it.

She'd tried to explain it to Hay. He had come to watch her in a competition once before they were married, but had left, white-faced, halfway through. When she saw him leaving, she handed Irish's reins to another competitor and ran after him.

"Hay, what's wrong?" she'd said, when she caught up to him at the car.

He still looked pale. "I can't watch," he'd said. "If you got hurt—"

She'd been touched. "I won't get hurt," she assured him. "Irish is a splendid jumper. He's never fallen." That wasn't quite true, but she didn't see any reason to upset Hay any more than he already was.

He wasn't reassured. "I'll just wait here," he'd said.

She didn't need to think about it. If he was going to worry like this, no competition was worth it, she decided, and said immediately, "I'm going to withdraw. I'll be right back."

She'd never forgotten his response. She had begun to turn away, but he grabbed her arm and stopped her. "No, you won't," he said.

"It's not important—" she started, falling silent when she noticed his expression. She had never seen him look so fierce.

"If you do withdraw now," he said, "you'll disappoint both of us. This is *my* problem, Briar, not yours. I don't ever want you not to do something because of me. Please, darling, I mean it. *Never hold back!*"

"But—"

"No. Your courage and daring are the reason you've come so far, accomplished what you have. If you let my fear or worry stop you from doing the things you should—from doing the things you want to do, then I'll have destroyed the qualities that make you what you are. I won't be responsible for that, Briar, I won't. Do you understand?"

Thinking that she had never loved him more, she gave him a kiss. Then she'd gone back and won the competition. But she had never competed again during their marriage.

Irish started prancing a little just then, bringing her thoughts back to the present. Thinking with fond exasperation that she couldn't take her attention off her horse even for a minute, she collected him up and cued him for a shoulder-in to give him something to think about, and in this mannerly fashion they finally arrived at the warm-up area. The jumping ring was just beyond, empty at present, and when she saw that the last person in had put all the jumps up to over four feet, she smiled.

"Well, let's just see what we can do about all this excess energy, my boy," she murmured, and bent down from the saddle to push open the gate.

Irish had been in this arena many times; he knew what was about to happen, and because he loved to jump, he snorted and side passed smartly through the opening. It had been a while since he'd been out, so Briar couldn't blame him for being excited, but she wasn't about to let him jump without warming him up thoroughly. A trot and canter in both directions accomplished that, then she rode him over a few ground rails to stretch his back. He never had any problem picking up his feet or watching where he was going, so after a while she set him at a low cross rail from both directions. Two small verticals were at one end of the warm-up area, and when he took those with ease, she moved into the jumping ring.

One of the reasons she had decided to board Irish at the Riding Club was because of the excellent practice jumps that were always set up. In the ring were the typical verticals, a large triple bar spread, a liverpool—one with water before the jump—and an unusual four-part combination that required some tight striding, finishing with a fan jump at the end. It was a good test of ability, she thought, and something that would give them both some much-needed exercise. Mentally deciding on her course, she turned Irish and set him at the first jump.

As always, she barely had to regulate his stride, and they sailed over with room to spare. The next one was just as easy, and the next, and the one after that. Irish hesitated a little at the water jump; someone had added tin foil to the bottom of the pool, and the late afternoon sun reflected right into their eyes, making it hard to see the top bar. One of his hind hooves just ticked the rail, but long experience told Briar it wasn't going to fall, so she didn't look back. Irish never had liked water jumps, and neither had she.

The next jump was the wall, and to her surprise, one of the papier-mâché bricks rattled as they went over. But the in-and-out was directly ahead, and Briar barely had time to gather him again before they were practically on it. Irish shortened his stride without direction from her, and she was so surprised at the unaccustomed move that she allowed him to take off, and then was sorry she hadn't asked for more speed. They went up and over awkwardly, which forced her to hold him only one and a half strides before they had to meet the other fence. This time as they went over, she heard the ominous clunking sound that meant a rail was about to go down, and when it did thud to the ground behind her, she wondered if she should finish the rest of the course. Either she wasn't concentrating, or her horse wasn't in the mood for this after all. It wasn't worth getting hurt, and she was just pulling Irish up to assess the situation when she heard someone shout. Surprised, she looked around.

A man dressed in jodhpurs and scuffed riding boots had vaulted over the fence—vaulted over? He couldn't open the gate and walk through like anyone else? she thought, instantly antagonized. She didn't recognize him at first, but then she saw his mustache, and her eyes narrowed. So this must be the new riding instructor. She had already decided she didn't like him when Amber and Gretchen had told her about him; she liked him even less now. Even his walk annoyed her, and she was irritated that he had intruded on her ride.

"Sorry to interrupt," he said, in a faint accent that, to Briar, was not divine at all, but as aggravating as his deep, sexy voice. "But I couldn't help notice—"

"Yes? What?" she said coolly.

He didn't seem to acknowledge her frosty tone. "Well, it's probably none of my business, and you certainly didn't ask my help, but it seems to me you're allowing this horse to rush those fences. With the rails so high, I was worried that one of you might get hurt."

As Briar looked down at him, she thought that Amber had been right about one thing, at least. He did have deep blue eyes. But his thick blond hair was too long for her taste; he looked like he hadn't had a haircut in months. And even if he did have a good body, with a broad chest and muscular arms and long, strong legs, she didn't like lean, tall, arrogant men. She disliked them even more when they dared stop her in the middle of a course.

Completely forgetting that she had pulled up before he called to her, she said icily, "The way to get hurt is to have someone shouting at you from the rail. It's very distracting, in case you hadn't noticed."

He was taken aback. "Yes, you're right," he said, for some reason irritating her even more with his apology. "Sorry," he added. "Maybe we should start over. The name's Stefan Yager. I'm the new instructor here . . . well, temporarily, anyway. I'm helping out a friend. You know Stan Taber, of course."

Stan Taber was a former member of the USET, the United States Equestrian Team, who owned the Riding Club. "Yes, I know him," she acknowledged.

"And you are . . . ?"

It was pointless not to introduce herself. "Briar McKenna."

"And Irish," he supplied, giving her horse a professional glance. "That's a nice animal you've got."

Wondering why she was disliking this man more and more with every comment, she couldn't help an acid, "Apart from his tendency to rush his fences, you mean?"

He was still giving Irish the once-over. "Oh, that's always the fault of the rider," he said, seeming not to notice Briar's outraged glance as he bent down to inspect the slight thickening over the big gelding's left front tendon, the injury that had ended Irish's chances at the racetrack forever.

"I see he's hurt himself at one time," he commented, straightening. "He must have had good care, because it doesn't show in his stride."

Was the man oblivious to her annoyance? Briar had always thought the English had excellent manners; now she was beginning to wonder. Still seething at his previous comment about rushing being the rider's fault, she was tempted to challenge him to take the horse and prove he could do better. Prudence stopped her. Aside from the fact that she never allowed anyone else to ride Irish, she couldn't take the chance. Irish hated all men. Having been abused by the man who had owned him previously, the big gelding barely permitted males to work around him; the one time she'd tried to let someone ride him Irish had pitched such a fit that the man had been thrown. The same thing happened on the second, and the third, and the fourth, tries. By that time, both the prospective rider and the horse were drenched with sweat, and Briar didn't think it was worth it just to prove a point. Since then, she had politely but firmly rejected all offers, male and female, to ride her horse.

"Say," Stefan Yager said just then, "d'you mind if I try him?"

"As a matter of fact—" she started to say, but to her renewed annoyance, he grinned at her again.

"I'll understand if you say no; it's a bit forward of me to ask to ride someone else's mount, but I really would like to try. Not that I think I could do any better, I assure you," he said hastily, seeing her expression. "But he's a fine animal, and I do admire good horseflesh."

Well, really! That boyish grin might influence airheads like Amber or Gretchen, but Briar wasn't fooled. It was right on the tip of her tongue to tell this arrogant so-and-so that Irish didn't like men and wouldn't let one in the saddle for a second, but then she suddenly decided to teach him a lesson instead.

"Of course you may ride him," she said, kicking out of her irons and swinging over to drop gracefully to the ground. With a sweet smile, she handed over the bridle. "Be my guest."

"I won't take a minute, I promise," he said, and vaulted lightly into the saddle. Gathering up the reins, he looked down at her. "D'you mind if I take a few fences with him?"

Irish rolled his eyes the instant he felt the man's weight on his back. Catching a glimpse of her horse beginning to pin his ears as well, Briar felt guilty enough to say, "I wouldn't—"

She was too late. Irish had gone from rolling his eyes and pinning his ears to humping his back. Briar could tell that he was getting ready to throw a fit, and she started to warn Stefan, but the man just laughed and winked down at her.

"A bit keyed up, I think, wouldn't you say?" he said, sitting there calmly, not moving an inch in the saddle as the gelding suddenly leaped forward, trying to unseat him.

This wasn't funny now, and Briar said worriedly, "I think—"

"Oh, we'll be all right," Stefan said unconcernedly, as Irish lunged forward again. Unruffled, he gathered up the reins, giving the glossy neck a pat. "Now then," he said. "Let's see what a fine, strong horse like yourself is made of."

He barely touched his heel to Irish's flank before they were off. Fighting the urge to put her hands over her eyes, Briar forced herself to watch. But the rodeo she had cringingly anticipated failed to materialize. To her amazement, after lunging around and fighting for his head for a moment or two, while Stefan just sat there waiting him out, her big horse settled down into his beautiful long-strided canter. Briar was so entranced at the sight that she forgot to be fearful or angry and just stared. She had seen videos of herself on Irish, but she had never seen anyone else ride him, and as he literally sailed over the first jump Stefan set him to, she drew in a sharp breath. Irish had never jumped like that, even with her.

The rest of the course was just the same. Irish took every jump as if he had wings on his heels, while Stefan crouched gracefully over his back like he'd been born there. Briar couldn't even see him asking for an adjustment in stride or a change in lead; every cue was so subtle that it was as if horse and rider were reading each other's minds. She had never seen anything like it, and when Stefan set Irish at the last jump, the difficult fan that was five-foot-ten on one end, with a seven-foot spread at the other, it was as though a camera clicked behind her eyes. She knew she would forever have that beautiful picture in her mind of horse and man rising to meet the jump over the highest part; even after it was so quickly over, she could still see Stefan Yager leaning effortlessly forward, his hands loose on the reins, giving Irish his head in the air . . . and her horse with his ears pricked and his front legs curled beneath him, powerful haunches lifting them both up and forward. It was as if they had been sailing toward the sky.

Then it was over, and Irish had cleared the jump, and they were coming around toward her. Even before Stefan pulled him to a halt a few strides away, Briar saw his expression; she knew just how he felt. She had been impressed just watching; how much more glorious the feeling to have been in the saddle.

But if she had expected Stefan Yager to rhapsodize, the illusion vanished the moment he opened his mouth. Instead of telling her what a magnificent ride he'd had, or what a beautiful animal Irish was, Stefan kicked out of the stirrups, swung a leg over, and dropped lithely to the ground.

"Here," he said, handing her the reins. "You try. I think if you just check him a little about a half stride ahead of the place where you did before, he won't rush those fences so much. What d'you say? Would you like a leg up?"

Briar couldn't believe that he could dismiss an experience like that so lightly. Her horse had been glorious, magnificent. If Stefan Yager lived to be a hundred and ten, he would *never* have a ride quite like that again.

"No, I don't want a leg up," she said, outraged. "I think my horse has had enough for the day, and I know *I* certainly have. Good day, Mr. Yager. I wish I could say it's been a pleasure."

And with that, she turned on her booted heel and left the ring, leading Irish behind her. She could feel Stefan's puzzled glance on her back, and she lifted her chin, refusing to give him the satisfaction of looking around again, thinking that if he was going to treat everyone here so cavalierly, he certainly wouldn't last long.

But after she had cooled off her horse, brushed him down, put him away, and left the club, she was still thinking about that encounter with Stefan Yager. Increasingly irritated with herself, she seemed preoccupied with a man she had thoroughly disliked.

"Arrogant bastard," she muttered, on the way home. But she knew she would never forget that breathtaking sight of Stefan Yager and Irish taking that last jump. It was a picture that was ingrained in her mind forever, and most annoying of all, she wasn't sure which had entranced her most: the horse . . . or the rider.

---

# CHAPTER SIX

Stefan Yager was tired as he finished up at the riding club that night. But he couldn't leave without doing a last "walk around," as he had called it when he'd managed Lord Bowen's racing stable in England, so despite his weariness, he finished his chores by walking slowly down one side of the big barn aisle, and then up the other, looking in at the horses contentedly munching the remnants of their dinners. When he came to the large corner stall at the end, he stopped to study the big bay gelding inside nosing his hay. He'd always had an eye for good horseflesh, and this one had caught his eye the first day. But then, he thought wryly, this particular horse would have been hard to miss. In addition to his size and near-perfect conformation, Irish Coffee possessed that rich, black-cherry-colored coat so prized in bays—and an attitude that made him stand out even more. Of all the horses here, only Irish seemed to feel he *deserved* the best stall on the place. Every time Stefan had seen one of the grooms leading the gelding out to the hot walker for exercise, he'd been arching his neck and prancing along as if saying, Hey, look at me. Amused at such antics, Stefan had idly wondered who owned such a beautiful horse.

Well, now he knew. His smile turned into a wince when he recalled what had happened out at the jump ring earlier today. He stepped away from the stall and glanced once more down the length of the aisle to make sure everything was as it should be. All was quiet, so he switched off the main lights. Floodlights, one at each end, and another in the middle, still provided illumination; unlike their counterparts in the wild, these expensive, pampered, elegant creatures did not sleep in the dark.

Wearily rubbing the back of his heck, Stefan left the barn and went through the gate to the private path that led to the employees' quarters. Although he had protested that he didn't need an entire trailer to himself, Stan had insisted that he take the one the former instructor had used. He would have been just as happy bunking down somewhere in the big house up the hill where Stan and his friend, Gary, lived, but Stan wouldn't hear of it.

"It's not that Gary and I wouldn't love your company," Stan had said, giving him the key and pushing him in the trailer's direction. "But you need your privacy, and we need ours." He paused. "If you know what I mean."

He had, so he accepted the key. If Stan and his lover wanted to be alone, he wasn't about to argue. The horse world was filled with homosexuals, and he had learned long ago that if he left them alone, they'd return the favor. Besides, he liked Stan, and there was no denying that in his heyday on the USET, Stan Taber had been a great rider. They had met at a polo match outside London, and while Stan denied it to this day, it had been Stefan's ragtag team that had soundly trounced the fancy Americans. Of course, that had been many years ago—and about thirty extra pounds around Stan's middle—but they'd been friends all the time since.

He was feeling every one of those years tonight. Two of his lessons today, Amber and later another blonde—he never could remember her name—had made him question just how far the bounds of friendship with Stan should go. One of them had coyly allowed her overmatched horse to run away with her, and then sat there, screaming her head off, holding on to the saddle and letting the reins fly while he tried to catch the damned thing. The other woman had nearly come off during a minuscule jump, stopped the horse, then proceeded to fling herself right into his arms, shrieking that she'd nearly been killed. It had been exhausting.

Wondering what had been in his mind when he told Stan he'd be glad to take over while his old friend looked around for another instructor, he knew he was stuck for a while now.

After all, Stan was doing him a favor by letting him stay here
until he decided what to do next, so the least he could do was
return the courtesy by giving a few lessons. But these women
here, he thought, shaking his head. Amber and the other woman
weren't the only ones; the place was filled with females who had
elegant horses and expensive tack and extravagant outfits—all
the right accoutrements—but he'd swear that if some of them
hadn't had a groom to help out, they'd put the saddle on backward and try to bridle the horse's tail. And once they *were*
mounted, it was bounce, bounce, bounce, and *squeal* over a
two-foot jump, letting the horse have its head and run out, so
that he had to ride the beast afterward to correct all those
bad habits before they came around full circle with the next
lesson. To make matters even more exasperating, he knew that
all the while he was telling them during their lesson to straighten
their back or drop their heels, or for God's sake, look *up*, what
they were really interested in was how fetching they looked in
their tight jodhpurs and black boots and stylish hats.

All except one, he thought suddenly, coming to an abrupt stop
on the top trailer step. Today out at the jump ring, Briar Mc-
Kenna hadn't seemed to care what anyone thought, least of all
him. Jesus, what a fool he'd made of himself with her; every
time he thought about it, he wanted to crawl right into a hole. I
think if you just pull him up a half stride he won't rush his
fences, he'd said. Or, even worse, D'you mind if I have a go?
This type of thing is always the fault of the rider, you know. . . .

Remembering it now, he squeezed his eyes shut. No wonder
she had acted as if she'd turned up a rock. He'd deserved that
acid in her voice, and more. What in the blazing hell had he
been thinking?

Well, he knew what he'd been thinking of, didn't he? If he
hadn't been so surprised to see a rider of her caliber, he would
have just minded his own business. But when he'd seen her in
that jump ring, he hadn't been able to help himself. Even now
he had a mental picture of her taking that Liverpool calm as
you please, she and that beautiful horse rising into the air in
perfect form, almost as if they had been one. He hadn't even
seen her face until then; he had been so impressed by her riding
that he'd stopped to stare. Then, when she had turned Irish
toward him and he saw her fully for the first time, something
had come over him. . . .

Yes, and what? he asked himself caustically. You couldn't

have acted more the schoolboy if you'd tried. Did you show off enough for her, lad? Did you make a big enough fool of yourself trying?

Muttering a curse, he reached for the trailer door. Even though he had the key, he rarely locked it; after years of travel, going back and forth to races, living "down under" for a while, and then coming to America earlier this year, he had learned to travel light. In fact, he'd often been amused at the notion that the horses who traveled with him packed more gear than he did; it had been enough trouble worrying about their stuff without keeping track of his.

The only thing of value he owned in the trailer, besides some tack and his good boots, were the papers he'd found in the attic of his grandmother's house in Kent after she died earlier in the year. But since he was the only one who understood the significance of those, he wasn't worried they'd be stolen, especially when he had put the really important documents, the marriage certificate and such, in a safe deposit box at the bank. After all this time, he wasn't going to take the chance that those would be taken, not until he cleared things up. When he had found those documents and decided to come to America to see for himself if what he'd learned that day in Nona's attic was true, he didn't know what kind of people he'd be dealing with, so he'd taken precautions. It turned out that it was just as well he did; one meeting with that family was enough to make him glad he'd put those papers safely away.

But it was just as fruitless thinking about that meeting as the one he'd had with Briar McKenna today. What was done was done, as Nona would have said, and on that thought, he pulled open the screen door and went inside.

As always, it was like an oven in this tin box; no matter how wide he cranked the windows, sitting in the sun all day even with the ocean breeze, the trailer seemed to soak up the heat like a sponge. He could feel beads of sweat popping out on his face, so he grabbed a beer from the tiny refrigerator and went outside again, pulling the top as he went. Some battered lawn furniture was scattered about on the tiny patch of grass that served as a lawn, and he sat down in one of the chairs, reaching out with his heel to drag another closer so he could put his feet up. His legs were tired from riding those spoiled horses all day and getting them back into form—except Irish, he thought with a brief smile, who didn't need retuning at all, only a firm hand.

He wanted to take his boots off, but he just didn't have the energy. Throwing his head back, he drained half the beer in one swig and settled deeper into the chair with a heavy sigh.

Lord, he was tired, he thought, and it wasn't because of all the lessons he'd given that day; that was nothing compared to the hard work he used to put in every day training his runners. It wasn't so much a physical weariness as a tiredness of the spirit, he thought, resting his head on the back of the chair. Looking up at the sky, he wondered what in the hell he was doing here. Now that he'd seen a glimpse of what he was up against, it seemed he'd come on a fool's errand after all, just as Samantha had said.

Then he was impatient with himself again. Now, why'd he have to think of Samantha right now, on top of everything else? Didn't he have enough problems without recalling all that? He could still remember their last quarrel. Even though he'd known long before then that it was over between them, he wished things had ended differently. He hadn't wanted to hurt her, but what could he do? And admit it, he thought: in his heart of hearts, he knew that she'd been relieved, too. His coming to America wasn't the last straw; it was the excuse they'd needed to let it go and get on with their lives. They weren't suited, never had been; it had been a mistake to think otherwise.

"You're a bloody fool if you think diggin' into the past is going to make any difference now!" she'd flung at him bitterly as he was packing to go. Her pale skin was blotched from crying, her pale blue eyes red from tears. Seeing her mouth an ugly, hard slash, he'd looked at her, wondering how he'd ever thought her beautiful. It must have been her thick, honey-colored blond hair that reached all the way to the small of her back, swaying mysteriously when she walked.

But no longer, he'd thought. When she realized he really meant to go to America without her, she'd raced to the hair-dresser who had hacked it all off. Now it was sticking up in spikes about an inch from her scalp, as hard and stiff as she'd become herself. He couldn't understand it; she had always been so proud of her hair.

"That may be so," he said as she faced him with her hands on her hips, looking hateful as could be. "But I have to try."

"For what?" she'd cried. "D'you really think those stories your granny told you were true? Even if they are, what d'you think you'll gain? Is it money, is that what you want? Do you think they'll give you a pile just because you show up on their doorstep? You're daft if you do; they'll never go for it!''

He finished packing his bag. It was only a duffle; he'd either sold or given everything else away. If he was going, he meant to make this a clean break, so he wouldn't be tempted to come back with his tail between his legs.

"You wouldn't understand," he said, hefting the bag. "It's something I have to do."

"You're a bloody fool!" she shrieked.

On some level, he had agreed. "You're not saying anything I haven't thought of myself, but I still have to go."

"Why? Because of that crazy old woman who just died? You don't owe her anything!"

"Leave Nona out of it!"

His ferocity silenced her, but not for long. Her voice rising again, she cried, "She asked you to do this didn't she? Well, if she did, you're a bigger fool than I thought for believing such rubbish! You of all people should know that she didn't know what she was saying half the time—and the other half she just made up whatever came to mind! You said it many times yourself!"

He couldn't argue, especially when over the past few years, his grandmother Nona, who had cared for him ever since his parents had died in a bombing raid over London during the war, had become increasingly confused. But then, she'd never really been right since the time when the country was at war; he knew it, and the rest of the neighborhood knew it, too. But she was a harmless, gentle old lady, and he owed her everything. If she hadn't taken him in, God knew what would have happened. So who cared if she told her stories? He had always listened, only pretending to believe . . . until he had found the trunk in the attic after she died.

At first he hadn't paid much attention, he remembered; the trunk just seemed like an old box filled with odd things. He'd been tempted just to put the whole thing in the trash, but it seemed irreverent to do that, so he had forced himself to sort through the contents. Later he was glad he had, and not just because of the papers he had found at the bottom. The faded dance programs, the brittle ribbons, the papery petals from some long-forgotten but treasured bouquet assumed an even greater poignancy that day. As he had carefully held delicate items so old they nearly crumbled at his touch, he could almost see his grandmother as a girl with hopes and dreams and a future that had been destroyed in one swift raid during the war.

More than his parents had been killed that night; Nona's husband, his grandfather, Rudy, had died, together with Stefan's mother, Maura, and his father, Retton, home briefly on leave. Nona had told him that she'd nearly lost her mind when she'd returned from watch duty that night and found the entire neighborhood in ruins; if she hadn't discovered him in the rubble, barely six months old at the time, she said she didn't know what she would have done.

There was so little in the wreckage that had once been a block of flats. The only things Nona had saved were some singed baby clothes, a few crocheted doilies, a crib quilt with stitches so tiny and perfect they were almost invisible—and those startling documents, carefully put away in a tin box that had survived the bombing.

But it was the quilt that had made tears come to his eyes. Even up to the end, he couldn't recall a time when Nona hadn't had something in her hands, knitting or mending—some kind of sewing. She was the perfect grandmother, soft and round and endlessly sweet and patient—a woman who might be confused about other things, but never about her love for him.

And he loved her, he thought, remembering all the childish battles he'd waged on her behalf. As children will do of someone they don't understand, who seems . . . not quite right in the head, an occasional schoolmate made fun of her—but only once in his hearing. He couldn't count the fights he'd been in defending Nona's honor; to the day she died, he'd felt that he was the parent and not the other way around.

Then he had found the tin box, tucked away in a corner of the trunk. It had held pictures, tintypes even, of stern, unsmiling people he didn't know, but who had obviously meant something to Nona. He had even found a faded announcement of his own birth and some pictures he knew were of his parents, although he'd been far too young to remember them.

At the bottom of the box, he had found the papers. He'd known they were important even before he took out the faded, stained, heavy envelope. The glue was brittle and old, and when the envelope fell open, he was almost afraid to look. He had never admitted it to anyone, even Samantha, but he had always hoped, somewhere deep in his heart, that Nona's stories were true—for her sake, if nothing else. When he saw the papers that day and realized what they meant, he'd been so excited he hadn't known what to do. To think that his dear, sweet little grandmother had been right about this all these years! He wasn't conscious of making the decision at that moment, but that was when he knew he had to come to America. Nona had loved her husband—his grandfather, Rudy—dearly; she would have wanted Stefan to try to put things right.

Samantha hadn't believed he was serious about giving up everything and going to America; when she realized he really meant to do it, she was appalled and then outraged.

"I can't believe you're actually going to leave," she'd cried. "How can you just give everything up because a crazy old woman filled your head with fairy tales?"

He was tired of talking about it, fighting about it, feeling he had to explain about it. If Samantha didn't understand now, when his bags were packed, he thought wearily, she never would.

"She was right about this," he said as he went to the door of the flat.

"You're really going to go?"

He turned to look at her one last time. "I'm sorry, Sam," he said.

"Sorry! *Sorry!* I'll show you sorry!" she screamed, and grabbed the nearest thing to hand, the tea mug out of which she'd been drinking before the quarrel started. She flung it as hard as she could toward him, and he just barely skipped out and slammed the door when it crashed against the wood. Unscathed outside, he debated. He and Samantha had loved each other once; they'd talked about spending the rest of their lives together. Maybe he shouldn't walk out without giving it another chance. Then he shook his head. It was no good; they both knew that. He'd given it chance after chance, and it still hadn't worked. It was time to call it quits.

Thousands of miles and weeks away from that last quarrel with Samantha, Stefan sighed and crushed the beer can in his hand. He supposed he should go in and do something about dinner, but he didn't have the energy to see what there was to eat, and he wasn't really hungry anyway. Remembering Samantha had spoiled his appetite, and he sat back again, wishing he had another beer, or at the least, that he hadn't given up smoking. Thinking a cigarette would taste good right now, he tried to distract himself by looking up at the tall pines around him. Through the dark green branches he could see the sky already being tinted gold by the setting sun, and he felt affected by the sight despite his gloomy mood. This close to the beach, the sunsets were glorious things when the fog wasn't in, and it was so clear and beautiful tonight that he wished he had someone to share it with.

Then a face popped into his mind, and he frowned. Now what had made him think of Briar McKenna again, he asked himself irritably. Wasn't it enough that he'd relived the hash he'd made of things with one woman? Why torture himself with how big a fool he'd looked in front of another? Suffice to say, he thought darkly, that that was the last time he'd engage in a manly little display to prove how superior he was. The damned horse had almost unseated him, and if it had, he would have had only himself to blame.

He was just about to go inside and see about making a sandwich or something after all when he heard footsteps crunching the pine needles on the path to the trailer. It was almost dark by that time, and he turned curiously just as Stan Taber emerged from the trees.

"You forget to pay the light bill, or are you communing by yourself in the dark?" Stan asked, as he came up.

Still tall, but no longer lean, Stan didn't ride much anymore. Thoroughbreds were too high-strung, he claimed and Warmbloods took too much energy. He preferred to lounge at the sidelines and shout instructions in case anyone was listening. Much easier on the body, and on the nerves. Stefan still thought it a pity; in his younger years, Stan Taber had been one of the best riders he'd ever seen, and he suspected that it was lingering memories of a bad accident that kept his old friend out of the saddle rather than his increasing girth. Years ago, a bad fall at a seven-foot wall had effectively ended his competitive career when he'd had to be carried out of the arena with a crushed pelvis, broken hip, both legs broken in several places, and various cuts and bruises. Even at that, he'd fared better than the horse, a big-hearted mare named Silvana Simone, who'd had to be put down immediately. Even after months of recovery and painful therapy, he had walked with a slight limp. He had bummed around Europe for a while, eventually settling here and starting the stable after he'd met Gary, an investment counselor who put up the money.

"Hi, Stan," Stefan said. "Would you like a beer?"

Even in the darkness, Stan looked horrified. "You're offering me *beer*? I'll take a glass of Montrachet, if you have it, chilled to a temperature of—"

Stefan smiled. "Sorry, old boy. It's beer or nothing."

"Well, in *that* case—"

"One beer coming up," Stefan said, standing.

As Stefan headed toward the trailer, Stan glanced around for a chair that didn't look as if it would collapse as soon as he sat on it, and said, "Good heavens. I didn't realize things were so shabby here. What did the last fellow do, use these as part of a cross-country course?"

"Take heart," Stefan said with a grin. "The inside of the trailer is even better."

"And to think I forced you to accept my hospitality," the other man replied, gingerly sitting down. "How grateful you must be."

"I've lived in worse."

"Not much, I'll bet," Stan said, and sniffed. "Well, it's obvious that I'm going to have to have a little chat with Gary about this. We can't have our members thinking the club has gone to wrack and ruin."

Stefan came out with the beers. Laughing, he tossed one over. "I don't think you'll have to worry. This is employee territory. No self-respecting member of the club would be caught dead down here."

Stan popped the top of his can. "Oh, I don't know," he commented. "I'm sure I've seen a few feminine glances following the new trainer as he makes his rounds. I doubt you'd have much trouble persuading some of the more . . . er . . . *curious* down to your lair. Tiffany Ginsmore, for one . . ."

"So that's her name," Stefan muttered, sitting down again. "I don't know why I can't remember it. The blonde, right?"

"Aren't they all?" Stan said, sipping delicately from the can. "Except one, of course."

"Oh, who's that?"

"My, my, such a casual attitude. Do you really think you're going to fool *me*, my boy? You and I go back a lot of years."

"So we do. I still don't have any idea who you're talking about."

"*Whom*. The correct pronoun is *whom*," Stan said loftily. "And you know very well *whom* I'm talking about, so don't be coy. It doesn't suit you nearly as well as it does me."

Laughing, Stefan gave in. "All right, I do know *whom* you're talking about. Briar McKenna, right?"

"Right!" Stan said approvingly. "I knew if I gave you enough time, you'd come up with it. Well, what do you think? I saw you in the jump ring with her today—"

"What do you do, scan everyone with binoculars?"

Stan smirked. "Well, one can hardly miss that gorgeous horse of hers." Innocently, he added, "I have to admit, I was surprised to see you up. Until now, Ms. McKenna has never let anyone else near her saddle, much less her horse. You two must have hit it off."

"Hit it off? I wouldn't say that. For a minute there, I thought she was going to deck me."

"But she did let you ride her horse, and that's never happened before—not to my knowledge, anyway."

"Yeah, well don't get excited. She was probably hoping the beast would kill me."

"Ah, the infamous Yager charm at work again, I see. What did you say to her?"

Embarrassed, Stefan growled, "If you must know, I told her she was rushing her fences a little, that's all."

Stan raised an eyebrow. "That's *all*?" He shook his head. "Well, I must say, you do know how to make an impression."

"I wasn't trying to."

"Obviously. I take it you have no idea who our Ms. Briar McKenna really is."

"No, I don't."

"And you're going to try and tell me you don't care, either, right?"

"Right."

"Okay."

Stefan waited a minute, but when Stan just sat there, companionably sipping at his beer, he said impatiently, "All right. Who is she?"

Stan shook his head dolefully. "You Brits. Don't you ever pay attention to what's going on over here?"

"No, we've got enough of our own problems. Besides, we have the royal family, so it's you Yanks who are more interested in us."

"Not true, not true."

Stefan didn't want to argue the silly point. "So tell me," he said. "What's so special about Briar McKenna?"

"Apart from the fact that she's a beautiful woman who knows how to sit a horse, you mean?"

"Yeah," Stefan said dryly. "Apart from that."

"Well, in addition to being quite a successful woman in her own right, our Ms. McKenna was married to Hayden Lord, of Lord Industries," Stan said, and paused. "And please don't tell me that you haven't heard of Lord Industries, or my faith in you will be shattered forever."

Despite himself, Stefan was impressed. He remembered reading an article some time ago about Hayden Lord, the industrialist who had rocked the business world back in the early seventies with his blistering indictments on industrial waste. In fact, if he recalled correctly, Lord Industries had been a pioneer in recycling and alternate energy sources, as well as instituting new guidelines for pollution control.

"As a matter of fact, I have heard of Lord Industries," he said. "I've even heard of Hayden Lord. But I didn't realize Briar McKenna was his wife."

"Was is the operative word," Stan said. "Hayden Lord died a couple of months ago. Leaving, I might add, his entire estate to his wife."

Stefan sat back. "Wow."

"Wow, indeed," Stan said, and looked at him curiously. "It was in all the papers. Didn't you see it?"

Stefan was still feeling a little taken aback. "No, I don't have time to read," he said. "You've got me working from sunup to sunset."

"That reminds me, I did come to ask you something."

"What's that?"

For the first time, Stan seemed uncomfortable. "I know we said when you took on this job that it would be only temporary, but I . . . er . . . Well, that is—"

Stefan had never known Stan Taber to be tongue-tied about anything, and he said, "Don't keep me in suspense here, Stan. What's up? Do you want me to push on, is that it? Have you found another instructor? If so, that's—"

"No, no, it isn't that!" Stan said quickly, appalled. "Oh, dear, I knew I'd make a mess of it! I wanted Gary to ask, but he said it would be better from me, because you and I are friends—''

"Stan!"

"Yes, yes, get to the point, right? Well, the point is that we were both wondering if you might consider staying on permanently," Stan said, and held up his hand. "Now, just hear me out, all right? You've always said that teaching wasn't your thing, but I've been watching you, and you're damned good at it. I'm not the only one who thinks so, either. Every one of your students has nothing but praise for your methods."

"That's a surprise," Stefan said dryly. "Since I haven't gone to bed with any of them, despite those come-hither looks."

"Your private life is your own affair," Stan said primly.

"My private life is nonexistent," Stefan retorted. "But aside from that, I have to say that praise from the bored, rich women who alternate between taking riding lessons, shopping at Rodeo Drive, and suntanning to mummydom at the beach, isn't something I regard as a high achievement. For your sake, I'm glad they're pleased with the way I give lessons, but I—''

"You were going to hear me out," Stan said, injured.

Closing his mouth, Stefan sat back. "Sorry. Go ahead."

Stan leaned forward. "Now, I don't know why you felt compelled to leave your very successful racing stable over *there*," he said, and added hastily, "and I don't want to know. That's your business, after all. But the fact is, you're here, and since I've known you the better part of twenty years, I really can't see you just drifting around the rest of your life."

Despite their long-standing friendship, Stefan hadn't really told Stan the entire truth about why he had come. Now he started to say, "I hadn't either, b—''

"Do I still have the floor, or don't I?"

"Sorry," Stefan muttered with a sigh. "Go on."

"All right, thank you, I will. Now, after talking it over with Gary, who agrees absolutely with me, I've come to offer you a proposition."

Warily, Stefan asked, "What's that?"

Stan took a deep breath. "First, I want to say that no matter what you decide, Gary and I are very grateful for the way you've helped out. In fact, we both feel that you're such an asset here that we . . . that we want to offer you a partnership."

Stefan was totally taken aback. This was the last thing he had expected, and he stammered a little when he said, "Well, Stan, I . . . I don't know what to say."

"Don't say anything yet," Stan said. "I know it's sudden, but I want you to think about it. If you agree—and both Gary and I hope you will—we can work out the financial details later. Right now, I just wanted to present you with the offer." He paused. "You *will* think about it, won't you?"

What could he say to that? Touched more than he wanted to admit, Stefan put out his hand. "Sure, I'll think about it. Thanks."

Returning the handshake with a relieved grin, Stan said, "Whew, I'm glad that's over. I wasn't sure how you'd take it."

"What do you mean? It's quite an offer."

"You haven't heard the financial details."

Smiling Stefan said, "You might have been a fierce competitor, but you always were a sportsman."

"You never saw the times when I lost. I'd leave the ring and go back to the hotel and throw myself on the bed and cry."

"Well, you never did it in front of anyone else."

"What? And have my adoring public think I was a piece of fluff?"

Stefan laughed. "Well, you never lost that many times."

"Nor did you, my friend," Stan said, and paused. "Now that I've humbled myself in front of you, d'you mind if I ask a personal question?"

"Ask. I might not answer."

"First, let me say that I know you have every right to be annoyed, because it's really none of my business, but we have been friends for a long time, and when you said you'd just *left* that racing stable in England, well, I have to admit that my curiosity was aroused, so I did a little checking—just a few phone calls to a few old friends, that's all," Stan explained hastily. "But I did find out that Lord Bowen apparently doted on you, and you were beating everything in sight with those horses of his, and doing very well, so it seemed, if you'll pardon my saying so, inexplicable of you to just leave like that, and I wondered if . . . if you were in trouble, or something. If you are, let me help, Steve. As I said, we've been friends for a long time, and you've helped me out of a jam or two."

Exasperated and touched at the same time, Stefan shook his

head. But he still wasn't ready to tell Stan everything. "I appreciate the offer, I do. But I'm not in any trouble, and I really don't need any help. It was just . . . time for a change, I guess."

In the growing darkness, he couldn't see Stan's expression, but he knew he'd hurt his friend's feelings when Stan repeated, "Time for a change. I see."

Now he felt like a heel. Leaning forward, he said, "Look, Stan, it's just that I . . . I had something to do here, and I couldn't do it and run the stables over there, too."

Stan was silent for a moment. Finally, he said quietly, "Do you want to talk about it?"

"Not right now," Stefan said honestly. "But when I can, I will."

"And you're not in trouble."

"No, it's nothing like that, I promise you. It's just . . . something I have to do."

As Stan had pointed out, they had known each other for a long time. When Stefan didn't offer anything more, he nodded and got to his feet. "All right. But if you need anything— anything at all—you know where to find me."

Stefan stood, offering his hand again. "Thanks, Stan, I'll remember that."

"And don't forget about our offer."

"I won't."

"All right, then, I can't ask for more than that," Stan said. "Good night, I'll see you tomorrow."

"Right," Stefan said, and watched his friend take the dark path through the trees. But even after Stan had disappeared, he didn't go inside. At this time of night, the darkness seemed to mute the endless roar of the surf, but he could still hear its comforting sound in the background, and for a moment he debated about taking a late ride on the beach. A quick run or gallop always cleared his mind, and he'd often taken one of the horses out at home and ridden up to the moor and let the animal have his head. He didn't have such luxury here, and just for an instant he was hit with a wave of homesickness so strong he wondered again what he was doing here. Stan was right, he thought; he had burned all his bridges behind him . . . and for what?

"You think they'll open their arms and take you in, just 'cause of who you say you are?" Samantha had sneered. "When they realize what it is you've got up your sleeve, they'll fight you all the way, boyo. It won't be as easy as you think, you'll see! You'll see!''

Stefan sighed. Samantha had been more right than she realized. It wasn't going to be easy at all. In fact, he thought, remembering that one meeting he'd already had with Rupert and Carl Jaeger, if he'd read them right, things could get downright ugly if he persisted. It might be better just to forget about it and take Stan up on his offer, he thought. He could do worse, far worse . . . and probably would, before this was over.

Sighing heavily, he was about to go inside when he heard a far-off nicker from the barn. It came carried on the breeze that had blown up, and suddenly a face flashed into his mind again, and he was remembering Briar McKenna as he'd first seen her. He'd come around the path to the jump ring just as she was taking that vertical, and he'd stopped instantly, nearly transfixed. He'd jumped a few in his time before he got involved with running horses; in his career, he'd seen the finest horses and riders in the world. In addition, he had watched awesome competitions that challenged even the finest over the toughest courses man could imagine.

But he had never seen a sight that thrilled him more than his first glimpse of Briar and Irish Coffee taking that particular jump. In his mind's eye, he saw that big bay gelding again, rising powerfully into the air in perfect form . . . and Briar leaning over his neck, her lips slightly open. There had been such a glow on her face that to watch her had almost made him ache.

---

# CHAPTER SEVEN

Briar had just finished getting dressed when the doorbell rang. The annual fund-raiser for the American Horse Owners Association was tonight, and because she'd served on the board before, and had supported the organization during the days of her own competition, she hadn't been able to beg off. Because Hay had gone with her the past five years, many of the people who would be there tonight were sure to speak of him, and the thought of facing another gathering where she would be the recipient of all those pitying glances and sympathetic pats made her shudder. But when the president of the association had called personally to ask if she'd be there, he'd sounded so sincere that she hadn't had the heart to refuse him. Before she knew it, she had agreed to go.

The doorbell rang again as she was finishing her lipstick, and she frowned, thinking that she didn't have time for visitors. If she didn't leave soon, she was going to be late. Besides, she wasn't expecting anyone. Hoping this wasn't another of those sympathy calls designed to keep her from feeling depressed, she stepped back from the mirror and gave herself a last, quick inspection. The fund-raiser was a formal one, so she was wearing a floor-length gown in a sheath design that tonight emphasized how much weight she'd lost. But her figure wasn't what caught her eye; she was looking at the gown itself—a silver-beaded black velvet that had been one of Hay's favorites. She hadn't thought of that until now, but once she remembered how complimentary he had been when she first wore it, she wanted to take it off and select something else. Standing in the middle of the room, she briefly shut her eyes. Damn it, it was these little things that caught you unawares, she thought.

The doorbell rang a third time while she was standing there, and when she glanced quickly at the clock, she realized she didn't have time to change anyway. She'd just have to wear this and hope that no one else commented on how much Hay had loved her in black. She grabbed her beaded evening bag and a heavy silvery silk shawl—she had always refused absolutely to wear fur, a decision with which Hay had concurred—before going downstairs.

To her surprise when she opened the front door, her stepson Jaz was there, dressed to kill in a tuxedo with a magenta cummerbund and matching tie. With one hand, he flicked away the cigarette he'd been smoking; with the other, he held out a gold foil corsage box with the grin that seemed to drive so many women wild. Tanned and blond, with a lean jaw and a devilish look in his blue eyes, Briar's stepson was thirty years old, but sometimes seemed to Briar to be more like eighteen. Technically a junior vice president in charge of production at Lord Industries, he spent most of his time at various beaches or ski slopes around the world, although he'd been careful when his father was alive to put in an occasional appearance at one of the company offices scattered throughout the country. Hay hadn't been fooled, but Jaz was his only son, and, as he had confided to Briar, at least he could keep an eye on him this way. Briar thought it was a waste, but she had wisely kept her opinions to herself.

Still, while she and Jaz were poles apart in everything from work ethics to political beliefs, she had always liked him. Unlike his sister, Fredrica, Jaz didn't care what anyone thought; he wouldn't have minded if the entire world believed he was an unproductive, spoiled, pampered, rich ne'er-do-well. He was; he readily admitted it. Furthermore, he enjoyed indulging himself; otherwise, what was the point? One had to smile, Briar thought, in the face of such blithe disregard. And if she wanted to be honest, a part of her envied him.

Still holding out the foil box, which Briar saw contained a black orchid corsage, Jaz bowed. "Your driver is here, madam," he drawled. He gestured over his shoulder at his silver Lamborghini parked in the drive. "And your carriage awaits. Shall we be off?"

Jaz always had been able to make her laugh with his nonsense. But then she had always been immune to his charm. How could she not be, having been married to the master, while Jaz was only an apprentice? Every man had seemed to pale in comparison when Hayden Lord had entered a room, even his son, Briar had always thought, and maybe that was a clue to Jaz himself. Perhaps he had always subconsciously known that he could never compete with his father, so he had decided not to try. Smiling, she accepted the corsage.

"It's beautiful, Jaz," she said, admiring the expensive black orchid. "But I told you I didn't need an escort."

He raised an eyebrow. "I know what you told me, but if I let you go to something like this without taking you myself, Dad would rise up out of his grave and smite me on the spot."

Jaz had always been irreverent, and Briar had enough of a sense of humor to smile at that, too. Hay had always been a stickler for protocol and manners, and when Jaz was so inclined, he had the most beautiful manners she'd ever seen. Still, she felt obliged to offer a token protest. "Well, you've put in your appearance. I appreciate it, Jaz, but I'm sure you've got better things to do."

He gave her his mischievous look. "You know, that's what Freddie said when I told her we were going."

Remembering her last encounter with Fredrica, she said dryly, "Is that all she had to say?"

Jaz grinned. "Well, as a matter of fact, what she really said was"—He raised his voice in a perfect imitation of his sister—"It's a disgrace! Daddy hasn't been dead a month, and she's out partying!"

Despite herself, Briar felt her hackles rise. Fredrica always had known how to get her goat, and even though Briar knew she didn't have to explain herself, especially to Fredrica, she felt defensive. It didn't do any good to remind herself that Hay had been gone two months now—two months, four days, and six hours, to be precise, she thought grimly—and that this fund-raiser wasn't a party, but a worthy cause that Hay himself had supported.

"How does she do it, Jaz?" she asked.

"What's that?"

"Spoil the evening without even being here?"

Jaz laughed. "Don't worry about Freddie. She wouldn't know what fun was if it came up and bit her on the ass. Besides, tonight's for a good cause, right? So, come on—let's go. You got your keys and everything?"

With an effort, Briar shook off her annoyance. It was ridiculous to allow a comment by a vindictive, spiteful woman to affect her this way, and she managed a smile. "Yes, I'm ready. But are you *sure* you want to do this?"

"Positive," he said. "Tonight I'm all yours."

"I'm sure there's a legion of female fans out there who are going to be bitterly disappointed."

"Well, anticipation increases savor, or something like that," he said, reaching around and locking the front door. "Shall we go?"

Pinning the black orchid to her evening bag, Briar smiled. "We can take my car if you like."

He looked scandalized. "I said I'd escort you to this shindig tonight. I didn't say anything about arriving like a pauper. No, thanks, we'll take my car if you don't mind."

"Only if you promise to go the speed limit and not your usual hundred and ten miles an hour."

Opening the Lamborghini's side door for her, he dramatically crossed his heart. "Tonight, I'll be the epitome of decorum."

"I'm sure the Highway Patrol will be glad to hear that," Briar commented, while Jaz blithely slammed the door.

As he'd promised, he did go the speed limit back to the city, although he couldn't prevent an occasional mutter about the snail's pace. "The thing will be over before we get there," he grumbled once.

"Good," Briar replied. "I didn't want to go anyway."

His hand casually on the wheel, he grinned across at her. "We could cut out and go down to Monterey. I know about this beautiful little place—"

She didn't doubt that he did. "Spare me the details," she ordered, "and just keep driving."

Pretending injury, he said, "If I didn't know better, I'd think you'd been taking lessons from Freddie on how to avoid having fun."

"Well, that's a low blow."

"You're right, I'm sorry. I shouldn't say things like that, especially since Freddie is so intent on hauling you into court over Dad's will."

Hoping that Fredrica would change her mind after all, she hadn't discussed the court case with anyone but Spence. Cautiously, she said, "We've never talked about that, Jaz. How do you feel about it?"

"It's none of my business."

"But Hayden was your father."

He stared straight ahead. "Yeah, that's true. But I never expected shit from him, if you want to know the truth. I know how he felt about me."

Briar knew that Jaz and his father had never been close. In fact, every time they'd gotten together, there had been arguments, shouting, slamming of doors—on Jaz's part, she remembered. Hay just maintained a stony silence for a while, locking himself in his study until he had control again. He had never really discussed his son with her, but because she knew Hay, she had guessed how he'd felt.

"Whatever you might think, Jaz," she said quietly, "your father loved you."

Jaz barked a laugh. "Oh, yeah, right. He thought I was a good-for-nothing fuckup who had to be kept out of the way, and you know it."

"That's not true—"

"Oh, yeah, it is," he said, and looked across the seat again. Suddenly, he put his hand briefly over hers. "It's okay. I accepted long ago that I'd never measure up to what he wanted of me, so I just gave up trying. Just like he gave up trying to be a father to me. But we still got along—as long as we didn't try to get too heavy, you know. And we had some good times. It could have been worse."

How? she wondered, and was silent. This was an old argument, but to her, who had never known her family and who had dreamed so often of belonging to one, Jaz's attitude was incomprehensible no matter how many times he tried to explain it. She knew that Hay had been demanding, that his standards were high, but she couldn't fault him for that. He had wanted the best for his family, that was all, she thought; he had recognized that both his children had potential, and he had wanted to encourage that quality, not destroy it. But was that what he had inadvertently done in the end? Maybe he should have allowed Jaz to fend for himself for a while after he'd gotten kicked out of college. Maybe he shouldn't have supported Fredrica through her divorces. And what about the trusts he had established for both of them in his will? With those, Hay's children could live in luxury the rest of their lives even if they never worked a day.

But it wasn't enough, Briar thought. Now, despite her father's generosity, Fredrica was going to court to try to prove that he'd been incompetent to manage his own affairs, while Jaz simply shrugged, as if his father's memory had no value or meaning to him at all. She couldn't understand it. Was this a typical family? Maybe, she thought sadly, she'd been more fortunate being an orphan than she knew; after being a member of the Lord clan, it seemed to her that families caused more pain than even loneliness could. Perhaps it was better to belong to nothing than to be a part of something that caused grief.

"I'm still sorry you feel that way."

"Hey, life's a bitch, right?" he said with another shrug. Then he gave her an irrepressible grin. "And there have been compensations, I can't deny. The name 'Lord' does . . . er . . . open certain doors."

"Yes, I'm sure it does," she agreed. "Any new conquests lately?"

"There's always new horizons," he replied with an elaborate sigh. "So many girls, so little time, you know."

"I'll take your word for it."

"But hey, you've been busy, too, haven't you? I heard about all that property you just inherited in the wine country."

"How did you hear about it?" she asked, surprised. She wouldn't have thought Jaz was aware of anything but the condition of the surf in Waimea, or whether there was new powder at Squaw Valley.

"Oh, I have ways," he said mysteriously. "And, despite everything, I am a Lord, too, you know. So. What do you think about your windfall—or landfall, as the case may be? Have you seen it yet?"

"Yes, I drove up a few weeks ago."

"You don't sound very impressed."

"Oh, the land's beautiful, there's no denying that."

"And plenty of it, I hear. What'd you get—a hundred acres or so?"

"About that," she said, still wondering where he'd gotten his information. She hadn't discussed this with either Fredrica or Jaz, and as far as she knew, no reporter had gotten hold of it—yet. Still, she realized, everyone in the office knew, as did Spence and that investigator, Weitz. And there had been court appearances and documents and affidavits. Jaz could have found out any number of places, she decided, and shrugged it off.

"So, what are you going to do with all that acreage?" he asked, still curious. "Keep, or sell?"

"I don't know. I haven't decided."

"I'd heard it was once a horse ranch of some kind. Is that true?"

"A Thoroughbred breeding farm," she said absently, still thinking about what he'd asked earlier. She'd been putting off the question in her own mind, but she realized she'd have to face it sooner or later. What *was* she going to do with that land?

"Maybe you could build the place up again—use Irish as the foundation stallion, or something."

She burst into laughter. "Irish is a gelding!"

"Oh. That's right. Well, then he could be eunuch to a bunch of mares."

Smiling, she said, "I don't think so."

"Why not?"

"Because I have a business to run, in case you've forgotten.

Even if I were so inclined—which I'm not—I can't just drop everything to build a horse ranch.''

"I repeat. Why not?"

She shook her head. How to explain? "You haven't seen the place. It's in such disrepair that it would take months—not to mention—''

"Money?" he said carelessly. "You've got plenty of that.''

Was there just a trace of spite in his tone? Quickly she looked at him, but his face was in profile as he signaled for the turn off the freeway, and before she could ask him what he'd meant, they were pulling up in front of the Civic Center Plaza. Two valets, their eyes gleaming when they saw the silver Lamborghini pull in, came running to open the car doors. Briar got out, but Jaz waved them away.

"I'll park it," he said. "Just tell me where.''

A protest rose. "Aw, mister!"

Ignoring the valets, Jaz leaned over the seat and looked up at the amused Briar. "I'll meet you.''

Waving, she left him to care for his car and went inside. Immediately, as she had anticipated, she was engulfed by a group of well-wishers, and by the time she accepted their sympathies and managed to work her way across the main ballroom, the place was so full that she couldn't have found Jaz if she'd tried. Hoping he hadn't decided to skip the fundraiser in favor of the bar, she was wondering how soon she could decently leave when she saw a man approaching her. Lean and white-haired, with sharp features and unsettling pale eyes, he was impeccably dressed in evening clothes, as were the other men here, but there was such an . . . air about him that he seemed somehow set apart. Wondering if she was supposed to know him, she waited while he made his way toward her.

"Good evening, Ms. McKenna," he said, coming up. "I'd hoped we'd see each other here.''

Sure that she'd never seen him before, she smiled politely. "Forgive me," she said. "I don't think—''

"No, we haven't met," he said, and added as a much more familiar man came up beside him, "My name is Rupert Jaeger. You've met my son, Carl.''

Briar had already recognized Carl as the man who had annoyed her with his offer for her land that day in Sonoma.

Wondering what they were doing here, she wished she'd had time to do more than skim the report her investigator, Albert Weitz, had sent over yesterday to her office. The file was thick, filled with newspaper clippings, notes, and about a dozen typed pages. Just glancing over it, she had quickly realized there was too much material for a brief run-through, and she had put it aside to peruse more slowly when she had time. Thinking that she would have made time if she'd known the Jaegers would be here, she nodded coolly at Carl.

"Yes, I remember," she said. "What a surprise to see you here, too."

Her pointed remark wasn't lost on the younger Jaeger. Glancing at his father, he said to Briar, "If I'm not careful, you'll think I'm following you around."

Since she had been a member of this association for the past five years and hadn't seen either of these two men here before, she couldn't help asking, "*Is* that what you're doing?"

Rupert spoke up. "I hope you don't think the Jaegers are quite that rude, Ms. McKenna," he said, and then smiled disarmingly. "But I have to confess that we *did* hope you would be here tonight, so we came, too."

"And what does one have to do with the other?" she asked. She didn't know why, but she didn't like this man. He was too . . . smooth, like a crocodile slithering noiselessly down a riverbank into the water.

Rupert glanced around at the press of people. The big room was even more crowded now, and the conversation buzz had gone up several volumes, making quiet discussion impossible. "Would you mind finding a place where we can talk a bit more privately?" he asked.

Thinking that she minded a great deal, Briar was tempted to refuse and excuse herself. She suspected what he wanted to talk about, but she was curious about his approach. The son had already tried; now the father was making an attempt. What did he plan to say to convince her to sell him her land? They had already made an outrageous offer; he couldn't possibly top it.

While she debated, Carl gestured. "There's a balcony just over there."

Before she could object, Rupert took her arm. Although his head barely came to her shoulder, he gave her a courtly bow, murmuring, "Allow me."

Briar was so intrigued that she allowed him to lead her forward. With Carl opening the way, they had just started toward the balcony when Rupert leaned close to her and said, "Please accept my sympathies on the passing of your husband. He was a giant of industry, and he'll be sorely missed."

Briar looked down at him. "Thank you. Did you know Hayden?"

"Unfortunately only by reputation," Rupert replied. "Although my company and his were peripherally involved in several of the same areas, our paths never quite crossed. A regrettable circumstance, I believe. I'm told he was a fine man."

"He was," Briar agreed, and in spite of the charm, felt her guard going up. His advanced age aside, there was no doubt in her mind that Rupert Jaeger was a dangerous man, and she was wary. She had run across powerful men like him before in business, and she was keenly aware that, beneath the undeniable charisma, lurked an entirely different personality. She already knew that he desired her land; what she couldn't gauge yet was how determined he might be to get it.

"Would you like something to drink?" Rupert inquired politely, once they were outside.

To Briar's disappointment, the balcony was empty. She had hoped someone else would be here, giving her an excuse to slip away after a moment's polite conversation. Now that she was here, she was sorry her curiosity had nudged her this far; she wasn't going to discuss selling her land, not with this man, not here, not without Spence, anyway. As gallantly as he tried to disguise it, Rupert Jaeger could not hide the cold, calculating look in his pale eyes, and it disturbed her. She wasn't sure now that he wouldn't threaten her in some way if she refused to sell, and she didn't want things to get ugly.

"No, thank you," she said. "I rarely drink."

"Admirable. I wish I could say the same for Carl," Rupert commented, giving the flushed Carl a quick glance. "However, because tonight might be a cause for celebration, I think we should have champagne. Would you mind, Carl . . . ?

With a look in Briar's direction, he said tightly, "A good idea, Father. I'll be right back."

He disappeared through the doorway before Briar could object, and Rupert sighed. "I knew it was a mistake to send him to see you," he said regretfully. "When I found out how crass he'd been with that offer . . .'' He shook his head. ''No wonder you were put off. I don't blame you for refusing.''

Briar wasn't going to be taken in by the man's charm. ''If you don't mind my saying so, Mr. Jaeger,'' she said, ''that sounds suspiciously like a prelude to another offer for my property.''

Something flashed in his pale eyes, but Rupert's voice was as smooth as ever when he replied, ''I'd heard you were direct and to the point, Ms. McKenna—a trait I do admire. When a man gets to my age, time becomes even more precious—far too much to waste bandying around. Yes, you're right. I am prepared to make another offer.''

''In that case, let me save you even more time, Mr. Jaeger. I don't intend to sell.''

''Ah, but you haven't heard my proposal.''

''I don't need to hear it. I don't want to sell.''

''Every man—and woman—has her price.''

''Not in this case.''

Something gleamed in his eyes again—dislike? Briar wondered. Impatience? Or something deeper, more dangerous? Whatever it was, it was gone again in a flash, and he was saying suavely, ''Then perhaps we're not negotiating in the proper coin. I'm well aware that your husband was a wealthy man, Ms. McKenna, and California *is* a community property state. Equally important, perhaps even more so, is the fact that you are a successful businesswoman in your own right. It's obvious that you don't need the money.''

''Whether that's true or not, it's not a question of money.''

He gave her a thoughtful look. ''Indeed,'' he said. Then, ''Forgive me if I have been insulting.''

She shrugged. She knew he didn't give a damn if she forgave him or not—just as long as she sold him her land. ''Not at all, she replied. ''You made an offer; I refused. It's as simple as that.''

''Is it?'' he murmured. ''I wonder.''

Before she could ask him what he meant by that cryptic remark, Carl Jaeger returned with a waiter in tow, bearing a tray with three glasses of champagne. As the waiter bowed and offered Briar a glass, she saw the quick glance that passed between Rupert and his son. It was obvious that Carl correctly interpreted his father's expression, for he shot a dark look at

Briar, who merely gave him a cool smile. She was trying to think of a graceful exit line when the waiter departed, and Carl turned to her.

"It seems that my father was equally unsuccessful in convincing you to sell, Ms. McKenna," he said.

"That's true," she agreed calmly. "I'm just not interested in any offers right now."

"You don't understand how much this means to us!" Carl blurted. "We've been after that property for years—!"

"Now, Carl," Rupert murmured. He sounded calm, but Briar had seen the flash of anger in his eyes. "That's not really Ms. McKenna's concern."

Carl turned in outrage toward his father. "How can you say that? The property is rightfully ours, and you know it! You've been saying that for years, and if it hadn't been for that crazy old woman, things would be settled by now!"

Rupert looked coldly furious. "That's enough!"

Carl's voice was loud. "No, it's not enough! Goddamn it, I'm tired of this pussyfooting around! We did it with Juliet, and we're doing it now. The truth of the matter is that property belongs to us, and has for sixty-odd years! I'm not going to—"

Briar had heard enough. "Excuse me, gentlemen," she said. They both turned to her with surprise, as though they'd forgotten she was there. Wondering why she was even bothering with this, she asked, "What makes you think that property belongs to you?"

"We don't think it, we know it!" Carl said angrily. "We had an agreement with—"

"That's *enough*, Carl!" Rupert commanded, so sharply that the younger man immediately broke off. In furious silence, he glared at his father, but Rupert merely looked at him, and in the end, it was Carl who dropped his eyes. Draining his champagne, he set the glass angrily on the balcony rail and went out without excusing himself.

As soon as he was gone, Rupert turned smoothly to Briar. He had himself under control again, and he said calmly, "Forgive my son, Ms. McKenna. As you can see, this property of yours means a great deal to us."

"So it seems," Briar replied coolly. "Well, I'm sorry, but that's just too bad."

The muscles tightened around his eyes. "I don't think you understand. We do have a vested interest in those acres—"

"It's a little more than that, isn't it?" Briar said. "But if you truly believe that property belongs to you, why haven't you been to court about it?"

"It's not that simple."

"Why not?"

Carl returned just then, carrying a highball glass filled with dark amber liquid. From his expression, it seemed this glass wasn't his first. Buoyed by alcohol, he said aggressively, "Why are you making this is so difficult? We made you a fair offer—more than fair. You wouldn't get half that much selling it on the open market, and you know it!"

Briar could feel herself getting angry. She was tempted to try to push past him, but he was deliberately blocking the way, and she doubted that he would politely step aside. Coldly, she said, "That might be true, Mr. Jaeger—if I was interested in selling. Which, as I've said repeatedly, I am not. Now if you will excuse me, I have some people to see."

He wasn't going to let it go. "Why won't you sell? Damn it, until a few weeks ago, you didn't even know that property existed! What could it possibly mean to you?"

She was really tired of this. Her eyes flashing, she retorted, "Even if it meant nothing at all, I don't see that it's any business of yours. Now if you don't mind—"

She was annoyed enough to start brushing by him, but to her amazement, he actually grasped her arm. "You're not leaving until we settle this!"

"Take your hand off my arm," she said, her voice frigid.

His face was suffused. "We want that property!"

She looked down into his eyes. "And you think this clumsy attempt at intimidation is going to get it?"

"There are other ways."

"Is that a threat?" she asked incredulously.

"It better not be," a new voice said. They'd all been so intent none of them had heard anyone come out onto the balcony. Startled, Briar looked toward the doorway. To her amazement, Stefan Yager was there, lounging against the door frame. She only had time to register how good-looking he was in his tuxedo before Rupert turned and saw him there, too.

"You!" he exclaimed.

"Yes, me," Stefan said calmly, pushing away from the

door. He came to stand beside Briar, who was so nonplussed at his sudden appearance she didn't know what to say. He glanced down at her, his sun-bleached blond hair looking almost silver in the light spilling onto the balcony from inside. "Are you all right?" he asked.

"I'm . . . fine," she said faintly. She still didn't have the slightest idea what he was doing here, and why.

Stefan glanced at the two men. "Gentlemen, you were saying . . . ?"

Despite the restraining hand Rupert put on his arm, Carl elbowed his way forward. His chin thrust out aggressively, he said, "I don't think that's any of your damned business. This is a private conversation!"

Stefan raised an eyebrow. "Really? Was that why everyone within shouting distance could hear what was going on out here?"

Carl's face suffused again; to Briar's horror, he looked ready to start throwing punches. She tensed, but beside her, Stefan seemed relaxed, almost anticipatory. She looked from one to the other. Stefan was clearly hard and fit, Carl obviously overweight and out of condition. Surely Carl wouldn't be foolish enough to start a brawl! Quickly she said, "I think this discussion is finished."

Rupert clearly agreed. His cold, pale eyes resting on Stefan with active dislike, he put his hand on Carl's arm. "It's time for us to leave," he said. "We can continue this discussion at another time."

Briar had no intention of meeting either of these two men again, even if Spencer Reed were there to assist. "No, I don't think so," she said. "As far as I'm concerned, we've said all there is to say."

Rupert turned to her. His face was half in shadow, half in light, his expression menacing. "I don't think so," he said quietly. "I imagine we'll be talking again."

"If we do," she said coolly, "it will have to be through our attorneys."

Rupert bowed. "As you wish, Ms. McKenna," he said, and then he turned and left the balcony. After an ugly glance in her direction, Carl followed. As soon as they were gone, Briar let out the breath she'd been holding. Shakily, she reached for the rail. It seemed absurd, but she felt as if she'd just been in the presence of evil.

Stefan waited until she pulled herself together. Then he asked quietly, "Would you like me to take you home?"

With an effort, she got herself in hand. Straightening, she shook her head. "No, I've got a ride——" she started to say, and then looked horrified. She'd forgotten all about Jaz!

Stefan was still looking at her with concern. "If you don't mind me saying so, you look a little pale. Are you sure——"

"No, I'm fine," she said, thinking that she had to find Jaz and drag him away either before he forgot *her* and found someone else to leave with, or before he started to drink too much. She knew how he was about his car; even if he were falling-down drunk, he wouldn't let her drive, and she'd have to take a cab home.

"Maybe we should find a place to sit down for a bit," Stefan suggested.

"No, no, I'll be all right," she said, and looked at him fully for the first time since he'd come out on the balcony. Reminded of something Rupert had said, she asked, "Did you know those men?"

Stefan glanced away, out at the misty San Francisco night. Tendrils of fog were working their way inland through the Golden Gate; soon the city would be overlaid with silver-gray mist that blanketed sound and made it difficult to drive. "Not really," he said evasively. "I just heard all the shouting, and thought I'd better see what was going on."

"I'm glad you did. Things were getting a little . . . tense."

"So I gathered," he said, and smiled. She hadn't noticed before what a nice smile he had—perhaps because the other time they'd met, she'd been so infuriated with him. As though he'd read her mind, he shifted position, and started to say, "About that day at the riding club——"

But he was interrupted by Jaz, of all people, who suddenly appeared on the balcony, saying, "There you are! Damn it, Briar, I've been looking all over hell and gone for you! I thought you'd found some——" He stopped abruptly realizing that Briar wasn't alone. "Oh," he said. "Sorry. Didn't mean to interrupt."

"That's all right, Jaz," Briar said quickly. Now that she'd found him, or vice versa, she didn't want to let him get away again. Grabbing his arm, she said, "Jaz, I'd like you to meet Stefan Yager. Stefan, this is my . . ." She'd been about to say, "stepson," but changed it hastily to, ". . . this is Jarris Lord."

Grinning, obviously giving Stefan the once-over, Jaz held out his hand. "Call me Jaz," he said lazily. "Everyone does." He looked mischievously in Briar's direction. "Even my wicked old stepmother here."

"Thanks a lot, Jaz," Briar muttered, as the two men shook hands. There was the usual exchange of pleasantries, then Stefan turned to her again.

"I don't think they'll bother you again," he said. "But if they do—"

"Wait a minute," Jaz said, immediately turning protective. "Was somebody bothering Briar? Who?"

"It doesn't matter," Briar said quickly. Jaz didn't work out daily at a gym or take karate lessons twice a week for nothing, and she could just see him sailing out in a misguided attempt to defend her honor.

"The hell it doesn't!" he exclaimed. "If someone was threatening you—"

"It wasn't exactly a *threat*," she said, and she knew by his aggressive expression that she'd better explain. "Look, it's just that these two men approached me about buying the land I just inherited in Sonoma. They offered me quite a bit of money, and I refused. End of story. See how simple it was?"

Jaz looked at her suspiciously. Then he glanced at Stefan. "Is that true?"

Stefan shrugged. "That's what the lady says."

Still doubtful, Jazz searched her face again. Then, abruptly, he relaxed and grinned. "So, I guess this means you decided, right?"

"Decided?"

"Yeah, on the way in, you said you didn't know if you were going to sell or not. I guess this means that you're going to keep it after all."

"Yes," Briar said slowly. "I guess it does."

"Uh-oh," Jaz said, his grin widening as he winked at Stefan. "I know that expression. You've got something up your sleeve, don't you, Briar?"

Briar didn't answer. She was busy thinking, debating, trying to decide. She hadn't consciously realized it until now, but she knew that the idea had been at the back of her mind all the time. The conversation with Rupert and Carl Jaeger had crystallized her thoughts; the veiled threats had suddenly made her determined.

"Well?" Jaz prodded.

She'd made her decision. Even though she knew it was folly to commit herself to such a big project when she had so many other things to attend to, even though she really didn't know what was involved, or have the faintest idea what she was doing or even how to begin, she had to go ahead. She had known all along that she had inherited this property for a reason, and suddenly everything became clear.

"You're right, Jaz," she said, while Stefan looked on, his handsome face unreadable. "If those men hadn't approached me tonight and tried to intimidate me into selling that land to them, I probably would have just let it sit. But now . . ."

"Now?" Jaz asked.

Her eyes suddenly taking on a glow, Briar lifted her head. "Now," she said, "I'm going to rebuild Caulfield Farm."

"Right on! Jaz exclaimed giving her a hug.

"Congratulations," Stefan said. But when she turned to him, he had gone.

---

# CHAPTER EIGHT

Once Briar decided to renovate Caulfield Farm, she plunged into the project with a vengeance. Jaz had been amused by her new quest, but she was serious and immediately proved it. Before the month was over, she was elbow deep in blueprints and designs and contracting ideas, and she had contacted and interviewed several big construction firms—all in addition to her already heavy workload at the office. Inundated with endless details, she was starting to wonder what she'd gotten herself into.

Of course, Patsy was always eager to help. Swept up by the

romance of what Briar was trying to do, she was constantly coming into the office with questions or offering suggestions or perkily asking who else she could call. Gabe was more philosophical; he accepted all this additional frenzied activity on Briar's part as proof positive that the boss was just another of your typical superwomen dynamos—while Spence just shook his head when she had told him about her decision. It irritated Briar to find herself wondering at times what Stefan Yager would think of all this—but then, she didn't have the chance to ask him anyway. For some reason he was making himself scarce at the riding club these days, and she hadn't seen him since the night of the fund-raiser when he had inexplicably vanished.

But she was far too busy to dwell on the activities of her self-appointed rescuer from that night, and she certainly wasn't going to ask what had happened to him when she did go out to the club. Resolving both to put him out of her mind and simply thank him again when she did happen to see him, she got on with her work.

And she had plenty of that. She was also suddenly deluged with new clients and prospective accounts. As she moaned to Gabe one time, it seemed that the more she tried to set aside for her private business, the more people called wanting her professional services.

"Briar, listen to me," he said one night after she'd exhausted herself coming and going all day. "If you don't slow down, you're either going to have a heart attack or make yourself sick. Why don't you let me take some responsibility? I can screen new clients and keep these preliminary appointments. And I can do the final proposal for Kibbe Discount. You've been saying for a while now that I was ready. I think it's time."

She didn't have to think about it at that point; in addition to welcoming the prospect of sharing the heavy burden she was carrying, she agreed with him. He had been taking more and more responsibility all along; it was time he had the authority to go with it. She needed his help more than ever, now that she was going to be so involved getting her own pet project off the line, and so she made one of her usual quick decisions that she'd actually been debating about in the back of her mind for some time.

"You're absolutely right," she said, formally holding out her hand. "As of this minute, I'm promoting you to vice president. How's that sound?"

"It sounds just fine," he said, solemnly returning the handshake. But he couldn't prevent a grin from spreading across his face when he added again, "Just fine!"

"Good. We'll work out the details later. Right now, I've got another appointment."

And another, and another. It wasn't until the end of that week, when she finally had time to interview a local Sonoma contractor named Ted Skerrit, that she knew she'd finally found the person to rebuild the ranch. Skerrit was a big, burly man with a no-nonsense manner who met with her in his cubbyhole of an office in Sonoma late Friday night. Over a strong cup of coffee he'd made for her with a battered coffee maker sitting on the window sill, he listened politely to what she wanted to do, told her outright what was possible and what wasn't, offered a few suggestions, and ended up by saying how much it was going to cost—barring complications, price hikes for supplies, weather delays . . . and her changing her mind halfway through the job, of course. She was so impressed by his directness that she hired him on the spot.

A month later, she hadn't stopped congratulating herself on such a lucky find as Ted. He was not only familiar with the local building codes, but the various suggestions he'd made so far had improved on her original ideas and were saving them both time and money besides. She had already decided that when he and the crew were finished, she was going to give them all a big bonus. Almost before her eyes things improved at the ranch; if she let a day or two go by without driving up to see the place after he started work there, she was amazed at the changes she saw the next time. She hadn't believed such a transformation could take place so quickly, despite various complications they'd been dealing with, and she told him so one Saturday when she drove up to spend the morning discussing new plans. He had called her apologetically that Friday night to say that he needed to talk to her about the next phase of construction, so she had driven up early the next morning, arriving with coffee and doughnuts for all the crew.

"You'll spoil 'em, Miz McKenna," Ted had said, scooping up three of the crullers before any of his men had a chance.

Then he spread one set of plans on a makeshift table set under the trees. "Now, this is the problem," he said loudly, speaking over the competing noise from a backhoe. Pointing with a thick, calloused finger to a place on the blueprints, he traced the irrigation line that had been drawn. "We can't put the irrigation lines here because of the serpentine rock we found during the drilling. So we're gonna have to move 'em over here. . . ."

Briar nodded, following the movement of his finger, but feeling frustrated at another delay. Sometimes it seemed that it was one thing after another. First it had been problems with the water. The existing well had been found to be dry, so another one had to be drilled; then a new septic system had to be engineered, designed, and approved. Then they couldn't get power because all the lines had to be moved underground, and the power company couldn't do that until they could schedule a crew—a seemingly impossible feat for some reason, although Briar had tried. Aggravated at the bureaucracy, she had gone to visit the power company's district manager himself, only to be told that they were twelfth on the list, and a crew would get to them as soon as possible. Briar had offered to absorb the cost herself, but for some reason, that, too, seemed to be against the rules. Ted had told her it wasn't a problem; the crew could continue with just the generators, but there were moments when Briar thought that if she heard a generator power up just one more time, she was going to scream.

Now Ted was telling her that the irrigation lines they had worked out so carefully in relation to the newly fenced pastures had to be moved because of something called a serpentine. Not quite sure what that meant, she was just about to ask Skerrit to explain when she realized that she had company. A man she didn't recognize as one of the crew was walking around, and when she realized he was speaking into a hand-held tape recorder, she knew he was a reporter. Now what? she thought, and straightened. When he saw her staring at him, he started guiltily and quickly came over.

"Ms. McKenna?" he said as he came up. "My name's Mason Ahern, and I'm from the—"

The last of the sentence was lost in a renewed roar from the backhoe, and before he caught himself, he cringed and ducked as though he expected to be run over.

Amused in spite of herself, Briar said loudly, "I'm sorry, I didn't hear you."

Giving the huge machine a dirty look, he turned back to her. Raising his voice over the appalling noise, he shouted, "I said, I'm from the *Chronicle*. I'd like to talk to you for a few minutes, if that's all right."

During Hay's illness and the horrible aftermath, Briar had had enough of reporters to last her the rest of her life. "I'm sorry," she shouted back. "I don't have time."

"This won't take long, I promise!" he yelled.

Someone turned on one of the big table saws just then; the high-pitched whine seemed to go right through her head. "No interviews!"

"But I came all this way!"

She had learned long ago, and painfully, that she just couldn't be nice to them. "Then you'll just have to go back!"

His face flushing with annoyance, he started to say something, but just then another tractor started up, adding to the din from the table saw and the backhoe. He broke off, his hands to his ears.

"Jesus Christ! How does anyone stand this infernal din!" he shouted, dropping his little recorder in the dust. Smiling nastily, Ted bent down and picked it up for him.

"If you don't like the noise, maybe you'd better leave, like the lady says," he said in a loud voice that could easily be heard above all the clamor. Pointedly, he held out the recorder.

The reporter glared at him. "I wasn't talking to you."

"You're not going to talk to Miz McKenna, either," Ted said. Suddenly, without even trying, he looked bigger. "The lady said she didn't want to talk to you. Now, beat it. This is private property."

Looking as if he'd rather turn and run, the reporter stood his ground. "You don't understand!" he shouted over the din. He said the magic words proudly. "I'm from the *Chronicle*!"

Ted took a step forward. "I don't care if you're from the Angel Gabriel!"

Briar had always fought her own battles. Placing a hand on Ted's arm, she said, "It's all right, Ted. I can handle this. You go ahead with that irrigation line. I'll be right there."

He looked down at her. "You sure? 'Cause I could throw this little guy off the place with no trouble, if you want."

As the reporter glared balefully at him again, she smiled. "I'm sure you could," she said. "But really, it's all right."

He still seemed uncertain. "Well, if you need me, just shout."

"I'll do that," she promised, and waited until he had walked reluctantly away before she turned back to the reporter again. Before he could start in about her obligation to the public, she said loudly, "Now, listen, Mr. Ahern, I told you, no interviews. As you can see, I'm very busy now, so I would appreciate—"

"But you don't understand!"

She sighed. "I know. You're from the *Chronicle*."

"No, it's not that. Well, it is, but . . . this is big news here. If you give me half a chance, we could do a great story about the rebuilding of the Caulfield Farm!"

She stared at him. "What do you know about the Caulfield Farm?"

"Hey, I've done my research. I know this used to be a big Thoroughbred breeding place. Come on, won't you give me a chance?"

She had been mistreated too often at the hands of the press to be taken in now, even by a fresh-faced, eager young reporter. "Why?" she asked suspiciously. "Why are you so interested?"

"Are you kidding? This could be a big story!" He gestured, his arm sweeping around to include her little valley. "Imagine the header! 'Widow of Hayden Lord, of Lord Industries, rebuilds ancient family farm.' It's got everything, intrigue, history—"

"What it's 'got' is going to be of no interest whatsoever to you or your readers," Briar interrupted. She was not going to have this turned into a circus by the press.

"But that's not true! When we print that you're the long-lost heir to this property, and that the first you knew of it was when a private detective tracked you down, th—"

"How do you know about that?" she interrupted sharply.

"It's a matter of public record, Ms. McKenna. So is the fact that your stepdaughter, Fredrica Lord Hudson, has gone to court in an attempt to have her father's—your husband's—will declared void. If you won't talk about Caulfield Farm, maybe we could talk about that."

"We're not going to talk about anything! Now, I'd appreciate it if you would just leave the way you came in. As I said before, I'm very busy.''

"It's a bad mistake not to talk to the press," Ahern warned.

Briar had turned back to the blueprints Ted had left spread out. Slowly, she straightened. "Are you threatening me?" she asked.

"You're news, Ms. McKenna," he said, shrugging. "No matter how much you might want to deny it. Your husband was a very wealthy man; Lord Industries alone rakes in—"

"I know what Lord Industries is worth, Mr. Ahern."

"Yes, well . . . A fortune is at stake, and as I say, that's news." He paused. "If you don't want to talk to me, perhaps your stepdaughter will."

Mentally damning Fredrica, who had started all this, Briar furiously rolled up the blueprints. "Talk to whomever you like, Mr. Ahern," she said. "Now please excuse me."

"Just one quote . . . one, and then I'll leave, I promise," he wheedled.

"No," Briar said shortly, and went to find Ted.

The reporter caught up to her before she'd gone two steps. "Wait!"

She stopped. "What now? I told you, I have nothing more to say!"

He looked at her with guileless blue eyes that didn't fool her for a minute. He might be young, but he had a tape recorder and a pencil in his hand, and he represented a major newspaper. "All right," he said, "if you won't talk about the property you inherited, or your stepdaughter going to court, would you comment on this business with the Jaeger family?"

She'd started walking away again, nimbly hopping over the cables snaking around, moving out of the way for two workmen carrying a load of two-by-fours on sawhorses. He was following, vainly holding out his little tape recorder, and when she stopped suddenly, he almost ran into her.

"What about the Jaeger family?" she demanded.

"You haven't heard? It was in the paper this morning."

She hadn't had time to read the paper. Eager to get here to talk to Ted, she'd left the house with barely a cup of coffee. Definitely not a morning person, she didn't like noise when she first woke up, so she hadn't listened to the morning news on the radio, either. Now she wondered if she should have. Since that confrontation at the fund-raiser, she'd managed to put the Jaeger family out of her mind. Despite their veiled threats, she hadn't been intimidated, just angry that they had tried to frighten her. But had that escalated into something more now?

Seeing that he had her attention again, Ahern said, "Could we discuss the article in the paper, Ms. McKenna? I wondered if I could have some comments from you about that."

Briar took his arm and moved him out of the way of another workman who was trying to get by with a load of electrical wire. "I don't know anything about an article," she said impatiently. "Now, if y—"

"It was in the *Chronicle* this morning, Ms. McKenna. During an interview yesterday, Rupert Jaeger stated—"

But Briar didn't have a chance to find out what Rupert Jaeger had said. Just then, Ted Skerrit approached, and with a glance in the reporter's direction, he said to Briar, "Can I talk to you a minute? We found something I think you should look at."

Relieved to have an excuse to get rid of the reporter, Briar said good-bye to him without giving him a chance to ask if he could tag along. Then, not looking back, she followed Ted into the house.

"What is it?" she asked the big foreman.

"It's in the kitchen," Ted answered. "You'll see."

Briar didn't realize Ahern had followed them until they were inside, but by then it was too late. Because of the termite and dry rot problem, two carpenters had been in the kitchen tearing up the old floor, preparing to put in a new one. When she saw the big gap off to the side of the floor, she turned uncertainly to Ted. "Is this what you wanted me to see?"

He turned to one of the sawhorses. "No, these," he said, and he handed her a stack of books. There were half a dozen, and Briar looked at them in surprise.

"Where did you get these?"

One of the carpenters pointed toward the hole. "We found 'em right there after we took up that old linoleum. Place was covered up just as pretty as you please. Don't think we ever would have noticed it if we hadn't been tearin' the floor apart. Musta been there for a long time."

Peering over her shoulder, Ahern asked, "What are they?"

Briar hardly heard him. Perching on the sawhorse, she ran a hand over the peeling cloth backing of the top book. *JOURNAL* was written in faded script on the front. Carefully, hardly daring to breathe, she opened the cover. On the frontispiece, written in a beautiful hand that must be copperplate, Briar thought absently, was a name: *Marguerite Kendall Caulfield*

And underneath the name: *My Journal*

And the date: *1890*

A thrill raced through Briar, and she quickly put the book aside to examine the others. Except for different recorded years, they were all written in that same fine hand, and she looked up dazedly. What a miracle this was!

Abruptly, she realized that all the men in the kitchen were staring at her. "I think . . . ." she started to say, but her throat felt so constricted that she had to start all over again. "I think these journals belonged to my great-grandmother," she finally managed.

Now that her first shock was over, she was so excited that she could hardly breathe. To think that after all these years, after all this time of wondering and dreaming and hoping, she finally had a link—a direct link—to her family! She could hardly wait to gather these precious notebooks up and take them someplace to pore over privately. She wanted to read every word—again and again and *again*.

"Good grief, if they're genuine, they might be worth something!" Ahern exclaimed.

Briar looked at him. She had forgotten the reporter was even here, and when she realized what he had said, her expression changed. "I told you before to leave, Mr. Ahern," she said. "I'm not going to tell you again!"

"Hey, I didn't mean—"

Flanked by his men, Ted took a step forward. "You heard what the lady said."

Ahern looked uneasily from one man to another, taking in the little half circle that had formed protectively around Briar. "All right, all right, I'm going," he said. "But can I have one quote from you Ms. McKenna? Just one?"

Briar's mind was on the journals. "No, I told you—"

With one desperate eye on the advancing carpenters, Ahern said beseechingly, "But our readers are going to be interested in your response to what Mr. Jaeger said!"

Briar couldn't have cared less at the moment if Rupert Jaeger had declared all out war on her; she was too eager to go somewhere alone to revel in this unexpected, thrilling discovery. Even *touching* the journals made her tingle, and when she thought of how old they were, and how long ago her great-grandmother had written in them, she felt awed and exhilarated at the same time. What would she find inside? Right now, she didn't care if all Marguerite had written down were grocery lists. The books were a precious connection to her great-grandmother, and through Marguerite to the rest of her family, and no matter what was inside, to Briar the journals were more precious than gems. She couldn't wait to sit down and read every one.

Still clinging tightly to the cherished books, she looked vaguely at the reporter. Was he still here? As if that were a signal for him to proceed, Ahern said eagerly, "Jaeger's claiming that you're a fraud, Ms. McKenna, and that you have no claim to this land. Furthermore, he says he can prove it. *Now* can I have a quote from you?"

Briar thought of all she had yearned for, and all she had gained. Standing in the torn-up kitchen of the old farmhouse with construction going on all around, on land that had been in her family for generations, and now in possession of these precious journals her great-grandmother had left behind, she felt something she had never felt before. Not about anything, not even the company she'd built, or the possessions she had earned, or the distance she had come in so little time. *This* was what it felt like to belong to something, she thought fiercely; *this* was what it meant to have roots.

It was an emotion she'd never thought to experience. It made her feel as if she had wings, as if there was nothing, *nothing* she couldn't do. To belong to something, to have a link to the past, people to descend from, memories to share . . . The feeling was indescribable.

"A quote, Ms. McKenna?" Ahern asked again.

She looked at the reporter, her new realization blazing in her green eyes. "I'll give you a quote," she said. "You can tell Mr. Jaeger if it's a battle he wants, that's what he'll get. I don't care what proof he thinks he has; I don't care what he tries to do to get this land. I've got resources too—resources I haven't even tapped into yet, and I'll use them all—all!—to keep what is mine! Mine," she repeated, her voice shaking. There was something in her face that made even the seasoned carpenters look at her in awe.

Ahern didn't see her expression. His tape recorder wasn't working after he'd dropped it in the dust, so he was writing frantically on a crumpled piece of paper he'd found in his pocket. Briar grabbed his hand, forcing him to look at her. "Did you get that? Did you write down what I said?"

Now that he saw her face, he paused. Briar looked so fierce that he nearly took a step back. "I . . . got it," he said. "But you . . . you realize that you're going up against Mondragon Enterprises, don't you?"

She drew herself up. Blessing Hay, and thinking that no matter what happened, she would never forget the gift he had given her, she gazed directly at the startled reporter. "And he's going up against the full weight and power of Lord Industries, which *I* own now," she said. "Tell him that."

Then, as Ahern turned to go, practically running before he even reached the door, so eager was he to get back and file his story, Briar heard something no one else seemed to hear. With all the construction noises roaring around her, and the men getting back to work, and even Ted giving her an admiring look, she was sure—wasn't she?—that just for an instant, she heard the ghost of a delighted laugh.

---

# CHAPTER NINE

With an angry exclamation, Rupert Jaeger threw down his newspaper and snatched up his coffee. Spying his untouched breakfast, he shoved the plate away as if the bacon and toast were at fault, then he took a quick sip from the cup, burning his tongue. The morning was not going well.

The article he had been reading concerned Briar McKenna and how she was going to rebuild Caulfield Farm come hell or high water, and when he caught sight of the headline again, he felt the rare desire to curse. How like the media, he thought scathingly, to turn things around and make the poor, downtrodden little widow the heroine. Angrily, he grabbed the paper again and reread the section that had infuriated him the most.

"In response to what seems to be an escalating feud between Briar McKenna, widow of Hayden Lord, of Lord Industries, who died several months ago at age sixty-five, and Rupert Jaeger, of Mondragon Enterprises, Ms. McKenna reacted angrily yesterday to Jaeger charges that she was a fraud and therefore unentitled to the Sonoma property known as the Caulfield Farm, once the site of one of the foremost horse breeding establishments in California. Readers of this newspaper will recall a recent interview by this same reporter, during which Mr. Jaeger was quoted as saying he has proof to back his claim. When questioned, Ms. McKenna's reply was unequivocal. 'Rupert Jaeger has tangled with the wrong woman. . . . He's going up against the full weight and power of Lord Industries, which *I* now own. . . . If he wants a battle, that's just what he'll get. . . .' "

His expression even more aggravated now that he'd read the article a second time, Rupert threw the paper down. If he didn't know better, he'd think that Marguerite Caulfield herself had come back in Briar McKenna's form to bedevil him all over again. It wasn't difficult to believe: when he had first seen Briar McKenna in person the night of the fund-raiser, he'd felt as if he'd been jerked back in time. The McKenna woman looked so much like her great-grandmother that they could have been twins.

In more ways than one, Rupert thought. They not only resembled each other physically, but they were both stubborn, obstinate, *irrational* creatures, as well. If he hadn't been before, he was determined to stamp them both out of his life this time once and for all.

"If she wants war," he muttered, tapping his fingers against the table, "I'll be pleased to oblige."

"What's that, Father? Talking to yourself again?"

Rupert looked up angrily as Charlotte came breezing into the dining room. Dressed in breeches and boots, she had obviously been out riding, as she often did in the morning, risking life and limb to take one of the untrained two-year-olds up into the hills behind the ranch for conditioning. Settling into her place at the table despite his frown at her attire, she smiled unfeelingly and said, "What's wrong, Father? Are we going to be involved in another hostile takeover, or something?"

Instead of answering, he said irritably, "I wish you wouldn't wear your riding clothes to the table. It puts off my appetite."

Refusing an offer of orange juice from the maid with an absent wave of her hand but accepting coffee instead, Charlotte annoyed him further. "There's nothing wrong with the good, clean smell of horse, especially when the horse is as well cared for as one of ours." She looked at him over the rim of her coffee cup. "Don't you want to know how the new colt is doing?"

"No," he said, and shoved the offending newspaper as far away from him as it could get.

"But Father—" Charlotte started to say slyly.

He gave her a quelling glance. "Leave it be, Charlotte," he said.

She subsided, smiling into her coffee. Well, let her smile, he thought; he had other fish to fry. It was no secret that he had never liked horses—a paradox, because he, through Mondragon Enterprises, supported the Stud. He knew that Charlotte had always suspected that his dislike stemmed from some incident in his childhood, but it was much less complicated than that. The truth was that he had never had any use for the great, stupid creatures whose only attributes were eating large quantities of expensive hays and grains and running around an oval track; the only reason he supported the Stud was because his father had established it. And the only reason his father had done that, Rupert thought coldly, was because of Sloane Caulfield.

Carl came to the table just then, looking as dour as his sire. It was obvious he'd already seen the morning paper, for he had it rolled under his arm. Smelling of the strong cologne he insisted on using, although Charlotte had repeatedly told him he smelled like a still, he was dressed for the office in a navy and magenta pinstriped suit, one of many he had tailored regularly in Tokyo. Unfortunately, he had gained more weight since this one had been ordered, and he insisted on wearing a vest. The waistcoat strained across his middle, drawing creases and making him, Charlotte thought, look like a stuffed pig.

"Well, good morning," she said. "I see that you're in the same good mood as the rest of the family."

Glaring, Carl tossed her the paper. "You've seen this, I suppose?"

As the rolled paper landed beside her plate, it unfolded to the article about Briar McKenna. To one side of the column was a black-and-white picture of the new owner of Caulfield Farm. Charlotte looked down at the photo, noticing Briar's resemblance to photographs she'd seen of Marguerite. In fact, it had been all the publicity after Hayden Lord's death that had caused Charlotte to hire Albert Weitz in the first place.

Charlotte had always wondered if Ariana and Duncan had had a child, and when the investigator came back with the report of who Briar seemed to be, Charlotte had been elated. She had immediately realized what an impact another Caulfield heir would have on her father's state of mind, and she had gleefully imagined turning the tables on him at last. She wanted satisfaction for all the hurts he had dealt her over the years, and she believed she could achieve it by having Briar identified so she could take over Caulfield Farm. She hadn't thought beyond that . . . well, that wasn't true. She *had* wondered how she would feel about Ariana's daughter, but seeing her father squirm had been so much more important.

Queasily, Charlotte averted her eyes from the paper. Before, it had seemed so easy. Now things were getting complicated. She had always believed that if she ever met a child of Ariana's and Duncan's, she'd feel nothing but anger and resentment, but now she didn't know what she felt. Briar was no longer a nonentity, an object to be used for revenge. To Charlotte's chagrin, Briar was becoming a person instead.

Even so, she was not about to let her father know her feelings. "She looks so much like Marguerite, doesn't she?" she said casually.

Carl immediately puffed up. "The *likeness* isn't the point! Did you even bother to read the article?"

"An article with a title like, 'Another Clash of the Titans'?" she said, feigning disinterest. "Don't be ridiculous."

Practically choking with indignation at the reminder, Carl threw himself in his chair as Rupert said severely, "This isn't funny, Charlotte."

"Oh, I don't know. And after all, you started it."

Carl came to life again. "That's not true! This is all your fault! If you hadn't hired that damned *detective* to find her, none of this would be happening right now!"

Languidly, she turned to her brother. "I might have known *you* would blame me for doing the right thing."

"You've never done the right thing in your life!" Carl exploded. "You only did this to . . . to get *back* at us!"

"That's absurd. You don't know what you're talking about."

"You said it yourself, and now look what's happened! She's giving interviews to the paper!"

"Well, what did you expect when Father said all those outrageous things to that silly reporter? Did either of you really think she'd just fold up her tent and go home to San Francisco?"

"I certainly didn't expect her to attack us in print!"

"Why not? Father attacked her."

Carl half rose in outrage from his chair. "Why are you *defending* her?"

"That's enough, Carl," Rupert said, and turned in Charlotte's direction again. "What I told that reporter was true."

"Oh, really?" Charlotte scoffed. "Are you saying that you actually *do* have proof that she's a fraud? Because if you do, I'd like to see it. If that were so, why didn't you use it to stop her from rebuilding Caulfield Farm?"

His expression unreadable, Rupert gestured for the maid who had just come in to refill his coffee cup. "Because it wasn't time yet," he replied, lifting the cup.

"Teresa, bring me a Bloody Mary," Carl ordered the maid as she started back toward the kitchen.

Charlotte was still engaged with her father. "What do you mean, it wasn't time?"

Rupert took a sip of coffee. "Just what I said."

Recognizing that she wouldn't get anywhere this way, Charlotte tried another tack. "And now?" she prodded. "You've called her a fake, a phony, and an imposter. What did you expect her response to be?"

"Not this!" Carl exclaimed angrily. "We thought she would realize just who she's up against!"

She looked at her brother disdainfully. "And instead you're finding out just who *you're* up against. Or did you happen to forget that she's the widow of Hayden Lord? I'd say that gives her a weapon or two, wouldn't you?"

"Well, *of course* you'd take *her* side!" Carl muttered, savagely accepting the hastily made Bloody Mary. He took a big swallow, and then another, draining nearly half the glass.

"Who says I'm on her side?"

"Well, you're certainly not on ours, are you?" Carl exclaimed, slamming down the glass. Drops of tomato juice splashed out onto the pristine white tablecloth, but he didn't notice. "Honest to God, Charlotte, sometimes I don't think you belong to this family at all! What is this Briar person to you, anyway?"

Charlotte felt something twist inside her. But the feeling was gone in a second, and she answered with a shrug, "She's the rightful heir to Caulfield Farm, that's all. I just wanted to see justice done."

"Justice!" Carl exploded. "The only *justice* will be when that property becomes ours, as it should have been all along!"

"You know, that's another thing," Charlotte said. "I never have understood why you think that land should be ours."

Carl erupted again. "You known damned well why we feel that way!" he said. "Sloane Caulfield was supposed to deed all that land to Father in payment for a debt. It's been common knowledge for years."

"Common to whom?" she scoffed. "*We've* always said so, but who else? Juliet certainly didn't believe it."

"Juliet was crazy as a loon!" Carl snapped. "And furthermore, she was a usurper!"

Charlotte burst into a laugh. "A usurper! She'd lived on that land since she was a child! She was *born* in that house! How can you possibly say she had no right to live there?"

"Because it's true," Rupert said, calmly sipping from his coffee cup. "She forfeited that right the night her father agreed to give that land to me."

"Yes, well, if that's so," Charlotte said, "why is it that no one's ever seen any official papers or documents?"

Rupert's pale eyes rested on her face. "It was a 'gentlemen's agreement.' "

Charlotte smiled nastily. "It's a pity there weren't two gentlemen present, then."

"Sloane Caulfield was the one who reneged!" Carl said angrily. "Father never should have trusted him!"

She turned to him. "Father has never trusted anyone," she said flatly. "Least of all a Caulfield."

"And he was right, too!" Carl insisted with a quick glance in his father's direction. "Just as grandfather was!"

"Oh, please, you're not going to start in about that match race, are you?"

"That and a dozen other things," Carl retorted, dismissing for the moment the infamous match race between Caulfield Farm's great stallion, Fane, and their own family's Ulrich. He looked at Rupert. "Isn't that right, Father?"

But Rupert seemed not to hear; his light eyes fixed on Charlotte, he was watching her with a narrow smile curving his cruel lips. What he was thinking, it was impossible to say, but Charlotte didn't care for his expression, and when she saw him looking at her, she said, "You know, Father, maybe Juliet was right, and it wasn't an accident. You do remember her saying that, don't you? I do. Oh, not when they took her away—she wasn't saying anything then, was she? But years later, after she came back . . . after the fire, and Ariana and . . . and Duncan left, she was saying it then, I know. In fact, I'm sure she was saying it the day she died. What do you think about that?"

"I think," Rupert said, wiping his lips with his napkin before setting it aside, "that I've had enough of this ridiculous conversation."

"Me, too," Carl said belligerently, joining his father as he prepared to leave the table. "You want to know what *I* think?"

"Not particularly," Charlotte answered, reaching for her coffee cup.

He didn't care whether she wanted to listen to him or not. "I think you're just trying to stir up trouble, as you always are, Charlotte. But in the future, maybe you should just mind your own business."

"But this is my business, baby brother," Charlotte said, her eyes following the men as they started out. She raised her voice. "Briar McKenna isn't going to go away, Father, you might as well accept that. I think this time you've bitten off more than you can chew."

Rupert turned to look at her from the doorway. A thin, cruel smile curved his mouth again. "We'll see about that, won't we?" he said, and left the dining room without looking back.

Carl was still there. "Father's right," he said, his expression ugly. "We haven't even begun to deal with this woman, and you'd better believe that!"

Charlotte laughed. "We'll see who deals with whom."

Carl still stood there. "I thought we were a family, Lottie," he said finally. "But I just don't understand you. Why are you doing this to us? I've asked you this before—what is Briar McKenna to you?"

Charlotte didn't answer for a moment. Then, scraping her own chair back, she stood and started to leave the dining room, too. As she passed her brother, she paused. "Maybe," she said, "one day you'll find out."

Charlotte took another horse out later that afternoon, a big chestnut mare named Proud Dana. The mare was older and more mature than the colt she'd ridden this morning who had given her such a wild ride. That one had shied at everything, refusing to walk through a muddy spot on the trail until she gave him a quick swat with the bat, then practically falling while trying to get away from a menacing squirrel. She had a lot to think about, and she knew the experienced mare wouldn't disgrace herself as had the unruly two-year-old, and she took another fork in the road when she got up into the hills, allowing the mare to follow it along without much direction from her until they came to the crest of one particular hill. Once she had ridden this way so often that she could have found it in the dark.

It was late afternoon now, and lengthening shadows from the westering sun were gilding the tips of the oaks and pines and bathing the little valley below in a golden light. She'd always thought this place one of the prettiest she had ever seen, and as she slid out of the saddle and looped the reins over one arm, her expression changed. Walking with the mare to the crest of the hill, she looked down.

From her high perch, the men working far below looked the size of dolls, but even so, the slight breeze carried the noise of the buzz saws and even a faint hammering sound to her ears. Miniature trucks and tractors and other heavy equipment were moving back and forth like little toys playing in the dirt, and she could see a lilliputian red Mercedes parked off to the side under the trees.

Work had been going on for weeks, and because she had come here so often as a child, a glance told her that soon the house would be ready for habitation again. Like a Phoenix rising from the ashes, Caulfield Farm was coming to life: the newly erected fences blocked out the pastures that had recently been reseeded and were already showing a faint green, and the fresh asphalt drive curved like a new black ribbon. As she stared somberly down at all the activity, she couldn't help wondering how soon horses would fill the pastures and the new barn.

Her eyes narrowed as she looked for the barn. The last time she had ridden this way, she had come later still when no one was around, and she had gone down to see if a barn had been planned. When she found the stakes marking out a large area, she shivered. It had seemed like an omen, for although Briar couldn't possibly have known, the new barn was going to be built exactly where the old one had been.

She hadn't been able to prevent a quick look around that day she'd gone there alone. But as she had already guessed, too many years had passed for any sign of the previous barn to exist. The grass had long since grown back. Standing there in the middle of that big square, it was hard to believe that the fire had ever happened.

But now there was going to be a new barn and a new owner for the Caulfield Farm, Charlotte thought, and she was smiling as she climbed into the saddle again and turned Proud Dana toward home.

At last, she thought, after all these years, justice was about to be done.

Rupert took out the gun that night before he went to bed. Dressed in his pajamas and slippers with a burgundy-colored velvet smoking jacket tied around his lean middle, he locked the door of his private suite, then he sat down at his desk to unlock the secret compartment. He hadn't looked inside this drawer for years—longer than he could remember, in fact. He slowly pulled on the knob that fitted so cleverly under the top, and the drawer slid noiselessly out; the little derringer was still nestled inside, just as he remembered. The short engraved silver barrel caught the light and glinted back at him, and as he reverently took it out of its hiding place, the mother-of-pearl handle felt cool and smooth against his palm, just as it always had. His expression unreadable, he hefted the little gun in his hand, then closed his fingers around the grip for a moment. The gesture took him back over the years, and he could remember. . . . Hastily, he put the little gun down on the desk top.

Even though he had never cared for guns—for violence of

any kind—he had to admit that this one was an elegant deadly weapon. It had originally been part of a set, but the other one had . . . disappeared. He had never known where, and it hadn't mattered. The important thing was that he had kept this one all these years. As a . . . memento, of sorts, he thought, and smiled for the first time until he realized how long it had been in his possession.

*Good Lord,* he thought, sitting back with the little gun still gleaming innocently on the desk, *could it be over sixty years ago now?*

It didn't seem possible; time had a way of speeding by too fast. He could still remember the day his father, Heinrich, had brought the set home. The two derringers were fitted into a carved rosewood box with a red satin lining, the stubby barrels pointed toward each other, the fancy handles facing out. He could recall to this day how pleased his father had been to have come across such a find, but Heinrich had been less proud of the fact that the weapons had been used in a duel between a New Orleans aristocrat and a titled Englishman than he was at the knowledge that they had originally been manufactured by Henry Deringer himself, a gunsmith of German descent.

"Such craftsmanship, eh, Rupert?" he'd said to his then young son. Giving one to Rupert, he had held the other up to the lamp, admiring the meticulous engraving along the barrel as it caught the light from one of the lamps at the summer house where Heinrich kept his office. Rupert still remembered his amazement as he watched his father lovingly stroking the weapon; until that moment, he hadn't even suspected that Heinrich liked guns. How ironic, he thought now, that one of the derringers had been the instrument of his destruction.

Rupert's expression even more thoughtful, he picked up the gun again and carefully set it back in its hiding place. As he shut the drawer and checked to make sure that all was as it should be, he thought about the conversation that morning at breakfast. Resting his elbows on the chair arms, he tented his fingers and tapped his lips with the tips. Charlotte might be a silly fool, playing a game she thought she could win, but she had been right about one thing, he mused. Briar McKenna was never going to give up; she was too much like that damnable Marguerite.

He was not a superstitious man, but he still recalled his

amazement that night of the fund-raiser when he had seen Briar enter that ballroom. Her coloring, the way she carried herself, that proud lift to her chin . . . It was as if Marguerite Caulfield herself had come to life. The pictures he'd seen of Briar hadn't done her justice, he had realized then. He'd thought he was prepared for the likeness, but to meet her again in the flesh . . .

Without warning, he shivered. Marguerite had been a formidable opponent in her own right, he recalled with a frown. To her dying day, neither he nor his father had been able to break her iron will—and they had tried; they had tried. Would the great-granddaughter be the same? he wondered, and then threw off his sudden gloom by barking a laugh.

*Ah, but this time things are different,* he thought. This time he was no callow lad, half afraid of the game. He had all the power and wealth of Mondragon Enterprises behind him, and he would use all the resources he had to crush his enemy the final time. No longer would he hear, even down through the years, the whispers about his father and what he had done; no longer would he feel the same humiliation Heinrich had felt at the hands of someone named Caulfield. At long last, the victory would be his alone.

Because no matter how much the great-granddaughter looks like her, he thought, Briar is no Marguerite. He had waited a long time—a lifetime, it seemed—for that crazy old woman, Juliet, to die—but finally it had come to pass, and now she was no longer a threat. In the end he had bested Marguerite Caulfield, and he would do the same all these years later with the last of her damnable clan. By the time he was done with Briar McKenna, the mortal blow he dealt would finish the Caulfield line for all time. Only then would he be satisfied and free of his terrible dreams.

---

# CHAPTER TEN

Briar moved to Caulfield Farm in July. The finish work wasn't done yet on the house, but she was too impatient to wait for every last detail to be completed. As much as she had loved the place in Pacifica while Hay was alive, the beach house seemed so empty now, too big and hollow, and she was growing to hate it. Without Hay to fill up the spaces, she felt as if she were rattling around in echoes of the past, and she had to get out. Sonoma drew her more and more as time went on, and by the end of June she couldn't wait much longer. She was so eager that she asked Ted Skerrit to double his work crews.

By this time, Ted was accustomed to her quick decisions, and he didn't even mention the added expense of bringing in extra men to finish; he just nodded and did it. With all those additional hands, work proceeded much faster than even she expected.

"Ready or not," she told Ted, "I'm going to move in July 1."

"It won't be ready then, I'm telling you," he said.

She dismissed his complaint with the wave of her hand. "It'll be habitable, won't it?"

"Habitable," he retorted, "doesn't mean finished."

"That's good enough for me," she answered, smiling at his protectiveness. She knew he was stalling because, as he'd said more than once, he didn't think it was a good idea for her to live alone. "All the way at the back of beyond," as he direly put it.

"Something could happen," he insisted.

"Something could," she agreed serenely. "But if it does, I've got Jaime to help out."

Like Ted had been, she believed finding Jaime Salazar was another stroke of luck. Small, well-built, with a thick shock of coal-black hair and dark-chocolate eyes, the twenty-year-old young man had come looking for work one day—anything, he said; it didn't matter. When she found out that he was not only handy with his hands but had grown up around horses, she had hired him immediately, and she was glad she had. Jaime was such a hard worker that both she and Ted had to tell him to slow down at times; even when the rest of the crew knocked off for lunch, Jaime could be seen out in the hot sun, working away. Briar had asked him why one day, and he had smiled, showing even, white teeth.

"I work to bring my Isabella to this country," he said to Briar in his heavily accented English.

"Isabella?"

Jaime's smile broadened. *"Mi esposa,"* he explained. "My . . . wife. She work for a rich family now in Mexico City, but one day, we be together, *sí*?"

"Maybe sooner than you think, Jaime," Briar said, smiling in return. She liked Jaime, and she couldn't deny that he worked harder for her than any five people. Because she needed someone to stay at the ranch while she was gone, she had asked him to live on the place—a plan he had eagerly accepted—so she had bought him a little house trailer. But the trailer would be too small if she brought Jaime's wife up from Mexico, so she got together with Ted, and soon plans were being drawn for a new caretaker's house.

"If you're giving away houses," Ted told her with a shake of his head at her largess, "my brother-in-law could go for one, the bum. I'm sure he wouldn't mind livin' here for nothin'." But he smiled when he said it, and Briar just grinned.

But even though Ted agreed that Jaime was quite a hand, he still told her stubbornly, "I think you should let the finishing carpenters come in before you move in. That way, we'll be sure things are right. They could pick up something the others missed."

Briar laughed outright. He was really searching for excuses, she thought. She knew he had already gone over the place with the proverbial fine-tooth comb. "Stop worrying," she told him fondly, and she handed him a thick ham sandwich to go with his beer.

To the crew's surprise—including Ted's, because she had kept her plans a secret from him, too—she had breezed in late that afternoon followed by three catering trucks and a half dozen people who quickly proceeded to put up long tables and set up a scrumptious buffet. It was her present to Ted and his crew, for even though she had already included a generous bonus check, she wanted to show them in another way how much she appreciated all their hard work.

Her gesture was well received, for one by one, even the shyest members of the crew came up to thank her. Then, after a lot of hemming and hawing and self-conscious milling around, two men disappeared around the back of the house, returning with a bulky oblong object covered by painting tarps.

"What's this?" Briar asked, as they formed a circle around her. Feeling embarrassed and pleased at the same time, she glanced at Ted, who just shrugged and pretended he didn't know what was going on, either.

They were all standing in front of the house, which itself stood, as it always had, on a rise overlooking most of the property, except for what extended to the hills in back. As she looked around proudly, she thought how different the place looked today than when she had first come. Now, newly fenced five-acre pastures rolled down and away on either side of the house, and the new barn was the centerpiece to it all, long and low, resplendent in the old Caulfield "silks," colors of green, amber, and gold.

She had researched those racing colors and reapplied to the Jockey Club and had been delighted to learn that Caulfield Farm was still registered, along with the distinctive design of an amber and green field split by a lightning bolt of gold. They had sent her a picture, in fact, of the silks as they had originally been registered, and if she did get into racing, that was the design her jockey would wear.

For now, she had carried that color scheme through the ranch, and as she intended for all the other buildings still to come, the new barn was painted similarly, although she had lightened the amber to a dramatic pale beige that better suited the topography of the land. As she stared critically at it, she had to admit that her choice had been a good one; with the pale siding, the green-shingled roof, and the gold trim, the barn was indeed the showplace she had planned.

She still didn't know why she had insisted that the main stables be built on that exact place. Ted and the surveyor had gone out and come back with other, more suitable, sites, but for some reason, she felt that the barn *had* to be raised where she had first indicated, and as the foundation was put in, she had known deep down that she had chosen right. What had happened to the original, she still didn't know; she'd had Albert Weitz researching to find out, but he hadn't come up with anything yet.

For the time being, she was content with what she had built, and the new barn—with the herringbone-patterned brick aisle, the tongue-and-groove pine for the stalls, two-inch-square, covered-wire mesh for the grills—stood waiting for occupancy. She'd been so busy running back and forth that she hadn't even had time to bring Irish up to his new home, much less order the sign she intended to put up over the big gates at the end of the road. The gates were repaired now and were opened and closed by an automatic mechanism, even though she intended them always to stand open in welcome.

Smiling at the thought, she looked in that direction now, beyond the newly seeded pastures and the straight-as-a-die chocolate-brown fences that enclosed them, and she thought that the only thing missing was the sign. Ted and his men had accomplished a lot in a very short time, but as pleased as she was with the way everything was turning out, she had told the crew several times during the lunch breaks she had shared with them that she wouldn't feel the ranch had come to life again until that sign went up, announcing that Caulfield Farm was in business again.

"All right, you guys," she said, when the two men stopped in front of her with the bulky tarp-covered object. "What's going on?"

Motioned by the rest of the crew, two men came forward. "Ms . . . ah . . . McKenna?" one of them said. With the exception of Ted, she had never been able to talk any of them into calling her Briar. Red-faced, he looked around and then just blurted it all out. "We . . . er . . . well, shoot, this here's for you."

With that, they whipped off the tarp to an accompanying huzzah from the crew. Briar caught Ted grinning widely before she turned to look at what the men had done, then she blinked in surprise. For a moment, she couldn't believe her eyes. It was a sign. *The* sign, she thought, and just looked.

"I-I don't know what to say," she stammered, overcome.

Someone called out, "Just say you like it!"

She looked up, her eyes shining. "I do! Oh, I do! It's . . . beautiful!"

It was. It was also huge—at least twenty feet by five feet, so heavy that several men came forward to help the first two. Briar couldn't stop looking at it—the colors of Caulfield Farm that had come to life. On a pale beige background, with green border trim, the intricately carved and raised initials, CF, stood out in elegant gold relief. It was the logo for the farm—the same logo that had existed for nearly a hundred years, she thought with a lump in her throat. Suddenly emotional, she found herself blinking back tears. She had seen these letters so many times—in her dreams, in her thoughts, on the locket she had carried close to her heart. She had traced the elaborate pattern so often on her gold pendant that she could have drawn it with her eyes closed. To see it come to life again in front of her, well . . . she didn't know what to say.

"Hey, guys," Ted said, as she fumbled for a tissue. "I think she likes it."

Tears shining in her eyes, she tried to express what she was feeling. "I don't . . . if you only knew how much this means to me. . . ." Still feeling overwhelmed, she looked helplessly around. "I can't thank you enough," she said finally. "It's the most beautiful present I've ever received in my life."

Looking a little misty himself, Ted handed her his handkerchief, a big blue bandanna that he pulled out of his back pocket. "We found it out back," he said awkwardly, as she quickly dabbed at her eyes. "We knew as soon as we saw it that it had to be the original—or close to it. How it got there, I don't know. But we decided to refinish it. We . . . we thought you might like to hang it up in the barn, or something."

"Hang it in the barn!" Briar stuffed Ted's bandanna in her back pocket. "We're going to put it up over the front gates. Right now! Come on, guys—let's go!"

With whoops and hollers, they all piled onto one of the flatbed trucks and roared down the hill. The front gates were almost a half mile away, and as they screeched to a halt, Briar was the first to jump down. The big pillars on either side were sturdy enough to carry the weight of a sign, and she pointed to the arch that rose high over the center of the driveway. "There. Right there. That's where I want it."

They gave her the honor of driving the last nail and tightening the final bolt, which she did with a flourish while sitting on two of the crew's shoulders. The ceremony over, she made them all drive up the hill again, where she broke out the champagne she'd been saving as a final surprise. Holding a glass aloft, she made a toast.

"To Caulfield Farm," she said.

"To Caulfield Farm!" they all cried.

The revelry lasted until nearly dark, when Ted finally pointed out that they had to be on a new job up the coast at seven the next morning. Reluctantly, after saying good-bye, the crew left in their trucks and four-wheel vehicles and Jeeps, honking and shouting and generally raising hell all the way down the hill. Briar stood on the porch, feverishly waving until everyone had gone. But finally, the last faint horn sounded, the last rumble of an engine died away, and silence descended.

Alone, she glanced tremulously around. Attuned as always to the slightest vibration, Jaime had tactfully disappeared as well; the light in his trailer down by the barn glowed yellow in the twilight. Far up on the hills at the back of the house, the last glow of the sun was gold plating the trees. As she stood on the porch watching, soft purple shadows moved down the hill, and the air took on a new tang—the scent of ownership, Briar thought, breathing in deeply. Closing her eyes, she couldn't remember ever feeling this way—so satisfied and pleased, so *content* deep down, as if this had always been meant to be. The only thing that could have made it better was if Hay had been here to share the triumph with her.

And triumph it had been—and would be, she thought, opening her eyes. She loved this place already; she had felt proprietary from the moment she had first set foot on the property. Now the house was nearly complete, and soon the horses would begin arriving. Irish first, she thought guiltily; she would have to drive back right away and trailer him up or he would never forgive her. But after that, she would begin some serious searching. She hadn't renovated the ranch only to live on an empty showplace. Once committed, she knew she was going to have to bring horses in—to breed and raise and train. The thought scared and exhilarated her at the same time; she loved horses, and she knew how to ride. But what did she know about a breeding farm?

*I'll learn*, she thought fiercely, looking forward to the challenge. Whether she had a ranch manager or not by then, she planned to attend her first Thoroughbred sale in a few weeks, where she intended to buy the first of the brood mares that would fill her pastures with strong, healthy foals. That reminded her to call Stan Taber again; he had promised to try to find her someone to manage the place and to help guide her through the sales. As much as she thought she already knew about horses, she realized she still had a lot to learn for this new venture.

One thing at a time, she told herself, and looked around again, hugging her waist. She had plans for this place, and she smiled again.

*Well, great-grandmother,* she thought, *what do you think of the ranch right now?*

But she knew what her great-grandmother would think; all along, from the moment she decided to reconstruct the farm and make it the showplace she knew it had been, she hadn't had any doubts that she was doing the right thing. Without being able to explain it, even to herself, conviction had grown. Fate and circumstance had brought her here at this time for a reason, and although it sounded corny and absurd, she knew deep inside that she was fulfilling a purpose she had been headed unknowingly toward all her life. She didn't know why she knew, or how it was intended to be, but she felt that she was here to finish what her great-grandmother had started so long ago.

*It's a circle,* she mused, and again she couldn't say why she was so certain; she just knew it was true. Maybe tonight she would find out, she thought, when she reread the first journal.

She knew it was silly, but after reading the first two journals so quickly she hardly knew what they had said, she had put them away with the rest. Despite her eagerness to devour them all at one sitting, it seemed more fitting to wait until she moved in, so that she could read them in the very house in which they had been written—the house that would span four generations and nearly a hundred years now in her family.

Her *family,* she thought, and hugged herself again.

Thinking of the set of six volumes she had put upstairs by her bed, she went quickly inside. She felt breathless and excited and so filled with anticipation that she was almost sick. She couldn't wait any longer to get started, and she was just locking the front door from habit when she thought of something Albert Weitz, the investigator, had said to her the other day, when she told him she'd soon be moving.

"You be careful out there," he'd warned, sitting across from her at the office. A city-boy to the core, he'd been as protective as Ted, worried about her staying alone so far back from the road. "God knows what kind of kooks are wandering around."

"In Sonoma?" she'd asked, amused.

"You laugh," he said direly. "But things happen, you know."

She'd been touched by his concern, as she had been by Ted's. "Don't worry," she said, reassuring him. "I have Jaime."

He already knew about her young caretaker. "A boy!" he scoffed. "If anything happens, you'll have to protect *him*."

"I can do that, too. I took your advice and bought a shotgun."

He wasn't as impressed as she thought he'd be. "Do you know how to use it?"

"Of course I do," she said indignantly. "You said yourself that all I have to do is point and pull the trigger."

"Oh, great. You're going to shoot yourself in the foot, I can just see it."

"Thanks so much for the vote of confidence."

"Just want to make sure you're alert," he said, then he grinned at a sudden thought. "Well, it don't matter anyway. One of those barrels will blow a person all the way to kingdom come, and then some, so I guess you'll be all right."

"Lovely thought," she murmured, and opted to change the subject. "So. What have you found out for me this week?"

As he pulled out his battered notebook from a coat pocket, she thought how glad she was that she had hired him. Albert, as she called him now, had become a gruff friend in addition to doing her investigative work, and she wasn't sure what she would have done without him these past weeks. After that unpleasant confrontation with Rupert and Carl Jaeger, she had called him and told him she needed everything he could get about the Jaeger family. He knew by this time that she wanted more than public record, but getting that kind of information took time, and when he called back and said it was going to be a little more difficult than he had anticipated, she tried to be patient. She already knew that a family as obviously influential and powerful as the Jaegers seemed to be was capable of hiding what it didn't want others to see. And she knew from things Hay had confided to her how easy it was for large companies to hide what they didn't want discovered.

Still, as Albert tried to find a way inside Mondragon Enterprises, Briar couldn't help thinking that if it was this difficult getting information about the Jaegers, it was going to be much harder to find out about her own family. Despite their combined efforts so far, she still knew little more than what Albert had started with, and sometimes it was hard to contain her impatience. She wondered what had happened, for instance, to cause such a schism in the fortunes of the two families. At one time her great-grandfather, Sloane Caulfield, had been one of the most influential men in California; he was even listed in some of the history books on the state. But while the Jaeger star continued to rise, first with the establishment of the Mondragon Stud, then with the formation of Mondragon Enterprises, the Caulfields seemed to . . . drop out of sight.

At first she speculated that the reason had something to do with the demise of racing across the nation around 1909 to 1910, when the antiwagering laws were passed. But she knew now that wasn't the entire answer because both the Jaegers and the Caulfields had been in the business of breeding and raising racing horses at that time, and if Caulfield Farm, which supposedly had been producing horses superior to those at Mondragon, had been affected, the Jaeger clan would have suffered as well. Obviously, the fall of racing wasn't the cause. But what was? Why had her family's fortunes declined, while Mondragon's rose?

Hoping that Marguerite's journals would help her find her way through the puzzling questions that continued to crop up the more she tried to unearth her family's history, she went into the living room and turned on the lights. Basking in the warm glow from the genuine Tiffany lamps for just a moment, she looked around. To her regret, most of the furniture her great-aunt Juliet had left behind had been invaded by moths and mice, and she'd had to get rid of it and bring in new. But the lamps still worked, and in the soft light they cast, the big living room looked warm and inviting—quite a change from the abandoned canvas-and-sheet covered appearance it had had the first time she'd seen it. The overstuffed genuine cotton sofa she'd chosen looked wonderful in cream against the windows, and the glass-topped coffee table and end tables gave the room an open feeling. She'd had the giant fireplace painted white, as well, and the low slab hearth redone in slate. Unfortunately, the original India rug couldn't be saved, so she had replaced it with a rug of Southwestern design, this one in muted tones of green and orange and light blue on a pale background; the rug emphasized the glow from the hardwood floors that had also been redone. In addition, all the curtains had been replaced; the dusty, ragged heavy satin draperies were removed and the windows were now flanked by gauzy open-weave drapes in pale orange that emphasized the cream-colored walls. With light blue and green and orange accents, the room looked elegant and inviting at the same time, and she was pleased at the effect.

She was just about to turn off the lights again when the big front window caught her eye. It was dark now, and she couldn't see much, but she knew, because she had stood here so often the past two months, that from this vantage point she could see practically the entire ranch. Ted had found her here once, just gazing out, a dreamy look on her face. As though he understood, he quietly asked, "Well, how does it feel?" And she'd turned to him with a smile and answered honestly, "Just great."

Smiling again at the memory, she left the window and gave a last satisfied look around the living room before she went toward the kitchen. She wasn't really hungry; whether from too much excitement or still full from the buffet, she couldn't think of anything she wanted to eat. But she wouldn't mind a cup of coffee, and as she pushed through the swinging doors into the kitchen proper, she wondered how her aunt Juliet had managed with the antiquated appliances that had been here before. Briar had taken one look and decided that the ancient sink, the stove, and washing machine had had to go. She had replaced them with their more modern cousins, adding a dishwasher, garbage disposal, trash compactor, and matching washer and dryer for the service porch. After making a quick cup of coffee, Briar headed upstairs.

The master bedroom was, as it should be, the biggest bedroom in a house of big bedrooms. The dark green silk wallpaper that had covered the walls when she'd first seen it had been so stained and blotched and curling in places that she had ordered it replaced with something more modern—flowers on a pale background. Although she wasn't exactly a "flowery"

type, somehow the room seemed to demand it. There was also
a four-poster bed she'd brought in, and matching bed tables,
and carpet in a rose color that complimented the flowers in the
paper. It was an old-fashioned room in an old-fashioned house,
and Briar smiled again as she thought of what Hay would have
said if he could see her now. He'd always called her the most
modern of women, and he'd loved the fact that she not only ran
her own company, but also her life—and their marriage—with
efficiency and dispatch.

But something in her that she hadn't suspected until now
appreciated these quaint touches, and as she ran her hand over
the moss-green velvet bedspread, she shook her head. *Who
would have thought?*

Twenty minutes later, after a quick shower, she climbed into
bed. The moment had come at last; she'd done all she could to
put it off, but if she waited any longer, she was going to
explode with excitement. Reaching out, she carefully took the
first of her great-grandmother's journals from its protective
jacket. Then as she looked down at the faded cloth cover, she
was suddenly reluctant to open the book. If Marguerite's journals *did* hold the key to so many mysteries surrounding the
family, did she really want to know the answers? She already
knew her aunt Juliet had been mentally ill—or so Albert had
told her—but suppose there was more? What if the Jaegers
were justified in the hatred they obviously still felt toward
anyone named Caulfield? Perhaps the competition between
them had been more than that, she thought; maybe the bitter
rivalry had been born from acts better left in the past.

No, no, she knew that wasn't true, she told herself, and she
remembered what Albert had told her just the other day about
her great-grandfather, Sloane.

"He was supposed to have been quite the fella," Albert had
said. "But you already know that."

"Yes, I do—thanks to you," she said. She even had a
picture of Sloane, who had been such a handsome man that
he'd taken *her* breath away. No wonder Marguerite had married him, she'd thought; she would have been a fool to let him
get away.

According to what Albert had found out, Sloane had already
made a fine reputation for himself as an attorney in his native
Kentucky when he decided to come to California during the
mid 1880s. He had been twenty-seven to Marguerite's seven-

teen when they married in 1890, already a self-made million-aire because of his canny investments.

"But your great-grandmother very nearly didn't marry him," Albert told her. "It's hard to believe, but I just found out that until she and Sloane eloped, Marguerite was going to marry Heinrich Jaeger."

Recollecting that conversation now, Briar could still recall her shock. That had been a twist, all right, she remembered, and decided she wanted to find out what had happened to change Marguerite's mind.

She opened to the first page. The date at the top was 1890, and, Briar calculated, Marguerite would have been just seventeen years old. The facing page was thick, of good stock, but the book had been put away for so long that the page stuck to the one behind it. As Briar reached out to separate it, she wasn't surprised to see her hand shake. She was so afraid of ruining the paper, tearing it, or something equally awful, that it took her a moment to get the pages apart. Then, abruptly the book fell open, and there, right at the top, written in that elegant copperplate, was the first line of Marguerite's diary. Instantly, it seemed to Briar, her great-grandmother leaped to life. Even the way the words raced across the paper sounded like a cry from the past.

---&---

# CHAPTER ELEVEN

*Marry Heinrich! Heinrich Jaeger? I'd sooner throw myself into the river!* Marguerite had written tearfully, her hand flying across the paper. *Oh, how could Papa even think such a thing? He must be out of his mind!*

But Jacob Kendall wasn't joking, it seemed, and, to Marguerite's shocked dismay, he appeared in full possession of all his faculties. For the first time since he had broached the subject, in the drawing room of the Kendall farm outside Sacramento, she felt real alarm.

*It can't be!* she thought, and tried not to panic. She hadn't heard her father correctly; it was all a horrible misunderstanding. Perhaps she was having a dream—a nightmare! she thought in sudden hope—and seized on the explanation with abject relief. Of course, it *had* to be that. Her father, her darling papa, would never ask such a thing of her—never! She had known the Jaeger family since childhood—and why not, since Claus Jaeger had been her father's business partner for longer than she could remember?—but no one had ever mentioned the possibility of marriage before, and not even her recent disgrace, which had precipitated her family's move out of the city and back to the farm, was cause enough for life imprisonment! Oh, surely her parents wouldn't be so cruel! Heinrich, the only child of Claus and Frieda Jaeger, was so cold and controlled, so . . . *passionless!* She would never marry him—never! She would sooner marry a toad!

But she knew from past bitter experience that she could only push her father so far, and now that she was over her first shock, she remembered that she was usually able to change his mind if she tried hard enough. Hadn't she wriggled her way out of her last escapade? True, things hadn't worked out *quite* the way she wanted—her mother *had* insisted on moving the family out of the city and back to the ranch for the time being—but at least she hadn't been sent to Iowa to live with Aunt Hortensia. She had begged and pleaded and wept so piteously that her father had finally relented, and if she had been able to change his mind then, she certainly could now. She would *not* marry Heinrich, and that was final!

She had just been out riding, and her cheeks were still flushed from galloping her father's new young stallion, Saxon. She knew Jacob would be angry if he discovered she had taken the horse out, but she couldn't worry about that now. This other problem was too pressing, and she was just in the act of tossing aside her plumed riding hat and running across the room so she could fling her arms around him and beg him to reconsider, when her mother appeared in the doorway.

"You've told her, then?" Anna Kendall said, looking at her husband.

Unhappily, Jacob nodded.

Caught in the middle, Marguerite looked from one parent to the other. When she saw her mother's face, she felt a chill. She knew that intractable expression, and she had never been as adept at winning her mother to her side as she was her father. Only her cousin Mariel, who had come to live with them last year after her parents died, seemed to be able to do that—but then, why not? Butter would melt in Mariel's mouth, the little sneak, but Marguerite knew how two-faced she really was. Mariel ran to her aunt Anna over every real or imagined slight, and Marguerite thought blackly that if she heard her mother say one more time that she had to treat her cousin with kindness because of her recent loss, she was going to *scream*. It was Mariel who had informed the headmistress at their academy about the escapade at the Governor's Ball. No one ever would have found out Marguerite had slipped in without an invitation if Mariel hadn't told, and look what had happened. Now she was disgraced, and it was all her cousin's fault.

Still, Marguerite thought distractedly, she would do it again. The Governor's Ball was where she had been introduced to Sloane Caulfield for the first time, and now she was in love. Like everyone else in California, she thought, she had been hearing exciting stories about Sloane, the young lawyer from Kentucky who had come West to make his fortune, and when one of the girls at school told her that someone had told *her* that Sloane was invited to the ball because he was a friend of the governor's, well . . . of course she had to go, invitation or not.

And what a success she had been! Even at seventeen, she knew when a man was smitten, and Sloane Caulfield had surely been smitten with her that night! They had danced practically every dance; they had had supper together at midnight. They hadn't lacked for things to talk about. They had laughed endlessly, and when she learned that he planned to settle near San Francisco, she nearly swooned. She *loved* San Francisco; she had been begging her father to relocate there from dull old Sacramento for years! To think of it—the parties, the theater, the social affairs—and the *racing*! To be a part of that would be a dream come true!

She had decided that night that Sloane Caulfield was the man she was going to marry, and she had been planning how she was going to introduce him to her father when the world caved in. Mariel found out she had gone to the ball and had immediately rushed to the headmistress of the school with the tale. Before Marguerite knew what was happening, she was being dismissed in disgrace from the school, and her tight-lipped mother was supervising the family move back to the ranch, where, she said with a baleful look in her daughter's direction, she could supervise Marguerite's activities more closely.

Compelled to withdraw from the academy as well, Mariel was furious with her, but Marguerite didn't care. In fact, she'd often thought smugly, it served the little telltale right. None of this would have happened if it hadn't been for Mariel, and in any case, she was far more preoccupied with how to see Sloane again.

But even then it seemed that fate was on her side, for just when she was thinking that she was doomed to spinsterhood, her father announced that Sloane Caulfield was coming out to look over some of the bloodstock her father had for sale. In addition to the prosperous mercantile business Marguerite's father owned with his partner, Claus Jaeger, Jacob dabbled in breeding running horses—one reason why Marguerite hadn't been more distraught about her exile than she might have been. Like her father, she loved the horses, and—although her mother would have been horrified if she had learned of her daughter's plans—intended one day to own a ranch herself. For years she had been pumping her indulgent father for information, and he had patiently answered all her questions; indeed, pleased by her interest in his avocation, he had even allowed her to participate in many of the breeding decisions, and he often admitted to her that she knew as much now about the horses as he did.

Then Sloane Caulfield came out to look at the horses. Marguerite was in heaven, especially when that first visit turned into several, then several more, until Sloane became almost a regular fixture. Nearly giddy with delight at how well her plans were coming along, Marguerite failed to notice for a long while that she wasn't the only one interested in the handsome lawyer from Kentucky. Bored and unhappy at the ranch, Mariel decided to set her cap for their eligible visitor, and by the time Marguerite noticed what her sly cousin was up to, she was alarmed to see Sloane eyeing Mariel with what she thought was more than polite interest. She had come too far to lose now—especially to her disagreeable cousin—and so, as brazen as it was, she came right out and asked Sloane what his intentions were during one of their rides along the river.

At first her mother had objected to these excursions, as innocent as they were, but as always her father had indulged her. "What could happen?" he'd said fondly. And then, seeing his wife bristle, added hastily, "I'll see that Manuella goes with them."

Since Manuella was the fat cook and disinclined to ride, she followed at a discrete distance behind Marguerite and Sloane in the pony trap when they rode out together. It wasn't what Marguerite had in mind—she would much rather have engaged in a wild gallop across the flatland—but she had to admit it was better than enduring those stiff talks in the parlor under Anna's watchful eye. As they trotted sedately along in front of the pony trap, she did get a chance to talk privately with Sloane, who always seemed amused. With her parents, or even with Mariel, he was always unfailingly courteous and proper and very reserved, but with her for some reason, he'd often throw his head back and laugh aloud.

Hoping that was a good sign, and aware that time was running out—Sloane was, after all, a *very* eligible man, and soon he would be leaving for San Francisco—Marguerite screwed up her courage one day and broached the subject of the future. Thinking herself very clever, she approached it obliquely, as she did most things she wanted.

It was a beautiful day, that afternoon; one of those lovely springs, not too hot or too windy. The river flowed along peacefully, green and serene, and behind them, Manuella prodded the slow little pony. Glancing over her shoulder to make sure that their duenna couldn't overhear, Marguerite took a deep breath, smiled across at Sloane, and said, "I never thanked you for not telling my father when you first came out to the farm that we had already met."

Sloane was riding beside her, holding the reins easily in one hand. He had started out dressed formally in black riding boots and fawn breeches with a white shirt and red cravat and black jacket, but because the day was warm, he'd asked her permission to remove the coat. Much to the following Manuella's disapproval, he had also rolled up his sleeves, as well, and as they rode, Marguerite had trouble keeping her eyes off his strong forearms. Transferring the reins from one hand to the other, he slapped at a fly on his mount's neck, and then glanced at her with a devilish grin.

"You asked me not to, remember? I was just rescuing a lady in distress."

"Yes, I remember," she said, and then couldn't help smiling, too. A dimple appeared in her cheek as she looked mischievously at Sloane. "And I *was* in distress. Oh, my parents were *so* angry when they discovered I attended that ball! Sometimes I wish . . ." She stopped.

Sloane shifted in the saddle. His eyes suddenly seemed very blue. "That you hadn't defied decorum and gone to that ball? But if you hadn't, we wouldn't have met."

"Oh, I doubt that," she said demurely. "After all, my father met you soon after that and invited you out to see his horses."

Sloane chuckled. "Do you think *that* meeting was an accident, too?"

She gave him a quick look from under her long lashes. His eyes were twinkling, and he was smiling. She smiled, too. Then, realizing what he had said, she laughed outright. He laughed with her, and then, before she knew what he was doing, he reached for her gloved hand.

"I love your laugh," he said. "I've loved it from that very first night. It's like music. . . ."

Suddenly confused, very aware of the warmth of his fingers on hers, even with the protection of her glove, she glanced hastily away. Since entering her teens, she had always had the upper hand where callow young boys were concerned, but, abruptly, she was very much aware that Sloane was no boy. He seemed overwhelming to her, overpowering, experienced, a man of the world. While she . . . she seemed only a disgraced schoolgirl living in a fantasy world. What did she know about Sloane Caulfield, really?

"Marguerite," he said softly, and reached up to take her chin in his hand. Manuella be damned. Gently forcing her to turn and look at him, he said, "Forgive me if I said something I shouldn't have."

She looked into his face. "No, it . . . it wasn't that," she stammered.

"You must know that as much as I enjoy your father's company, and your family's hospitality, the real reason I come so often to visit is . . . you."

She felt like a fool. To think that she had planned so brazenly to ask his intentions! Now that the moment was here— and gone—she felt so embarrassed she wanted to spur her horse and disappear. What had ever made her think she knew how to deal with men?

"Perhaps I spoke too soon," Sloane said, rescuing her. He paused. "Or out of turn."

Marguerite might be impulsive, foolish at times, but she had courage. "No," she said. "You didn't."

He looked at her for a moment, then he smiled—a slow smile that she had already grown to love, or thought she had. She wasn't sure what she felt at the moment, except disoriented and confused, and she was very glad that Manuella, seeing Sloane's hand-holding gesture of a moment ago, had slapped the reins against the pony's fat back, urging him to trot reluctantly a little closer to her charges.

"*Señorita*," she called anxiously. "Is everything all right?"

Marguerite looked back. Manuella was bouncing up and down in the pony trap as the plump little creature hurried to catch up. The amusing sight made Marguerite forget her own discomfort, and she laughed. Then, abruptly, she remembered what Sloane had said about her laugh, and she felt embarrassed again. "Everything is fine, Manuella," she said, avoiding Sloane's eye. "Just fine . . ."

She hadn't told anyone about that tantalizing, unsettling conversation during her ride with Sloane that beautiful spring morning, not even her best friend Cecilia. And she certainly hadn't breathed a word to Mariel, who she already knew listened at doors and stood behind corners, appearing suddenly when one thought she was elsewhere. She'd had such high hopes when she first learned that her cousin was coming to live with them; she had always wanted a sister, and she and Mariel were so close in age that she had imagined they'd have all sorts of things to share. But it hadn't worked out that way at all, and as time went on, it became obvious that Mariel not only disliked her, but was jealous and resentful as well, especially of her friendship with Sloane Caulfield. She intruded rudely at every opportunity; she constantly tried, figuratively or literally, to elbow Marguerite aside, until even Anna was embarrassed.

"Well, I don't care!" Mariel cried one night when Anna took her to task yet again after Sloane had visited recently and Mariel had shrilly insisted on sitting next to him at supper. Her black eyes flashed, and she tossed her long, black hair. "I'm going to marry him one day, see if I don't!"

Marguerite had been so shocked she couldn't think of anything to say. *In a pig's eye!* she had thought angrily, wondering why she was thinking of all that now, when she had another emergency to deal with. Thrusting thoughts of Mariel aside, she looked at her parents again. As she stood there uncertainly, tall and slender like her mother, with a luxurious mane of thick chestnut hair that would escape its pins, and flashing green eyes that betrayed her feelings no matter *how* she tried to hide them—but much more vivacious and headstrong than Anna, she knew instinctively that an appeal to her mother would be a waste of precious time. Jacob might call her his spirited lass, but because of her quick temper and volatile nature, her mother had too often despaired of her. Anna Kendall believed, even in this modern year of 1890, that women—if they wished to be ladies—were demure and retiring and self-effacing. None of which remotely described Marguerite.

It did, however, describe Mariel, Marguerite thought resentfully, remembering the conversation she had overheard between her parents just the other night. Her mother had been berating her father when she—borrowing a page from her cousin's book—had crept up to their bedroom door to listen. She was supposed to be in bed, but when she had heard the raised voices, she *knew* they were talking about her, and she couldn't help herself. The bedroom door had been ajar, and, since she had come this far to listen, she decided she might as well try to see what was going on, as well. Tiptoeing up, she put her eye to the crack in the door just as her mother turned from her dressing table to speak to Jacob, who was sitting on the bed.

"Mariel would never have engaged in such disgraceful behavior that it resulted in being dismissed from the prestigious Sacramento Academy for Girls," Anna was saying to her unhappy husband. "And she would never hunker down like a common milkmaid to watch a new foal being born now that we've all been forced to retire to the farm. And Mariel certainly would not race around like a hoyden on that dangerous stallion you just bought, that . . . that *Saxon*!"

"Now, Anna," Jacob had said placatingly.

Anna wasn't in the mood to be soothed. "Don't you 'now, Anna' me! This is supposed to be a punishment for Marguerite, not an opportunity to do exactly as she pleases while we all suffer the consequences of her thoughtless behavior! Now, I want you to talk to her about riding that horse. It's intolerable and . . . and unseemly for a girl of seventeen to be riding a stallion, and I won't permit it!"

Jacob reached to take his boots off. "It's little enough to ask," he said indulgently. "After all, there's not much for her to do out here."

Anna had been very angry then. "Not much for her to do!" she cried, and then deliberately lowered her voice because she thought the girls were in the next room. Listening outside, Marguerite held her breath. She didn't know what she'd do if her mother found her there, but she couldn't leave now, especially when Anna pointed the hairbrush she'd been using at her husband. "As you might trouble yourself to recall, Jacob, the reason we had to move back to the ranch was because of Marguerite's disgraceful exhibition in town. *Flaunting* herself uninvited at the Governor's Ball, when she should have been safe in her room at school . . . Going to the *races* when she was supposed to be attending class—and heaven knows what else! The only reason I didn't object to having to uproot the entire family—not to mention withdrawing poor, innocent Mariel from school—was because our daughter was developing a reputation for being—" her lip curled—"*fast!*"

"Oh, now—"

"No! I will not have Marguerite think this is some kind of holiday, where she can do as she pleases! Do you understand me?"

"I do, but I've got more important things on my mind right now than my daughter's lack of decorum."

Anna looked at him incredulously. "What could be more important than that?"

Oblivious of Marguerite, riveted, outside the bedroom door, Jacob had told his wife about the investments he'd recently made that had failed, about the losses he'd sustained in his horse-breeding business, about the bets on races he'd lost trying to recoup, and about the tremendous sums of money he had borrowed from his partner Claus Jaeger against his half of their once-prosperous mercantile business.

Anna was so shocked that she could hardly speak. "You . . . you can't mean we're—" she hardly seemed able to say the word aloud—"*destitute!*"

Jacob winced. "There is a way," he had muttered. And then he told Anna what Claus had proposed. Heinrich was in love with Marguerite, he said. If a marriage could be arranged . . .

Listening, Marguerite was so frozen with horror that she

couldn't think, but Anna grasped the implications at once. "You mean that if Marguerite marries Heinrich, Claus will forgive you your debt?"

Unhappily, Jacob nodded. "And pay off all my creditors."

"Then we have no choice!"

"But it seems so unfair—"

"Unfair! *Unfair?* After all we've done for that ungrateful girl?"

Jacob tried again, but he was sinking fast. "But you know how Marguerite feels about Heinrich."

Marguerite thought of Heinrich Jaeger, lean, ascetic Heinrich, with his straight posture, blond hair so pale it was nearly white against his narrow skull, and eyes the color of a wintry sea. Then she pictured Sloane Caulfield, so young and handsome with his thick gold hair and warm blue eyes, and she put her hand over her mouth to stifle a cry. *No, it couldn't be!* she thought, and she would have burst in to confront both her parents if she hadn't been so paralyzed with fear. Caught, she had to listen.

"Heinrich has an . . . unfortunate manner," Anna was saying carefully. "But I believe he's a good man. And if there is no other way. . . ?"

Jacob's shoulders slumped. "There is no other way," he said, rubbing his eyes. "God help me, but there is no other way."

Remembering that conversation this morning as she stood in the drawing room between her parents, Marguerite looked wildly from one to the other. Her eyes met her mother's, and Anna looked away.

"I'll be in the garden," she said tersely, and left them.

Alone with her father, Marguerite turned to Jacob. Now that her mother had gone, she knew she could take matters into her own hands. She would *not* marry Heinrich; she could not. Surely she could make her father see that.

"You can't be serious, Papa," she said, her voice trembling.

But to her dismay, Jacob said unhappily, "Sit down, Marguerite."

"I don't want to sit down!" She knew her father, and this wasn't a good sign. Turning her back to him, she said angrily, "And I don't want to talk about this anymore!"

"We have to talk about it, Marguerite. You must understand—"

Whirling around again, she clenched her hands. "Well, I *don't* understand! Oh, how can you even think such a thing, Papa? You *know* how I feel about Heinrich! Why, you . . . you didn't even consult me! If you had, you would have known I was going to refuse outright!"

"I'm afraid it's not as simple as that."

"Why not?" An appalling thought occurred to her, and she paled. "You haven't told him I *would* marry him, have you?"

Jacob looked, if possible, even more miserable. Dressed impeccably as always in a black suit, with a starched high collar and subdued cravat, he suddenly seemed to wilt. "Not in so many words," he admitted reluctantly.

Color flooded Marguerite's face again. "Well, then! You'll just have to tell him I can't!"

"But I promised Claus."

Marguerite couldn't believe they were having this conversation. Confused and angry and hurt, and beginning to think that this might be real after all, she pressed her nails into her palms to stop herself from screaming. She wanted to run from the room, but her pride wouldn't allow her such craven behavior. Instead, her eyes glittering with her unshed tears, she said, "And what does *Claus* have to do with this?"

Jacob looked away in shame. "It's too complicated to explain."

"You owe him money, don't you, Papa?" she said. *"That's* what all this is about!"

"It's not quite as simple as that. . . ." Jacob started to say again, but then he saw the knowledge in her eyes. Miserably he looked away. "It's not as simple as that," he repeated, his voice choked.

Despite her dire situation, Marguerite's generous heart went out to her father. He looked so sad, so . . . beaten. She wanted to rush over to him and have him enfold her in his arms and tell her that it was all a mistake and that somehow they'd work something out. But even she knew that such simple, childish solutions had gone forever, and she had to swallow over the growing lump of fright in her throat to say, "But . . . *Heinrich,* Father! He's never even indicated by a . . . a *word* that he wanted to marry me! There has to be some mistake!"

"There's no mistake, Marguerite," Jacob said. "He told me himself."

"Why didn't he tell *me*?"

But perhaps he had, she thought suddenly, her mind going back to the last time she had seen him. It had been three weeks ago, when the entire Jaeger family had come to dinner here. That was a monthly ritual Marguerite hated, for if the Jaegers weren't coming out to the farm, the Kendalls had to go into town and return the favor at their mansion at the corner of Third and Broadway. She disliked the big, cold house; everything—from the hard horsehair sofas in the parlor to the plain, white china and heavy, unadorned silverware in the dining room—seemed to symbolize the meanness of spirit she had always associated with anyone named Jaeger. Claus and his wife, Frieda, might have been cut from the same miserly bolt of cloth, and Heinrich was just like them.

Thinking of the Jaeger's only son, Marguerite closed her eyes. She had never suspected for an instant that he was remotely interested in her, much less that he desired to *marry* her. And why should she have? Who had ever been able to see beyond those wintry gray eyes of his, or that stiff manner? Even his voice made her shiver, and she couldn't imagine why he would want her for his wife, or think that she would even consider marrying him.

Then she thought of the conversation they had had the last time he was here, and she felt another stab of alarm. She hadn't thought much of it at the time; Heinrich was always saying inexplicable things to which she rarely paid attention, but it seemed that she should have listened. Feeling the need for some air after the heavy dinner Anna always insisted on preparing when the Jaeger family came on Sundays, she had excused herself and gone to the stables to check on one of the mares. She hadn't realized Heinrich had followed her until she turned and saw him behind her. Instantly, she became annoyed.

"My goodness!" she exclaimed. "You startled me. Why didn't you say something to let me know you were here?"

Heinrich was wearing a fawn-colored suit that day, she remembered, which, with his pale blond hair and light lashes and brows, made him seem all of one color. The late afternoon sun slanted through the open stable doors, enveloping him in a halo of sorts, and to Marguerite, always a little unnerved in his intense presence, he looked almost like an apparition.

But it was no apparition who said, "I wanted to talk to you, Marguerite."

She wasn't interested in what he had to say. Turning back to the mare who had come to the stall door and put her head out, she stroked the silky nose. "Oh? What about?"

"I'm serious, Marguerite," Heinrich said in his chilly, flat voice. "I want you to listen to me."

Briefly, she looked at him again. "I am listening. Go ahead."

He watched her for a moment, something passing behind those steely gray eyes. Was he angry? she had wondered, and then dismissed the silly thought. She couldn't imagine Heinrich passionate enough about anything to become angry; even at twenty-three, he always exhibited such perfect control.

At last, he said, "You don't like me, do you, Marguerite?"

The question startled her. Heinrich getting personal? Intrigued, she said, "What a strange thing to say. Of course I do. You're the son of my father's partner. Why wouldn't I like you?"

He sensed that she was mocking him in some subtle way, and his eyes narrowed. But she should have known better than to play games with him, for he said, "I'm glad to hear that, Marguerite. It makes things so much . . . easier."

She didn't like the sound of that. "What things? What are you talking about?"

He drew himself up, if possible, even straighter. But instead of answering her directly, he asked, "What is your heart's desire, Marguerite?"

She was so caught off guard by the question that she answered flippantly, "To marry a handsome, rich husband and to live in a beautiful house near San Francisco."

"I see," he said. "Anything else?"

Some demon seemed to take hold of her, and she wanted to see if she could shock him out of his usual stiff imperturbability. "Yes. To have my own stable, and to raise running horses who will win big purses and make me the most famous woman horse breeder in the world."

"I see," he said again. "Anything else?"

Uneasily, she wondered if this was really a game. Deciding

she didn't want to play anymore, she smoothed her skirt. "No, nothing else. Isn't that enough?"

"For now," he said. "I just wanted to be certain."

"Certain of what?"

He gave her a stiff little bow. "You'll know soon enough," he said. "After I make my . . . er . . . arrangements."

"What arrangements? I don't know what you're talking about, Heinrich." She was really getting irritated. How like him to be oblique and secretive! she thought. Did he really think she would find him more interesting if he pretended to be mysterious?

Apparently he did, for he refused to say more, and soon after that, he and his family departed in their carriage. She hadn't thought any more about that strange conversation until this moment. But as she reviewed it now, she wondered if he could have been talking about marriage that day. If he had been, she thought angrily, he'd certainly been obtuse about it!

"I won't marry him, Papa!" she said again. "You can't make me!"

"Please don't fight me about this, Marguerite," Jacob said wearily. "It will only make things even more . . . unpleasant."

"Unpleasant! *Unpleasant!* You're telling me I have to marry a man I loathe and despise and you ask me not to be *unpleasant* about it?"

Marguerite had a quick temper; she was often impulsive and rash, but she was not a violent person. But something came over her and she wanted to dash at him and beat at him with her fists, she was so angry. With an effort, she unclenched her hands. She had to think. She had to think!

"You can't do this, Papa," she said, her voice shaking despite herself. "We're living in the Middle Ages, where daughters were sold to pay off their father's debts."

Jacob turned quickly toward her, misery etched on his face. "It isn't like that."

Her eyes flashed. "Then why are you making me do this? Why don't you sell some stock? We have an entire crop of foals coming—they alone will be worth a lot of money. And then there's the business. I can't believe—"

The look on Jacob's face begged her to understand. "Even if I sold everything—everything, Marguerite, even Saxon—"

She blanched. "You wouldn't sell Saxon!"

"Even Saxon," he repeated, knowing how much she loved the horse, which she had nursed herself earlier in the year through an infection that nearly took its life. "Not even that would . . . would begin to cover what I owe Claus."

Feeling faint, Marguerite groped for the back of the sofa to brace herself. Black spots circled before her eyes; there was a roaring in her ears. *This isn't happening!* she tried to tell herself, and wondered what she was going to do.

Jacob had been holding himself up by the fireplace; now he came over to steady her. Despite herself, she stiffened when he tried to put his arms around her—she, who had always found comfort in her father's embrace.

"It won't be as bad as you think, my darling," Jacob said, his voice breaking a little. It was almost as if he were trying to convince himself as much as her. "I know you'll be far away, but we can come and visit you—"

That penetrated her misery. "Far away! What do you mean?"

"Why, what do you think?" Jacob said, sounding surprised. "Heinrich has promised to buy you a mansion near San Francisco, and to allow you to have your own stable there. He says those were your conditions—"

Marguerite jerked away from him, a look of horror on her face. "Conditions! I never said those were conditions to *marriage*!"

"But he . . . he said he talked to you about these things."

"It was only a joke, Father! A joke! I only said that because I . . . because I . . ." She didn't know why she'd said it; she only knew how sorry she was now. "I won't marry him, Papa. I won't!"

"I'm afraid you have no choice—"

Wildly, she cried, "Oh, yes, I do!"

If possible, he looked even more alarmed. "What do you mean?" he asked. Then, as she ran out of the room, he cried after her, "Marguerite, wait! What do you mean?"

She didn't answer. She ran straight to the barn, where one of the hands was rubbing Saxon down from his morning ride. Grabbing her saddle, she quickly threw it on the horse and had the girth buckled before the startled groom could comprehend what was going on. Intent only on escaping this intolerable situation and getting away before her father came out and tried to stop her, she threw the bridle over Saxon's head and launched herself into the saddle.

The groom came to himself as she wheeled the horse around. Seeing Marguerite's white face and brilliant green eyes, he made a grab for the reins. "Miss! Wait!"

But Marguerite couldn't wait. Digging her heel sharply into Saxon's side, she grabbed hold of him as he bolted out of the barn. They were in a full gallop by the time they passed the front of the house, where Jacob had just come running out onto the porch.

"Marguerite!" he cried. "Stop!"

She couldn't stop. Riding as if the hounds of hell were on her heels, she fled at a dead run all the way to Sacramento. When she reached the town house where Sloane was staying, she pulled her lathered mount up and threw the reins around the hitching post just as he came to the door.

"What . . .?" he exclaimed on seeing her.

"Oh, Sloane!" she cried, and threw herself, weeping, into his arms.


Sloane and Marguerite were married three days later in a special ceremony brought about by the intervention of his friend, the governor. Sloane's wedding present to his bride was her beloved stallion, Saxon, which he had bought from her distraught father. She didn't find out for a long, long time that the purchase price Sloane had insisted on paying Jacob more than covered his debts to Claus and enabled him to get out from under and establish his own mercantile business without his former partner.

Heinrich had reacted violently to the news. "You'll regret this to the end of your days, Marguerite!" he had thundered, in the first real display of emotion that she had ever seen from him. He had just learned about the marriage and had arrived in a cloud of dust, demanding to see her. He'd been so loud and strident that she had agreed to talk to him just so he'd go away, but she regretted it when she saw his face. Wishing too late that Sloane hadn't gone to look at property near San Francisco, she was forced to listen to his tirade.

"I never said I'd marry you!" she cried once when he took a breath.

His face was crimson with anger; she was glad the servants were close. At that moment, he seemed so unlike himself that she was almost afraid of him. "Your father and I had an understanding!" he shouted.

"Then it's unfortunate that neither of you consulted me!" she shouted back. She was beginning to get angry. How dare he shout at her like an ill-bred peasant?

He seemed to realize how he was behaving then, himself. Controlling his anger with an effort, he lowered his voice, which was even worse. "I'll never forget this, Marguerite," he said, his pale eyes holding hers. His voice shook a little again with his rage. "Never! You made a laughingstock out of me, and I'll go to my grave without forgiving you! I'll make you rue the day you ever heard the name Heinrich Jaeger!"

She slammed the door in his face, but the threat—and the look in Heinrich's eyes—had shaken her, and she could hardly wait for Sloane to return so she could tell him how frightened she'd been and demand satisfaction. But when she told him about Heinrich's visit, Sloane dismissed it with a wave of his hand. He wasn't afraid of Heinrich Jaeger, he told her, and he had more important things to talk about. Enthusiastically, he related his news: his buying trip had been a success, and they were now the proud owners of a hundred and fourteen acres in the Sonoma Valley, some distance north of San Francisco.

The news distracted her, all right. "But you said we were going to live near the city!"

"We are," he replied. "Sonoma is only sixty miles or so north of the Golden Gate."

"Sixty miles!" she cried, outraged. "It might as well be on the moon!"

She was so angry that she locked him out of the bedroom and then threw herself on the bed, sobbing piteously—and as loudly as she was able. But instead of kicking the door in, as she had secretly hoped he would, or throwing himself against it and begging her forgiveness, as she had also imagined he might do, all she heard between her sobs was silence on the other side. Finally, too exhausted to keep up her tantrum any longer, she threw herself off the bed again, flung open the door, and went looking for him.

She found him calmly sitting in the front room, reading the newspaper. As she stood on the threshold, her hair in unruly tangles, her face blotched and ugly red from all her tears, he looked up.

"You said we were going to live near San Francisco," she muttered. "You tricked me!"

He looked at her with those blazing blue eyes of his, and

said, simply, "We are, and I'd never do that. I love you."

She was too exhausted and emotionally spent to argue any more. He held his arms out, and as she climbed wearily into his lap and he held her tightly to his fast-beating heart, she tried to cling to the last vestiges of her pride.

"I married the wrong man," she said, sobbing.

With one lithe movement, he stood, holding her in his arms. Looking down, he smiled. "No, you didn't," he said, and carried her upstairs.


The phone rang, startling Briar so badly that she nearly dropped Marguerite's journal off her lap. Grabbing for it as it started to slide off the bed, she reached for the telephone receiver on the table. She felt disoriented, caught between two time zones, still with her great-grandmother and Sloane on their honeymoon. Letting out the breath she hadn't even realized she'd been holding, she shook her head slightly and spoke into the phone.

"Hello?" Her voice sounded hoarse, even to her ears.

"Briar?" The voice at the other end sounded uncertain. "Is that you? I didn't wake you, did I? I mean, it's not even eleven o'clock yet."

"Is it that late?" She'd been reading for three hours, lost in Marguerite's world, longing to go back to it as quickly as she could. Trying to come back to the present, she gave herself a little shake and then recognized the voice. "No, you didn't wake me, Stan. What can I do for you?"

"Haven't you got that backward? Didn't you ask me to do something for you?"

Yes, she remembered. Long ago, in another life, it seemed, she had asked Stan if he knew of someone with experience who might be available to manage her ranch.

"Yes, you're right. I'm sorry. I was just—never mind. Don't tell me you've found someone so soon!"

"I did," he said, sounding proud of himself. "Didn't I tell you that old Stan gets things done? Listen, you're going to love this. He was right under our noses all the time."

"Who?"

"Stefan Yager, that's who."

She sat up in dismay. "Stefan!"

"Why do you sound like that? He'd be perfect for the job."

"No, he wouldn't!" She was certain about that. Suspiciously, she demanded, "What does he know about running a ranch?"

"Are you kidding? He's had his own racing stable."

"That was in England," she replied. "Things are different here."

"Do I detect a little hostility?"

"I'm not being hostile," she denied, feeling flushed at the lie. "I . . . I just don't understand why he would even consider—wait a minute. Have you asked him about this?"

He sounded affronted. "You don't think I'd suggest it otherwise."

"And what did he say?"

"He said he'd be willing to give it a try if you were, of course. What do you think?" He paused. "Are you?"

"Willing to give it a try?" she repeated, stalling for time. "I don't know. I don't think he's—"

"Oh, he's perfect, and you know it—despite your little dust-up a while ago."

"You know about that?"

"He told me, of course."

What exactly had Stefan said? Sharply, she said, "It was more than that!"

"All right," Stan said agreeably. "He insulted you. But he's sorry about that."

"Then maybe he should tell me that himself."

"He tried."

"When?"

"The night of the fund-raiser. When he was kind enough to put in an appearance for me, that's when. And if you don't remember, let me put him on."

"Wait!"

But Stan had already handed over the phone. She could hear it being transferred from one hand to another, and she had the irrational impulse to slam down her own receiver. Marguerite's journal caught her eye just then, and she suddenly knew how her great-grandmother had felt about Sloane: confused and disoriented, and . . . attracted. They were very much alike, Briar thought, her great-grandfather and Stefan Yager; they were both blond, blue eyed, handsome . . . and stubborn. She knew just why Marguerite had been intrigued by Sloane, for, unwillingly, she felt that same pull toward Stefan Yager.

Appalled at the thought, she thrust it immediately away. I

don't even like blond-haired, blue-eyed men, she told herself, and she wondered what she was going to say to Stefan about the ranch manager's position.

She'd tell him that it just wouldn't work, she decided. She'd say that she wanted to wait . . . that she had changed her mind and planned to run the place herself. No, no; he'd never believe that, she realized in a panic, but before she could decide on any excuse, even the most feeble, he was already on the line.

"Ms. McKenna," Stefan said, "Stan tells me you're looking for a ranch manager."

"Yes, I am," Briar said, her composure entirely deserting her for once. Instantly, she forgot everything she'd planned to say—or was going to try to say. The gold lettering on the front of Marguerite's journal glinted up at her in the lamplight, as if enjoying a joke. Shutting her eyes, she pushed the journal away. Her hand tightened on the receiver. What are you doing? she asked herself, and said, "If you're interested in the job, I guess we could give it a try."

---

# CHAPTER TWELVE

Stefan Yager came out to Caulfield Farm two weeks later to talk to Briar in person about taking on the job of ranch manager. He had barely set foot on the place before they were involved in another argument, but she knew before then that it would never work. Part of the problem was that Stefan seemed even more attractive to her at this meeting than before. She hadn't anticipated this, and because she felt something between them right from the first, she was too defensive. She didn't realize until afterward that she was unconsciously trying to establish some emotional distance; she only knew at the time that Stefan could mean something to her, and at this point in her life, she just wasn't ready. Maybe she would never be.

So she already felt hostile when she began showing him around and telling him about the new foaling barn Ted was just finishing. She *wanted* him to be critical, or sarcastic, or to say something out of turn, because that would give her an excuse to send him away. But when all he did was look around with that keen blue glance of his and nod at the appropriate times, she began to feel exasperated and not a little foolish. Obviously, she was the only one who felt something here, and she was trying to get herself under control when it finally happened.

She wasn't expecting it, and that made it even worse. Ill at ease because of all her emotional turmoil about Stefan, she was still enthusiastic about the foaling barn when she began to show him around. After all, she had researched all the latest equipment and techniques and procedures, and was proud of the results: the closed-circuit television; the "belly bands" for the pregnant mares that sounded an alarm the instant they lay down; the generous size of the stalls, so mother and baby wouldn't be crowded; the two-inch-square rubber-coated mesh that would replace the entire front wall of every stall so an attendant could see directly into each, from his own "waiting room" overlooking the entire area. . . .

"Wait a minute, wait a minute," Stefan said, interrupting her. They had already inspected the main barn, with its twenty stalls and immaculate bricked aisle; now they were standing inside the newly framed foaling barn. Other structures around the ranch were in various stages of construction, as well; she had asked Ted to finish Jaime's caretaker's cottage first so she could bring Isabella from Mexico, and then she wanted another house built for her ranch manager—who at this point, she was thinking, was not going to be Stefan Yager, after all.

"What is it?" she asked, practically spoiling for a fight so she could get rid of him before she made a fool of herself.

Stefan glanced around. As a job interviewee, he certainly didn't get an *A*, Briar reflected irritably. Not that she had expected him to be wearing a suit, of course, but the jeans and boots and sportshirt were just a little too casual for someone who was supposed to be applying for a job. If she hired him, she would expect him to wear something more . . . appropriate, she decided. What that might be, she wasn't sure; she just didn't like his nonchalant attitude. Or maybe what she really didn't like was the way those jeans fit him.

But of course that was absurd, she told herself quickly. And she really didn't care *what* he wore, because he wasn't going to work for her.

"This is a nice place," he said politely, interrupting her

black little reverie. "But you seem to be shooting off in all directions here. Maybe you'd better decide first which kind of ranch you want to have."

She didn't like his tone, and she was about to snap back a haughty reply, when she suddenly reconsidered. She hadn't come as far as she had in business by refusing to listen to advice, and what he said struck a note inside her despite herself. Since he was supposed to be the expert, maybe she should at least listen to what he had to say before she sent him on his way.

"What do you mean?" she asked coolly. "I've told you that I intend to breed and raise racing Thoroughbreds."

"Yes, so you said. But as I'm sure you already know, there are several approaches you can take in the horse business—especially with running horses. One is to become a home breeder—"

Was he being sarcastic? She could be a little obvious herself. "I don't want to raise horses solely to run in my own colors," she said. "I've no intention of trying to compete with names like Green Tree or Calumet or Claiborne—"

"Good," he interrupted again, setting her teeth on edge. "Because you won't be able to do it. Those farms have been in existence, in some cases, for generations—"

Stung, she snapped, "Caulfield Farm is not exactly an unknown in the world of racing!"

"That might have been true a hundred years or so ago," he pointed out, unruffled. "But it doesn't have a name now, and you can't raise a reputation from the dead just by putting up a new sign. You have to prove yourself all over again."

Despite the thought that if he knew about Caulfield Farm's former reputation, he had at least done his homework, she said icily, "I'm aware of that. But as I was saying, I don't intend to compete with the big names in racing—or at least," she couldn't prevent herself from adding, "not yet."

He didn't respond directly to that. "In that case," he said mildly, "you should be aware that few racing stables show a profit. Expenses are high: stud fees, transport, vet fees, buildings, maintenance, tack, and repair. . . . All those consume a whopping part of the budget. I've heard that some farms spend more than a quarter of a million dollars in fencing alone because it all has to be painted every three years."

Briar knew all that; did the man think she was a complete

idiot? Unable to disguise the acid in her voice, she said, "It might surprise you to know that at this point, I am less concerned about the cost of painting my fences than I am in acquiring a good band of broodmares. So, why don't we leave the maintenance problems to me, while *you* give me some idea how you might go about fulfilling a job as ranch manager here. If that's what you are."

To her annoyance, he laughed. "It sounds as if that last is in serious doubt."

His smile altered his entire face. His eyes crinkled charmingly at the corners, and even a dimple appeared briefly in one lean cheek. Under his well-trimmed but bushy mustache, his lower lip was full and generous, and his teeth seemed very white against his tan. Adding to her irritation, Briar suddenly realized that despite her own height, she still had to look up at him. Deciding that was another thing she didn't like about him, she took a step back. Reminding herself that she didn't care for blond men, and that she had always detested mustaches, she said coolly, "On the contrary, it sounds to me as if you're not seriously considering the position, Mr. Yager. Perhaps you're the one with doubts. Obviously you don't think I know what I'm doing."

His smile vanished. "That's not true," he said right away. "If anyone seems to know what she's doing, I'd say you do. I'm sorry if I gave you the wrong impression. . . ." His eyes left her face; he glanced around. "I guess I just didn't . . . expect all this."

She wasn't going to let him off the hook as easily as that. "What did you expect? Some flighty racing enthusiast who thought it would be fun to see her own colors out on the field while she held a champagne party in her owner's box?"

"Well . . ."

"You *did* think that!" She was annoyed, and her expression showed it. Wondering why she felt the need to explain, she heard herself sweeping on. "Well, fine! But I want you to know that even though I've never been involved in breeding horses before—and certainly not racing Thoroughbreds—I take this very seriously. I know I've got a lot to learn, but I've been in that position before, and it doesn't frighten me. I also realize I'll make mistakes—which is just another reason why I need an experienced ranch manager to advise me and handle things on a day-to-day basis while I attend to my other business in the city. But—and I mean this—no matter what you or anyone else thinks, I view this as a unique opportunity—a legacy, if you will. This property belonged to my family—*my* family, Mr. Yager, and I intend to do right by it. Caulfield Farm will rise again. I'll see to that with or without you, but I *will* see to it.''

With that, she turned dramatically on her heel, intending to leave him standing flat-footed and chagrined while she marched regally away. It didn't happen as she expected. Her foot slipped on something, and she turned her ankle awkwardly and nearly fell. With the quick reactions of the natural horseman, Stefan instantly reached out to steady her. His hand tightened on her elbow, and their eyes met . . . and suddenly she could hardly get her breath. Something electrified seemed to zing between them as they looked at each other, and when she saw his eyes darken, she knew he was feeling it, too—this inexplicable, overwhelming desire that was rising up, demanding release. She could almost feel his hard body moving over hers; she could sense the swift pounding of his heart against her breasts, and she wanted . . .

Horrified at the direction of her thoughts, she jerked quickly away. She was furious with herself for her clumsiness, and terribly shaken by what she'd just felt, and for an instant she didn't know what to say.

''Thanks,'' she muttered, wanting to pick up the rock that had tripped her and fling it to kingdom come. How inanely *trite*! she thought scathingly, and wondered what was wrong with her.

Stefan didn't seem to know what to say, either. Then, finally, he cleared his throat. ''If you're still hiring,'' he said, ''I'd like to apply for the job.''

He moved onto the ranch the following weekend. Despite her protests that she wanted him to wait until the ranch manager's house was ready, he insisted that the trailer Jaime had just vacated for the caretaker's cottage would suit him just fine.

''But I haven't had time to get anyone in to clean!'' she exclaimed, when he called from Pacifica to tell her he was coming right away.

As always, he dismissed her objections. ''It doesn't matter,'' he said. End of discussion. ''Now, when I bring my stuff on Saturday, do you want me to bring your horse or not?''

She hadn't had time to move Irish in, and she missed him

terribly. She knew he would enjoy exploring the hills behind the ranch as much as she would, but she couldn't impose on Stefan like that. "Oh, I don't know. . . ." she said. "He's so hard to load. . . ."

It was a weak protest, and they both knew it—especially because he was going to be responsible for handling all her horses in the future. With a comfortable laugh, he said, "Don't worry, I'll get him into the trailer if I have to use a crowbar—that, or a two-by-four across his rear."

She was horrified at the thought. "You wouldn't!"

"Trust me," he said. "Isn't that what you hired me for?"

She knew what she had hired him for, and it wasn't to transport stock. But she was still glad to see her horse when Stefan brought him up that weekend, and she was so delighted at the reunion that she didn't realize for a few minutes that Irish wasn't wearing his leather hat when he came out of the trailer. She never trailered him without that head protector, and she turned accusingly to Stefan.

"Why isn't he wearing his cap?"

Stefan took one look at her proud bay Thoroughbred and shook his head. "We both felt too ridiculous with that silly thing so I left it off."

"But he could have been hurt!"

"With my driving? Not a chance."

"But he never goes anywhere without it!"

"He does now," Stefan said unperturbably, and led Irish to one of the pastures. Removing the halter with a flourish, he gave the horse a whack on the rump and then grinned as the animal took off. Leaning against the fence, the halter and rope dangling from his arm, he watched as Irish snorted at the grass for a second or two, then suddenly whipped his head up and took off, flying across the field like Pegasus. When he got to the opposite end of the pasture, he slid to a stop, then raised his head again, and let out a whistling snort before he began running again along the fence.

Stefan laughed. "I think he knows he's home."

Briar joined him at the gate. She hadn't expected to feel such a thrill, but as she watched Irish galloping around, switching directions, turning this way and that, squealing with delight, and generally making a fool of himself, she found herself smiling, too. "I know just how he feels," she said.

Stefan turned to look at her, and their eyes met. Just then, she caught a whiff of his after-shave—Old Spice Lime. It filled her nostrils, stirring something inside her that was confusing and dismaying and definitely improper. Dismayed, for she was sure she'd gotten her attraction to him under control, she glanced quickly away from him, back to Irish, who had stopped running long enough to paw the ground. She knew that sign, and she exclaimed, "Oh, no!"

Stefan turned to look just as Irish went down. "Too late now," he said, and laughed again.

They watched as the horse dropped to the ground to roll back and forth with utter abandon, grinding as much dirt as he could into his shining coat. By the time he heaved himself to his feet again, he was covered with dust, and when he glanced their way, Briar could almost swear that he was hiding a grin.

"I'll get you for that!" she called, but Irish just shook himself and took off again. He was quivering with delight, filthy as sin, and enjoying every minute of his new-found freedom.

Briar suddenly became aware that Stefan was watching her instead of the horse. Feeling uncomfortable again, she said the first thing that came into her mind. "He needs company, I think."

Whatever Stefan had been thinking was lost. Pushing himself away from the fence, he said, "I agree. And since that's what I'm here for, maybe I should start earning my money. I showed you that catalogue from the sale in Southern California this week. If you agree that those mares would be worth going to take a look at, I could fly down and check it out." He paused. "If that's all right."

Briar couldn't tell if it was a concession or a sarcastic remark. But she had studied the catalogue he'd given her, and she realized that if she was going to be so sensitive to everything he said, this would never work, so she nodded. "That's fine. If you think they're worth buying, go ahead. As I said, you've got a blank check, but I want to hear about it first."

"Can't ask for more than that," he said. "Anything else?"

She hadn't intended to say it; after all, it was none of her business. But for some reason, the words were out before she knew it, and then it was too late. "Yes, there is. I've been wondering. If you're from England, how come you don't have much of an accent?"

" 'Cause I've worked damned hard to get rid of it, that's

why,'' he said, and then he grinned, adding in the broadest possible cockney, ''But if you don't think I've got one, miss, well, that's a bitta awraight. I'd hate to put ya t'shame, speakin' like a Limey.''

Briar knew she was blushing; she could feel heat in her cheeks that had nothing to do with the warmth from the sun. She didn't like being laughed at, even when she deserved it—as she did now. ''I'm sorry,'' she said stiffly. ''I don't know why I said that. I didn't mean to be rude.''

She began to turn away, but he quickly put his hand out and took hers. She was so startled at the touch that she turned back. He was too close; she turned right into him, and as though it had been planned—which of course, it hadn't—he put his arms around her and pulled her toward him. Confused and alarmed by the unexpected embrace, she looked up into his face. He seemed just as surprised as she was, just as helpless.

''Stefan . . .'' she said, not knowing what to do. He smelled like horses and aftershave and another indefinable scent that was wholly Stefan, and her heart began to pound so hard in her ears that it was all she could hear. Slowly, as if something were compelling him to, he began to lean toward her, his eyes intent on her face.

*No! It's too soon!* she thought in panic. She wanted to pull away—and couldn't. One part of her wanted those strong, lean arms of his to hold her close; one part wanted to feel his mouth on hers, for his kiss to take her to some place she'd never been before.

But she was afraid. She couldn't explain it, didn't want to try. She felt paralyzed with indecision, torn with longing. She couldn't move. He was going to kiss her, changing everything forever, and she . . . couldn't . . . decide what to do.

His breath fanned her hot cheeks, his mouth was only inches from hers when, from some far distance, she heard a thundering sound. Confused, she thought at first that it was the furious beat of her heart. But then Stefan looked up, his eyes widening slightly, just as there was a loud crash against the gate. The whole fence shuddered, and before she could react herself, Stefan pulled her out of the way. Disoriented, she looked up. Irish, tired of playing alone and wanting some attention, had come dashing up. Obviously, he had intended to come to a dramatic sliding stop before he reached the fence, but a slight miscalculation had caused him to crash into it instead. Now, looking abashed and embarrassed as only a horse can, he had backed away, pawing the ground.

Briar couldn't help it; the big gelding looked so ridiculous that she had to laugh. Stefan laughed with her, and, as naturally as if it had been planned, they stepped away from each other, and the moment that had been fraught with danger passed.

"Well," Stefan said, not looking at her, "I guess I'd better get ready for Los Angeles."

She was so unnerved she almost forgot they had talked about his going to the sale. "I'll drive you to the airport," she said.

"No, that's not necessary. I'll just take the truck."

She was relieved, but she tried not to show it. She needed some time away from him, to think about what almost happened. "If you're sure."

"I'm sure," he said.

He looked as if he wanted to say something else, but she didn't give him the opportunity. Grabbing Irish's halter, she quickly slipped inside the gate. "I'll just put him away now," she said. "You go ahead. I'll see you when you get back."

He left that afternoon, driving off, as he'd said, by himself in his battered truck. He'd called from the trailer before he went, telling her he would phone again after he'd arrived in Los Angeles and checked out the sale mares; if they decided to buy, he'd arrange for transfer of ownership and transport back to the ranch. She wasn't to worry about anything. He'd handle it all from his end.

She was sure he would, Briar thought, waiting until the sound of the truck's engine had died before she went back inside. She had already made a mental note to supply him with one of the ranch vehicles she intended to buy; if he was going to represent Caulfield Farm, he had to have a suitable vehicle, not that awful old truck. How she was going to convince him of that, she didn't know, and she wrapped her arms about herself as she went upstairs to get some papers she'd left by the bed. She didn't want to think about Stefan; it was too confusing right now, and she had other things to worry about. With Jaime to take care of the place, and her ranch manager off to Los Angeles to—hopefully—bring the first of the broodmare stock back, there wasn't much for her to do here, and she had already neglected her work long enough. She didn't think she'd been into the office five days out of the past thirty. Although she had installed a computer and modem and fax machine in her new office down at the broodmare barn, as well as duplicates here in the den in the house, and was in touch constantly whenever any of her staff needed her, she couldn't continue to let Gabe handle things on his own. As good as he was, the business needed her touch, and she'd been away far too much.

She had also left the Pacifica house empty, she reminded herself, and she still had to decide what to do about that. She knew she should either give it to Fredrica, as she had once intended, or put it on the market for sale, but she seemed unable to make a decision about either plan. Was it because Hay's presence still lingered there?

Disturbed by the thought, she went to the bedroom window—one that gave a panoramic view of the pastures and paddocks and the barns below. As she pulled aside the curtain and looked somberly out, she realized suddenly that Hay had been gone six months now. It didn't seem possible, especially when she recalled the terrible sense of loss she had felt after he had died. Recalling the first board meeting at Lord Industries after Hay's will had been read and everyone discovered that she had inherited control, she closed her eyes. How difficult that had been! If Hayden hadn't already taken care of things in his customary thorough manner, she didn't know what she would have done. She didn't want to step in as chairwoman; she had no intention of trying to run such a vast and far-flung enterprise. Fortunately she didn't have to. Along with a battery of Lord Industries' lawyers, Spencer had reassured her that Hayden had set up a sound corporate structure; with him looking over things for her, the company could go on indefinitely, as it had before. Hayden had taken care of that for her, too.

As he'd taken care of so many things, Briar thought, dropping the curtain back into place. She was glad she didn't have to try to handle Lord Industries along with her own company; even without the added pressure of Fredrica's lawsuit against her, it would have been too much. Spencer had told her a while ago that things would soon be coming to a head and that she had to prepare herself for a long siege, but she didn't want to think about it just yet. The thought of Fredrica actually going to court to have her father declared incompetent was too painful. If it weren't for Hay's memory—and the tremendous financial drain of renovating and starting up Caulfield Farm again, a project of which she knew Hay would have approved—she would have given up all claim to Fredrica. But now she was committed to something deeper, and she couldn't simply hand it all over to her husband's grasping daughter. She needed what Hay had given her to make her dream come true, and she knew that her loving husband would have applauded her.

But she didn't want to have his name dragged through court, even if, as Spence had assured her, she would be vindicated. She was determined to do everything she could to avoid that, and so she had instructed Spence to throw up every kind of legal roadblock he could find to stop Fredrica's suit. So far, fingers crossed, he'd been successful. Briar didn't know what he was doing, and she didn't want to know. She trusted Spence to do his job, and so far he had. She had no illusions that her stepdaughter would tire of the game and drop the suit, and she didn't believe that Fredrica would ever accept the settlement she periodically directed Spence to offer. Jaz was more than willing to settle; he hated confrontations, and he was content to take Briar's additional offer on top of what his father had already given him and go off to his fun. But not Fredrica; she wanted everything.

Maybe she *should* sell the company and just divide the profits, Briar thought, turning back to her bedroom. Maybe that would make Fredrica happy.

But nothing was going to please Fredrica unless she won, Briar realized; no offer, no proposal, no solution would be acceptable to someone determined to have it all. And, in the end, could she just sell off everything that Hay had worked for? She shook her head. No, she couldn't do it, not even in the hopes of establishing a fragile peace between her and her stepdaughter.

So now what? she asked herself, and she knew the answer. As Spence had told her, they'd start as they meant to go on. And if Fredrica wanted a court battle, well, that's what they'd give her.

But Fredrica was only one of her growing list of problems, she thought, as she found the papers she was looking for and went downstairs again. Even in the few weeks since she had moved to Sonoma, she already thought of the ranch as home, and it was obvious that she was going to have to make some important decisions about the direction her life was taking. It was getting more and more difficult to juggle her work at the office with what she wanted to do here, and it would be even harder when the horses started coming and Caulfield Farm became a full-time breeding operation again.

Her expression somber, she thought about what she wanted to accomplish with the ranch and knew that she couldn't do so and continue to put the same energy into her company. After burning a lot of midnight oil and reading catalogues and pedigrees and sales charts and racing results until she was groggy, she had decided to start with a broodmare band of twenty-five good mares—not a lot of horses for a ranch her size, but it was a good beginning. If most—or even some—of the mares she bought as foundation stock were in foal when they came, and then sent out for breeding again after the babies were born, it wasn't inconceivable that by next year she would have almost twice as many horses as she'd started with. The numbers would change depending on how many she was able to sell—and what she decided to buy to add to her stock and what she just culled because the results had been disappointing. But on balance, she'd have a good number of mares from which to choose for future breeding.

Then there were the "lay-up" horses she intended to board here, and the "retirees," she thought, and winced as she remembered Stefan's scathing reply to that particular idea.

"You're going to what?" he asked disbelievingly.

She'd thought he had been questioning her decision to board "lay-ups," those horses that had injured themselves either while running a race or training for one, and subsequently had to be rested for weeks, months sometimes. If the horse was valuable enough, or its racing potential hadn't been compromised by whatever ailment had temporarily halted his racing career, it was laid-up until the injury was healed sufficiently for the horse to return to training. Someone had to take care of the animals during that time; it was too cost-and-labor prohibitive to keep them at the track, and many farms and ranches had special laying-up facilities. She had been in the midst of explaining her logic when Stefan had interrupted her.

"No, no, I don't mean injuries," he said impatiently. They were still working out the details of his employment, and they had been sitting in her office down at the main barn, where she had just set up the new computer system and the fax machine.

The chairs and the couch were green leather, and the desk was a massive thing she had brought down from the Pacifica house. It had been Hay's, and she enjoyed having it here with her.

She sat forward. "What do you mean, then?"

"This . . . retiree program you mentioned. What the hell is that?"

Here they went again, she thought, and said, "I take it you don't think that it's a good idea."

"Not if you're going to be running a rest home for horses," he said flatly. "I thought this was going to be a breeding ranch."

She could feel herself getting stubborn. Besides, she thought, if she wanted to turn the ranch into a goat farm, it wasn't any of his business. "It is," she said. "But I've plenty of room, and I always promised myself that if I had the chance, I'd open up a place for old show horses—or any kind of horse that's given service and is just too old to give more. They deserve something more than being sent to the glue factory or sold to someone who might mistreat them because they're so cheap." She drew herself up. "What's wrong with that?"

"What's wrong?" He sat back, still looking as if she had proposed something outrageous. "I just hadn't pictured you as a bleeding heart, I guess."

Offended, she said, "I'm not a bleeding heart!"

"A romantic, then," he said, and leaned forward again, ignoring her outraged sputter. "Look, Ms. McKenna, you hired me to manage your ranch. Presumably that means that you're prepared to take my advice."

She was still indignant. "Not if you're going to call me a fool!"

"I didn't call you a fool, I said you were a romantic. That, or you're planning on running some kind of orphanage here."

Her expression changed; even he saw it. Between her teeth, she managed to say, "Go on. You were about to give me a piece of advice."

For some reason, he didn't seem quite so sure of himself. "Look, if I—"

"Never mind," she interrupted. She didn't want to talk about it. "Just say what you were going to say."

He hesitated again, but then he gave a slight shrug. "All right, then. I was just going to say that it costs just as much to feed a bad horse as it does to feed a good one. If you're in this business to make a profit—and I presume you are—you can't be taking in old, broken-down horses and trying to take care of them, too. It'll cost too much in time and labor, and it'll eat into your profit—assuming there is any, of course. In my experience, very few ranches ever see the black. Even without taking care of the Good Ol' Clems of the world, you'll be lucky to break even. It'll be impossible if you try to take that on, too.''

Briar sat there stiffly. "Thank you for your advice, Mr. Yager," she said, in a tone that indicated she meant no such thing. "I'll think about it. In the meantime, do you think we can discuss something more . . . *profitable*, such as the purchase of some broodmares?"

His lean face only slightly flushed at her acid tone, he nodded and reached for the catalogue they'd been discussing before they got sidetracked. As he began to discuss possible purchases, pointing out the black print in pedigrees and performances—the more black print, the darker it was, and the higher up it was on the catalogue page, the more valuable the horse—she made an effort to put aside her pique. She knew that if she was going to succeed in this venture, she couldn't afford injured feelings, so she forced herself to concentrate.

But once she got past her annoyance, she had to admit that Stefan did know his stuff. His comments about the sale horses seemed shrewd and astute to her, and they indicated that he not only knew what he was doing about the buying and selling of horses, but he had taken the time to study exactly which mares would be a good investment for Caulfield Farm. As much as she hated to admit it, she'd been impressed.

But there was another reason why she felt so off balance inside, so confused and distressed. As she paused in the living room, she knew she had to face it. No matter how much she wanted to put it out of her mind—to deny that it had even happened, in fact—she couldn't ignore the embrace she and Stefan had shared this afternoon. She'd been more shaken than she had wanted to admit, and just thinking about it made her feel horribly disloyal to Hay. After all, it had only been six months since he died, and she couldn't understand how she was even remotely interested in another man—even one as undeniably attractive as Stefan Yager.

She had never felt like this, muddled and flustered and unsure about what her true feelings were. Even when she had finally accepted that she loved Hay, she hadn't felt so off kilter. The idea that she could be intrigued by another man so soon after Hay's death made her cringe; it seemed such a betrayal.

I'm thirty-odd years older than you are, darling, Hay had said, tenderly holding her face in his hands one night and looking deep into her eyes. If something happens to me—and I don't intend it to for a long, long time—I want you to get involved again. Oh, I don't expect you to marry—not unless you want to. I know how difficult it was to persuade you to marry me, so I won't ask that. But don't shut yourself off, Briar. You're too loving, and giving, and passionate a woman to do that. His fingers had traced her jaw before he kissed her. Promise me, darling. It's all I ask. . . .

And she had promised; of course she had—why not? She couldn't refuse Hayden Lord anything. As he had pointed out, she had even abandoned her *own* iron-clad rule, not only to remain uninvolved, but not to marry. Many years before, when she was a child with those second foster parents and had seen what marriage did to people, she had vowed never to marry. She had abandoned that vow for Hay, but she didn't think she'd be able to keep her promise to allow herself to become involved again, even for him.

She left the living room to scrounge something in the kitchen for dinner. She planned to go back to San Francisco in the morning; as she'd already admitted, she had neglected the office too long, and she had a few things to say to loyal Gabe and Patsy about the work they'd been doing in her absence. Being in touch by phone or modem wasn't the same as being there in person, and after all these years together, she owed them more. Patsy had sent some papers down by courier, and she returned to the living room with a sandwich on a small plate. She had intended to work in here until it was time to go to bed, so that she'd be prepared when she got to the office in the morning, but instead of settling in to read, she put the plate down and went out onto the porch.

The sun had set by this time, and the fading light had triggered the automatic lights out at the barns. To her left, she could see a yellow square of light in Jaime's cottage; he was making plans to bring Isabella to America at last. Smiling at the thought, Briar wrapped her arms about herself; the evening air carried a chill. But she didn't go inside right away; instead, she turned and looked in the direction of Stefan's trailer. It was only a dim outline, the windows dark, but she stared at it for a long time, thinking of its new occupant and wondering if she'd done the right thing hiring him to manage the ranch. She had no doubts about his ability; she knew that despite their constant fencing about practically everything, with his help she could make Caulfield Farm rise again.

But was that all she needed from him? Thinking of that crooked smile of his, and the lean, athletic body, and the blue of his eyes against his tanned skin, she wondered.

What would Hay think of Stefan? she wondered again, and knew the answer already. Hay had always respected strength, and there was no doubt that Stefan Yager had that in abundance. And Hay would have approved of the fact that Stefan was obviously competent and knowledgeable in his field. He would have liked Stefan, Briar mused; in fact, she decided that they probably would have become friends.

Oh, she knew how Hay would have felt about Stefan, she thought. The question was, what should *she* think of him?

He might be a little sure of himself—well, all right, down-right arrogant at times, I admit, Stan had told her. But the man knows horses, and I'd trust him with the Crown Jewels and anything else. He'll do right by you, Briar, even if you grow to hate him in the process.

But growing to hate him might not be the problem, Briar thought, and with a heavy sigh, she turned to go back inside.

---

# CHAPTER THIRTEEN

Briar attended her first big sale in Kentucky that November. It was the Keeneland Breeding Stock Sale, and she had been excited about going for weeks ahead. She needed a break; the four months before had been more hectic than she ever would have believed, for in addition to what seemed like never-ending decisions about the ranch, she had been forced to spend more time than she had been prepared to at the office. All the publicity that had surrounded her since Hay's death, including Fredrica's court challenge, the news about her inheriting Caulfield Farm, and her reported decision to rebuild the place with Lord money, had contributed to a surge of business at McKenna TimeSave. Before she knew it, she had been inundated with more phone calls and requests than she could handle, even with the help of her efficient staff.

She had always had more than enough clients; in a society where CEOs and other top executives raked in astronomical salaries and bonuses unheard of in a different era, *time* had replaced money as the most precious commodity. She had never been so much in demand as these past months, and sometimes, when she was wearily leaving the office at midnight—again—long after everyone else had gone home, she wondered if she should hire her own company to reorganize her life. Time was becoming so dear to her that she was seriously thinking of bringing in a cot and just sleeping there to save the increasingly wearing commute.

Her only respite was her time at the ranch. As weary as she might be from all her long hours at work, she never tired of coming home; just driving up the road and catching a glimpse of the sign over the gates seemed to give her strength, and once the pastures had begun filling up with horses Stefan was buying for her on his trips across the country, she felt even more satisfied at what she had accomplished. But she'd been so busy these past few months that she rarely had time to enjoy the place; she was up early and gone, and so many of those nights she came home long after dark. She really should, she thought wryly, try to figure out a way to take some time off.

Stefan called one afternoon while she was hard at work. She'd had a busy morning with meetings back to back, and the mound of paperwork on her desk seemed to have grown again since the last time she'd looked at it. She was resignedly working her way through the stack when Patsy buzzed through to tell her Stefan was on the line, and when she heard the excited note in her secretary's voice, she shook her head. She knew now that it had been a mistake to ask Stefan to stop by those two times he'd come in from his horse-buying trips; ever since seeing him, Patsy hadn't been the same.

"He's *so* good-looking, Briar!" Patsy had said that first time, practically in a swoon when Stefan had gone. "Those blue eyes of his, that smile, that sexy mustache! Oh, when I think about how he just kind of sat on the edge of my desk to talk to me—well, I nearly fell into his lap! If I were you, I would have done something about him *months* ago!" Then she seemed to realize what she'd said, for she turned red and blurted, "Oh, God, I'm so sorry, Briar! I didn't mean any disrespect to Mr. Lord. I know how much you loved each other, and how wonderful he was, and how it hasn't been that long since he . . ." She blushed again, looking as though she wanted the floor to open so she could sink through. Flustered, she said, "I'm sorry, I shouldn't have said that, either. It's just—"

"It's all right," Briar assured her. Then, because Patsy still looked embarrassed, she added gently, "As Hay himself would have said, life goes on. I still miss him—and probably always will. But you shouldn't feel you can't be natural around me. That only reminds me what a loss it's been."

"Oh, Briar!" Patsy had nearly been in tears, her halo of red hair seeming to stand out around her head. "I feel like such a jerk. I'm really sorry. I won't mention Stefan Yager again!"

And she hadn't—not directly. But Briar could still hear that thrill in Patsy's voice when she buzzed through to tell her Stefan was calling, and as she reached for the receiver, she wondered why her own pulse had suddenly begun to pound. *Ridiculous*, she told herself as she picked up the phone. If she was excited, it was because she suspected he'd have good news. He had gone to Arizona this time to look at a couple of mares for her, but even if those hadn't panned out, she wouldn't be disappointed. After Arizona, he had continued his trip back East to check out stallion candidates for the upcoming breeding season, and she was eager to find out what he had decided.

She could say what she liked about how difficult and stubborn and aggravating he could be, but she couldn't deny he knew what he was doing. Caulfield Farm now owned a broodmare band of almost twenty horses, and it was all due to Stefan's hard work. He worked so hard, in fact, that she rarely saw him anymore. With Jaime to take care of the ranch and the horses while she was at work, Stefan had been away scouting prospects most of this past month. When he did stop by to change his clothes or meet a van bringing the newest horses in, very often she herself wasn't home. They'd been reduced to communicating by phone—or more commonly, through messages here or on her answering machine at home, and all she knew was that he was somewhere back East. The mares she was so proud of were to be bred this coming year, and decisions had to be made. Glad that he had called because there was something else she wanted to talk to him about, she pulled off her earring and spoke into the receiver.

"Stefan? This is Briar. I'm glad you called; there was something I wanted to ask you. Are you home, or calling from the airport?"

"No, I just got in. I thought I'd give you a call to let you know I was back."

"You sound exhausted," she said, and remembered guiltily that he hadn't taken any time off for himself in months. There was always a sale or an auction or a dispersal he had to attend; he spent so much time away that she had applied for a new credit card in the ranch's name, on which he could sign.

"Well, the weather wasn't the best," Stefan said. "My flight was delayed four hours in Louisville, then we had a mechanical problem when we finally got to Chicago. It would have been faster to walk, I think. But I did see some good horseflesh. Are you going to be here this weekend? If you are, we can discuss prospects then. I don't have any plans to be gone, unless something comes up. What did you want to talk to me about?"

Briar had seen in the paper that Edgar Harriman, owner of Harriman's Kentucky Oakes, one of the leading Thoroughbred farms in the country, had decided, at age seventy-nine, to get out of racing. Harriman's decision had been a shock to the racing community, for the crimson and silver silks of his farm had long graced winner's circles both in this country and on the Continent. Famous for his "blazing ladies," Harriman was consigning all his stock to a dispersal sale in conjunction with the November Keeneland Breeding Stock Sale a few weeks hence.

As soon as she saw the article, Briar decided to attend the sale. She had never been to Keeneland, and it would be a good opportunity to meet some of the most noted names in racing and to introduce herself as well. The dispersal was open to the public, but she wanted to reserve a seat, so she made a few phone calls to friends in Kentucky, with whom she had competed during her show-jumping days, to a few other people they recommended, and so on. As Hay had so often said, it wasn't what you knew, it was who, and Briar knew a lot of people. Those she hadn't met through her own business, or those she didn't know through Hay, were hooked immediately when she mentioned Lord Industries, and soon she not only had her reserved seats, but an open line of credit and a sale catalogue on the way.

Now it was a matter of telling Stefan of her plans. She wanted him to come with her—she wasn't afraid of meeting these people by herself, but she wanted Stefan to be there to advise her. Edgar Harriman was the winner of four Eclipse awards as the nation's leading owner, and his dispersal stock was some of the most elite in the country. She already had her eye on a couple of horses and she wanted Stefan's input.

"You move in some elite circles," he said when she told him what she had done.

"Not yet," she replied. "But I intend to."

Even in November, when all the grass was brown and the trees bare, Keeneland, in Kentucky, was an absolute delight. The instant she and Stefan passed through the limestone gates trimmed in green and drove toward the renowned old racecourse, Briar felt as if she'd stepped back in time. Huge, graceful trees lined the road, ivy and vines draped the limestone buildings; the elegant paddock area, with the wrought-iron fences and the brick pathways, seemed to represent gracious elegance at its best. At this time of year, the famous bluegrass had gone into hiding, but Briar could imagine a carpet of blue-green covering the rolling hills, and everywhere she looked were those noted white fences—miles and miles of them, marching absolutely straight into the distance. Of course, many of the fences were painted a black-brown now, but the illusion somehow remained the same; seeing the endless pastures with not a stray leaf or twig in sight, she was sure an army of elves came out every night to vacuum.

The Sales Pavilion itself was more modern, a vast structure with conference rooms and sales offices, a press box, a bar, a terrace, reserved seats, a holding area, the sales ring, and the auctioneer's stand. To Briar, seeing it for the first time, empty and waiting and hushed with reverential silence, it was almost like walking into a church. The sales ring, around which the horses paraded during the auction itself, seemed very small. Electronic boards were placed high up on each side of the

auctioneer's booth; during the sale they would show the hip
number of the horse being sold and the selling price.

Out in the barn area were the horses—thousands of them, it
seemed—but Briar was only interested in Harriman's bloodstock, and she and Stefan had arrived several days early to give
them plenty of time to view the one hundred and twenty-five
horses that were set to go on the block. Of that number, three
of Harriman's greatest distaff runners captured her interest—
and that of the rest of the crowd. These were last year's Kentucky Derby winner, the magnificent Incandessence, now
retired from racing because of a serious injury; her half sister,
Horse of the Year, Heat of Night; and *their* half sister, the
winner of this year's Distaff Cup, the spectacular, never-
beaten, Night Fever. Together, these three comprised the so-
called "blazing ladies," of which Harriman was so proud.

He had reason to be, Briar thought. She had already decided
to bid for all three, for each of them—a daughter of the great
broodmare sire, Feel the Heat, himself a multi-stakes winner in
his time—could hardly have a more outstanding pedigree or
performance record. But buying a horse on paper was different
entirely than seeing it in person, and once Briar saw the "blazing ladies" in the flesh, she was entranced.

Viewing of the horses took place twice a day in the barn
area, and at every appointed time, she was there with the rest
of the growing crowd, gazing in awe. Each one of the three
great distaff runners seemed to recognize the nobility her sire
had passed on; from the challenge in their eyes to the finely
tuned muscles under their shining coats, they were truly the
aristocrats of racing—and had proven it, time after time.
Watching them parade back and forth on the grass between the
barns, Briar became even more determined to take one or more
of them home.

But there was one other horse in the sale that she had her eye
on, as well: a coal-black yearling filly named Touch the Fire,
who didn't have the elite bloodlines, and whose progenitors
had had less than spectacular careers, even at so-called bush
tracks, out of the major leagues. She never would have known
the filly was here if someone hadn't tipped her—and that had
been curious itself, she thought with a frown. She'd been standing by the Sales Pavilion waiting for Stefan one morning when
a wizened old man sidled up to her, and, with a touch of two
fingers on the brim of his flat cap, whispered that she might

want to look at a filly named Touch the Fire. When she asked
why, all he'd say was that she'd be interested because of
Caulfield Farm. He'd disappeared into the crowd before she
could stop him, and she hadn't seen him again, but she'd been
curious enough to look up the filly's pedigree. She'd been
riveted at what she found. From that moment on, she knew that
if she only came home with one horse, the black filly would be
the one. She had never seen the old man again, and although
she had asked, no one seemed to have heard of him or seen him
before. It was puzzling, but she wasn't going to question good
fortune. Not even the other three were as important to her as
this one yearling, and no matter what happened, she would not
leave Kentucky without her.

With that in mind, she was standing by the stall watching the
restless occupant and promising that, if all went well, soon
she'd be on the way back to Caulfield Farm, when Stefan found
her after what had been an exasperating search. Because the
filly was one of the least important in the sale, she had been
consigned to the farthest barn, out of the main thoroughfare.

"There you are," Stefan said when he found her. "I've
been looking all over for you. What are you doing, hiding back
here?"

"I'm not hiding. I'm just looking over this filly."

"Who is it?" he asked, squinting in at the horse pacing
inside. The filly was black as night; in the dim light, it was
difficult to see her—until she rushed the door, her ears pinned
and her teeth bared. Stefan jumped back, cursing mildly.
"Friendly little thing, isn't she?"

"Her name's Touch the Fire," Briar said, and took a deep
breath. She already knew what his reaction was going to be,
but she had made up her mind. "I'm going to buy her."

He looked shocked. "The hell you say! This is the first I've
heard of it. What for?"

She didn't want to explain, not now. "Because of her pedigree."

"Her pedigree?" Quickly, he flipped through the catalogue
pages until he came to the filly's name. There wasn't much to
see; from her spectacular lack of black print, it was difficult to
understand what she was doing here in the first place. Looking
up again, he said flatly, "She doesn't seem to have one. As
your bloodstock agent, not to mention your ranch manager, I
strongly advise against it."

"Noted," she replied. "But I'm still going to buy her."

He knew that look by now. Cramming the catalogue into a pocket, he said, "Well, since you're probably going to be the only one bidding, it shouldn't be too difficult. From the looks of things, they're likely to give her away just to get her out of here. The question is why you'd want her to begin with."

She looked again at the filly, who had gone back to her restless pacing. "Maybe one day I can tell you."

"Well, fine. In the meantime, maybe you can explain why you want to buy all three of those Feel the Heat daughters tonight. At the price they're sure to go for, you'll never recoup your investment—especially since one of them can't race any longer. Maybe you should reconsider."

"I thought we decided."

"No," he said meaningfully. "*You* decided. Sometimes I wonder what I'm even doing here."

"Because I need your advice, of course."

"I don't know why," Stefan retorted. "You never take it."

"That's not true. I trust your judgment implicitly. Now, do you think we should go back to the hotel to get ready for tonight's sale?"

"You're the boss," he said, obviously disgruntled. Then, as they started walking back toward the car they had rented, he said, "You're not really going to buy that black demon, are you? You're pulling my leg."

"No, I'm serious," she said, handing him the keys. "I'm going to have her, come hell or high water."

By the time Edgar Harriman's dispersal sale began that night, there wasn't an empty seat in the entire Sales Pavilion. Racing's glittering elite had gathered to pay homage to the grand old man of the sport—and to buy his horses—and everywhere Briar looked were the Beautiful People. All the men were wearing tuxedos, including Stefan, who—to her secret dismay, looked even more handsome in evening dress than he did in jeans and polo shirts—while the women were equally formal. As everyone got settled, sequins glittered under the spotlights and millions of dollars of jewels and gems seemed to shoot off sparks. Briar herself was wearing a gown that Hay had particularly liked; beaded in deep green from the plunging neck to the slitted skirt that exposed a great deal of delectable thigh, she looked like a tall, green flame. Because the gown required it, she had put up her dark, chestnut hair for the occasion, and emeralds and diamonds flashed at her ears. Unlike so many of the other ladies present, she wasn't wearing fur, but the green velvet cape that swirled around her ankles seemed even more elegant and sophisticated because she handled it with such flair.

"You still plan to bid for all three of those fillies?" Stefan whispered, leaning toward her.

She glanced at him. His eyes seemed more black than blue in this light, and he wasn't smiling. "Those and Touch the Fire," she answered.

He started to say something more, but just then Edgar Harriman entered with his entourage, and at his appearance, spontaneous applause broke out and Stefan's remark was lost. Glancing at him again, Briar saw his expression, but she just smiled. This was her first big sale, and she intended to enjoy it to the fullest.

So, it seemed, did everyone else present. An expectant hush fell, and into the ringing silence, the auctioneer reeled off the terms Edgar Harriman required. Most of his other horses in the sale catalogue had been sold at this point; only the crème de la crème was left. The procedure would be that, as each individual horse was paraded in the show ring for the crowd's approval, the announcer would provide swift details about pedigree, history, racing performance, and anything else deemed necessary for purchase. The horse would stay in the ring until the gavel came down, and the auctioneer would announce a floor price before the bidding began in earnest. Even before he finished his remarks, his tuxedoed associates had taken their places, and the dark-suited assistants were fanning out, ready to pass along a bid that had been raised by a nod or a lifted finger.

"And now," the auctioneer said with a flourish, when he had finished with his presentation, "Lot Twenty-five!"

An obviously frightened chestnut filly was brought into the ring, the number "25" taped to her hip. As her handler started to circle her around so that people in the audience could get a good look at her from all sides, the auctioneer began listing her pedigree, and then gave a concise summary of her so far sparse racing history. When he had finished, the bidding began very quickly.

"And we are bid, ladies and gentlemen. . . !" he cried, and that was the last thing Briar understood for the next five minutes. She assumed that the bidding had started at fifty thousand dollars, for she thought she heard the word "fifty" once or twice, but then, just as suddenly, the gavel banged down and the auctioneer was crying, "Sold! To Harvey Lymon of Lime Tree Farm!"

The next lots went even more swiftly; everyone present seemed eager to get to the high point of the evening, the last five horses in the catalogue. Briar raised eyebrows when she outbid everyone on Night Fever, the first of the "blazing ladies" to come up. By the time the gavel came down, she had paid over a million dollars for the never-beaten three-year-old filly. Heads started to turn. Who *was* this newcomer?

Next up was Heat of Night, Horse of the Year, half sister to the filly Briar had just purchased. In a furious spate of rapid-fire bidding, where the board flashed increments in the six figures from the first offer, Briar finally saw who was bidding against her, and she tightened her lips. Now she knew why the price was rising so high, and with the merest jerk of her head added another hundred thousand dollars to the ante. When it was swiftly topped, she nodded again . . . and again . . . until the tote board read a quarter tick over one million dollars. By this time, people were turning in their seats, and as she made her decision, she couldn't help noticing that Stefan was looking a little pale. The man on her other side was giving her sideways glances, and as the auctioneer turned in her direction again, and one of his helpers came to stand right near her chair, Stefan leaned over and said, "Briar, don't you think—"

"I do," she said, and lifted her chin. The tote board ticked again at one million five. Delighted, the auctioneer turned to the other side of the pavilion where the person trying to outbid her sat. Stefan couldn't see from his position, but Briar was able to see him clearly. Their eyes met for just the briefest instant, and when he lifted a finger to the waiting auctioneer and the board flashed one million three hundred seventy-five thousand, Briar smiled. This time when the auctioneer turned to her, she shook her head and stood down.

"Sold!" the auctioneer cried, while her opponent half rose in anger at being outbluffed, and the filly was led off.

Stefan leaned toward her again. "I couldn't see. Who—"

But Briar didn't have time to tell him. An instant later, the high point of the evening was announced: Lot Number One. A profound hush settled over the crowd; even the auctioneer's voice changed, became deeper, almost reverent.

"And now, ladies and gentlemen," the auctioneer said, his voice actually trembling with emotion, "we come to the last of the great ladies of Harriman's Oakes. This filly we're about to present to you tonight stands beside her sisters in history, from the great Kincsem who won all *fifty-four* races in which she was entered, to the bold Gallorette, and that crowd pleaser Dark Mirage, to the tragic Ruffian herself! In seventeen races, this magical creature has proved herself worthy of racing's crown, capping her spectacular career with the winning—*by three lengths*—of last year's Kentucky Derby."

He took a breath, wiping his brow with a flourish with the handkerchief he took from his pocket. Like the showman he was, he let the tension build. Then, finally, he leaned forward and spoke into the microphone, his voice starting as a whisper, and then beginning to soar with every word until he was practically shouting, "Ladies and gentlemen, let me introduce the country's most brilliant distaff runner in a decade and more . . . the magnificent *Incandessence*!"

Into the ring, accepting the wild applause of the well-heeled crowd as if it were her due, stepped the dainty bay filly that had wowed racing audiences from coast to coast for the past three years. With her fine legs and little feet, she looked far too fragile to be the tough competitor she was, but Briar had seen videos of her in contests with the colts, pushing her way between horses in a space too small to admit a gnat, driving to the finish despite another jockey's whip right in her face, outshouldering stronger colts who looked as if they'd knock her right over. She raced in mud or sun, on fast tracks or grass; it didn't seem to matter. If ever it could be said of a horse, this filly had been born to run.

But as magnificent as she was, standing there in the spotlight, with her ears pricked forward, Briar could easily see her misshapen right front leg. A broken pastern bone had ended her racing career; it was held together now by five pins. A champion to the end, she had run despite the crippling injury that happened, as near as endless viewing of the videotape of the race could ascertain, at the sixteenth pole. No one, not even the jockey, could be sure when the bone broke, for the gallant filly had battled her way to the finish line without pause, pulling up dead lame only after coming in first.

That had been her last victory. The tearful jockey had thrown himself over her neck when he finally realized what had happened. He hadn't even been aware she was injured. Like those other great champions—the 1947 Triple Crown Winner, Assault, who raced with a malformed foot, the horse they said ran on three legs and a heart; or the gallant Dark Secret, who ruptured a tendon a sixteenth of a mile before the finish and forced all his weight onto his good foot, shattering it, too, only a step away, but crossing the line to win the 1934 Jockey Gold Cup—such was the indomitable will to win that had forced Incandessence to race through her pain first to the finish line.

Briar knew the history. Watching this filly parading about the ring, every muscle quivering, her great nostrils flared, nearly pulling her handler off his feet from time to time despite her obvious impairment, Briar knew what it meant to be in the presence of greatness. She had already made up her mind, but she reinforced her decision again. No matter how foolish it might be, or how improvident, or how unjustified an expense, she had to take this filly home.

The bidding opened at a cool one million. The man beside her murmured to his companion, "Pretty high, if you ask me. She'd be worth more dead. They should have put her down and run with the insurance, like they did with Ruffian."

The woman he was with whispered back. "That's only a story. Nobody ever proved that."

The man shrugged. "Something could have been arranged. It's been done. . . ."

Briar turned and looked at him. He seemed to sense that she was staring, for he glanced her way. When he saw her expression, he shifted uncomfortably and looked away again. Beside her, Stefan looked grim.

"Welcome to the real world," he murmured.

"Not at my ranch," she murmured back.

He shook his head. "You and your orphans. You know this horse is never going to run again."

Briar smiled. "Who said that?"

As Stefan looked startled, the auctioneer started to chant. "So what am I bid, what am I bid, ladies and gentlemen? We've got one . . . one . . . come on, what am I bid, what am I bid? We've got one . . . one . . . one . . ."

Briar turned toward the sales ring. One of the auctioneer's helpers was standing in the aisle, waving his rolled-up program frantically about, as if exhorting someone to make another offer. Instinctively, it seemed, just as she looked his way, his eyes flicked to hers, and he looked expectant.

Almost imperceptibly, she nodded. Instantly, he turned toward the stage and waved his program. Suddenly, the race was on again. Briar knew this time before she looked who was bidding against her; she was also aware that by outbluffing him last time, he was even more determined now to beat her. Did he really want Incandessence? Or was he just going to drive the price up higher and higher? Either way, she decided, it didn't matter. Before the gavel came down again, she was going to own this filly; she didn't care what price she had to pay for her.

The bidding progressed so furiously that finally, once again, only Briar and her opponent were bidding against each other. As the price climbed higher and higher, one million five, one seventy-five, two, then two-ten, and finally two million two—coming from the other side of the pavilion—Stefan clutched her arm.

"Let it go," he hissed. "You've got the best filly here already. It's too much, and I've got a feeling that whoever that guy is, he's been paid to drive up the price."

He still hadn't seen who her opponent was, but she didn't have time to explain. The auctioneer's helper was practically standing in front of her now, his face red, sweat running down his cheeks and dripping onto his starched shirt. People all around were staring, and at the podium, the auctioneer was chanting incessantly. Briar felt surrounded by noise and confusion and shining lights and movement, but she really didn't see or hear anything; her attention was solely on the horse, that gallant filly she was going to have at any price. Like Incandessence herself, she would *not* be beaten.

"And we've got a bid of two and two, two and two, two and two, do I hear two and a half? Two and a half? the auctioneer cried, looking at her. She didn't move. "Two and a half?" he asked again.

The helper leaned down, waving his program—but not, she noted, in her face. "Come on, you can't let that beautiful horse go now!" he pleaded.

"Two and a half?" the auctioneer cried.

Briar didn't respond. Beside her, Stefan murmured, "Thank God."

She hardly heard him. She was staring at the stage, her glance moving between the high-strung horse jigging around the handler, her ears twitching back and forth, and the auctioneer, who was chanting again, exhorting the crowd not to let this filly go at such a ridiculously low price.

"All right, all right, all right," the auctioneer said finally. Reluctantly, the gavel came down. "Going once . . ." *Bang!* "Going twice!" *Bang!* He looked hopefully in Briar's direction. "This is your last chance," he wheedled. "Two and a half? Just two . . . and . . . a half." He picked up the pace, as though by changing the rhythm, he could lull her into raising the price. "It's your move, now, your move, your move . . ."

He waited expectantly. Again, Briar didn't respond. Unwillingly, the auctioneer sighed. "All right, then . . ."

Imperceptibly, just as he raised the gavel for a third and final time on that other bid, Briar gave the barest nod. The auctioneer saw it even before his quivering helper whirled toward the stage, jumping up and down and waving his program frantically.

"Two and a half!" the auctioneer cried triumphantly. "I've got two and a half, two and a half!" He looked in the other direction; hundreds of heads swiveled with him, as if at a tennis match. Briar didn't follow the movement; she only had eyes for that filly . . . *her* filly.

Stefan leaned toward her. "This is insane. If he bids against you, you'll have to go to three—"

"He won't," Briar said, without looking at him. She could feel his glance on her, and knew he was wondering what in the hell she was doing. She couldn't explain; she only knew that she had to go on to the end.

Sounding exasperated, Stefan asked, "How do you know?"

"I know," she said, never taking her eyes off the horse.

"And I suppose you know she'll race again," he said, his voice dripping sarcasm.

Still gazing at that beautiful horse, Briar nodded. "I think she will."

She could feel him looking at her as if she'd lost her mind. "What, a little genie told you that?"

Briar shook her head. "No. She did."

And up at the sales ring, Incandessence suddenly let out a shrill challenge. Her great nostrils flared, her sides quivered, and as if it had been ordained, she seemed to look directly where Briar was sitting. At her seat, Briar smiled.

But just then, the tension began to build again. Up at the stand the auctioneer was pleading with Briar's opponent in the bidding war, begging, cajoling, wheedling. It was his job to wring the last of the juice from the grape, and he was giving it his all.

"You *can't* let a beautiful filly go at this price!" he cried into the microphone. He was leaning over the podium as if mortally wounded at the thought of gaveling down on two and a half million dollars for a horse who was standing majestically in the ring, looking out over the crowd at something only she could see.

Taking a deep breath, the auctioneer began working the crowd again. His voice dropping like an evangelist invoking the help of the Lord to make these people see the light, he whispered, "It's a *sin!*"

He raised his voice. "It's a crime!"

He went to full pitch again, bugling, "She deserves better than that, yessir, she does, she does, she does! So . . . *what am I bid, what am I bid, what am I bid,* ladies and gentlemen? Do we go two and three-quarters, two and three-quarters, two and three-quarters?" He hesitated, glancing around. "All right, then, how about two-two-six, two-two-six, two-two-six?"

Without realizing it, Briar was holding her breath. She could almost feel Stefan's anxiety, and on her other side, the man sitting next to her had moved to the opposite edge of his seat. She knew he was staring at her, but she didn't care. People were turning to look at her, craning their necks, whispering again behind their hands, and up on stage, the auctioneer seemed about to go to his knees to get his two-two-six. The tension was so thick she could hardly breathe, but she didn't take her eyes off that horse. The groom circled the filly again just as the auctioneer lifted the gavel. Even from this distance, the horse's limp was noticeable. No wonder people believed she was crazy, Briar thought; she was beginning to wonder herself.

"All right, then!" the auctioneer cried suddenly, startling the high-strung horse, who jumped and spun, nearly knocking the handler off his feet. Well aware of what would happen to him—not to mention the horse—if he let go of the halter, the groom grabbed tightly onto the lead shank and wound it around his fist.

At the podium, the auctioneer was shouting. "Going once . . ." *Bang*. "Going twice . . ." *Bang*. There was a deep hush as he looked around, seeming to search every face in the entire place. "All bids in? You won't get a second chance! This is it? No more?" His eyes swept the tense audience again while his helpers jerked their heads back and forth, searching for the slightest movement, the barest nod, the most imperceptible wink.

After an interminable wait, during which the tension level jumped at least another three notches, the gavel came crashing down a third and final time, and the auctioneer was warbling into the wild applause, "SOLD FOR TWO MILLION FIVE HUNDRED THOUSAND DOLLARS TO MS. BRIAR MC-KENNA OF CAULFIELD FARM!"

How or when he'd gotten her name, or found out who she was, Briar didn't know. In any event, she was too delighted to wonder about it, for under cover of that frenzied applause, and people actually coming to their feet in excitement, the auctioneer's helper who had been standing next to her, practically trembling with eagerness to relay her bidding, leaned down and whispered that she was supposed to go up to the stage this time so Edgar Harriman could have some last pictures of his horse with her new owner. It was a little unorthodox, but one did not refuse one of the men who had defined the sport of racing in this country from his simple office at Harriman's Oakes.

Even that sophisticated, elite and jaded crowd went wild again when Edgar Harriman graciously greeted Briar on stage after all the necessary documents were signed and contracts had changed hands. Honored to be standing there with him, she was touched when he smiled at her, took her hand, and then looked pink and pleased when, feeling emotional herself at the moment, she leaned down and kissed his cheek. Like a slender, green flame in her beaded gown, she remained behind while his people helped him off the stage so that she could be photographed with her new purchase. Clearly afraid that the overwrought filly would spin and fire, kicking the old man before he could get down or knocking her new owner right off her feet, the filly's handler looked so frightened that Briar took pity just as the photographer was trying to line up the shot.

"Here," she said to the groom. "Let me hold her."

The handler's eyes bugged out. "Oh, no, ma'am . . . miss . . . missus, I'm beggin' your pardon, but I doan think that's such a good idea. This here filly's a little high-strung, if you get my drift."

"I do," Briar said, smiling. She held out her hand for the lead shank. "It'll be all right."

"Oh, lordy," the man moaned, and he closed his eyes as he handed it over.

Excited by all the noise and confusion, Incandessence had lived up to her name, jumping around so much that her bay coat glistened with sweat. Like all fine Thoroughbreds, she was thin-skinned; blood vessels close to the surface had been pumped up, looking like a fine lace tracery beneath her skin. Her eyes were a little wild, and those large nostrils quivered like every other muscle in her body . . . until Briar took the shank.

"Hush," Briar whispered, and put her hand on that fine muzzle. The filly snorted, and for an instant it seemed as if she might strike. Briar simply held her hand in place. Then, with everyone watching anxiously, the horse visibly relaxed. The agitated little dance she'd been doing in place became a step or two, then she stood still. The champion filly with the look of eagles stood quietly, snuffling into Briar's hand.

"Lordy," the handler murmured unbelievingly. "Ain't *never* seen her do that! She's so full o'herself even now that she'd just as soon take your head off as *breathe*!"

Applause began to swell again, and flashbulbs started to pop all around, while Briar held on to the filly and posed for picture after picture. She tried to peer into the darkness to where she and Stefan had been sitting, but all she could see was a crowd of faces looking at her, and those damned flashbulbs going off in her eyes. Hoping that Stefan had gone to check on the other filly she'd bought, she reluctantly handed the horse back to her groom and went to the post-sale party.

The party was held in one of Kentucky's famous landmarks, the huge, round show barn at Harriman's Oakes. The barn had been a symbol of wealth and affluence even back in the late eighteen hundreds, when it had first been constructed. In addition to twenty stalls encircling a riding area in the center, the domed ceiling lofted to three stories and included a widow's walk around turreted spires. Gingerbread and scrollwork abounded, and each stall was a minor work of art. The riding ring inside had been converted for the party tonight, and along the perimeter were vast buffet tables groaning with every conceivable kind of food. Most of the people were congregated around the open bar at one end. Along with bluegrass and fine Thoroughbred horses, Kentucky was known for its bourbon, and it was flowing freely tonight.

Briar had heard it said that there were three ways inside the charmed circles of racing: money, connections, or name. A fourth way, she thought ironically, as she was surrounded again by well-wishers who wouldn't have given her the time of day just a couple of hours ago, was to acquire in one evening two of the finest horses in the racing world. Admittance to the sale might have been open, but actual participation had required an advance line of credit in the seven figures. What she had paid for her two horses caused comment that night, and suddenly everyone wanted to know more about the newcomer from California. It hadn't escaped attention that, in his excitement, the auctioneer had linked her to Caulfield Farm; when word flashed around that she was also the sole heir to that proud old name that had once belonged to one of Kentucky's own, Edgar Harriman sought her out again and kissed her hand.

"My father knew Sloane and Marguerite Caulfield," he said in his quavery voice as astonished guests looked on. He had eyes for no one but Briar, and he smiled. "He always said that Marguerite had an eye for good horseflesh, and I see that that talent has been handed down to her—?"

"Great-granddaughter, Mr. Harriman," Briar supplied.

He nodded. "The resemblance is uncanny, even to me, and I only saw her once. Oh, she could ride a horse, could that girl! She had a magic touch with them—just as you had with Incandessence tonight. So, congratulations, my dear. I hope you enjoy my ladies as much as I have. If you treat them well, they'll give to you until they can give no more."

Choked with sudden emotion, Briar squeezed the liver-spotted hand holding hers. "I'll treasure them always, Mr. Harriman," she said. "I'll make sure they do you proud."

"They already have, Ms. McKenna," he said, his rheumy old eyes alight with memories of victories past. Softly, he repeated. "They already have."

When he moved on, Briar suddenly knew what it felt like to be knighted. The little visit by the king of racing, that private conversation right in the midst of the party as it was, had been like the touch of Excalibur on each shoulder. She could have worked years to reach the level of acceptance that Harriman had just granted her by his presence and a few words; and as she looked into the faces that surrounded her again in their host's wake, she knew that they realized it, too.

*One for us, great-grandmother*, she thought fiercely, and she knew this was only the beginning. Tomorrow she would buy that little filly called Touch the Fire, and then they'd all go home, where they belonged.

She still hadn't seen Stefan, and, hemmed in by well-wishers, she nodded and smiled and said all the right things, but she began surreptitiously to look around. Before she could spot him, she turned—and looked right at someone else she was beginning to know all too well.

"Good evening, Ms. McKenna," Rupert Jaeger said politely. As always, like an appendage, his son Carl was by his side. "I see that congratulations are in order. You certainly made your mark tonight."

Rupert was the one who had been bidding against her for Harriman's top fillies, hoping, she knew, to make her look like a fool by paying too much for the horses. Because they were both aware that she had finessed him by deliberately dropping out of the bidding on Heat of Night, she decided she didn't need to make more of it, so she replied courteously, "Why, thank you, Mr. Jaeger. It was very exciting, don't you think?"

An aggressive expression on his doughy face, Carl stepped forward. But before he could say what was on his mind, a woman appeared at his side. She was as tall as Briar, but lean to the point of looking spare. Dressed in a long white sheath of a gown with a silver spray of beads down one shoulder and across one meager breast, she looked even more like her father in person than she did in her photo.

"We haven't met, Ms. McKenna," the woman said, holding out her hand. "My name is—"

"I know," Briar said, returning the handshake. "Charlotte Jaeger."

Charlotte seemed surprised, almost uneasy. "You know who I am?"

"Of course," Briar said graciously. "Who wouldn't recognize the woman who breeds the magnificent horses of Mondragon Stud?"

Charlotte gave her a quick glance. "Why . . . thank you," she said uncertainly. Then she quickly recovered. "I do apologize," she said. "You've been right next door all this time, and I haven't even gone to welcome you. I would love to show you the Stud. Would you like to come for tea one day?"

Before she could answer, Carl sputtered. In his tight tuxedo, he looked like a fat little penguin as he turned angrily to his sister. "You can't be serious!"

Charlotte glared at him. She seemed almost taken aback by the invitation herself. "Of course I'm serious, Carl. What a ridiculous thing to say." Then her expression turned sly. "After all, we should give Ms. McKenna a proper welcome. As Father himself said, she's made quite a splash tonight, so it's only right."

Carl was so furious that he couldn't speak. Rupert's attention was claimed just then by someone else, and after excusing himself, he grasped Carl's arm, and they both walked away, leaving Briar alone with Charlotte, who waited a moment before she spoke.

"You're not what I expected," Charlotte said finally.

Briar wasn't sure what to say to that. "Oh? In what way?"

Charlotte shook her head, her eyes suddenly far away. "I'm . . . not sure. Perhaps I thought you'd be . . . older."

Briar couldn't help smiling. "To tell you the truth, I feel I've aged years since moving to Caulfield Farm. The only saving grace was that I had no idea how exhausting it would be. If I had known before I started, I might not have tackled such a demanding project. Or at least," she amended, "not in such a big way."

Charlotte's gaze was unreadable. "Perhaps you should have accepted my father's offer to buy the property."

Something flashed in Briar's eyes. "I know how much your family wanted that land—"

"Not I," Charlotte interrupted. *"I* never wanted that land. I'm quite preoccupied with the Stud."

"As I intend to be with Caulfield Farm," Briar said evenly.

"In that case," Charlotte said, her eyes never leaving Briar's face, making her feel uneasy without knowing why, "you've made a good start tonight. With Edgar's approval, you could go far. Far indeed."

Briar returned Charlotte's stare with one of her own. "And how would you feel about that, Ms. Jaeger?" she asked.

Uncertainty darted quickly across Charlotte's lean face. But she said, "I wouldn't feel one way or another about it, Ms. McKenna. As far as I'm concerned, there's room for all in this business. All who can afford it, anyway."

"Just so,"Briar agreed. "And in fact, Stefan Yager, my ranch manager—"

Charlotte drew in a hiss of a breath. "Did you say . . . Stefan Yager?"

"Yes, that's right," Briar said, startled by Charlotte's reaction. "Why . . . do you know him?"

It was as if a curtain had come down over Charlotte's face. "I don't know him, no," she said stiffly. "Let's just say . . . we've met."

Briar was surprised. She was sure Stefan hadn't mentioned that he'd met Charlotte. But then why should he? she asked herself. They had never discussed the people at Mondragon Stud; there had been no need to. But she was still curious, and she said, "Oh, really? I had no idea. When was that?"

"I . . . I really don't care to discuss it, Ms. McKenna," Charlotte said, and quickly added, "Now, will you excuse me? It was nice meeting you, and we will get together . . . at a convenient time."

Perplexed, Briar watched Charlotte disappear into the crowd before she again began looking for Stefan. It hadn't occurred to her before, but she suddenly realized now how similar were their surnames. She didn't know why the Jaeger family used the Teutonic spelling but the anglicized pronunciation for their last name—with a hard *J* rather than the softer *Y* sound—but of course it was just coincidence that Stefan's last name was Yager—and that his was the anglicized spelling but with the Teutonic intonation.

She was still puzzling about it when she saw Stefan. He was leaning against one of the stall doors that had been decorated with ribbons and fancy foil for tonight, and he was holding an untouched glass of champagne. She knew at once by his expression that he had seen her talking to the Jaegers, and as their eyes met, his lean, handsome face changed to an expression she couldn't interpret. She was wondering what he was thinking when he slowly raised his glass in a silent toast. With a look that could have meant anything, he drained the glass and set it down. Then, to her surprise, he turned and left the barn.

---

# CHAPTER FOURTEEN

Stefan was not about to allow over three million dollars and three thousand pounds of valuable horseflesh to travel without him, no matter how good the airline pilot was, or how many grooms Edgar Harriman offered to supply. It was his job to supervise the transport of Caulfield Farm's precious new cargo, even Briar's inexplicable purchase of that hot-tempered yearling, Touch the Fire, so that's what he was going to do. Consequently, he was there on the tarmac at the airport two nights after the last sale, waiting for the van to arrive with the horses so they could load and go home.

Remembering the almost-empty sale yesterday morning during which Briar had bought the filly no one else seemed to want, Stefan shook his head. Who could figure women out? After handing over millions for the other two horses, the purchase price on the black filly of five thousand dollars seemed almost ludicrous. As he shifted from foot to foot with impatience, he decided that if he lived to be a hundred, he would never understand Briar McKenna.

But that didn't mean he wasn't going to do his job. He shoved his hands in his jacket and glanced at the men waiting with him. He couldn't take care of three horses himself on a flight, so he had arranged for three grooms to travel with them, and now they were all standing around waiting for the truck.

The night was chilly; they were huddled in their coats, with collars pulled up around their ears against the cold wind that had come up about an hour ago. Hands under his armpits, one of the grooms had a cigarette between his lips; when Stefan saw it, he was tempted to take it out of the guy's mouth and inhale a drag. There were times when he wished he hadn't given up smoking, and this was one of them.

He couldn't figure out why he was so nervous. He'd flown horses before, some just as valuable as these; it wasn't as if he were a complete novice. And two of Briar's new fillies had been on a plane before, traveling without incident. The only unknown quantity was Touch the Fire, but even so, most horses seemed to travel better on a plane than in a trailer anyway, so what was he worried about?

Well, for one thing, he knew how easily—and how frighteningly quick—something could go wrong. He had seen horses who had traveled placidly for thousands of miles by trailer suddenly refusing for unknown reasons to load—and determined to fight to the death to avoid being put inside a van. He had been there when a horse with more flying hours than the pilot had suddenly gone berserk right at takeoff and had to be put down. With horses anything could happen, and he'd hate like hell having to explain to Briar why he'd had to use the humane killer.

"Hey, man, the van's here!"

Preoccupied with dire thoughts, Stefan hadn't seen the truck arrive. But the big nine-horse van was pulling to a stop, the driver getting out, his assistant already going around to the back to let down the hydraulic ramp. As the three waiting grooms went to help, the driver waved at Stefan. Lighting a cigarette and pulling his cap further down over his ears against the cold, he called, "Where do you want these mares?"

Stefan pointed. The three horse boxes were already lined up; the first one was on the cargo lift that would raise it level with the plane. Made of stout tongue-and-groove pine, the boxes were just wide and long enough to allow the horses to stand comfortably but not to move around. Pilots didn't like sudden massive shifting of cargo; they complained that unexpected movement made it difficult to fly the plane. Every box was bedded deep with straw for sure footing and less strain on delicate ligaments and tendons; the box sides reached to about the height of a horse's withers, allowing the animal to look out and around but effectively cutting off escape—or so Stefan hoped.

Once on board, each horse would be given a hay net—a big ball of alfalfa stuffed into a rope webbing and hung in front of the box. Some horses—experienced travelers, or gluttons who would eat through anything, even their stall bedding—munched all through the flight; others wouldn't even drink. It depended on the horse, and Stefan wasn't about to force-feed or water these high-strung fillies tonight. He wanted them to remain calm at any cost, so they could do what they liked. Anything, so long as no one got into a lather, including him.

The driver's assistant had the back ramp lowered by this time, and one of the grooms went in to help unload the first horse. Bundled up to the eyes in a quilted blanket with a hood, wrapped in thick shipping boots that came up to her knees and hocks and protected those delicate legs, the filly looked like an equine mummy as she emerged rear first from the back of the van. Despite her padding, she came gracefully down the ramp, carefully putting one foot behind her, then another, testing every step of the way. When she finally felt the tarmac under her, she stopped and looked around.

She was so swaddled in blankets and wraps that Stefan didn't recognize her. Then the groom removed the hood, and as she pricked her ears and looked his way, Stefan saw that it was the four-year-old, Night Fever. Under the floodlights, her chestnut coat—what he could see of it—seemed more brown than red, but it was her manner he was concerned about. He was glad to see that she looked calm as could be when the attendant led her to the first horse box and put her in. Under the hood, she'd been wearing the leather cap that covered her poll—the area at the top of her neck, between the ears, it was one of the most vulnerable parts of the horse—and when he saw that, he was reminded of Briar's reaction when he'd brought Irish down to the ranch without his protective headgear.

But he didn't want to think of Briar, not right now, anyway, and so he distracted himself by supervising the loading of the other two horses. To his relief, the temperamentally volatile Touch the Fire, who had already thrown a fit at the barn before being put into the van, came out of the trailer like an angel, delicately picking her way down the ramp and then standing quietly as her hood was removed. After Briar's inexplicable announcement that she intended to buy this filly, Stefan had gone back to study her, and he'd had to admit that, even more than the other two, her bearing was truly regal. Even now, she made the ridiculous-looking leather headgear she was wearing look more like a tiara than the protection it was, and with queenly grace, she allowed herself to be put in the second box for her trip to the plane.

The horse that gave them the bad time was the usually most well behaved of the three. Incandessence decided to be difficult tonight; she came out of the van as if she were on fire, kicking and rearing, and striking terror into everyone who was present, including Stefan, who was so afraid she was going to rip the pinned pastern apart that he leaped forward to help the groom, nearly losing his own footing in the process.

"I'll take her," he panted, grabbing for the lead shank. He was quick to thread the chain part of the shank up under her lip and over her gums before she knew what was happening. The so-called "lip chain" method might look cruel, but when a thousand pounds of valuable and temperamental Thoroughbred was at the other end of the line, it was by far the best and most humane way to control. All it took after that was a slight jerk to get the filly's attention. As most racehorses are, this one had been trained to the chain, and respected it.

"Now," he said, as the horse gave one last toss of her head to show him who was *really* the boss before she subsided, "shall we act like a lady, or would you prefer to sleep your way home on a little Ace?"

Ace-promazine was a tranquilizer, sometimes used for horses in transport. Unlike other tranquilizers, which sometimes produced opposite and unpredictable behaviors, Ace was much safer in these situations. Stefan preferred not to use it. But he was still prepared to give her a shot if she gave him any more trouble. Better a sleepy horse than a dead one, he thought, and when the third horse box was brought up, he led her in himself. She came but not as willingly as he would have liked, and he wouldn't let himself think what could happen if she threw a fit once they were in the air.

"Be good now," he murmured, bringing her carefully along. It was cramped in the box; it had been designed for horse or man, but not both. He entered first and prayed that she wouldn't lunge in on top of him before he could escape. A stout circular steel ring was set deeply into the front of the box, and when she came forward he tied the lead rope there with a quick release. One of the worst things that could happen would be if she had a tantrum and fell and they couldn't untie her head. He had seen horses strangle that way, or even worse, break their necks.

Of course, they could do that standing, too, he thought, and remembered a time in England when he had been transporting a horse for the Prix de l'Arc de Triomphe, or French Arc, as it was called. The horse, a favorite, no less, called Incapacitating, had suddenly gone crazy at twenty thousand feet. It had tried to rear, but, being tied to the box, succeeded only in getting its front legs caught over the top. Then the frenzied animal had jerked back with such force that it broke its neck before anyone could get there and release the rope.

He'd never forgotten how that horse looked, dangling with its neck crooked. He shuddered again from the memory. Telling himself not to think such happy thoughts, he decided maybe he'd better make the ride to the plane with the filly, so he signaled to the forklift driver, who engaged a few levers. With the tiniest of jolts, the truck started moving forward.

Everyone connected with this operation knew how dangerous it was to be riding in the box—and how quickly things could go wrong—so the driver was very careful not to bounce them around any more than absolutely necessary. Even so, as soon as she felt the box moving, Incandessence flung her head up and looked fearfully around.

"Come on, girl," Stefan soothed, placing a calm hand on the filly's quivering shoulder. "You've done this before, and you've got a long way to go. If you keep this up, we'll both be nervous wrecks by the time we get home."

Whether it was the sound of his voice or the steadying touch of his hand, the filly quieted. The short ride seemed to take forever, but finally they were aboard without incident. Thinking that now all they had to do was get through the next two thousand miles, Stefan climbed out of the box so it could be attached to the rails running down the center of the cargo plane. With someone's help, he finished lashing it to the floor and then glanced around.

The other two attendants were already fussing around their assigned charges; they had the hay nets ready and water at hand, and as Stefan checked everything one final time while the third groom came up to take over Incandessence, he crossed his fingers. All seemed quiet and calm.

Takeoff proceeded without a hitch—not even Incandessence seemed disturbed. Stefan was alert for about an hour into the fight, but finally, the quiet sounds of all three horses munching at their hay and the steady droning of the plane's engines started making him sleepy. The three grooms had retired to the front of the plane where they could still keep an eye on their charges and gossip over a card game; they asked Stefan if he wanted to join them, but he shook his head.

"No, I'm going to catch some shut-eye," he said. "Wake me if you need me."

"Will do," said the groom who was taking care of Night Fever. He sounded cheerful. Why not? He had already won a hand, and his horse was acting like an old veteran.

"You can count on that," said the man who was in charge of Incandessence. He didn't sound nearly as cheerful and relaxed, and it wasn't because he'd lost a bet. Nervously he glanced over his shoulder at the placidly eating Derby winner. As if she knew she was being watched, she cocked an ear in their direction but kept on nibbling.

"You won't go far?" asked the third, who was taking care of Touch the Fire. He didn't sound merely anxious; he was more in terror. He'd been back at the barn when she'd had her fit. It had taken four men—one at each ear and two more in back to literally pick her up and lift her into the van, and even then she'd managed to fight her way out twice. Finally, they'd just thrown her in and slammed the door shut.

"Only over there," Stefan said, smiling and gesturing toward a couple of hay bales that had been pushed toward the back of the plane. They would make as good a cot as any, and be a lot more comfortable than some of the other places he'd had to sleep over the years.

But once he settled down, three of the quilted horse hoods bundled up under his head for a pillow, he couldn't sleep. After fidgeting for twenty minutes or so and not being able to get comfortable, he finally sat up. Longing again even for just one cigarette, he ducked down and looked out the little port window. The only thing visible was black sky with a smattering of stars; below was just darkness. Thinking it was almost hypnotic—the drone of the engines as the plane sped through the night, the horses munching contentedly on their hay, the three grooms playing cards and joking quietly among themselves—he turned to brooding.

He'd thought he'd miss the routine of running a racing stable—the early morning gallops on the downs to condition the horses; the hustle and bustle of getting each horse to the racecourse on time, and having each ready to run; the late afternoon feedings; arranging for the veterinarian or the farrier; the paperwork—no, he knew he'd never miss the paperwork. Of all the headaches associated with running a stable, that had been the worst. He could read form charts and pedigree records and past-performance listings until kingdom come and never got bored, but sit him down in front of a ledger or accounts book, and his eyes immediately glazed.

But aside from doing the books every month, he thought, everything else had been a cherished and familiar routine. He'd been doing it so long that he'd thought he'd feel out of kilter, a spoke gone from a wheel, when he'd chucked it all to come to America. Now the only thing he really missed was that last look-see along the shed row at night before going to bed. Seeing the horses safely in their boxes, warm and comfortable in their rugs, had always given him pleasure; only after he'd checked every one did he feel he could retire for the night as well.

It had been a busy life, a full life, all right, but basically satisfying. He'd been content . . . until he found that trunk in his grandmother's attic. If he hadn't gone through it, he might still be at Epsom, setting the alarm for four A.M. to rouse the lads for the first of the gallops. Instead, he was sitting in a chartered plane watching over two *very* expensive mares and one orphan and working for someone else—he, who had always cherished his independence. If anyone had told him a year ago that he'd be in this situation, he wouldn't have believed it.

"Are you going to tell her?" his friend, Stan, had asked, after he had accepted the job as Briar's ranch manager. They had been sitting in the living room of the house at the riding club; it was late, and the only sign of life down by the barn was a single horse moving around its paddock. Everyone had long since gone home, and with Gary away for the night somewhere, Stan had invited him to dinner. They were having a last brandy before Stefan started back to his trailer, and as he watched the horse moving back and forth with its head down, looking for a good place to roll, he shook his head.

"I don't know," he said. He'd finally told Stan the real

reason he was here; he'd felt it only fair after everything his
friend had done for him. It had been Stan's idea to ask Briar
about the ranch manager job; in addition to everything else, it
was close to Mondragon, and, as Stan had so astutely pointed
out, if Stefan was there, he could keep an eye on both parties.
But Stan was the only person he'd told so far, and he wanted
to keep it that way. The fewer people who knew his true
purpose here, the better.

"Don't you think you should?" Stan had asked. His eyes on
his glass, he swirled his brandy and took an appreciative sniff.

Stefan turned away from the window. The horse he'd been
watching had just rolled, enjoying himself thoroughly but getting his blanket askew in the process. Stefan would go down
and straighten it on his way back to the trailer.

"No, I don't," he said. "There's no reason for her to know,
and if I tell her, it will look suspicious."

Stan took a sip of the brandy. "It *is* suspicious, my friend.
And if you *don't* tell her, and she finds out—or even worse,
figures it out—she's going to be furious that you tricked her,
and I wouldn't blame her."

Put that way, Stefan wouldn't blame Briar either. But he still
stubbornly insisted, "There's no way she can find out." He
frowned in Stan's direction. "Unless, of course, you tell her."

"Your secret's safe with me, old boy. But what if one of that
Jaeger family tells her? You're bound to run into each other
sooner or later. You have to, living practically in each other's
pockets out there, *and* in the same business. You'll be going to
sales and races and things. And since you've already had one
altercation, don't you think that when you do meet up next, it
will be—to say the least—a trifle awkward?"

It had been more than that, Stefan thought, shifting position.
He'd been expecting to see the Jaeger clan at Keeneland, and
he'd kept a sharp eye out, but by some miracle, their paths
hadn't crossed until that last night. Thank God, he thought,
Briar had been so preoccupied. She'd been so flushed with
success that she hadn't seemed to notice something amiss, but
you never knew with her. Just because she hadn't said anything
didn't mean she hadn't picked up on the fact that he'd been
avoiding her at that post-sale party, and the reason he'd done
so was because he had seen Rupert and Carl and Charlotte
come in. He hadn't wanted Briar to connect him with them for
any reason, and because he knew he'd never be able to avoid

a confrontation if he joined them, he'd stayed off by himself.

He had listened to the conversation, and when he recalled those snippets he'd overheard, he smiled to himself. Oh, she was clever, all right, he thought. Until he realized who had been bidding against her for those two fillies, he hadn't understood why she had deliberately driven up the bidding on Heat of Night before dropping out.

"One good turn deserves another, eh, mate?" he murmured, and laughed softly, picturing Rupert's face when he realized he'd been finessed. He hadn't wanted that filly anymore than he wanted to run naked through Keeneland, but because Briar had turned the tables on him, now he had an expensive horse he'd paid far too much for, and worse, had to figure how to pawn off without looking the fool. Just thinking about it made Stefan laugh all over again.

Then he remembered his current predicament, and his smile faded. He'd suspected it before, but now he'd had a good demonstration, and he knew that it was a mistake to underestimate Briar McKenna. Worse, now that he'd worked for her these past few months, he was beginning to realize he shouldn't have taken on the job as her ranch manager, no matter how tempting. As much as he hated to admit it, the attraction he felt for her, not to mention the admiration, was making it difficult for him to do his job.

At first, he thought he'd handle it by just getting away, figuring that as long as he wasn't at the ranch when she was, there was less chance of his making an ass of himself and spilling the beans in the process. But that wasn't working either. Now in addition to everything else, he was feeling like a traitor. She didn't deserve to be lied to, he told himself, but what other choice did he have?

*You could come clean and just tell her,* a little voice whispered. *Wouldn't that be easiest?*

Yes, yes, it would, he thought. But unfortunately, things weren't so simple. He couldn't tell Briar why he was really here, not now, after all this time. She'd want to know why he hadn't told her before; she'd accuse him of obtaining the job under false pretenses, and he couldn't argue. She'd be right. He had.

He couldn't understand what was happening to him; he'd never felt this way about a woman, not even Samantha. But with Sam, things had seemed so simple; with Briar, somehow they were a lot more complicated. And it wasn't because they had an employer-employee relationship.

Irritably, he shifted position on the hay bale again. He didn't know what he was feeling, and it annoyed him. After all, Briar *was* his employer. And, despite that one near kiss all those months ago, she had never indicated that she wanted things between them to be anything more than that. So what was he going on about? He was paid to run her ranch, to oversee the horse operation, to give her advice about her horses, and that should be it.

He laughed sarcastically. After this recent experience, it was obvious that Briar didn't want, or need, his advice about buying horses. The only thing she hadn't done, thank God, was buy a stallion to go with these mares. On that, at least, she had listened—but only after he'd driven the point home. He'd finally convinced her that, while the best racing, with the highest purses, was in California at Santa Anita and Hollywood Park, the best racing *stock* still came from Kentucky. Until that changed, through California's breeding incentive program and others like it, it wouldn't pay to have a stallion, no matter how good.

Briar hadn't liked the logic, he remembered, but she had accepted the argument. For the time being, he amended. With Briar, one was never sure. He could go home right now and find ten stallions stabled on the place.

Shaking his head, Stefan gazed out the plane's port window. What an optimist he'd been to think that she was learning to heed the advice for which she was paying him so well. Remembering how avidly she had sought his opinion at this last sale, he shook his head again. Oh, she had listened there, hadn't she? The proof was right here in front of him, all three eating their heads off.

But then a picture of Briar as she'd been that night of the auction flashed into his mind, and without realizing it, his irritation vanished. She had been beautiful, he thought, in that green gown with the sparkles, and the slit up the leg, her hair off her neck. She'd looked so lovely that she'd taken his breath away. It had been all he could do to keep his hands off her; he'd wanted to . . .

Well, it didn't matter what he'd wanted to do, he thought hastily; the point was he hadn't done anything—and wouldn't. They'd established an employer-employee relationship, and he was going to keep it that way. Bugger all, he thought, remembering something else. He really didn't have a choice. She'd been a widow for less than a year; what was he thinking of? He knew by the way she spoke of Hayden Lord at times that she had loved her husband. And why not? From what he'd heard, the man had not only been rich as Croesus but a good-looking bloke, and he'd been charming as hell even if he had been old enough to be her father.

Guiltily, he thrust the thought away. Briar's relationship with her husband wasn't anyone's concern, least of all his, he told himself. His job was to mind his own business.

But when her face flashed into his mind unbidden again, and he pictured that glorious smile of hers, and those beautiful eyes, he felt something stir inside despite all his vows. She had easily been the loveliest woman in that elite gathering at Harriman's Oakes, he thought, and then hated himself.

Oh, bloody hell, he was doing it again, thinking of her as though he had a right. Restless, he got up and headed toward the galley at the back of the plane. Maybe what he needed was some coffee to get her out of his mind, he thought—that, or a shot of Ace himself, so he could sleep the rest of the flight.

The coffee looked like thick brown ink when he finally found it, but he poured some anyway. He was just taking a sip when the plane hit an air pocket, and he ended up burning his lips.

"Damn it to effing, bleeding hell!" he shouted, jumping back and holding the cup out as the plane dipped again. Coffee cascaded all over the front of him, and as he reached for a towel, he happened to look up.

Touch the Fire had apparently heard him curse, for she was looking curiously back in his direction. Just for a second, their eyes seemed to meet—man and horse—then, as if she were laughing at some private joke, she blew out a breath and turned her back again. Watching her, wondering what had just happened, Stefan stood there with drops of coffee still burning his hand, until the plane hit another pocket and he reached for the towel again.

# CHAPTER FIFTEEN

Charlotte Jaeger was furious when she drove into the parking lot at Mondragon Enterprises in San Jose at five to eleven in the morning. She had just come from a meeting in San Francisco with her accountant, who had told her, among other infuriating things, that her father was cutting the budget for the ranch. Rising costs, he'd said . . . too much overhead . . . too slim a profit margin. . . .

What her father was *really* trying to do, she thought in a fury, was save face by making her pay the cost of that filly he'd been forced to buy when Briar McKenna outsmarted him at the Breeding Stock Sale in November. As if it was *her* fault that Briar had pulled a coup! If he hadn't been venting his spleen by taking it out on her, she'd think it was hysterically funny—not to mention well deserved—that the great Rupert Jaeger had been bested by the enemy.

But she wasn't laughing now; she was too angry. She had never felt so humiliated in her life as she had this morning, being lectured as if she were a wayward child who had to be taught a lesson about the value of money. She had been running the Stud over twenty-five years now, and no one, not even her father, had a right to tell her how to manage the ranch. *She* hadn't bought that filly; *he* had. Let him take the money out of the company; it would serve him right! She shouldn't have to pay for his mistake; why, he hadn't even had the courtesy to confront her face-to-face but had gone through an intermediary!

Whipping into a parking space reserved for some executive vice president or other, Charlotte rocked the Cadillac to a halt. Jerking the key from the ignition, she opened the door and got out. For her appointment this morning with that cretin accountant Harold Swensen, she had worn a cream-colored business suit made of imported merino wool jersey. The wool was the softest kind imaginable, but she felt so agitated now that it was like wearing a hairshirt, and she irritably straightened her skirt while glancing toward the building. As always, she had to pause a moment and just stare. Ever since her father and Carl had moved to this place from the comfortable old offices down on Geary, she felt as if they'd vaulted into some ugly twenty-first century. These days, the corporate offices of Mondragon Enterprises were housed in a building made of awful bluish mirrored glass with concrete struts. Supposedly designed to reflect the sky and the clouds, all the glass reflected was an irritating glare, Charlotte thought.

To make matters worse, the building stood five stories, and as she went quickly up the curving walk toward the front doors, she tried not to look. The sight reminded her of how little power she had when her father chose to excise it. Even though she supposedly held twenty-five percent of voting stock, she was only allowed to affix her signature now and then to incomprehensible legal documents. She had never paid much attention; she was too busy running the ranch. But it still made her angry when she thought about it, especially at times like this. It was infuriating to feel so powerless.

The receptionist, a silly girl dressed in a sapphire-colored dress that was supposed to match her eyes, but which only made her look sallow, glanced up when the front doors were thrown open. Her eyes widened when she recognized Charlotte, and she half stood.

"Miss Jaeger!" she exclaimed.

Charlotte was in no mood to be civil to a chit of a girl she had already discovered didn't have a brain in her head. "In person," she said. "And don't bother to announce me. This is a surprise visit."

The girl—whose name Charlotte had forgotten, if she had ever bothered to find out what it was—had already reached for the complicated phone system on her desk. Confused, she looked up. "But—"

"It's simple enough," Charlotte said, reaching over and taking the receiver from the girl's hand and slamming it down again. "I said I wanted to surprise them. You can tell me though, are both my father and brother here?"

That seemed to fluster the girl even more. "Well, yes . . . That is, they came in earlier, but I don't know—"

"I know it was a difficult question, my dear. Just go back to whatever it was you were doing, and I'll see myself up. Do you think you can manage that?''

Looking ready to cry, the receptionist sat down with a thump as Charlotte turned toward the bank of elevators. She had already forgotten the girl as she punched the elevator button. Now that she was here, she wanted to say what she had to say and then be on her way. She had a lot to do; it was time to order feed, and the shavings bin needed replenishing. Then there were the two-year-olds to bring in and start saddling, and the yearlings had to be moved to another pasture. She had her eye on some new tack, and—

Reminded that her budget had supposedly been cut, her face set. She'd see about that!

As she waited impatiently for the elevator to arrive, she glanced over at the huge portrait of her grandfather that occupied one entire downstairs wall. She'd always thought the thing was indecently ostentatious, for the painting was at least twenty feet tall by ten feet wide, and it dominated not only the wall but the entire marbled entryway. She knew it was the first thing anyone new coming into the building would see, and sometimes she cringed at the thought of what visitors would think.

She had never known her grandfather, who had died before she was born—well, he hadn't actually *died*, he'd been shot, she amended, in some mysterious incident involving, of all people, Juliet Caulfield. But as she gazed up at the pale, ascetic painted face, with the glacial eyes and the thin, cruel mouth, trying not to think how much she and her father both looked like Heinrich Jaeger, she thought that she would rather *not* have known him. She was grateful that his interest in horses had led to the establishment of the Mondragon Stud, but unlike Carl, who worshipped the grandfather he had never known, she hadn't been able to summon even a scrap of feeling for Heinrich. By all accounts, he had been ruthless, dictatorial, egotistical, and practically inhuman.

Staring at the man in a typically nineteenth-century pose—one long-fingered hand gracefully resting on the back of a chair, the other carefully inserted into a waistcoat pocket as he gazed haughtily into space, she wanted to laugh. Had he really believed he was fooling anyone? Even the tales that circulated about him in his own family weren't inspiring stuff: there were stories in abundance about his merciless business tactics and his callous treatment of friends and associates. He had been consumed with the need for power, but what had haunted him to his dying day had been his complete and utter obsession with Sloane and Marguerite Caulfield. Heinrich had hated Sloane with a vengeance that was still felt three generations later, and all because of a woman named Marguerite.

Charlotte knew all about her grandfather's passion for Marguerite Caulfield, but what she'd always thought much more intriguing was Heinrich's famous—or infamous, she thought snidely—three-day disappearance. It was one of those mysteries that had spanned generations and caused endless speculation and conjecture and comment—at least by Charlotte, who had been fascinated from the moment she had heard it. What had happened? Where did he go? *Why* had he disappeared? And what did he do while he was gone? No one knew, and she remembered discussing the great mystery many times with her brother when they were young. As a girl, she had thought it endlessly engrossing, and she had imagined all sorts of reasons why her grandfather Heinrich, who was so painstaking and meticulous and controlled and precise, should have simply *vanished* for three days back in 1890.

She had always been sure that there was some connection between her grandfather's disappearance and Marguerite's marriage. Even Heinrich couldn't deny that he had asked Marguerite to marry him. But when she had spurned him by eloping with Sloane Caulfield, Charlotte believed that he had tried to still the gossip by marrying quickly—Marguerite's cousin, Mariel Kendall.

Heinrich had never forgotten what he believed was the ultimate betrayal by the two lovers, and it was no secret to anyone that he had vowed to destroy them. Sometimes, when she was feeling charitable, Charlotte could understand just how her grandfather had felt. After all, she had been in love once, and the same thing had happened to her. Only in her case, the woman's name had been Ariana, and the man had been . . .

Well, it didn't matter, she decided, dismissing the past with the arrival of the elevator. As she stepped in and pushed the button for the top floor, she decided that perhaps she had better marshal her thoughts and plan what she was going to say to her father. Even though Rupert consistently underrated her, Charlotte had never made the same mistake about him. He might be nearly eighty now, but he was no doddering old man. People might look at the spare, white-haired, dignified visage and believe that because of his courtliness, his impeccable manners, his fastidious dress, that he had mellowed, but Charlotte knew from bitter experience that wasn't true. Rupert was every bit as ruthless as he'd always been—a true son of Heinrich Jaeger, whom he had always emulated. Charlotte had had proof of her father's devotion only a few months ago, when he had driven a family off land that had been theirs for over fifty years. A construction company had approached Rupert about building a mini-shopping mart on some property he owned, but he had immediately calculated how much greater value that property would have if he also owned the adjacent land. The fact that it belonged to the DeLindsey Dairy family made no difference; Rupert knew that most farmers operated in a continual state of debt. It was a simple enough matter to check around and find out which bank held the DeLindsey note, even simpler to buy the note and call it in. When the inevitable happened, as Rupert had known it would, he hesitated long enough just to arrange the earth movers. Oh, Rupert was no sweet, little, white-haired man, Charlotte thought, and she felt herself tense as the elevator doors opened.

When she emerged, another girl was decorating the desk right in front of her; this one had dictaphone headphones clamped to her ears, but she immediately removed the headset when she saw Charlotte open the glass doors to the inner office. Like those below, these doors sported the company logo, the Mondragon coat of arms, which showed a crimson chevron rising over a black mountain, the initial "M" emblazoned over the chevron. Charlotte remembered how angry her father had been with her long ago, when she had discovered that the name Mondragon really meant "serpent mountain," and she had asked him nastily why the coat of arms didn't have a snake in it.

Although Charlotte had seen the Mondragon design many times, she stopped suddenly and looked at it fully today. For some reason, she had just remembered seeing the logo for Briar McKenna's TimeSave Corporation. Picturing the sun rising, or setting—she had never been sure which—over the mountain depicted in that motif, she smiled. Was that prophetic? She almost hoped so.

"Miss Jaeger!" the secretary exclaimed, diverting her thoughts. "I didn't know you were expected!"

"I'm not," Charlotte said, and looked toward her father's closed office door. "Is he in?"

"Well, actually—" the girl started to say.

Charlotte had heard enough. "Don't bother to announce me," she said. "I'll just go in."

"Oh, but you c—"

But Charlotte had already flung open the office door and stalked inside. As soon as she realized her father wasn't behind the desk, or even, it seemed, in the room, she paused. The only occupant besides herself was a woman who had been standing near the window. She turned at Charlotte's abrupt entrance, and they both stared at each other in surprise for a moment.

Then Charlotte took charge. "Who are you?"

The unhappy secretary had followed her in. "Miss Jaeger—"

The woman by the window drew in a hiss of a breath. "So!" she said. "*You're* Charlotte Jaeger!"

Charlotte turned just long enough to gesture the dismayed secretary out. Closing the door firmly in the girl's face, she turned back to the other woman, who was dressed in black, from her wide-brimmed hat to her well-shod feet. Her red lipstick looked like a slash on her pale face, and Charlotte wondered if she was in mourning or just sick. "I am," she said. "But you have the advantage, because I haven't the slightest idea who you might be."

The woman drew herself pompously up. "I," she said, "am Fredrica Lord Hudson!"

"Well, all fall down," Charlotte said carelessly as she walked over to the desk. Casually, she dropped her purse atop the shining surface. "Would you mind telling me what you're doing here? This *is* my father's office."

"Not that it's any of your business," Fredrica said, "considering what you've done, but your father and I have an appointment."

"I see." Charlotte was disliking this woman more and more with each second. Wondering what in the world her father would want to talk to her about, she gave Fredrica an appraising look. "Ah . . . Fredrica *Lord* Hudson," she said, comprehension dawning. "*Now* I get it." She paused, then leaned forward conspiratorially. "Tell me. What exactly are you accusing me of?"

Fredrica looked at her as though she'd lost her mind. "Oh, this is too much! After what you've done, you dare to ask me that?"

Slowly, Charlotte took off her gloves, finger by finger. When she was finished, she dropped them casually near the purse on the desk and then perched on the edge herself. "You would save us both a lot of time and energy by just telling me what you think I've done . . . and why it could possibly concern you."

"I don't have to tell you anything. As I said, my appointment is with your father."

Charlotte looked deliberately around the room. "Who appears not to be present at the moment. Is there anything *I* can do for you?"

"You've done quite enough, thank you!" Fredrica snapped. "If it weren't for you, none of us would be in this mess!"

"Oh, please, you give me too much credit," Charlotte said modestly. She was enjoying herself for the first time all morning. "I really didn't have that much to do with . . . what is it you think I did, anyway?"

Fredrica's hands clenched into fists. "You found her, that's what," she said. "You *found* her."

"Who?"

"Who? Who do you think I'm talking about? Briar McKenna, that's who. And if you hadn't interfered, she never would have inherited that property, she never would have gotten involved in that preposterous scheme to restore the Caulfield Farm, and she wouldn't be spending all my father's money! You're to blame for this, only you!"

Charlotte pretended to examine her nails. "Well, as I said, I really can't take all the credit. Technically, *I* wasn't the one who found her; it was a private investigator named Albert Weitz."

"Whom you hired." Fredrica scathingly pointed out.

"Well, yes, that's true, I did. But it was only fair—"

*"Fair?"* Fredrica looked at her in outraged disbelief. "I can't believe you'd say that. If it weren't for you, *your* father would have his property, and I wouldn't be watching *my* father's life work go down the drain. Two and half million dollars for one horse, Miss Jaeger—two and a half million dollars! It's outrageous, inconceivable, utterly and absolutely. . . *outrageous!*"

Fredrica was so overcome that she gasped to a halt. Her fingers shaking, she reached into her purse and took out a handkerchief that she used to blot her brow.

Charlotte wasn't impressed by the melodrama—if that's

what it was. Just for an instant there, she'd thought she'd seen real fear in Fredrica's eyes, and she wondered just why Fredrica was so rabid about Briar spending money. Idly, she speculated that it might be financial trouble, but if it was it was no business of her own. And because she had problems at the moment with finances herself, she could hardly spare any pity for someone whom she'd just met and didn't care if she never saw again. "Oh, I don't know," she said. "I thought the price quite fair. After all, the horse *is* a Derby winner, and—"

Fredrica's head jerked. "I don't care if she was Horse of the Year!"

"No, that was the filly my father bought, actually. Her name is—"

"I don't *care*!" Fredrica cried, wadding the handkerchief into a tight little ball. "*I don't care!* The point is that she has no *right* to be spending that money! She—"

"I beg your pardon," Charlotte said with raised eyebrow. "But it seems to me that she has every right."

"We'll see about *that*!"

"Well, at least now we've come to the real reason why you're here to see good old Dad," Charlotte said, getting up from the desk. She smiled coldly. "If you're plotting something, he's the best. By the way, where is he? I came to see him about something myself."

Gathering her things, she decided to look for him elsewhere. She had tired of baiting this ridiculous woman; she had more important things to do. But Fredrica came up swiftly behind her and grasped her arm. "Don't you care?" she demanded.

"Care?" Charlotte repeated. "About what?"

"About what that . . . that woman has done?"

Charlotte wasn't sure *what* she felt about Briar McKenna. Meeting her at Keeneland had been an unsettling experience, one she still hadn't completely sorted out yet. She had been prepared to dislike her thoroughly. After all, she was Ariana's daughter, and if it hadn't been for Ariana . . .

Hastily, she thrust those thoughts away. She didn't want to think about Duncan and Ariana; she didn't even want to think about Briar, whom she'd found impossible to dislike, and whom she actually, grudgingly, almost admired. Who else could beat Rupert Jaeger at his own game? she thought in wonder, and she remembered wanting to cheer the night Briar brought her father to the brink about buying that filly before she abruptly stepped down and left him holding the bag.

A very expensive bag, she thought. Forgetting Briar for the moment, she remembered again why she was here, and her anger rose once more. She was *not* going to pay for that filly out of Stud funds, and that was that.

But first she had to get away from this tiresome woman. "As far as I'm concerned," she said coldly, "the only thing Briar McKenna has done is commit the unpardonable sin of succeeding in a man's world. She manages her own company, which is very successful, I hear; she's the widow of one of the lords of industry—oh, sorry, no pun intended—and she's sole heir to Caulfield Farm, which, in its day, despite what my father might say to the contrary, produced some of the finest racehorses in the United States. And now she *owns* two of the best mares this country has ever produced. What more could we ask of an orphan who started out with nothing and rose to such lofty heights?"

"Why are you taking her side?" Fredrica demanded shrilly. "What is she to you?"

But before Charlotte could answer—if she was even sure what the answer was anymore—the office door was opened from the other side, and her father came in, closely followed by Carl. Both men stopped when they saw her, and Rupert exclaimed in obvious annoyance, "Charlotte! What are you doing here?"

Charlotte certainly didn't intend to discuss her business in front of Fredrica. For all she knew, this woman might run to Briar with the news; she certainly hadn't been adverse to discussing her problems in front of a virtual stranger. "I came to see you, Father," she said. "I had something I wanted to talk to you about." Her eyes met his. "I'm sure you know what it is."

Rupert looked even more irritated. "Can't it wait? As you can see, I'm busy just now."

Charlotte glanced in Fredrica's direction. "Yes, indeed. You can't imagine how surprised *I* was to discover that you all not only know each other, but that you were carrying on secret meetings right under my nose."

"This isn't a 'secret,' and Father certainly doesn't have to explain his office appointments to you, Charlotte." Carl snapped.

"That's true," she agreed calmly. "However, I imagine there are certain people who might be interested in knowing that you are meeting—secretly or not."

Outraged, Fredrica gasped. But before she or Carl could say anything, Rupert said coldly, "That will be all, Charlotte. As I said, I'm busy right now. Whatever it is you want to discuss will have to wait until I get home."

"To Mondragon, you mean, Father?" Charlotte said, holding his glance again. "I've been to see Harold, you know. And I won't put up with it, not for one minute. I think we'd better get that straight before we do anything else, don't you?"

Rupert glanced at the avid Fredrica, who, for once, seemed more interested in someone other than herself. When he saw her speculative expression, he moved his head toward Carl, who quickly stepped in and muttered something about finding a cup of coffee. Reluctantly, Fredrica left the office with Carl, who closed the door behind them.

As soon as they were gone, Charlotte turned back to her father. "There's no need for discussion about this," she said. "I merely came to tell you not to try this with me because you'll regret it."

Rupert was at his most supercilious. "Are you trying to threaten me?"

"Not at all," she shot back. "But just remember one thing. I still have twenty-five percent of Mondragon stock in my name."

Condescendingly, he said, "Since between us Carl and I own the other seventy-five percent, that's hardly enough to swing a vote, dear girl."

"I haven't been a girl for years, Father!" Charlotte snapped. "And I wasn't thinking of trying to swing any votes! I just wanted you to know that under certain circumstances, I wouldn't be adverse to offering them up for sale."

He was shocked. "You wouldn't!"

"Oh, I would, Father," she said, reaching for the door. "If I thought the Stud was threatened, I'd do it in a minute. Bet on it."

He looked incredulous. "But that stock has been in the family for years—since the company began!"

Charlotte opened the door, vaguely surprised that her brother wasn't crouched with his ear against it on the other side. Fredrica was still keeping him occupied, she thought, no doubt crying pitifully into her crumpled handkerchief about how mean Charlotte had been. She smiled. So far they hadn't *seen* mean.

"Then maybe it's time we diversified, Father," she said, looking back at him. "You think about it. And while you're doing that, you might put in a call to Harold Swenson. I'm sure he'll be glad to know that you've reconsidered those budget restrictions."

"I won't put up with this, Charlotte! You can't talk that way to me!"

"I just did," she said, and closed the door firmly on his outraged expression.

Down at her car again, she tossed her purse and gloves onto the passenger seat, then glanced back at the building. She'd gotten what she'd come for, she was sure. So for the time being, that problem was solved. Now all she had to do was decide what to take care of next. Her expression thoughtful, she climbed into the Cadillac and got out her keys. Something was going on, all right, she thought. She knew her father, and Fredrica hadn't been paying a social call. Maybe it was time to pay someone a long overdue visit.

———❦———

# CHAPTER SIXTEEN

Briar returned home from Kentucky feeling both troubled and triumphant. As thrilled as she was about the new mares she had purchased, she couldn't understand what was wrong with Stefan. After the sale, he'd been avoiding her. And, as she peered out the front windows toward the dark drive two nights later waiting for the transport van, she wondered why. He had disappeared at the post-sale party, and she hadn't seen him until he dashed in at the hotel to say he'd made arrangements to fly the horses home and would get in touch with her later. He was in and out so fast that she couldn't pin him down. It had started right after she'd had that conversation with the Jaeger family at the party, and she was sure his behavior had something to do with that.

Annoyed with herself for not insisting that they work it out right there, she dropped the curtain and decided to make a cup of tea. It was going on one A.M., and she had no idea when the van would arrive, but she wanted to be awake when it did.

Not that anyone would need her help, she thought irritably as she went into the kitchen; Stefan had made it clear that he didn't need, or want, her assistance in this matter. The only thing he *had* told her in Kentucky was that getting the horses home safely was his responsibility, and that he'd take care of it. She had been annoyed with him for avoiding her, so she had booked the first flight out. As soon as she was on her way back, she felt guilty. She should have stayed behind; she should have pursued what was wrong; she should have seen those horses safely onto that plane. There were a lot of things she should have done and hadn't, but that was about to change. The more she thought about Stefan's odd reaction that night, the more certain she was that something was going on.

Briar didn't like mysteries, especially when they seemed somehow to involve her, and as she held a cup under the instant hot water tap, she decided this had gone on long enough. She didn't care how tired Stefan might be when he arrived with the van tonight; as soon as the horses were settled, she'd have it out with him. She didn't like the idea of her manager having secrets from her, not when it might affect her ranch.

She stood by the sink, staring blankly down at the cup of water she'd just drawn. Maybe she was more tired than she'd realized. Why else was she making such a big deal out of this? She was acting as if Stefan were engaged in some kind of . . . of plot against her, for God's sake. Feeling ridiculous, she got down a saucer, then fetched a tea bag from the canister on the counter. What did she think he was hiding? Did she really believe he'd managed to get himself hired on here so he could spy for the Jaeger family? The idea was ridiculous, and she felt like a fool. No one had ever worked harder for her than Stefan Yager, and if she doubted that, all she had to do was think about the way he'd run himself ragged ever since he'd come. He had been on the move from the first day, crisscrossing the country, attending sales and auctions, constantly checking out horses for her. How could she possibly doubt him?

*But something was wrong all the same*, she thought, frowning. Her instinct told her so, and she had learned over the years to trust her instincts. There had been times when she'd had nothing else to guide her.

A little bell by the stove tinkled just then, startling her until she realized what it was. Thoughtful Isabella, who had taken such good care of her from the moment she had arrived from Mexico, had left a light dinner for her in the microwave. But as she reached up to turn off the alarm, she thought for once not even Isabella's homemade soup and crusty *pan Mexicano* could tempt her; with all these other things on her mind, she just wasn't hungry. Putting the pot in the refrigerator, she carried her tea into the living room instead. She sat down on the couch by the big front windows, curling her feet under her, so she'd see the truck's headlights when it came.

Except for the floodlights over the barns, the ranch was dark and quiet. Jaime, who always got up before dawn to check the horses and feed them, and Isabella, who usually arrived at the house no later than seven, both went to bed early. Of course Stefan wasn't home, so his house was dark as well. She saw it as a dark shape tucked into the curve of the drive down by the foaling barn, set well back under the pines that she'd forbidden anyone to cut down. She had always loved trees, and had asked Ted Skerrit, who was carrying on with the rebuilding she wanted done, to save as many as he could. As always, amused and resigned at the same time, he had planned the ranch manager's house in such a way that a tall pine grew out of the deck in back, shading the house and dipping over the creek that ran behind all year round. To Briar's surprise, Stefan had commented on how much he liked it. "Only in California," he'd said with a shake of his head, but he admitted to putting a chair out there so he could admire the view.

Thinking of Stefan again reminded her of her disagreeable conversation with the Jaegers at Keeneland. She still hadn't forgotten her first meeting with Rupert at the San Francisco fund-raiser, or the time Carl had visited the farm. Even though Charlotte was an unknown quantity so far, it was obvious that the men in the family, at least, didn't want her here, and she was starting to wonder just how far they'd go to see her gone. Carl was not nearly as subtle as his father, but she knew that of the two, Rupert was much more dangerous.

Not that she was afraid of either of them, she thought, and felt silly again at the idea of their trying to drive her out. This wasn't the Wild West, where powerful ranch owners retained hired guns to force someone out over a property dispute, and she did have legal title. Thanks to her own thriving business, and Hay's generosity, she was more than able to hold her own against anyone, even after the tremendous amounts she had spent so far both on the renovation and the horses—not to mention this most recent sale. She smiled when she thought of that. Spence had blanched when she'd told him the news about Keeneland, but he knew how determined she was to do this properly, so he'd just transferred more funds and wished her well.

So even if Rupert and Carl wanted her out so much they decided to play dirty, she wasn't without resources. With the business concerning Fredrica still pending, she really didn't want to get involved in another confrontation, but if pushed, the Jaegers would soon discover that she was no debutante ignorant of street fights.

*But what was Stefan Yager to them?*

Irritated by the thought of Stefan that swept in again out of nowhere, she put her teacup on the coffee table. Earlier, she'd left Marguerite's journal there, and, after glancing out the window again and seeing only the dark drive, she decided to read another segment while she waited for the damned van to arrive. She was sure they should have been here hours ago, but she knew Stefan would have called if there was a real delay. She hated waiting of any kind; it made her restless. But Marguerite would distract her, so she picked up the book.

As always, her great-grandmother began each "chapter," as it were, with an exclamation point, a sign of her own vibrant life. The moment Briar opened the journal and read the first line, she was transported back in time. The power of Marguerite's personality swept her up and took Briar with her. Instantly absorbed, she forgot the late hour and started to read.

*"So many exciting things have happened since I last had time to write,"* Marguerite had written, her words flying across the page, *"that I scarcely know where to begin! My darling Sloane has bought the most beautiful property in the world; we're to travel to Los Angeles to meet Lucky Baldwin, and—I can hardly believe it myself—Heinrich Jaeger has disappeared!"*

But despite her curiosity about where Heinrich had gone to,

Marguerite was too excited about the pending trip to Los Angeles, where she and Sloane would visit Mr. Baldwin's Santa Anita Rancho, to think about him. When Sloane announced that they had been invited to visit the Baldwin place, she had rushed out to the dressmaker and ordered a dozen new gowns. Then it had been a visit to the milliner to confer about matching hats . . . and then to the shoemaker and . . . heaven knew who else. She had been so busy getting ready that she hadn't had a minute to herself until she and Sloane were on their way.

To her secret relief, Sloane hadn't been annoyed, as she'd thought he might be, about the ten trunks and as many hat boxes she'd brought along with her. He only seemed amused at the huge pile of luggage that was assembled outside their private car when they got to the rail station.

"Marguerite, we're not going to India, you know," he said, watching for a moment as the porters trudged back and forth loading bags and boxes and her ten trunks inside. Humorously, he glanced at her as she supervised. "You can't possibly *need* all this!"

"But of course, I do!" she exclaimed. "Do you want your wife to look like a beggar? We're going to visit Mr. Lucky Baldwin, and I have to be prepared for everything!"

Sloane glanced significantly at a porter hefting yet another trunk. "I think you're prepared, my dear," he said dryly. "The only conceivable surprise on this visit would be an audience with the Queen."

"If I thought there was danger of that, I'd rush out and order ten more," Marguerite told him smugly, leading the way into their car.

Once inside, she forgot everything else but her pleasure at such luxury. For this journey, Sloane had hired a private car, which was luxuriously appointed with red velvet seats, crystal chandeliers, curtains at the windows, and even carpet on the floor. Sleeping quarters were toward the back, and when she had peeked in earlier and saw the double bed, she had blushed. But she was far too excited to be embarrassed for long, and when they were finally underway, she again professed her excitement and awe at meeting the man whose name was synonymous with racing.

"Baldwin isn't royalty, Marguerite," Sloane said with a smile. "He's in the business of breeding horses, as we're going to be. And I'd advise you not to let him hear you use that nickname of his. He detests being called 'Lucky.' "

"But he is—lucky, I mean," she protested. "How many men do *you* know who started out as a livery stableman and a few years later sold an interest in a mine for five million dollars?"

"Not many, that's true," he admitted. "But still, it would be more politic to call him Elias—or E.J., as he much prefers, don't you think?"

"For the time being, I think I'll call him Mr. Baldwin," she answered primly. Then she was struck with another thought. "Oh, Sloane," she said suddenly. "Do you really think he will sell us one of his horses?"

But Elias Jackson Baldwin sold them not one, but three horses during their visit, and by the time they returned home, Marguerite didn't know whether she had been more dazzled by the superb horseflesh she had seen at the Baldwin Rancho, or by the place itself. She had heard that the Rancho was becoming known as a beauty spot as well as a working ranch, and she had been amazed by the sheer numbers of things: five hundred acres of orange, lemon, and almond groves, thirty thousand sheep, three thousand cattle—and a stable of horses that numbered close to five hundred. Only about seventy of those horses were racing stock, but to Marguerite's eyes, they were seventy of the most beautiful Thoroughbreds she had ever seen. And of them all, she fell in love with Baldwin's pride and joy, the Emperor of Norfolk.

"Oh, Sloane!" she breathed, as the great horse was brought out for their inspection. She felt as if she were in the presence of royalty.

And she was. Widely regarded as the best California-bred racehorse of his day, the Emperor of Norfolk was an animal of tremendous power, even in his retirement. Deep through the heart, wide of girth, and possessed of powerful quarters, the great stallion had reigned as the champion of his division in America each year he had run. And run he had, Marguerite knew, having memorized the statistics: the Emperor had gone any distance from five to twelve furlongs, over any sort of track, in any part of the country. More, he had given away enormous amounts of weight to his rivals, sometimes up to thirty-five pounds, and had won every time, no matter what the condition.

"He's simply beautiful, Mr. Baldwin," Marguerite said to her host, as they all stood in the aisle watching the groom lead the stallion around.

"Thank you, my dear," Baldwin said, and looked sad for a moment. "It's a pity he won't run again."

Marguerite knew how he felt; she would have felt the same way about her beautiful stallion, Saxon. She had heard rumors of how the Emperor had been ruined during a stupid wager between exercise riders one day at Washington Park. Baldwin went on to tell her the details.

"The world record for a mile was then one minute, thirty-nine and three-quarters seconds," Baldwin said, his eyes clouded. "A record that hadn't been approached for years and didn't look like it would ever be broken. At the time, my horse was in his finest form and had never been better. But one morning, his regular exercise rider bet a friend that the Emperor could not only tie the mile record, but lower it as well. Naturally, the bet was taken. . . ."

He paused for a moment, obviously pained by the memory, and Marguerite, moved to tears herself, put a sympathetic hand on his arm. "You don't have to go on. . . ."

"No, I want to," Baldwin said. "The story bears telling, so maybe it won't happen again. The Emperor smashed the previous record that day, you know. With several watches on him, he traveled the distance in one thirty-eight, unofficially slashing nearly two seconds off Ten Broeck's long-standing record. But in the process, he destroyed his tendons." He paused painfully. "I knew when I heard that, he'd never race again."

Tears glittering in her eyes, Marguerite turned to look at Baldwin's magnificent big bay stallion. Even then he still had the look of eagles, she thought, and she knew that no matter what happened, she *had* to have one of his get.

They came home with three. One was a filly sired by the great stallion called Lady in Waiting; the other two were mares in foal to him. As Marguerite anxiously supervised them being unloaded from the train, she thought excitedly that she could hardly wait until spring. "I want to breed the filly to Saxon," she said, watching the delicate young creature prance gracefully down the ramp.

"Oh, you do, do you," Sloane said, his arm around her waist.

She looked up at him. He had already promised that she

would have equal say in running the horse ranch they intended to build, and she intended to hold him to his vow. "Yes, I do," she said, and added with a defiant look in her eye, "This year."

Laughing, Sloane held up his hands in surrender. "Then that's what we'll do," he said. "I know that look. I'd be a fool to argue."

"No one ever said you were a fool, Sloane Caulfield," she said, her eyes twinkling. Then, because she was so happy and life was so good to her, she burst into laughter. "Oh, Sloane, it's going to be wonderful!" she exclaimed and, casting decorum aside, threw her arms around him.

Laughing in delight at this exhibit, he hugged her in return before he kissed the tip of her nose. "I suppose you've already thought of a name for the cross between this filly and your stallion."

"I have," she said, before she noted his use of the pronoun. Loving him even more for it, she smiled and traced his lean jaw with her finger. "But since I already know it's going to be a colt, I give you the honor. What do you say?"

He thought about it for a moment, then he said, "I've got just the thing."

"What?" she said eagerly. "Tell me."

"We'll call him Fane."

"Fane?" she repeated. "I don't think I've ever heard that name."

"It means a person whose laughter is as contagious as a wild bird's song." Holding her away for a moment, he looked deep into her eyes. "It also means glad, joyful—which is exactly how I feel whenever you're near. I never tire of hearing you laugh, Maggie, so I think it suits you both. How do you feel about that?"

She felt as if she had never loved anyone more. "I think it's perfect," she whispered, her green eyes brilliant. "Because that's how I feel about you . . . glad, joyful . . . and so very happy to be your wife."

They moved out to the ranch from town soon after that. Marguerite was so anxious to start her breeding program that she insisted on resettling even though the house wasn't quite finished. When Sloane protested that she wouldn't have all the comforts she was accustomed to at the hotel where they had been staying, she airily dismissed the thought. She wasn't made of Dresden china, she claimed; she could live in a tent if necessary, just as long as they got started.

"I don't think it will come to that," Sloane said mysteriously, and he drove them out to the property in a smart landau. As they came around the last bend, and Marguerite saw what had been done during their absence in Los Angeles, she gasped.

"Sloane! How did you ever manage—?" She turned to him, wide-eyed. "I'm speechless!"

"That'll be the day," he replied dryly. He had pulled the horses to a halt by the side of the road so she could gaze at the house—*her house!*—she thought with a thrill. She was so excited that she could hardly speak. "Oh, Sloane, I don't know what to say!" she finally managed. "It's beautiful!"

"Just say you love me," he suggested, and he laughed aloud when she threw her arms around him and gave him a heartfelt kiss. "Whoa, now!" he protested, holding her tightly with one hand while he held on to the reins with the other. "You'll scare the horses."

"I don't care!" she exclaimed. "This is the best surprise I've ever had!"

She could still hardly believe her eyes as they drove through the big gates with the huge sign overhead—an elaborately scrolled "CF" for Caulfield Farm—and followed the gently curving drive up to the house. It stood on a rise, overlooking the five-acre fenced pastures, the vast show barn down in front, the paddocks, the working ring, and the half-completed half-mile track. There was so much to see that Marguerite couldn't take it in all at once. When Sloane pulled up in front of the house, she just clasped her hands and looked. It was the place of her dreams, two full stories with an attic, all painted white, with a dark-green steeply pitched roof and a porch that ran the entire front length. There was even a swing at one end where she could sit and gaze out at the horses at pasture and a vast spread of lawn in front, upon which several white geese waddled.

"Oh, Sloane, how did you ever—?" she asked, as he climbed down and came around to help her out. With her foot on the step and her hand in his, she gave him a suspicious look. "You said just the other day that the house wouldn't be finished for weeks!"

Tossing the reins to the groom who had come running out,

Sloane laughed. "I lied," he said. "Would you like me to have it all torn down so we have to wait to move in?"

"Don't you dare!" she exclaimed, racing up the front steps.

The house was everything she could have dreamed of and more. Sloane had seen to every detail, even those Marguerite wouldn't have thought of herself. New furniture filled the front rooms, the parlor, the sitting room, the dining room; the kitchen had every convenience. The banisters were polished walnut; the stair treads covered with new carpet. And upstairs. . . .

"Oh, Sloane!" she exclaimed, clasping her hands under her chin when she saw the view from the master bedroom. It seemed the only thing she was capable of saying. "It's beautiful! But how did you know. . . ?"

"That you would want to keep an eye on the horses?" he teased. "Oh, I just guessed."

She looked at him with shining eyes. "Can we go see the barn?"

Smiling indulgently but pleased at her excitement, he led her outside.

The barn was made of oak, with a wooden floor and thirty stalls large enough to be kind to foaling mares. The three mares Sloane had bought from Mr. Baldwin were scheduled to arrive later, but a dozen others that Sloane already owned before he and Marguerite married were already settled. At the end, separated from the mares but already presiding like King Tut, stood Saxon, Marguerite's pride and joy. The young stallion nickered when he heard her voice, and she rushed to see him before she remembered that in her haste she had forgotten to bring him a treat.

"Oh, dear, I forgot—" she started to say to Sloane, and then she saw that he was silently holding out two cubes of sugar for her to take. Laughing, she took the sugar from him and fed it to the eager horse.

Later, after a supper prepared by the housekeeper Sloane had temporarily hired, pending Marguerite's approval, they watched the sunset from the front porch. Still later, Marguerite not only told her handsome husband how happy she was but proceeded to demonstrate fully.

After such an arduous, exciting day—and night—Marguerite was still in bed late the next morning. She was thinking how wonderfully happy she was when her cousin arrived and demanded to speak to her.

The housekeeper, a large, comfortable woman named Leona Bevins, whom Marguerite had already decided to keep on, came to tell her that Mariel was downstairs in the sitting room waiting to see her. When Marguerite heard the news, she frowned. How like her cousin to arrive unannounced and uninvited, she thought irritably, and said, "I really don't feel like seeing anyone right now—especially my cousin. Please tell her that I am . . . indisposed."

"As you wish, Mrs. Caulfield," the housekeeper said doubtfully, and went away.

Marguerite had just settled back again when she heard a commotion downstairs. She suspected that Mariel was putting up a fuss at being sent away, but she knew Mrs. Bevins could handle it, so she snuggled into the pillows, smiling at the thought of how irate Mariel must be. She was just pulling the covers up when she heard rapid footsteps on the stairs, and before she knew what was happening, her bedroom door burst open and an infuriated Mariel appeared.

"Well, really! Have you become so high and mighty that you instruct your *housekeeper* to send me away? How *dare* you treat me in such a manner!"

"Do come in, cousin," Marguerite said.

Mariel obeyed, slamming the door behind her. Immediately, there was an agitated knocking from the other side. Mrs. Bevins called, "I'm sorry, Mrs. Caulfield. I tried—"

"It's all right, Mrs. Bevins," Marguerite said. Sighing, she levered herself to a sitting position in the bed and pushed her hair out of her eyes. Dark-haired and dark-eyed, petite and delicate-looking, but with a will of iron and a tongue that could cut sharper than a knife, Mariel was glowering at her from the other side of the room. Marguerite said impatiently, "Well, as long as you're here, you might as well come and sit down."

"If I'd known this was the sort of reception I would receive, I wouldn't have come!" Mariel retorted, but she swished over and flung herself down on the chair near the bed.

Hoping that whatever Mariel wanted could be accomplished quickly and without their usual fierce quarrel, Marguerite resigned herself and said, "What do you want, Mariel? Didn't Mrs. Bevins tell you I wasn't feeling well?"

"Yes, she did, but I certainly didn't believe her. You've never had a sick day in your life, Marguerite. You just didn't want to see me!"

Thinking how true that was, Marguerite threw back the covers. If she had to deal with her cousin, she needed some coffee. "Well, now that you're here, what do you want?"

Obviously torn between what she had come to say and indignation at the way Marguerite was treating her, Mariel debated—but briefly. Tossing her dark curls, she said, "I have news."

Marguerite yawned. "Oh, really? What?"

"I'm getting married."

Whatever Marguerite had expected Mariel to say, it wasn't that. She had just reached for her wrap when she stopped and looked at Mariel in astonishment. "I beg your pardon?"

"So. I have your attention at last!"

"Indeed you do," Marguerite said, shoving her arm into the sleeve, and belting the silk wrapper around her waist. "And I have to say, that isn't funny."

"Do you think I'm joking?"

"Of course I do. You're only sixteen, a schoolgirl. You can't possibly be thinking of marriage."

"Well, I am. And here is the proof!" With a flourish, Mariel removed one of her gloves. A large sapphire ring surrounded by diamonds glittered up from her finger. "You see? Now do you think I'm joking?"

Marguerite didn't know what to believe. The safest thing seemed to be to go to the dressing table to brush her hair. As she sat down, she wondered what her parents were saying about this, and she said, "I suppose I should ask who the lucky man is."

Mariel drew herself up haughtily. "Indeed you should. It's Heinrich Jaeger."

Marguerite was so astounded that she dropped her hairbrush. She was still looking at Mariel in disbelief when Mrs. Bevins knocked and then came in with a tray of coffee that she put on the table by the window.

"I took the liberty—" the housekeeper started to say.

"Yes, yes," Marguerite said vaguely. She was still staring at Mariel. Mrs. Bevins obviously noticed something amiss, for she quickly withdrew. As soon as she was gone, Marguerite found her voice.

"I don't believe it," she said. "You dislike Heinrich as much as I do! You would never marry him—never!"

"Oh, yes, I would!" Mariel said, her black eyes snapping. "I'm going to!"

"This is . . . this is . . ." Marguerite was so stunned she hardly knew how to react. "What did Mama and Papa say?"

For the first time, Mariel looked uneasy. Smoothing her gloves, she admitted, "They don't know yet."

"*What?* You're engaged to be married, and you haven't told them?"

Mariel turned back fiercely. "No, I wanted to tell you first!"

"Why?"

"To show you that I could get married, too!"

Marguerite wondered if she were having some kind of dream. None of this made sense, and she said, "But why—"

"Oh, you fool!" Mariel cried in a sudden rage. She jumped up, startling Marguerite, who looked at her, wide-eyed. "You don't understand anything, do you? *I* wanted to marry Sloane, but you stole him from me. You—"

This was too much. Marguerite shot to her feet in outrage. "I did no such thing! Sloane was *never* interested in you! Why, you're just a . . . a child!"

Mariel clenched her hands. "I'm only a year younger than you!"

"Chronologically, perhaps," Marguerite flung back. "But this latest stunt of yours proves you're years younger than that. Do you really think you can exact some kind of childish revenge on me by marrying Heinrich? Heinrich *Jaeger*, of all people? You're the fool, Mariel, and this has gone far enough. I'm going to go right now and talk to Mama and Papa. You have obviously lost what little sense you were born with, so we'll just see what they have to say about this."

"Go ahead, tell them!" Mariel cried in a fury. "It's too late. I'm going to marry Heinrich, and that's final!"

Marguerite saw that it was useless to continue the conversation—such as it was. Her lips tight, she whirled around and went to her dressing room, intending to get dressed and ride as fast as she could to Sacramento to speak to her parents. Mariel had obviously lost her mind; nothing else could explain it.

But Mariel followed her. "You're just jealous!" she cried, as Marguerite flung open her wardrobe and started to reach for the first thing at hand.

"Jealous!" Marguerite was so indignant that she turned to look at her cousin, her hand still outstretched. She started to say something, then realized how futile it was. Turning back to the wardrobe, she selected something green at random. She was so upset she hardly knew what she was doing anyway. "That's the most ridiculous thing I've ever heard you say."

"No, it isn't; no, it isn't! You've always been jealous of me. I knew it when I first came to live with you and your parents. I could see it in your eyes."

"That's absurd." Throwing down the green dress, Marguerite turned to her lingerie drawer, but Mariel reached out and grabbed her arm. Digging her nails in painfully, she forced Marguerite to turn and look at her. Her black eyes looked like ink.

"Yes, you are jealous! That's why you eloped with Sloane—because you were afraid he would ask *me* to marry him. That's it, isn't it? Oh, I knew all along how much you hated me, and this proves it."

Wincing with pain, Marguerite tried to free herself from her cousin's tight grip. "For heaven's sake, Mariel!" she cried, beginning to lose her temper despite herself. "This idea you have that Sloane wanted to marry you is . . . is as outrageous as your engagement to Heinrich. How can you say you love one man one minute and then turn around and marry another the next? It doesn't make sense."

"Yes, it does, when the man I love is married to someone else!" Mariel cried. "And when Heinrich asked me to marry him after he got back—"

She stopped abruptly, a look of fear flashing through her dark eyes. Abruptly, she dropped Marguerite's arm and turned away. But Marguerite had seen that frightened look, and now it was she who grabbed Mariel and forced her to turn around.

"You said when Heinrich got back," she said. "When he got back from *where*?"

Mariel tried to jerk away. "Never mind." she said. "I'm not supposed to tell you."

But Marguerite was remembering Heinrich's strange disappearance. It has been the talk of the town after she had married Sloane; rumors had still been flying when they had gone to visit

Los Angeles. "What do you mean, you're not supposed to tell me?" she demanded.

"You have no right to question me!" Mariel cried, shaking free of Marguerite's grasp. "The important thing is that he came back and asked me to marry him."

"No, the important thing is why you said yes!"

Mariel whirled around on her. Marguerite had never seen such a look of hatred on anyone's face. To think it was directed at her made her blanch. "Why do you *think* I said yes?" Mariel demanded shrilly. "Do you think you're the only one who should ever get her way? Heinrich is going to be a rich man one day; he'll be able to give me things that you are only going to be able to *dream* about. And together . . . together," she repeated, her lips drawing back malignantly, "we're going to destroy you."

Despite herself, Marguerite felt a chill. "This is absurd!" she said sharply. "I won't listen to such rubbish."

"You've always underestimated Heinrich, Marguerite," Mariel said, black eyes holding hers. "But now you'll be sorry."

With that, she whirled around and started toward the door. Marguerite wanted to scoff, to tell her cousin that she wasn't in the least intimidated, certainly not by such childish threats, but something stopped her. Just for a moment, she had seen something in Mariel's face.

No, the whole thing is ridiculous, she told herself as Mariel slammed the door on the way out. She's just being her usual melodramatic self. She didn't mean it, and she certainly isn't going to marry Heinrich. Heinrich, of all people!

But despite her certainty that the whole thing was just a fantasy concocted by her imaginative cousin, Marguerite made a quick trip to Sacramento to talk to her parents—only to find on her arrival that Heinrich had already formally asked for Mariel's hand, and that Jacob Kendall had accepted.

"But why, Papa?" she asked, bewildered at the suddenness of the proposal—and the acceptance.

His expression pained, Jacob had glanced away. "Because your mother did so want one of you girls to have a big wedding," he said awkwardly. "And Mariel said that if we didn't give our permission, she would elope, as you did."

So it was all her fault, Marguerite thought angrily, and she refused to stand with the wedding party four months later when her cousin married Heinrich Jaeger. She hadn't forgotten Mariel's threat to destroy her and Sloane, but that only made her angrier. What could they do? she scoffed, and she put all her energies into making the Caulfield name in horses one to be proud of.

The sound of a van pulling in interrupted Briar's reading. Her mind still back in Marguerite's time, she looked vaguely out the window, and then half stood when she saw the headlights of the big transport coming up the drive. She had been so intent on Marguerite's story that she had completely forgotten about Stefan's arrival, and she quickly set aside her great-grandmother's journal and reached for her coat. With the driver's help, Stefan was already unloading the first of the three mares by the time she ran down to the barn, and he stopped with his hand on Night Fever's lead rope when she saw her.

"Are you all right?" he asked.

"Yes, of course," she said. But she was still feeling a little dazed, and she shook her head slightly to clear it. Reaching for the rope so she could take the horse while he helped with the other two, she tried to smile. "Why?"

He frowned. "I don't know. You're so pale. You look like you've seen a ghost or something."

"It's just late," she said, glancing at her watch, surprised to see that it was after two A.M. "I was worried. How was the trip?"

"Long," Stefan said. He hesitated. "Are you sure you're all right?"

For some reason, Briar shivered. "Yes," she said again, and met his eyes directly for the first time. "I'm glad you're back. When you have time, I'd like to talk to you."

He shifted position. "About avoiding you, right?"

She was a little taken aback at his perception. "We could start with that, yes."

He glanced off, as if debating something, then looked back at her again. "Look, there's no big mystery. I just didn't want to get into a hassle with Carl or Rupert Jaeger. If you remember, we didn't really hit it off so good the first time, and . . . and I didn't want to spoil your night. You were so excited, so happy. So I just stayed away. It's as simple as that."

She didn't know why she said it, but the words were out before she thought. Maybe because she was tired, too. "But I wanted to celebrate with you," she said. Now she had embarrassed them both; she could tell by the way he reddened.

"Well, we can celebrate another time," he muttered. "Right now, I've got to get these horses settled and pay the driver so he can get home."

"Yes, you're right, of course," she said quickly, feeling like a fool. "Here, I'll take this filly and come back for one of the other two. Jaime and I already have some stalls prepared. The first three on the right."

Wanting to get away, she turned with the horse, but Stefan called out, "Briar—"

She didn't know if she wanted to turn back or not. She already felt as if she'd said too much, but she reluctantly looked over her shoulder. "What?"

Now that he had her attention, he didn't seem to know what to say. Just then the driver, who was inside the van, shouted, "Hey, we going to be here all night?"

"No, I'm coming," Stefan called back, and looked quickly at Briar again. "Really," he said awkwardly. "I . . . didn't feel comfortable there that night. I was thinking about getting the horses home, and I . . . I just had to get out."

She searched his face, but all she could see were lines of fatigue. He'd been traveling all night, responsible for these valuable horses, and now she wondered again if she'd been making too big a deal of it. Maybe all he'd been the whole time was concerned about getting the mares home safe and sound. That was his job, after all, and she knew he took it seriously. And if he hadn't felt comfortable, she couldn't blame him for that. She didn't feel so comfortable herself at the moment, and she was glad when the driver shouted impatiently again so she could take the filly she was holding into the barn.

# CHAPTER SEVENTEEN

The breeding shed at Ridgeway Farm in Santa Ynez in Southern California wasn't really a shed at all, but an immaculate cement-floored room larger than a three-car garage and twice as high, complete with double ceramic sinks, hot and cold running water, breeding stocks, teasing stall, and rubber mats on the floors. It looked more antiseptic than a hospital operating room, and the people assembled were almost as highly trained for this operation as surgeons were for theirs. Everybody wore long blue lab coats over their clothes, including Briar, who had been granted permission to observe the mating between her maiden mare, Song of Splendor, and the new Ridgeway stallion, Silver Reign, a Stakes winner imported from Kentucky.

Ridgeway's owners were Matt and Marla McCue, and they were transplanted Kentuckians themselves, forced to move to the milder climate of California after Marla was diagnosed with rheumatoid arthritis. Briar had known them both for years through their daughter Megan, against whom she had once competed in horse shows; their acquaintance was why she was permitted in the breeding shed with the other staff this morning. She hadn't asked to be here, but when Matt had offered, of course she had accepted. She had seen mares covered before, but she had never ceased to feel awed at the sight of such powerful creatures mating. Song of Splendor was a "maiden" mare—never bred or in foal before—and she wanted to be here in case there was trouble.

Not that she'd be needed, Briar thought wryly. As they had at their farm in Kentucky, Ridgeway had a huge staff: there were two resident veterinarians, a brood mare crew, a stallion crew, a farm manager, an *assistant* farm manager, a foaling foreman, two secretaries—one for stallion records alone—along with maintenance people, office workers, accoun-

tants. . . . It was almost a small self-contained city in itself,
much bigger than her operation, but then, she didn't have six
resident stallions booked to forty to sixty mares each a year.

Today, along with the stallion and brood mare crews, only
one of the veterinarians was present, a husky man named Duke
Pritchard, who had palpated Splendor again that morning and
pronounced her breedable. The broodmare crew had gotten her
ready, and she was standing in the center of the shed facing the
wall, her tail wrapped, breeding hobbles on her hind legs, a
stout halter over her head and people standing by with extra
hobbles, a twitch for the mare's upper lip, if needed, and
various other equipment. All this was for the stallion's protection more than the mare; when a stud was worth between forty
and fifty million dollars, every precaution was taken.

When everyone was in place, Silver Reign was brought in.
As soon as Briar's normally placid mare saw the great stakes-
winning stallion, she pinned back her ears and let out a piercing
squeal. Not an auspicious beginning, Briar thought, watching
from the sidelines, and she wondered how successful this was
going to be.

The stallion seemed confident. He was wearing a thick
leather halter with the ever-present chain shank wrapped over
his nose. With the breeding manager holding tightly to the
shank, Silver Reign stretched his neck out as he came up to the
mare and blew out a great noisy breath right onto her flank. As
most well-trained, experienced stallions do, he was courting
her, but Splendor was having no part of it. Pinning her ears
again, she squealed once more.

"Oh, boy," Briar muttered, and shoved her hands deeper
into her pockets.

On the mare's other side, one of the helpers quickly picked
up Splendor's left front leg, figure-eighting the leather strap he
was holding around her upper leg and shin, getting ready for
quick release once the stallion was safely aboard. Until then,
even though she was restrained by thick breeding hobbles in
the back, he'd hold that leg off the ground so the mare couldn't
possibly kick him or the stallion. Standing to the other side at
the mare's head, and holding on to a second lead rope, was
another helper, ready to restrain her if she tried to jump despite
all the other precautions. Everything was ready, Briar thought.
Was the mare?

Pulling against his own handler, the stallion extended himself and strained closer to the mare. He blew out another whistling breath. It sounded like the roar of a freight train, and Song of Splendor flattened her ears. Suddenly, the stallion squealed himself and struck out with a front leg—but carefully out of hitting distance—just to show her who was boss. Unimpressed, Song of Splendor squealed in return and humped her back.

Watching, Briar crossed her fingers. Another reason she'd wanted to be here was because of the trouble they'd had bringing the mare into heat. Maiden mares, especially right off the track, often remained transitional unless their reproductive tracts had a chance to quiet down and get regular—to "quit horsing," as the veterinarian called it. To help her do that, she'd been given ten days of progesterone therapy. Just this morning, she had finally produced a breedable follicle, so if she was going to be bred the time was now.

The stallion seemed to think so, too. After another blistering exhale through quivering nostrils, he came forward to nuzzle Splendor's flank. This time just one ear went back. Encouraged, he nuzzled her again. She looked around.

"Okay, big guy," the stud manager murmured, and pulled the stallion around.

Unlike other young stallions Briar had seen, who in their eager inexperience tried to mount from the side, or who became so frenzied that they attacked the mare even when they finally did get to the right position, Silver Reign was an old hand at this. He was here to do his business and not fool around; he had other dates to keep. So now that he was sure the mare would accept him, he positioned himself behind her without further ado and reared up for the cover. Like the well-rehearsed team that they were, everyone went into action with him: the stud manager guided him in; the handler with the leather strap released Splendor's hobbled front leg; the header steadied her as the stallion mounted; and then, almost before it began, it was over.

Like the gentleman he was, Silver Reign dropped his head against Splendor's withers for a moment before he dismounted. Briar had always thought this a little romantic—until someone had told her that most stallions expended so much energy in breeding that they had to rest before they got down. A few got so caught up in things that they actually passed out up there, then had to be held up until they came to so they could sheepishly crawl off on their own.

Silver Reign didn't need any help. As soon as he dismounted, one of the helpers ran forward with the buckets to wash him, and then he was led away while other members of the team unhobbled Briar's mare and began walking her in a circle so she wouldn't lie down. With stud fees in the hundreds of thousands, no one wanted one precious drop of semen to be lost.

As always, no matter how many times she had seen two horses mating, Briar felt awed. Deciding that she should get out of the way, she went out the side door and took a deep breath. Someone came up beside her, and when she turned she saw it was Dr. Pritchard.

"We'll cover her three more times in the next day or so," he told her, "and that should do it. She's got a good follicle, so I don't anticipate any problems."

"Do you think we should continue with the progesterone after we take her back?" Briar asked.

"Well, progesterone levels do decrease during shipping due to stress," he said. "So we'll giver her ten ccs before she leaves, and I recommend another ten when she first gets home. Then back off to five ccs for the next few days. Maybe it's overkill, maybe not. But once she's in foal, you want her to stay that way."

Briar fervently agreed. "Whatever you suggest."

"Of course, you can always consult your own veterinarian."

"I'll tell her what you recommended," Briar said, and held out her hand. "Thank you, doctor. I appreciate all you've done."

"No problem," he said with a smile. "It's my job."

"Now I've got to do mine," Briar said, and waved goodbye. Since the McCues weren't there this morning, having gone into Los Angeles to see the doctor, Briar stopped by the office to make sure the secretary knew to thank them.

"Will do, Ms. McKenna," the woman said cheerfully. "And if there's anything else we can do . . ."

"Just give me a stakes winner," Briar said with a grin.

The secretary winked. "We do that all the time," she said, and waved good-bye as Briar pulled out and left the farm behind.

As she headed to the airport to take the plane back, Briar turned on the radio for company, then impatiently switched it off again. The past few weeks had been even more hectic than usual, and now that she had a little time to herself, she realized how tired she was. It seemed that she'd had one problem after another crop up after getting back from Kentucky, both at the office and at the ranch. She'd been so frustrated at one point that she had even been sharp with Gabe—the first time in their association that had happened.

It had been the day when she had found out they'd lost two clients. Since that was the first she'd heard of it, naturally she wanted to know why. When Gabe had hinted that it might be because she was burning her candle at both ends, she had been really furious. The fact that she knew he was right made her even angrier, and she had taken her frustration out on him.

"You *are* my executive vice president," she had sharply reminded him. "I thought you could take care of these things! If you couldn't handle it, you should have told me!"

If she had reached out and slapped him, he couldn't have looked more stricken. Angry and hurt, he had said tightly, "I *can* handle things—most of them, anyway. But the problem is that your clients are accustomed to your personal attention. What am I supposed to do when they refuse to deal with me?"

"Convince them!" she'd snapped. "And if that fails, use the telephone! That's why we have a direct line, you know—in case you have problems!"

Looking as if he didn't trust himself to say more, he had left the office. She'd been too angry—and too guilt stricken—to follow and apologize right then; she had decided to approach him at the end of the day, after they'd both had a chance to cool down. She'd used the time to reevaluate what was happening and hadn't liked what she was seeing. Although it was no excuse at that point, one of her problems was exhaustion. She'd been up three nights with a sick horse. Both Jaime and Stefan had insisted they would stand guard and call her the instant there was any change, but she couldn't let them watch over the mare by themselves. The horses were hers, ultimately *her* responsibility; she couldn't just . . . sleep . . . when one of them was sick, so she had taken over her share of the watch until the mare got better.

But that meant she was short-tempered and impatient when she came to work, and finding out they'd lost two clients because she wasn't paying as much attention to business as she should was the last straw. Overworked, exhausted, trying to do too much, and running herself ragged, she had lashed out and blamed Gabe when it was really all her fault. McKenna Time-Save was *her* company; she had only herself to blame if it wasn't being run properly.

If only she could clone herself, she thought as she left Ridgeway Farm. Then she could spend the necessary time at the office and run the ranch, too. She felt so torn; both businesses needed her, but she couldn't be in two places at once. It was turning into a hoary Catch-22.

Idly, she wondered if she had to give up one, which would it be? She'd pondered that before and still didn't have an answer. Giving up the company and running the ranch was just as unpalatable as vice versa. Why couldn't she do both?

She could become a absentee owner, she thought; that was one solution, all right. She had seen a lot of farms like that when she had toured Kentucky; there were places were the owners were only in residence two or three weeks a year. The rest of the time the farms were kept fully staffed and running just as if the family was there, leaving the owner to concentrate on other things—like the businesses that had enabled them to own the farm in the first place.

But if she did move back to the house in Pacifica—which for the past few months had been watched over by the caretaker she'd hired to live in the guest house—what would be the point of having the ranch? She didn't *want* to be an absentee owner. To her, Caulfield Farm wasn't just an investment, a toy, a bauble, or something she had because she was bored. It was a legacy, a tradition, a responsibility to her family that she was only just beginning to know through the reading of her great-grandmother's journals.

"Maybe you'd better get your priorities straight," she muttered, coming to the airport turnoff and switching to the lane for rental cars. As she waited in line to turn in the car, she wondered just what her priorities were these days. Everything had been so clear once; now the waters seemed so . . . muddied.

Or maybe the water was clear after all; maybe she was the one who was muddled, she thought. She felt so protective about the ranch, but was she really needed there all the time? Between them, Jaime and Stefan could certainly take care of the place; they were both competent, they knew what they were doing. And, she thought with a grimace, remembering that she'd said the same thing to Gabe in another context, if there was a problem, she was always as close as the phone.

By the time she got home, she still felt restless and frustrated at her unresolved conflicts. She decided to go for a ride. Irish had his own five-acre pasture to run around in, but they hadn't been out together in some time, and as she changed into breeches and boots in her bedroom, she thought that she needed a gallop more than he did.

Irish was feeling his oats this afternoon. Although gelded, he was still the only male horse on the ranch, and he had somehow gotten it into his head that the band of broodmares belonged to him. To everyone's amusement—even Stefan's—her big bay horse had begun to act a little studdy when "the girls" were around, running up to the fence, rearing, and shrieking out a comical challenge now and then across the pastures, as if to warn any foolishly roaming wild young stallion that these mares were *his*.

What wasn't so funny was that he was becoming difficult to catch. As humiliating as it was, she'd had to resort to using a grain bucket as a bribe. She'd always thought that he should come when he was called, but who wanted to chase a horse across a five-acre pasture on foot? It was easier to drag out the grain when he was being stubborn, but even that didn't work all the time, and there had been nights when Irish simply refused to come in. She'd left him out all night a time or two to teach him a lesson, but to her chagrin, he hadn't seemed to mind a bit.

She didn't need the grain today to catch him; for once he seemed as eager as she was to explore. In fact, he was so eager to get going that he started dancing in the cross ties while she was trying to groom him, and she had to speak sharply to him.

"You know better than that," she grumbled, pushing him out of the way so she could brush his legs. "Now just stand still!"

She was still muttering when Stefan came into the barn. Preoccupied with brushing what had once been a long, silky tail, but what now had grass and burrs stuck to the hair, she didn't notice Stefan standing there until Irish fidgeted again, and she gave him a whack with the brush.

"Need some help?" Stefan asked.

Startled, she jumped around. "Oh, it's you," she said, and

then, because she was embarrassed, added, "You shouldn't sneak up on me like that!"

"I didn't sneak," Stefan said. "I've been standing here for five minutes, watching you try to groom that horse. If I'd known you were going to ride, I could have worked him a little to take the edge off."

Now she felt guilty for being sharp. Wondering why he always seemed to bring out her worst side, she went back to picking out the burrs in Irish's tail, muttering, "Thanks, but he's going to get his exercise in a few minutes.

Stefan looked over his shoulder to a fenced circular area behind the barn. One of the first things Briar had requested once the major building was done was a riding ring, and Ted had called in an expert to level the ground and bring in load after load of fine sand mixed with a special kind of dirt. Plans called for the ring to be covered eventually, so they could use it in all weather when they started training the yearlings and two-year-olds that were due to come. But for the time being, it was still open.

"I don't know," Stefan said. "The ring's still pretty wet after that last rain. It might not be such a good idea to ride in there."

Briar stopped what she was doing. Irish was so tall that she had to rise on tiptoe to see over his withers to where Stefan was standing, but she glared at him all the same. "In the first place," she said, "that ring is supposed to have excellent drainage—"

"Even so—"

"And in the second," she said, "I'm not going to ride in the ring. I'm going up into the hills."

"There's a lot of country up there. What if you get lost?"

Why was he bugging her like this? "Would you like me to take a ball of string?" she asked.

As always, sarcasm was lost on him. Today he was wearing boots, jeans so old they were more white than blue, a checked shirt, and because of the breeze in the chilly February air, a down vest, open in front. Shoving his hands into the back pockets of his jeans, he shrugged and said, "You're a big girl."

"Thanks," she said acidly, and reached for her saddle. It was an old Stubben, not her best saddle but one of her most comfortable; it had a sherpa pad underneath, already attached.

As she heaved it up onto Irish's back, she started to say, "By the way, things went just fine with Splendor today. In fact—"

That was all she had time for. Irish, who had been saddled literally *thousands* of times before, and knew this particular saddle like his own back, chose exactly that moment to act like an unbroken two-year-old. As if he'd never in his life felt such a thing, he leaped forward when she reached underneath to bring up the girth. Since he was cross tied in the aisle, he hit the ends of both chains at the same time, and when they went taut, he reared straight up.

"Oh, for heaven's sake!" Briar exclaimed, reaching for the halter when her horse came down again. For some reason that seemed to alarm him even more, and he went up again. She was already holding on to the halter, and because she was too stubborn to let go, the big horse swung her up with him. For a second or two, her feet dangled in midair.

"Let go!" Stefan said, grabbing her by the waist just as Irish started to come down again. Pushed off balance by the big horse's heavy body as his front feet hit the ground, Stefan stumbled back, still holding on to Briar. Caught in that awkward position, she couldn't catch her balance either, and together they tumbled back into the nearest open stall, landing with a crash on the thick straw bedding inside.

"Oh, this is too much!" Briar cried, trying to free herself. She'd fallen on top of Stefan, and either he was out of breath or something was wrong because he wouldn't let her go. She grabbed at his hands around her waist. "Stefan! What are you—"

He released her then, so quickly that she nearly fell back on him again. She immediately rolled away, jumped up, and tried to catch her breath. She was so furious with Irish that she could have beaten him senseless with his own lead rope. Then she felt even more chagrined when she looked down and saw Stefan still lying there.

"Are you hurt?"

Straw sticking to his blond hair, Stefan got to his feet. "No, I'm all right," he said, brushing off his jeans. "How about you?"

"I'm fine," she muttered, glancing at her innocent-looking gelding, who was now standing placidly in the cross ties, looking as if he'd died there. Furious with him, and thinking that might not be such a bad idea, she shook her fist in his direction. "I'm going to kill that horse!"

"I told you, you should have worked him. He's too high from not being ridden in so long."

Was that a subtle criticism? She was so unnerved at this point that she couldn't tell. She had been careful around Stefan since the day when he had first come to the ranch and they'd found themselves in that awkward embrace; she'd gone out of her way not to touch him. It wasn't that she didn't trust herself, she thought hastily; it was just that she felt it was better to maintain a certain . . . distance. So why she should still be thinking of how Stefan's hands had felt on her waist or how strong his body had been under hers when they fell, she didn't know. Because she was angry and embarrassed and not at all certain of her feelings, she glared at Irish again, the cause of all her emotional disarray.

"He won't be high by the time I finish with him," she threatened, climbing out of the stall.

Stefan followed, but at a discreet distance, as if he, too, were having second thoughts. Briar hardly noticed; she was too busy trying to get herself under control. Stefan offered to help her finish saddling up, but she muttered something about doing it herself, then sighed with relief when he went away. Alone in the aisle with her horse, she grabbed the bridle, just *daring* him to give her another bad time. Irish stood still as a statue—he knew when he was in the doghouse—and allowed himself to be bridled without further incident.

Chastened, the big gelding didn't even give his customary little crow hops after Briar mounted, and they started out of the barn. Irish behaved like a perfect gentleman and trotted sedately up the drive, around the back of the house, between the two big pastures behind the house, and finally onto a deer track Briar had discovered some time ago.

Briar waited until she got that far before she dared to look back. As always, she felt she hadn't handled herself well with Stefan, and she was annoyed and frustrated with herself, unable to understand why she acted like a . . . a teenager whenever he was around. She certainly wasn't this way in business; and even as a young woman, she'd always known how to handle herself with men. Not even Hayden had put her into this bumbling state, she thought. It was inexplicable, but where Stefan was concerned, it seemed that years had dropped away and she *was* an uncertain teenager who didn't know what to say or how to act. What was wrong with her?

Stefan certainly wasn't any help, was he? she thought with a flash of irritation. He seemed to disagree with her about everything at times, and she suspected that he often took the opposite position just to see her reaction. Did he get some perverse satisfaction out of needling her?

*Oh, face it,* she told herself impatiently. *You're attracted to him, and you don't want to be. That's what the problem is; you might as well admit it. You never allowed yourself to be really attracted to a man until Hayden; you were too busy being an adult, responsible for yourself. And then when you did allow yourself to get involved, it was to a man much older. Stefan is too close to your own age.*

Wondering why that should matter—or even more important, why she was trying to make excuses for herself, she decided that she didn't want to think about it anymore. She had too many other things on her mind right now, and with her horse beginning to pull on the bit, it might be better to forget the whole thing and just go for a simple, uncomplicated gallop. She was tired of trying to find the answers, and when she came to an old fire road, she gave Irish his head and told him to go for it.

As if he'd been waiting for the signal that meant she had forgiven him, he engaged his powerful hindquarters. His stride lengthened to a canter, and then to a gallop, and Briar started to smile, then laugh aloud. She'd been right: this was what she needed, she thought, as the wind began to whistle in her ears and her eyes to tear. Bending over Irish's neck, she urged him on faster, not quite into a run. She knew the road, but there was no sense taking chances; if he shied at a squirrel or something, she wouldn't have to worry about a ball of string. She'd probably never be seen again, period.

It was a good thing she'd been prudent. As they swept around a bend in the road, she caught a glimpse of someone up ahead. There was just time to sit up and tighten her reins before Irish came to a screeching halt all by himself. Only the fact that she was such a good rider prevented her from catapulting right over his head, and when she finally got her balance she was startled to recognize Charlotte Jaeger.

True to the rules of the trail, Charlotte had pulled her horse over when she heard someone coming behind her. She and the big chestnut mare she was riding were by the side of the road when Briar regained control, and she said, "Hello, Ms. Mc-Kenna."

"Miss Jaeger!" Briar was momentarily confused; she couldn't believe she and Irish had come so far. Was she on Mondragon property? "I'm sorry. Am I trespassing?"

Charlotte shook her head. "Please call me Charlotte. And no, I'm afraid I'm the culprit. How embarrassing that you caught me."

So she was still on her own land. That was a relief. She said graciously, "It seems to me that these hills are big enough for the both of us."

Charlotte seemed startled. "Why, how nice of you to say," she murmured, and then looked nostalgic for a moment. "I confess that I miss coming this way. I used to ride all through here when I was a child, but . . ." She shook herself, and then shrugged as if embarrassed. "Old habits die hard, I suppose. This area is so lovely."

Briar agreed. In contrast to great areas of the country where grass died to dry brown in the winter, here in California winter meant green. Now that it was February again, the hills had a slight green sheen, a sharp contrast to the deciduous trees that had lost their leaves. Bare oak trees festooned with lacy moss and round balls of mistletoe were everywhere on the slopes, and the hard red wood of Manzanita provided another contrast. Pine trees added to the green, with certain varieties just starting to reveal the chartreuse-colored tips that signaled new growth. Birds moved busily through bare branches looking for insects, and a flicker at the corner of Briar's eye meant that a gray squirrel had seen them and dashed for safety. Far above their heads, a red-tail hawk was circling, and as Briar glanced around, she thought Charlotte was right. It was a beautiful place, and she certainly didn't mind sharing it. After all, she had over a hundred more acres on which to ride, and besides— she had wanted a chance to talk to Charlotte Jaeger privately ever since they'd met.

"I can't blame you for wanting to ride through here," she said. "It *is* a lovely area."

"You're very kind, Ms. McKenna. Thank you."

She didn't see any reason for the formality. "Briar, please."

"Briar, then. That's such an unusual name. So . . . distinctive."

"My mother's name was Ariana," Briar said carefully. "But I imagine you know that."

"Yes, I do. And I used to think her name was beautiful, too."

Briar couldn't help herself. Eagerly, she leaned forward. "Then you knew my mother?"

Charlotte seemed wary again. "Of course," she said. "The Jaegers have lived here as long as the Caulfields. And back then, the community was so small, like a family."

From what Briar knew of the history, she doubted that. But she certainly didn't want to offend Charlotte at this point, so she said, "I imagine it was." Then, trying not to be obvious, she had to ask, "Did you know my mother well?"

Some emotion flashed across Charlotte's face but was gone too quickly for Briar to identify it. Her manner changed, and she said distantly, "Everyone knew Ariana Caulfield."

Without realizing it, Briar's hands tightened on the reins, but when Irish jerked his head in response, she hardly noticed. The thought that she might actually learn more about her mother made her feel almost faint, and she had to take a firm grip on herself. She wanted to beg Charlotte for every scrap of information, but she also realized that this woman was a Jaeger, after all, a member of the clan that had sworn undying hatred for anyone named Caulfield.

"I realize now isn't the time," she said carefully. "But perhaps some day in the future, we could meet and you could tell me what you know about my mother." Then, because she was so excited at the thought, she pressed too hard. "And my father," she added eagerly. "Did you know my father?"

Again, that flash of emotion, just as quickly hidden. "Your father?" Charlotte repeated. "No, I . . . didn't know your father."

Briar tried to swallow her disappointment. She'd been so sure that if she found someone who had known her mother well, she would also be able to learn more about her father, who she knew now had been named Duncan McKenna. Then she realized she shouldn't be discouraged; Charlotte hadn't been acquainted with Duncan, but she *had* known Ariana, and anything she could tell her, Briar would treasure.

"You'll have to excuse me now," Charlotte said, to Briar's dismay. "It's late, and I should have been back an hour ago."

"But—"

Effortlessly, Charlotte wheeled her horse around. "We'll talk again, I'm sure," she said. "Good-bye."

"Wait!" Briar called, but Charlotte either didn't hear or pretended not to. Touching her heel to the chestnut's flank, she moved away at a brisk canter. Briar could have followed on Irish, but what was the point? It was obvious that Charlotte wasn't going to talk to her, and she stared after them in bitter disappointment.

Well, what had she expected? she wondered, as she dejectedly turned Irish in the opposite direction. The Jaeger men had made no secret of their enmity toward her just because she was a Caulfield. Had she believed Charlotte would feel differently?

Knowing that she wouldn't make that mistake again, she started back to the house. Her enthusiasm for a ride had vanished, and now she felt even more tired than she had before. Getting away for a while certainly hadn't solved any of her problems—either at the ranch or at the office. She was still in the same muddle as she had been. Worse, in fact, because Charlotte had held out a tantalizing carrot only to snatch it away again. Depressed, she let Irish find his way home again, and, as if he sensed her mood, he dropped his head and plodded back like an old hack.

She had to pass her office in the barn to put Irish away, and as she went by, she glanced in the window and saw the red light blinking on her answering machine. Freeing Irish in the big pasture to go and roll, she was just starting toward the office to see who had left a message when Jaime came running.

"Miss Briar, there's a man on the phone!"

She really didn't feel like speaking to anyone. "Take a message, please, Jaime," she said, hefting the tack she was carrying.

"I asked if I could, but he said he had to speak to you," Jaime said, taking her saddle and bridle from her to put away.

Briar sighed. "Who is it? Did he say?"

"Sí, sí, his name is Spencer Reed."

Briar knew it had to be important for Spence to call her at this hour; he usually waited until she was at the office. However, there had been additional problems with Fredrica lately, who had been making a lot of noise about how much of her father's money Briar was spending. Spence had successfully delayed going to court, but Briar had the sudden feeling that they'd just run out of time.

*Oh, Hay!* she thought mournfully. She had done everything she could to spare his memory, but it seemed that they'd gone through all their options.

"Thank you, Jaime," she said, turning toward the office and reaching for the phone. "Spence?" she said. "What's wrong?"

Spence didn't waste words. "I'm sorry, Briar, it's bad news. I'm afraid we're going to have to go to court, after all."

Sighing, she sat down. "Well, we knew it was going to happen sooner or later."

"No, it isn't that," Spence said, sounding very strange. "This isn't just a competency hearing now—"

Something in his voice warned her. "What, then?" she asked, sitting up.

He hesitated. Then he said, "I'm afraid Fredrica has managed to get a judge to freeze all moneys to you from Lord Industries. Now I know how this sounds," he went on quickly. "But I'm sure it's just a temporary situation."

She couldn't believe what she was hearing. "I don't understand," she said, her voice sharp. "How could she do that?"

He sounded more unhappy than ever. "Briar, why didn't you ever tell me about a prenuptial agreement?"

She felt as if someone had hit her between her eyes. "A . . . a prenuptial agreement?"

"Briar, you've got to tell me," Spence said. "*Was* there one?"

She had never mentioned it because she didn't think it mattered. It hadn't meant anything, after all; she'd been the one who suggested it. She didn't want Hay to think that she was marrying him for his money.

"But darling," he'd protested, amused and delighted. "I'm the one who asked *you*!"

Nevertheless, she had persisted. And so to please her one night—as a joke, he insisted—he had allowed her to draw one up while they were sitting in the hot tub, drinking champagne and toasting their engagement.

"Now are you happy, my darling?" he'd said. "You have your piece of paper—"

"But you haven't signed it," she'd answered.

"And I don't intend to," he'd said, and kissed her.

Remembering that scene now, Briar fought back both tears

and panic. "Yes, there was one, but it was a joke to Hayden, Spencer," she said. "He never signed it."

"Did you?"

She closed her eyes. "Well . . . yes," she said reluctantly.

Her attorney groaned. "Well, that does make things difficult."

"Why? It wasn't legal—"

"No, but it does establish that you didn't want Hay's money, so now Fredrica can get it by proving that she *needs* it."

"That's absurd. Fredrica's husband is a very successful plastic surgeon!"

"Was," Spence said succinctly. "He's declaring bankruptcy."

*"What!"*

"My guess is that he got too cocky in the stock market and overleveraged himself out of business. Regardless of the cause, he's in big trouble financially, so if Fredrica can prove she needs the money . . ."

Briar couldn't believe it. Bennett Hudson on the verge of bankruptcy? No wonder Fredrica had been so wild. Status was everything to her; for her husband even to hint of financial trouble was catastrophe. The money was bad enough; the loss of face and position would be intolerable.

"Wait a minute," she said, seizing a thought out of all the others whirling through her mind. "How did Fredrica know there was a premarital agreement—even one that was a gag? Hay put that paper in the safe. . . ." Her voice trailed away. Fredrica had the key to the house in Pacifica. Did she know the combination to the safe, as well?

"What are we going to do?" she asked, trying not to panic.

"I don't know. I just now heard about this; I'm going to have to get together with her lawyers. I'll call you tomorrow. And in the meantime—"

"Yes?"

"Try to figure out how she got hold of that paper, will you?"

"Why?"

"Just do it. At this point, anything we find out will be helpful," he said, and broke the connection.

After she hung up, Briar sat in a daze just staring into space. Finally, the little blinking red light on the answering machine caught her eye, and, hardly realizing what she was doing, she pressed the button.

The tape rewound and then played automatically. At first, Briar didn't recognize the voice; it took her a few seconds to realize that it was the man she had hired as caretaker for the Pacifica house.

"Miss McKenna?" the voice said. "I don't mean to bother you, but something happened today that I think you should know about. Mr. Lord's daughter was here. She insisted on going into the house, and as she had a key, I couldn't stop her. She was in there a long time, and when she finally left, I went in to check around, you know, to see if something was missing?"

Briar closed her eyes; she knew what was coming next, and right on cue, it did.

"I'm really sorry to tell you this, but I think she got into the safe. I can't be sure, 'cause it was all closed up again, but you know that picture that's in front of it? Well, it was still down on the floor when I came in, so I'm thinking . . . Do you want me to call the police or something?"

But Briar knew it was too late for that. Sitting back, she rubbed her forehead. Suddenly she had a splitting headache.

"Well," her caretaker was saying, "I'll just wait until you tell me what you want. I'm real sorry, Miss McKenna. I really couldn't stop her, and she did have that key. 'Bye for now. I'll be waiting to hear from you."

The tape switched off by itself, while Briar sat there in stunned silence.

---&---

# CHAPTER EIGHTEEN

The more Briar dwelt on it, the angrier she felt. Fredrica had gone too far this time, she thought. She had tried to be patient, to give her time to overcome her "grief" at her father's passing, but going into the house, breaking into the safe, and taking something she had no right to touch was too much. Briar was so angry that she had to wait until the next afternoon after she'd put in a morning's work to call Fredrica's house in Palo Alto. It was time, she thought, to fight fire with fire.

Fredrica's husband, a pompous plastic surgeon named Bennett, whom Briar had never liked, answered the phone. Briar wasn't in the mood for pleasantries; she identified herself and asked to speak to Fredrica.

"I'm sorry, but Fredrica isn't here," Bennett said in an affected tone. Briar had always thought it made him sound like a pretentious jerk. Stuffily, he added, "And at any rate, I'm not sure she should be talking to you. Aren't we all due in court soon?"

*Not if I can help it*, Briar thought grimly, and said, "That's exactly what I wanted to talk to her about, Bennett. Is there a number where she can be reached?"

"No, I'm afraid I don't have any idea where she is," he said, sounding smug.

"Then maybe you'd better find her, Bennett," she said, her voice steely. "Because I'm going to talk to her one way or another, and the way I feel now, it had better not wait until we get into court."

"Isn't that rather an empty threat? It seems to me that with a prenuptial agreement in Fredrica's hands, you're the one who should be treading softly, not the other way around."

"Don't try to intimidate me, Bennett. Just tell her that I want to speak to her—today."

"Oh, I'll tell her, certainly. But I doubt that it will do any good. She doesn't want to talk to you—except through our attorneys."

"That can be arranged, too," Briar said curtly, and hung up the phone.

Now that she'd made the call, she sat at her desk for a moment, drumming her fingers against the blotter, trying to control the anger that had been building ever since she had talked to Spence the day before. Because she faced things squarely, her anger was directed mostly at herself. It had been a stupid thing to do, leaving that facsimile of a premarital agreement around; if she hadn't had such a sentimental attachment to it, she would have gotten rid of it long ago. Now it was too late.

The only reason she had kept it was because Hay had gotten

such a kick out of it, she thought, smiling briefly despite her concern. Sometimes when he wanted to tease her, he'd threaten to get it out of the safe and sign it so that she'd have to do what he wanted. Usually, what he wanted was to take her to an island somewhere so they could relax and be alone. When she protested that she had too much work to do, he'd say that if she didn't do as he asked, he'd take everything away, and then where would she be? He never would have done it, of course; it had been a joke between them.

Some joke, she thought bitterly, and wondered how in the hell Fredrica had found out about it. She couldn't imagine, but maybe it didn't matter now. The point was that Fredrica *knew*, and now she had to do something about it.

"What a fool I've been!" Briar muttered. This was turning into a circus, and she had only herself to blame.

She had never believed in feeling sorry for herself; since this was her fault, she had to think of a way out. Spence had told her he wouldn't be sure until he and Fredrica's attorneys met to discuss it, but there was a good chance Fredrica could win if this went to court. Wearily, she put her head in her hands. Maybe she should just give it all up and let her have her victory, she thought. The way she felt now, she didn't want anything—and she certainly didn't want to go before a judge. It would have been bad enough to defend Hay's state of mind, to prove his competence; to battle Fredrica over money would be absolutely abhorrent. Even if she did win, she would still look like an opportunist, a younger woman who had married a wealthy older man pretending not to want his wealth, only to change her mind after he had died and try to keep everything.

What a mess! she thought. There had to be some way out of it, some compromise, some—

Abruptly, she lifted her head. Why hadn't she remembered this before? She had wanted to make this offer long ago, but when Fredrica had initiated that suit, Spence had counseled her to wait before doing anything. He'd been sure that once Fredrica realized the futility of what she was trying to do, she'd drop the lawsuit, but Briar knew now that wasn't going to happen. Everything was changed now that Fredrica was really threatened by what her husband had done, and now that she had that stupid piece of paper in her possession, anything Briar offered would look like a bribe. Her lips tightened. Still, she had to try. She knew what Spence would say, but she had been wanting to do this for a long while anyway, and it seemed clear she'd waited too long. Before she could change her mind, she reached for the phone and dialed her attorney's office.

Spence sounded somber when he answered the phone. "What did you find out?" he asked, and then was ominously silent when Briar told him about her caretaker's message on the answering machine.

"But that's not why I called," she said quickly. "Listen, Spence, I have an idea. . . ."

"No, no! Absolutely not!" he said when she told him what she intended. "I won't hear of it! You simply cannot offer to divide the entire estate three ways! It's out of the question!"

"Why?"

"Well, for one thing, it's not what Hayden wanted!"

"That's true. But you know I never thought it was fair that I inherited everything."

"Your husband thought it was fair—"

"Yes, but . . ." She sighed. "Spence, we both know that Hayden had a blind spot where his children were concerned. He was so sharp and smart and sophisticated in every other way, but when it came to Jaz and Fredrica—"

"Whom he took care of very well!"

"Not well enough, according to Fredrica," Briar said. "And I have to admit, one some level, I agree with her. I never have felt comfortable with things this way, and maybe if I divide everything equally, Fredrica will be . . . appeased."

"That woman will *never* be appeased," Spence said blackly. "She was born a malcontent. No, I can't let you do it, Briar. In addition to the fact that it's not what Hayden wanted—"

"Hayden is dead, Spence," she reminded him quietly. "And now I have to deal with this in my own way." She paused. "Will you help me?"

He was silent. "Even if I make the offer, she might still want to break the will—"

"Yes, but if she goes ahead, she takes the chance of losing everything. This way, she'll have a third."

"With her, it might not be enough. She still has that damned piece of paper you signed, which, as I've already told you, she could use to prove that you didn't want the money in the first place."

"Does that mean she should get it?"

"That's what she's going to claim."

"And in all the time she's taking to go to court over this, she could be receiving an income from her third of the estate."

He was silent again. Then, grudgingly, he said, "Well, she *is* greedy enough not to want to miss out on all that. But Briar, have you really thought about this? You're giving away a hell of a lot, and all because of that stupid woman's threats."

Briar had thought about it. But she, of all people, knew how it felt to be left out. "Not because of her threats, Spence," she said quietly. "But because it's right."

He sighed heavily. "I hate it when you're like this. All right, I'll present the proposal to her attorneys. But not without a few guarantees from both her and Jaz, Briar, and that's not up for argument. If we go forward with this, she has to withdraw all claims, period. Furthermore, they both have to agree not to sell their interests in Lord Industries unless they approach you first."

"No," she said.

"What?"

"I said, no. I'll agree to her having to drop the suit, but not to that last."

"Why not? It's for your own protection. If you insist on doing something like this, at least you ought to have some guarantee that the company won't be sold out from under you."

"I know, Spence. But I don't think that will happen."

"And if it does?"

"No. If I'm going to do this, I don't want any strings attached."

"No *strings* attached?" He sounded as if he might come right through the phone. "Do you realize—"

"I know what they could do, Spence. But don't you see? Hayden gave me everything to do with as I wished. I can't offer to share, only to attach conditions of my own. That's like giving with one hand and holding the other one out."

"It is not! Briar, I don't think you understand the implications here."

"Yes, I do," she said quietly. "And I mean it, Spence. No strings."

"This is crazy!"

"It's what I want," she said. "Will you call me when you've drawn up the papers—or whatever it is you have to do?"

"Before I jump off the Golden Gate Bridge, you mean?"

She smiled briefly. "It's not as bad as all that, Spence," she said. "You'll see. Now, how long do you think it will take you to arrange everything?"

"Weeks, months, years, if I have anything to say about it," he growled. "Why?"

She smiled again. "Because before we sign, I have to talk to Jaz."

"Do you even know where he is?"

She'd seen in the papers the other day that he had attended some function with one of San Francisco's socialites, so she knew he was in town, probably at his apartment in Sausalito. "I think so," she said. "I'm going to visit him today."

"Jaz always did like you," he said slowly, as comprehension dawned. "Ah, I think I see the plan. He's going to be your ace in the hole, so to speak."

"I certainly hope so, Spence," she said fervently. "I'll let you know."

"In the meantime, I'll contact the interested parties, who I'm *sure* are going to be very interested in what I have to say. Then I'll start drawing up the articles of doom. Remember, until you sign them, you can change your mind."

"I won't change my mind," Briar said, already relieved that she'd made the decision.

Instead of calling Jaz, as she had intended, Briar decided to go to see him in person. He rarely answered his phone anyway. Hoping they'd have a chance to talk so she could explain what she was doing, she told Patsy and Gabe where she'd be and headed out of the city.

On the way, she could feel herself getting tense again, so she tried not to think of what she was going to say to Jaz and concentrated instead on what was happening at the ranch. She'd left too early this morning to check on all the horses, but she remembered seeing one called Dancin' Light out on the pasture as she drove out. She couldn't put her finger on it, but something about the horse didn't look right, and she hoped that either Stefan or Jaime had brought her into the foaling barn this afternoon. They hadn't put her in yet because she wasn't waxing up, but she had been bred to a Kentucky Stallion named Barishnakov, and Briar didn't want to lose that foal. With a breeding agreement that didn't guarantee a live foal, just that the mare had been *in foal* when she left the Kentucky farm, Briar was well aware that if something went wrong, the stud fee of nearly a quarter of a million dollars went down the drain. It would be a big loss—especially now that she was about to reduce her current income by two-thirds—but then she told herself not to dwell on it. If she started thinking like that, she *would* drive herself crazy. Confident that Stefan was watching the mare more closely than even she would be if she were home, she crossed the bridge and went on into Sausalito to see Jaz.

She had been to Jaz's condo only twice before, but she had a good memory for details like names and streets, and she found it without any trouble. Parking the Mercedes on the cramped street in the picturesque old town, she got out of the car and looked up at the new cluster of town houses. They seemed incongruous in this setting of old-fashioned, vine-covered cottages; rising high above their dusty little neighbors, the ultramodern duplexes looked out over the bay through walls of smoked glass windows. How like Jaz, she thought with a shake of her head, and started up the steps.

The front door—a misnomer, because the door was actually around to the side of the two-story condo—was reached by going through a small wooden gate. The previous owners had apparently liked a lot of shrubbery and flowers, for the low fence that separated the place from the street was almost hidden. Jaz kept saying he was going to have the whole thing ripped out and cement put in, but he never had—another of the conundrums about her stepson that Briar had always found fascinating: the most modern of men, Jaz had an old-fashioned streak that softened his hard edges and made him more accessible than he seemed. He'd spent a lot of time trying to eradicate that part of him, but like the shrubbery and flowers that surrounded his town house, he had never quite managed it. Briar was glad because it made her present request easier.

She was so preoccupied with what she was going to say to him that she forgot to check in the street-level garage to see if his car was inside. By the time she got to the door, the street was out of sight, and because she didn't want to battle her way through the bushes again, she reached for the doorbell when she thought she heard a man's voice around back. A deck ran the whole length of the house, wrapping around from the place where she was standing, so, thinking Jaz was out there, she went around the corner—and stopped cold.

The voice hadn't belonged to Jaz. Another man was standing

on the deck, someone vaguely familiar. But Briar didn't have time to wonder if she knew him because someone else was there, and as they all stared at each other, Briar didn't know who was more surprised: herself, the stranger, or Fredrica, who, after a few transfixed seconds, drew herself up defiantly. From the telltale flush that spread quickly on her pale cheeks, Briar was sure she had stumbled into a rendezvous.

"What are *you* doing here?" Fredrica demanded. She stepped in front of her companion, who turned his face away as if he didn't want to be recognized.

Briar didn't care who Fredrica's lover was; she had come for another purpose, and she really didn't want her stepdaughter to interfere. "I came to talk to Jaz," she said.

"He's not here."

"I gathered that," Briar said dryly.

The man still had his face half turned away. From the little Briar could see, she was sure he looked familiar. "Excuse me," he muttered, and disappeared into the house through the back door.

As soon as he was gone, Fredrica came forward. "Why didn't you call first?" she said angrily. "Are you just in the habit of *dropping* in on people? Don't you ever knock?"

"I could ask the same thing about you, Fredrica," Briar said evenly. "Or perhaps you think you have an excuse because you have a key."

Fredrica flushed but held her ground. "I had every right to go into that house."

"What's your excuse for breaking into the safe?"

Fredrica's color rose even higher. "I didn't break in. Daddy gave me the combination long ago, so there."

Briar knew it would be futile to argue. Controlling herself with an effort, she changed the subject. "I don't want to fight with you, Fredrica; I came to see Jaz. Do you know where he is?"

Fredrica glanced swiftly toward the house and then back to her face again, making Briar wonder if Jaz was inside after all. "No, and if I did, I wouldn't tell you, of all people," she declared. Her eyes narrowed. "Why did you want to see him anyway? If you think you're going to inveigle him over to your side, you've got another thing coming."

"I don't intend to inveigle anyone. I just wanted to talk to him."

"About what? It's too late for that. We've got you now, Briar. That piece of paper proves I was right all the time. You're nothing but an opportunist, and I'm going to prove it."

"We'll see," Briar said, holding onto her temper by a thread. Briefly, she thought Spence was right. Did she really want to share everything with this woman? What was the point?

"We'll see, all right." Fredrica snapped. "It's not a joke now, is it? The truth is that if you *really* didn't marry my father for his money, you'd give it all up right now—just like you said you would in that agreement." Her lips twisted, and Briar thought she had never seen a more malignant expression on anyone's face. "I know you for what you are, Briar McKenna. And by the time I'm finished, the whole *world* will know it, too!"

"Do what you have to, Fredrica," Briar said. "And so will I."

Incensed, Fredrica came toward her. With her face only inches from Briar's, she hissed, "What did you do to him to make him give you everything, Briar? Screw his brains out every night and twice on Sunday?"

Repulsed by the vulgarism, Briar drew back, but Fredrica only laughed contemptuously. "Oh, don't pretend to be offended, Briar. We all know where *you* came from."

Briar's eyes turned very green, a portent that she was close to losing her temper after all. "Don't push me, Fredrica," she said. "I'm warning you."

"You think I'm scared of *you*? Even if I were, I'm not alone in this, you know."

"If you mean Jaz—"

"Jaz!" Fredrica laughed. "*Jaz*? You think he cares how this comes out? As long as he's got his skis in one hand and some young blonde on the other, he couldn't give a damn less."

"Then I don't know who you're talking about."

"No, you don't, but you will. And when you find out, you're going to be sorry."

On that note, she pushed Briar aside and stomped off. Briar could have followed, demanding to know what she had meant, but to what purpose? She didn't care what friends Fredrica thought she had on her side; it really didn't matter. She didn't want to continue this battle with her stepdaughter; she just wanted to reach an agreement and get it over with.

Disappointed that Jaz wasn't home, she waited a few minutes to make sure Fredrica had gone, then she went out to her own car again. She'd just have to call Jaz tomorrow or stop in again, she decided, as she climbed wearily in and started the engine. One way or another, she had to talk to him soon. Hoping that he hadn't left town again, as he often did on the spur of the moment, she got back on Highway 101 and headed toward Sonoma.

It was after dark by the time she drove through the big gates to Caulfield Farm. When she came around the curve in the drive and saw the lights on in the barn, she drew in a breath. Something was wrong; she knew it even before she saw the veterinarian's truck parked outside the foaling barn.

"Oh, no!" she muttered, thinking immediately of Dancin' Light and the foal she was due to have. She'd meant to call Stefan and ask him about the mare, but with everything else today it had slipped her mind. Pulling up beside the truck, she jumped out of the car and slammed the door. Hurrying inside, she went to the stall where the lights were on and looked inside. Her heart sank.

The veterinarian, a competent dark-haired young woman named Denise Roberts, five-foot-three and a hundred and ten pounds soaking wet, was kneeling beside Stefan on the straw. A mournful-looking Jaime was also with them, and even before Stefan turned in her direction, Briar realized what had happened. The exquisite Dancin' Light, with her blaze like a star and her four white socks . . . daughter of the Stakes winner, Blazin' Light, winner of six Grade I stakes races herself, lay on the deep bed of straw. Beside the mare lay the foal, a filly the exact image of her mother, except the star on her forehead was larger—and brighter, Briar thought distractedly. She didn't have time to notice much else. Both the horses were as still as . . . death.

Denise was busy with something, so Stefan slowly got to his feet and joined Briar outside the stall. "I'm sorry," he said, his voice low and strained. "Denise did everything possible, but it . . . it happened so fast. There wasn't anything we could do."

Briar couldn't look at him; she knew if she did, she would start to cry. The day had been such a strain, and now . . . this. "What happened?" she managed.

Looking even more unhappy than Stefan or Jaime, if that were possible, Dr. Roberts glanced up from her position near the mare. Her gloved hands were covered with blood, and dark smears marked the jumpsuit she was wearing to protect her clothes. She even had a streak of red across one cheek. "She ruptured," she said. "It had to be through the main uterine artery. I'm sorry, Briar, but there wasn't anything I could do. She . . . would have bled to death even if I'd had her on the table."

Briefly, Briar closed her eyes. She had loved this mare, with her great liquid eyes and her gentle manner, and as irrational as it was, she felt this was all her fault. If only she had stopped this morning; if only she had called Stefan to make sure the mare was all right. But life was filled with "if onlys" sometimes, she thought, and over the lump in her throat, she started to say, "I know y——"

But just then, before her astonished eyes, the foal that had been lying so quietly on the straw gave a little snort and lifted her head. Too weak to hold it up for long, she flopped back down on the straw and lay still again, but Briar saw the little ribs moving, and she looked quickly from the baby to Stefan. "I thought . . ."

"No, the foal made it—or will, once we find her a surrogate," he said. "She's a little weak, but Denise says she should be just fine."

Quickly, Briar looked for confirmation toward the veterinarian, who gave her a tired smile as she brushed a hand across her forehead. "He's right; she should be okay," she said, but then her smile faded when she looked back down at the mare. Sadly, she added, "Some good came out of this, at least."

Briar glanced away from the inert body on the straw toward the foal. She couldn't allow herself to grieve for her gentle Dancin' Light just yet, so she forced her mind onto practical things. "Do you have any colostrum on hand?" she asked Denise.

Colostrum was the first milk from the mare. It was packed with antibodies from the mother, along with other important components necessary to give the baby a good start. Foals who didn't receive the enriched colostrum within a short time after being born didn't thrive as well as those who did, and Briar wanted to make sure that after losing its mother this baby had every chance. To do that, she was prepared to drive to the University at Davis, if she had to.

Denise was gathering her equipment. "Yes, I have some at the office. I'll go and get it."

"I'll bring it back," Jaime said. He was clearly anxious to help.

"Thanks, Jaime," Stefan said, and looked at the pale Briar. Putting his hand on her arm, he said, "She'll be okay. We'll supplement her if necessary."

Dr. Roberts had finished collecting her tools; she added encouragingly, "Orphan foals can do very well. It's just a matter of making sure they get enough to eat."

Briar opened the door so Denise could get out with her stuff. "That won't be a problem," she said quietly. "I'll feed her myself if necessary."

The young woman smiled wearily. "Let's see if we can't find a foster mother to do it for us first, shall we? Feeding a foal can be very time-consuming."

Briar glanced at the baby. Tears filled her eyes despite herself when she saw the little foal nudging the still body of her mother. "Do you know of anyone who might have a mare they can lend us? If I have to, I'll buy one."

"When I get back to the office, I'll call around."

"But it's so late."

Denise smiled. "Would you object if I called you at this hour?"

Briar shook her head. "No, of course not."

Stefan helped Denise take all her equipment out to her truck. Jaime had gone to get one of the ranch vehicles so he could follow the vet to her office. For the meantime, Briar was alone with the dead mother and her baby. Fighting tears again, she slipped inside the stall and dropped down on the hay. Heedless of her designer suit, she gathered the filly to her. Confused, the baby bumped her arm, obviously searching for food, and Briar stroked its neck. Because she had been an orphan herself, she knew how this little one felt.

"Soon," she told the foal, and then reached out to touch the still mare's shoulder. "I'm sorry," she whispered, her voice breaking again. "I should have done something sooner."

"It wasn't your fault," Stefan said. Without her noticing, he had returned to the barn. "There wasn't anything anyone could have done. I brought her in earlier, and we had a watch on her until she went down. Denise was here, but . . . when she ruptured, it was like a fountain."

Still holding the foal, who seemed content for the moment to

huddle practically in her lap, Briar brushed away her tears.
"But I thought something was wrong. I should have—"

"We were here, and we couldn't do anything," Stefan said,
coming into the stall. He squatted down beside her, forcing her
to look at him. "It wasn't your fault," he repeated.

Briar looked at the foal she was holding. Exhausted, the filly
was sleeping, her delicate head nodding up and down with each
little breath, but she looked so vulnerable that Briar felt her
heart contract. So much had happened today that she felt delicate herself, her emotions had swung from one pendulum to
another, and suddenly, she didn't feel strong enough to go on
by herself. She needed someone to hold her, like she was
holding this foal, but she didn't have anyone, no one at all.

Without realizing it, a sob escaped her, then another. It was
too much, she thought; she couldn't be brave and courageous
and strong all the time; she couldn't just go on as if nothing had
happened. She needed someone to share it with. She needed to
depend on someone besides herself.

Stefan put his hand on her shoulder. At his touch, she looked
up. "Oh, Stefan!" she choked, and held the foal tighter.

Without a word, Stefan reached out and put his arms around
her. It was awkward with the foal in her lap, but at Stefan's
touch, she felt as if a tremendous burden had been lifted from
her. Dropping her head onto his shoulder, she closed her eyes.

"It'll be all right," he whispered, one hand coming up to
stroke her hair. "Everything will be all right. . . ."

She knew she shouldn't allow this, but she couldn't help
herself. She felt so alone . . . so in need of comfort. "I'm
not sure," she said weakly, thinking of all that had happened, and all she had before her. "I just don't know anymore, Stefan. . . ."

"You're not alone," he murmured, holding her closer. "I'm
right here beside you, and I'm not going anywhere."

She didn't know how she felt about that; she was too drained,
too exhausted to think straight.

"Just hold me," she whispered, and when his arms tightened around her and she felt his heart beating strongly under
her cheek, she closed her eyes again and sighed. She'd never
thought she'd feel this comforted again, this safe. It was a
blissful feeling, and yet as her tension melted away and she
began to feel something else stirring deep inside her, she knew
she should pull away from him.

"Stefan—"

As if he sensed it, too, he shook his head. "Shhh," he whispered, his lips in her hair. "Don't say it."

So she didn't. They sat like that until Jaime came back, and then, because the foal was much more important, and, because, after all, the both knew it wasn't time for them yet, they warmed the colostrum and fed it to the little one together. The filly was hungry by this time, and as she greedily sucked at the bottle in another stall far away from where her dam lay so still, Briar's eyes met Stefan's over the filly's head. They both knew that something had changed between them that night, and as Briar gently stroked the foal while the baby finished the milk, she felt stronger again, sure that somehow, someway, everything would work out.

---

# CHAPTER NINETEEN

Stefan and Briar went to Los Angeles a month after Dancin' Light died. Long before that time, however, Briar had regained the composure that had slipped the night she lost her mare. She never mentioned it, so Stefan pretended nothing had happened between them, either. When she announced that she wanted to enter some of her horses into race training, he didn't know what to think. She had heard of a good man at Santa Anita Racetrack, in Arcadia, and she wanted them both to go down to interview him.

Feeling as if he'd missed something, Stefan rallied enough to argue against it. Putting his own personal feelings aside, it was too soon for her to get involved in racing; she needed more time to establish the ranch. Briar of course argued back that she wanted to see what the trainer thought, but Stefan knew what he was going to think: only a fool would refuse to take on new horses—especially those of the caliber Briar intended to train. She couldn't take the unbeaten filly that she had bought at Keeneland, Night Fever, because she had sustained a hairline fracture of the cannon bone one day just playing in the paddock. But she could take Touch the Fire, who had turned two with the coming of the new year, and another new horse she'd bought, a big, powerful mare called Ten Diamonds. The third candidate was Incandessence.

When Stefan heard this last, he nearly went through the roof. "And what's she going to train on—never mind *race*—three legs and a prayer?" he'd demanded, thinking of those five pins in her pastern.

"She's been cleared by four veterinarians, including two leg men at Davis," Briar replied. "And look at her—she *wants* to run."

He couldn't deny that. If ever a horse was coming out of her skin with eagerness, it was Incandessence. She obviously felt she had been laid off too long and wanted to get back into harness. It was a trial to get her from the stall out to the hot walker for her daily exercise, and she was like a dynamo in the new swimming pool Briar had had installed just for her. Only Touch the Fire, the filly from hell, as Stefan now called the temperamental horse, showed more promise. Stefan wouldn't mind sending that black demon out in the world to have some sense knocked into her, but the Derby winner, well, that was another story. He didn't like those pins in her leg, and he didn't care what the vets said. He thought she'd be better off taking her place as a broodmare, and told Briar so.

"But Stefan," Briar had said with that innocent expression he had never trusted. "Didn't you say that if she didn't race again I'd never recoup my investment?"

"You'll never recoup it if she breaks that pastern again and has to be destroyed," he'd said tactlessly and been rewarded by a flash of green eyes.

"She won't break it. Everybody tells me that leg is stronger than ever. And she deserves another chance, you said so yourself."

"I don't remember saying that."

"Well, you did. You said it was a shame her race career was cut short."

"Yes, that's true. But I never—"

"Well, now it won't be," she'd interrupted. "So. When would be a good time for you to come to Los Angeles with me?"

He knew it was useless to argue further, so he said there was no time like the present, and before he knew it, she'd made her arrangements to meet with the trainer, a man named Wayne Kaminsky. Stefan had heard of Kaminsky before and grudgingly approved.

As they waited at the airport for their flight to be called, Briar buried herself in the paperwork she had brought while Stefan roamed restlessly around the concourse, casting covert and dire glances in her direction. He couldn't understand her. The night that mare had died, he had really believed . . .

Well, it didn't matter what he'd believed, he decided, watching her as she concentrated on the work in her lap. She was in control of herself again and pretended that she hadn't been vulnerable that night, even for a minute. If she wanted to forget it, that was fine with him. He'd never intended to get involved anyway; he still had problems of his own to work out.

For some reason, the rationale only made him feel even more restless, and he decided to take another turn around the airport. When was the damned flight going to be called?

Some activity on the tarmac out by the plane they were due to take caught his eye, and he stopped by the windows to watch. It was just the ground crew, but after a moment, Stefan didn't even see the hustle and bustle and hurrying about. He was thinking that he wished he had never come to America in the first place. Why couldn't he have stayed in his own little stable at home? he wondered. Taking two lots up to the downs every morning, doing evening stables every night, and dealing with owners and paperwork and form books and everything else in between seemed child's play compared to what he was engaged in now. He'd been his own boss then—or nearly. Lord Bowen, who had owned both the stable and the horses, had given him free rein, so to speak; he could do as he liked, without having to worry. He had been happy, he'd thought—or at least a damned sight happier than after he'd opened that trunk in his grandmother's attic.

*You're got to tell her*, a little voice said at the back of his head, referring to Briar. *The way you're starting to feel now, it isn't fair if you don't.*

Wincing at the voice, he tried to rationalize. He knew he should say something, but what could he say when he wasn't sure what it was he felt? Even if he decided he was flat-out in love with Briar—and he wasn't sure at all that was the case— what made him think she would give a good damn anyway?

He'd thought the night she lost the mare that they'd crossed some barrier, but she had gone up to the house alone after they got the orphan settled, and when she'd been her cool self again the very next morning, he didn't know what to think. Afterward, he couldn't tell her that he was here under false pretenses. Perhaps if everything worked out today, he'd come clean and tell her the truth. He could just imagine her reaction. If she didn't kick him off the place, she'd probably demolish him with one of her looks.

And for what? he asked himself. He had been here almost a year and wasn't any closer to what he'd come for than he had been when he first arrived. If he hadn't felt he owed this debt to his grandmother—and through her, to his great-grandmother, Flossie—he would have given it up a long time ago and just gone home.

He was startled by the thought. But home was increasingly *here*, he felt, and he looked over his shoulder again to where Briar was still sitting. As he watched her frowning at her notebook, he felt annoyed with himself. Things were getting bad when her simplest action stirred something in him. Just now, he'd been thinking how beautiful she looked in the morning light, even dressed in a business suit like all the other efficient-looking women executives waiting to fly to Los Angeles. Maybe the difference was that he knew how Briar was at home, in her jeans and boots, her hair down, a tender expression on her face as she made the rounds of the horses and gave them all a carrot and a pat, saying something to each one, as if they could understand her. And who knew? he thought to himself, maybe they did.

As if she sensed his eyes on her, Briar glanced up just then and their eyes met. Without warning, he felt a warmth inside him spread, and because he didn't like to be feeling something she obviously wasn't, he gave her a brief nod, then turned quickly away again. She had no right to look like that so early in the morning, he thought with sudden irritation. It was just on seven now, and they'd been on the road since five to make sure they got through the commuter traffic in plenty of time to make their flight. He was already feeling gritty and impatient, while she sat there, composed as a princess, getting work done. Jamming his hands into his pockets and trying not to notice the shape of her calves in high heels when he went by, he headed toward the magazine kiosk. Just then the clerk at the gate took up the microphone to make an announcement.

"Good morning, ladies and gentlemen, we are now ready to begin boarding United Airlines flight five-twenty-four, nonstop to Los Angeles. At this time, we invite all those passengers who need special attention, or those traveling with small children, to board first at Gate Ten. First-class passengers may board at their leisure. Please have your boarding passes ready for flight five-twenty-four. . . ."

With people getting up eagerly and starting forward, Briar started to put away what she'd been working on. She was just snapping her briefcase shut when Stefan returned to help.

"No, I can get it," she said, when he offered to take the briefcase. "But I wouldn't mind if you carried my overnight bag."

The overnight bag near her feet was a Louis Vuitton done in a paisley print that Stefan thought suited her perfectly. His own scuffed and battered valise was right beside it, and he picked both up, struck by the unconscious symbolism of it. Like his duffel, he was starting to feel a little buffeted himself by his proximity to Briar McKenna.

Tickets in hand, they got in line. Standing slightly behind her, Stefan caught a whiff of Briar's perfume, a light, spicy exotic scent that went right to his head. Wondering how he was ever going to get through this without doing something stupid, he tightened his grip on the suitcase and reminded himself that they were going to Los Angeles to talk to a trainer about racehorses. That was all. She'd made that clear, and he had to accept it.

But then he caught another whiff of her perfume and wondered who he was trying to kid. Ever since the night they had tended the orphan foal together, he had regretted a thousand times not following through on his instincts. She had been so vulnerable that night, clearly needing something he had been longing to offer. Even now he could remember what it felt like to hold her, to feel her pliant body in his arms, to know that all he had to do was tip her chin up to kiss her.

But some vestige of common sense had told him that if he had done it, they couldn't go back. She might not have rejected him that night, but what about the next, and the one after that, and the one after *that*? God knew he'd wanted to push her down in the straw and make love to her right there, but he hadn't, and he wasn't sure now whether he was sorry or not.

It didn't matter anyway, he told himself as they moved forward to the plane; he'd lost his chance. Maybe it was better this way. Less complicated, anyway. He supposed he should be grateful for that.

"You're still not happy about this, are you, Stefan?" Briar asked, after takeoff. The flight attendant had just served coffee, and he'd been so preoccupied that he'd asked for sugar when he took it black. Grimacing at the sweet taste, he put the cup down on the tray again and wished to hell he had a cigarette.

"It doesn't matter whether I'm happy about it or not," he said, looking out the window to avoid her glance. "You're the boss, and if you want to get into racing, it's none of my business."

"But why are you so against it?" she persisted.

He finally looked into her mezmerizing eyes and sighed. "I've told you before, racing's a fool's game. No one makes money, not really, and besides, I thought you wanted to be a breeder."

"I do. But we've decided that Caulfield is only going to retain fillies with broodmare potential, so don't you think I should see how they perform before I breed them? What good's a racehorse if she's never run?"

Stefan had no ready answer; Briar always had had a quick tongue. Fortunately for him, the attendant came by again offering breakfast, and he pretended to be occupied with that for the hour it took to fly down the coast. Before he knew it, the plane was starting a descent into LAX, and when they claimed the rental car, he was too busy trying to find his way out of the airport maze to talk much. After the relative serenity of Sonoma, being on the freeway system in Los Angeles was like entering the Indianapolis 500 with a Volkswagen, and by the time they reached the racetrack in Arcadia, they were both tense.

The trainer had remembered to leave their names with the guard at Gate Seven, where they'd been instructed to go to get onto the backside of the track. Satisfied with their identity, security waved them in. They followed a winding road to the barn area. Stefan glanced at Briar. Seeing her rapt face as she looked around, he knew he didn't have a chance in hell, but he had to try again.

"Briar, are you *sure* you want to do this?"

She turned to look at him. "You keep asking me that, Stefan. Why?"

He hadn't said it before, but now was a good time. "Because there're a lot of things that go on behind the scenes in racing. Are you sure you're ready to take your lumps with the cream?"

"I'm not a child," she said. "I know there are abuses, things that go wrong. I . . ." She hesitated, and he knew she was thinking of Dancin' Light, who had died so unexpectedly. "I know that high hopes can change to disaster in the blink of an eye."

"Then why do you want to put yourself through this?"

She glanced around; so did he. As unhappy as he was about this whole thing, he still had to admit that Santa Anita was about as pretty a track as he'd ever seen. Here on the backside—or the "backstretch" for those more eloquently inclined—all the aisles were raked and swept every day, some with a herringbone pattern. Not a stray wisp of hay or weed was in sight after the pickup trucks went by at noon. The only time there was any kind of disarray was in the early morning when stalls were being cleaned. But there was a kind of beauty even then, he knew, about the huge piles of used straw mounded up at the ends of the aisles waiting for the trucks to haul them away; even then, it all was neat and pristine.

It truly was like walking into another world—something out of the past. All the shed rows were painted in two shades of green, with roofs that extended out over passageways in front of the stalls to provide shelter and shade. Big, old trees rose high over the barns, and here and there a stable dog—or a companion goat—was tied to a post, keeping guard or just hanging out. They weren't needed now, but in full summer, big fans would be set at each end of the aisles to cool the horses, who would stand with their heads hanging out. Santa Anita might be a beautiful old place, but it lacked the modern air circulation of the later barns or the insulation of the brick and cement shed rows at the newer part of its sister track, Hollywood Park.

Spying Wayne Kaminsky's training barn sign up ahead, just as the guard had told them, Stefan slowed the car. At this hour, nearly ten o'clock now, "tracking"—the morning workouts from easy gallops to fast breezes for the clockers to record times—had almost ceased, and the frantic early morning activity of the backside had slowed to a walk. Only a few horses were tied to the rotating walking machines; here and there a horse was being bathed before it was put away from its morning workout. The trucks that belonged to the track veterinarians, made distinctive by big vet packs on their backs, were seen here and there, but many of the vets had already gone over to Hollywood Park to check in with clients there.

"Just take a look around, Stefan," Briar said. "Don't you want to be a part of this? Come on, what do you think?"

"I think you're nuts," he said flatly. He still wasn't ready to give up. "Mishaps and accidents aside, as your ranch manager, I have to point out—"

Briar sighed. "You're going to talk about money again."

"Damn right," he said. "Now, I know you've got all the money in the world—"

She glanced away. "I wouldn't say that."

"What?"

She shook her head without looking at him. "Never mind. Go on."

He hesitated a moment, then decided it was none of his business. What *was* his business was pointing out some of the mathematics of racing. Patiently, he said, "Briar, you said that eventually you want to test every filly you have with brood-mare potential in actual racing. Now, I know you're fully aware that it can cost upwards of twenty-five thousand dollars a year just to keep a horse in training, but have you considered some of the other factors?"

She was watching one of the exercise girls walk a long-limbed, graceful bay by the car, which Stefan had stopped near the side of the road. Keeping her eyes on the horse whose stride seemed to flow like water, she said, "Such as?"

"Such as the fact that during a typical year, about eighty thousand Thoroughbreds compete at tracks in the United States, Canada, and Mexico. They earn about six hundred million in purses—"

Briar still had her eyes on the horse that had gone by and was now walking up the road, its beautiful head bobbing slightly, ears pricked forward as it looked back and forth. "An average of seventy-five hundred dollars per horse," she supplied.

"Yes . . . er . . . that's right," he said, surprised by her quick arithmetic. Winding up again, he went on, "Which as you can also calculate, is not enough to support a horse at a major track.''

''That's true,'' she agreed absently, looking down the shed row by which they were parked. A groom had just brought out another animal and had put it in the cross ties, preparing to change a leg bandage. ''So what's your point?''

''My *point*,'' he said, wishing she would pay attention to him, ''is the average horse rarely pays its way.''

She turned to smile at him. ''But I don't have average horses, do I, Stefan? Even you have to admit that.''

He didn't have to admit anything, he thought, irritated as hell. Besides, what business was it of his how she spent her money? If she wanted to have a bonfire in the backyard with piles of thousand-dollar bills, why should he object? Why should he even care?

He didn't know, he thought blackly, but he did. He had a bad feeling about this, a *bad* feeling, and if he could talk her out of it, he would. One last time, he said, ''Since you're so quick with numbers, you've obviously figured out that an estimated ninety-eight percent of racing stables lose money each year—and that you're going to be one of the two percent that doesn't,'' he added, when she looked quickly at him. ''All right, so be it. But there's something we haven't talked about before that I think you should consider.''

''What's that?''

''I know this Wayne Kaminsky comes highly recommended, so what I'm going to say might not apply to him. I hope it doesn't. But it's a fact of life that horses are entered every day in races they cannot hope to win except by sheer accident. They're outclassed or put at the wrong distance; they're off their feed, or sore for some reason, or bleeding, or short of wind.''

''Go on.''

''Racing is a business, after all. Tracks have to fill nine or ten or sometimes as many as twelve races a day. Fields of fewer than eight horses are unpopular. Have you thought about what happens when there aren't enough fit and ready horses to go around? They don't cancel races; that isn't good for revenues. So what they do instead is expect trainers to keep their stock active. A trainer who refuses to run as frequently as possible soon discovers that the track would rather give stall space to a more cooperative stable. Under these pressures, only stables owned by the big names of racing are permitted to train horses the proper way—racing their horses when they're ready to run and not before. But even they sometimes get sucked in.''

Briar looked at him for a long moment. Finally, she said, ''And you think that might happen with Wayne?''

Stefan looked away from that intense green glance. Trying not to think what beautiful lips she had, he stared at the plain wooden sign hung at the end of the shed row right in front of them. It said Kaminsky Training, and he shook his head.

''I don't know,'' he said honestly. ''I just want you to be aware.''

Without warning, she put her hand over his. He nearly jumped at the contact and looked at her quickly. ''Thank you,'' she said. ''I appreciate your concern.''

His *concern*? What he was concerned about was this inexplicable desire he felt to take that hand of hers and pull her toward him. What he was *concerned* about was this feeling of wanting to put his arms around her and feel her next to him. But most of all, he was *concerned* about . . .

With difficulty, he reined in his galloping thoughts. On the pretext of taking the keys out of the ignition, he took his hand out from under hers, muttering, ''Well, I just wanted you to know what you're getting into.''

''I do,'' she said, much more in control then he was—or ever would be. ''But it doesn't change my mind. I know I may be making a mistake, but I have to try. I have to try,'' she repeated.

Hearing the passionate note in her voice, he wondered why she felt so intensely about this, so determined to forge ahead, despite the difficulties and heartaches. Then, suddenly, he realized the answer had been right in front of him all the time. As she'd said, these horses were bred to run. And like these horses, he thought, racing was in *her* blood. It was so obvious, he wondered why he hadn't thought of it before. Briar wasn't playing at this; she was profoundly serious about success. It wasn't a game to her; she was carrying on a legacy begun nearly a hundred years before by her great-grandparents, Sloane and Marguerite Caulfield. It was obvious that she hadn't inherited only their love of horses but their passion for racing them, as well. And if anyone should understand that, he thought, it should be him. Hadn't he felt the same joy, that swelling excitement at seeing a horse do what it had been born and bred to do—run? There was no more thrilling sight than seeing a field of horses rounding the turn for home, watching them drive toward the finish, putting everything on the line. Oh, yes, he thought, if anyone should understand Briar's desire to be part of that, he should.

He opened the car door while Briar looked at him in surprise. "We came all this way," he said. "We might as well go listen to what the man has to say."

Wayne Kaminsky had a lot to say, and all of it quickly. When Briar and Stefan came up to his office at the end of the barn, he was standing on crutches inside the office talking to a young man whose diminutive stature indicated he was a jockey.

"Listen, Pat," the trainer was saying, "I'd appreciate your coming in to work Refractory early tomorrow morning before we race him on Saturday."

"Sure thing, Wayne. What time you want me here?"

"Oh, not before six. I've got a couple others I want to track before him, and—oh, hello," the trainer said, spying Briar and Stefan coming up to the doorway.

"Hello," Briar said with a smile. "I'm Briar McKenna, and this is Stefan Yager. Are you Wayne Kaminsky?"

"In the flesh," the trainer said. "Come on in."

"We didn't mean to interrupt—"

"No problem, Pat and I were just talking strategy. Oh, this is my jockey Pat Shannon."

Briar held out her hand to the black-haired, blue-eyed young man who barely came up to her shoulder. "I've seen your name in the paper many times," she said.

Briefly, with a shy smile, Pat took her hand, then Stefan's. Then he turned to the trainer. "Well, I'll see you tomorrow, Wayne."

"Right. Don't be late," Wayne called as the young man left. Pat waved without looking back and disappeared around the edge of the barn. Watching him go, Wayne shook his head. "A lot of talent in that boy, but sometimes . . . Well, that's not your problem, is it? Come in, come in. Excuse the crutches, horse stepped on me." He glared down at the big bandage covering his foot. "That'll teach me to get out of the way."

"I hope it isn't serious," Briar said.

"Nah. Another couple days and it'll be good as new. But for the time being, do you mind if I sit? I'm supposed to keep it up as much as possible, but don't worry, as my staff always says, I can order them around just as well on my butt as I can on my feet. Training doesn't stop just because I pulled a stupid trick.''

Briar smiled, and Stefan had to grudgingly admit that he was starting to like the guy himself. He liked him even more after Wayne gave up the best chair to Briar despite her protests and took a seat on a battered old tin thing that had clearly seen better days, gesturing to Stefan to take the mate.

''Now,'' Wayne said, propping his foot up on the desk. ''Let me tell you what I have to offer in the way of training, and then you can tell me what you have in mind.''

For the next twenty minutes, he outlined his training program, handing out printed sheets of expenses and costs and stressing that every horse that came into his barn was trained as an individual. ''I don't know if you got colts or geldings or fillies or what,'' he said at one point. ''But it don't matter to me. I'll train everything that has potential, although I have to admit—'' he grinned abashedly—''I've also trained a few in my time that didn't.''

''Who hasn't?'' Stefan commented, and when Wayne shot him a look, he explained about his time in England.

''Oh, so you trained across the water, did you?'' Wayne said. ''You must find it a mite different here.''

''Not really,'' Stefan replied. ''Horses are horses the world over. They either run or they don't.''

''That's true,'' Wayne said, and added with a wink, ''the trick is finding out which day they want to do what.''

''Amen to that.''

Still grinning, Wayne turned toward Briar. ''Now, Ms. McKenna—''

''Briar, please.''

''Briar, then,'' Wayne said. ''God, that's a pretty name,'' he commented, then suddenly looked embarrassed. ''Well, as I was about to say,'' he went on quickly, ''I don't mind taking people's money for doing what I'd do for free any day, but if I have an animal here for a couple of months and I see he just doesn't have what it takes, I'll tell you, make no mistake. I don't have time in my barn to fool with luggers or those lazy bones that just aren't interested. Let the dressage people have 'em, or the jumpers.''

Stefan noticed Briar's amused lift of an eyebrow and knew

she was thinking of Irish. "Yes, I see," she said. "Please, go on."

Wayne obeyed. "There's an old adage that says bad horses eat just as much as good 'uns, but the good 'uns pay out better. And I'll be honest with you, Briar, economics bein' what it is, I've got to fill my barn with horses that have potential." He paused, then smiled again. "I guess it all boils down to this. I love what I'm doin', and they should, too. Otherwise, neither of us belongs taking up space here at the track."

"As it happens, I agree," Briar said, and leaned forward. "And now that you've told me what you've got to offer, let me tell you what I expect."

For the next twenty minutes, she proceeded to do just that. By the time she finished reeling off the pedigree and race record of Ten Diamonds, Wayne was definitely interested, but when she started to tell him about Incandessence, he held up his hand. "Beggin' your pardon, Briar, but unless I'm mistaken, that mare has a leg held together by iron. I'd need a vet's certificate—"

Calmly, Briar pulled out the necessary documentation, along with the latest X rays, and handed them over. "I want her in training, Mr. Kaminsky—" she began.

"Wayne," he murmured absently. He was already holding up one of the X rays to the light. The five pins holding the mare's pastern together were clearly visible even to a novice, which he wasn't. Letting out a whistle, he shook his head. "I don't know."

"I only want her started, Wayne," Briar said. "She's ready, I know she is. But if you don't think so, or if she shows up the slightest bit lame at any time—and I mean at *any* time—I'll take her home and she'll—" she glanced at Stefan "—become a broodmare. But I have to give her this chance. She deserves it, and she . . . I know you'll think it's silly, but she wants to race again. I know it."

Slowly, Wayne put down the thick, black X ray. "I don't think it's silly," he said quietly. "There are some horses that'll just wither away if they can't race. I've seen it myself." He hesitated. "All right, bring her in. We'll start her slow, *real* slow. And if she goes on, well, we'll discuss it from there. Is that acceptable?"

"Perfectly," Briar said with a dazzling smile.

"Now, what's this third horse? Touch the Fire, you say?"

Briar's smile turned mischievous. "My demon horse from hell, as Stefan calls her. Yes, she's a two-year-old, and I'd like to get her started, too."

"What's her breeding?"

When Briar told him, he looked blank. "I . . . uh . . ."

"That's all right," Briar assured him. "She doesn't have the fancy bloodlines that the others do, but I think you'll be surprised. This filly can run. I'm sure of it."

Stefan could almost feel what the other man was thinking. If he'd been in the trainer's position, he'd have been thinking it himself. Glad to see someone else trying to deal with Briar when her mind was made up for a change, he sat back as Wayne said, "Well, I'll surely be glad to give those three a try. Anything else?"

"I'd like to send Night Fever down as soon as she's ready to train again," Briar said. "If that's all right."

Wayne's eyes gleamed. "That's just fine. When do you want to ship the others?"

Briar turned to Stefan. "When can you arrange it?"

"I'll get to it as soon as we return to the ranch," Stefan said, meeting Wayne's eyes with amusement. As he knew from experience, it was difficult, if not impossible, to refuse Briar anything when she wanted it, and they both knew that of the three horses Briar was offering him right now, only Ten Diamonds had potential because of her pedigree. Touch the Fire was an unknown quantity, and with her injury, Incandessence was chancy, more likely to break down than anything, no matter what anyone said. Stefan knew as well as Wayne did that if that happened, despite the care he was sure to take bringing her along, he'd still be known as the trainer who had taken a has-been Derby winner and ruined her completely.

Still, one did not refuse an owner of Briar's potential; she had money, and she had a lot of horses. If Wayne played his cards right, theirs could turn into a lucrative partnership after all.

"Fine. I'll be ready," Wayne said gamely. "Would you like a tour of the place? I could show you a few of the horses I've got in training."

"I'd like that very much," Briar said, but then looked doubtfully at the crutches. "But are you sure you can manage?"

"No problem," Wayne said, and led them out for a tour of the barn.

The first horse they stopped to see was a bay colt called

Cherry Ridge. "By Riva Ridge out of a mare called Cherry Pie," Wayne said. "You'd never know this sucker could run by the way he stands here with his head in the sky, but he can blister a track, I'll tell you that."

The next was another colt called My Preference, who made Briar laugh when he put his head on her shoulder as she was scratching his nose. "He'll do that all day if you stand there," Wayne said sounding exasperated, but he gave the horse a fond pat as they went on down the shed. By the time they completed the tour, Wayne looked a little pale on his crutches, but Stefan was impressed. He hadn't said much as they were going along, but he'd taken careful note of the way the horses looked, how they were cared for, what they were fed, and how much they were raced. Although he'd tried, he couldn't fault the trainer on anything he'd checked, and he said so before they left.

Wayne seemed pleased but not surprised at the compliment. "Horses are my life," he said simply, and then glanced at Briar. "That sounds silly, too, don't it?"

"No, it doesn't," Briar said quickly. "In fact, if you didn't feel that way, my three wouldn't be on their way here."

"I'll take care of them, I promise you that."

She grinned mischievously. "And let me know if any of them should be sold as jumpers?"

Wayne laughed. "We'll give it a couple months, and I'll let you know for sure."

"Can't ask more than that," Briar said, and shook his hand. She was just getting into the car when a grizzled old black man appeared from a shed row across the way and came hesitantly toward the car.

Wayne instantly looked irritated. "Damn it, Gillie, not now!"

The old man ducked his head, but he shuffled forward anyway. Curious, Briar got out of the car again and waited until he came up. "I'm sorry, Mr. 'minsky," the black man said, taking off a battered hat that looked as old as he was. "But I saw this lady, and I has to know—"

"What?" Wayne said impatiently.

The old man looked at Briar, his rheumy bloodshot eyes lighting up when he saw her face. "You're Miz Marguerite, ain't you?" he said wonderingly.

"No, she's not—" Wayne started to say, but Briar reached

out and grabbed his arm. Her grip was so strong that he looked at her in surprise, but she only had eyes for the old man.

"What did you call me?" she demanded.

Gillie's gnarled hands tightened on the brim of his soiled hat. "I'm sorry," he said, ducking his head again. "I didn't mean no disrespect—"

"No, no, it's not that," Briar said quickly. "It's just that I was . . . surprised. My name is Briar McKenna. Why did you think I was called Marguerite?"

" 'Cause you look just like her," the old man said, looking frightened now. "I'm sorry, I didn't—"

"No, no, that's all right," she reassured him hastily. "Er . . . Gillie, did you *know* Marguerite?"

"Yassum, I did," the man said, looking fearfully from one of them to the other. "A long, long time ago, I worked at Caulfield Farm, for her and Mr. Caulfield."

Briar was stunned. "I . . . I don't believe it!"

"Oh, come on, now," Stefan started to say. He didn't know what game the old man was playing, but he didn't like the way Briar was acting.

She hardly heard him. Her eyes tight on the old man, she said, "Gillie, are you saying you knew my great-grandfather?"

"If he be Sloane Caulfield, I did, oh, yes indeed," Gillie said, and nodded vigorously. "The finest man I ever did work for, yessiree. And that Miz Marguerite—"

Wayne spoke up again just then. "All right, Gillie, I think that's enough—"

"No!" Briar said sharply. "I want to hear what he has to say."

Wayne looked as surprised at her vehemence as Stefan did. "He doesn't have anything to say, Briar. He's just an old drunk who likes to hang around the track, making a buck when he can by brushing down horses. He doesn't even know where he is half the time."

Briar looked at the old groom, who was twisting his hat again. "Gillie," she said. "Listen carefully. Is what you just told me true?"

"Oh, yassum, it is!" There was no doubting the old man's sincerity, but whether he was telling the truth or only thought he was was another matter. Listening to all this, Stefan thought it unlikely. How could this man have known Sloane Caulfield? It just didn't seem possible.

Apparently Briar didn't think so. "If you knew Sloane and

Marguerite, you must have known others in my family. Can you name anyone else?''

Gillie gave her an anxious look. Pitifully, he said, "You don't believe me?''

"Well, Gillie, I have to admit, it does sound a little—''

"Her name was Juliet," Gillie said, his hands tightening on the brim of his hat so that it crumpled under his swollen, arthritic fingers. "An' praise the lord, she was the most beautiful angel who ever did live."

Briar actually swayed. "You . . . knew Juliet?" she said faintly.

Stefan knew he should have just thrown up his hands at that point and given up, but he couldn't help himself. He tried. And so did Wayne. They'd both been around enough racetracks to know when someone was being hustled, and it was obvious that this Gillie, whoever he was, had other problems besides an active imagination. The bloodshot eyes told a whole other story, Stefan thought, and Wayne agreed.

"Briar, you can't—" Stefan started to say.

"Really, Briar, I know this guy, and he—"

She didn't listen to either of them. She was adamant. If Gillie had worked for her family all those years ago, she owed him something.

"Gillie," she said, as both Wayne and Stefan looked at her in dismay, "Would you like to come to Northern California and work for me?"

"Me?" Gillie said, looking as if she had handed him the moon and the stars and a bottle of Johnny Walker Red all at the same time. "Me?"

"You," she said, smiling. "I promise you, the work won't be too hard—"

"Oh, nothin's hard for me, Miz Briar. I may be old, but I still know horses. I can take care of how ever many you want."

"Uh, Briar," Stefan said. "Could I talk to you for a minute?"

Briar turned to him. "What is it?" she asked impatiently.

He practically hauled her out of earshot. "What do you think you're doing?" he demanded. "You don't even know that man!"

"He knew my great-grandparents."

"You don't know that. He could just be making the whole thing up."

"Why would he do that?"

Stefan felt like pulling at his hair. "What's wrong with you? You're not usually this naive. You can't just . . . just *hire* someone you don't even know."

Her eyes were turning that deep green warning color. "What's the matter, do you think he'll steal something?"

"No, I think he'll be too drunk to do that! For God's sake, Briar."

"He's an old man, Stefan," she hissed. "He's obviously down on his luck."

"For good reason."

"I want to give him a job."

"What makes you think he'll work and not just drink it down?"

"He just needs someone to give him a chance."

"What he *needs* is a detox unit and then a long stay in an old folk's home."

"I can't believe you're acting this way," she said. "He knew my *family*!"

"So he says. Anyone could say that."

"But he knew about Marguerite, and Sloane, and Juliet."

He realized he wasn't getting anywhere. "Listen, Briar, you heard Wayne—"

"Wayne's like you. He thinks Gillie is just an old drunk."

"He is! And even if he weren't, just what do you have in mind for him? Is he going to buck hay? Help break the two-year-olds?"

"He can help with the broodmares," Briar said stubbornly.

"You don't even know if he's any good around horses."

"Then let's ask Wayne and find out."

To Stefan's obvious disappointment, when they did ask him, Wayne reluctantly admitted that Gillie had the finest healing hands of any groom he'd ever seen. But he also said, during a frantically whispered conference in Wayne's office, with Gillie waiting patiently outside, "I don't think it's a good idea, Briar. We tolerate Gillie on the backside because he's always around. I don't think he has any other home, to be frank. But he goes on binges that'd make your hair stand on end. Do you really want someone on your ranch like that?"

"Do you think he worked once for Caulfield Farm?" Briar asked.

Wayne shook his head. "He says he did. In fact, it's all he

talks about at times. Once you get him started on that, you won't be able to shut him up. But—''

''Good,'' Briar said. To Stefan's dismay, Gillie came back with them on the plane, sitting wide-eyed in the first-class seat across the aisle from them, his fingers clamped so tightly to the arm rests that Briar had to gently pry him loose when they touched down at San Francisco International again.

But he took to the horses as if they were old friends, and after a while, even Stefan had to admit that Gillie was a big help. He was the one to call to calm a restless mare; he always seemed to know, even before any other sign, when one was ready to foal. He was the best hand even Stefan had ever seen with a sick horse. And, as time went on, and Gillie stayed sober, Stefan withheld final judgment. Briar was happy, Gillie seemed to fit right in, and after a while, it was as if he'd always been there.

---

# CHAPTER TWENTY

When Charlotte saw the headlines splashed across page one of *The Daily Racing Form*, she threw down the paper with a curse. It had been bad enough several months ago with a banner screaming: INCANDESSENCE RETURNS IN TRIUMPH!, praising the first successful outing—one of several, it turned out, Charlotte thought blackly—of the former Kentucky Derby winner that Briar had bought last year. Now this recent victory after a string of seven previous by Briar's so-called Cinderella filly was too much. Muttering to herself, Charlotte snatched up the paper again. This headline read: CAULFIELD FARM'S TOUCH THE FIRE BLAZES HER WAY INTO THE WINNER'S CIRCLE— AGAIN!

''Touch the Fire, the spectacular two-year-old distaff runner who burst onto the racing scene in May by winning Santa Anita's restricted La Contessa Stakes by four lengths, has once again proved she's more than a match for the boys.

Yesterday, during the running of the mile Burton Oaks, the Cinderella filly took charge right out of the starting gate, racing wire-to-wire and easily holding off a late stretch drive by Stone Martin Farm's formidable colt, San Marcos. Owned by Briar McKenna, of Caulfield Farm, the coal-black Touch the Fire has never been headed in eight impressive outings. Purchased for five thousand dollars at last year's Keeneland Breeding Stock Sales, this filly has proved to be first-class all the way. . . ."

With another annoyed exclamation, Charlotte threw down the paper. She was in the living room with her father and her brother, who was sitting, as always, with a drink in one hand while he pored over some boring papers from the office. Rupert was reading an edition of the *Chronicle*, but when he heard her disgusted sound, he looked over the top of the page in her direction.

"You have a comment about something?" he inquired mildly.

Aggravated, she gestured with the *Racing Form*. "That filly of Briar McKenna's has won another race."

"Oh, yes," he said, returning to his paper. "I saw that."

Charlotte sat where she was for a few seconds. Finally, she couldn't stand it any longer. "Don't you care?" she demanded. "For Christ's sake, Father—"

He didn't even put down the section he was reading. Maddeningly, his voice came disembodied from behind it. "There's no need to swear, Charlotte."

"No need to—!" She looked furiously at his newspaper for a moment, tempted to leap up and snatch it from his hands. "I just don't understand you," she exclaimed. "How can you sit there so calmly when Briar is racing the filly of the decade?"

"What's the matter, Lottie?" Carl said from his chair. He grinned slyly. "Jealous?"

"Of course not. Don't be absurd." she snapped. But she was; she couldn't help it. She'd been breeding horses for twenty-five years, and only two years ago managed to produce a colt that was probably the only two-year-old in the entire damned country of either sex who could *touch* Briar's damnable Cinderella filly. Why shouldn't she be jealous? It was maddening, infuriating—and what was a hundred times worse was that, despite her envy, she couldn't help feeling a grudging admiration for this upstart. That alarmed her even more. She didn't want to admire Briar McKenna; she didn't want to like her. She wanted to hate the woman, to revile and despise her. When the time came—and it would—she wouldn't give a damn that she, Charlotte Jaeger, was the one who had put the unsuspecting new owner of Caulfield Farm in position for Rupert to destroy. Jealousy warred with admiration and guilt, and she was in such a state that she didn't even know how she felt anymore, just that she wished to *hell* she'd never gotten involved. Oh, why had she ever tried to be so smart?

"Well, I wouldn't worry about it, Charlotte," Rupert said, slightly lowering the paper so that he could look at her. "She won't be getting those headlines long—at least not that kind, anyway."

She wasn't in the mood to be baited, especially by him. "Oh?" she said witheringly. "I suppose you know something I don't?"

"I do," Rupert said, glancing at Carl, who had gotten up from his paperwork to freshen his drink.

"Well, in that case, would you *mind* sharing it with me?"

"It's too early to talk about it yet."

"What's that supposed to mean?"

"It means," Carl said, turning from the bar, "that you can just mind your own business."

She glared at him. "I *am* minding my own business," she told him. "In case you hadn't noticed, *I* run Mondragon Stud, and I don't like just sitting by while you two hatch some kind of plan. I'm involved in this, too, you know."

"Oh, indeed we do," Carl said nastily. "Considering that it's all your fault."

"Are we going to get into that again?" she cried, infuriated. "What's done is done. When are you going to accept that?"

Carl's expression turned even uglier. "When that woman is destroyed utterly."

"Well, it certainly doesn't look like *that's* going to happen in the near future, does it?" Charlotte sneered back as a finger of dread ran down her spine. "In fact, it wouldn't surprise me if she gets an Eclipse award. Or even more to the point, if that damned filly is nominated Horse of the Year!"

Setting aside his paper, Rupert said calmly. "Neither is outside the realm of possibility, I agree. I see that bothers you."

"Doesn't it bother *you*?" she countered. "Or are you trying to tell me that you've put aside this stupid vendetta of yours so that you can become a good sportsman?"

Her jibe scored; she had the satisfaction of seeing him flush. But all he said was, "I've always admired good horseflesh."

"Really?" she said acidly. "You certainly have a strange way of showing it. Perhaps you've forgotten that *I* have a contender, too, in my two-year-old colt, Galland."

"On the contrary," Rupert replied, carefully folding the newspaper he'd been reading into a neat square. "In fact, after his last stakes victory, he has been much on my mind."

"Oh?" she said sharply. She didn't care for his tone. "And why is that?"

Calmly, Rupert set aside the paper. "In time, my dear," he said. "In time."

She definitely didn't like that. "I'm afraid that's not good enough, Father."

"And I'm afraid it will have to be," he countered, taking out his pocket watch and pressing the spring to open the ornate case. As she always did whenever he took out the watch to end a conversation, Charlotte had the urge to snatch it out of his hand and grind it to pieces under her heel. She hated the watch; it always seemed to be keeping something other than time.

Still at the bar, where he was lounging like a lout on the counter, Carl commented, "Whatever else we might think of her, she certainly seems to have the Midas touch."

Charlotte turned to look at him. "Strange words from you, who regard her as a dire enemy."

Carl shrugged. "True, but even I confess a sneaking admiration for someone who can turn lead to gold."

She didn't know why, but she felt an absurd obligation to try to convince them that Briar wasn't as good as they all knew her to be.

"It's luck, that's all it is," she said. "Just plain luck! Who could have guessed that a horse with no breeding, no background, no . . . no *nothing* could have come as far and fast as this?"

"She did," Carl said.

His words stopped her, but only for an instant. Another thought occurred to her, and she said, "You know, I just don't understand you, Carl. I would have thought you'd be furious at her success, but instead you're practically gloating about it. In fact,'' she said, narrowing her eyes, ''you both are. Now, why, I wonder, is that?''

''It's for us to know and you to find out,'' Carl said, smirking into his drink.

But Charlotte had already forgotten him. She had just thought of something, and she was too preoccupied to joust with her brother. Thinking back to what had happened at that Breeding Stock Sale at Keeneland, when Briar had made such a splash buying Incandessence, she said slowly, ''Father, did you know that Briar was looking at Touch the Fire during that breeding stock sale at Keeneland?''

Snapping the pocket watch shut, Rupert smiled. ''Of course I knew.''

''Then why didn't you bid against her on that horse, as you did with the other three?''

''Bid against her on the black filly? Are you out of your mind, Charlotte? What would I want with that thing? As you said yourself, she has no breeding, no pedigree—nothing. Why would I have wanted her?''

Charlotte didn't know, but she decided that as soon as dinner was over, she'd go upstairs and begin searching through her extensive library of breeding and pedigree reference books. Her father never did anything without a reason, and the answer had to be there. She was sure of it. All she had to do was look in the right place.

One of the maids, Mona, appeared in the doorway to the living room. ''Dinner is served,'' she said in her soft voice, and disappeared.

Thoughtfully, Charlotte glanced at her brother as they all got up to file into the dining room. Carl was taking this news about Briar in stride, too, and she wondered why. Despite his indifferent attitude about the horses, she knew her brother was hardly detached about the revenues they generated. He insisted on going over her books every month himself, and he was always on the lookout for ways she could save a penny here, or shave a dime there, in the running of the ranch. But as for the horses themselves, she knew he wouldn't have been able to group them by sex, let alone recite their names, and he certainly wouldn't have recognized any of them even if he'd had a list. He'd always been that way; even as a child he preferred to be anywhere but at the barn.

But that was her fault, wasn't it? she thought guiltily, as she accepted the soup but waved away the fish. She was the one responsible for her brothers' lifelong fear of horses, and she'd never been able to deny her responsibility. But for her, Carl could have been killed, and it would have been her fault.

It had been early March, she remembered, the time when the fruitless plum trees were just starting to display pink and purple flowers, and in the fields the mustard grass was beginning to turn yellow. She recalled that it had been a wet winter, and the ground was still mushy and treacherous. At twelve years old, Charlotte was considered far too young to help out with the training—a decision she bitterly resented, especially after her father had installed a half-mile training oval around the perimeter of the property so the horses could be worked before sending them down to train at the big racetracks.

Unfortunately, because of the rain, no one had been able to use it that winter; in fact, Rupert had forbidden anyone to ride there because he didn't want the surface pitted. Charlotte still remembered many a day that winter when she had been stuck inside the house staring out at the enticing strip of track and wishing the rain would stop so she could go out and saddle one of the horses. At her age, she had been riding for eight years and had never been afraid of any horse, even their premier stallion at the time, a mean-tempered seventeen-hand Thoroughbred named, appropriately, Mad Jack.

On that day the horses seemed restless as well; too much rain and too much inactivity were taking their toll. Finally, Charlotte decided to brave her father's wrath and take one lap around that tempting track. When Carl, two years younger, discovered her sneaking out, he had to know what she was doing. When she told him, he immediately yelled that he was going to tell.

"Don't you dare!" she'd hissed, dragging him inside the barn so that no one would hear. It was midmorning, and because of the endless downpour no one was there. The hands had come in at their usual time at dawn, hurried through the feeding and cleaning of stalls, and then gone home again. All the tack had long since been cleaned and repaired; even on a ranch their size, there was nothing more to do but wait until the storm passed. The twenty-stall barn was quiet except for the comforting sounds of horses chomping away on what was left of their breakfasts—and, far down the line, Mad Jack pacing back and forth, restless as always.

Charlotte knew that her father had ordered that Jack be left in; the fields and pastures were so wet he didn't want to take the chance of letting the horse out to run. Last spring one of the colts had broken a leg—just snapped it at the knee—when it stepped into a gopher hole, and even though he didn't seem to care much about the horses except for what they produced, Rupert didn't want the same thing to happen to his best stallion.

But Charlotte reasoned that nothing could happen on the training track, which had been graded and leveled and carefully constructed with seven kinds of dirt and gravel. As she grabbed Jack's bridle from its peg in the tack room, Carl's eyes had widened.

"You wouldn't dare!" he exclaimed, titillated and frightened at the same time. Because of the stallion's uncertain temperament, Charlotte had been expressly forbidden to get near the horse much less ride it. There had been no need to issue similar orders to Carl, who, much to his father's disgust, had always been timid around horses. Charlotte had never understood Rupert's attitude about Carl, since her father never rode, either. In fact, she didn't really know why he kept the horses; he rarely went out to the barn, and he certainly never touched them if he could help it.

But because she loved them so, she was glad he continued the operation—for whatever reason—and this day, she had been determined to ride the stallion.

"I'm going to," Charlotte had said, starting down the aisle. "You can't stop me."

"Oh, yes, I can!" cried her tattletale brother. "I can call Father!"

Charlotte knew what would happen if he did; furiously she rounded on him. Her father was at work in the city, but he was as close as the telephone. "If you try," she said, advancing, "I'll lock you in Jack's stall myself, and then what will happen?"

Even at ten, Carl had been doughy. His round face paled. "You wouldn't. . . ."

But she had. She remembered it so clearly, even to this day, and that had been forty years ago now. Without even trying, she could recall the sweet hay smell that surrounded them as she dragged Carl down the aisle, possessed of some devilment she couldn't explain. Probably it had been prompted by restlessness and boredom, or maybe the mean-spiritedness that all children possess at times. Whatever it was, Carl was forever terrified of horses after that; Charlotte had completely lost any chance of her father's respect; and worst of all, Mad Jack had paid the ultimate price.

Even now she didn't know what had possessed her to unlock the stall door and push Carl. Maybe she'd thought to teach him a lesson. She wasn't sure herself even now, but she remembered feeling sorry the instant she slammed the stall door with Carl inside. When he screamed in terror, her blood actually ran cold. She had never heard a sound like that; she hoped never to again. Faced with the huge seventeen-hand horse in a confined space, Carl had taken one look and become absolutely hysterical.

As frightened and terrified as she was at that point, she still thought of herself. What if someone had seen? In her instant of indecision, she heard Jack paw the floor, then he squealed. She didn't remember until then that Carl was wearing his precious baseball cap, the one he'd gotten at the only ball game Rupert had ever taken him to. Mad Jack hated stall cleaners; the stallion especially hated stall cleaners with caps on. A long time ago one of the grooms, wearing a cap similar to Carl's, had nearly beaten Jack to death with a pitchfork because the horse had bitten him. As horses do, the stallion had never forgotten; every time he saw a man with a cap in his stall, he squealed like that—just before he attacked.

All this Charlotte remembered—too late. Terrified now for her brother—and for her own endangered hide if her father found out what she had done—she threw herself against the stall door, shouting for Carl not to panic and tried to get in. But with Carl continuing to scream bloody murder, and Jack squealing like mad, she was so scared that she couldn't get the door open. The latch resisted her shaking fingers, and she began shouting for help as she pulled frantically at the unyielding iron. No one heard; the rain was coming down too hard. Everyone was inside. She knew if Carl was going to be rescued, she had to do it herself.

Somehow she unfroze the latch and desperately opened the stall door just as Jack started to charge. Carl had crumpled into a tight little ball in one corner of the stall to protect himself from the heavy hooves. As the stallion reared up, preparing to strike, Charlotte screamed at the horse to get his attention and began waving her arms wildly, trying to divert him.

She was more successful than she realized. In her terror and confusion, she had forgotten to shut the door again. When Jack saw the path to freedom, he took it. Already agitated by the storm and all the screaming and shouting, the horse charged right through, tossing Charlotte aside as if she were straw, thundering down the aisle and out of the barn.

Flung to one side of the aisle, her head meeting the edge of the door with a sharp crack, Charlotte saw stars. With a quick look to make sure that Carl was all right, she hauled herself up and charged after Jack. She had to get help; a stallion running wild was a thought too awful to contemplate. If he didn't hurt himself, he'd terrorize the other horses. When she suddenly remembered another story about a gentle old gelding he'd savaged to the point where the poor thing had to be put down, she started screaming her head off as she pelted down the aisle. She was beyond worrying about what was going to happen to her; she had to get help before something even worse occurred.

She was too late. Half a dozen hands came rushing out from their cottages when they saw the stallion burst out of the barn at a dead run; horsemen all, they managed somehow to turn him in the direction of the training track where they hoped he would run until exhausted. No one mentioned the possibility of his jumping the rail and racing off. Clinging to the fence with everyone else, Charlotte was just beginning to hope that things were going to turn out well after all when the stallion suddenly stumbled. Before their horrified eyes, Mad Jack went down with a shrill whinny. When she saw him thrashing trying to get up, she knew what had happened.

"No." She had whispered, terrified. She was responsible for this; she couldn't believe her eyes. Rain was still falling, mingling with the stinging tears running down her cheeks. When she saw the men start to run toward the fallen horse, she wanted to go away someplace forever and hide. "No!" she cried when someone turned and ran back for a rifle. She put her hands over her face. How was she going to explain to her father?

She jumped down off the rail and whirled around—right into Rupert. She hadn't known he was there; she hadn't expected him. He was always at his office in San Francisco at this hour; the storm must have prompted him to come home early. Practically fainting with fear and fright, she looked up into his cold, set face. She had never been so scared of him, not even the time she'd locked Carl in the grain bin and he had found out about it. He wasn't looking at her; his eyes focused out across the field where the little group of men stood huddled around the flailing horse. When the shot rang out, Charlotte cried out and cringed, but Rupert didn't move a muscle, except for his eyes. When he looked down at her, she wanted to die.

Sitting in the dining room nearly forty years later, Charlotte relived that day as if it were yesterday. Every detail was engraved on her memory, for nothing had ever been resolved from that incident. Her father had never spoken of it, had never blamed her, had never *reacted* with so much as a flicker of an eyelid. All he had done was turn around and go inside to call his lawyer. He told the man that he wanted to sue the contractor who had built the training track; one of his horses had just broken its leg there, so obviously the work had been shoddy and he wanted his money back. That was all. There had been no emotion in his voice, no anger, no pain—nothing whatsoever.

Huddled in misery by the doorway, thinking only that her father would never forgive her now because of what she had done, Charlotte had been too young then to realize that she hadn't been on Rupert's mind at all. In fact, once the call to the lawyer had been made and the carcass of the horse hauled away in the rain, he had forgotten the incident completely. And she, she realized later, was so concerned with her own fate that she had completely forgotten about her brother, who was found by someone still curled into a tight frozen ball in Mad Jack's empty stall. Because he had been incoherent and unresponsive, the doctor had been called.

But Rupert didn't believe in coddling his children. When his wife, Hermione, either refused or was unable to deal with the emergency he dismissed the physician and threw out all the soothing medicines the man had ordered, maintaining that there was nothing wrong with Carl other than the fact that he had yet to learn how to be a man. And as for Charlotte . . .

For a young girl who dreamed only of living forever at home, taking care of her beloved horses and running the ranch, she had received the ultimate punishment. Without recourse or discussion, her father had banished her to a boarding school in Chicago where she served out her term until she graduated. The school had no stables, and there were none for miles around. It wouldn't have mattered anyway; during those years she was not allowed to leave the grounds, not even for holidays or school vacations. The only time she was permitted to come home was when her mother died—and then, only for the funeral. Still wearing the black dress she had worn to the cemetery, she returned to Chicago to finish her education.

All during her long, lonely exile, Charlotte had believed that she was being punished for what had happened that rainy day she shut her brother in that stall. It took her years to realize that the incident had just been a convenient excuse to send her away. She had never gotten along with her mother, a tall, unhappy woman who was given to bouts of gaiety that quickly turned to fits of depression, but she had loved her father, whole-heartedly and without reservation, even though he was a cold, withdrawn man.

But during her stay in Chicago, all that changed. An excellent student because she had no choice in the matter, she had few friends and much time to ponder many things. As year after year went by without her being allowed to come home, she was finally forced to accept the inescapable conclusion that her father didn't love her in return. As time went on, she began to realize that Rupert Jaeger was incapable of loving anyone. The only thing he seemed to live for—other than making Mondragon Enterprises more powerful each year—was his obsession with the Caulfields. Long before she reached adulthood, she had accepted that nothing in this life or any other mattered as much to Rupert Jaeger as the chance to avenge himself against his old enemies. Not even his wife's suicide seemed to have much impact on him; nor did Carl's later brushes with the law when, at sixteen and seventeen, he started drinking and joyriding and picking up girls all over town. Wordlessly, Rupert paid the tickets and hired a lawyer when necessary to keep his son out of jail. He brought Carl into the company as his right-hand man when Carl turned twenty-one. But through it all he was untouchable, emotionless—except when the name of his enemy was mentioned.

When Heinrich had died, Rupert had inherited everything: the ranch, the horses, Mondragon Enterprises. But he had also inherited his father's hatred and profound mistrust of anyone named Caulfield. Charlotte knew that her father lived for the day when he would redress old injuries, when he would finally, and with pitiless satisfaction, take back what he felt had been stolen from him. Now she wondered if she had done the right thing in finding Briar McKenna and returning her to Caulfield Farm. She'd thought she was so clever; she had wanted a little revenge of her own after the way her father treated her. At least by finding Briar and installing her close by she'd get her father's attention, but now it seemed she had more than that. What had he meant about Galland? He surely wasn't thinking of taking him over!

She had never consciously admitted it, but she had always secretly harbored the dream that if she only proved herself where the horses were concerned—making Mondragon Stud a name to be reckoned with and respected as a breeder of fine horses—she would one day win her father's approval. She'd thought that if she once bred a true champion, a Triple Crown winner, Rupert would finally be proud of her and would finally forgive her.

Well, now she had her contender—the big chestnut colt called Galland. The young stallion was just two, but he had been so impressive in his first outings that she knew he could only get better. She had brought him along so carefully, spacing his two-year-old races with care, thrilled every time he came home first at the wire. With Mondragon's trainer, Laine Magree, down at Hollywood Park, Galland had made his debut in January at Santa Anita and won. In February, he had easily taken the Santa Teresita Stakes, then romped home to victory in two more stakes races. He had scored by five in the San Bruno Handicap, and then, in his most impressive outing yet, had blazed home in the Hollywood Juvenile. Already Laine was being asked if Galland was headed East to the Belmont Futurity or the Saratoga Special. They hadn't agreed on anything yet, but she and Laine had discussed it the last time she'd gone down to see him.

But she still hadn't liked her father's earlier remark, and as dessert was served, she said, "What did you mean a while ago when you said you'd been thinking about Galland?"

"Didn't you hear me, Charlotte?" Rupert answered. "I told you, all in good time."

She hated being spoken to in that way, as if she were still a terrified twelve-year-old child. Her lips tight, she said, "And

I told *you*, that's not good enough, Father. Galland is *my* horse, and I decide what's best for him.''

The only one to accept dessert, Carl looked at her from his place across the table, his fork raised. ''Aren't you forgetting who supports the ranch, Lottie?''

She might have to endure that patronizing tone from her father, but she wouldn't put up with it from Carl. ''And aren't you forgetting to whom you're speaking? I pay the bills for Mondragon Stud, so I'll thank you to stay out of this.''

''I'll stay out of it when you review the books again, Lottie. Or have you conveniently forgotten that outstanding loan you have with Mondragon Enterprises?''

''I told you—'' she began hotly, but just then, Rupert tapped his spoon against a glass. ''Children, children,'' he said. They looked at him with similar expressions of annoyance. ''Please, let's not argue at the dinner table.''

''Tell Carl that,'' Charlotte muttered. ''I don't know why he has to bait me!''

Rupert ignored her. ''I believe the subject was what we were going to do with Galland.''

Infuriated all over again, she demanded, ''Why do you keep saying 'we'? There is no we where Galland is concerned. I bred him, I raised him, I helped to train him, and—with Laine's help—I'm going to race him. When and where I choose. And that's final!''

''And Touch the Fire?'' Rupert asked, calmly dabbing at his lips with his napkin.

''What about her?''

''Do you think she and Galland will race against each other?''

She felt a flash of fear. She'd wondered that herself . . . wondered if even her swift colt could beat the filly who seemed to have wings on her heels. But she wasn't about to admit it, so she said, ''If they do, we'll see just how little that filly is made of. Why, she'll burn herself out in no time at all, just fizzle down to a little ember, and then—'' she snapped her fingers''—poof! Like so many of these so-called wonder horses, she'll be gone, never to be heard from again!''

''You're sure of that.''

''Yes, I am. I've seen it too many times not to know otherwise.''

''Perhaps people are saying the same thing about Galland.''

She was outraged. ''Who told you that?''

"No one," he said with a shrug. "I just wondered."

"Well, wonder no more. Galland is pure quality, with generations of excellent breeding behind him!"

"And in poor little Touch the Fire's pedigree, there is only . . . Fane."

Abruptly, Charlotte paused. Her father so rarely paid attention to bloodlines and genealogy that it took her a moment to absorb what he'd said about the filly. "How do you know that?" she asked sharply.

Rupert smiled. "I'm not so out of touch with these things as you'd like to believe, my dear," he said. "I may have given you the responsibility of running the ranch, but that doesn't mean I don't keep an eye on things."

Things were becoming clear. "You knew about the filly's background as far back as Keeneland, didn't you?" she demanded.

"Certainly."

"You knew—and all this time you never said anything?" She could hardly wait to run upstairs and check to see if he was right. Touch the Fire was distantly related to Fane? To *Fane*, the horse her grandfather had stolen from Sloane Caulfield in their notorious match race? Feeling feverish, she looked at her father again. "Why?"

Rupert gave his lips one last dab, then set aside his napkin. But instead of answering her directly, he said, "Tell me about this Wayne Kaminsky, who's training the McKenna filly."

"Kaminsky is a pompous, know-it-all, arrogant jerk," she lied. She was still trying to put two and two together. She knew her father had his reasons for this, and she wanted to know what they were. "However," she added grudgingly, "I've never heard even a word about him, and that's quite a feat in the racing world."

"Yes, but does he know how to train horses."

"You've seen his results with Incandessence and Touch the Fire. Judge for yourself."

"Can he be bought?"

"Bought?" Charlotte straightened. "Why do you ask that?"

He shrugged. "No reason. It was just of mild interest."

She didn't believe him. "Well, the answer is no, Kaminsky can't be bought." Then she gestured irritably. "But why are we having this discussion, anyway? It's all academic. If they ever do meet, Galland is going to beat Touch the Fire, and that's all there is to it!''

"You're sure of that."

"Of course I'm sure," she exclaimed.

"You say this Kaminsky can't be bribed. I'm assuming that Laine can't be, either.''

She couldn't believe him. "Surely, you don't think Briar—''

"I think the Caulfields are capable of anything, Charlotte.''

"But Briar isn't a Caulfield!"

"She has the blood," Rupert stated. "And there are always . . . ways . . . to win races, aren't there?''

Before Charlotte could reply, Carl finished the last of his wine. "Like there was in that other match race between Sloane Caulfield's Fane and our own Ulrich, Father?'' he said, carefully setting down his glass.

Neither Charlotte nor Carl had been born at the time of the famous match race between the foundation stallions for their two ranches, but the story had been preserved and passed down. Charlotte had heard it so many times herself that she could have repeated it from memory. Her grandfather Heinrich had challenged Sloane Caulfield to a race between their stallions, in a match where the winner had his pick of the other's stock . . . and Sloane had accepted the challenge, only to accuse Heinrich's jockey of cheating when Mondragon's Ulrich won. Charlotte knew the tale so well that in her mind's eye she could practically see the horses take their marks that day and could hear the bell signaling the start of the race. She had pictured it so many times that she could hear the thundering of hoofbeats as the two great horses leaped off the line and flew down the road toward the old tree and back. She could see them: one bold and black, the other, her grandfather's esteemed Ulrich, a pale gray, racing side by side until, inch by inch, one started to pull away. The race had been a true test of courage and endurance—two miles over the hills, each horse carrying weights of over one hundred and thirty pounds. Clockers and impromptu stewards had been stationed along the way to make sure that the race was run cleanly. But there was a lot of territory to cover, and anything could happen—or so she had heard tell.

Because she was a Jaeger, she wanted to believe that Ulrich had been the bigger, the stronger, the more fleet. But she had heard once from an old man who had been there at the time that no horse on this earth could match Caulfield's Fane.

Charlotte knew the outcome of the race; everybody knew. But what had really happened even the old man wouldn't say. He'd only told her that men raced horses for the thrill of the game. All sorts of factors came into play when horses met on the starting line, and maybe, for some reason, one of those great stallions just hadn't wanted to run that day.

"You never know," the old man had told her, "what gets into a horse's mind when he takes his place at the gate. It could be his day, or it could not. It's all up to him when the flag goes up."

What would be in Galland's mind if he ever met Briar's spectacular filly? And what fate might decree that the race be a match race? Charlotte wondered. And then, in sudden awful comprehension, she turned to look at her father. "You're not thinking . . ." she said, her voice choked. She couldn't finish.

Galland was the product of an entire life devoted to raising Thoroughbreds, and she hadn't spent all her days designing and refining and fine-tuning her breeding program to lose out on the chance of a lifetime like a shot at the Triple Crown. Behind Galland was all her experience and knowledge, her reputation as a horsewoman and as a breeder. A colt like hers came along just once. Like every other horsebreeder who ever stood over a mare in labor and waited for the dream to emerge, she knew instinctively that this was the one. Oh, yes, there was only one dream horse, Charlotte thought—just one, if you were lucky. For Sloane and Marguerite Caulfield, it had been Fane. For her grandfather, Heinrich, it had been Ulrich. And for her, it was Galland.

"Now, then, Charlotte," Rupert said calmly, rising to leave the table. "Have I said anything?"

Much later that night, when, too restless to sleep, she had thrown on a coat and had gone to check the horses in the barn, Charlotte thought about the pedigree on Touch the Fire that she had traced all the way back. She felt a chill. Once again, she heard Carl's mocking voice in her mind.

*Like that other match race, Father?*

The words echoed in her head, and she shivered. Without warning, she suddenly felt sick.

---

# CHAPTER TWENTY-ONE

One of the worst things that anyone working on the backside of the track could hear during or after a race was the cry: Horse broke down! Briar heard it one October day when she and Stefan were in Los Angeles for the running of the Norfolk Stake, a prestigious race for two-year-olds, in which Touch the Fire had been entered. It would be the filly's last race of the season before she came back for her three-year-old year, and Briar was glad it was over. Caulfield Farm had had a spectacular racing season so far, and she didn't want to break her lucky streak by having something happen now when things had gone so well. She had recently retired her magnificent Incandessence, who had won four major stakes races after her triumphant return to the track, and who was home now preparing for motherhood in the coming year, and Ten Diamonds had done very well. But it was Touch the Fire, her little Cinderella horse, as she was called by the press, who had preformed beyond Briar's wildest imaginings.

But enough was enough, and she and Wayne and Stefan all agreed that they couldn't ask the gallant black filly for more this year. If she won today, she would come back as an unbeaten three-year-old, along with her stablemate at home, Night Fever, who was still recovering from the hairline fracture she had sustained the first week she'd been at Caulfield Farm. Briar had been distraught when the accident occurred, but as Wayne—and Stefan—both had assured her, these things happened with horses, and they were all lucky it hadn't been worse. She tried to be as philosophical as they were, but she just wasn't able to manage such savoir faire. Her horses were important to her, and when something happened to one of them, it was as if it had happened to someone in her family.

But everything was fine this day as she and Stefan waited for the running of the big race. Or as fine as things were going to get, Briar thought, glancing at Stefan as they walked toward the stable entrance to the track so they could watch the next race. She'd kept herself so busy these past months since Dancin' Light died that it was starting to be obvious even to her that all her activity was a front to keep Stefan at arm's length. She still felt badly about the way she had shut him out, but she had been so frightened of her feelings that she couldn't do anything else. She hadn't been ready for a relationship then, she knew; maybe she still wasn't. So she kept herself so occupied at the office, at the ranch, with the horses, with traveling back and forth to the racetrack, that she didn't have to think about it . . . or at least, not too much. But she knew she wasn't being fair to Stefan, who deserved an explanation, if nothing else, and she had just drummed up enough courage to say something when that dreaded cry, "Horse broke down!" went up.

The second race had just been run, and as soon as she and Stefan heard the shout, they stopped where they were. Briar knew by this time that it could mean anything from a fractured leg to a pulled muscle, but no matter what was ultimately decided, the reaction was the same: a horse was hurt, and people started moving—fast.

As soon as word flashed down the line, the barn where the injured animal was stabled came even more alive than it had been during the busy morning. The stable manager emerged from his office at a run; grooms went racing toward the track armed with blankets and halters and wraps of all kinds; the stable veterinarian was paged over the loud speaker; the horse ambulance was put on alert. When a horse broke down after a race, the best thing was if it could leave the track under its own power; spectators didn't get so upset, and things went smoother. But if the injury was very serious, the ambulance was summoned and the victim carried off.

They were still standing there when the horse came hobbling out. As soon as Briar saw the poor thing, tears came to her eyes. She had seen this horse being led to the saddling enclosure only a few minutes before the race and had been impressed with the way it pranced, ears pricked forward, looking eager and ready to run. Now, little more than half an hour later, the transformation was pitiful. No longer bursting with life, the suffering animal limped along, eyes glazed, head hanging down. Sweat still gleamed wetly on its shiny coat; a network of swollen veins snaked under its thin skin—still pumped from the exertion of the race, and now, from pain.

Seeing her expression as the horse slowly went by, Stefan tried to lead her away. "Come on," he said, taking hold of her arm. "You don't need to see this."

Briar loved horses, not only her own. She wanted to be able to help this one even though she knew there was nothing she could do. Three grooms surrounded the animal; farther along, waiting at the entrance to the barn, one of the track veterinarians, a young blond woman named Kara Voss, had just pulled up in a cloud of dust and raced around to the back of her truck. Pulling open the doors to the big vet pak that held all her equipment, she began dispensing medication. While she selected different drugs and filled syringes, she cast a quick professional eye over the horse as the grooms led it carefully into the barn.

Her own glance still following the sad little procession, Briar said to Stefan, "What do you think happened?"

"Maybe a tendon," he said with a shrug. "Can't tell without a closer look."

Her face troubled, she met his eyes. Beyond the buildings, the shrubbery, and the fence lining this back part of the track, she could hear the murmur of the grandstand crowd, low at first, and then swelling with excitement as another race went off. As cruel as it was, racing went on, no matter who was hurt. "Do you think he'll be all right?" she asked.

"It depends," Stefan said, shoving his hands in his pockets. In honor of the race today, he was wearing slacks and a shirt topped by a tan corduroy sport coat. The blue in his shirt matched his eyes, and with his longish hair and mustache, he looked masculine and stylish and—she hated to admit it—sexy as all get out. She had seen some of the exercise girls eyeing him as they walked along, and she couldn't blame them for looking. She'd cast a few glances his way herself.

"On what?" she said, trying to distract herself by thinking of the injured horse.

"On how valuable he is to the owner, of course. If it was a stallion or a mare . . ." He shrugged.

She knew what he meant, but she didn't like to think about it. Geldings like Mi Flor Amor, who had just been hurt, lived on borrowed time at the track. If a breedable horse—a stallion or mare—was injured, there was at least a chance that the owner could recoup lost racing revenues by breeding it back. For a gelding that option didn't exist, of course, and so it depended upon how serious the injury was, how much potential the horse had compared to how it might race in the future, or, finally, how compassionate the owner was. But as Wayne himself had once so eloquently put it, "To a lot of owners around here, Briar, sentiment is just a word in the dictionary between senile and shit."

Slowly, Briar turned and looked in the direction of the barn where they'd taken the horse. Another muted roar from across the track floated back to her; vaguely she realized that an inquiry had been resolved or a photo finish decided. Maybe the crowd was just cheering for the fact that some of the smog seemed momentarily to have lifted. Santa Anita was one of the most beautiful racetracks in the country, perhaps in the world, if one could see it. Nestled against the foothills that sometimes trapped fumes from the freeways, Briar had been here on days when the smog was so thick she couldn't see across the track. Today was one of those days; a vile yellow-brown haze hung over everything like a pall, making it hard even to breathe. As she debated about what she wanted to do, she wondered how the horses felt, going all out.

Stefan saw the look on her face. "Briar," he said, "it's none of your business."

She supposed it wasn't, but then she saw Kara come out to the truck again, and on impulse she started over. "I'll be right back," she called over her shoulder to Stefan, and she could just feel his look of exasperation as he reluctantly followed.

Kara was filling more syringes and writing things down in a leather-covered book when Briar came up. Brushing blond bangs out of her blue eyes, she gave Briar a smile and held up a finger while she finished writing. They knew each other, for Dr. Voss was also Wayne's veterinarian, and she had kept a careful watch on all Briar's horses, especially Incandessence, to make sure the valuable mare was running sound on that pastern.

"Hi, Briar," she said, obviously distracted. "How's it goin'?"

Briar knew Kara's time was valuable, especially right at the moment, so she didn't waste words. "I just saw that horse come off the track," she said. "Is he going to be okay?"

Kara shut the book she was writing in. She hesitated for a

moment, then pushed her hair behind her ears with a sigh. "Given time, and about eight months off, he would be—in any other business. But the owner doesn't want to fiddle around with a torn tendon, so no . . . I'm afraid not." Throwing down her notebook with a thud, she said, "We got a date in the Blue Room after the last race."

The Blue Room was a walled-in area across the turf course and behind a high hedge where horses were taken to be euthanized. As Briar stood silent, Kara stood up abruptly, turning to arrange the back of her truck again. Shoving drawers containing medications, bottles, bandages, syringes, and all sorts of other necessary paraphernalia back into place, she quickly washed her hands in the little portable sink. Briar could tell she was upset, as all good veterinarians are when they're contemplating putting a horse down—especially for such little reason. As she watched Kara finish up, she knew what she had to do. The thought of Mi Flor Amor being put to sleep simply because the owner didn't want the expense or the bother of letting him get well again was too much, and she said, "If that tendon had a chance to heal, would the horse be serviceably sound?"

Behind her, Stefan knew what was coming, and he groaned, but she ignored him.

Kara looked from one to the other. "Sure. I'll have to x-ray to be sure, but with care and some time off, he'll go sound." A fleeting look of disgust crossed her face, the only emotion she permitted herself to show. "All it takes is a few months," she said, and then paused. "You're not thinking of . . . offering to buy him, are you? I said he'd be sound for riding. I didn't say he'd run again."

"I know that," Briar said. "But there are other things in life than racing. Will the owner sell?"

"Instead of taking a flat loss by putting the horse down? You've got to be kidding."

"No, she's out of her mind," Stefan said. "Briar, have you really thought about this? What are you going to do with a gelding who can't run?"

She had thought about it. "Put him in with Irish," she said at once. "He never gets out with any of the mares, and I bet he'd love the company."

He looked at her as if she were crazy. "You don't even know this horse—"

"Oh, he's a love," Kara contributed, smiling despite herself. All the good track veterinarians not only knew the names of the horses they cared for, but also their quirks and characteristics. To keep body and soul together, it behooved them to know which horses they could treat themselves, and which had to have a header; they needed to know who turned tail to an intruder and who only threatened by pinning his ears back. "A real character," she went on. "He likes to put his tongue out and let you play with it. He'll do it all day if you stand there and tickle him. In fact, we used to say that if he was ever in a dead heat sometime, he could just put his head out and win by a tongue."

Stefan didn't think it was so funny, but Briar laughed in delight. Kara laughed with her, until she remembered that Mi Flor Amor's racing days were over, then she sobered. "Are you really serious about this?" she asked. "Because if you are, I'll have Joe get in touch with the owner."

Joe Mendoza was the stable manager for this barn. Briar glanced at Stefan, who, after all, would have to make arrangements to care for another horse. Resigned, he lifted his hands. "Go ahead. It's your ranch."

Smiling, Briar went to see her new horse. Kara had given Mi Flor Amor pain-killing medication, and he was now standing in a huge tub of ice, his head down, and—as Kara had said—the pink tip of his tongue hanging out.

"You want to come home with me, big fella?" Briar murmured, gently stroking the gelding's neck. He really was a beautiful animal, she thought, and when he blew out a breath, and then stuck his tongue out for her, she laughed. "I think you and Irish will get along just fine," she said, giving him a final pat. "I'll be back later to check."

Outside, she made arrangements for Kara to find her after she'd talked to the owner. As an owner herself, Briar had boxes at both Santa Anita and Hollywood Park, and since Touch the Fire was due to run soon, she told Kara she'd be at the grandstand until after the race. "If I haven't heard from you by that time, I'll come back and check here," she promised.

Kara grinned. "After you leave the winner's circle, you mean," she said. "Good luck today—even though you won't need it. I went over Touch the Fire this morning with the proverbial fine-tooth comb. She's ready to bring it home again, probably with a new track record."

Briar glanced at the barn, where Mi Flor Amor was just

visible with his tub of ice. "You never know," she said soberly, "but thanks."

"No, thanks goes to you," Kara said, suddenly somber as she followed Briar's glance. "I didn't want to say anything, but I hated like hell the thought of putting this one down."

"Me, too," Briar agreed, and waved as Kara got in the truck and went off. She was smiling and happened to look at Stefan. When she saw his expression, her smile faded. "You don't approve, do you?"

"It's not up to me to approve or not. As I said, it's your ranch."

Suddenly annoyed with him, she said, "Stop saying that!"

"Why not? It's true."

"I know it's true. Still—" Irritably, she turned away. She knew she was deliberately allowing herself to get angry with him because she didn't want to say what was really on her mind, and a part of her knew she wasn't being fair, but she didn't seem able to help herself. She had grown up hiding her emotions, keeping her thoughts locked away in a private place, and even now, she wasn't sure what had happened to her that night Dancin' Light had died. Sometimes she thought she had sought the comfort of Stefan's arms because she was so lonely. Even though it hadn't been a year since Hay had died, it felt so long . . . so long. And apart from those five years she had been married, she had been alone much of her life. She had felt very alone that night, and she was sure Stefan had sensed it.

But he hadn't taken advantage of her, and she wasn't sure whether to be relieved or annoyed. Maybe she had wanted him to, she thought, so the decision would be out of her hands. But he hadn't, and she was left with the unwelcome conclusion that maybe he didn't want a relationship himself. How would she know what he wanted? Stefan never talked about himself or his feelings; except for the horses, he rarely offered an opinion about anything.

Did she want him to? She wasn't sure. She did know that once they crossed this invisible barrier they had both put up, they couldn't go back. What frightened her even more was that she didn't know how much she had to give anymore. She believed that what she'd had with Hayden had been something special, a once-in-a-lifetime miracle; she had never expected—or wanted—to feel like that again. Hay had been husband, lover, mentor, confidant, friend. She had believed she'd never have that again with any other man.

But then Stefan had come into her life, and everything got confused. She didn't like the little thrill she felt when she saw Stefan unexpectedly somewhere around the ranch—but she still felt it. She didn't like it that her heart leaped at the sound of Stefan's voice—but it did. She didn't want to listen for his footsteps or hope he'd be standing there when she looked up— but she did those things anyway, too. It was even more foolish when she realized that she knew nothing about his personal life; she really knew nothing about him at all except that she didn't want him to walk out of her life.

She couldn't explain it even to herself. Night after night, aching with loneliness, missing Hay, missing their physical closeness, missing the feeling of being with someone, a part of his life, she had tossed and turned in her big empty bed, thinking of Stefan asleep at his place, so near, and yet so damned far away. It wasn't a matter of physical distance; if she'd wanted, she could have gone down there and knocked. He might even have let her in. But she couldn't do it, not even to assuage the overwhelming need she felt. She couldn't be the only one who needed; if there was to be something between them, they both had to want it.

And did he? Realizing she'd been quiet too long, she glanced away, saying quickly, "Well, maybe we'd better get going. Isn't it almost time for the race?"

"No, we've got time," he said. Earlier, on the way in, he'd bought a racing program; now he had rolled it up and was slapping it distractedly against his thigh. "Damn it, Briar—" he said suddenly, and stopped.

At his outburst, she turned to look back. The slight breeze that was struggling to blow away some of the smog lifted his hair, stirring a sun-streaked lock across his eyes. Like the breeze, he looked as if he were struggling with something, too.

His expression made her aware that they were alone on this part of the shed row. Now that the excitement about Mi Flor Amor had died down, the area had emptied. The sporadic clip clop of horses being led by on the way to the paddock area was the only sound. That, and the sudden hard pounding of her heart. She was seeing something in Stefan's eyes that she hadn't seen before, and she didn't know what to think.

"What is it?" she asked. Maybe he was upset about her

buying the horse, she thought, and then realized how absurd she was being. Why should he care? It was nothing to him.

"I don't know," he said, crumpling the racing program in his hand. "It's just . . . just when I think I have you figured out, you go and . . . do something like this!"

She didn't know whether to laugh or be irritated. He wasn't the only one having problems figuring things out, she thought, and said, "Why are you so upset? It's not as if we don't have room at the ranch, and Gillie will be thrilled to have something to take care of besides broodmares and babies."

"I know, I know, it's not that."

She was beginning to feel a little exasperated. Why were they arguing? What were they arguing *about*?

"Then what?"

Shaking his head, he threw his crumpled program into the nearest trash can. "Never mind. Let's go and see Wayne before the race."

She still wasn't sure what was going on. "I can't believe you're angry about my buying that horse."

"I told you, it isn't that." He took her arm and tried to tug her along. "Why should I care if you buy a thousand crippled geldings? It doesn't matter to me."

"Then I don't understand why you're so upset."

"I'm not upset! It's just . . . oh, hell!" he said in exasperation, and stopped. Facing her, he said, "It's just that I've never known anybody like you, Briar. You keep a man off balance, you know? You're all business one minute—hard headed as hell, knowing exactly what you want and how to get it. And the next—the next, you're buying a horse you've never seen before and don't know beans about, because you feel *sorry* for it! Wouldn't anybody be confused? Wouldn't you?"

She had never seen him like this—not cool, composed, collected Stefan Yager, she thought. He looked so aggravated that she started to smile. He instantly looked furious.

"So you think this is funny?" he demanded. "I knew I shouldn't have said anything. Just forget it, all right? Just forget it."

To her dismay, he turned around and started walking away. She knew by the stiff set of his shoulders that she had offended him. Feeling guilty, she called his name and started after him. When he didn't stop or even look around, she grabbed his arm, forcing him to halt.

"Stefan, please, I'm sorry. I didn't mean to offend you."

He jerked away and kept walking. "I said, forget it."

She reached for him again. "No, I won't. I want to explain."

"There's nothing to explain."

"Yes, there is. I . . . Damn it, will you *stop*?" she finally cried. She didn't like having to trot along beside him while she was trying to apologize, and because she felt foolish, she began to feel angry as well. When she was angry, she too often said things she was sorry for later. Now, it seemed, was going to be one of those times.

"You're not the only one who's felt off kilter here, you know," she told him. "You said that you can't understand me—well, I've been trying to figure *you* out for months now!"

That stopped him. "Me? Why?"

"*Why?* Because you're so damned private, that's why! I never know what you're thinking—if you like working at the ranch, for instance. If you like your job, or the horses, or any of a hundred other things you have to do for me. If—"

"If I didn't like the job, do you think I'd stay?"

"How do I know? You keep so much to yourself that I don't know *what* you think!"

"All right. What do you want to know?"

How could she say that she wanted to know how he felt about her. If he felt anything at all? She didn't want to have to *ask*, she thought irately; she wanted him to *tell* her. To say something, anything at all.

"Never mind," she said angrily. "I don't want to know a damned thing, after all!"

With that, she turned around and started back down the aisle. She hadn't gone two steps before he caught up with her. "I'm sorry, Briar," he said. "That was . . . stupid. I shouldn't have baited you."

She wouldn't look at him. "No, you shouldn't have," she said coldly, and kept walking.

"I'm sorry," he said again.

"So am I," she said, her tone still frosty.

"Briar, listen to me."

"No."

"Yes!"

"Damn it, Stefan—"

She turned to face him just as he reached for her. She had a split second to decide. She could have pulled back and kept walking; it would have been simple. But her glance flashed up to his, and in that instant, what she saw in his eyes mirrored her own feelings. Then his arms went around her, and she stepped into him.

The touch of their bodies seemed to dissolve all her resistance and anger. When he put one hand behind her neck, spreading his fingers in her hair and looking down so briefly into her face, she didn't have time to think. A second later, his mouth came down hard on hers, and she was transported instantly to another place where every sense seemed heightened. In one moment, she felt the hard pound of his heart under the hand she put on his chest, the smoothness of his lips, and the tickle of his mustache. His after-shave was in her nostrils; his tongue was deep in her mouth; his body was hard against hers, demanding everything she suddenly wanted to give. His thighs pressed against hers, and she felt his burgeoning erection against her pelvis. Her answering response raced right through her entire body like wild fire. She made a strangled sound. It didn't seem to matter; all she could taste, feel, touch, and smell was Stefan.

With his mouth still hard on hers, he pulled her with him into the shadows of an empty stall. His breathing rasped in her ear; his hands roamed all over her body. He couldn't get enough of her, and she didn't want him to stop until he had touched every inch of her.

But then, dimly, from someplace outside, she heard a shout and realized they weren't alone here, after all. She knew then that if she didn't stop this somehow, her shaking legs wouldn't hold her; she'd fall to the floor and pull him with her. She wanted to, oh, she did. But then a shrill alarm went off inside her head, demanding an answer. *Do you really want it this way? Do you?*

Yes, yes, she did; she wanted him any way she could. It was ecstasy feeling his hard body against hers. She was pressed tightly against him, her breasts crushed against his chest, her hips locked into his. Their thighs trembled together, and when she put her hands on his tight buttocks and felt him move against her, she wanted to pull him deep, deep inside. The hardest thing she ever did was pull away and look up.

His hands shook at her waist. "Briar . . ." he said hoarsely, his eyes dazed. "What . . . why did you stop?"

She wasn't sure. She didn't know how she had. Stefan's kiss had released an intolerable tension inside her, a pressure that had been building ever since Hay's death. She had grieved; she had. But so many other things had happened this past year that she hadn't had time to put everything in its place. And through it all, she had kept herself so busy that she hadn't had time to realize how terribly lonely she had been.

No, that wasn't true, she thought as she looked up into Stefan's handsome, troubled face. She had known; she just hadn't wanted to admit it. Loneliness made her vulnerable, and she had always hated weakness. On some level, she knew that once she admitted her need for Stefan, something like this would happen, and she hadn't been ready. Was she ready now? She wasn't sure. She hadn't been prepared for the intensity of her reaction to him; it had been like a hurricane, an avalanche. She had been helpless, and she didn't like it.

Silently, she extricated herself from Stefan's embrace. She wasn't certain what to say, and she felt awkward just standing there.

Stefan obviously felt the same way. Running a hand through his hair, looking as if he'd just come through a storm himself, he said disjointedly, "Briar, I . . . I know—"

"Don't apologize," she said. "For God's sake, don't apologize!"

"I wasn't going to. I was going to say that even though I didn't mean for that to happen, I—I'm glad it did." He held her eyes. "I've been wanting to kiss you ever since I first saw you that day at the riding club."

She glanced away; the look on his face was too intense. She felt her body yearning toward him again. "I . . . I don't know what to say, Stefan," she confessed. "It's too . . . new."

"I know what you mean."

She looked quickly at him. "You do?"

He shook his head, as if to clear it. "What do you think? Do I look like I know what I'm doing? So, now what?"

She was more relieved than she knew. "Now," she said unsteadily, "we go watch a race."

"And then?" he asked.

"And then," she said, "we'll see."

Relieved to have the race to distract her, Briar briefly visited the saddling enclosure to see Touch the Fire before she went out and to wish Pat Shannon, the only jockey ever to ride the dazzling black filly, the best of racing luck.

"Oh, we won't need it, Ms. McKenna," Pat said with a grin as Wayne tossed him up into the saddle. "If ever a horse was born to run, this filly is it. Ridin' her is like flyin' without wings, I swear. We'll meet you in the winner's circle again, for sure."

"Just be careful out there," Briar said, giving the horse a pat. The filly blew out a whistling breath, dancing under her rider. Serious as always before a race, Wayne led her out and handed them off to the outrider. Seconds later, Briar heard the bugler announcing that the horses were on the track, and because Wayne liked to watch down by the rail, she and Stefan went alone to her owner's box so they could view the race from high up.

Despite that emotional moment with Stefan, Briar was still transported when she saw her coal-black filly out on the track, cantering easily along with Pat standing in the stirrups, for the warm-up. She had never gotten over it; every time she saw any of her horses race, she felt excited, thrilled, elated. But Touch the Fire, who had never been headed in any of her races, who seemed to blaze over the ground as Pat had said, a creature of another world who flew without wings, touched something deep inside her, a fierce pride she wasn't able to explain. She loved her gallant filly, and she had never told anyone—not even Stefan—why she had been so certain Touch the Fire would make her mark on racing. One day she would tell him, but for the time being, the secret was her own—and Marguerite's.

Watching this horse race was the greatest thrill of Briar's life; being called to the winner's circle time after time was almost an anticlimax after the heart-stopping excitement of her brilliant stretch runs. Briar's Cinderella horse had taken the racing world by storm, and as far as Briar was concerned, her filly deserved every accolade. She knew that no matter how many other horses she bought, raised, or bred, she would never have another like this one; even the spectacular Incandessence couldn't compare with her black filly. Horses like this one came along once in a lifetime, if that, and she felt both humbled and honored and ecstatic that she was part of the moment. It was a privilege to witness the greatness of this filly, and Briar knew now that what was born in the blood runs true. Far back in the past, the filly's great-great-great grandsire had been born to run, and many years later this daughter of his was fulfilling the promise he had never been allowed to reach. As post time was announced, she sent up a quick prayer for a safe race.

The announcement came: The flag is up!

Still keenly aware of Stefan beside her, Briar turned toward the gate. The horses were all loaded, and she could see Touch the Fire standing still in stall three. A horse down the end of the line suddenly reared, holding the start; as soon as its feet hit the ground again, the flag came down, the gates sprang open, and ten horses leaped like thunder onto the track.

Briar knew her horse so well; when she saw Touch the Fire take just the slightest bobble coming out of the gate, she unconsciously clutched Stefan's arm. "Something's wrong!" she exclaimed, holding him tightly.

He was watching, too. "Just a bad step," he said, his eyes following the horses as they stormed past the grandstand for the first time. "She's all right."

Briar watched as Touch the Fire took the lead even after the slight misstep. The filly's coal-black coat shone in the late afternoon sun, and as they made the first turn, the Caulfield lightning bolt on the green and amber silks Pat was wearing seemed an omen.

"She's all right," Stefan said again. Briar realized only then that she was still clutching him.

Quickly, she removed her hand and put her binoculars up to her eyes, focusing only on her horse. She didn't care about the rest of the field; her eyes were on Touch the Fire. She didn't know why she was certain something was wrong; the filly was leading the field as she always did, running easily, it seemed, with Pat still taking hold of her. Obviously, the jockey didn't feel anything was wrong, and yet . . . and yet . . .

The murmur of the crowd swelled as the field roared around the backstretch and turned for home. People leaped to their feet, straining to see, cheering the horses on. Touch the Fire always gave her audience a magnificent stretch run, and she didn't disappoint today. All the horses in this race were stakes winners; all had class. But Wayne had told them that if anyone could beat her, he thought it might be the strong, dun-colored colt called Que Card. Briar saw him making his move at the head of the stretch, coming on strong to challenge her black filly, who responded with almost contemptuous ease, extending her stride effortlessly, pinning her ears as if to say, Keep away, you'll never catch me.

The crowd was going wild now, leaping and shouting and screaming themselves hoarse. Que Card was still coming on strongly, but Briar had faith in her horse. Leaping to her feet, she didn't even realize she was shouting along with everyone else. Then the scream died in her throat. She thought . . . she knew . . . that the filly had bobbled again at the eighth pole.

"Stefan!" she gasped. Now she knew something wasn't right.

Stefan had seen it, too; he put his hand over hers and gave her fingers a tight squeeze.

Whatever had happened, Touch the Fire recovered in a split second; her stride evened out. In the saddle, Pat was crouched down, his hands high on the filly's neck, giving her a hand ride home. Nearly matching her stride for stride, came the dun horse. It was going to be close.

The crowd was going wild; the screaming was intense. Inch by inch, Que Card started to gain, but then Touch the Fire stretched her neck out, and the race was finished. Pat stood high in the stirrups, waving his whip in the traditional signal of triumph, but Briar hardly noticed the big PHOTO sign light up. Grabbing her binoculars, she left the box, Stefan right behind her.

"Wait—" he said, grabbing onto her arm. "Let me—"

He must have known something was wrong, too. People were milling all over, waiting for the official results of the race, and as they hurried down toward the track, Stefan practically made a battering ram of his body. Briar came close behind, holding on to him tightly. Only once he turned and said, "She's all right."

Briar couldn't say anything; she just nodded, praying it was true. Just as they reached the winner's circle, another roar went up from the crowd. Briar glanced at the tote board and saw that number three was first. Touch the Fire had won the race, but she felt numb. Only moments had passed since the horses crossed the finish line; Pat and the outrider were still bringing the filly back around. Her heart in her throat, Briar was straining to see when someone came up to her.

"Ms. McKenna, if you'll follow me to the winner's circle, please."

She only wanted to see her horse. Dragging Stefan with her, she followed the official into the charmed circle and waited anxiously for Touch the Fire to come back. Wayne was already there, slipping under the rail onto the track, and when she saw the trainer's expression as he got a clear shot of the returning horse, Briar's heart sank. Then she saw what he was looking at, and she nearly swayed. Pat was trying to say something to Wayne, but all Briar could see was blood. . . .

It seemed to be everywhere, on the filly's feet, on her front legs, under her belly, splashed across her chest. Red, red . . . everywhere.

"No!" she screamed. She didn't even see the flashbulbs popping off around her or hear the sportswriters yelling for attention; she only had eyes for her gallant filly and for the ambulance coming around. Kara was already racing out onto the track, followed by two grooms. Briar saw the state vet appear and couldn't wait. Running with Stefan close behind, they joined the little group.

"What is it?" she cried, reaching Wayne. "What happened? Oh, God, what happened?"

Pale and trembling, Pat was trying to explain. "I felt her stumble out of the gate, but she seemed just fine, honest, just fine. I never thought to pull her up, she wanted to go on. She *wanted* to go on!"

Wayne was hardly listening; dropping to one knee, he looked at the filly's leg. White-faced, Kara was already holding it up.

"Damn it," Stefan muttered.

"What is it?" Briar cried, shoving someone aside. She couldn't see what they were looking at; everything, everywhere, seemed to be covered with blood. She felt dizzy and sick, and suddenly the ground shifted.

You can't faint! she told herself fiercely, and took a deep breath. Pat was taking off the saddle and bridle so that someone could put a halter on the stricken filly. Grabbing him, Wayne shoved the shaken jockey toward the scales.

"Go get weighed," he commanded. "We're not going to default on the race after all this."

Gulping, Pat ran off so the race could be declared official. As soon as he jumped down from the scales, he was surrounded by reporters, but he had ridden for Wayne long enough to know to keep his mouth shut, and with his head down, he disappeared in the direction of the jockey's quarters. Disappointed, the sportswriters turned back to the drama still being enacted on the track.

To Briar's relief, the horse ambulance had arrived. Tight-lipped, Kara issued orders right and left. Her eyes met Briar's just for an instant, and she said, "She must have clipped part of a hoof on the gate when she stumbled. That's where the blood is from. This other's more serious."

"What other?" Briar cried, but they were already trying to get the horse onto the van. Still holding the filly's leg up by herself, Kara went with them, barking at someone when he wanted to take over.

"Just hold her up on the other side!" the veterinarian snapped as they all disappeared inside. "Come on, move it! She's still pumped, and I don't want this leg to hit the ground again."

The ambulance went off, leaving a limp Briar behind. Stefan took one look at her face and said, "I think—"

"No, I want to be there. As long as it takes," Briar said fiercely, and shoved her way through the crowd again, heading toward Wayne's barn. His hand on her arm in silent support, Stefan followed close behind.

The next few hours were the longest of Briar's life. With a white-faced and silent Pat Shannon, who just squatted outside the stall with his head down, Briar and Stefan waited, first outside the stall, then outside X ray, and then back to the barn again, until she felt as if she were going to fly into pieces. People went in and out, Kara and Wayne, and the hastily summoned horseshoer, Roy Guerrero, who had performed such miracles shoeing Incandessence when she had returned to racing. With a nod in Briar's direction, he disappeared into the stall as well.

Only Stefan's calm presence, his hand on her arm, then his arm around her shoulder, and his arms around her, kept her from screaming. All she could think of was that she was going to lose her gallant horse.

"You won't lose her," Stefan whispered, reading her mind. His arms were tight around her, holding her close. Part of her numbed mind marveled that they become so intimate in such a short time, but she couldn't think about it; she was too grateful he was here and too worried about her horse. "Kara's a good vet," he said, stroking her hair. "If anyone can fix her, she can."

Briar hated to cry, but tears filled her eyes as she looked up at him. "But what if she can't?"

In answer, Stefan held her even more closely. His lips in her hair, he murmured, "She will. It'll be all right, I know it. She'll run again."

With a shuddering breath, Briar put her head against his chest. She wanted to believe him; she did. But at this point, she wasn't even sure the filly would live, much less race again.

"She's a fighter," Stefan said, putting a hand under her chin and forcing her to look up at him. He gave her a brief kiss. "Just like you are."

Looking drained and exhausted, Kara and Wayne finally emerged from the stall with Roy. Darkness had long since fallen, and the stable lights were on. As if sensing the drama going on, the barn area was quiet, the night very still. As soon as she saw them, Briar tensed even more. From their expressions, she expected the worst, and it nearly was. The only thing more catastrophic, Briar felt, was if Kara had come to tell them she advised putting the horse down.

"It's what we call an avulsion fracture of the sesamoid bone," the veterinarian said, giving her the bad news up front. "It happened when the distal sesamoidean ligament—"

"Kara," Briar said tersely, "just tell me what it means."

It meant that Touch the Fire might never race again. In a complex arrangement of bones and ligaments, the distal sesamoidean ligament attached to the bases of the sesamoid bones in the fetlock. When the filly had stumbled out of the gate, shearing off part of her front hoof—the cause of all that blood—she had put such stress on the leg that the ligament was strained beyond endurance. When it gave, it took a piece of sesamoid bone with it—the avulsion fracture Kara had described.

"I'm sorry, Briar," Kara said. "I wish it could have been better news."

Briar forced the words out. "Will she be all right?"

Kara gave her an unhappy look. "Are you asking if she'll race again? Because if you are, I can't tell you that yet. If you're asking if she'll heal from this, the answer is yes, she will, but it will take time."

"Time, she'll have," Briar said, tears filling her eyes again in relief. "What do we have to do?"

"The first thing is talk to the gate man and find out what the hell happened," Wayne exploded. "She's never stumbled coming out of the gate, and I want to know why she did today.''

Briar realized then that the filly hadn't broken as well as she always did. Even so, she couldn't dwell on that now; Wayne could take care of it. At the moment, she wanted to hear what Kara had to say about the filly's care.

"She's going to need rest—at least four to six months in a stall," Kara said. "And good shoeing," she added with a tired smile at Roy. "Because she sheared off part of the weight-bearing wall of her hoof when she came out of the gate, I've had Roy give her some support on the foot with a glue-on shoe. We can't nail anything on right now because of the fracture. But she's going to need special shoeing all the way—bar shoes with wedge pads . . .''

Briar looked quickly at the horseshoer. "I'll pay anything you ask, plus expenses, but will you be willing to come up to Caulfield Farm to shoe her when she needs it?''

"I'll go anywhere to help that horse, Ms. McKenna," he said. He sounded so fervent that despite the tension of the moment, they all smiled.

Briar was grateful and told him so, but Kara had a last warning. "She's a tough patient, Briar. You're going to have your hands full.''

Briar didn't care if Touch the Fire tried to tear the barn down. She didn't care about anything, as long as her horse was going to be all right. She'd think about racing later; at present, she just wanted to get the filly safely home.

"I have someone who's a wonder with horses," she said to Kara, picturing Gillie, who could calm the most fractious horse just by his presence. Thinking that they were going to need all his talents and abilities over the next few months, she shook the vet's hand. "Thanks, Kara. I'm glad you were here to take care of her.''

"I'll be on call if you need me," the veterinarian said, and on impulse, gave Briar's arm a squeeze. "Good luck, Briar. I hope we see her here again.''

They took the filly home in a hired van that night, along with another patient, the gelding Briar had impulsively bought earlier. Until they were making arrangements, Briar had almost forgotten about Mi Flor Amor; that incident seemed so far away, as if it had happened in another lifetime instead of just this afternoon. When she did think of the horse, she blessed whatever whim of fate had directed her decision; the trip was going to be long enough, and Touch the Fire hated to travel alone. The gelding would be good company—for all of them.

Telling herself that this was an omen for things getting better, not worse, she sent someone back for Mi Flor Amor, and then she realized that Pat was still there, standing by the van, looking ready to cry. Seeing his expression, she drew him to one side.

"It's not your fault, Pat," she said.

Dolefully, he shook his head. "I should have felt something, I *should* have. I could have pulled her up."

"And you would have if you'd felt her go wrong, but you didn't, did you?"

Tears filled his eyes. "No, after that misstep out of the gate, she came on so strong. She was ready to run, she *wanted* to. I didn't even *ask* her until the sixteenth pole, and even then, I just shook my whip a little and she went on. Jesus!" He ran a hand through his dark hair. "I can't believe this happened! I'm so sorry, Ms. McKenna, believe me!"

She did believe him, but she couldn't do more than say so; he'd have to fight his own demons these next few months, just as they all had to. Sadly, she shook Pat's hand and thanked him for waiting. Then she went back to Stefan and announced that she was going with him in the van.

Stefan knew better than to argue with her; he had already told her he was going to ride with the horses, and it was obvious that she didn't have to come as well. But he couldn't prevent himself from saying, "Are you sure you want to? You look exhausted, and it will be a long trip."

"I know," she said. "But I have to."

Then she went to say good-bye to her unhappy trainer. "She'll be back," she said bravely to Wayne. "I know she will."

"I know it, too," he said, but he wouldn't meet her eyes. When she turned to go, he added softly, "Take care of her."

Although she hadn't intended to, Briar fell asleep as the van was laboring up the Grapevine, the mountain passage that separated the Los Angeles basin from the San Joachin valley. She never noticed when Stefan used his jacket to cover her, and she woke just briefly when he put his arms around her and pulled her close.

"Are we home yet?" she asked drowsily.

"Not yet," he said, putting her head against his chest. "Go back to sleep."

"I'm not asleep," she protested, but she felt soothed by the strong, steady beat of his heart under her cheek. The sound kept at bay those nightmare words she had always dreaded to hear, yet had now heard twice that day: Horse broke down!

Shuddering involuntarily, she fell into an uneasy sleep.

---

# CHAPTER TWENTY-TWO

Briar awoke near Bakersfield, about two hours later. Because of the noise of the van and the endless jolting, she hadn't been able to do more than doze, and when she came awake with a start and sat up, she realized that Stefan had fallen asleep with his arm around her, his head crooked awkwardly against the wheel well. Muscles protesting, she carefully moved away from him and stood up. Grimacing, she stretched.

The van she had hired was a nine-horse, with space, of sorts, in the form of an empty shelf in front for any grooms traveling inside, and most of the room down the length for the horses. Touch the Fire and Mi Flor Amor had been put side by side in the first two stalls. She was relieved to see that they looked comfortable. Giving each a pat, she checked their bandages.

She turned to look at Stefan, who hadn't moved. Seeing his uncomfortable position, she was tempted to shift him a little, but she was afraid he'd wake up, and she didn't want him to. She already felt as if she had gone through an emotional wringer today, and she just wanted to sit by herself for a while and calm down.

Cautiously moving with the swaying of the van as they drove up Interstate 5, she took a seat on the shelf that ran the entire front width of the inside. Bringing her legs up, she wrapped her arms around them and rested her chin on her knees. Rocking back and forth with the rig's movement, she watched the play of light on Stefan's lean face as the occasional truck went by.

At this time of night, there weren't many cars on the highway, mostly trucks and trailers going by, their drivers sometimes blinking their headlights in the code of the road. One blink meant it was okay to pass; two meant thanks. Briar didn't know more than that, and maybe she'd got those wrong. She wasn't interested in how truckers amused themselves on these long night drives, anyway; she was more intrigued with watching Stefan sleep. The same lock of hair had fallen across his forehead, and she wanted to reach out and brush it away, but she didn't disturb him. She had to think about what had happened between them today and decide what to do from here on.

But she didn't seem capable of making any decisions about anything; as she sat there, swaying with the motion of the van, her mind wandered, and she found herself thinking, for some reason, about Jaz. She couldn't imagine Jaz spending all night locked up with two injured horses back here; the idea was so absurd she nearly laughed. Jaz was all flash and dash, a handsome ne'er-do-well who meant well when it suited him, but who might not be counted on to come through in a pinch. At least, that's the impression she'd first had when she met him. Now she knew differently, and she thought back to the conversation they'd had when she'd finally tracked him down a couple of months ago to explain her position about dividing Hay's estate. To her surprise, Jaz had been appalled; he immediately tried to talk her out of such craziness.

"Why on earth would you want to do that?" he demanded.

They were sitting in the luxurious living room at his Sausalito town house, with a picture-perfect view of the fog-shrouded Golden Gate Bridge, having espresso that Jaz had proudly made himself on the machine in his own almost unused kitchen. Briar had called first this time to make sure he'd be home and had stopped by after a long day at the office. With the anticipated drop in her finances, she was working harder than ever at McKenna TimeSave; despite the drain on her resources, she still felt her decision to divide the estate three ways was the right one. Difficult for her, in view of her high expenditures on the horses and the ranch these past months— but right all the same. It would be a squeak now the rest of the year, and into the next, but she had been in tight financial spots before, and with the foal crop she expected in the spring, she anticipated that within the next year or two the ranch would stop being such a big financial drain.

But even if things didn't work out quite as she expected, she still had McKenna TimeSave to shore things up; she could expand, as she had planned to do before inheriting the ranch, and use the added revenue from that to support Caulfield Farm. There were ways, she thought, to make things work.

"No, no, I can't let you do that," Jaz said agitatedly, when she had explained her reasons.

She smiled. "You don't have any say about it, Jaz. It's already done."

"Then undo it!" he exclaimed. He was so distressed that he actually got up to pace, an elegant, handsome man dressed in slacks, with Ferragamo loafers on his feet, and a custom-tailored long-sleeved shirt with the cuffs oh-so-casually rolled back. He made quite a picture against the big windows, with the Bay as a backdrop, and Briar could see why he always had women hounding him. Men, too, if she recalled correctly, but that wasn't unusual in this town.

"Why are you so upset?" she asked. "After all, it's only fair."

"Fair?" He stopped in midstep. "What's 'fair' is the way Dad wanted it!"

"Yes, I know, but I never felt right about having it all, Jaz—"

"You didn't have it all. Dad was very generous with the trusts."

"Not according to Fredrica—"

"Fredrica is my sister, but she's a greedy bitch!"

"Now, Jaz—"

"No, no, don't 'now Jaz' me," he said, coming over to sit by her on the couch. He took her hands, his handsome face a mask of concern. "You don't have to do this, Briar," he said earnestly. "Freddie will never make that prenuptial agreement stick. I know how Dad felt about it, and I'll . . . testify, or whatever the. hell it is I have to do."

She was touched. "Thanks, Jaz, but I'm not really worried about the legality of that agreement. It's not even the issue. I would have done this even if Fredrica hadn't forced my hand, because I'd been thinking about it for a long time, anyway. I just hadn't found a way to convince Spence."

He knew who Spencer Reed was, and he sat back. "That's another thing," he muttered. "I'm surprised Spence is going along with this."

She smiled again. "He's going along, but he doesn't like it, I'll tell you that."

Abruptly, Jaz sat up again. "And I don't like it, either, Briar. Listen, you don't know Freddie like I do. She won't be satisfied with this; she won't stop until she gets the whole damned pie."

"Well, she's only going to get a third, which is better than what she has now. She's going to have to be content with that."

He still wasn't convinced. "I don't know, Briar—"

"I do," she said, and carefully set aside her espresso cup. She had come to the real purpose of her visit. "But that's why I wanted to talk to you about this before we actually signed the agreement, Jaz. I'm aware of what Fredrica thinks of me, but I also know how your father felt about Lord Industries. If I'm giving away two-thirds, I need to know—"

"How I'd vote if push came to shove?" he said, and then smiled wryly when she looked at him in surprise. "It's obvious that I'd be the swing vote, Briar; it doesn't take a giant intellect to figure it out. You want to know whose side I'd be on, right?"

"It isn't a matter of *sides*, Jaz—"

"Oh, yes, it is. We both know it. So, while I think you're crazy to be doing this—*I* certainly wouldn't, in your place—I'd be a fool to turn it down, wouldn't I? But I also know how Dad felt about the company, too. And despite the fact he always thought I was such a loser—"

"He didn't think that!" she protested.

"Oh, yes, he did. I know it, and he was right. But as I was going to say, despite all that, I do feel a certain loyalty to the old bastard, just like you do, so if it came to a power fight, I'd support you, of course. I'll make sure the company stays in family hands, and if Freddie tried to pull a fast one, well, she'll have to fight both of us. Does that set your mind at ease?"

It did, and it had. Jaz was many things, but she knew he wasn't a manipulator, and she believed him. Spence thought she was a fool to put such trust in someone who roamed the world looking for kicks, but she had always suspected there was more to Jaz than that. She had faith that if the time came, he would do what was right. She practically had to force Spence to draw up the agreements, but when it was all done, she felt relieved.

Especially, she thought, since she hadn't heard a peep from Fredrica. Spence thought Hay's daughter had capitulated too quickly, but Briar knew what a greedy opportunist she was, and she hoped that Fredrica had realized she could lose everything if it came to a bitter court fight. In that sense, one-third was better than none, but even if Fredrica still wasn't satisfied, Briar was confident she could handle whatever Fredrica might come up with next. After all, she had Jaz's promised support if there was some kind of power play, so she would just have to handle it. Until then, she wasn't going to worry about it; she had too many other things on her mind.

"What are you thinking about?"

Startled out of her introspection, Briar returned to the reality of the van and the realization that Stefan was awake. She didn't know how long he'd been watching her, but for some reason she felt strange about it, and she jumped down from her position on the shelf.

"I was thinking about my stepson, Jaz," she said.

He grimaced. "Oh. Him."

She remembered then that Stefan and Jaz had met at that fund-raiser. Smiling despite herself at Stefan's expression, she said, "I take it you didn't like him?"

He shrugged. "I didn't have an opinion one way or the other."

"Somehow, I don't think that's true," she said dryly, and glanced around. "Would you like some coffee? I had a thermos put in here somewhere."

He rubbed his eyes. "Yeah, coffee would be good right now. How're the horses?"

"See for yourself."

Both Touch the Fire and Mi Flor Amor were watching them interestedly, and when Stefan got up to check their bandages, as she had done earlier, she found the thermos and poured some coffee into the top.

"We'll have to share," she said. "I didn't think to bring another cup."

"God, what a day this has been," he said, after he'd taken a couple of sips and handed the cup back. He hesitated. Then, "Are you all right?"

She glanced at the quietly riding horses. "I will be when we get home."

"Where are we?"

"Somewhere outside Bakersfield."

He grimaced. "We've got a long way to go. Lord, I could use a cigarette."

She'd been thinking the same thing. "Me, too."

"You don't smoke!"

"I used to," she confessed. "Almost two packs a day. I quit over five years ago, but sometimes I still miss it."

"Yeah, I do, too. Especially at times like today. When that guy walked by with a cigarette right before we left, I nearly knocked him down and stole it right out of his hand."

She laughed. "I know how you felt. I was tempted, too."

He shook his head. "Sick, isn't it?"

"Well, we didn't. I guess we should get credit for that."

"You should get a lot of credit," he said, suddenly serious. "You handled things really well today, and I admire you for it."

Embarrassed by the compliment, she protested, "I didn't have a choice."

"Yes, you did. You could have fallen completely apart. I've seen owners do it before when a horse gets hurt."

She glanced away from him, toward the black filly who was still watching them. "I couldn't have let her down like that," she said, and looked back at him. "Besides, you didn't do so bad yourself."

He shrugged. "That's my job."

"I can't believe that's all it is to you—a job. I've seen the way you are around horses, and I know you care about them, too."

Now he was the one who seemed embarrassed. "Well, that's true, I do. But in this business, you can't let your feelings interfere with what you know you have to do."

She was silent a moment. They had come to the issue they'd both been dancing around all this time, and she made herself say, "Is that what happened today? You let your feelings interfere with your job?"

He paused. "I don't know what happened today, Briar," he said finally. "Do you?"

Slowly, she set the empty thermos cup down. "No," she said. "I thought . . ." She shook her head. "I don't know what I thought, Stefan. I feel so confused, pulled in so many different directions. When Hay died, I didn't think I'd ever be attracted to another man, but now . . ."

"Now?"

She had to say it. "Now things are complicated, and I . . . I feel almost guilty, as if I'm betraying Hay's memory. He was so good to me, Stefan; he was such a good man."

"And you still mourn him, is that what you're saying?"

She looked into his eyes. To find the coffee, she had switched on the interior lights, but the bulb was dim, and his face was all planes and shadows. "A part of me will always mourn him," she admitted. "But maybe . . . maybe I just need more time. Does that sound foolish?"

He smiled, that wonderful smile of his that had attracted her without knowing it, almost from the first. Reaching out, he drew her close to him. "No, it doesn't sound foolish," he said, his lips against her ear. "You've been through a lot this past year, I realize. Losing your husband, inheriting his estate—"

"Only a third," she said distractedly. She was enjoying the feel of his arms around her as he held her to his chest. He smelled good, like horses and hay and an indefinable scent that was individually him.

"A third?" he said curiously. "But I thought I read in the papers that you inherited the whole shebang."

"I did. Well, except for the trusts, of course. But a couple of months ago, I divided the rest among the three of us—Jaz, my stepdaughter Fredrica, and me."

"That was . . . generous."

"No, it was fair," she said, and looked up at him, only half-teasing. "Why? Would it make a difference? Were you only interested in me for my money?"

"Well, as a matter of fact, yes," he said solemnly, his arms tightening around her as she reared back in protest. Holding her firmly, he grinned. "That's why I allowed Stan to persuade me to take the job at the riding club. I knew the membership was comprised of rich women just looking for a handsome young stud like me, and when I saw you, well, it all fell into place. That's why I was so charming and suave that first day. I wanted to snare you right away."

She couldn't help smiling. "You certainly had an interesting approach, I grant you that."

"Reverse psychology," he replied. "It only works on certain women."

"I think," she said dryly, starting to extricate herself from his embrace. "I'll have more coffee."

"Wait," he said, suddenly serious again. Still holding her, he said, "You know I'm speaking nonsense, Briar. I would have been attracted to you if you hadn't a dime to your name."

She knew this wasn't about money, and she said, "I know, Stefan."

"We both know something is happening here," he went on. "But if it's too soon, or you want me to make things easier by backing off, just say the word. I know there's no time limit on grief, and I respect that."

She was so touched she felt the sting of tears. "Thank you, Stefan," she said. "I . . . appreciate it."

"Good," he said, and then deliberately sought to lighten the mood. "As I said, I'm willing to wait, but not too long. I'm pretty wonderful, but I'm only human, after all."

She laughed, brushing tears quickly from her eyes. "Deal," she said shakily. "I'll let you know. But in the meantime, how about more coffee?"

He looked around bleakly. "How about if I make us a couple of cigarettes out of this straw and some of those paper towels in back?" he said. "After baring my soul, I could use a smoke; it doesn't matter what."

Laughing again, she handed him the cup.

After swinging wildly on an emotional pendulum, first with Stefan then with Touch the Fire, Briar felt exhausted and worn-out by the time the big van lumbered through the gates to Caulfield Farm early the next morning. As she looked through the van window and saw Gillie and Jaime running out, she felt eager to hand over the responsibility for the two horses and escape to a long, hot bath and an even longer nap. The way she felt now, she would never wear these clothes again.

She had called before they left Santa Anita to tell Jaime what had happened and ask him to prepare, and when he and Gillie helped pull down the ramp, she thought she'd never been so glad to see anyone in her entire life. Then Stefan spoke up, and before she knew it, they were disagreeing again.

"I don't think we should let that old man take care of Touch the Fire," Stefan said to her in an aside, as Gillie and Jaime helped with the horses. "The gelding, okay, but not the filly. She's too valuable."

Briar was distracted, watching the elderly groom talk to the filly before gently untying her from her place. Since Stefan hadn't said anything about Gillie in a long time, she thought he had finally accepted the old man's presence, and she looked at him in surprise.

"Why do you say that?"

"Well, look at him."

She obeyed, turning to see Gillie running his gnarled old hands carefully down the black horse's neck and over her shoulder, giving her a chance to get acquainted with him again before he tried to move her.

"Yes, so?" she said. She could hear the impatience in her voice and tried to disguise it. She didn't want to fight with Stefan, not when they seemed to have reached a new level in their relationship.

"See how his hands shake?"

"He's an old man, Stefan," she said. Was he talking about Gillie's drinking? But the aged groom had promised her faithfully that his drinking days were over now that he had another chance to prove himself, and she had never doubted him. Besides, with Jaime so busy with chores, and Stefan occupied with the other stock, and she herself running back and forth to her office, she needed Gillie to care for her two sick horses—a task he seemed not only willing, but able, to take on. As he turned with the filly's lead rope in his hands, Briar saw even inside the van, his eyes were alight. Chirping encouragingly, he let the injured horse find her own pace down the ramp, and then he began leading her slowly toward the barn. Because of her injury, Touch the Fire had been bandaged from foot to knee on her left front leg, and when she heard what he said after giving the bandage a professional glance, Briar smiled despite herself.

"You don't need that big, bulky thing, do you, love? To my mind, a good dose of Mississippi mud will be just the thing. . . ."

Briar had heard of Mississippi mud, a secret combination of actual mud—not necessarily from Mississippi, either, she'd found out—and other bracing ingredients that only the old-timers seemed to know how to make. It was used for all sorts of ailments—as a poultice, a heating pad, and a means to reduce inflammation among other things. She intended to ask Dr. Roberts' advice first before she allowed him to use it, but she wasn't really worried about what Gillie might do. During the time he had been at the ranch, wide-eyed and grateful at having a room to himself in the living quarters over the barn, instead of having to find a cramped space inside someone's tack room at the track, she had seen him with all the horses. She knew that no matter what he was, there was no way this old man could ever hurt one of the horses.

Besides, Gillie knew this filly. He had been the one to take care of her when she'd first come in from Kentucky, and Briar had seen how good he was with her fractious horse. No matter what Stefan felt, she trusted Gillie completely. After watching him walk with infinite patience beside his hobbling charge, she turned to observe Jaime leading the other patient, the equally lame Mi Flor Amor, down the ramp.

Jaime saw her looking at him and dolefully shook his head. "*Aiee*," he said, "with these two horses, we should start a hospital ward, don't you think?"

"I think we already have," she said somberly, and then breathed in deeply. It was good to be home, she thought. Then she looked at Stefan again, and saw that he was still watching disapprovingly as Gillie slowly walked into the barn with the black filly. Seeing his expression, she felt herself tense. "You don't mean that about Gillie not being able to take care of Touch the Fire, do you?" she asked. "Not after the way he just handled her."

"I saw an old man leading a horse out of a van, that's all," Stefan said stubbornly. "It didn't take much talent. It's going to take a hell of a lot more than that to care for her in the next couple of months."

Was this the man who had tenderly given her his coat in the van, who had held her in that awkward position because she'd accidentally fallen asleep against his shoulder? Was this the same person she had joked with, and teased, and who had teased her back to help relieve the boredom during the long drive? Maybe she'd been dreaming the whole time, she thought, exasperated.

"Well, why don't we just give him a chance and see how it goes?" she said, telling herself she would not lose her temper just because she felt as though she'd been dragged through dirt.

He shrugged, irritating her further. "Whatever you say. It's your—"

"Why are you doing this?" she demanded. "What's wrong with you?"

He glanced away from her. "Nothing. I guess I'm just tired."

"We both are."

"Look, I'd better go check the horses," he said, obviously wanting to get away before they got into an argument out of sheer weariness.

She was too tired to think about it further. Deciding for once to leave things in the hands of the three men in charge, she paid the van driver and then went up to the house, where Jaime's worried wife, Isabella, immediately started fussing over her. Soothed by the comforting attention, Briar nearly fell asleep in the hot bath her housekeeper drew for her, and after refusing anything to eat, she fell on the bed intending to sleep—and was instantly, grittily, awake.

"Damn it," she groaned, and knew that Stefan's conduct just now was at the root of her restlessness. But she didn't want to get dressed and go bang on his door demanding an explanation when he was probably just getting to bed himself. Still debating what to do, she saw her great-grandmother's journal on the bedside table. Marguerite always made her feel better, she thought; maybe what she needed was to lose herself in another life for a while. Already anticipating her return to that gentler time, Briar pulled herself up to a sitting position and reached for the journal.

---

# CHAPTER TWENTY-THREE

*The worst possible thing has happened!* Marguerite had written agitatedly across the page. *Heinrich and Mariel have bought property next to ours, and they've named it the Mondragon Stud! They're going to raise Thoroughbreds, too, and Mariel has promised to—oh, it's too melodramatic for words!—'Drive us out'!*

Marguerite still couldn't believe that her cousin had actually said such a thing. Imagine! she thought in outrage. Resorting to threats!

"Oh, I always *knew* she was nothing but a . . . a peasant!" Marguerite stormed one night as she and Sloane were getting ready to retire. Sloane was already in bed; dressed in her nightgown, Marguerite was pacing the floor, her hairbrush in hand. The long, chestnut-colored hair that Sloane loved to run his hands through swung like a curtain every time she turned, and finally, he reached out and drew her gently down onto the edge of the bed.

"If you're not careful," he said, nuzzling her ear, "the baby's going to hear you."

Distracted, Marguerite glanced guiltily in the direction of the nursery door, down the hall and across the corridor. For a moment, distracted by thoughts of their son Kyle, sleeping peacefully nearby in the connecting room, she forgot her agitation. Even now, almost two years after Kyle's birth, she could hardly believe that she had brought someone so wonderful into the world. Sometimes she went in to look at him at night, just to convince herself he was real.

She had never pictured herself the devoted mother. In fact, whenever she had thought about motherhood as a young girl, she had imagined it to be a rather undesirable state that, mercifully, was far into the future. She hadn't had time, or interest, in children; she was far too involved with horses. Then, when she had failed to become pregnant during the first five years of her marriage, she couldn't help but wonder if she were being punished. She hadn't wanted children, she'd thought, so now a vengeful fate was complying with her girlish wishes just at a time when she was *desperate* to conceive. As the years passed, she began to believe she was destined to be barren, and she had spent many a night sobbing in Sloane's arms about the injustice of it all.

But then the miracle had happened, and she had become pregnant with Kyle. It hadn't even been a difficult pregnancy; she had breezed right through, in fact, and at the end had emerged triumphantly with a beautiful son. Except for her wedding, that had been the happiest day of her life. Sloane had been so proud, and so was she. With chestnut curls and green eyes, Kyle had her coloring, but Sloane's bone structure, and even though she felt compelled to demur when visitors exclaimed over her handsome son, she still felt a thrill of pride.

She and Sloane had talked about another baby, and she hoped she would find herself in a certain condition soon. Her first pregnancy had been so easy that she was actually looking forward to another, and since Kyle was about to celebrate his second birthday, she didn't want to wait too long. A brother or sister would keep him company, and although she hadn't said anything, she secretly hoped the next one would be a girl. She dearly loved her son, but she couldn't help thinking of all those darling little dresses and froufrous she'd be able to buy for a daughter.

But first she had to get pregnant, she thought, and how was she going to do that when she was so upset by this latest move on her cousin's part? Reminded once more of Mariel, she felt herself getting angry all over again. Oh, she should have known Mariel would find another way to bedevil her! From the time she had come to live with the family, Mariel had always caused her trouble, and this time it was even worse. *Now* they were going to be in each other's pockets again, and she just couldn't bear it!

It wasn't fair, she thought resentfully, that she should have to worry about what Mariel and that stick Heinrich might do to compete. Heinrich had always been interested in horses, too; she remembered very clearly the trotters and the carriage horses he'd had. He had always prided himself on perfectly matched teams and had used to show off every Sunday by hitching a different pair to take him to church. He'd come flying along in the handsome phaeton he'd imported from England, driving the bays or the grays or those chestnut Hackney horses that stepped so high it seemed as if they might hit their noses with their knees. Down the road they'd come, legs pumping in absolute unison, necks arched, ears pricked, and behind them would be Heinrich, dressed in suit and bowler, waving his whip, acting like the lord of all he surveyed. Even she, who had always detested Heinrich, had to admit that it had been quite a sight.

It wouldn't be so bad if he was going to be breeding trotters, she thought; at least they wouldn't be in competition. But Mariel had smugly told her when they met in town earlier that now Heinrich was interested in racing horses so they were going to raise Thoroughbreds, just like she was. Standing on the sidewalk in the middle of the town square as they had been, Marguerite wasn't about to give Mariel the satisfaction of making a scene. Instead, she had confined herself to a haughty, "In that case, you'll be out of business in a year, dear cousin. Neither of you know the *slightest* thing about racehorses!"

"Oh, we don't have to know," Mariel had retorted in that breezy, *superior* way that made Marguerite want to gnash her teeth, "my darling Heinrich has hired someone to manage all that. He's so busy with all his other interests, you know. The stud farm will be just a . . . toy."

She had managed to escape without telling Mariel what she thought, but she had seethed all the way home. She spent the rest of the day in a tizzy, waiting for Sloane to get home from Sacramento, where he had gone to discuss business with James Ben Ali Haggin, of Rancho del Paso. Finally, in the afternoon she had gone down to the barn and requested one of the mares be saddled. She needed a gallop to clear her head; otherwise, she felt as if she would scream from sheer frustration.

She couldn't ride Saxon any longer because they had been using him solely for breeding, but she gave him a fond pat as she went by his paddock. Because of him Caulfield Farm was building a reputation for fine bloodstock; during the five years since establishing the farm, Saxon's get were already making their mark. His sons and daughters had raced back East, and here, as well, both at Ingleside, and at the older Bay District. In fact, one of his colts had won the Haggin Stakes at Ingleside just this year, when unruly horses and jockeys had delayed the start for more than an hour and a half. That fiasco had prompted more talk about what was being called the Australian Barrier, or the Gray Gate—which Marguerite understood wasn't really a gate at all, but a long, thick webbing stretched across the track, set to be drawn up quickly once the horses were in line to signal the start of a race. She didn't care what it looked like; at this point any device would be an improvement.

Riding out that day on a gangly mare named Amber Light, Marguerite began to feel more peaceful. She shouldn't allow Mariel to upset her. Even if Heinrich was successful in his new venture, she and Sloane still had Caulfield Farm, and as she looked around with satisfaction at the green pastures, the fences marching in perfectly straight lines across the rolling hills, and the horses placidly grazing, she no longer felt threatened, but fortunate. She *was* lucky, she thought; she not only had a beautiful son and a handsome, attentive husband, but a lovely home, as well, with pastures and barns filled with horses that were starting to do the Caulfield name proud.

And what did Mariel have? A calculated marriage to a man who would never love her or anyone else because he was obsessed with hatred. Far from being resentful of her cousin, Marguerite decided, she should pity her instead.

But she still told Sloane about that irritating conversation she'd had when he finally came home that night, and now she had agitated herself all over again.

"Marguerite," Sloane said, nuzzling her neck and bringing her back to the present, "why don't you come to bed?"

Normally she would have given in; Sloane whispering in her ear was always hard to resist. But despite her ride that afternoon, she still felt too restless to sleep. It was all very well for Sloane to say—and for her to tell herself—that Mariel and Heinrich were harmless irritations, but if that were so, why couldn't she rid herself of this feeling of dread?

Disturbed by the thought, she jumped up again and went to her dressing table. Sitting down she began to brush her long hair. Back at the bed, Sloane sighed.

"All right," he said, "let's talk about it. What exactly did Mariel say?"

Marguerite halted in her furious brushing to think. "It wasn't what she *said*, it was how she said it," she replied, slamming down the brush. "Oh! Every time I think about it, I could just—"

"Why are you so concerned?" Sloane asked curiously. "You know there's nothing Heinrich can do that will affect the ranch."

"How can we be sure? You don't know him like I do, Sloane! And you don't know my cousin at all!"

He got up and came to where she was sitting. Unconventionally, Sloane never wore anything to bed, and as she watched him walk across the room, lean and long legged, she found herself distracted. Flustered by the thoughts that arose in her mind, she hastily glanced away from him, but just as quickly her eyes were drawn back again. From the beginning, she and Sloane had always had a passionate private life, and when she was alone with him, she couldn't pretend otherwise, especially when he halted in front of her and slowly drew her to her feet. Smiling, he put his hands on her shoulders.

"I know," he said, gazing down into her eyes. "Heinrich

Jaeger—and Mariel—can bluster and threaten all they like, but that's all it is—bluster.''

She didn't agree, but she couldn't tell him why. She had never told him Heinrich had threatened her; she knew what he would do if he ever found out. She said instead, ''But they bought that place next to us, Sloane. It wasn't bad enough that I had to endure Mariel when I was growing up; now I'm going to run into her every time I turn around!''

Sloane smiled again. ''Oh, I think with two hundred acres between the two farms, you can manage to avoid each other, don't you?''

''No,'' she said, still fighting the feeling of dread. She didn't know what she expected Sloane to do, but she couldn't help saying, ''She'll find a way to plague me, I just know it!''

He laughed softly. He was always amused by her displays of temperament when they were directed toward someone else, and with his arms around her, he drew her gently into his embrace. ''Well, we'll just have to think of a way to keep you occupied so you won't have to think about it, won't we?''

She was too preoccupied with thoughts of her cousin. ''Sloane, I really—''

Without saying anything more, he gently slipped the nightgown off her shoulders. Her former pregnancy had swelled her breasts, and they were still full; the silky material clung to her for a second, giving an enticing glimpse of cleavage and rounded flesh. Glancing down, Sloane audibly caught his breath. In the lamplight, Marguerite's skin looked like cream, smooth and oh so inviting. Slowly, tantalizing them both, he pulled the ribbons away from where they had caught on her nipples, and the nightgown whispered to the floor. She was as nude as he was now, and he held her away from him for a moment, gazing at her body. Marveling, as always, at how beautiful she was, he reached out and traced the line of her torso down to her belly. As large as she'd been with Kyle, she had quickly gotten her figure back, and she still had the body of the young woman he had married. She was breathtaking, and he let her know it by his expression.

''Come to bed,'' he whispered, putting his hands on her waist.

All thoughts of Heinrich and her troublesome cousin vanished. Gazing up into his face, Marguerite smiled. She knew she was being brazen, but she couldn't help herself. Stepping close to him so that her breasts just touched his chest, and their thighs barely met, she put her arms around his neck. "I don't know if I should," she murmured, beginning to move her hips slightly back and forth. "It could be dangerous."

With one hand on her waist, he wound his fingers in her hair, gently pulling her head back. Bending to kiss her throat, he murmured, "I hope so."

She could feel his bulging manhood pressing against her thighs, and a warm feeling started to spread inside her. When his lips left her throat and traveled to the swell of her breasts, the warmth intensified, and she tried to press against him, but he held her back. Kissing first one breast, then the other, he sucked on one nipple until she moaned.

"Oh, Sloane . . ." She knew it was shameless, but she reached down to cup him in one hand, part of her marveling that she could do such a thing, another part wanting to drop to her knees and . . .

Tantalizing pictures rose in her mind of the nights they had spent exploring each other by flickering candlelight, her long hair spilling over him, arousing sensations in her that she had never dreamed of with his hands, his mouth, his tongue. She knew that she should be ashamed of such wanton behavior, but how could it be wrong when they loved each other so?

She had tried to talk to him about it once, haltingly, and with flushed cheeks because she was embarrassed. She had tried to cover her face, but he had taken her hands and forced her to look into his eyes.

"Nothing two people in love do is wrong, Marguerite," he said softly. "Unless they hurt each other. You are a beautiful, desirable, passionate woman."

It was the passion that bothered her; she had been raised to think it wasn't right for a woman, a *lady*, to display such . . . ardor. Not that she had ever been told in so many words; her own mother would have died before even hinting at what really went on behind closed marital doors. But the implication had been there, all right, drilled into every young girl's head. Married women must perform their conjugal duty; it was a responsibility to their husbands and the only way to create a family. But no lady would *ever* enjoy such a necessary and repugnant act; that was left to tarts and loose women of no virtue, who were doomed to damnation because of their shameless behavior. After being married only a few weeks, Marguerite had had the heretical thought that if loose women were sent to hell for enjoying being in bed with a man, they certainly enjoyed themselves before getting there.

But her ardent response still disturbed her, until that conversation with Sloane. After telling her that whatever two people who loved each other did was right, he had taken her upstairs and proceeded to demonstrate.

"But Sloane!" she had protested, but faintly. "It's the middle of the afternoon—full daylight! What will everybody think?"

Slowly, he had unbuttoned the two dozen buttons down the front of her gown. "They'll think," he murmured, "that we're in love."

"But—"

She couldn't say much more, for with each article of her clothing that he removed and tossed casually to the floor, he stopped her increasingly faint protests with another kiss until she felt breathless. Only then did she realize that she was naked while he was fully clothed, and as her cheeks flamed and she quickly reached for something to cover herself, he gently stopped her hands.

"No," he whispered, "let me look at you."

She didn't want him to look at her; embarrassed and uncomfortable and sure she was going straight to hell because she was allowing him to do such immodest things to her, she stood in agony while he bent his head and kissed her—gently on the eyelids at first, then the tip of her nose, then her lips. She wanted to reach out and pull him to her, but he held her hands and kissed her throat, her shoulders, her breasts, her nipples. Then, kneeling, he put his arms around her and ran his tongue down the line of her torso to the swell of her stomach, and then even lower. His hands kneaded her buttocks for just an instant until she closed her eyes, then, gently, he spread her thighs.

Her eyes opened. "Sloane!"

"Shhh," he murmured, and touched his tongue to her.

She wasn't prepared for the feeling that shot through her at that intimate caress. For a second or two, she wasn't sure her trembling legs could hold her, and when a moan escaped her she put her hands on his shoulders to stay upright.

"Sloane . . ."

His response was to probe deeper with his tongue. She had never felt this way; it seemed that every inch of her was on fire, and without realizing it, she began swaying her hips, pressing his head into her. Her own head dropped back and she moaned again as a fire spread wildly inside her. She forgot where she was. All she could feel was that swift sensation of raging desire sweeping through her and a hunger so savage that without realizing it, she wound her fingers in his hair and pulled his head up. Just for a second, they looked into each other's eyes, and then, with a strangled sound himself, Sloane got to his feet. Sweeping her up, he carried her to the bed and ripped off his clothes. His weight sliding over her was the most blissful feeling she had ever felt, and as she took him inside and wound her legs around him to draw him in even deeper, their shared passion exploded at the same time. She knew then what he had meant when he said this couldn't be wrong.

After that, they had spent many an afternoon alone upstairs, and she had never wondered what their hired help might think again. Tonight, she gave no thought to it, either. How could she, with her handsome husband looking at her like that? But she had learned a few things herself since that first cataclysmic afternoon, and when Sloane led her back to bed, she went willingly.

Much later that night, she awoke for a moment and smiled to herself. Sloane was lying on his back with his arm around her; he had flung off the covers in his sleep, and as she lifted up a little to rearrange the blankets, she saw something and smiled. In the shaft of moonlight streaming in through the window, her forgotten nightgown still lay in a crumpled, wanton little heap alone on the floor, and she went back to sleep, leaving it there.

Sloane and Marguerite's daughter, Juliet, was born almost nine months to the day after that night. This second birth was much more difficult than the first, and after a twenty-six hour labor, the doctor warned her against having another child. Marguerite paid little attention to the warning; she was too delighted that her daughter was whole and healthy—and here at last. Even at just a few hours old, it was obvious that with her fine blond hair, blue eyes, and pale skin with just the hint of rose, Juliet was going to be a beautiful child. The passing months proved that prediction right. By the time of Juliet's third birthday, Sloane and Marguerite's daughter seemed to have bypassed the chubby, awkward baby stages all children go through and had emerged a willowy, ethereal creature who looked at the world with solemn blue eyes and a serious, gentle manner. Marguerite worried at times that Juliet was too delicate; she remembered keenly the last months of her pregnancy when she had been confined to bed for fear that she might lose the baby. She had trusted Dr. Morgan completely, but she had sensed his apprehension, and although Sloane had been careful to keep worry from his eyes, she knew from the way he snapped at the help, and even at Kyle, that he had been concerned as well.

She hadn't discovered, of course, until after the long, difficult birth that both men had been even more worried about losing her than they were the baby. But by then it was all over; she and Sloane had their darling little girl and their bright, handsome boy. And as the old century ended, and a bright new one began, there arrived at the ranch a man from Sloane's past.

His name was Andrew McKenna, and he was originally from Balleyshannon, near Donegal Bay, in Ireland. Although they hadn't seen each other for a long time, Andrew and Sloane had known each other for years, it seemed. Sloane's interest in horses had taken him far afield, and Andrew's family raised some of the finest hurdlers and 'chasers to be found in all Ireland. That had been before "the trouble," which was the only way Andrew would speak of it, and Marguerite wasn't to find out those details for quite a while.

Long before, however, she had welcomed Andrew with his small son, Angus, with her characteristic generosity, opening her house and her heart to the taciturn red-haired man with the haunted eyes and his little boy. Soon both McKennas, father and son, had responded to her vivacity and loving care, and quickly they became part of the family. Sloane gave Andrew more than a job; he built father and son a house nearby and asked Andrew to manage the ranch. Marguerite, who had already seen how Andrew handled the horses, was delighted, and she completely approved when Andrew hired a very shy, quiet local young woman named Ula to watch the baby while he was at work. Soon Ula was cleaning the house and preparing meals for him; the only thing she didn't do was spend the night. As was proper, she left at the end of each day, escorted by her father, who came to pick her up in the wagon from where he worked at a nearby vineyard.

The new year came, and with it, a brand-new century. A

child was born to Heinrich and Mariel the year following, a boy they named Rupert. From the beginning, the child was difficult, pale and sickly, always fussing. Mariel endured for two years, but then, not having the time nor the temperament for children, the impatient mother handed the boy to a nanny and proceeded to visit one health spa after another for over a year, complaining that she had never recovered from the difficult birth and that the child had ruined not only her health but her good looks. In an attempt to recover both, she took herself off to Europe for two years more, causing a scandal that Marguerite felt she richly deserved. With her troublesome cousin gone, she felt sorry for the little boy, even though Heinrich provided the best of care in the form of nannies and nurses and tutors. But she didn't miss Mariel, and she was uncharitable enough to hope her selfish cousin stayed away forever.

Marguerite was granted her wish, but in such a horrible manner that she had guilty nightmares about it for years afterward. Having recently returned for a quick visit, Mariel had stopped in San Francisco to stay with friends the night of April 17, 1906. By morning, after a devastating earthquake, in which hundreds were killed and property damage soared to the millions, the city was destroyed. Fires claimed more property and more lives; the devastation was horrifying and incalculable. The house where Mariel had slept was leveled, and Heinrich Jaeger was suddenly a widower, and little Rupert without a mother, even one who had been absent for several years. Marguerite blamed herself, until Sloane put his foot down. It was ridiculous that she should feel anything but grief for a neglected little boy, he declared. If Mariel had been with her family . . . with her son, like she was supposed to be, according to him, she needn't have died.

Since Marguerite could hardly deny his logic, she wiped her eyes and offered to take care of little Rupert until Heinrich could make other arrangements. Her offer was not only summarily refused, but Heinrich coldly stated that he didn't need any help raising his son from anyone named Caulfield.

Life had been somber since the Great Earthquake, as everyone was calling it; even then, a year later in 1907, damage was still being calculated. And she had still felt a little guilty every time she thought of Mariel. But life had to go on, she realized, and so she had decided one day that she wanted to give a party.

They all needed a little gaiety in their lives; it had been so long since she had danced, or entertained, or had *fun*.

Sloane had been reading the paper when she came in with her announcement; cautiously, he glanced over the top of the page. "A party?"

Now that she had thought of it, it seemed the perfect solution to the doldrums. "Yes, you old stick! A party. You've heard of those, haven't you?"

He put down the paper. In the chair with him was Juliet, sitting quietly as always, reading a book of her own that she had brought down from the nursery. Her heart-shaped face was solemn as she looked up at Sloane and then toward her mother. She had been nearly ten years old then, Marguerite remembered, and wondered where the time had gone.

"Is it someone's birthday?" Juliet had asked, her gray-blue eyes widening at the thought. She was looking forward to her next party, when she would finally have permission to wear her beautiful new blue-satin dress.

Her expression mischievous, Marguerite smiled at her daughter. "No, this is a grown-up occasion where the host and hostess—that's your father and I—invite people to our house and entertain them with gracious hospitality and sparkling wit."

Juliet thought about that for a moment, then she looked downcast. "Oh, I see," she said. "Then I guess that means Kyle and I aren't invited, and I won't be able to wear my new dress."

"Oh, I think something can be arranged," Marguerite said, smiling as she reached for Juliet's hands. Pulling her up, she began dancing them around the room. She had long ago lost the pallor and look of strain that had so worried her doctor and her husband, and she was the picture of health whirling around with her daughter. She said gaily, "But first we have to convince your father to come. What do you think?"

Solemnly, Juliet looked back at Sloane, then up to her mother's face. She always considered everything, even the simplest question, and after a moment, she said, "I don't know, Mama. Doesn't Papa like parties?"

Even Sloane had to smile at that. "I'm sure your mother doesn't think so," he said, tossing aside the paper so he could give his two favorite women a hug. "But I could give it a try."

"Really, Sloane?" Marguerite asked her eyes bright.

Sloane looked at her tenderly for a moment before shooing Juliet out of the room. "When could I ever refuse you anything?" he asked, and then proceeded to whirl her around the room himself.

Breathless, Marguerite had finally extricated herself. Giving him a push in the same direction as Juliet had gone, she sat down at the desk to begin planning. She and Sloane had entertained before, but she had never designed an affair of the scope she intended to arrange now, and everything had to be exactly right. She wanted this party to be the event of the year, something all who were invited would remember for a long, long time. She was already in the midst of her second list when Sloane came in. She had been so preoccupied that she hadn't realized he had gone outside and then come in again. Her expression questioning, she looked up when he paused in the doorway.

"It's time," he said.

She was still thinking in terms of how much food and drink they should have on hand and how many they should invite to stay over.

"Time for what?" she asked blankly, and then threw down her pen. Springing up, she exclaimed, "But Cantata isn't due to foal for two weeks!"

"Tell her that," Sloane said, and held out his hand. She took it, and together they sped down to the barn to watch the birth of the foal Marguerite had planned for so long. Twice now, the mating of Saxon and Cantata, their Emperor of Norfolk's daughter, had produced only fillies. But this time—this time! Marguerite thought, crossing her fingers—their luck was going to change. She desperately wanted a colt to carry on the lines she had established, and if this foal was a male, and he was as good as she planned for him to be, he would become the foundation sire for Caulfield Farm.

Andrew was already in attendance when they arrived, crouched in one corner of the big foaling stall, where the straining mare was lying down, preparing to give birth. The stall was bedded two feet deep in straw, for this was no ordinary mare, and she wasn't carrying an ordinary foal.

*Oh, please let it be a colt!* Marguerite thought. Touching Andrew on the arm, she whispered, "How long has she been down?"

"About thirty minutes," he whispered back tersely.

That was dismaying news, and Marguerite met Sloane's eyes. They all knew that the longer the mare was down without giving birth, the poorer the chances were for both mother and foal. The prevailing wisdom dictated waiting for at least thirty minutes before interfering with the natural process, but Marguerite was in a fever of impatience, wondering if something was already wrong.

Sloane knew how much this meant to her; busy with his law practice and his investments, he had long since handed over the running of the horse farm to his wife. He liked horses, but hers was the passion, and she had proved it in the fine quality stock she had already brought to market.

"It's early yet," he said, trying to reassure her.

"She's straining," Marguerite replied, her eyes on the laboring mare. "We can't just sit here and watch her. We've got to do something—now!"

Andrew agreed. Motioning to Sloane, he said, "You hold her, and I'll see what I can find."

"I'll help," Marguerite said at once.

Neither man argued. They had both given up trying to protect the willful mistress of Caulfield Farm from some of the more distressing sights that went on, so Andrew said, "All right. You hold her head."

Without further ado, they all inched into place, being careful not to disturb the mare any more than necessary. As Andrew and Sloane went around to the rear, Marguerite sat down on the straw and cradled Cantata's head in her lap. Oblivious to ruining the dress she was wearing, she stroked the mare's sweating neck, crooning softly while the men worked behind. With Sloane holding the horse's powerful hind legs, Andrew very carefully reached inside. After a moment, he withdrew his arm.

"One of the forelegs is turned back, blocking the exit," he announced tensely.

Marguerite looked up. "Can you move it?"

He hesitated. "I'm afraid it will tear her inside."

Both men looked at her; Marguerite knew the decision was hers alone. She barely hesitated. If they didn't help, both mare and foal would surely die. She said, "Do it."

Andrew didn't ask if she was sure; they all knew the chances. Nodding grimly, he reached inside again. Sweat broke out on his face as he worked, and several times the mare thrashed.

The muscles in both men's arms bulged: Andrew's from trying to turn the foal's leg, Sloane's as he fought to keep the horse from kicking Andrew in the head, or worse, trying to get up. In front, Marguerite was using all her strength to keep the mare's head down. Horses had less leverage in this position, and as she leaned over, using her weight, she didn't realize that tears were running down her face. She wanted to scream at Andrew to hurry, but she knew he was doing what he could, so she bit her lip and did what she was told.

At last, Andrew grunted and moved back. Her own face running with perspiration, tendrils of hair clinging to her cheeks, Marguerite looked at him. "Andrew?"

Using his forearm to wipe his face, Andrew said, "I think—"

But just then, the opaque white sack that surrounded the foal emerged. A tiny foot was inside . . . then the muzzle showed . . . then the other foot appeared. Helped along by Andrew, the rest of the foal's body slid out onto the straw, and with a grunt of her own and a heavy sigh, the mare struggled to look around. Marguerite let her head go this time, and after Andrew had cleared away the sack so the foal could breathe and gave it a quick check, they all moved back.

"Is it. . . ?" Marguerite whispered, hardly daring to ask as the new mother nudged the still-wet body of her baby.

Andrew grinned. "Aye, it 'tis," he said in his lilting brogue. "You've got a fine colt there, Mrs. Caulfield. None finer I e'er did see."

Her eyes shining, Marguerite clasped her hands under her chin and looked in delight at Sloane. Smiling, he put his arm around her waist and bent to kiss her cheek. "Congratulations, my love," he murmured. "It looks like this time you finally got your wish."

"Oh, I did!" she exclaimed, drinking in the sight of the foal trying even now to struggle to his feet. "He's just perfect, Sloane. Just perfect!"

"What are you going to call him?"

She couldn't look away from that wonderful sight. "Fane, of course! Just as you suggested! Fane!"

As if he already recognized the name, the new colt suddenly made it to his feet. Wobbling and swaying and taking two steps forward and then a bobbling series back, he finally managed to find a precarious balance on all four tiny feet. His coat had dried just enough now after a few rough licks from his mother so that they could see that he would be coal-black, and with his little bobtail whipping furiously back and forth for balance, the future foundation sire for Caulfield Farm lifted his head and proudly surveyed the world for the first time.

Then, with mama nickering softly nearby, reminding him that he had to find his first meal, he emitted a shrill baby whinny to let everyone know he had arrived . . . and promptly fell down.

Caulfield Farm gave another party the year the colt named Fane—meaning joyful—turned three. As Marguerite intended, it was an event, for everyone who was anyone in racing on the West Coast came: James Ben Ali Haggin arrived from Sacramento; Colonel Daniel M. Burns came from his Candelaria ranch near Hopland, and neighbors poured in from all around. People were everywhere, and no matter where Marguerite turned she seemed to be accepting one compliment after another: about the house, the barns, the horses, her husband, her beautiful children—handsome Kyle, who was nearly fifteen now, almost as tall as his mother, and Juliet, thirteen, shy and solemn in her white party dress and long, fine, blond hair. Because they were of an age now when they were expected to conduct themselves properly in public, they were on hand to welcome the guests and be polite—and nothing else.

Marguerite's other pride and joy was in his paddock, showing off for the guests who were watching by racing along the fence. Fane was a leggy black colt with a beautiful body and fine head. In addition to nearly faultless conformation, large, luminous, intelligent eyes, and that glossy coat, he also possessed the elusive quality so prized by horsemen the world over: presence. There was no doubt in *his* mind, or in the minds of anyone who saw him, that he was destined to make his mark in the racing world, and Marguerite's one regret was the current trend of racing horses younger and younger. Soon she would have to make a decision about sending him for training, and because she didn't believe in straining young horses, she was torn. He had to prove himself on the racetrack before he could do so in the breeding shed, but it was too soon, she thought, too soon!

Naturally, everyone who came to the party wanted to see Caulfield's colt, and so finally Marguerite suggested that all the guests repair to the barn so Fane could be brought out. She had already prepared Andrew for this event, and he had spent hours brushing and currying Fane until he shone. Both were ready when the party trooped down, Fane in a patent-leather halter to show off his black coat, Andrew in a tight suit, proudly holding on to the line.

"Beautiful!"

"Excellent conformation!"

"Look at the depth of his girth!"

"And the length of his shoulder!"

Thrilled by the awed comments, Marguerite was just about to say something in response when she turned and looked directly into Heinrich Jaeger's cold eyes. Without realizing it, she tensed. She had invited him to the party, of course; being neighbors, even she couldn't have snubbed him by ignoring him so pointedly. And he had formally accepted, sending along a chilly little note saying he'd be delighted to come. But she hadn't really expected him to appear, and since she had barely seen him since Mariel died, it was a shock just to turn and see him standing there. She and Sloane hadn't been invited to view the magnificent mansion he was building just over the hill; it was supposed to be quite a flamboyant showplace, with fountains and gazebos and guest cottages—even a man-made lake. When he had started rebuilding, speculation had been that he was about to take another wife, but so far that hadn't happened, and Marguerite doubted it would. She didn't believe that Heinrich would ever marry again.

Heinrich smiled coldly at her when he saw her looking and gave a little bow. As always, he looked remote and withdrawn despite his polite greetings, but he was immediately included in the group. With Caulfield Farm, Heinrich's Mondragon Stud was making a name for itself, too, and he had sent some horses back East that had done quite well. No one knew what was going to happen with racing if the new antiwagering bill that was before Congress was passed, but those involved here in California had vowed to band together and fight it to the death. Since Heinrich was one of their own, he was greeted—if not warmly—with respect, before everyone turned to observe Fane again.

"That's a fine colt you've got there, Marguerite," Heinrich said. "As I was saying to Sloane just a moment ago, it would be interesting to see how he and my Ulrich compete."

"Then you'll have to wait until they're both in a race, Heinrich," Marguerite said. She suspected he was trying to bait her in some way, and she was just turning to someone else when he spoke again.

"How coincidental you should say that, dear Marguerite. Sloane and I were just discussing that very same thing."

Slowly, Marguerite turned back. Sloane had appeared at the edge of the group, and when she glimpsed his face she didn't know what to think. She knew he was furious about something; his eyes were dark, and a muscle ticked his cheek, but she couldn't imagine why he was angry, unless—

"Discussing what?" she asked abruptly, turning to look at Heinrich.

Heinrich smiled, reminding her of a snake. "A match race, of course," he said, and deliberately glanced around the big group. "Between Fane, and my own three-year-old, Ulrich, who has just come back from the East. Don't you think that would be exciting?"

Instantly a clamor arose, and above it Marguerite's alarmed green eyes met Sloane's furious blue. What was going on? she wondered. She knew Sloane would never have agreed to such a preposterous thing; why, Fane wasn't even in training. He had never even raced!

"Please!" she said shrilly, over the hubbub. Instantly, the babble died, and curious eyes turned toward her. Fiercely, she willed herself under control. She didn't know what was going on here, but she knew Heinrich never did anything without a purpose, and she didn't trust the look in his eyes. But she couldn't make a scene here that would be repeated, embellished, and she certainly couldn't do anything that would make it worse. Already she was seeing speculation on the faces of her guests—racing enthusiasts, all—and she knew it would take very little encouragement for them to join Heinrich in supporting a race. It was the kind of thing they would all enjoy, and in other circumstances, she might even enjoy it herself. But not with Fane, she thought. Not with Fane!

"Please," she said more calmly, and by a magnificent effort even summoned a gay little laugh. "Aren't we jumping the gun here a little? Fane is just three, and unlike Ulrich, he hasn't even raced!"

Heinrich's glance was like a chill wind in her face. "Does that mean you refuse my challenge?" he asked.

"Of course, it does!" she said merrily, holding on to her

control by sheer will. "Why, I can't imagine you were even serious!"

"Oh, but I am," Heinrich said, to the renewed enthusiastic murmur of Marguerite's guests, whom she hated at the moment, every last one. "And once again, I invite you to compete. My colt Ulrich, against Fane. The winner to have his choice of the other's stock."

"But that's absurd!" Marguerite cried, losing control at last. "Ulrich is older—"

"Only by a month. I'll give you a weight allowance."

"Can't be fairer than that," someone murmured.

Marguerite whirled around to glare at the speaker, but from the other side of the group, someone else said, "I'd like to see it."

She whirled around again. "Well, you won't! This has gone far enough! Fane will *not* race Ulrich in a match, and that's final!"

"Final, my dear Marguerite?" Heinrich said. Calmly, he turned to Sloane. "Do you allow your *wife* to speak for you, Caulfield?" he asked. "Or need I remind you again of the name . . . Ian McConachie?"

Despite her preoccupation, Marguerite heard someone behind her gasp at the mention of the name. Instinctively, she turned to look back and saw that Andrew's face had paled and he looked sick.

"Andrew!" she exclaimed. For a horrified moment, she thought he might faint, and she reached for him, but he shook his head. His eyes like bruises, he kept them on Heinrich's face.

Heinrich was clearly enjoying himself. "There was a time," he said, "when you were man enough to make your own decisions, Sloane."

Someone gasped again; this time it was Marguerite. Quickly she looked at her husband. She didn't know why the name Heinrich had used should cause such a reaction, but when she saw the look in Sloane's eyes, she hastily stepped forward. "Sloane!"

But for the first time in their entire married life, he paid her no mind. His eyes hard on Heinrich's face, he said, "So. That's the price? The match race against the . . . other?"

This time, before Heinrich could answer, it was Andrew who came forward. "Sloane, don't. It's not—"

Sloane didn't even look at him. "Stay out of it, Andrew," he said. "It's done."

"Done?" Marguerite cried. "What do you mean, *done*? You can't do this, Sloane! Fane is mine!"

She reached for his arm, but he shook her off. Still facing Heinrich as if they were the only two people for miles around, Sloane said, "I have your word?"

Heinrich bowed. "My word is my bond, Caulfield."

"Then," Sloane said, before the horrified Marguerite could protest again, "I accept."

"No!" Marguerite cried.

But as Sloane had said, the decision had already been made.

---

# CHAPTER TWENTY-FOUR

*Word of the match race spread like wildfire.* A contest between an untried son of the great Saxon, and Ulrich, the lightly raced, once-beaten powerful gray colt from Mondragon Stud was too good to be missed, and on the appointed day—a month after the challenge had been issued and accepted, people came from miles around.

It was scheduled to be an old-style race—two miles down a newly surfaced dirt road between the Caulfield and Jaeger ranches, up a hill, around a big oak tree on the other side, dipping down toward a lay-by, and then back to the finish line. Since Heinrich had issued the challenge, Sloane had answered by designing the course, which was to be a test of more than speed. Endurance, and the indefinable quality of "heart," which enabled a horse to run beyond its ability, would come into play, as well. And if Sloane was betting his colt—not to mention his marriage, he thought—he wanted a race worthy of the cost. With the gauntlet well and truly flung down, Heinrich could hardly refuse, and so it was agreed.

The rest of the racing world was not so disposed. From the moment the rumors started flying about the proposed match, promoters had hounded both Sloane and Heinrich, offering everything but the Crown Jewels for the race to be held at a recognized California track. Ingleside had been destroyed in the '06 quake, but Tanforan was still running, as was the elegant Emeryville in Oakland, which was considered a vacation paradise, complete with elaborate gardens and a modern stables. It would be the perfect showcase, they all pleaded, especially in the face of this antiwagering threat. It might be the last time anyone had a chance to bet on his favorite.

But neither of the participants could be swayed, not even by offers of large purses and a cut of the take. For once, Heinrich seemed to speak for both himself and Sloane when he said coldly, "This isn't about money."

What it was really about wasn't quite certain, either. Even though the feud between Sloane and Heinrich wasn't news, no one seemed to know what the dispute was about. Marguerite, who could have shed some light on the subject, absolutely refused to discuss it when approached, and of the upcoming race, she would not speak to anyone at all—even Sloane. She was too angry at him.

She and Sloane had been married twenty years; until the day of the party, she'd thought of all the people in the world, except her children, she knew him best. But her husband had become a stranger to her when he accepted Heinrich's challenge, and after a fierce quarrel that same night, their relationship was still strained as the day for the fateful race loomed. For Kyle's and Juliet's sake, she maintained an icy politeness with Sloane. She answered any question he put to her; they ate their meals together as always.

Beyond that, she wouldn't go. She had moved into one of the guest bedrooms and refused all social requests at which they would be expected to appear together. She was angry, yes, but more, she was hurt at what he had done. She just couldn't understand how he, who had always treated all the horses well, could have accepted such a risky challenge with the colt she had spent years breeding for, and which was hers alone. He hadn't even discussed it with her, he, who had always discussed every detail concerning them. She had trusted him; until he accepted Heinrich's challenge, she'd had his confidence, too. Now she had nothing, and she didn't even know why.

It wasn't for lack of trying, she thought. She had screamed at him to explain; she had begged and pleaded and demanded and cried. By an inhuman effort of self-control, she had managed to wait until after all their guests had gone from the party before she confronted him, but when they were finally alone, she demanded an explanation.

"But why?" she'd cried, already in tears. She knew that even if Fane did win the race, there was a good chance he might get hurt; he was too young, too inexperienced. He had never raced against a real opponent before, especially a powerful colt like Ulrich, who had already been to the track and knew how to run. It was worse than folly; it was criminal to expect her colt to compete successfully against a stronger, more experienced opponent. They had to wait.

"There isn't time for that," Sloane said flatly. They were in the living room, where she had found him after the last guest had gone. To Marguerite's astonishment, he had poured himself a stiff whiskey. He rarely drank, and she knew that was a further sign of trouble.

"Why not?" she demanded, her voice rising. "Why the big rush? Just because Heinrich—"

"I don't want to talk about it."

"Well, you're *going* to talk about it!" she cried. "I have a stake in this, too—or have you forgotten?"

He tossed down half the drink in one gulp. "I haven't forgotten. It's just that I can't change things now."

She couldn't believe what he'd said—not Sloane, who was never swayed by anyone, especially a man he despised. "That's absurd!" she said. "Of course you can. You can say you changed your mind!"

"No, I can't."

"Why not?" she said shrilly. "Sloane, I don't understand!"

"I can't explain," he said, and turned to pour himself another drink. When she saw that, she nearly dashed across the room and flung the decanter from his hand. Getting drunk wouldn't help the situation; they had to find a way out of this mess or the only one to suffer would be Fane.

Barely controlling herself, she said tightly, "Well, maybe you'd better try."

When he looked at her again, she almost recoiled. Where was the man she had married, the husband she had loved and lain beside, the man whose children she had borne? She didn't recognize this stranger; she had never seen the cold, furious look in his eyes. For a moment, it almost seemed as if the hard planes of his face were set in stone.

"I told you," he said, his voice low and dangerous. "I can't."

She wouldn't accept it; he owed her an explanation, and she intended to have it. "Why not? Sloane, this is madness! We don't owe Heinrich anything, and he's said for years that he'd ruin us. He's just trying to—"

"It's done, Marguerite, can't you understand that?"

"No! I can't!" she'd shouted. She was so furious now that she didn't care if she did wake the children; she didn't care if she woke the whole ranch. "Fane is *my* colt. You have no right!"

"Leave it be, Marguerite!" he thundered. "Goddamn it . . . leave it be!"

She looked at him in total shock. He had never spoken to her like that, not in the twenty years of their marriage. She was so upset she hardly knew what she was saying. "If you do this, Sloane," she said, her voice shaking with emotion, "you'll regret it."

"And if I don't, I'll regret it more," he said. Then he relented enough to say, "I wish things could be different but they . . . can't, Marguerite. I'm sorry."

She saw the haunted look in his eyes, and in any other circumstances she would have run to him and thrown herself into his arms, sure they could work it out. But she couldn't do it, not tonight, not when a good colt—the best colt the ranch would ever produce, she was sure—was in danger of being destroyed because of his pride.

"Not as sorry as you're going to be, Sloane," she said, her voice shaking with rage. "Now, I'm going to ask you one more time. Are you going to change your mind?"

The look on his face gave her the answer, and, her head high, she swept out of the room without looking back. She slept in one of the guest rooms that night, and every night thereafter, crying herself to sleep and wondering what had happened to the man she loved and to her marriage.

Andrew had taken over Fane's training, and seemed more confident than she that the black colt could win. "And how could he not?" he'd say in his lilt, "when he knows those hills like the back of his hand?"

Every day Andrew would take Fane up into the hills behind the ranch, first walking him up, then trotting, then cantering, and finally, galloping full speed. As he had planned, the colt's strength and agility and confidence grew day by day, and soon he was jumping everything in his path—fallen branches, creeks, whatever they came across. Once on the crest of the highest hill, Andrew would loosen the reins and give Fane his head, and they would race like the wind. Watching from the ranch far below, Marguerite would close her eyes when she caught a glimpse of her fleet young colt. There was no doubt about it; Andrew's methods of training were unorthodox, but even she had to admit that he was getting results. In those moments when she saw them running full tilt, there was no more beautiful sight than her colt racing on the rise.

But running the hills was different than a match race against a seasoned colt like Ulrich, and even when she was most struck by Fane's beauty and speed and grace, Marguerite couldn't rid herself of her feeling of dread. As good a horse as he was, as great in heart, Fane was still green and inexperienced, and she knew how easily a young horse could be ruined. If Ulrich's jockey bumped him, or knocked him off his stride, if something frightened him, or he felt intimidated by the other colt's sheer size, his racing career could be over before it began.

And if Ulrich won . . .

She quaked at the thought. The bet was that the winner of the race had his pick of the other's stock, and Marguerite had no doubt which horse Heinrich would choose. She tried not to think about it, but sometimes at night the insidious thought would creep in, and she would lie there awake, cursing all men. How could Sloane have done such a thing? she wondered again and again.

At last, no matter how much she wanted it not to, the day for the race arrived. Marguerite had prayed for a terrible storm so the match would be canceled, but the fates were against her still, and the day dawned bright and clear and warm. Even the air smelled fresh and clean.

Crowds of people began arriving as early as dawn for the ten o'clock race time, but long before the hour, a picniclike atmosphere prevailed. The hills were dotted with the throngs who had brought baskets of food and blankets to rest on; some enterprising gypsies had set up tents along the road and were plying their trade, reading fortunes for coins, or offering to predict which horse would win for those who paid. Children swarmed, playing with hoops or running around in other games, and even though Marguerite had forbidden both children to leave the house, Kyle risked punishment by sneaking off to join the parade.

Her lips tight, her body stiff, Marguerite watched the circus unfold from an upstairs bedroom window. She was so intent— and trying hard not to burst into tears at the sight of all the revelry going on below—that she didn't realize her daughter had slipped in to join her until she felt a small, thin arm around her waist. When she saw Juliet, she summoned all her control. "What are you doing here, darling?"

Her blue-gray eyes solemn as always, Juliet looked up. "I came to comfort you, Mama," she said. "I know how worried you are."

Marguerite, who had been willing herself not to cry, felt a sob break at the back of her throat. "You're such a comfort, Juliet," she said, grabbing her daughter tight. "Where is your brother?"

Juliet glanced away, out the window. "I don't know, Mama," she said, avoiding Marguerite's eyes.

But a mother knew, Marguerite thought, and she tightened her lips. "He went out to join the crowd, didn't he?" she asked.

"I . . . I'm not sure, Mama."

Marguerite was certain then, but it didn't matter. Nothing seemed to matter at the moment except getting through the day in one piece. At this point, she wasn't even concerned about winning or losing, only that her beloved Fane wouldn't be injured.

"Mama?"

Marguerite had been staring out the window again, looking down at the gathering crowd. She hadn't asked, but Sloane had volunteered the information this morning that a coin toss had decided that the race would start and finish at the front gates to Caulfield Farm. Throngs of people were already there, and she savagely hoped that they'd fill the road and make it impossible to run the damned race.

"What is it, darling?" she asked absently.

Juliet hesitated. Both children knew, because Marguerite didn't believe in lying to them, how she felt about this contest. But her father had sent her up with a message, and because she was a dutiful little girl, she reluctantly repeated it. "Papa wants to know if you'll come outside for the race."

Marguerite's lips tightened. *So, you coward*, she thought, angrily. *You send one of your children with a message you're too craven to come with yourself.*

"Absolutely not—" she started to say, and then changed her mind. She had decided before that she would not dignify this event with her presence, but suddenly she knew she had to be there, no matter how she felt. *For Fane*, she thought. She couldn't let him do this without sending him off; if nothing else, he deserved her support.

"Yes," she said. "You can tell him that I'll be there."

The timid Juliet had always been afraid of horses—or so Marguerite had thought. But now she smiled shyly and gave her mother a hug. "Oh, Mama," she said. "I knew you wouldn't let Fane down. With you there, he's sure to win!"

But Marguerite wasn't at all sure that her presence would be the deciding factor, especially when she forced herself to go down to the barn a few minutes before ten. Since the race would begin and end here, Heinrich had brought his colt over earlier that morning; the big gray was standing in the cross ties at one end of the barn, pawing the floor, while at the other stood her beloved Fane. Seeing Heinrich standing by Ulrich when she came in, Marguerite turned her head, refusing to recognize him.

She did the same thing when she went to the opposite end of the barn, where Fane was being attended to by Sloane and Andrew and two other grooms. She met Andrew's eyes, but she would not look at her husband; she knew if she did, she wouldn't be responsible for what she might say. Instead, she concentrated on her colt.

In contrast to the controlled energy of his opponent, Fane was standing quietly; only a slight quiver to his muscles and his flared nostrils hinted that he sensed something important was about to happen. Her own heart beginning to pound with her fear, Marguerite put her hand out, and Fane gave her palm a quick snuffle before he lifted his head to stare at the gray colt opposite him.

"Miz Caulfield?"

Marguerite felt someone pluck at her sleeve. When she turned and saw Fane's jockey for this race, a local boy named

Danny Sturmer, she tried to smile, but her face felt too tight. "Hello, Danny," she managed.

He was already dressed in the Caulfield Farm colors of green, gold, and amber. He looked so anxious that Marguerite took pity on him and reached out to pat his arm. The silks felt cool and rich under her fingers, and she had a bittersweet memory of the night Sloane had chosen these colors.

"Green for your eyes, Maggie," he'd said, tenderly using the diminutive only he was permitted to use. They'd been in bed, and she was cuddled close, his arms around her, her head on his chest. She could feel his heart beating under her ear, and she lifted her head so she could smile at him. As she did, he reached up and crushed a handful of her hair in his fist. "And amber for your glorious hair. And finally, a lightning bolt in gold to show the impact Caulfield Farm is going to have on the sport."

Then he had pulled her down on top of him, and they had made passionate love.

"Miz Caulfield?"

The images of that glorious night vanished; Marguerite looked down at the anxious jockey again. "What is it, Danny?"

"I just want you to know that I'll take care of 'im, Miz Caulfield," Danny said. "I'll do my best."

"That's all I can ask, Danny," she said, and bent to give him a kiss on the cheek before she burst into tears.

"Jockeys up!" the man who was keeping time said. "It's almost ten o'clock."

Danny turned toward Fane, but Marguerite touched his arm. "Good luck," she managed to say, and then Andrew gave him a leg up. She was so upset that she couldn't listen to the last minute instructions Andrew was giving the boy as they all filed out of the barn and onto the road. She didn't realize for a moment that Sloane was standing by her side. Trying desperately to control her tears, and her growing dread that this was all wrong, she clasped her hands tightly, hoping she wouldn't disgrace herself by making a scene after all.

"Marguerite . . ." Sloane said softly.

She didn't want to talk to him; she couldn't. "Not now," she said, without looking at him. Her heart was pounding so furiously that she thought it might jump into her throat. "You wanted me to be here, and I am. That's all I can give you right now.''

Somehow she made it to the forefront of the crowd. Only once did she involuntarily clutch Sloane's arm for support; it was when they all came in sight of the big front gates and the great throng roared and seemed to surge forward. To Marguerite, tense already, it was a frightening sight, and she reached for her husband. Instantly, he drew her to his side. ''It's all right,'' he assured her.

But it wasn't all right. As she waited for the race to start, she had the feeling that things would never be all right again. *Two miles!* she thought, and couldn't prevent an anxious look at Fane.

As nervous as she was, she had to admit that her colt had never looked better. Andrew had done a marvelous job conditioning him, and muscles bulged under his glossy black coat. He wasn't ''washing out,'' sweating all his energy through nerves; indeed, ears pricked forward, he was practically prancing to the ribbon that had been stretched across the road for the starting line.

In the saddle, Danny seemed relaxed, if a little grim, she noted, and looked at his hands. His fingers were light on the reins—the reason Andrew and Sloane had chosen him out of all the other jockeys who applied—and he barely gave the other horse a glance, concentrating instead on his own mount.

Tearing her eyes away, Marguerite glanced at Heinrich's colt. She deliberately hadn't looked at Ulrich when she entered the barn, but what she saw now made her heart sink. The big gray looked equally fit and much more powerful than the lighter Fane. His haunches were well muscled, and his chest was a greater depth. His rider was Gilbert Hickey, a fearless jockey who had been disciplined by the stewards several times already at various tracks, and when she recognized him, she looked quickly at Sloane.

''You didn't tell me Gilbert Hickey was riding Ulrich,'' she accused.

He didn't say that she hadn't given him a chance. Instead, his eyes on Fane, he answered, ''There are spotters every foot of the way. Hickey won't dare try anything.''

Marguerite wasn't reassured. She knew there were ways for jockeys to control a race: causing another horse to bear out so it had to cover more ground than the rest, or shifting his weight just slightly in the stirrups on a turn, preventing the horse from changing leads. And when there were only two horses running, anything could happen if a jockey was ruthless, and determined, enough.

But it was too late to protest. Helplessly, she watched the two horses surge toward the ribbon stretched across the road. The starter was holding up a red flag signaling that the race was about to begin, and when the crowd saw the flag, it quieted. In those endless seconds before the start, Marguerite felt dizzy. She was so nervous she thought she might faint, and despite her anger at him, she clutched Sloane's arm for support. He was just looking at her in concern when the bell clanged. At almost the same time, as if it had been planned, there was the loud report of a shotgun, and Marguerite looked in horror with everyone else as Fane, panicked by the unexpected sound so close to him, went straight up into the air. Only Danny's skill kept him in the saddle; as it was, he had to grab for a fistful of mane so he wouldn't slide off backward. It took her a few seconds to realize that Heinrich's gray hadn't been affected by the noise; leaping off the starting line with Gilbert shouting at stragglers to get out of the way, Ulrich was already five lengths along the road when Fane came down again.

Marguerite's black colt needed no encouraging; the gun had frightened him, but the blood of champions ran in his veins, and his front feet had hardly touched the ground before he shot forward like a bolt of black lightning. Fortunately, Danny was still holding on to the hank of mane or he would have been left behind. Despite her shock at what had happened, even Marguerite thought she had never seen a horse take off like that. He seemed to shoot forward, disappearing after Ulrich almost before she could blink.

Andrew appeared at Sloane's side. "If I find who e'er shot that gun, I'll have his hide," he growled.

"It wasn't your fault," Sloane said.

"But I should ha' trained him with a gun," Andrew said, enraged. "If I'd known—"

Marguerite was watching Sloane's face. "You think Heinrich has something to do with that, don't you?"

The look he gave her was all the answer she needed. She was about to say something else, but then she realized by the distant roar that went up that the horses had almost reached the halfway point. Grabbing her skirts, she said hurriedly, "I'm going up to the widow's walk to watch the race."

Sloane took her arm. "I'll come with you."

There wasn't time to argue. Together, they practically ran up the steps to the narrow platform high atop the barn roof. From there they could see for miles around, but it wasn't necessary to know the route of the race. People lined the entire course, and as Marguerite emerged breathlessly out onto the platform, she saw two specks, one black, one gray, just coming around the big oak that marked the halfway point. Even without binoculars, she could see that the two horses were neck and neck, and when the black speck slowly started to pull away, she dug her fingers into Sloane's arm.

"He's ahead!" she cried. "Oh, Sloane, he's ahead!"

"Here, here, take the binoculars." He had them on a strap around his neck; jerking the strap over his head, he handed the glasses across to Marguerite. It took her a moment to focus— her hands were shaking so—and when she finally managed to adjust the lenses, the horses were disappearing into the dip down the hillside, before the trees.

"Oh, Sloane! I can't see them!"

"Was Fane ahead?"

"Yes, yes, he was when they disappeared." Andrew claimed that if Fane were ahead at this point, he would win.

"He won't be headed long, I tell ye," Andrew had said, after he had practiced racing Fane against several of the other, older horses on the ranch. "He hates to lose. He hates it!"

Marguerite clung to that thought during the tense few seconds she couldn't see the rivals. But finally there was movement against the hillside, and when the horses emerged, straining up the slope, she gave a cheer along with hundreds of others.

"He's ahead!" she screamed. "Oh, Sloane! He's ahead!"

She couldn't believe it; he was going to win, to win! A last line of trees blocked the horses from view before they swung around again for the finish line, and then it was a clear shot down the road again to the ranch gates. Just for a second or two the flying, driving horses disappeared from view; when they emerged again, the cheer in Marguerite's throat died with a choke. Horrified, she saw that Danny was struggling to stay in the saddle.

"No, no!" she cried. But Fane had been thrown off stride

just long enough for Heinrich's big gray to pass, and then both horses were flying toward home. Wild cheering rose as they raced down onto the road, the gray in front but Fane closing fast again. Marguerite could see the shine of sweat on her colt, his ears pinned flat, and then Ulrich's jockey glance back.

"Faster, Fane!" she screamed, but it was too late. Ulrich flashed by the finish line, a blur of gray and white, and a second later Fane thundered in. The horses had barely been pulled to a halt before Danny flung himself out of the saddle and pulled Gilbert out of his irons. Dragging him off Ulrich, he threw the other jockey to the ground and started to pummel him as hard as he could, shouting like a banshee all the while, tears and sweat flying off his face and hair with each blow.

Marguerite and Sloane raced down to the ground again. Already men were trying to separate the two jockeys, while the grooms had grabbed the horses and leaped up into the saddles to trot them around the pasture so they could cool down.

"Here! Here!" Sloane shouted, wading in. With one powerful arm, he reached down and grabbed Danny by the back of his silks and pulled him off Gilbert, underneath. Gilbert's face was covered with blood, and Danny already looked as if he were going to have a black eye, but he tried to fight his way free of Sloane's grasp anyway.

"I'm going to kill him!" Danny shouted, livid and enraged. "Let me go! I'm going to kill the cheating son of a bitch!"

Gilbert Hickey was known as a bully; like all bullies, he rapidly backed down when confronted. Still on his back, he scuttled out of the way of Danny's flailing feet. If Danny couldn't punch him, he was going to kick what he could.

"I don't know what he's talkin' about!" Gilbert wailed. "What's the matter with him? Is he crazy or somethin'?"

That sent Danny into a renewed frenzy. Even Sloane couldn't hold him this time. Breaking free, Danny launched himself toward Gilbert once more, getting off a couple of punches to the other man's ear and his eye before Sloane and Andrew grabbed him again.

"Here, here, what's it all about?" Andrew demanded, seizing him by the arm. Trying to get his attention, he shook him violently, and at last Danny calmed down.

"He cheated!" Danny cried, bloody and bruised and still so furious he was almost in tears. "He tried to pull me off my horse when we went through those trees back there!"

In the sudden, ringing silence that fell, all eyes turned toward the disheveled Gilbert. Blood and sweat mingled on his red face, too, dripping pinkly down onto the Mondragon silks of black and red. He flinched when Sloane advanced, scrambling back toward Heinrich, who put a proprietary hand on his shoulder. Sloane didn't even flick a glance in Heinrich's direction; his eyes on Gilbert's face, he demanded, "Is that true?"

Reassured by that hand on his shoulder, some of Gilbert's bravado returned. "Nah," he said, wiping his face. "Ol' Danny boy lost control o' the horse. That's all there is to it."

Struggling ferociously against Andrew's strong arms again, Danny shouted, "I didn't lose control, you lyin' son of a bitch! You tried to get me off the horse!"

"Yeah, you're just tryin' to blame me 'cause you lost the race," Gilbert sneered. He glanced slyly at Sloane. "You had spotters up there. Whyn't you ask them?"

But no one had seen anything—or claimed they hadn't—and Sloane was hard put to argue, when the entire route had been lined with spectators. The only blind spot had been for just that second in the trees, but everyone had seen Fane enter first, followed by the gray. Could Ulrich have put on that burst of speed at just the right moment, catching up to let Gilbert tug on the saddle cloth? Even Andrew had to admit that it didn't seem likely.

Everyone but Marguerite—and Danny—seemed to feel that Ulrich had won the race. But Marguerite knew her horse, and for those critical few seconds, she had seen him off stride. She believed Danny, who was practically beside himself with fury and outrage. Her jockey hadn't made a mistake; she would have bet her life on it. Inexperienced he might be compared to Gilbert Hickey, he could ride a horse, and only death would have stopped Fane, who had performed beyond her wildest dreams.

"Then I guess it's official," Heinrich said, when a consensus of sorts had been reached. He glanced around, a glitter of triumph in his eyes. "Ulrich came in first, and as the winner of this match race, I claim as my prize . . ."

Her face white, Marguerite rushed forward. They were all standing in a circle in the courtyard, with the now-cool, blanketed horses still being walked by the grooms somewhere behind them. The crowd was waiting, craning over the fences and the gates, trying to hear the results. Marguerite didn't care; as far as she was concerned they could wait forever. "Sloane, do something!" she cried. "You can't let him do this!"

In the center of the circle, Heinrich looked at her reproachfully. "Ah, Marguerite, my dear. I hadn't expected you would be a poor loser."

She whirled around on him. Her face had been pale before, but now it was flushed with anger. Her eyes fairly blazed. "If Fane had truly lost this race, I would admit it. I've never cheated in my life! But Fane didn't lose, Heinrich Jaeger! You know it, and I know it. Ulrich did not deserve to cross that finish line first!"

Heinrich had involuntarily taken a step back before Marguerite's fierce green eyes. With an effort, he managed to say, "Come now, Marguerite, if you can't admit that your beloved Fane lost, at least give credit where credit is due. Ulrich is a fine horse, which he has just proved."

She clenched her hands, afraid that she might attack him. In a fury, she cried, "The horse is not the issue here, and you know it!"

"Ah, but I'm afraid he is," Heinrich said, and glanced around for confirmation. Uneasily, the men surrounding him nodded, but they wouldn't meet Marguerite's eyes.

Marguerite was so enraged that if someone had handed her a gun, she would have shot him. She stepped forward again, but Sloane took her arm and held her back. His grip was like iron. "Enough, Marguerite," he said, his eyes on Heinrich.

She turned to look at him contemptuously. "Let go of me, Sloane," she said. "If you won't defend the honor of Caulfield Farm, I will!"

Someone gasped. But whether it was that, or the look on Heinrich's face that turned Sloane to stone, Marguerite never knew. Thrusting her behind him so roughly that she nearly lost her balance, he said to Heinrich, "You won the race. Now claim your prize."

Heinrich's eyes blazed coldly in triumph. Glancing around to make sure that everyone there appreciated his victory over his old enemy, he said loudly, so that all could hear, "As the winner of the match race, I claim . . . Fane."

"*No!*" Marguerite cried. The sound was so anguished, so filled with pain, that several of the men who had acted as judges turned away.

No one would help her; she saw it in their eyes. Feeling as if a knife had stabbed her, she jerked away from her husband's grasp. Blindly she ran through the little group surrounding Heinrich and Sloane all the way up to the house. Her heart breaking, she left the ranch that night, taking both children with her, fleeing from the man who had betrayed her, flying from the knowledge that her cherished colt was gone from her forever, all because of something she didn't understand. Filled with grief for all she had lost, she couldn't even weep.

She went to Sacramento. Her father had died several years before, but her mother was still at the house, and when Marguerite arrived in the middle of the night with two sleepy children and only a single suitcase, Anna took one look at her daughter's face and silently took them in. She didn't say anything that night as she prepared the guest rooms for the children, but the next day when she found Marguerite agitatedly sorting out the few clothes she had brought with her, she came into the room and shut the door.

"A good wife does not leave her husband," she said.

"Then I'm not a good wife," Marguerite retorted.

"It is nothing to be proud of, Marguerite."

Marguerite looked out the window. Her children were outside by the now-empty paddocks, looking as bewildered as she felt herself. "I don't want to talk about it, Mama," she said. "This is between Sloane and me. You don't know what happened."

"I don't have to know what happened," Anna replied severely, maddening to Marguerite as always. "It is wrong for you to abandon him."

Marguerite threw down the clothes she had just taken from the suitcase. "Do you want me to leave, then?" she cried.

"No," Anna said stiffly. "A mother does not turn away her child."

With that, she left Marguerite alone. Grabbing the clothes she'd thrown down, Marguerite started putting them away. Her movements became jerky, and she dropped one or two articles before she slammed the drawer shut and burst into tears. Throwing herself on the bed, she cried until she couldn't cry anymore. Not even Juliet could comfort her, nor Kyle, who came in from outside and heard her storm of weeping. Awkwardly, they patted her shoulder, murmuring words of endearment, only half understanding what was wrong. Their gestures touched her heart, but as she gathered them to her, she sobbed even harder. As much as she loved her children, she couldn't help wondering why Sloane hadn't been the one to comfort her.

Andrew came riding in two weeks later. Marguerite was in the kitchen with her mother snapping beans for supper. When she heard the excited cries of her children, she got up to look, then quickly untied her apron and hurried out onto the porch. Trying to hide her disappointment when she saw that he was alone, she came down the steps, holding out her hands.

"Andrew!" she said, thinking how glad she was to see him even though Sloane obviously hadn't come with him. She hadn't heard from her husband the entire time she'd been away, and she wasn't sure how she felt about that. Sometimes she hated Sloane, but at others, when she was calmer, she knew he'd had a reason for what he'd done. She just wished he had explained it to her.

"Sloane doesn't know I've come," Andrew said, giving a nod to her mother, who was peering out the window. He took her hands in his. "Marguerite, I've got to talk to you—alone."

Because she was trying to choke back bitter disappointment, she thought that might be best. If she were going to break down, she didn't want to do it in front of the children, and she sent them back to the house despite their protests. Sure that Andrew had come to tell her some dreadful news—that Sloane was so angry with her he wanted a divorce, for instance—she suggested they take a walk down by the river.

He accepted eagerly, obviously anxious to tell her whatever he had come to say. "Mind you, I'm not supposed to know meself," Andrew said, when they were out of sight of the house. "But I know what a blow it was to you, losin' Fane, and when I found out why, I had to come."

She didn't know what he was talking about. Still disheartened because Sloane hadn't come himself, she stopped under one of the willow trees that grew by the riverbank. The day was hot and humid, the Sacramento River sluggish, like her heart. "Andrew—" she started to say.

He took her hand again, placing it between his own rough

palms. "No, please hear me out, Marguerite. I only pieced it together last night when Sloane let something slip about a man I . . . knew once."

She had to force herself to keep her mind on the conversation. "What man?"

Andrew actually shuddered. "Ian McConachie."

She'd heard that name before; even in her preoccupation with her own misery, she frowned. "Now, why does that sound so familiar?" she said. Then she remembered. Heinrich had said that name to Sloane the day of the party, the day he had challenged Sloane to the race. But what did that have to do with Fane? She still didn't understand.

"He never would ha' said it, if he hadn't been drinkin'," Andrew said earnestly. "He misses you somethin' fierce, Marguerite. He's not been the same man."

Dourly, she said, "I don't deny that. If he'd been the man I married, he never would have agreed to the race."

"But he did it for me, Marguerite," Andrew said. "It's what I came to tell you."

That's when she learned the true story of why he had left Ireland behind. For generations, Andrew's family had raised horses on their farm there, but Andrew had been restless, and he had come to America to see something different, he said sheepishly. But it was there he'd met Sloane in a most dramatic way—helping him stave off some would-be robbers, who, because of the way Sloane was dressed, thought him an easy mark. One of the robbers had unsheathed a knife and Sloane was fighting him for it when Andrew came along and pitched in.

"He got nicked, all right," Andrew said, his eyes lighting with the memory before he remembered he was talking to the man's wife. "But it was only a small wound," he said hastily. "The blade hit his shoulder instead of his heart."

Marguerite felt a little pale. Her hand at her throat, she leaned against the willow tree. "My goodness," she said. "You saved his life!"

Andrew looked embarrassed. "Well, I just happened to be in the right place at the right time," he said, and then his expression changed. "Another time, I wasn't so lucky."

That had been when he'd gone back to Ireland to take over the horse farm. His mother had died some years before, and his ailing father was trying to work the place alone. With no one else to help, Andrew had been forced to give up his dream of living in America.

"I was angry, oh, indeed, I was," Andrew said grimly. "And how I resented the end to all my grand plans. But me da needed me; there had been some funny goings on. One of the townsmen, a fine swell named Ian McConachie, wanted our land, but me father wouldn't sell. The land—and the horses— were all he knew, don't you see? And he wouldn't give it up for nowt." His blue eyes turned sad. "But it cost him, it did; in the end, his fightin' for that land killed him."

Marguerite put out a hand. "Oh, Andrew, I'm sorry," she said.

"Oh, if only the story would end there, it would be bad enough, but it doesn't," Andrew sighed. Bending down, he picked a long stem of grass and stuck it between his teeth. After a moment, his eyes far away, he said, "Sometimes I think the only good thing to come of that time—aside from my Angus, I mean—was my Eileen."

"Eileen?"

"My wife," Andrew said, biting down hard on the blade of grass. "Oh, you would have liked her, Marguerite," he said dreamily. "She was so beautiful, was my Eileen—eyes blue as the sky and hair like fire, and the most beautiful smile I ever have seen."

Marguerite was almost afraid to ask. "What happened?" she said gently.

Andrew tossed aside the blade of grass. Staring out across the river, he said, "Well, it wasn't enough for McConachie that he'd killed me da. Oh, I couldn't prove it, y'see, and he knew he was safe. Soon things were happenin' to the horses, and a fire had sprung up once in the barn. Two of the dogs were killed, their carcasses left in the yard for my Eileen to see. I was white with fury, for by then she was carryin' Angus, and she didn't need to deal with such things. I knew he'd never give up, and I wanted to confront him, but she wouldn't let me. McConachie was a powerful man, and with the baby due soon she didn't want any trouble."

But trouble had come anyway, the night Eileen was attacked on the way home from evening service at the church. By the time she was found, the doctor was only able to save the baby. Eileen died that night, and Andrew went crazy. Out of his mind with shock and grief, he went to see McConachie.

"E'en then, I might not ha' done what I did," Andrew said bleakly. "But he admitted it to me, Marguerite, he *admitted* it to me. He said he'd sent those thugs around, that they were supposed to frighten her, so that she would convince me to leave." He paused, expelling a heavy breath. "Well, that convinced me, all right," he went on finally. "But I couldn't go, not without gettin' some o' my own back." He looked down at his thick, strong hands. "I beat the man to a bloody pulp, Marguerite. With these fists, I beat the man senseless. But I didn't mean to kill him, I swear before God, I didn't mean to kill him."

But he had. When word came quickly to him in the early hours of that dawn, he knew what he had to do. McConachie was a powerful man; Andrew McKenna was a nobody. With no other choice, he took his son and ran.

He ran all the way to America, smuggling himself and the baby aboard a steamer bound for New Orleans. But California was the land of opportunity, and he knew that if he could get to Caulfield Farm, his old friend would give him a job until he got on his feet.

"But I couldn't ask him for anythin' until I told him the whole sorry tale," Andrew finished. He shook his head. "How that man Jaeger found out, I don't know," he said bleakly. "But he used it to force Sloane to agree to the race, Marguerite. And Sloane, big, blithering fool that he is, thought he owed me a debt." He looked anxiously into her face. "Can you forgive me, Marguerite? If I could undo what's been done, I would, you know I would. But all I can do is pack up and go before I cause more trouble. So I'm takin' Angus, and we'll be on our way. I just wanted you to know before I went that what happened wasn't Sloane's fault." His voice broke. "Never a better friend did a man have than Sloane Caulfield."

"And never a better husband for a foolish woman," Marguerite said, her own voice suddenly choked. Now she understood. She had known all along that Sloane had had a powerful reason for doing what he had; she just wished he had shared it with her. Fane was gone; she had to accept it. But that didn't mean she had to lose everything. Reaching for Andrew's hand, she said, "You're not going anywhere, Andrew McKenna. Except back with us to Caulfield Farm."

Andrew looked at her disbelievingly. "You mean you don't want me to leave? After . . . after all the trouble I caused?"

Marguerite thought again of her beloved Fane, gone now to

Heinrich Jaeger. *But not forever*, she thought fiercely. One day, she didn't care how long it took, she'd get him back. But right now she had something else to do—her own fences to mend. She had misjudged Sloane, who deserved more than an apology, but her wholehearted admiration as well. Could she have been so selfless? she wondered, and hoped she'd never be put to the test.

"I think," she said, smiling shakily at Andrew, "that it's time we all went home. . . ."

---

# CHAPTER TWENTY-FIVE

Two months after Touch the Fire came home, the holiday season arrived. Briar had been wanting to throw a party to celebrate Caulfield Farm's return to the racing world, but after the filly's injury at the track, she hadn't felt like celebrating anything. But when the horse was doing so well by Christmas, she decided she could at least invite some of the people she had met through racing for cocktails, so she planned the party for one weekend in December.

Naturally, it was raining that night, but she had almost expected it, and she actually thought it would work out best this way. She knew at least some of her guests would want to go down to the barn to see the great race mares, the beautiful Incandessence and her Touch the Fire, but the black filly was in such a black mood herself after her long confinement that Briar didn't want her disturbed. Even Gillie, who never had trouble with any of the horses, was having difficulties with her, although he had become so protective of his charge that he would find an excuse even for the worst behavior.

"Don't you worry about this little girl," Gillie had told Briar just the other day. He patted the filly's glossy black neck, smiling even when the temperamental horse laid back her ears. She looked as if she wanted to nip, but Gillie smiled again and cradled her head against his chest for a moment before he released her. "She'll be jus' fine, jus' fine," he said proudly. "She'll race again, I guarantee it."

Briar wished she could be as certain. But Denise, her vet up here, and Kara, who had been consulted by phone from Santa Anita, as well as two other leg men from the renowned equine center at the University at Davis, were still cautious about the final outcome for the filly as far as racing was concerned. True, she was healing well, and with Roy flying up from Santa Anita every four weeks or so to shoe her with the special glue-on shoes, she could put weight on the leg now. But with an injury like hers, doing well wasn't enough; if Touch the Fire were to race again, the leg had to heal completely and be as strong as, if not stronger, than it had been before.

Every time Briar went down to the barn to check on the horses and saw the leg bandages on the filly and Mi Flor Amor, she was reminded of her ambivalence about the sport. She'd had mixed emotions from the beginning about racing and the demands made on the horses. On the one hand, she felt there was no sight in the world more thrilling than a Thoroughbred doing what he had been born and bred and raised and trained to do. But there was a dark side to that glorious picture, and during the time she had been directly involved in racing as an owner, she had learned more about the sport than she ever wanted to know. At times it had made her almost physically ill to discover what was going on: the doping, the insurance scams, the medication given to mask illness or injury, the bets that were taken, the deals that were made. . . . The list went on and on.

"It's no different than any other sport," Wayne had told her one afternoon when she and Stefan had flown down to watch Ten Diamonds race. "It's no better or worse than any of 'em."

"That doesn't make it right," Briar said. "There are rules to protect the horses—"

Wayne had given a philosophical shrug. "But it's not about horses, Briar; it's about money. Horses are only the tools to make the game run."

"Horses shouldn't be tools!" she exclaimed, and then saw the glance exchanged between the two men. "All right, I know I sound like a naive, silly fool," she said, "but I can't help it. Horses can't defend themselves; someone has to do it for them."

"And you're about as good an advocate as I can imagine," Wayne had said gallantly. "But you're not going to change the system, no way, and if you can't accept that, you don't belong on the backside—nor anywhere else at the track."

Intellectually, she agreed. In her heart, it was a different story. Stefan saw her stormy expression and said, "Come on, Wayne. You know what she means. Things do happen, and it's always the horse that suffers."

"Yes, that's true, but it's the way of the world," Wayne insisted. "Mind you, I'm not defending it, and I'm not a part of it myself. But I know for a fact that when the newest hop comes along, a lot of trainers leap at it."

Briar had heard about "hopping," an expression that originated early on when trainers started using heroin on horses. It had happened on the best racecourses, not only the bush tracks. Even around the barns at Belmont Park, trainers from the old days who won many major stakes races were remembered with admiration—in some cases—for using heroin on horses better than anyone else.

Briar hadn't believed it, but Wayne told her it was true. "In fact," he said, "even the legendary Man o' War, who was so popular in his time that crowds attended his burial and there were live national radio broadcasts, was spoken of by some as the 'greatest hophead horse of all time.' "

She felt sick. "It's hard to believe."

"And what about the time that a federal narcotics agent found a veterinarian about to give Whirlaway—a Triple Crown winner—cough syrup saturated with morphine?" Stefan asked. "That was at Calumet Farm, if you can imagine. Didn't he later plead guilty in court?"

"But why would he do such a thing in the first place?"

"Morphine can either sedate or stimulate a horse, depending on the dose," Stefan said with a shrug. "I guess it depended whether he was supposed to lose or win."

Briar shook her head. "Cough syrup," she muttered.

"There were lots of so-called tonics back then," Wayne said. "In fact, as far back as the eighteenth century, stimulating a horse with whiskey was as common as using vitamin B today. And I remember reading about one mixture that everybody used—a combination of heroin, cocaine, and nitrate of glycerin, I think."

"Good lord," Briar said. "That's horrible!"

"Yeah, it is," Stefan agreed. "But take heart, things are even more sophisticated today."

She was almost afraid to ask. "How?"

"Well, now instead of simply trying to make a horse run faster, the fad is to minister to an animal's specific physical or psychological weakness," Wayne said. "We've gotten so fancy that we have drugs to reduce pain in a specific area of a sore or stiff horse, and drugs to increase the stamina in a fast but weak horse, who might otherwise tire in the stretch. Then we have other things that can relax, without depressing, a talented but highly nervous horse. The stuff comes out so fast there isn't even time for the chemists to identify it before they're on to something else."

"And I thought all a horse had to do was run," Briar said, shaking her head. "What a sap I am."

Stefan smiled sympathetically. "No, not a sap. Just someone who cares about horses and likes to see them do what they do best."

"Yes, but now I'm not going to know which ones are fit to be out on the track, and which have been . . . hopped up to race."

"Well, I'll tell you one thing," Wayne said, ending the discussion. "Every horse in *my* stable runs honest. I don't tolerate drugs, except legitimate ones, either for my horses or the people who work for me. And you can bet on it."

Remembering that conversation as she started getting dressed for her party, Briar wondered if she really wanted Touch the Fire to return to the track. She trusted Wayne implicitly, and she knew he would never be part of doping a horse, but she also was aware of the abuses that went on, and she hated the thought of encouraging it, even indirectly, by her own participation in the sport.

"If you can't handle it," she muttered to herself as she sat at the dressing table to do her hair, "you should just get out. It's as simple as that."

But it wasn't simple at all, and she knew it. Life rarely was. She'd known even before she got involved in racing that she would see things she wouldn't admire. It was the same way in anything. There were always those who would try to get an edge any way they could, morals or ethics be damned, and sometimes all you could do was refuse to go along—or look the other way.

As much as she hated the last alternative, she thought, she might just be reduced to that. She couldn't fight a system that had been in force for over three hundred years—since the colonists cleared quarter-mile paths through dense forests over which to race their horses. Maybe the only thing she could do was, as Wayne said, race honest.

But it was early as far as Touch the Fire was concerned, she told herself. She had several months still before a decision had to be made, and it might even be out of her hands, at that. In the end, she thought with a pang, it was all up to her gallant black horse.

As she started to do her makeup, she thought about her great-grandmother and Fane. She didn't like to think about Marguerite's account of the match race and the tragic after-math; whenever she did, she felt enraged all over again. What Heinrich had done was unfair and unjust, and although she believed that no one had ever promised that things would be fair in this life, she still seethed. Because she felt the same way about Touch the Fire as Marguerite had felt about Fane, she knew the pain her great-grandmother had suffered when she'd lost her young colt, and after reading the heartrending account, Briar wondered if maybe the vendetta between the two families hadn't gotten turned around. To her way of thinking, Marguerite was the one who had been wronged, and she should have been the one seeking redress and revenge. Why, then, all these years later, was Rupert Jaeger still obsessed?

The thought gave her pause, for she didn't know what she would do if she were ever put in Marguerite's position. The idea of losing her own magnificent horse to anyone, but especially a man like Rupert Jaeger, was too awful to contemplate, and she shivered suddenly and reached for her robe. She'd better hurry if she wanted to go downstairs and check on things before her guests started to arrive. She quickly finished her makeup and put on the heavy cream-colored satin shirt and long forest green velvet skirt she'd bought for this occasion. With emeralds at her ears and the Christmas corsage Stefan had sent up earlier, she was ready.

But as she paused in front of the mirror to check her appearance one last time, her glance went to the corsage she had pinned to the blouse, and she slowly reached up to touch it. She had been surprised when Isabella brought it up before she started to dress; at first, she hadn't the faintest idea who might have sent it. Then, when she saw the card, signed with a simple *S*, she actually felt herself flush.

"Oh, isn't it *beautiful*!" Isabella had said, giggling and looking significantly at Briar from under her lashes. "And see the red roses! According to your custom, does not that mean love?"

Briar knew what a romantic soul Isabella had, and she took the silver box with the cellophane top a little too quickly. "It's Christmas," she said. "Red is a Christmas color. That's all it is."

Isabella's bright black eyes twinkled. "If you say so, señora. But the *red* roses are still beautiful, are they not?"

Briar took the corsage out of the box. Deep green holly leaves framed the three roses, with delicate white baby's breath clustered around them, sprinkled with glitter. Remembering flamboyant Jaz with his black orchid for the fund-raiser, she thought guiltily that she much preferred the roses. But then maybe it had something to do with which man had sent them.

"Yes, they are beautiful, Isabella," she agreed, feeling a little pink herself. "I. . . I didn't dream Stefan would think of this, but it will look nice with my outfit tonight, won't it?"

"Oh, *sí*, very nice," Isabella said, carefully closing the box. Without looking at Briar, she added, "The only thing better would be if the señor could be here himself, don't you think?"

Briar did think so, but Stefan's absence couldn't be helped. Stan Taber had called earlier with a real emergency: the storm was worse down in the Bay Area and had caused flooding in both big barns at the club. With the water rising, he was having to relocate horses and was desperate for enough trailers and competent drivers to handle the task. Since Briar had recently acquired a nine-horse van herself, he had called to ask if he could borrow it—and Stefan, too, if he could be spared. Of course Stefan had gone down to help evacuate.

"I'm sorry, Briar," Stefan had said, when he'd hooked up the rig. He was wearing a yellow slicker and a hat whose brim was already dripping water. They were standing outside the barn, Briar with a coat thrown over her shoulders. "I'll try to get back as soon as possible, but I don't think I'll be able to make the party."

"That's all right," she said, wondering how he could be so good-looking in any circumstances, in any kind of weather. She had really looked forward to having him at the party tonight, but she couldn't be selfish. "Helping Stan is more important. And don't hurry. I don't want you to get into an accident."

He grinned. "Why? Isn't the rig paid for?"

She grinned back. "One more crack like that, and I'll give another party so you *have* to be there."

They both knew she was referring to the discussion they'd had about his attending this one. When she had first proposed the idea of a holiday party and said she wanted him to come, he had protested with all sorts of excuses.

"I don't know, Briar," he'd said immediately. "I'm not much on parties."

"Neither am I, but I'll try to make this one as painless as possible for you."

"Well, who are you going to invite? I really don't want to spend an entire evening listening to a bunch of swells bragging about how little they know about horses."

"Neither do I," she'd countered. "I promise I'll invite people who can talk about other things than horses."

He'd pretended horror. "You mean there are other things to talk about?"

"We could talk about why you don't want to accept," she said. "Why don't we discuss that for a minute?"

"It's not that I don't *want* to come. It's just that if you're inviting owners, it'll make things difficult."

"How?"

"I have a different relationship with those people than you do. If they have to socialize with me, or me with them, it'll change things the next time I try to negotiate a deal for you."

"That's ridiculous. You're coming."

"Is that an order?"

"Do I have to make it one?"

"If you do, I won't come."

"Then I won't. Are you happy now?"

"I'd be happier if you didn't expect me to attend this party in the first place."

"How about if I make it worth your while?"

"Even *you* don't have that much money."

"I wasn't thinking of money."

There was a silence. "What were you thinking of then?"

She smiled, catlike. "I was thinking of having our own party after."

"After what?" he said suspiciously.

"Why don't you come and see?" she said, and added for good measure, "By the way, a suit is fine; this isn't black tie."

"Oh, darn, and here I was hoping that in addition to everything else, the damn thing would be formal."

"I could arrange it if you like."

He glowered at her. "A suit will do just fine."

"I thought so," she said, and left it at that.

Now he wasn't coming after all. With rain beginning to drip down her neck, she clutched her coat more tightly about her and said, "It's all right, Stefan, it's not your fault."

Under the hat brim, his grin was evil. "You mean you don't think I ordered the storm on purpose so I wouldn't have to come tonight?"

"The thought occurred to me, I admit. It's a good thing I like Stan, or I wouldn't have loaned him you—or the trailer."

"How about the other invitation?" Stefan asked, with an even more wicked glint in his eye. "Is that still open?"

She laughed. "I don't know, we'll have to see what time you get back. . . ."

The party started out well, Briar thought. At the risk of hurting Isabella's feelings, she had suggested hiring caterers to prepare hors d'oeuvres and special holiday canapes, and Isabella had been so happy she had practically gone down on her knees in thanks at being relieved of the responsibility. That taken care of, and with a chef from one of the best restaurants in Sonoma busy in the kitchen, two maids circulating with trays, and a bartender and one waiter to serve drinks for the twenty invited guests, Briar was able to relax and enjoy her role as hostess. Dressed in her cream and forest green, with the red rose corsage, she looked elegant and composed and confident as she moved among her guests with a glass of white wine she rarely touched. As Stefan had predicted, the conversations she overheard or took part in were about—what else?—horses.

"I had to fire my trainer just the other day," one man, whose family had been breeding Thoroughbreds for three generations in Maryland, was saying when Briar came up to see if anyone needed fresh drinks. "When I caught him giving water to one of my horses right before a race."

"The oldest trick in the world," commented someone else

in the group. "Untraceable—nothing easier if you want to cheat."

In another group, a woman who had been in the business for fifty years, was saying, "I remember when, even on major tracks, strong men were needed to start races. There was one mixture everybody used—a combination of powdered caffeine, applejack brandy, and wild cherry wine."

"Whiskey was simpler, in my granddaddy's time," said someone else. "Of course, you had to have a decent horse to wake up, even at that."

And in yet another little group: "Yeah, I remember one hop—what was that, Milton? Something concocted of hydro-chloride and apomorphine that was secretly used for ten years at Belmont Park."

"What on earth for?" Briar asked.

"Supposedly, it instilled the same aggressiveness in a fast but timid horse as two martinis would do to a shy man."

"What will they think of next?" she murmured, and moved on.

"I think that colt's a cinch for the Ambergris Stakes," someone was saying when she joined the next group.

"If it were me, I'd prefer a mortal lock," another commented.

"What's the difference?" Briar asked.

The man grinned. "A cinch is just that—a sure thing. A lock is a horse that has to fall down to lose. And a mortal lock is a horse that can't lose even if he *does* fall down."

In the accompanying laughter, someone said, "Or, we can always hope to be 'on the Bill Daly.' "

Briar turned to him. "Bill Daly?" she said.

"He was a trainer who was fond of telling his jockeys to go to the front and try to improve their position," the guest explained, to another round of laughter.

Still smiling herself, Briar was starting out to the kitchen to check on the flaming cherry dessert she had ordered when she noticed Charlotte Jaeger standing by herself at the front of the room. Motionless in black velvet, she was staring out the window at the night, and when Briar saw the expression on her face, she paused, wondering what the older woman was thinking about. Charlotte looked so . . . sad, she thought, and on impulse she went over.

"We haven't had much chance to talk, but I wanted to thank

you for coming tonight,'' Briar said as she came up. She glanced out the window at the rainy night and shivered. ''It's not a very good night for a party, I'm afraid.''

As if coming back from a faraway place, Charlotte blinked and looked at her. ''For some people, any night is a good night for a party,'' she said, distracted.

Briar smiled. ''But not for those of us who have to get up early to take care of a horse ranch, right?''

Charlotte returned the smile with a faint one of her own. ''That's true,'' she agreed, and then glanced somberly in the direction of the barn again. ''I doubt you'll believe me, but I was sorry when I heard about your filly. I hope she's coming along well?''

''Yes, she is,'' Briar said, and then had to add, ''But why wouldn't I believe you? I would no more wish one of your horses ill than I suspect you would one of mine.''

Charlotte seemed almost surprised by Briar's comment. ''That's true,'' she said again, her pale glance turning speculative as she looked into Briar's face. ''But how can you know that?''

Briar held her glance. ''We're both horsewomen,'' she said, glancing toward Charlotte's father, who was surrounded by people on the other side of the room. She couldn't resist adding, ''And I've never believed animals should suffer because of the foibles of their humans.''

Unwillingly, Charlotte followed her glance. ''Nor I,'' she muttered, and without warning, a cold curtain seemed to come down over her face. ''Excuse me,'' she said abruptly. ''It's been a lovely party, but I really must go.''

''So soon!'' Briar couldn't hide her dismay. She'd thought that in a social setting, she and Charlotte might have a chance to talk.

After her last comment, Charlotte seemed anxious to leave. She'd brought her own car, Briar had noted earlier, and now she reached for the coat she'd left on a chair. ''I'm sorry, but I have a horse with colic at home, and I really must check on her,'' Charlotte said hastily, throwing the coat around her shoulders. ''You understand, don't you?''

There wasn't much Briar could say to that. Trying to disguise her disappointment, she showed Charlotte to the front door. But Charlotte paused before she went out.

''Thank you again for inviting me,'' Charlotte said, and

then, as if on reluctant impulse, she reached out and touched Briar's hand. "You're so like—" she said, and then caught herself. Quickly, she turned and went down the steps to her car.

Wondering what she'd meant, Briar was still standing in puzzlement by the doorway when she heard the party stir. As she glanced around, she saw that Rupert Jaeger, whom she had also felt compelled to invite despite her better instincts, had gone to the fireplace. Loudly, he cleared his throat.

"I'd like to make a toast," he said. Everyone turned expectantly, glasses in hand. He was drinking champagne, and he raised his flute. As his eyes met Briar's, she wondered if she was the only one who noticed that the smile didn't reach his wintry eyes. Taking a glass of champagne herself from a waiter, she waited to hear what he had to say.

"To Briar McKenna, our gracious hostess," Rupert said. "And to the reemergence of an old name in racing: Caulfield Farm."

"To Caulfield Farm . . . Caulfield Farm . . ."

As Briar acknowledged the echoes of her guests with a smile and a lift of her own glass, she decided that she was not going to be outdone. Waiting until everyone had drunk, she raised her glass once more.

"And to Marguerite and Sloane Caulfield," she said clearly, "who made possible what Caulfield Farm is today."

"Hear, hear!" someone said, while before the fireplace, Rupert Jaeger's eyes narrowed. He was the only one who did not drink to Briar's toast, but set aside his glass. Briar should have known he had something more up his sleeve, but he waited until her flaming dessert had been served, to the appreciative murmurs of her guests, before he brought up the subject of Touch the Fire.

"And when, Miss McKenna," he said, into a brief silence, "will we be allowed to see that great filly of yours?"

"Oh, I don't think . . ." she murmured. "After all, the rain . . ."

But it was too late. Rupert had sowed the idea, and everyone else joined in. They would take their cars down to the barn to have a quick look at her black horse, and then they would depart. It would be such a fitting end to a wonderful party. Wasn't it possible . . . ?

Gracefully, she gave in. She had expected this, after all, and had prepared Gillie earlier for the influx of guests whom she was sure would want to see her special horse.

"And they should, they should," Gillie had said proudly, when she had asked if he wouldn't mind standing by. "Don't you worry, Miz Briar, I'll have her ready. She'll *shine*!"

And so she did, when everyone drove down to the main barn and dashed in from the rain. As he had promised, Gillie was waiting, and when Briar saw him, standing straight and at attention, right by the filly's stall, she was touched. He was wearing the new suit she had bought for him and looked proud as punch.

"You look just fine, Gillie," she whispered to him.

His smile nearly split his face. "I tried, Miz Briar. I wanted you to be proud of me."

"I am, G—" she was starting to say, when suddenly he looked beyond her and gasped. His eyes widened, and he looked so frightened that Briar thought he was having some kind of attack. Quickly, she put her hand on his arm. "Gillie! What is it?"

He couldn't seem to answer. His eyes strained and wide, he continued to stare at some point beyond her, his mouth making involuntary movements, as if he wanted to say something but was unable. Wondering if she should call the emergency number, she glanced quickly over her shoulder, trying to see what he was looking at.

The rest of her guests had fanned out down both sides of the aisle, occupied with looking at the other horses until Touch the Fire was ready to be brought out. The only other person close by was Rupert Jaeger, who was staring at Gillie with such a strange expression that Briar didn't know what to think. Did they know each other? Quickly, she looked from one man to the other.

"Gillie?" she said.

The old man broke out of his trance. "I'll jus' get the filly now, Miz Briar," he said hurriedly. "I'll jus'—"

She couldn't pretend she hadn't noticed anything, and as Gillie tried to lunge away, she took firm hold of his arm. Urgently, she said, "What is it? What's wrong?"

She could feel him shudder. "Nothin', Miz Briar," he said, clearly anxious to get away from her. "Nothin' at all. If you'll 'scuse me, I'll jus' get the horse now."

Before she could stop him, he jerked away from her. Clutching a leather halter in his hand, he quickly opened the filly's stall door and slipped inside just as Rupert came up.

"What was that all about?" he asked, unconcerned.

"I'm not sure," she said. "Do you . . . know each other?"

"Never saw him before in my life."

"Are you sure? He looked as if he knew you."

"He's an old man," Rupert said with a shrug. "He's obviously confused."

Briar was about to tell Rupert that when he was a boy, Gillie had once lived right here on the ranch. But something about the way Rupert was acting stopped her; he seemed too unconcerned, too impassive and detached. Deciding that now was not the time to get to the bottom of it, Briar murmured something, and then stepped back as Gillie, eyes downcast, but shaking visibly, brought Touch the Fire out of her stall. Despite her obvious injury she emerged like a queen, gazing with that look of eagles over their heads at something only she could see.

"Oh, Briar, she looks just wonderful!" someone said.

Briar said something in response, but her attention was on Gillie. He looked . . . she wasn't she how he looked, but he obviously wasn't well, and she took the filly's halter rope from him. "I'll take over," she whispered. "Why don't you go on upstairs?"

She was even more disturbed by the way he was acting when he didn't protest but quickly handed her the horse. This was so unlike him that she barely heard the rest of the comments from her guests. Unable to understand why he hadn't insisted on showing off his beautiful girl, as he called the black filly, Briar watched as he quickly sidled by the people crowding around and disappeared up the stairs to the loft.

Her eyes troubled, she turned back to her guests in time to hear, "Will she race again, Briar?"

Briar felt the quickened interest in the group. This was the question that had been on everyone's mind since the filly had been injured. Even now, the general public didn't know the full extent of the horse's injuries; Briar had refused to give out statements.

"It's early yet," she said. "We're just taking it one step at a time."

"A pity, isn't it? She was so promising as a two-year-old," Rupert said.

With her mind still on Gillie's strange behavior, Briar wasn't as cautious as she should have been. "I wouldn't say her racing career is over yet, Mr. Jaeger. She and your own Galland may yet meet one day in a race."

"Boy, that would be some contest, Touch the Fire against Galland!" someone said.

"Yes," Rupert said with that crocodile-like smile. "It would be, wouldn't it?"

"Don't tell me you'd consider it!" another voice said excitedly.

Alerted too late, Briar started to speak up, but no one was paying attention to her, for Rupert had seized the floor.

"Before she was sidelined by her . . . er . . . injury, Touch the Fire was at the top of her class, just as Galland is now," he said. "In fact, I think it's fair to say that neither horse has been truly challenged by any other animal in their age group. I do think it might be interesting to see how well they'd perform against each other, yes, I agree."

"But no one knows whether your horse will run again, isn't that so, Briar?" someone asked.

Briar hardly heard the question; she was fighting a sudden wave of dizziness, an appalling sense of déjà vu. This wasn't how it had happened in her great-grandmother's time, but she still remembered reading Marguerite's journal, and she knew she was experiencing the same trapped feeling Marguerite had felt then.

Fiercely, she willed herself together. Marguerite had been compelled by circumstances to agree to the match race between Fane and Ulrich; no such forces were at work here tonight.

"This discussion, as fascinating as it is, is all academic, don't you think?" she said, forcing herself to speak lightly despite the hard pounding of her heart. "We still don't know if Touch the Fire will return to racing. We'll just have to wait."

Rupert said, "But there's plenty of time. As you all know, our Galland came back with sore shins earlier this week; he won't be able to race for at least a month, and—" he paused to look craftily in Briar's direction"—by that time, Ms. Mc-Kenna will be in a better position to judge her filly's recovery. Why don't we wait until then?"

Briar couldn't believe this might be happening again. Was it true that history repeated itself? No, no. She would not be railroaded into a match race as Marguerite had been, not to satisfy this cold bastard of a man who thought he could play games with whomever he chose. Even if her filly did race again in the future—and that was still in doubt—Rupert couldn't *force* her to participate. She would not be goaded into doing this just because of an age-old vendetta she didn't even understand.

"No," she said, "I'm sorry. I will never agree—"

She was interrupted by a renewed buzz, as her guests excitedly digested the idea Rupert had proposed. "Imagine, a match race between the filly of the decade and the colt who might be Horse of the Year!" someone exclaimed. "It would generate as much interest or more than the race between Ruffian and Foolish Pleasure—"

"I'm sure it would, but—" Briar started to say loudly.

No one seemed to have heard her, except Rupert Jaeger. Standing to one side, a cold smile playing around his thin lips, he was watching her—much, she imagined, the same way his father had watched Marguerite when Heinrich had proposed the match race between Ulrich and Fane.

*No!* Briar thought, trying not to panic. It wasn't happening again. She wouldn't let it. Even if her filly did race again, she wouldn't agree; not again. It was insane!

She held herself together until the last of her guests had finally gone. Once he had planted the seed and done what damage he could at present, Rupert Jaeger was one of the first to leave, eloquently polite as always, as he thanked her for a good time. But she knew by remarks everyone else made as they departed that she hadn't heard the last of this match race business. She was in a tizzy as she rushed upstairs to change into jeans and a sweater after everyone had gone. As late as it was, she had to reassure herself about Gillie.

But Gillie wasn't in his room over the barn when she dashed back down there and knocked. His little studio apartment was empty and dark when she opened the door, and she knew immediately that something was wrong. Feverishly she paced until Stefan got home again, wet and dirty and exhausted from moving all those horses to safe ground. By that time, it was after two in the morning, and Briar was ready to call all the hospitals.

"Gillie's disappeared!" she cried, running out to the truck as Stefan pulled up by the barn. She didn't even give him a chance to get out before she jerked open the door. "We've got to find him!"

"Wait, hold on!" he exclaimed, surprised by her sudden appearance out of the dark. He had circles under his eyes, and his jeans were wet to the knees. "Let me change, and you can tell me what's going on."

"There's no time for that," she said frenziedly. "Gillie's gone—just disappeared—and we have to find him!"

He'd never been fond of the old man, and he was so tired he had almost fallen asleep on the way home. Firmly, he said, "Briar, I'm cold and wet and tired, and I need a shower and a brandy and some time to get warm. The last thing I want to do right now is run around like a fool trying to find an old drunk in the dark."

"Then I'll do it myself!" Briar said, and whirled away. Sighing heavily, he got out of the truck and pulled her into the relative warmth of the barn.

"Just calm down," he said. "Even if I intended to, we can't just go running around like chickens with our heads cut off. We have to have a plan. First, tell me what happened."

"I don't know what happened!" she said, trying to control her growing panic. She knew he was right, but she felt it was all her fault. She never should have let Gillie leave. She should have followed him. But with Stefan looking at her like that, she couldn't go off half-cocked, so she took a deep breath and said, "It started when everyone wanted to see Touch the Fire. . . ."

"Go on," Stefan said, rubbing his hands together. He had a smudge of dirt on one lean cheek and even his mustache looked bedraggled. Seeing how pale and tired he was, she had a change of heart.

"I'll tell you while you change," she said. "Come on."

He didn't argue and led the way at a run through the driving rain toward his house. He never locked the door; he saw no reason to, and after switching on the living room lights, he said, "I'm going to take a quick shower. Why don't you make some coffee?"

Thinking that was an excellent idea, she had two cups made by the time he came into the kitchen again, his hair still wet, but the smudge gone from his cheek. He was dressed in dry jeans and a heavy Irish sweater. As he sat down at the table and put his hands around the mug, he said, "All right, now start from the beginning."

The thought of Gillie being out somewhere in the storm, frightened and cold, clawed at her nerves, but she was calmer by this time, so she told him what had happened as succinctly as possible.

"We all came down to the barn to look at the horses—especially the black filly," she said. "I knew everybody would want to see her, so I had already warned Gillie to have her ready, and he was here when we came." She smiled tightly, thinking of how proud he had looked. "He was wearing his new suit, and everything was fine—until he saw Rupert Jaeger. Then . . . I don't know . . . it was as if he had seen a ghost. He looked so frightened that I thought for a minute he was having a heart attack. I asked him what was wrong, but he insisted he was all right. He wanted to show the horse, but I told him I'd take care of it, and then I sent him upstairs. I . . . I didn't know what else to do, Stefan. You should have seen him; I've never seen anyone so scared."

"What was he scared of?"

"I don't know. It had to be Rupert; he was the only one around, and Gillie was looking right at him when he froze. But when I asked Rupert if they knew each other, he denied it, so I . . . I don't know."

"So then what happened?"

She was starting to relax in his soothing presence. "Well, I waited until everybody left, and then I came down here again to talk to him. I was worried. I knew he was sick, or something was wrong. But by the time I got here, he . . . he was gone."

Suddenly, she didn't feel so serene after all. Terribly worried that Gillie might be ill or hurt, she clutched Stefan's arm. "We have to find him, Stefan! I don't want him wandering around in the storm!"

"He's not wandering around in the storm."

"How do you know that? How do you know *where* he is?"

Stefan sighed. "Oh, Briar, you and your orphans."

"My orphans! What do you mean?"

He shook his head. "Well, first there was Jaime—"

"Jaime? He needed a job!"

"And then there was Isabella."

"She was Jaime's wife! They were miserable, having to live apart!"

He wasn't going to let her off the hook easily. "You even

rescued your so-called stepchildren, what are their names? Oh, yes, Jaz and Fredrica, isn't that right?''

"I didn't rescue them. I only did what was right.''

"By dividing your husband's estate?''

What was he talking about? "That was only fair—''

He shook his head. "More orphans.''

"No, that's not it,'' she said. "Stefan, this is—''

"Silly? What about Gillie?''

She flushed, because even she was beginning to see a pattern. "Gillie used to work here,'' she said defensively. "I couldn't ignore that.''

"Nor can you ignore the fact that he's a drunk,'' Stefan said. "You're worrying yourself sick about him, and I bet right now he's cuddled up to a bar somewhere, drinking himself stupid.''

"He wouldn't do that!''

"What makes you so sure?''

"He promised me.''

"And you believed him?''

"Yes, I did. And he hasn't had a drink since he got here. Deny that, if you can. Have you ever seen him drunk?''

"I knew it was only a matter of time.''

"Why are you so hard on him?'' she cried.

"Because I knew he'd hurt you,'' he said, reaching for her cold hands. She tried to pull away, but he held her tightly, forcing her to look into his eyes. "Look, I don't want to fight about this—''

"I don't either, but you're wrong, Stefan. You're . . . wrong.''

"Am I? Well, that's all right. Because this orphan syndrome of yours doesn't just include people; you rescue animals, too.''

"That's absurd!''

"What about the gelding we brought back from the track?''

"I couldn't let him be put down! And besides, he's company for Irish!''

"Then there's Cocoa.''

She wasn't sure what to say about that. Cocoa was the brown stray mother cat who had wandered into the barn one night, heavy with kittens, her tail rotting off. Briar had cleaned her up, taken her to the vet, and given her a box in her office when she went into labor. Now in addition to Cocoa, there were three half-grown cats running around the ranch.

"Cocoa is a barn cat," she said defensively. "She keeps the mice out of the grain."

"All right, then," Stefan said. "What about Touch the Fire?"

Suddenly aware that the atmosphere had changed, Briar got up abruptly from the kitchen table. "She wasn't an orphan," she muttered.

Stefan turned to look at her. "Nobody wanted her."

"That's not true," she said. "I did."

Stefan was silent a moment, sensing something going on here that he didn't understand yet. "Why?" he asked quietly.

She had never told anyone. She wasn't sure she wanted to tell Stefan. He saw too much at times, she thought. He understood her better than she did herself. It was unnerving; it made her feel . . . vulnerable. She could be hurt when she was vulnerable; it had happened when she'd lost Hay, and she didn't want to feel that same pain again. Because Hayden had made her love him, she had allowed herself to depend on him—she, who had never depended on anyone, ever, in her entire life. Now she could feel it happening again with Stefan, and the thought scared the hell out of her. It had been so hard . . . so hard . . . when Hay had died. How could she bear to go through it again?

"Briar?" Stefan said softly.

She couldn't look at him. Standing at the sink with her back to him, she drew in a deep breath, then she let it out again. It was too late, she thought bleakly; what she had feared the most had already taken place. Slowly, she turned around to face him.

"Touch the Fire traces back to a horse named Fane," she said. "She's a direct descendent of the horse my great-grandmother planned to make Caulfield Farm's foundation stallion."

Stefan knew bloodlines and pedigrees better than anyone. She could almost see him mentally reviewing stud books and stallion registries. "Fane," he said. "I don't—"

"No," she said, "you wouldn't. Years ago, Heinrich Jaeger challenged my great-grandparents to a match race: Fane against his stallion, Ulrich." She paused. "Ulrich won." She paused again. "The prize was my great-grandmother's stallion."

He didn't say anything for a few seconds. Then, his voice quiet, he asked, "Briar, what happened here tonight?"

She dropped her head. It was a moment before she answered. "It's happening again, Stefan," she said finally. "Tonight, Rupert Jaeger challenged me to a match race himself. This time he wants my filly to race against Galland."

"But no one knows if she will ever race again," Stefan said. She looked at him. "Rupert knows that," she said.

Seeing her expression, he got up and put his arms around her. Drawing her close, he said, "There's no force on earth that can make you run that filly if you don't want to, Briar."

She looked up into his eyes. "I'd like to believe it, Stefan," she said. "But sometimes I feel this is all a circle, and that it's coming around again. And if it does . . . I'm not sure I'll have a choice."

"And that's why you're so desperate to find Gillie?" Stefan said. "Do you think somehow he has the answer to all this?"

"I don't know," she said miserably. "But if you'd seen the look in his eyes when he saw Rupert. . . ." She shivered, remembering how terribly frightened the old man had looked. "We have to find him, Stefan. We have to try."

And they did try. But Gillie had vanished into the storm, and it would be a long time before Briar would see him again.

----&----

# CHAPTER TWENTY-SIX

Charlotte didn't know about the interview her father had given to *The Morning Line*, the racing industry's bible, until nightfall. It was February, two months after Briar's cocktail party, from which she had fled in total disarray. It was so confusing, she thought. Things changed every time she talked to that woman, and now, far from being just a tool Charlotte had hoped to use to avenge herself on her father, Briar had not only become a person to her, but someone whom she admired and . . . liked. She had heard from her father that Briar was too much like Marguerite, whom she had never known. But to her, she was more like Ariana, whom she had. *She's so like her mother*, Charlotte thought, chagrined. *All that effortless charm and beauty. It isn't fair!*

She felt muddled and uncertain about her course now. She thought the best thing was to keep herself busy. It wasn't difficult to do during this season, and the day the news broke she'd spent all morning and afternoon helping break yearlings and two-year-olds about to go to the track. Long before the men in her family came down to breakfast she was out at the barn; by the time they came home again from the office, she was up in her suite soaking in a hot tub. With all the activity, she hadn't had time to listen to the news or read the paper, so she was unaware of what Rupert had done until she came down to the living room just before dinner.

She was already in a bad mood; one of the colts that she'd thought had promise had injured himself badly by rearing up and backward in the starting gate they had here at the ranch. Her beloved Galland was still off work, nursing a swollen tendon sheath this time after coming back from the sore shins around Christmas. Since she and Laine were trying to get the colt fit for the Santa Anita Derby in April, and perhaps the Wood Memorial at the end of that month, before sending him on to Kentucky and the road to the Triple Crown, she was looking for someone to blame for her bad fortune. When she spied a vase of roses on the coffee table that should have been set on the sideboard, she exclaimed impatiently. No matter how many times she was told, Teresa never seemed to know where to put flowers; every time Charlotte came in, she had to rearrange things, and she was tired of it. Thinking that she would have to speak to the stupid girl, she was just moving the vase when Carl came into the living room and made a beeline for the bar.

"Well, you look pretty calm," Carl said, pouring himself a stiff shot. "I thought you'd be having a fit by now."

Charlotte stopped with the vase in her hands. "Why?"

He smirked. "Oh, my, you haven't heard. Well, that explains it."

She looked at him impatiently. "What?"

"The match race," he said, tossing back the shot he'd poured before reaching for the decanter again.

She felt a stab of alarm. "What match race?"

"Between Galland and Briar McKenna's Touch the Fire.

Father gave an interview yesterday to *The Morning Line*, saying we'd be glad to meet her, anytime.''

"*What!*" The vase slipped from her hands, crashing to the floor. The signed crystal had been in her family for over seventy years; her grandfather, Heinrich, had brought it back after his trip to Ireland in 1910. It was a treasured family heirloom— at least to Rupert—for to him it symbolized one of the family's most exalted triumphs over the Caulfields: the winning of the race between their stallion, Ulrich, and Marguerite and Sloane's foundation sire, Fane.

But as the heavy crystal smashed into pieces against the hardwood floor at Charlotte's feet, she didn't even notice the noise, or the mess, or the fact that the water from the roses was soaking the hem of her raw-silk slacks. She was staring at Carl, telling herself it couldn't be true. After the argument she and her father had had a few months ago, he couldn't be thinking of committing Galland to a match, especially when no one was certain Briar McKenna's filly would ever race again, anyway. And with their own colt barely holding together for the Derby . . .

"I don't believe you," she said.

Sneering, Carl tossed back the second shot. "Fine by me. Ask Father when he comes in."

"I'll do no such thing! The idea is preposterous. In the first place, neither horse is fit to race—"

"Not now, but they should be in the spring."

"By *spring*, Galland will be in Kentucky for the Derby!"

"Well, fine, maybe he can do both," Carl said with a shrug.

"He *can't* do both. The whole idea is ludicrous!"

"Tell that to Father; he's the one who's so damned set on this thing."

"I will!" she snapped, but she wasn't as certain as she sounded. She knew how obsessed Rupert had become with Briar McKenna, and she was aware of how much Briar's success ate at him. Oh, what had she done? she asked herself in renewed panic. She thought she was being so clever, bringing a Caulfield back to Caulfield Farm to bedevil her father, but it was all boomeranging back on her!

She was still standing there foolishly when Rupert came in. He had some office work with him, but he stopped abruptly when he saw what had happened to the vase.

"For heaven's sake, Charlotte," he exclaimed. "Look what you've done!"

"Never mind," she said, stepping over shards of crystal and crushed roses to confront her father. "Carl just told me you gave out some ridiculous story about wanting a match race between Galland and Touch the Fire. Is it true?"

Rupert was more concerned with the mess on the floor. Turning toward the doorway, he shouted, "Teresa! Teresa, come in here! And bring something to clean up!"

"I asked you a question, Father.'

He still wasn't paying attention. Muttering something about water ruining the hardwood, he shouted for the maid again.

"Father!" Charlotte demanded. "Will you please—!"

But just then the maid came hurrying in, carrying a broom and dust pan. When she saw what had happened, she stopped in dismay. "Oh, my, what is this?"

"Never mind!" Charlotte cried. "Just get it cleaned up and leave us alone!"

"Yes, yes, of course. But, oh my, all this water. I'll have to get some towels."

"Here, use these," Carl said. He was leaning against one end of the bar, obviously enjoying the upset, and he tossed a roll of paper towels to the maid. Teresa reached for it, but the aim was off, and the spool landed on the floor, rolling away from her and leaving a line of paper towels behind.

"For the love of God!" Charlotte cried. She was so irritated by the maid's clumsiness she nearly snatched the broom out of Teresa's hand and cleaned up herself. Then she realized that her shoes were wet, as were the hems of her slacks, and she became even more aggravated. Aware of the rising tension, Teresa hurriedly swept and mopped, then scuttled out of the room. She had barely disappeared before Charlotte turned back to her father.

"Now will you answer me?"

Having dismissed the problem with the appearance of the maid, Rupert had sat down in his high-back chair and started reading through his reports. He looked over the top of a page. "What was the question?"

Charlotte dug her nails into her palms. "You know exactly what I'm talking about, Father. Did you or did you not challenge Briar McKenna's filly to a match race with Galland?"

"I did," Rupert said calmly, and went back to reading his report.

Charlotte stood there a moment, struggling for control. She wanted to grab what he was reading and fling it right back into his face. Finally, she managed, "Is that all you have to say?"

With exaggerated patience, Rupert lowered the report to his lap. Carl leaned on the bar and sipped his whiskey, enjoying the confrontation. Charlotte knew he was smirking, but she didn't care. She was more interested in her father.

"What more do you want to hear?" Rupert asked, calmly inserting his papers back into the file.

"What *more*?" she said incredulously.

Rupert cut in sharply. "Charlotte, please lower your voice. It's unseemly for a woman of your years and position to shriek like that. The servants will hear you."

"I don't care if the entire *ranch* hears me!" she cried. "Father, you can't *do* this. Galland is just coming off a tendon injury—"

"Touch the Fire is injured, too," Carl said helpfully. His voice was muffled from the piece of ice he had in his mouth, but there was no mistaking the satisfaction in his face when Charlotte whirled around.

"You know nothing about it, and even less about horses, so I'll thank you to keep your puerile opinions to yourself!"

Chewing on the ice, Carl came to the couch. "I was only pointing out—"

"Well, don't," she said in a fury, and turned back to her father. "I won't permit this, Father, I won't!"

Rupert looked at her calmly. "I don't understand you, Charlotte. I would have thought you'd leap at such a chance. You're always boasting about how superior Mondragon horses are; this is your chance to prove it. What better showcase can you ask for? Millions of people will see this race. A Jaeger in the winner's circle will guarantee Mondragon's place in history."

"Mondragon already *has* a place in history. And contrary to what happened before, Father, there's no guarantee that *this* time it'll be a Jaeger in the winner's circle. Things aren't nearly as simple now as they were then—not with *millions* of people watching."

Rupert stiffened. "What do you mean—contrary to what happened before?"

"Oh, please! You know very well I'm referring to that other infamous match race in our family's past."

"This has nothing to do with that."

"Oh, doesn't it? Are you telling me that you haven't dreamed about having history repeat itself, with you as the captain this time? You've said for years that you'd give anything to—"

"That's enough, Charlotte! I won't have you speak to me this way."

"I'll speak to you any damned way I please, especially where one of my best horses is concerned. Aside from the fact that even if I permitted this absurdity, the Triple Crown would be in jeopardy, have you thought about what would happen if he didn't win? How would you feel if, instead of Galland, Touch the Fire was the horse who won the race?"

"That won't happen," Rupert said flatly.

"You can't be sure. Not unless you intend to fix this race, just like Grandfather fixed the first one!"

There was a silence, broken only by the sound of Carl spitting back into his glass what was left of the ice cube he'd been chewing on. Both Charlotte and Rupert looked at him as if he'd shot off a gun.

"Hey, sorry," Carl said, when he saw them glaring. "I'm just an innocent bystander here. I don't care whether the horse runs or not."

"He's *not* going to run!" Charlotte exploded. "Not against that filly—not in a match race!"

"That remains to be seen," Rupert said. "In the meantime, I'd like you to explain the remark you just made, Charlotte. Who told you the race between Ulrich and Fane was . . . fixed?"

"Oh, please, Father! Everybody's known it for years. Even Mama knew. She was the one who told me!"

"Mama knew?" Carl said, startled.

"Your *mother* told you that?" Rupert said, his pale face flushing.

Still defiant despite her father's expression, Charlotte lifted her chin. "Yes, she did. She told me, long before she . . . died."

Even under the best of circumstances, Rupert did not like to be reminded of his wife, a dour spinster five years older than he named Hermione Geiger. For reasons he had never fully explained, he had suddenly decided to take a wife at nineteen, and since Hermione had been seeking an escape from nagging parents who felt they had supported her long enough, arrangements had been made. Because Heinrich Jaeger had recently been shot to death, the abrupt marriage caused a small scandal in the community, but Rupert had insisted on going through with it anyway. The union had produced the two children, Charlotte and Carl, but little else, for Hermione soon developed the mental instability that had plagued her until her suicide fifteen years later.

"And what, pray tell," Rupert said acidly, "would your *mother* know about the match race? Hermione and I didn't even *marry* until long after that time. She wasn't even there!"

"But Alden was," Charlotte said, looking a little smug at the mention of her mother's father. "And because they were such good friends, grandfather Heinrich couldn't resist bragging about how he'd found a jockey who would fix things if he was paid. It was child's play for a rider of Gilbert Hickey's experience to reach over and jerk the saddle cloth on Fane at just the right time. Just a quick little flip!—" she snapped her fingers "— and what do you know? Fane was thrown off stride for just those few precious seconds Ulrich needed to get ahead of him." Her smile turned nasty. "The rest, as they say, is history—even if it was rewritten somewhat to change the outcome."

"That's absurd!" Rupert snapped. "Ulrich won the race fairly."

"No, he didn't," Charlotte said, looking, at that moment, very much like her father. She bent down so they were eye to eye. "Fane *deserved* to win," she hissed. "It didn't happen before, but if you persist in your foolish game, it just might this time. And then, how will you look? Will you relish being the laughingstock of the entire racing community?"

"You're forgetting one thing," Rupert said, coldly holding her gaze. "Galland is bigger than that filly. He's three inches taller and sixty pounds heavier."

Charlotte straightened, looking down at him. She said, "And last year, before she was injured, Touch the Fire was faster. She went three-quarters of a mile in a minute and nine seconds—on the same track that he ran a minute eleven. And at a mile, she was *still* a second faster than he was, proving she can go the distance."

Abruptly, Rupert stood. "I don't care to discuss it further. If I say he's going to race, then that's what he'll do."

"Oh, no, he won't!" she said sharply. "Galland is mine."

"Then you're as misinformed as your mother apparently was," he said indifferently. "Perhaps you'd better check the papers, my dear. You'll see that Galland, like *all* the horses, belongs to a subsidiary of Mondragon Enterprises called Mondragon Stud. And since I am the president of the company, it means that *I* own the horse, Charlotte, just like I do everything else."

"But you've always said the ranch was mine!"

"I said the ranch was yours to *run*," he corrected. "I didn't say anything about ownership. There's quite a difference. Even so, there is the little matter of the loan you took from the company, isn't there?"

Her face pale, Charlotte reached for the back of the couch. "*You* took that loan, to pay for Heat of Night!"

Rupert had started for the door, but once there, he turned back. Smiling his crocodile smile, he said, "But as you pointed out, my dear, *you're* the ranch manager. As I see it, the loan is your responsibility."

"But that doesn't have anything to do with this."

"Oh, I'm not so sure. For instance, if I found myself short and had to call in my notes, you would be hard pressed to come up with that much money in, say, a few days?"

"You wouldn't!"

"Oh, but I would. I wouldn't *like* to, mind you. But business is business."

Charlotte didn't look smug any longer, only sick. "You can't do this, Father!"

Rupert apparently wasn't ready to make an enemy of his daughter quite yet. "Now, now," he said, sure that they understood each other. "Isn't it all academic? You said yourself the horse isn't ready to run. And as your brother so astutely pointed out, neither is Touch the Fire."

"But you gave an interview to *The Morning Line*!"

"In which I suggested I wouldn't be adverse to having the two horses meet. You have to admit yourself it would be quite a race."

She tried to pull herself together. "And so would the Kentucky Derby and the Preakness and the Belmont Stakes," she said shakily, unable at the moment to see her way out of the noose. Desperately, she added, "You can't squander Galland's chances for the Triple Crown to support this . . . this vendetta of yours!"

Something flashed in his eyes, but Rupert was far more controlled than she. Calmly, he said, "I repeat, Charlotte, it's early yet. Why don't we wait and see?"

She couldn't let it go; she knew the extent of her father's obsession to destroy anyone named Caulfield, and she wasn't going to be drawn into his fight. Briar McKenna could take care of herself and her own horses; she had to worry about Galland, who was by far the best horse that Mondragon Stud had ever produced. She had spent years studying breeding records and pedigrees and performance charts and racing times; she had memorized so many facts and figures about every single horse in both Galland's sire and dam lines that she was a walking encyclopedia about every aspect of his bloodline. Long ago, she had set out to breed the perfect horse—or as perfect as genetics and nutrition and evolution and breeding and performance could be, and she had finally succeeded. Galland was her dream, her goal, the apex of all her achievements as a breeder and a horsewoman, and she could not let her colt's chances be destroyed because her father was obsessed with the name Caulfield.

"I really don't understand why you're so upset, my dear," Rupert said, interrupting her thoughts. "A match race with the Caulfield filly will only enhance Galland's reputation, don't you see? After all—"

Charlotte dug her nails into the back of the couch in sheer frustration. "The Caulfield filly! The *Caulfield* filly? Father, do you hear what you're saying?" she cried. "Touch the Fire has nothing to do with anyone named Caulfield. She belongs to Briar McKenna!"

"Of Caulfield Farm," Carl contributed.

She whirled around on him. "It would be the same difference if the place was called Hole in the Ground. One doesn't have anything to do with the other. It was a long time ago—a *long time ago*. It can't possibly matter now."

At that, Rupert's formidable control abandoned him for a moment. "You, a *Jaeger*, can say that?" he demanded harshly. "You *know* the Caulfield land should have been ours years ago!"

Charlotte was on firmer ground now. "Because of that business with grandfather? Nothing was ever proved."

"Sloane agreed to deed over the land, and then he reneged on the deal," Rupert thundered. "What more proof do you need?"

"Proof that Juliet really *did* kill him, as you've always said!" Charlotte flung back. "But if that were so, why did you tell the police it was a robbery? Juliet *was* attacked, we all know that. But who did it, Father? The supposed robber, or grandfather Heinrich?"

"How *dare* you! She was *there*!"

"And so that was the price for murder? Sloane handing over his land? I never did understand how you could justify it, Father, even in your own mind!"

"This is outrageous!"

"Why? Because I'm damned sick and tired of this whole ugly thing?" Charlotte cried. "I thought when Juliet finally died, we'd be rid of it, but now it's started with Briar again. I'm beginning to think it's never going to end!"

"It'll end when she gives me what is rightfully mine!"

Carl had been enjoying the shouting match. Getting a little carried away himself, he said, "And when Fredrica—"

"Shut up, Carl!" Rupert snapped.

Charlotte turned toward her brother. "What about Fredrica?" she demanded. She looked back at Rupert. "What have you done now?"

"It doesn't concern you."

But Charlotte knew that, somehow, it did, and she looked at her father as if he were a monster. She had never bothered herself with his business dealings; she had been happy staying out of the company and running the ranch. But she was being inexorably drawn into her father's obsession with the Caulfields now, and she had a sudden frightening glimpse of the future when her own foolishness in finding Briar would be her own downfall. She had always known her father was a ruthless man, but she'd thought herself charmed, safe. Now she didn't know what to believe. He was perfectly capable of taking the goal of her life's work—her beautiful Galland—and using the horse to his advantage without a thought to her own wishes. She, who had bred and raised him. She wondered suddenly what else he might be capable of.

"You'll never beat Briar," she said to him. "Never. She's too much like Marguerite."

Rupert lifted his head. "Marguerite didn't win!"

"No," Charlotte cried. "She died!"

Into the ugly silence that fell, the doorbell rang. Charlotte was so tense she jumped, and even Rupert looked startled. "Who could that be?" Carl muttered.

The front door was through an archway off the living room, where the family was gathered. Still frozen in position, Charlotte could see as Teresa came through and opened the door. When Charlotte saw who was standing on the porch, she drew in a quick breath. What was *he* doing here?

Rupert saw who it was, too. Teresa had just ushered their visitor in when he said, "You're not welcome here. Get out."

Stefan ignored him. "Not until I've said what I came to say."

Stefan had spent the short drive to Mondragon Stud composing his thoughts. He'd kept his mouth shut these past months while he worked for Briar, but he couldn't let this latest move pass without trying to help. Even if he hadn't started to feel so deeply about Briar, he knew as soon as he read the interview in *The Morning Line* that he couldn't stand by—not when he had the means to stop Jaeger in his tracks.

Briar rarely cried, but he knew how shaken she was by the challenge to her black filly, and he was familiar enough with the racing world to know that an idea like this could catch fire and soon run out of control, forcing her to participate whether she wanted to or not. If the filly never ran again, it would be one thing; but if Touch the Fire did return to the track without Briar having agreed to the ultimate test of her horse, conjecture about how good she really was would haunt her, and that would be even worse. Stefan's jaw tightened. Jaeger knew what he was doing, he thought. He had put Briar in an impossible position.

Or so the man believed, Stefan thought grimly, as he drove through the big gates to the Mondragon Stud. But in devising his little game, Rupert seemed to have forgotten one player. Stefan had stayed out until this point because he wasn't sure that he wanted to pursue it, but the die was cast now, and he knew that if he made a threat, he'd have to go through with it.

Was it worth the chance? He knew it was, without question.

He couldn't put his finger on when he had started to feel so protective about Briar, but now whenever he felt she was threatened, he wanted to do murder. *That's* what she had done to him.

Unconsciously, his hands tightened on the wheel as he headed toward the big house that blazed like a carnival at the end of the drive. There had been times in the past when he wasn't sure he could control his passion for Briar, he thought; he *ached* to hold her, to kiss her, to feel her skin next to his, to make love to her. But every time he thought he was getting close, she'd shy away again and he'd have to rein in his impatience a little longer. He'd told her that there was no time limit on grief, and he meant it. But there was only so long a man could hold out on desire, and if she didn't relent soon, he knew the best thing might be just to leave here. It was either that or go mad.

The problem, he thought, was that that damned husband of hers seemed to have ruined her for any other man. Briar had told him about Hayden Lord, and from what she had said, Stefan knew he probably would have liked him. But had the bastard realized that by dying he'd be elevated to deity status? How could he fight that? Sometimes he felt the odds would never be in his favor.

And now, just when he thought he was making a little headway, he was about to jeopardize it by interfering tonight. When Briar found out what he was doing—and why, and how—she was going to have a fit. She'd probably sack him, if she didn't kill him first, but he couldn't help it. If Jaeger was going to play hardball, he should find out just how fast someone else could pitch.

Long ago, when he'd first come here, he'd gone to see Rupert and Carl and Charlotte, just to say who he was. But right from the outset, they had made it clear that they regarded his claim as so much bullshit, and he'd been warned that if he tried to pursue it, they'd make him sorry he had ever heard the name Jaeger . . . or Jager, as his great-granny Flossie remembered it. Over the years a "Y" had replaced the "J," and an "e" had been lost, but it was there for all the world to see on the certificates he had found in the chest in his grandmother's attic.

The irony of it all was that he hadn't wanted anything from anyone, Jaeger or not. He'd only come over because he wanted to meet the family and explain what had happened; the last thing on his mind had been elbowing in with a claim. But now, he thought grimly, things were different. If he had to, he'd use whatever he could to make Rupert back off and leave Briar alone.

He didn't know what had happened to make Rupert so obsessed about anyone named Caulfield, but whatever it was, it had happened a long time ago and had nothing to do with Briar, who was fast becoming an innocent victim. He didn't like it; he didn't like it at all. The same thing had happened to his great-grandmother, and it was time the family learned they couldn't just ride roughshod. It was too late to do anything for Flossie, but if he could change things for Briar, he would. On that thought, he pulled up in front of the house and went to the door.

He knew the instant the little maid let him in that he'd just interrupted some kind of family argument; cousin Charlotte was standing by the archway on the other side of the living room, looking flushed and furious and a little sick; Carl was by the bar, pouring himself a drink. From his blotched face and slightly glazed eyes, Stefan judged that it wasn't his first of the evening.

But it was the patriarch he had come to see, and when Rupert so politely greeted him by telling him to get out, he decided just to say what he had come to say and leave as fast as he could.

"This won't take long," he said, his eyes on Rupert alone. "I've come to deliver a message."

From his position at the bar, Carl blearily waved a glass. "I'd offer you a drink, but the cirstan . . . the circanstun . . . the *circumstices* . . ."

His father flashed him an angry glance. "You're making a fool of yourself, Carl," he said. "Just shut up." He turned back to Stefan. "What is it you want?"

"I came to tell you to back off," Stefan said evenly. "I know what a power your name is, but you are not going to force Briar to race her filly."

Rupert lifted an eyebrow. None of them had taken a seat. "Is that a message from Ms. McKenna, or have you come to threaten me on your own?"

"Briar doesn't know I'm here," Stefan said. "But it's no threat. If you press it, you're going to regret it."

"Oh, really?" said Rupert. "And what, pray tell, do you think you can do about it?"

"You *know* what I can do about it," Stefan said. "So don't force my hand."

"If you mean to come forth with that spurious claim of yours in court, Mr. *Yager*, I'll—"

"I mean a hell of a lot more than that, and I think you know it."

Their eyes locked. "If you think you can come in here and threaten me . . ." Rupert said. His pale face was getting flushed, and deeper anger appeared in his light eyes.

"As I said, it's no threat," Stefan said. "I mean it, Jaeger, don't push this or you'll be sorry. I never wanted anything that wasn't mine; I told you. But if you continue to harass Briar, I'm going to decide suddenly that maybe I do deserve a share in all this, after all."

Rupert stiffened. "You can't possibly—"

"Oh, but I can," Stefan said. "And I can prove it."

"You're bluffing!"

"Am I? Try me and see. Try me again and see just how *much* I feel I deserve. If I have to, I'll take it all the way. And I'll win, Jaeger, believe me, I'll win. I've got the documents to prove it."

"You're lying, and you always were. What you claim could never have happened, never in a million years!"

"Are you willing to bet everything you have on it?"

"I don't believe you," Rupert said, but he didn't sound as confident as before. Suddenly he raised his voice. "I don't want you in this house. Get out. Get out!"

"I'm going," Stefan said calmly. But he paused before he left. "Believe me or not, Jaeger. That's your choice. But I'm warning you for the last time. If you harm Briar or anything of hers in any way, you'll regret it to the end of your days."

He started out then, but Rupert, compelled by rage, or pride, or sheer vindictiveness, Stefan thought, followed him. As he climbed into the truck, Rupert stood in the doorway, the living room light from behind shining clearly on his upraised fist. "You'll never beat me," he shouted. "And neither will she! Do you hear me? I'll get what is mine, you'll see! You'll see!"

Stefan didn't answer; he started the truck. But as he took the curve of the driveway, he briefly glanced over his shoulder and saw that Rupert was still standing in the doorway shouting something, with Charlotte vainly trying to pull him back inside. His skin crawling, he pressed down on the accelerator and drove on without looking back. There had been something . . . evil . . . just now in the old man's face, and as he quickly drove through the big gates again, he wondered if it had been a mistake coming here after all. The thought disturbed him so much that he pulled over to the side of the road as soon as he was off Mondragon property. Realizing with surprise his hands were shaking—but whether from anger or fear, he didn't know—he clutched the wheel. Somewhere along the line, he had committed himself, he thought; now he was destined to go all the way.

"Oh, granny," he muttered, thinking of Nona. "As you used to say, the fat's in the fire now, and my goose is cooked."

Then he started the truck again and drove back to Caulfield Farm.

---&---

# CHAPTER TWENTY-SEVEN

As the weeks dragged on with no sign of Gillie, Briar felt more and more discouraged. She couldn't stop blaming herself for his disappearance, and when he didn't even show up at Santa Anita Racetrack in Arcadia, or Hollywood Park out by the beach, she didn't know what to think. All she could do was pray he was all right and hope he would come back. In the meantime, she asked people to keep an eye out and then had to deal with Rupert Jaeger and the interview in *The Morning Line*. Stefan had told her not to worry about it, no one could force her to accept a match race for Touch the Fire, even if the filly did return to the track. But she couldn't shake the feeling that she hadn't heard the last of Rupert Jaeger yet, and as she stood near her living room window one night, she shivered. She was just thinking that maybe she would call Stefan and ask him up for a cup of coffee when she saw him come out of the house and get into his truck. Seconds later, his headlights swept through the darkness as he made the turn in the driveway and left. Well, that was out, she thought. Maybe what she needed was a little dose of Marguerite right now. The latest journal was on the end table. As soon as she sat down and started to read, she forgot her own problems and was once again transported back to her great-grandmother's time.

"*My beautiful Fane has gone to war!*" Marguerite had written, the words like an anguished cry. "*Oh, how could it happen? It's so unfair!*"

She couldn't write more. Tears filled her eyes, and she couldn't see. Sobbing, she threw the pen down and covered her face with her hands. Her heart was breaking; she didn't think she could bear the pain.

So much had happened since the ill-fated day her beautiful Fane was taken away that she hardly knew where to begin. In the four years since, she hadn't written in her journal; she just hadn't been able to take up her pen. Sometimes it seemed to her that part of her life . . . her heart . . . had just stopped when she lost Fane. She had days when it seemed impossible to go on—especially when she had learned that Heinrich was not going to race the colt, as she had feared, but had planned something much, much worse.

Just thinking about it tormented her, and she got up from the desk. At times like these, the only thing that kept her going was the fact that after she had returned from Sacramento, she and Sloane had regained the earlier closeness of their marriage. She would never forget the day Andrew drove them home; she could still see in her mind's eye, as clear as could be, Sloane waiting for her. She could remember just how she felt when she ran into his embrace and his arms closed about her.

"Oh, Sloane!" she'd wept against his chest, overcome with remorse. "I've been so foolish! I should have known!"

Gently, he had stroked her hair and turned her face up to look at his. "I couldn't tell you," he said, his eyes mirroring her own unhappiness. "I had promised Andrew—"

"I know!"

"Can you forgive me?"

But she already had. As much as she loved her young stallion, her good friend Andrew was more important, and she would never have forgiven herself, or Sloane, if they had failed to help him.

"But how did Heinrich find out?" she asked, when things were calm again and she was nestled where she should be—in her husband's arms.

She felt him tense. "I don't know," he said, sighing heavily. "I'd heard he'd taken a trip to Europe; I didn't dream it was Ireland. But when he told me that day that he'd found out about Ian McConachie, I knew he wouldn't hesitate to expose Andrew, so I—" He broke off. "I'm sorry you had to suffer, Marguerite," he said softly. "I know how much you loved Fane."

She did her best not to cry. "We'll get him back," she said, more confidently than she felt. "One day, somehow, we'll get him back. . . ."

But they weren't going to get him back ever, she thought mournfully four years later. Fane was gone, and she had to accept it. But it was so hard, she thought, wiping away her tears, so hard. It wasn't enough that Heinrich had cheated to get their horse; ever since, he had done what he could to destroy the colt's reputation. He couldn't kill Fane outright, although Marguerite would almost have preferred that to what happened. Instead, he had bred him to the most inferior mares he could find, utterly destroying whatever promise he might have had as a breeding stallion.

She sobbed again, just thinking of it. Sloane had told her over and over that she shouldn't dwell on it, that there was nothing she could do, and that if she continued to mourn, she'd make herself sick, but she couldn't help herself. Every time she thought of her beloved colt in Heinrich's hands . . .

But nothing Heinrich had done so far compared to what he planned now. Stifling another sob, she turned away from the window, where she had gone in an effort to compose herself. Her eye fell on the stack of newspapers near Sloane's chair, and she bit her lip to keep from bursting into fresh tears. The news from Europe was so bad now that Sloane had been saving the papers. The top one alone had headlines two inches high that leaped off the page: GERMANY INVADES BELGIUM; BRITAIN DECLARES WAR!

There was more, a dizzying collection of nations propelled into armed conflict that had all begun with the assassination of the Archduke Ferdinand and his wife at Sarajevo on June 28, 1914. Names and dates spun together in her blurred vision: Austria declaring war on Russia; Serbia and Montenegro declaring war on Germany. British troops landing in France; France declaring war on Austria; Britain declaring war on Austria; Austria declaring war on Belgium, Russia declaring war on Turkey; France and Britain declaring war on Turkey; the Russians invading East Prussia; the Germans occupying the Liege. . . . It went on and on until she could scream.

His face increasingly grim, Sloane had followed every new item, but with the world going crazy, she had paid little attention until Germany declared war on Russia and France. Only then had it occurred to her to wonder how Heinrich felt about his country in conflict. She knew that he had never really left the Rhine, and at first she thought he might go back and fight. She had never dreamed he would start supplying horses for the war effort, and when she had heard he had sent Fane, she had fainted.

She awakened on the living room sofa, with Andrew's Ula applying cold cloths to her forehead and Sloane hovering over her. When he saw her eyes open, he sat down beside her and began rubbing her cold hands. Only then did she remember why she had lost consciousness, and she began to cry.

But worse news was yet to come, for a year later, in 1915, Kyle celebrated his twentieth birthday by leaving the ranch to join the army. With the conflict still raging in Europe, cavalry units were begging for horsemen to take up the battle, and Kyle was young and eager to join in the excitement. He told his father what he intended, but they both agreed it would be better that Marguerite not find out until he was gone.

"I'll never forgive you for not letting me say good-bye. Never!" Marguerite cried to Sloane when he told her where Kyle had gone. Terrified for her son, she flew at her husband, beating at his chest with her fists. "I'll . . . never . . . forgive . . . you," she wept, before she broke down. Covering her face, she began to sob.

Wordlessly, Sloane held her close. Marguerite was too caught up in her own misery to see the tears glinting in his eyes. All she could think of was how afraid she was for her willful, handsome son. "You should have stopped him!" she choked finally.

"He's a grown man, Marguerite," Sloane murmured brokenly as he stroked her hair. "I couldn't have stopped him if I'd tried. . . ."

Of them all, Marguerite sometimes thought it was Juliet who

missed Kyle the most. The two had been inseparable; from the beginning, Kyle had seemed to sense his sister was delicate and vulnerable, and he had early on developed a fierce protectiveness that lasted through his teens—indeed, until he'd gone away. It hurt Marguerite to see her daughter haunting the post, hoping for one of Kyle's infrequent letters. As the months dragged on with only a note or two, hastily written and mailed, first from Colorado, where he had bivouacked, then from New York, before he went overseas, and then finally from England, before the letters stopped completely, Juliet, who had never been a healthy, robust child, became even more pale and quiet. As beautiful as she was in her ethereal way, with her long, fine, blond hair and great gray eyes and slender figure, Marguerite doubted that she would ever get married. The thought had caused her some anxiety before Kyle had went away, but with her son gone she clung to her daughter as never before. They had always been close, and often Marguerite would look up from whatever she was doing to find that Juliet had quietly entered the room and was sitting nearby, reading. There was something serene about her daughter's presence, and when the volatile Marguerite would look up and catch her daughter's calm gray eyes, she would feel comforted and smile before returning to her work.

By the time Juliet celebrated her twenty-first birthday in 1918, Marguerite couldn't help noticing that her shy and retiring daughter had collected two staunch protectors in her absent brother's place. One was Angus, Andrew's son, now a big boy of twelve, and the other was a shy child named Gillie, the son of the housekeeper, who had lived with them for years. Matilda Gentry was his mother's name, and she came from the deep South. Her accent was as thick as honey, and she worked hard to support herself and her young son, coming to Caulfield Farm after her husband had been killed in a thresher accident on a farm in Texas. It was easy to see that young Gillie adored the blond Juliet, and when he wasn't working—a seldom occurrence, since he helped his mother willingly from daybreak on—he could be seen squatting by the porch in case Miss Juliet wanted him to run an errand.

Juliet was embarrassed by such obvious worship, but in these years of sorrow and worry, Marguerite was amused. She liked the eager-to-please young Gillie, who was just as fond of horses as he was of Juliet, and she was often amazed at his talent with the animals. He could calm the most fractious colt; he could soothe a nervous young brood mare. He was such an asset that Marguerite insisted on paying him a dollar a week—an amount that scandalized Matilda, who declared he was going to be spoiled rotten.

The years of the war were slow and agonizing for Marguerite, who worried about her son while trying to keep the ranch alive in increasingly difficult times. In 1909, California had fallen victim to the antiwagering laws that had swept the rest of the country, and although the Walker-Otis Anti-Racetrack Gambling Bill had gone into effect, their old friends Thomas Williams and Colonel Burns had kept Emeryville in operation for two more seasons. In 1911, however, even they had been forced to bow to the legislation and close the last operating racetrack in California, and after that what remained of the industry in the state began to die a slow death. Only those with substantial outside incomes could afford to maintain their breeding operations in any capacity, and Marguerite constantly blessed Sloane's foresight in his other investments. But, sadly, the days of 40,000-acre showplaces like Rancho del Paso, and $150,000 stallions such as Ormonde, considered by many to be the "horse of the century," were over. Elias Baldwin, the man from whom Marguerite had bought her daughter of the Emperor of Norfolk, died in March of 1909, and although Marguerite missed him, she often reflected that he indeed had been lucky not to have seen the demise of racing in this state. Like a child, he had been happy with his new toy, Santa Anita Park, which he opened on December 7, 1907, and both of the two seasons it had been allowed had been phenomenal successes. Baldwin had died a happy man, not living long enough to see the gates close forever on his lifelong dream.

But in the meantime, with no Lucky Baldwins or Leland Stanfords left to build multimillion-dollar racing empires, a mass exodus ensued because of the antiwagering laws, and many breeders either sold out or moved out of the state, leaving only a loyal handful behind. Marguerite and Sloane joined with others who were left in an effort to keep the Thoroughbred business alive, but with no racing in the state, they were forced to breed for outside markets. Like their old friend, J. B. Haggin, who had exported more or less successfully for years when he sold his yearlings all over the world, they began marketing outside the States. But then, in 1913, the English handed them another blow by conjuring up something called the Jersey Act which, to Marguerite's angry dismay, labeled as "half-bred" any horse that couldn't be traced in every line straight back to certain foundation mares in the *General Stud Book*. This, in effect, branded most American-bred Thoroughbreds as mongrels.

Desperate to keep going, Sloane and Marguerite and others turned to alternative markets. During those black years of the war, and beyond, Caulfield Farm bred Thoroughbreds, but they also raised fine harness horses, carriage horses, stock horses, and pleasure horses. Through it all, Marguerite constantly thought of Kyle and prayed that he would be safe. His infrequent letters, often smudged and wrinkled and months out of date, found their way home only now and then, but she kept every one in a special drawer and took them out to read so often the thin paper became almost transparent.

The last letter the family received from Kyle was dated in the winter of 1917. After three years of fighting, the United States had entered the war on the side of the Allies, and Kyle had gone to France. He had written to them all, but had included a separate letter for Marguerite, which she waited to read until she was alone. In the meantime was the exciting news that Kyle had seen Fane.

Sloane had been reading the letter aloud to Marguerite and Juliet, but when he reached the part about Fane, Marguerite snatched the letter from his hand. "Where?" she asked excitedly, scanning the smudged page. "Where did he see Fane? How? Oh, can it be true?"

It was. Marguerite was nearly transported with joy. Taking up where Sloane had been forced to leave off, she read excitedly, ". . . saw Fane! I could hardly believe it myself! I was on a transport train when I saw him, and I only caught a glimpse, but I know it was him. He was being ridden by an English officer, but there isn't another horse in the world who has that look of seeing a future only he can see. It was Fane, Mama, I swear. And now we can rest easy, for if he belongs to an officer, he's got the best billet there is. Animals that go out to the field are gelded as a matter of course, but officers in town like entires; it makes them feel superior, I guess, when they dress up and go out to impress the ladies. So Fane is safe . . . safe as he can be in this horror they call war. I'll be so glad when it's over and I can come home. Until then, my love to you all. And when I come home, sweet sister," he ended, speaking to the blushing Juliet, "we're going to go out and get you a beau. . . ."

"Oh, silly," Juliet murmured, but there were tears in her eyes.

Marguerite felt emotional, too. Reading one of Kyle's letters was almost like having him visit in person. He wrote as he spoke, breezily and with supreme self-confidence. Holding his private letter to her heart, she waited until she was alone to read it. She knew she would cry, and she did.

The letter began in Kyle's bold, slashing handwriting—so like him, she thought, smoothing the paper as tears filled her eyes. For a moment, she couldn't see what he had written; she was seeing him in her mind's eye instead. He had been as tall as Sloane when he went away, so handsome, so much a man. Whenever she had looked at him, she had marveled that she could have borne such a son. She loved him so much. Before she could begin crying in earnest, she went on with the letter.

Dearest Mama,

I know how angry you must be that I went away without telling you, and I wanted to explain before I came home. I didn't want to hurt you, but this is something I had to do, and I knew that if I discussed it with you, you would talk me out of it. Like Dad, I never could refuse you anything, you know.

I've always felt so blessed—with my family, the horses, the ranch—and I felt so guilty just staying there, safe, when people were being killed and families such as mine were being destroyed. I had to do something to help. I wanted to give something back to show how grateful I was for all the privileges I had. I don't regret that part one minute.

And now, with the United States entering the war, I know it will soon be over. The German resistance is crumbling; the country and the people can't take much more. Pain and suffering are all around, and it's hard to believe the misery that man inflicts.

But enough of that. Soon we'll all be coming home, and I can put this experience behind me and get on with my life, knowing that I did my part to make the world a better place to live in. It's hard to believe that now, especially when I see the hardship so many must endure. It makes no sense, nor ever will, I fear. Just the other night I came across a young woman rummaging through the pockets of someone she had found dead on the street. Her name was Delia, she told me, and she was terrified that I would turn her over to the authorities. When I reassured her I had no such intention, she told me she had been looking for food, or money—anything to help her little brother, who was starving nearby. I offered to help, but the child had died just before we arrived. How can this happen to the innocent and defenseless, Mama? It makes me question the existence of God.

But soon we will all be coming home, if there is a God, and He's willing, and when I do, Mama, I'll bring Fane. I'll stay until I find him again, and then I'll steal him if I have to—you see how I've changed? But he belongs at Caulfield Farm, as, I've discovered, so do I. So we'll be coming home together; I pray it won't be long.

I think about home so much, Mama—the pastures, the barns, the horses . . . you and Dad and Juliet . . . and Andrew and Angus, and all the others. I miss you all so much. . . .

But until we meet again, remember that I love you. If a fellow's mother can be his best girl, well, then, I guess that's you. . . .

Marguerite saved the letter. She read it over so many times that the paper became brittle and the creases so thin she was afraid it would crumble. But she read it because that's all she had of her son. Despite his youthful promise, Kyle hadn't come home again, and neither had Fane. Marguerite never saw either of them again. No one was sure what had happened to her great stallion, but it was presumed he perished during a Luftwaffe attack over London. And as for Kyle . . .

He died during the Second Battle of the Marne, leading his men to the front. The Caulfields received his posthumous medals of Honor and Valor, and through the tears she thought would never end, Marguerite was proud. But she would have given them all . . . everything . . . to have her son back.

Then one day, just before the armistice was signed, Marguerite opened the door to a young woman named Delia, who barely had time to gasp that she was Kyle's wife before she fainted dead away in her astounded mother-in-law's arms. Delia had come a long way to be with her young husband's family, and that night she bore him a daughter she only had time to name Ariana. Before the doctor could save her, she died of massive hemorrhage. So through blessing and double tragedy, in his own special way Kyle had come back to Caulfield Farm.

Ariana was a year old when Caulfield Farm celebrated the birth of another baby. His name was Duncan, and his proud parents were Angus and Marta McKenna, who had been married only that year, and who had been eager to present Andrew with his first grandchild.

Andrew had never married again after Eileen; he and Ula, the woman who had begun as nanny to young Angus, and housekeeper to the McKenna men, seemed content with the way things were. And if Ula sometimes stayed over, no one commented or passed judgment or even paid any mind. Marguerite, for one, was pleased that Andrew had found someone to care for, and she wouldn't have objected if they had openly lived together, for the shadow that always lurked behind Andrew's kind blue eyes never quite disappeared. She knew that even after all these years, Andrew still mourned his Eileen.

But then Angus, who had grown into a tall, strapping young man every bit as good with the horses as his father, met Marta Kathleen Quinn at a dance at the county fair and was instantly smitten. He and Marta were married six months later in Marguerite's parlor, and for a wedding present Sloane gifted them with one of the cottages at Caulfield Farm. When young Duncan was born a year later—a spitting image of his father and grandfather, with his red hair and startling blue eyes—the McKenna family seemed finally to have overcome their tragedy. Often, Marguerite would glimpse Andrew playing on the lawn after the day's work with his grandson, and for the first time since she'd known him, he seemed happy. It was during those moments, when she stood at her favorite place on the front porch and gazed out at her beloved ranch, that she thought how bittersweet life would be. Sensitive as always to her mother's moods, Juliet would frequently join her, and they would stand with their arms around each other.

"I miss him, too, Mama," she would murmur, knowing that Marguerite was thinking of her handsome son, lost forever. And Marguerite would hold Juliet more closely to her, fiercely glad that she still had her daughter at least, and once more feeling blessed.

But then one day something happened that shattered the idyllic life at Caulfield Farm and changed everything forever.

The day began as any other; Sloane up with the first light, joining Andrew at the stables to decide on what needed attending to before he and Marguerite left for some business in San Francisco. Juliet was up early as well; the summer before, she had surprised both her parents by deciding to volunteer her time twice a week at the local library. She was involved in a book drive and wanted to get an early start into town. As always, the devoted Gillie was to drive, and he brought the buggy around exactly at nine. Dressed for the city, Marguerite met Juliet at the front door. She was about to kiss her daughter good-bye when she was inexplicably assailed with a strange feeling she couldn't identify.

"What is it, Mama?" Juliet asked. She was just pulling on her gloves, and when she saw Marguerite's expression, she paused.

But Marguerite couldn't explain herself. Looking at her daughter, so demure and elegant in dove-gray silk, with her white gloves and a circlet of pale roses around the crown of her hat, she opened her mouth to say something, then closed it again. A worried frown creased Juliet's pale brow; her huge, luminous eyes looked concerned.

"Are you ill, Mama?" she asked.

"No, I . . ." Marguerite had been about to say that she didn't want Juliet to go, but she stopped herself in time. She was being absurd, she realized. What harm could come to her at the library, of all places? she wondered. Gillie was an excellent driver, and she knew he would never allow anything to happen to Juliet. On that thought, she kissed her daughter's smooth cheek.

"No, I'm perfectly fine, darling," she said. "It was just . . . for a moment, I thought . . ." She forced a laugh. "I'm becoming fanciful in my old age, it seems. Gillie is waiting, so you run along, now. I know you don't want to be late."

But Juliet still hesitated. "Are you sure?" she asked. "If something is wrong, I could stay—"

"Don't be silly. Your father and I are leaving soon for San Francisco ourselves," Marguerite said, pulling on her own gloves. Then, without even knowing why, she added, "But please be careful today, darling. I . . . I don't want anything to happen to you."

Juliet smiled tenderly at her mother's concern. "What could possibly happen to me, Mama?' she said with a light little laugh. "I'm only going to the library, after all. I'll be back before lunchtime."

But Juliet didn't return for lunch, and she wasn't there by supper when Marguerite and Sloane returned from San Francisco. Long before then, the worried Andrew had sent Angus into town to find her; when Angus came back with the unwelcome news that Juliet had left the library at noon and hadn't been seen since, he immediately organized a search party and sent everyone out along the road and around the hills on the way to town and back. Of Gillie and the buggy, there was no sign either, and Andrew was beside himself with anxiety by the time Sloane and Marguerite arrived.

"No!" Marguerite exclaimed when she heard the news. She remembered her premonition that something was going to happen, and she clutched Sloane's arm, her face turning pale.

Sloane tried to be reassuring. "We'll find her, I know. She can't have gone far."

Her eyes were stricken. "I knew something was going to happen."

"What? What do you mean?"

But she couldn't tell Sloane about her inexplicable feeling that morning; it sounded ridiculous still, and besides, the time for acting on it was long past. Quickly, she shook her head. "Never mind. It doesn't matter now. I'm going to change and start looking, too."

Andrew already had all the ranch hands out, both on horseback and by foot. He had ordered them to report back the instant anything was found. Marguerite knew that there was very little she could do, but she couldn't stand by worrying and wondering and imagining all sorts of things; she had to help in the search, too. Sloane didn't argue with her.

Marguerite didn't waste any more time. She wouldn't even wait for someone to take her up to the house, but set off at a run. Because she was so worried about Juliet, she arrived in record time, flinging herself up the porch steps, throwing open the front door, and rushing toward the stairs. She had time to notice the house was unnaturally quiet; Matilda and the inside help must have volunteered to search, too. Sloane had long ago converted the place to the new electricity, but the interior was dusky by this hour, and Marguerite didn't want to take time to fumble for the light switches. She knew her way in the dark, and as she flung herself up the stairs, she was already taking off her hat and unbuttoning her jacket. She had almost reached the doorway to the master bedroom when she thought she heard something. Instantly, she jerked to a halt.

The upstairs hallway was crowded with shadows; she couldn't see clearly. Her hand on the door to the bedroom, she paused to listen. Her heart was pounding in her chest from her run and her fear for her daughter, and she couldn't catch her breath. She was just telling herself that she had imagined the noise when she was sure she heard it again.

She stiffened. The noise had sounded like a muffled sob, and it was coming from down the hallway. Stricken, she realized that it was coming from Juliet's room.

*No, that can't be,* she thought. Surely, the house would have been searched first. Uncertain, she reminded herself that Sloane was waiting, and she started forward once again. But instead of turning toward her bedroom, she took a step toward the end of the hall, and then another . . . and another. With each step, her thundering heart beat faster and faster until it was so loud in her ears that she couldn't have heard someone scream right beside her.

"Juliet?" she said. Then, louder, "Juliet, are you there?"

She had reached the doorway to her daughter's bedroom. The shadows had lengthened and thickened even more these past tortured moments; when she looked into the room, she couldn't see anything but bulky shapes in the gloom.

*You're wasting time!* her mind screamed at her, but she pushed the door open further and went in.

"Juliet?" she called again, and was just reaching for the light switch when she dropped her hand again. She didn't know why, but some instinct told her that if her daughter was here, she wouldn't want the light. "Juliet?" she said.

One door to the armoire was ajar; she could just barely see it in the murk. It was so unlike Juliet to leave anything out of place that she went toward it. Biting her lip, she reached out with a shaking hand and pulled the door open all the way. The tiny squeak the hinges made sounded like a gunshot to her taut nerves, and she nearly cried out herself when she heard another sob. Then she saw the shape crouching at the back of the closet and drew in a sharp breath.

"Juliet! What happened?" she cried, and reached in for her daughter.

Juliet screamed—a rending sound that echoed through the house and into the hills behind the ranch, causing even the searchers a mile or so away to stop and listen until it died out. Down at the barn, Sloane, who had one foot in the stirrup, preparatory to getting into the saddle, froze in position.

"What the hell . . . ?" he muttered, and turned toward the house.

The scream was the last sound Juliet made that day. By the time Sloane and Andrew and Matilda and the other women close by rushed into the house and pelted up the stairs, Juliet had lapsed into blank, staring silence.

When Sloane burst into the bedroom ahead of everyone else and reached quickly to turn on the light, the sight that greeted him was so shocking he actually reared back a step, bumping into Andrew, who was coming right behind him.

When Andrew saw Marguerite crouched on the floor, holding her bruised and battered and bleeding daughter, he spoke for them all when he exclaimed, "Holy Mother of God!"

Her arms tight around Juliet, Marguerite looked up at Sloane. Her green eyes were enormous, her face utterly without color even in the sudden harsh glow of light. She seemed beyond speech, the muscles of her throat working as she fought to say something. She wasn't sure what had happened, but she could guess. Juliet was still wearing the dove-gray dress she had worn this morning, but the dress that had been so immaculate and pressed when she left the house was rent now under one sleeve, and half the buttons were missing from the bodice. The skirt was torn in several places, and there was a dark stain on the hem that could only have been blood. Her pale blond hair, which she always wore in a chignon at the nape of her neck, had escaped its net and was disordered, trailing down her back in tangles. There were scratches on her cheek.

But as nightmarish as her appearance was, as frightening as was the blank, staring look in her eyes, the gun in her hand was the most terrifying aspect of all.

Everyone saw it at once, an ornate little derringer, elegantly engraved and inscribed, with a short silver barrel and a pearl handle. His eyes dilating, Sloane silently glanced at Marguerite. In that glance was the most horrific question a parent could ask, but Marguerite had no answer for him. Almost imperceptibly, she shook her head. She had seen the gun and tried to make Juliet give it to her, but her child's white fingers were clutched around the grip so tightly that gun and hand might have been welded together. Once Juliet had lapsed into the terrifying blank stare, Marguerite had been afraid to insist her daughter surrender it. Now she didn't dare think too much about the gun. She just wanted this nightmare to be over.

Carefully, Sloane bent down. "Juliet, darling," he murmured, while everyone held their breath. "Give Papa the gun."

It was as if she didn't even hear him; she just stared straight ahead, holding that derringer in her rigid hand. The girl didn't blink, and Marguerite had to tighten her embrace to make sure Juliet was breathing.

Sloane tried again. "Juliet, please give me the gun."

Marguerite felt as if she might scream from sheer tension. In her arms Juliet was unmoving, as rigid as she had been ever since her mother had managed to get her out of the closet. Behind them, holding everyone back, Andrew muttered into the frozen silence, "You're going to have to take it, lad."

Sloane nodded. Very carefully, he reached for Juliet's hand. "I'm going to take the gun, darling," he said, trying to pry apart her frozen fingers. "You don't have to be afraid. We won't let anything hurt you. . . ."

Somehow—it seemed an eternity—Sloane succeeded in getting the little gun away from his daughter. Everyone breathed a sigh of relief when he had it in his hand. But when he gave it up to Andrew, and Andrew sniffed the barrel, he frowned.

"This gun's not been fired," he said.

Sloane looked back at him. "What?"

"See for yourself."

As Sloane slowly straightened to check the gun, Matilda, who had been hovering anxiously in the background, pushed forward to give Marguerite a hand. Her handsome ebony features, usually so serene, looked carved from black stone now; her wide mouth was grim.

"Someone get the doctor," she said, as sensible as always. "This chile's been 'tacked." And with that, she simply reached down and lifted the waiflike Juliet in her ample arms and carried her to the bed.

Marguerite thought that things couldn't get worse during the long, terrible night, but they did. She didn't realize until after the doctor had come and gone and confirmed Matilda's diagnosis that Gillie was still missing. Ashamed of her preoccupation, she sought Matilda out in the big kitchen, only to learn Matilda didn't know where her son was. Andrew had the hands out searching, but so far no one had even caught a glimpse of the buggy Gillie had used to drive Juliet into town. The horse was missing as well, but that was a secondary consideration. After talking to the doctor, Marguerite still felt too numb to care much about anything but whether Juliet would ever recover from this experience.

"Juliet was attacked, there's no doubt about it," Dr. Morse told her and a murderous-looking Sloane privately in the parlor before he left for the night. "She's badly bruised, but I don't think there will be permanent damage. That is . . . er . . . I'm sure she will be able to have children."

At the moment, Marguerite was more worried about Juliet's emotional state. Plaintively, she asked, "When will she be able to speak?"

The doctor looked even more solemn. "I can't answer that, Mrs. Caulfield," he said. "Your daughter seems to have lapsed into a state of complete withdrawal, which is known as catatonia. I'm afraid there isn't much we can do about it." He paused, then added with determined hopefulness, "At this date, there is no cure as such, but time—"

"We don't have *time*, doctor," Sloane interrupted, his tone sounding as terrible as he looked. "We have to know what happened."

Marguerite knew he was thinking about the gun Juliet had been clutching and wondering where she had gotten it. It hadn't come from Sloane's collection, but that was almost a moot point. Juliet had always been frightened of anything to do with guns; as far as either of them knew, she had never even handled one in her life. The only hope she had was that Juliet hadn't fired it.

Marguerite put a hand to her mouth as Sloane went to the door with the doctor. Juliet had been given a sedative, the man said; he would return tomorrow to see her. Beyond that, it was in more powerful hands than his. He was sorry, but there wasn't any more he could do.

When Sloane came back from showing the doctor out, his first question was, "Has Gillie been found yet?"

Shocked at his tone, Marguerite looked at him. "You don't think that *Gillie*—"

Sloane poured himself a stiff shot of whiskey. Tossing it back, he said, "I don't know what to think."

Stunned, Marguerite groped for the back of a chair. "No, I can't believe it, Sloane. Gillie would never—"

"Then where is he?" Sloane demanded hoarsely. "What happened to him? Where did he go? Damn it, Marguerite, I want some answers!"

She was about to reply when she saw his face crumple. He turned away, but not before she saw the glint of tears in his eyes. Silently, she went to him and put her arms around him, placing her cheek against his stiff back. He stood there rigidly for a moment; then, with a muffled sob, he turned and pulled her close.

"She's so delicate, so fragile." he said hoarsely, agonized. "She'll never get over this, Marguerite, never."

"Hush . . ." Marguerite murmured, holding him close for a moment. Then she pushed him into a chair and sat in his lap, cradling his head to her breast. Now she was the one to comfort him, and as she stroked his hair, she whispered, again and again, "Hush . . ."

It was the nineteen-year-old Rupert Jaeger who found Juliet's buggy and horse. During the course of the frantic search, Andrew had sent two men to Mondragon Stud to ask if anyone there had seen Juliet, and according to Rupert, who told the story much later, he'd been concerned by then himself because his father, Heinrich, had failed to return from a trip to see his lawyer in Sonoma. Concerned when hours passed with no sign of his father, Rupert had joined in the search and his route had taken him past the summerhouse his father had built some years before for Mariel. Heinrich used it now for an office, and Rupert had been surprised to see the horse and buggy standing outside; naturally, he recognized it at once as belonging to Juliet Caulfield. He couldn't imagine why Juliet would be visiting his father in this remote place, and he was reluctant to approach. In fact, he said, he was about to simply go away when something—he couldn't say what—compelled him to stop after all. To his surprise, the door was open, and when he came in and saw his father in the chair behind the desk, he knew something was terribly wrong.

Heinrich was dead—shot through the heart with a bullet

from the ornate derringer he'd kept on display on the desk. At least, that's what he assumed. The gun seemed to be missing, and of Juliet, of course, there was no sign. But there was her horse and buggy abandoned, and so he came straight to Caulfield Farm.

"Without calling the police?" the white-faced Sloane asked, after Rupert had related his incredible story.

Rupert at the moment was in better control than Juliet's distraught father. "I thought we might keep this between the two of us, Sloane," he said. "I'm sure that if you don't have the derringer in your possession right now, Juliet knows just where it is. Perhaps we should ask her."

"You're not asking Juliet anything!" Sloane shouted. He didn't know what Rupert was after, but he himself was ready to do murder. Only Marguerite's restraining hand on his arm prevented him from attack. Barely able to speak over his rage, he said, "We're going directly to the police. According to the doctor, Juliet was raped. The way I see it, your father attacked my daughter, and whatever she did—if she did anything at all—was in self-defense!"

"Oh, I don't think so," Rupert said complacently. For a son who had just lost his father, he seemed remarkably calm. But then, Marguerite thought distractedly, their relationship had always been strained; nothing Rupert did had ever satisfied his demanding father. Now it seemed all that was behind him; with Heinrich dead, Rupert was the sole owner of Mondragon Stud. He went on. "After all, I did find Juliet's horse and buggy at the summerhouse. Who's to say she didn't go there voluntarily?"

"Why you—!"

Fortunately, Andrew was there to help Marguerite pull the enraged Sloane back from Rupert, who at this point didn't look quite as complacent. "She was obviously in the house, Mr. Caulfield. How are you going to explain it?"

"My daughter was attacked, you miserable little—!"

"You keep saying that. What proof do you have? After all, my father is the one who is . . . dead."

Sloane lunged in Andrew's tight grasp. "Let me go, Andrew! I'm going to kill the son of a bitch!"

"Oh, I don't think so, Sloane," Rupert said, backing carefully toward the door. "But I'll tell you what. We can make a deal, you and I, and both of us will be better off for it."

"A deal! I'd sooner make a deal with the devil!" Sloane yelled.

"As you wish," Rupert said calmly. "But I'm just thinking of your daughter, Mr. Caulfield. Juliet has always been . . . how shall we say? Delicate. Do you really think she could stand up under the strain of a trial? Wouldn't it be better to try to work this out between ourselves? In fact, we can keep poor Juliet out of it completely. How would you like that?" He actually smiled. "All you have to do is sign over Caulfield Farm to me, and in return, I'll say it was a robbery. In the course of a struggle, my father was . . . shot and killed. I can't be fairer than that."

This time not even Andrew could hold Sloane back. As the enraged father leaped at Rupert, he scuttled out the door. "You think about it, Sloane!" Rupert called, climbing quickly onto his horse. "Do you really want your daughter to be known as a murderess? Do you really want people to whisper that she killed her lover in a fit of jealous pique, perhaps? It's up to you, Sloane. But you'd better make up your mind quick. The offer's only good until dawn. After that, I *will* contact the police!"

Sloane nearly killed him right there. Instead, trapped by Rupert's duplicity and the sure knowledge that Heinrich's son would profit one way or another from his death, Sloane decided to play his own game. Long before dawn, he and Marguerite had made their arrangements. They couldn't know what had really happened at the summerhouse until Juliet recovered enough to tell them—that, or they found Gillie, who seemed to have disappeared without a trace. But they were not going to subject their daughter's delicate state of mind to inquiries, and possibly a trial, before they knew the truth. Fully aware that Rupert could take everything they had, they insisted on selling Caulfield Farm to Andrew. If the ranch was in Andrew's name, Rupert couldn't gain control. Andrew didn't like it, but he reluctantly paid over the dollar Sloane asked to make it legal. Then they said good-bye to their trusted friend, who promised to care for the place until they returned. Not knowing when that would be, but determined to protect their fragile child, they bundled Juliet and Ariana into their carriage and were on their way to Europe before Rupert realized they were gone. Leaving everything behind but memories of halcyon days when the future spread brightly before them, they vanished for five years.

---

# CHAPTER TWENTY-EIGHT

Briar closed Marguerite's journal with a shudder. Well, now she knew why Rupert was so obsessed with her family. Juliet might have been attacked, but Rupert's father had been shot and killed. When Sloane and Marguerite had sold the ranch to Andrew and fled to Europe, he must have seen that as the ultimate betrayal. Not only was his father dead, but Heinrich's death had never been fully explained, or the perpetrator brought to justice, or the family avenged. To Rupert, it would have seemed that Juliet—and by extension, Sloane and Marguerite, because they had taken her away—had never paid for what she had done, or been forced to testify even to what had taken place.

For her family, Briar thought, it was just as much a nightmare. The only person who might have been able to say what had happened was locked in her own silent world, withdrawn and helpless. Gillie had disappeared, and no one could be sure what had occurred that fateful afternoon. Lord, she thought, rubbing her eyes wearily, what a mess.

Still troubled, she got up stiffly and switched off the living room lights. She was just pulling the drapes over the front window shut when she saw something move down below, and she paused. The barns and the paddocks down below were illuminated in white pools of light by the timed floodlights, and as she watched, the tiny figure of one of the barn cats appeared, then crept around the corner and disappeared to hunt. She smiled briefly at the sight, thinking what Stefan would say about that. He claimed all cats were useless because they hunted on neighboring property instead of tracking down the mice in the barn where they belonged, and that hers were particularly spoiled because she fed them every day anyway.

Thinking of Stefan reminded her how strangely he'd been acting lately; he'd been so brusque and irritable that she tried to leave him alone. Then, today, when that damned interview appeared in *The Morning Line*, he'd really been angry. She'd been so irate herself that she had hardly noticed, but she wished now he hadn't gone out. He'd been jumpy long before the article showed up, and since he'd been so supportive of her these past months, she wanted to ask if she could help him for a change.

But she hadn't had the chance before she saw him leave earlier, and at this hour it was too late to go down to say she'd come to chat. She saw that his truck was parked in front of his house again, but all the windows were dark, and she sighed. She couldn't wake him up now; she'd just have to wait.

Transferring her glance to the line of dormer windows in the roof of the main barn, she counted to the one where Gillie had stayed. Like four of the other ranch workers, he'd had his own place up there, and as she gazed somberly at the darkened glass square, she felt sorry again that he was gone, and she wondered just how much he knew.

So many loose ends, she thought, frowning. Was Gillie the key? Remembering the journal she had read tonight, she wondered what had really happened the day Juliet disappeared. She simply could not believe that Juliet was having an affair with Heinrich—one explanation why her horse and buggy would have been found at the summerhouse—but what other reason could there be for her having gone there? Even Heinrich, bastard that Briar had seen him to be through her reading, wouldn't have had the nerve to force her to meet him in some way. Why had they both been there? Was Gillie the only one who knew for sure? He had been Juliet's driver; he must have driven her to the summerhouse.

No, no, she wouldn't believe he'd been a part of it, either, Briar thought. Marguerite had made a great point in her journals about how fond Gillie was of Juliet, how much he had worshipped her. Surely, if he had been there he would have protected her with his life.

Maybe Gillie had killed Heinrich, she thought suddenly, and then drew back from the idea. No, she couldn't believe Gillie could kill anyone. But if she didn't believe it, the alternative was that Juliet had done it after all.

Frustrated because she hadn't been able to illicit much information from Gillie himself while he'd worked for her, Briar turned away from the window. As eager as she had been to find out every detail from him about the Caulfields, he had always been reluctant to talk about it. She had hoped that when he felt more comfortable here, more secure, he would tell her, but that hadn't happened. Now she realized she should have pressed a little harder.

But there were other disturbing questions beyond the obvious ones. For example, how had Juliet gotten back to Caulfield Farm, and why was she carrying a gun that hadn't been fired? And with all those people looking for her, how had she managed to enter the house unseen? And even more important, where had Gillie gone, and why had he disappeared?

The questions went round and round, and Briar realized she had no answers. But one person might, she thought, turning to gaze down again at what had once been Gillie's bedroom window. There were only two people alive who might have a clue as to what had happened the day Juliet was attacked and Heinrich was shot. Gillie was one of them, but Rupert Jaeger was the other. Her eyes narrowed. What did Rupert know? Was he the reason Gillie had been so afraid that he'd run away from here a second time?

Oh, she didn't know, and she was starting to feel like she was going around in circles herself. She had a couple of important meetings tomorrow, so she should just forget it for now and go on up to bed. But she was still thinking about the puzzle through her shower, and she had just slipped into a nightgown and was putting cream on her face when she was struck by another sudden thought. Pausing with her hand halfway to her cheek, she stared at herself in the mirror.

She hadn't really thought about Rupert in connection with this incident, she realized. The nineteen-year-old boy Marguerite had described at that time was so far removed from the eighty-year-old man he was now that they seemed two separate and distinct people. But, remembering how he had come to Sloane and Marguerite with a deal right after his father was killed, Briar slowly capped the jar of cream. The boy had become a man, but she was still dealing today with the same person Rupert had been all those years ago, she told herself, and she felt a sudden chill. What kind of man was Rupert Jaeger, who could make bargains right after his own father had been killed?

She was still thinking about it when she woke the next morning, tired and out of sorts. After taking so long to drift off, she overslept and had to rush out of the house without even a cup of coffee. As she got into the car and started to drive down toward the barn, she thought of Touch the Fire and remembered a conversation she and Gillie had had right before he vanished.

"My medicine's workin' its magic, Miz Briar," he'd told her the day before he disappeared. He'd been rubbing some foul-smelling concoction into the filly's leg while he talked, and despite herself, Briar's nostrils had contracted. "It won't be long now before she's ready to run, I'll tell you that."

Briar had just smiled; both veterinarians who were following the filly doubted that she would be ready to return to training until next year, and maybe not then. Stefan had concurred, but she didn't want to tell Gillie that.

"I hope you're right, Gillie," she'd said, and then decided to tease him a little. "If I were her, I'd be eager to get back just to escape that awful-smelling medicine of yours."

"You laugh, Miz Briar," he said serenely, wiping his hands on a towel he had tucked under his belt. "But you'll see, you'll see."

"I'd like to think so, Gillie."

He looked up at her, an old man wearing a flat porkpie hat that had seen better days, his eyes rheumy and bloodshot. "You don't believe me?"

"Well, it's not that I don't believe you, Gillie," she said hastily. "It's just that Kara and Denise think—"

"Oh, those young women, yes," he said, dismissing both veterinarians with a complacent wave of his hand, as if between them they didn't have a combined education and experience total of perhaps thirty years. "They're good kids, but they got no sense. Everythin' they learned, they got from books."

Trying not to smile, Briar said, "I'm not sure that's true, Gillie. Kara, for instance, has been working at the track for years."

He thought for a moment before he reached for some cotton batting and began wrapping it around the black filly's leg. "Sure," he finally allowed. "But sometimes they still can't read horses. You take this filly here. She *wants* to run, and if we gave her the chance, she'd be off like she was shot out of a cannon."

"And probably do irreparable harm to her leg, too."

He grinned up at her. "Well, I never said horses was the smartest things, only just about the fastest."

Briar couldn't help smiling, too. "So what you're really

saying is that you don't know when she'll be ready to run."

"What I'm sayin' is that she's *ready* to run right now. Whether she should or not is a different story. But I'll be able to tell you better next week."

But he'd never had a chance to tell her the next week, Briar thought sadly. She'd given that stupid party the next night, and he'd disappeared right afterward. *Oh, Gillie!* she thought. Where are you?

Stefan came out of the barn as she drove by, riding one of the two-year-olds they were breaking for the track. The youngster was a big, gangly chestnut that hadn't been ridden much, and as the car came into view, the colt decided to test Stefan's mettle by throwing a fit at the sight of the strange monster.

Beginning to wonder if she was ever going to get to work, Briar braked to a stop until Stefan could get the colt under control. As she sat there watching the horse spin and dance and side pass all over the road, she couldn't help admiring the way Stefan rode—as if he were sitting on a rocking horse instead of an animal half-serious about trying to get him off. As always, Stefan just rode it out, moving easily with the horse no matter which way it went, letting it have its little fit, but making it realize at the same time that no matter what, it wasn't going to get rid of him. Finally, blowing hard, and obviously feeling a little foolish for putting on such a ridiculous show for so little gain, the colt settled down and Stefan was able to move to the side of the road so Briar could get by. A careful eye on the horse, she stopped again as she came up.

"I see *he's* coming along nicely." she said.

Stefan patted the colt's sweaty neck. He was wearing faded jeans under shotgun chaps that hugged his long legs, boots, and a red-and-white checked shirt. Instead of a Stetson, he had on a baseball cap to keep the sun out of his eyes, and he looked rugged and handsome and charmingly in need of a haircut. "A little too much energy, I think. He won't feel the same way after an hour or so up in the hills, I'll guarantee him that."

Briar smiled, but when she thought of all she had to do today, she felt a little wistful. She couldn't remember when she had last taken Irish up into the hills; could it really have been the time she'd met Charlotte Jaeger and they'd had that unsatisfactory talk? She had hoped when she moved here she'd have

more time to ride. After all, the hills were so close; all she had
to do was saddle up and go. But it hadn't turned out that way.
The best she'd been able to do lately was take Irish around the
training track three or four times a week or work him in the big
riding ring she'd had built down near the creek. Thinking how
ironic it was that she had so little time for herself when her
*business* was making time for other people, she said, "I envy
you. I wish I could go, too."

Stefan's eyes seemed very blue. "Well, come along, then.
I'll have Manuel saddle your horse."

Reluctantly, she shook her head. "No, I can't. I've got
appointments back to back today at the office and three new
accounts to set up. I'm already late as it is."

He looked down at her from the saddle, easily holding the
colt with light hands on the reins, gazing into her face. "You
work too hard."

"I'm beginning to realize that," she agreed wryly. "I never
dreamed it would be so difficult, trying to be in several places
at once."

"Maybe you should give up trying."

"Give up the ranch?"

"Or the business."

She was shocked. "I couldn't give up McKenna Time-
Save!"

"Why not?"

She had never seriously considered it, not even when she
had agreed to marry Hay, who had understood just how important her company was to her. Until they met, the business
had been her entire life, her reason for existence. Even after
she married, she had continued on; despite all the difficulties
and the drain on her energy, she couldn't picture not going into
the office on a regular basis. Aside from marrying Hay, and
perhaps rebuilding the ranch, McKenna TimeSave was her
greatest accomplishment. She had done it all herself, built it
from nothing. She couldn't let it go. It would be like giving up
her own beloved child.

"Well, I can't, that's all," she said. "I can't imagine not
going into the office. It would be like . . . like cutting off a part
of myself."

"So you've abandoned your idea of becoming just the gen-
tlewoman rancher?"

Something about the way he was staring at her made her heart race. He looked so damned handsome sitting in the saddle.

"When did I say that?" she asked lightly. "It must have been in a moment of weakness."

"I didn't know you ever had those."

She flushed. "Well, I do. Occasionally."

"Not often enough."

"Do you think that's true?"

"I do. Maybe we should talk about it."

"Maybe we should."

"When?"

"Well, I don't know," she parried, suddenly wary. "You haven't exactly been in the best of moods lately. If I didn't know better, I'd think you were trying to keep something from me."

"Why do you say that?" he asked. His tone was casual, but his hands had tightened almost imperceptibly on the reins. The colt responded by lifting its head slightly, and he put a leg into the horse's side to keep him in place.

"Why do you think? You haven't been yourself lately; that's why I've stayed away from you."

"That's funny. I was thinking the same thing about you."

"No, you can't blame me—" she started to say, but then asked herself if it was true. Wasn't this a little of her own fault, too? What *did* she want from him? Comfort when she needed it? Company when she was lonely? An escort when she wanted to go out? Someone to share physical intimacy with, and not much else? If he was giving confusing signals, what was she doing? It was time to face it. She couldn't hide behind widowhood much longer. Hay had always said that no one could—or should—mourn forever, and she was beginning to think he'd been right.

"Yes, maybe we should talk about it," she said, before she changed her mind. "How about if you . . . come up to the house tonight? We . . . we could have dinner. Unless you're busy, of course. In that case, we could make it another—" She was babbling from sudden nerves and didn't know why; she made herself stop. "I'd like for you to come," she said finally.

He didn't say anything for a long moment. Then, his eyes holding hers, he said, "What time?"

They agreed on eight, and as she drove carefully off, mindful of his skittish horse, she looked in the rearview mirror.

Easily holding the restless colt, she saw him staring after her until she made the turn and disappeared.

Patsy was waiting, wide-eyed, at her desk when Briar finally arrived. This morning the secretary was wearing a lime-green knit skirt and matching top that suited her rail-thin figure perfectly. Her curly hair was pulled up into a ponytail that cascaded down the side of her head, and she had a pencil stuck behind her ear. The first thing she said was, "Spence called. He wants to talk to you right away—"

"Fine," Briar said. "Give me five minutes, and get him on the line, will you? We've got a lot—"

"And—"

She'd started leafing quickly through the mail Patsy had yet to take into her office. Absently, she looked up. "What?"

"You've got a visitor. . . ."

"Now?" Briar couldn't remember an early appointment—not this early, anyway. "Who is it?"

"It's Mrs. Hudson," Patsy said, making a face.

"Fredrica?" Surprised, Briar looked toward her closed office door, then she frowned. "What is *she* doing here?"

"I don't know," Patsy said, lowering her voice. "But she looks pretty pleased with herself. And—"

"And what?"

Unhappily, Patsy finished, "Well, Spence didn't sound so happy when he called." She hesitated. "I hope nothing's wrong."

Looking grim as she headed toward her office, Briar said, "Where Fredrica's concerned, you can bet something will be. Hold all my calls, please. I'll try and get this over with as soon as I can."

It was over almost before she knew it. Fredrica was standing near the window when she came in, looking not only pleased with herself, but like the cat who had discovered the cream. Briar didn't pretend to be pleased to see her; she wasn't going to insult them both with spurious civility when they clearly despised one another. So she tossed her briefcase on top of the desk and said briskly, "Hello, Fredrica. What do you want?"

As always, Fredrica was wearing her favorite black today, but for this occasion, she had added a yellow scarf. Glancing at her, Briar thought that she looked like a malevolent wasp. Already feeling her patience wearing thin, she watched as Fredrica sauntered back to the desk.

"I came to tell you the good news."

"What good news?"

Fredrica hadn't taken off her hat, a large flat disk that hid half her face and was crowned by a big yellow bow that matched the scarf at her throat. Her voice acid, she said, "Well, as you know, despite your *generous* decision to divide Daddy's estate among the three of us, I still hadn't made up my mind about the will."

Briar couldn't believe it. The terms of their settlement clearly dictated that Fredrica had to withdraw all claims.

"Not that it makes any difference according to our agreement, but I'm curious," Briar said. "Are you here to tell me you've decided to go ahead and contest?"

"You *do* take the fun out of things, Briar. I was prepared to make my announcement, and now you've stolen all my thunder."

Briar didn't have time for nonsense. "Just get to the point."

"Well, all right, if you insist," Fredrica said, her black eyes gleaming maliciously. "As a matter of fact, I have decided that a long court battle would be just *too* boring—not to mention expensive. All those exorbitant fees to lawyers, and for what? So that we would have to keep meeting over and over, when the truth is that we never want to set eyes on each other again. I decided to pursue another option."

Thinking that she didn't have any, Briar said politely, "Oh? And what is that?"

"I know how you appreciate irony, Briar, so I'm sure you'll appreciate this. I've felt so powerless all this time that I thought it would be interesting to see you in the same position."

Briar didn't know where all this was going, and she wasn't sure she cared. She'd done everything she intended to for Fredrica—at great cost to herself, since she'd been in a financial pinch ever since—and she didn't want to waste any more time. Taking a seat behind the desk, she said, "I'm sure you find this amusing, Fredrica, but I really do have a full day planned, so do you think you could get to the point sometime during my lifetime?"

Fredrica's eyes flashed, but then she shrugged and stood back. "Your sarcasm no longer has an effect on me, Briar. *You* no longer have an effect. As of the start of business this morning, Jaz and I are no longer associated with Lord Industries.

You can thank me now or later, but we're finally out of your hair. Aren't you pleased?''

Slowly, Briar got to her feet. "What have you done, Fredrica?"

"What you wanted all along, when you seduced my father into cutting his children out of his will. Well, now you're rid of us, Briar. Jaz and I sold those shares you gave us—it amounts to two-thirds of the company, I believe, does it not? Leaving you a minority shareholder, it seems, but so what? You were never interested in Daddy's company, only for what it could do to finance that ridiculous horse ranch of yours. But just guess. Now you have a new partner, and I don't think he's going to indulge your whims much longer. In fact—'' She pretended to think. "I believe he said this morning that if the right offer came along, he'd sell it for . . . what was it? Forty cents on the dollar? Does that sound like too much?''

Briar couldn't believe it. "This is ridiculous," she said between her teeth. "No one in his right mind would sell for that! If this is your idea of a joke—''

"Oh, it's no joke, my dear. Call your lawyer and find out. I imagine he's been trying to get hold of you this morning— before your new . . . er . . . *partner* sells out.''

Briar grabbed hold of the edge of the desk to control herself. "I can't believe you did this," she said, her voice shaking with her sudden anger. "You *know* how much that company meant to your father!''

"Yes, but not to me or Jaz. How could it, when Daddy gave it all to you? We had to get *something* out of it, did we not?''

"You *did* get something! I divided everything equally!''

"Only when your back was pressed to the wall when that prenuptial agreement inconveniently surfaced. *That's* when you came forth with your oh-so-*generous* offer, remember? We certainly didn't hear a word from you before!''

"You won't get away with this!''

Fredrica smiled and wagged her finger back and forth. "Oh, don't think it isn't legal, my *dear* stepmother. I had my lawyers check it out thoroughly before Jaz and I signed those papers. After all, it was a *great* sum of money. But of course you know that already. You've certainly clung tightly to your share.''

Briar was so furious she wasn't sure she could speak. "You can't do this," she said between her teeth. "Not even you—''

"Oh, it's already done," Fredrica said, and pretended to

preen. "You haven't asked who your new partner is, Briar. Aren't you interested?"

"No."

"Well, I'm going to tell you anyway," Fredrica said vindictively. "It's Rupert Jaeger. Now what do you think of that?"

Briar felt a buzzing in her ears. Fredrica couldn't be serious. "I don't believe you. You're making it up."

"Oh, but Rupert and I are old friends, didn't you know?" Fredrica said. "He approached me months ago, when you started rebuilding your ranch."

It was possible; Briar knew it was. She wouldn't put anything past Rupert Jaeger. But she said, "I can't believe Jaz would go along with this."

"Oh, Jaz was no trouble."

Briar stared at her. Then she said, "You had something on him, didn't you? That's the only reason he'd do this. He might not have had much to do with Hay, but he respected his father. He'd never—"

Fredrica interrupted with a merry laugh. "But of *course* I had something on him, what do you think? I knew how much he liked you, but Jaz . . ." she shrugged. "Well, you know the saying. Blood *is* thicker than water."

"I know the saying," Briar said harshly. "But somehow I doubt it applies in this case."

"Because Jaz liked you so much?" Fredrica scoffed. "Well, that's true, of course. All right, let's put it this way. I used a little . . . incentive. And please don't ask me what it was," she added as she went to the door. "That's between Jaz and me." She paused with her hand on the knob. "I told you, I'd get you one day, Briar. Now I have. As I always said, it was just a matter of time."

The door had barely closed behind her before Briar reached for the phone. She intended to talk to Jaz if she had to hire Albert to track him down, but first she had to call Spence. She was just reaching for the phone when Patsy stuck her head in.

"Briar, are you—"

"Not now, Patsy," Briar said. "I've got to talk to Spence."

"But—"

"Not *now*, Patsy!"

"I just wanted to say that Spence is here, Briar," Patsy said quickly, before Briar could explode. "He's waiting to talk to you."

Feeling as if she were rapidly losing control, Briar slammed down the phone. "Well, why didn't you say so?" She had no time for niceties. "Send him in."

As soon as Briar saw her attorney's face, she knew she was in big trouble. Until then, she had hoped Fredrica had exaggerated out of spite. One look at Spence told her she was wrong, and she felt sick as she gestured for him to be seated. Ordering herself to be calm so she could try to think this through, she sat down again, too.

"It's bad, isn't it?" she said.

"I'm afraid so. I just passed Fredrica in the hallway. I assume she told you."

"That she and Jaz sold out to Rupert Jaeger? Yes, she did. Tell me she can't do it."

Spence didn't say he'd tried to warn her; they both knew it. "Well, she can. She did. I just came from a meeting with her attorney."

Briar slammed her hand down on the desk. "There must be a way to stop her!"

He looked even more unhappy. "I'm sorry, Briar. You didn't want strings, remember?"

Feeling close to tears, Briar stood and went to the window. Staring down at the street, she took a tight grip on her self-control. "I . . . I can't believe this, Spence," she said, when she was able. She felt more hurt by Jaz's betrayal than she would have believed. "I never thought Jaz would sell out. He promised me."

Spence was silent. What was there to say?

Still staring unseeingly down at the street, Briar said, "All right. What can we do?"

When Spence hesitated, she knew it was hopeless—or about as futile as it could be. "We can go to court," he said finally.

She turned to look at him. "And what will that do?"

He hesitated again. At last, he shook his head. "Not much, I'm afraid. There was really nothing but family ties—loyalty to their father, or to you—to prevent them from selling out."

"And to think she stood there, only a few minutes ago, and told me that blood was thicker than water!" Briar said contemptuously. "Thank God Hay isn't here to witness this."

"I'm sorry, Briar. I wish there was something we could do."

Her lips tight, she came away from the window and sat down at the desk again. "There has to be something," she said. "I am *not* going to allow Rupert Jaeger to profit from a lifetime of Hay's hard work. I'm not!"

Spence glanced down at his hands. "He now owns two-thirds of Lord Industries. He can do what he likes."

"I still own a third!"

He wouldn't look at her. "It won't be enough."

"It has to be!"

"It won't."

"What can I do?"

"You can sell out."

She looked at him as though he had lost his mind. "Absolutely not! I won't. Never!"

He looked even more unhappy. "You may not have any choice."

"What? What do you mean? Of course I have a choice!"

His eyes worried, Spence leaned closer to the desk. "Briar, listen to me a minute. Rupert Jaeger is an enemy—"

"I'm not afraid of him!"

"*Listen* to me! Whether you're afraid of him or not is beside the point! The point here is he can *hurt* you, Briar. With two-thirds control of Lord Industries, he can bring the company to its knees if he chooses, and you won't be able to prevent it."

"Oh, yes, I will! I'll fight him!"

"How? This man is out to destroy you, Briar, and now he's in a position to do it. Even if you could convince him to sell, could you buy him out?" Before she could answer, he went on, trying to make her understand. "And what are you going to do if he starts closing down plants, halting production, doing any of a hundred other things that can start a fatal downward spiral? Are you going to infuse dwindling assets with your own capital? How long can you sustain that? Don't you see, Briar? He's got you over a barrel. It's just a matter of time—"

"I can't believe you want me just to give up!"

"I don't want you to give up. I'm asking you to be prudent. If you sell now, he'll have to give you fair market value. But if you wait . . ."

She didn't have to think about it. Coming up from nothing,

having so little so much of her life, she had always been wary of giving anything of herself except hard work. But Hay had taught her about love and loyalty, and because of all he'd given her, she'd felt obliged to return some of it to Jaz and Fredrica. All right, in her desire to be fair, she had made a mistake that she was paying for now. But Lord Industries had been Hay's life's work; he had given it to her in trust, and no matter what his children did, she would not betray him, no matter the cost.

*And if the price was Caulfield Farm?*

She felt chill fingers down her spine. She knew that's what Rupert was after; he had made it clear right from the beginning. But she wouldn't sell, so he had taken another tack. He was going to squeeze her until she had no more resources to fight him, and then he'd take what he thought was his by right.

"I'm not going to sell, Spence," she said evenly. "And that's final."

Through sheer determination, she got through the rest of the day. But the effort exhausted her, and by four-thirty, she was ready to leave. She was just locking her briefcase when Patsy buzzed through.

"Rupert Jaeger is on the phone," her secretary said. "He wants to talk to you. Shall I put him through?"

Her expression turning to ice, Briar sat down again. "Yes, do," she said. "I've been expecting his call."

"Hello, Ms. McKenna," Rupert said, when she answered. "I take it by now you've heard the news."

"Yes, I have," Briar said.

"That's all you have to say?"

"Do you want me to grovel? Beg for mercy? Ask for your help?"

"Certainly not," he said reproachfully. "Especially now that we're going to be partners."

"We'll never be partners, Mr. Jaeger. You can count on it."

"Oh, you're intending to sell?"

"No, I intend to buy you out."

His amusement was genuine. "You don't have enough money, my dear!"

She clutched the phone tightly. "I'll get it."

"You don't understand yet, do you? What I want is not for sale."

Gritting her teeth, she said, "What do you want, then? Caulfield Farm? Because if you th—"

"Oh, mercy no, not that. Not yet, anyway. I had something much more interesting in mind at this time."

She wanted to reach through the phone and rip his black heart out. "What?"

"I want a match race, of course."

She had known it even before he spoke. "No!"

"Not even if I agree in turn not to disband Lord Industries? After that, we can negotiate."

She was holding on to her control by a thread. "Why are you so determined to force my filly to race?' she demanded. "What could it possibly mean to you?"

"A direct great-great-granddaughter of Fane against my best colt? Surely you jest."

She was too shocked to speak. Had he known all along? she wondered. But how? When had he found out?

As if he had read her thoughts, he chided, "You didn't think I knew. Who do you think arranged for that nonentity of a filly to be at the sale in the first place? She didn't belong there, and we both know it."

Her lips stiff, she said, "You couldn't know I would buy her—"

"Ah, but I did. You were hooked as soon as you traced her pedigree. And, being Marguerite's great-granddaughter, of course you'd do that."

She closed her eyes on a wave of sick fear. "You couldn't know she would be so good."

"No, that's true," he agreed. "But if she hadn't been, I would have just . . . thought of something else."

She didn't want to ask what. "Touch the Fire is not fit to race," she said. "But even if she were, I would never agree to a match. She will not race Galland, and that's my last word!"

His voice took on an edge. "I urge you to reconsider your stand."

"Are you threatening me?"

"I don't threaten, Ms. McKenna. I act. And I can destroy you when I wish, believe me. As they say, it's just a matter of time."

With those last words, he hung up. Feeling more shaken than she wanted to admit, Briar reached for her suit coat. She had to get out of here; she desperately needed some air. But then she looked at the phone again. First she had to call Jaz.

She dialed his number, praying he'd be home. At the other

end, the phone rang once, then again, and then a third time. His answering machine was set to pick up on the fourth ring, and she was just resigning herself to hang up when Jaz answered. He sounded breathless, as if he had been . . .

She didn't have to think what he had been doing. "Jaz?" she said. "It's Briar."

Instantly, he sounded guarded. "Oh . . . Briar," he said. "How . . . how'd you know I was here?"

"I didn't. I guessed." Then, before he could think of an excuse to hang up, she asked, simply, "Why Jaz? Why did you do it?"

He was silent for so long that she thought they'd been disconnected. Finally, he sighed. "It's sort of complicated, Briar," he said reluctantly. "There are things you don't know. Things I never wanted you to know."

She wasn't going to let him off the hook easily. Jaz had been avoiding responsibility for his actions all his life, but he was going to answer for this. "All I need to know is why," she said. "I'm not asking for anything more. When I came to talk to you that day, you—" Her throat threatened to close up on her, and she had to stop for a moment. "I trusted you, Jaz. How could you sell me out? Was it the money? If it was, I could have—"

"It wasn't the money, Briar," he said, his voice sounding flat. "It wasn't that at all. It was . . . oh, shit, if I tell you, will you promise not to tell anyone else? I mean it, Briar, you have to promise. It . . . it could ruin someone if it got out."

Thinking how like him it was to ask her for something after what he had done, she gave her promise. "Just tell me. I won't tell anyone else."

She heard him take a deep breath. "All right, remember that day you came here to talk to me and saw Fredrica and . . . and Arnie on the porch instead?"

Taken aback by the question, wondering what that had to do with it, she frowned, thinking back. Arnie? Oh, yes, the man she'd thought was Fredrica's lover. She had assumed they used Jaz's apartment. Thinking that there was still something familiar about the man, something she'd never been able to place, she said, "Yes, I remember."

Jaz sighed again. "Well, Arnie wasn't here to see Fredrica, Briar," he said, and paused. "He was here visiting me."

"So?" Briar said, and then straightened. "Are you saying . . ."

He sounded more reluctant than ever. "Yes," he said, his voice low. "Arnie and I have been seeing each other for quite a while now."

"I . . . see," she said. She wasn't surprised that Jaz was gay; she just couldn't understand how Fredrica could have used it against him. Knowing Jaz, she thought he'd just laugh and tell her to shout it from the rooftops.

"No, you don't see," Jaz said unhappily. "Look, I didn't care about myself. It doesn't matter to me who knows. After all, this is San Francisco, right? But Arnie . . . well, it's different for him."

She was still drawing a blank. "Why?"

Jaz sounded surprised. "You don't know who he is, do you, Briar?"

"No, who?"

"Arnie is Judge Arnold Pelletier," he said, and paused. "Now does it make sense?"

Briar closed her eyes. How could even Jaz have gotten himself into such a mess? In ultraliberal San Francisco, many of the residents, straight or not, couldn't have cared less if every judge on the bench was homosexual. They just wouldn't have wanted it bandied about.

"Oh, Jaz," she said with a sigh.

"I'm sorry," Jaz said, sounding near tears himself. "I know I promised. But Arnie—"

"I understand," she said gently, and hung up.

With a lover and a judgeship hanging in the balance, Jaz hadn't had much choice. Wondering how even Fredrica could have used such information against her own brother, Briar left the office and started to drive to Sonoma. Halfway there, just when she was feeling that if she didn't get home soon she was going to start screaming her head off from frustration, she ran into a traffic jam on Highway 12, the two-lane road that led to town. As traffic slowed, then slowed again to a mere crawl, she felt her anger mount. There was no other way home from this point; she'd have to sit it out. Oh, she didn't need this today, she thought; why couldn't everybody just get the hell out of the way?

Just then, even the crawl wound to a stop. Cursing, she rolled down the window and stuck her head out. Cars lined the road as far as she could see, and she knew there must have been an accident.

"Damn it!" she cried, and savagely switched off the idling engine. Ahead of and behind her other drivers were doing the same thing, and because she felt as if she wanted to smash something, she reached for the briefcase she had tossed on to the passenger seat. If she had to sit here, she might as well get some work done.

Snapping the locks on the attache, she was sorting through the papers stuffed inside when she saw Marguerite's journal. Snatching it out with a sound of relief, she pushed the briefcase aside. Thank God, she thought; she must have put the journal in with everything else this morning while she was going through her desk. The way she felt now, it would be her salvation; and even though there were only about a dozen more tightly written pages when she counted, she opened it eagerly. If nothing else, Marguerite would take her mind off these disasters today.

Turning to the place she had marked last night, she saw that one of the pages was marred by a big blotch of ink, as if Marguerite had lost control of her pen. This was so unlike her fastidious great-grandmother that Briar felt a chill—especially when she noticed the narrative had been continued in another hand. Whose was it? She didn't want to wait to decipher the mystery. Compelled by an urgency she couldn't explain, she quickly began to read.

---&---

# CHAPTER TWENTY-NINE

"*After an absence of five years,*" Marguerite wrote, the single sentence like a splash of tears across the page, "*I came home to Caulfield Farm to bury my husband.*"

The entry after so long a time away in Europe was dated 1925. It had been six months since Sloane had died, but Marguerite's hand shook even now as she wrote about the sad homecoming. As she lifted her pen from the journal, the nib dripped a great dollop of ink she felt too depressed to blot dry. Sitting there, staring at the black stain spreading across the page, she started to sob, and she bit hard on her lip.

Tragedy always followed her, she thought bitterly, and she would hate Paris the rest of her life. Paris was the place where Sloane had died, and now that it was far, far, too late, she wished she had never agreed to go there. She hadn't wanted to go; Paris was cold and damp, and Sloane had had a cough he couldn't shake. She was worried about him; she didn't want to go. But he insisted. A doctor, a famous Parisian psychiatrist named Jean-Luc Beauvais, was there, and he had agreed to examine Juliet.

But, like all the other countless doctors they had seen, Beauvais offered them no encouragement after he had tested Juliet. They had been to England and Sweden and Germany by then, and France had been their last hope. It had been a bitter blow when the great French psychiatrist had delicately suggested that an institution might be in Juliet's best interests. They had said good-bye to the man and hadn't spoken of him again; then they had returned to the hotel where the English nanny they had hired was keeping watch over Ariana. It was during the following days, when they were trying to decide what to do next, when Sloane's cough had taken a turn for the worst.

At first Marguerite hadn't been worried. The nagging hack of his had responded before to a syrup of horehound and honey. But she became increasingly concerned when the syrup didn't work, and Sloane soon couldn't catch his breath. When he began bending double with fits of congestion, she begged him to see someone, but as always, when his own health or well-being was at stake, he put her off. Juliet was more important, he said, and became so irritated when she insisted that she subsided uneasily. But when one day she saw blood on his handkerchief, she wouldn't listen to his protests any longer; she called the doctor, who came immediately to their hotel suite.

She had always thought until then that the view of the Seine from their balcony was one of the most beautiful sights she had ever seen. But over the next few weeks, the river, like her heart, seemed to turn cold and bleak. She would never see a river again, anywhere, without thinking of that lonely, desperate time, because by the time the doctor finally arrived, it was too late. Pneumonia claimed Sloane a scant two weeks later, and no one could tell her why. Even now she felt numb to think of it. Sloane had always been healthy as could be; during the entire thirty-five years of their marriage, she couldn't remember a time when he had even felt sick. She wouldn't let anyone else care for him; she nursed him day and night, refusing to leave his bedside, even though both the nanny and the nurse whom the doctor had insisted on begged her to get some rest. How could she rest, when her beloved husband was wasting away before her eyes? She couldn't leave him, not when he clung to her hand, so she sat there beside him the entire time, oblivious to anything but his labored breathing. Toward the end he seemed to be suffering so much that she longed for his trial to be over, only to be shocked and ashamed of herself for such thoughts. Oh, how could she wish him to leave her, sick as he was? He was her husband, her companion, her friend . . . her life!

When he died, late one night as the moon shone on the waters of the Seine and the world seemed tranquil except for his harsh gasping for breath, she had been able to look into his eyes one final time. Just once, so briefly she sometimes wasn't even sure it had happened, Sloane had come out of his restless and labored sleep and looked at her, really looked at her, for what she knew was going to be the last time. Overcome with emotion, telling herself fiercely that she would not cry, she forced herself to smile. She would not allow his last sight of her to be one of tears, she thought; she wanted him to know how much she loved him, how she always would love him, and how proud, so very, very proud, she had been to be his wife.

"Hello, darling," she said, willing her voice not to break. She smoothed the sweat-soaked hair back from his face, holding her smile. It took every single fiber of her will not to cry when he reached weakly for her face, and she kissed his fingertips that were even then turning blue. "I'm here, my love," she whispered, looking deep into his dark-shadowed eyes. "I won't leave you, ever. . . ."

He had so little strength left that she barely felt his fingers tightening on hers. "Ah, my Marguerite," he sighed. "How I have loved you . . . that wonderful, musical laugh of yours . . ." He coughed. "How I love you still . . ."

She could feel tears screaming for release. She couldn't let him go, not now, not like this, she thought, agonized. It was too soon. It was too soon!

Clinging to him fiercely, as if the grip of their hands could hold back what she knew was inevitable, she willed herself to be strong for him. He had always told her how much he loved her smile, and so she smiled for him.

"And I have loved you, my dearest, dearest Sloane—"

He was gone before she finished the sentence, closing his eyes for the last time, the slight grip of his fingers falling from hers. With a soft sigh, he went away to a place she could not follow, and as she clung to him and put her head against his chest in a gesture she had made so many, many times, she heard the last beat of his strong heart stumble . . . and fade into silence. It was the loneliest, most desolate absence of sound she had ever experienced, and when she wanted to scream out in her pain she couldn't make a sound. She couldn't even cry; her grief was too profound, her loss too deep. The nanny found her the next morning, still sitting by her husband, holding his hand and staring blankly out at the Seine as it flowed quietly along.

She brought him home to Caulfield Farm and buried him with a simple ceremony under one of the great oak trees at the cemetery. She thought he could look down on the ranch and the valley from there, and watch over his family. With the wind sighing through the trees and the long grass waving like the ripple of water on a verdant green pond, she knew it was a good place for him to rest.

She had managed the return from France in a state of suspended animation in which emotion played no part. But when she came home again and the sole burden she had carried alone was lifted, despair threatened to crush her. Sloane was everywhere she looked; he was in everything she touched. She had hoped the overwhelming grief she had felt all along would abate, so that she wouldn't feel as if her soul had been torn from her body, but every morning when she awoke—if she slept at all—the same grinding weight of heartache and despair threatened to crush her anew. It seemed then that she would never smile again, or laugh or even cry. She seemed bereft of all feeling save this paralyzing grief, and she wondered if she would ever stop listening for his footsteps or expect to hear his voice just one more time. Would she ever cease yearning for the blissful sensation of his arms around her? Would she stop expecting to see him standing beside her if she just glanced up at the right time? How she longed to touch his hand or see him smile or hear him say, just one more time, "Laugh for me, Maggie, my sweet. I always loved your laugh; it made everything right. . . ."

She knew she would never laugh again.

But the hardest thing of all, she thought, was having to lie in that vast, empty, cold bed, all alone. She hadn't slept well since Sloane had died; she doubted now she ever would. There were too many memories that crowded her mind, and to keep herself from going crazy with grief, she walked the floor for many a night until dawn, until she finally fell into an exhausted sleep, only to awaken and begin the same process all over again. Her arms ached to hold him; her body yearned for his touch. If only she could see him one more time, she thought. She missed him so much!

At those times when grief threatened to overwhelm her, she tried to think of the blessings she still had. People depended on her; she had responsibilities, she'd tell herself, and no matter how much she longed to give in to the terrible depression that crushed her down, she didn't have the luxury of giving in; she had too much to do. One of the first things had been to get through the funeral service after she brought Sloane home to rest.

Numbed with grief as she had been on the day of the service, Marguerite was vaguely surprised at how many people had come. Mourners arrived from miles around, friends, people she hadn't seen in a long time, some she had never even met. She had always been aware of how many acquaintances Sloane had, but the realization of how loved he had been only seemed to accentuate her own loss. She felt paralyzed that day, frozen with anguish, as she had been since Sloane had died.

She was brave through the brief, reverent ceremony; it wasn't until the end that her knees buckled and she nearly fell. She could not bear to see the coffin lowered into the grave. She could not make herself toss the clod of dirt on top of that shining, mahogany surface. To do so would be to accept that he was gone forever. She wanted to believe he wasn't really gone, just absent. Soon he would be coming home, tossing his hat expertly toward the hat rack, lifting her up effortlessly in his arms, swirling her around and giving her a kiss. They had been married for thirty-five years, she thought, but the time had flown by far too fast.

So she couldn't make herself end the ceremony, and finally it had been Juliet—beautiful, ethereal, fragile Juliet—who had reached down and taken a handful of fresh earth. Seemingly oblivious to the eyes upon her, including her mother's shocked glance, she had approached the edge of the grave and stood there for a moment, looking down. Marguerite, who didn't know what her delicately balanced daughter might do, started forward, only to be gently restrained by Andrew, who seemed to sense that Juliet needed to be left alone at this moment.

Her face working, Juliet, who hadn't cried once yet, who hadn't even seemed really aware that her father was gone, lifted her pale, white fingers and allowed the dirt to dribble down onto the casket. Then, her voice like the whisper of the wind, she murmured lovingly, "Good-bye, dearest, dearest Papa. I loved you so. Rest in peace."

Then, as if something momentous hadn't just occurred, and she hadn't just spoken her first words in five long years, she turned from the gravesite and came to stand beside the stunned Marguerite. Slipping her hand through her mother's arm, she waited with her head bowed and tears on her pale cheeks for the minister to conclude the service.

Those few words from her daughter broke through the frozen state Marguerite had been in ever since Sloane's death. She was able to cry then, with her daughter, and after everyone had gone, she escaped to her bedroom. Overcome with all the raw emotion she had been so fiercely holding back, she had just thrown herself across the counterpane in a spasm of uncontrollable grief when she felt a gentle hand on her shoulder. It was Juliet, whose huge gray eyes were filled with tears, and with something else as well: an awareness that had been absent since that last tragic day at the Jaeger summerhouse. Shocked out of her grief, Marguerite sat up and reached for her daughter's hands.

"Juliet?" she said carefully.

"Mama," Juliet said, sounding puzzled. "Have I been gone a long time?"

Marguerite swept her daughter into her arms. "A very long time, darling," she choked. As Juliet's arms tightened about her, and her daughter began to sob, she had closed her eyes in a renewed stab of pain and grief. She had prayed so many times for Juliet to come back to them, and now she had, but at what price?

Juliet's recovery was not complete; even after the breakthrough on the day of her father's funeral, she seldom spoke, and she spent hours just staring out the window, her hands still in her lap. But she was devoted to the vibrant, energetic Ariana, Kyle's daughter, who, even at six years old, was already demonstrating the quicksilver personality of her father. Ariana had Kyle's and her grandmother's coloring, with huge mischievous green eyes and thick dark chestnut-colored hair, but it was Juliet that she responded to best. As if Ariana sensed some deep pain in her aunt, she would often interrupt her play to come and sit quietly with her head in Juliet's lap, while Juliet would stroke the child's fiery curls with a serene smile on her delicate face. The two seemed to share a bond that no one else understood, and, watching them during those quiet times, Marguerite felt comforted. They would take care of each other if the time ever came, she knew, and was satisfied.

But as beautiful a child as Ariana was, and as thoughtful as she could be with Juliet, she was still a scamp at times, displaying the same spirit and mischief that had characterized Kyle.

"She puts me in mind of her father, himself a young rake," Matilda would say fondly, when either she or Marguerite had caught the impudent little girl in yet another of her pranks.

"She needs discipline," Marguerite would reply. "Everyone spoils her abominably."

The the two women would smile at each other and go to their separate duties. Marguerite often thought how glad she was that Matilda had stayed on during what she had come to think of as their European exile; there were days even now when she was comforted by the other's woman's strong, understanding presence. They had spoken only once of Gillie since Marguerite returned home—Gillie, Matilda's only son, who had disappeared in the aftermath of the tragedy at the Jaeger summerhouse hadn't been heard from since. Or so Marguerite had thought. Matilda finally confessed that Gillie had written to her once after he had run away, to tell her he was all right and not to worry.

"Thank heaven," Marguerite had breathed, genuinely relieved. She had never believed for an instant that Gillie had had anything to do with what had happened to Juliet, and for a long time she had harbored a secret dread that something awful had happened to him as well. She never had understood why he had disappeared, and because she was a mother herself, she knew how Matilda must have been suffering at his absence. Her hand on the big woman's arm, she asked tentatively, "Do you know where he is?"

Matilda shook her head. "He wouldn't tell me. He thought it was better I didn't know. But he tol' me to tell you he didn't have nothin' to do with what happen to Miz Juliet."

"I know that, Matilda," Marguerite said. "I never thought he did." Because she felt so distressed, she gave the other woman a hug. "I'm sorry, Matilda. So sorry . . ."

Matilda patted her shoulder. "Doan you worry 'bout me, Miz Marguerite."

"But it's so unfair."

"Nobody ever promised us fair, Miz Marguerite," Matilda said wisely. "And 'sides, can you 'magine what would happen if he came back? They'd string him up for sure, jus' to have someone to blame for Mr. Jaeger's death." She shook her head again. "Nobodys ever believed that cockamamie story Mr. Rupert put out about Mr. Heinrich bein' robbed, so it's bes' my Gillie stay away. Long as I knows he's all right, I be all right, too."

Marguerite understood, but she still wondered bitterly why so many women had to weep for their sons and mourn their husbands. "I wish Juliet could remember," she sighed.

"That girl has suffered enough," Matilda replied. "Leave it be, Miz Marguerite. There's nothin' you kin do now, so jus' let it res'. Besides," she said, smiling and gesturing toward the two children, Ariana and Duncan, playing outside, "you have those two to worry 'bout now. Wit' everythin' else, they keep you too busy to think."

"Thank God for that," Marguerite murmured, but she had to agree as time went on. While she was occupied with trying to rebuild the Caulfield breeding program, Ariana thrived. She charmed everyone she met, and even Andrew, who couldn't wait to sign back ownership of the ranch to Marguerite when she had returned, seemed to fall under the spell of the diminutive young minx. Now in his sixties, still a hard worker but more gruff and impatient than he'd been, Andrew worked his full days but found time to pay attention to the youngsters on the ranch. Soon two ponies appeared alongside the sleek Thoroughbreds in the barn, one for Ariana and one for her faithful companion, Duncan, the red-haired, blue-eyed son of Angus and Marta. To Marguerite's amusement, Andrew met the children every afternoon in the training ring behind the barn to teach them equitation. As she did everything else, Ariana took to riding as if she had been born to it, and soon she had progressed beyond the pony to a Welsh cross and insisted on competing in local schooling shows where she invariably returned home with the blue ribbon.

Watching her granddaughter grow, happy that Juliet had returned to her in some measure at least, Marguerite knew she was as content as she ever would be again.

And then came the day Rupert Jaeger came to see her, and Marguerite's tranquility was shattered.

She was out at the paddock looking over the yearlings when Rupert arrived. She heard the sound of the motor car, and she turned in surprise. She wasn't expecting anyone, and when she recognized Rupert behind the wheel, she tensed. It had been too much to hope that he would avoid her forever, she thought, even if he'd had the good sense not to come to the funeral. She hadn't seen him since she and Sloane had left for Europe, and when he got out of the car she was surprised to see that his hair had silvered along the temples. She had already heard about his marriage to the daughter of an old friend of the Jaeger family, an aloof woman five years older than he was, named Hermione Geiger.

"Good afternoon, Rupert," she said coolly, when he came over. "What brings you to Caulfield Farm?"

Removing his hat, he bowed slightly. "I came to tell you that I am truly sorry about Sloane."

Given their history, she doubted he had really come to offer his condolences, but she thanked him and turned back to continue assessing the yearlings. She and Sloane had been in touch with Andrew the entire time they had been away, telling him which horses to breed, which to sell, and which to keep on if they showed promise, and because their old friend had followed their instructions to the letter, she now had a good crop of youngsters from which to choose to reestablish her breeding program.

Rupert glanced over the horses milling around the paddock.

"Not quite up to Caulfield standards, are they?" he commented.

Marguerite didn't trust herself to answer directly. She could feel her hatred rise like acid bile in her throat, and she had to put a hand on the gate to steady herself. He had never reminded her so much of his father as he did at that moment; even his eyes held the same cold, deadly look she'd always seen in Heinrich. The illusion was heightened because they had the same coloring; like his father had been, Rupert was pale and blue-eyed, with thin blond hair that clung to his narrow skull. She had never forgotten the bargain he'd tried to make with them the night before they left for Europe, and, thinking how much she despised him, she asked, "Why are you here, Rupert?"

Reproachfully, he shook his head. "Ah, Marguerite, always direct and to the point."

"It saves time," she replied. "Don't you agree?"

"In point of fact, I do, madam. But I am truly sorry about your husband. I would have liked to have called him a coward to his face."

She stiffened. "My husband was no coward!"

"I beg to disagree," he said calmly. "We had an agreement. But like a thief in the night, he reneged on that contract and ran away. I would call that cowardly behavior, wouldn't you?"

Marguerite's hand tightened on the gate post, but she would not descend to his level. "That is not what happened."

"Then you disremember, madam," he said. "Your husband agreed to sell me this property—" he gestured with a long-fingered, pale hand"—in return for . . . shall we say . . . my discretion?"

She had anticipated this moment for years. "You are the one with the faulty memory, Rupert," she said evenly. "My husband would never have sold his ranch. He loved this place; it was his home. As it is mine." She held his wintry gaze.

Dislike flashed through Rupert's eyes. "Do not think I will take pity on you because you are a woman, Marguerite," he said, in a voice as deadly as night. "You and Sloane cheated me out of what is rightfully mine once; I won't allow it to happen again."

If he'd thought to frighten her, he had failed. Marguerite had always risen to a challenge, and now she had even more reason to fight. But for Rupert and his father, her beloved husband would never have died, and the thought gave her strength.

"I am not afraid of your threats, you little man," she said contemptuously, her brilliant green eyes hard on his face. "Remember, my husband was a prominent man; he had many powerful friends who are eager to protect both his memory and his family."

"They won't protect you, Marguerite," Rupert said. "I will destroy you, I promise. It's just . . . a matter of time."

"Is that so?" she replied. "Before you threaten me, you had best think of this. I am a brave widow raising a family without benefit of husband, running a ranch that has produced horses that outrival Mondragon. You can't fight me, Rupert. You will never beat me. Never!"

She saw the fury in his eyes, actually saw his hand clench as if he wanted to strike her. She wasn't frightened of him physically; a half dozen men would come running if she needed them, but it was the sight of his fist that surprised her. Until then, she hadn't thought him a violent man, and she wondered uneasily how many other things about him she had misjudged.

As if embarrassed by the gesture, Rupert dropped his hand and turned abruptly toward the yearlings playing in the paddock. Obviously trying to get himself under control, he pretended an interest in a well-put-together bay who was clearly in charge of the youthful pack. When the bay suddenly lifted his head and charged down the hillside and the rest of the herd followed hard on his heels, Rupert smiled coldly.

"If that's the best you have to offer, Marguerite," he said, "Mondragon need not fear any competition. Even the old plowhorse of a brood mare we bred to Fane before we sent him off to Europe produced better than that."

Marguerite would not talk of Fane to this man. The pain she had felt upon losing the stallion in the fixed match race had been nothing compared to what Heinrich and his son had done once they had stolen him. For those four years before they had sent Fane to war, Heinrich had bred him to the worst mares he could find. The plow horse Rupert had referred to was only one of those mares, and she had produced a filly Heinrich had derisively called Flame, who had been sent the way of her sire, to serve in the war effort. Neither horse had ever been heard from again, but that was not surprising; Marguerite had long ago bitterly resigned herself to Fane passing out of the record books. Now there was nothing left of her cherished horse except memories. And what did it matter? she wondered bleakly. With Sloane gone, it was all smoke in the wind.

But even so, she could not allow the slur to pass. Knowing in her heart how impossible it was, she lifted her head and said, "Fane is gone, I agree. But one day one of his get will bring glory back to Caulfield Farm, Rupert. You and I may not be here to see it, but I know it will happen. I know it will. As you say, it's just a matter of time."

"Oh, is that so?" he retorted. "And have you had a vision, or the second sight? Fane is *gone*, my dear Marguerite. My father and I made certain of it."

"And that is why you have come today, to gloat?"

He flushed, his pale skin turning an unattractive pink. "No, I came to tell you this business between us is not finished."

"We have no business."

"Indeed we do. I want Caulfield Farm, Marguerite, and I intend to have it."

"You won't get it. You've tried before, and you've failed. You'll fail again . . . and again . . . as long as any Caulfield anywhere is alive to fight you."

"Brave words from a woman whose daughter was found with the gun that shot my father," Rupert replied. Then, to her amazement, he actually smiled. "Tell me, Marguerite, what did you and Sloane ever do with the gun? You do have it, I know."

Marguerite never knew what had become of the gun they had found in Juliet's hand. Sloane had disposed of it and refused to tell her how or where. "For her protection," was all he had told her.

"And what do you know of a gun, Rupert?" she asked. "Unless you were there to see it?"

To her amazement, he blanched. She'd meant that he couldn't possibly know Juliet had returned home with a gun because he hadn't been here, but obviously he thought she'd meant something else.

"You have no proof I was there!" he said harshly, his eyes frightened.

The look in his eyes intrigued her. Deciding to press what little advantage she had, she stepped forward. "What would you say," she asked, "if I told you there was a witness to what happened that day?"

"A witness! Who?" He took a step back before he caught himself. "You're lying. You're lying to protect Juliet."

She didn't know why he was acting like this, but she sensed that she had discovered a weakness. "Try me," she said, not knowing what she would do if he did. "Try me and see."

"This is absurd!"

"So is your contention that I should simply hand over Caulfield Farm to you."

"Sloane made a deal!"

"Did he?" she asked. "Then prove it."

He had backed almost to where he had left the car. "You'll be sorry for this, Marguerite," he threatened, but without much conviction. "You'll be sorry!"

She was fighting not only for her daughter's sanity, but for their future, for the entire farm. Unrelentingly, she said, "And so will you, if you pursue this. You were the one who told everyone your father was murdered during a robbery. How are you going to explain if you recant now? Think about it, Rupert. People will wonder why you didn't come forward before. The police will want an explanation. There will be an investigation."

"In which Juliet will be involved!"

"Why should she be?" Marguerite pressed, her glance tight on his panicky face. "There's no proof she was there that day."

"We both know she was!"

"Do we?" she said. "Do we, Rupert?"

"You'd lie?"

He looked so outraged that she nearly laughed. After all he and his family had done to her. "Without a qualm," she said.

"You'll pay for this, Marguerite!" he cried, snatching open the car door. He threw himself inside. "You'll pay for this!"

"I already have," she said. "There's nothing you can do to me now that you haven't already done."

Marguerite's first crop of two-year-olds went to the track three years after her return to Caulfield Farm. It was a new decade, and while the last of the twenties had seen a return to normalcy for the country after the seemingly endless span of the war, Marguerite felt as if she were just emerging into the world again after a long absence herself. By then, headliners named Man o' War, Babe Ruth, and Jack Dempsey had taken entertainment-starved America by storm, and racing was thriving for the first time in years—everywhere but California.

Marguerite was not deterred. She and Sloane had worked tirelessly to fight the antiwagering legislation that had decimated racing in 1910, and she joined in the battle again to promote the sport. One way to fight, she reasoned, was to breed the kind of horses for which Caulfield Farm had once been famous, and she proceeded to do just that. Among her first crop of two-year-olds was the flying Taciturn, a blaze-faced filly who came in second in the Kentucky Derby the following year. Another was the spectacular colt, Without Wings, who had awed anyone with a stopwatch as he prepped to go East. His reputation had followed him, and at Aqueduct he continued to dazzle the clockers as he prepared for his racing debut. The first time out, he made a fine field of maidens look slow—and defeated, among others, the subsequent Preakness winner, Alexander Abbey. When the Caulfield colt came out next for Aqueduct's Tremont Stakes and won by ten lengths in a hand gallop, he proved his earlier win wasn't a fluke. And when he won his next three races as handily as the others, the colt Marguerite had bred and sold as a two-year-old seemed invincible. Once again, Caulfield Farm's reputation as a breeder of fine Thoroughbreds seemed secure.

Through all this, there was only silence from Mondragon Stud. Rupert never reappeared at the ranch, and Marguerite wanted to believe that her threat, as empty as it had been, had been enough to scare him off. But she had many friends in the racing world, and when she heard rumors now and then that Rupert wasn't happy with the reemergence of Caulfield Farm, she grew uneasy again. She knew he would never harm Juliet as long as the possibility of a witness to his father's death survived, but there was nothing to prevent him from harming the horses in some way, or even the farm. She tried to tell herself she was being ridiculous, but the feeling persisted, despite the news that after eight childless years of marriage, Rupert's wife, Hermione, had given birth to their firstborn, a girl they named Charlotte. Marguerite hoped that, if nothing else, she would appreciate an uneasy peace.

But peace between Caulfield Farm and Mondragon Stud seemed destined not to be. The higher Caulfield's star rose, the lower Mondragon's seemed to set, and the more resentful Rupert became. At a time when Marguerite seemed able to breed nothing but winners, Rupert lost several of his stallions to disease and injury. Three of his best brood mares suddenly came up barren, and his most promising runners were soundly defeated at the eastern race tracks—one of which had been entered in the same race as Marguerite's unbeaten colt, Without Wings, when he romped home ahead of all the rest.

Marguerite never experienced what came to be known as the Great Depression of the thirties. She was writing in her journal the last night of her life when she happened to look out the window and see a glow in the barn. Puzzled, she half stood to catch a better glimpse, and saw a figure running out, holding a torch. It was a man, and he happened to turn toward the house just as she looked out. The glow from the flaming torch he held illuminated his face for just a moment, and when she recognized him, she stiffened. It couldn't be! she thought. Not even Rupert would be involved in something so heinous.

She didn't have time to dwell upon the circumstances or on what she thought she had seen. As she watched, frozen with horror, the man tossed the torch aside and ran into the darkness. At almost the same moment, a tongue of fire rose up from one of the windows in the barn.

Even so far away at the house, Marguerite could hear the cries of terrified horses, and she scraped back her chair, dropping her pen on the open page. A blotch of ink spread out, fanning into what looked like a flame. She didn't notice. She was already out the door, running as fast as she could down the drive, screaming at the top of her voice.

Another hand had then taken over the narrative, but Briar was so riveted she hardly noticed. With the black blotch of ink spreading like fire down the page, she could almost imagine the scorching of the paper and smell the smoke rising into the night. Horrified, she quickly read on.

*I head Mama scream*, wrote the second hand. *And when I jumped out of bed and ran to the bedroom window, I nearly fell back. I couldn't believe my eyes: it seemed that a forest of fire had leaped up into the night sky, clawing its way to the stars. One look and I raced downstairs, so frightened I didn't even realize that I had left the house and was running down the drive in my bare feet. No one saw me; everyone was occupied. Smoke billowed everywhere, and the horses, trapped in the*

*barn, were screaming with terror. People were running
around, and the noise . . . !*

*Then I saw Andrew grappling with Mama, trying to prevent
her from running in, and I just . . . stopped. I knew there
wasn't a force on earth that could prevent Mama from trying
to rescue her horses, and I was so petrified with fright I just
stood there and watched.*

With her beloved horses screaming in panic and fright, no
one, not even Andrew, could hold Marguerite back. It was
obvious then, and afterward, that the fire had been set; in the
space of the few seconds, the entire barn was ablaze, and fire
streamed out the shattering windows above in the loft even as
Marguerite came down off the hill at a run. By then, everyone
was in motion; a line had formed at the pump, and hoses were
spraying, while buckets were filled. Two of the hands that slept
in the barn had managed to free a few of the horses from their
boxes before being driven back by the fierce heat, but with the
screams of the animals still trapped inside rending the night,
Marguerite didn't hesitate. She was just running in when Andrew appeared and nearly snatched her off her feet.

"You can't go in there, lass!" he shouted, holding her tight.
"It's madness. It's too late!"

Another scream from a terrified animal stabbed her heart,
and Marguerite whirled at him. "Let me go!" she cried, beating at him with her fists. She was sobbing and crying and
screaming above the crackling of the blaze. "Andrew! Let me
go! I can't let them die!"

A timber from inside, eaten away by the fire, crashed down
just then in a shower of sparks, cutting off another animal's
cry. The noise was horrendous; the spreading fire roared, and
inside the blazing barn . . .

"Let me go!" Marguerite screamed.

"You're daft, lass! You don't know what you're doing!"

But she did. As she wrenched her arm away from Andrew
and started inside before he could lunge for her again, she had
but one thought. She couldn't stand by and listen to her beloved horses die; she had to get them out. She didn't even see
the flames roaring higher and higher, painting the night sky
with scarlet; she only saw, through a shimmering haze, the box
of a mare who was the dam of Without Wings.

"I'm coming, I'm coming," she wept, throwing her forearm over her face, while outside, Andrew roared with helpless

anger and pain. His son Angus had come and was holding his father back so he wouldn't follow Marguerite into the conflagration. So frenzied was Andrew that Angus had to wrestle him to the ground, but even then the big man tried to get free.

Marguerite saw none of it, nor heard the cries of grief and horror as she disappeared into the flames. The heat was intense; everything all around was burning; flames shot up and sparks fell at the feet of the men who were standing helplessly outside, driven back by the heat. They could see that her slippers were burning, as was the hem of her robe; even the ends of her long hair were singed.

But inside the box in front of her, only a tantalizing few feet away, was the mare she had gone to rescue. Mad with fear and panic, the horse was whirling around and rearing and stamping her feet. Crazed with fright, she was seeking a way out that wasn't there until Marguerite, her lungs on fire and her eyes tearing, finally reached the glowing stall door and pulled it open with the last of her strength.

"Go!" Marguerite cried. All would be for naught if the horse panicked completely and bolted back into the fire, and Marguerite flapped her hands, bent sideways with a cough. The aisle was a shimmering golden red; everything was on fire now, every stick of wood, every blade of hay. There were no more sounds from the trapped horses beyond the wall of flame; the only noise was the roaring of the fire.

She never saw the horse leap over her on the way to freedom. The mare came thundering out of the barn, her mane on fire, just as the roof crumpled like a brittle leaf and fell in with a deafening crash. Held on the ground by his soot-blackened son, Andrew heard the collapse and buried his face in his arms, his body shaking with grief. Clutching his father, the stricken Angus looked at the inferno and closed his eyes, muttering a prayer. His hand reached for his father's, and they held tight.

Then, from somewhere behind them came a single, heart-wrenching cry. Standing at the edge of the bright illumination cast by the roaring blaze, Juliet lifted her tragic pale face to the crimson night sky. "*Mama!*" she screamed. "*Mama . . . !*"

Angus was the first to reach her as she sank to the ground in a faint.

"Miss? Miss, you'd better move along now. You're holding up traffic."

Briar looked up with a violent start. She had been so in-volved with the journal that it took her a moment to register the helmeted face looking in her car window. Still back at the fire, almost feeling the heat on her face, she looked at the highway patrolman blankly. She saw herself reflected in the mirrored lenses of his sunglasses.

"I'm sorry?" she said.

He took off his glasses. His eyes were bright blue, kind and concerned. "Are you all right, miss?" he asked.

Trying to pull herself together, she looked down at the jour-nal in her lap. Quickly, she closed the book and put it on the front seat. "Yes, officer, thank you. I'm fine."

"Well, it was a long wait."

"Yes . . . I guess it was. I'm sorry I'm holding things up."

"No problem," he said, and gestured. She hadn't noticed, but a flagman had appeared and apparently allowed other cars through, stopping in front of her while another line from the other side came along. "But if you're all right, you can go now," he said, and put the mirrored lenses back on with a smile.

Embarrassed, Briar quickly started the car. Nodding at him, and then at the flagman gesturing for her to go ahead, she started off, still feeling disoriented. She had been so involved that she had completely lost track of time and place. Shudder-ing when she thought of that terrible fire, she tried to put the vivid pictures out of her mind. But the fact that her great-grandmother had died in the blaze had shaken her to the core, and it was all she could do to drive on to Caulfield Farm. She was so upset that she didn't even stop to think why Juliet had written in Marguerite's journal. Feeling as if she had just lost someone so near and dear to her, it didn't matter who had finished the last chapter.

# CHAPTER THIRTY

Briar didn't stop at the main barn as she usually did when she came home. She was still so upset that she continued right on up to the house even when Stefan appeared in the barn doorway. He half waved as she drove past, but despite his puzzled expression, she nodded and continued on up the hill. Unfortunately, she didn't remember until she had pulled up in front of the house that she had invited him for dinner tonight; their conversation earlier seemed another lifetime ago, and she knew she wouldn't be up to company this evening, not even his.

She'd call him later, she decided, as she got out of the car and went inside. Right now, she just needed to be alone. She had to think, decide what she was gong to do.

*But you know what you have to do, don't you?* a little voice whispered. *You knew all along you'd have to choose.*

But not right now, she thought, holding down her panic by sheer force of will. Reaction was setting in, and she closed the front door just as Isabella come out from the kitchen, wiping her hands on her apron.

"*Señora!*" Isabella exclaimed, with a big smile. "Did you have a nice day?"

She couldn't go into it now. "It wasn't one of the best, Isabella," she said tersely, tossing down her purse and briefcase on the hall table. "Did I get any mail?"

"*Sí,* I put it there for you," Isabella answered indicating a neat pile on the table. Her warm brown face creased with the slightest of frowns. "You don't seem well, *señora.* Are you feeling all right?"

She was still disoriented from what she'd read about the fire. The scene had been so real to her that she was sure if she put a hand to her face, her cheeks would feel hot, and that if she looked down, she would find soot on her clothes. She knew it was absurd, but she could almost smell the smoke, and she wanted to put her hands over her ears so that she wouldn't hear the crash as the blazing roof of the barn fell in on itself. She didn't want to remember the terrified screams of horses being burned to death, or fragile Juliet lifting her hands in anguish to the fiery night sky.

"*Señora?*"

Startled out of her reverie, Briar jumped and then realized that Isabella was looking at her with concern. "I'm fine," she said, avoiding her housekeeper's bright eyes. "Just tired, I guess."

"I was about to go home, but I could stay if you like."

She appreciated the offer, but she just wanted to be alone. Her feelings of anxiety and apprehension were growing. In addition to her distress about her great-grandmother, she couldn't get the conversation with Rupert Jeager today out of her mind.

"No, no, I'm fine," she said quickly, just barely preventing herself from shoving the kind young woman out the door so she could be by herself. She felt a storm approaching, and she had to be alone. Summoning a smile by the fiercest effort of will, she said, "You go on home, all right? I'll see you tomorrow, first thing."

"But—"

"Really, I'm *fine*," she insisted. Reaching behind her, she opened the front door. "Good night."

Her expression still troubled, Isabella bade her good night, and as soon as the housekeeper was gone, Briar went into the front room and threw herself on the couch. She felt like crying and screaming and smashing something in sheer rage; she had never felt this way, as if she were about to come unglued at the seams. She bit down hard on her increasing panic and flung an arm over her eyes. What was she going to do? *What was she going to do?*

When the doorbell rang, she jumped as though she'd been shot. Bolting upright, she glanced at her watch and groaned. It had to be Stefan; she'd completely forgotten about canceling her invitation.

The doorbell rang again, demanding that she do *something*. She knew she couldn't just sit here and pretend she wasn't home, so she hauled herself off the couch, intending to tell him . . . what? She was sick? Well, that was certainly true. Feeling more emotionally fragile than she'd ever felt before in her life, she went to answer the front door.

It was Stefan, all right, but he wasn't dressed for dinner. "Hi," he said, when she opened the door. "Are you all right? Isabella said something was wrong."

Everything was wrong, she thought, and leaned against the edge of the door, clutching it tightly so he wouldn't see her hands shake. "I'm . . . not feeling well tonight, Stefan," she said, trying to hold herself together long enough to get rid of him. The last thing she wanted to do was break down and fling herself into his arms. "Could we do dinner some other time?"

"Well, sure. But—" He searched her face. Then, his voice quiet, he said, "Something *is* wrong."

"No, no," she started to say, but that look of concern in his eyes finally broke through the last of her defenses. The feelings she'd held back through sheer force of will today—the despair, the anger, the fright at what Rupert Jaeger might be able to do to her after all this—avalanched down on her at once. She could no more hold back the resulting emotional tumult than she could have flown by herself over Mount Everest.

"Oh, Stefan!" she said suddenly, helplessly. "It's all coming down on me, and I don't think . . . I don't think . . . I don't think I can fight him after all!"

Stefan didn't ask for explanations or reasons or answers to his questions. Instead he shut the door and took her into his arms—swept her into his arms—and carried her into the living room and onto the couch.

"No, this isn't—" she started to protest. Even she could hear the hysterical note in her voice, and she just wanted him to get out before she made a complete fool of herself.

But Stefan wouldn't let her go when she pushed against him. "Hush," he said, holding her tight while she feebly struggled. "Go ahead, love, and cry. You deserve it after all you've been through lately. It's a wonder you didn't break down long ago."

"I don't break down!" she cried, and then proceeded to do just that. The storm of emotions she had tried to hold back by will swept down on her like a fierce wind, and before she knew it, she was sobbing against him as if her heart would break. Disjointed thoughts surfaced and broke away, and she didn't know whether in her fear and confusion she was speaking them aloud or not. He wants everything. . . . He won't let up until he has that race. . . . He plans to destroy Lord Industries. . . .

I'll have to sell the company. . . . It's the only way to stop him, and even then it won't be enough. Oh, what am I going to do? What *am I going to do?*

And, holding her tightly, he murmured over and over, "We'll handle it together, as we were intended to from the beginning. He won't win, Briar. I'll see to it."

She shook her head wildly. "You don't understand! He's ruthless! He won't stop at anything!"

"Oh, yes, he will," Stefan soothed. "Now, don't worry."

She didn't ask how he could be so certain. At that moment, when she felt as if her world were falling apart, and the abyss was opening up beneath her feet, she didn't question him about anything. Instead, she clung to him helplessly, unable to halt her storm of weeping.

"Oh, Stefan!" she cried. "It wasn't supposed to be like this!"

"It never is, love," he said, his voice turning grim just for an instant. He stroked her hair. "It never is."

From somewhere deep inside her, she knew she had to get control of herself. But everything seemed to be happening too fast, and the thought that she could lose the ranch because Rupert Jaeger seemed obsessed in fulfilling an ancient vendetta against anyone related to a Caulfield increased her panic. Even with Stefan's arms around her, she felt as if she were being inexorably backed into a corner from which there was no escape, no hope, and she didn't know what to do or where to turn or whom to ask for help.

At last, her feeling of panicked desperation shamed her and gave her the strength to control herself. Abruptly, she sat up. "I'm sorry, Stefan,' she said without looking at him. "I didn't mean to drag you into this. It's not your problem."

"Everything that concerns you is my problem," he said. "Don't you understand by now? I love you, Briar. I—"

"Don't say it!" she cried, upset all over again.

He looked as if she had slapped him. "Why not? Because I'm not one of your orphans? I want to help, Briar. Damn it, let me!"

Without reason, she felt that he was cornering her, too, and her sense of desperation increased. She couldn't share this with him, she thought, and even if she wanted to, what could he do? She was so used to doing things on her own, to having only herself to depend on, she couldn't ask him to help her with this.

"I'm sorry," she choked, springing up. "I just can't—"

He jumped up, too. Taking her arm, he forced her to face him. "Look at me" he commanded angrily. "Tell me why you're doing this!"

"I'm not doing anything!"

"The hell you aren't! I can feel you going away from me even when you haven't left the room! Tell me why, Briar. Is it because my name isn't Hayden Lord?"

She was so shocked she jerked away from him again. "It has nothing to do with Hay!" she cried, dimly realizing that it was true. The whole time Stefan had been here tonight, she hadn't thought of Hayden once, not once.

"The hell it doesn't!" Stefan's face was red; he looked ready to break something in two. "From the beginning, it's been Hayden this and Hayden that. If you weren't so bent on making him a god, Briar, you'd see that he was just a man, like the rest of us. Just a man!"

"How dare you!" she cried, outraged. "How dare you say such things to me! I loved Hayden—"

"Fine!" Stefan shouted. "You loved him! You loved him! But he's gone, Briar. He's gone! Don't you think it's time to get on with your life now? Or are you going to—"

"I am going on with my life!" she cried. "I am! What do you think this is all about?"

"I think it's about you. What are you afraid of? That you only had so much to give, and you gave it all away to Hayden Lord so you don't have any left for anybody else? When are you going to trust someone besides him? Are you going to live the rest of your life alone, depending on no one but yourself?"

"I've never depended on anyone but myself!"

He looked angry enough to strike her. They were standing inches away from each other, practically screaming in each other's faces. "Then don't you think it's about time that you did?"

"Don't you dare lecture me!" she shouted. "Don't you dare! Get out of my house! Get out, right now!"

She was so upset she whirled around and headed toward the front door, intending to fling it dramatically open and order him out. She never got there. She hadn't gone two steps before he'd grabbed her arm again, spinning her around to face him once more.

"Damn it, Briar," he said, and pulled her tight into him.

"Damn it, Briar," he panted again, staring down into her furious, angry eyes. When she didn't fight him, something changed in his face, too. "Damn it, Briar," he said a third time. Then he kissed her.

She had always prided herself on being strong, on never giving in or needing help, but she felt right now that her world was coming to an end, and she wasn't able to fight it. She felt hopeless and bleak and despairing at the same time, and the instant his lips touched hers, she closed her eyes. She was so tired, she thought; how she longed to give in and let him take care of things. When Stefan lifted his head from their brief kiss and looked into her eyes again, he unhesitatingly turned toward the stairs. Feeling dazed and bemused, she went with him, only vaguely surprised at the top of the landing when he headed toward her bedroom.

"I can't count the nights I sat in my living room and just watched the light up here," he said, pausing on the threshold to look down at her. "I knew it had to be your bedroom, and I used to imagine you up here. So often I couldn't go to bed myself until your light went out . . ."

When she realized that while he had been watching her, she had been thinking so often of him, she said shakily, "And once my light was out, I used to sit in that window seat and just look down—first at the trailer where you stayed when you first came, then at the house where you are now."

Taking both her hands in his, he stopped just inside the door. His eyes holding hers, he said, "We've wasted a lot of time, haven't we?"

She reached up and wound her fingers through his thick sun-streaked blond hair. Hayden was a poignant presence to her now, a memory she would always love. But Stefan was real, and now that the storm had passed it was time to feel again. "It wasn't wasted if it led to this," she whispered, and stepped into his willing embrace.

In dreams and fantasy she had imagined this moment so many times, but nothing she had ever pictured approached the reality of making love to Stefan and his making love to her. She had imagined his body again and again, but when they undressed each other and she was able to feel and touch his bare skin, to trace with her fingers the muscles in his arms and shoulders, and to press her own naked body against his flat belly and trim hips, she closed her eyes blissfully. He was strong and lean and everything she had made him out to be, and when she ran her fingers down his spine and felt the hard curve of his buttocks, her own response surged within her. The warmth between her thighs grew to fire, and as they fell on the bed and she opened her legs to take him inside her, he groaned and said something about it all happening too fast.

"Later," she murmured, biting his ear. "Later, there will be time. . . . But not now. Not now . . ."

Desire was a fever inside her. It had been so long—so long! since she had given free rein to her passion—and she wanted him badly, not because she was starved, but because he was Stefan. She had waited for this moment; she had tantalized and teased herself and savored the anticipation. She had thought she'd be able to wait, to spend time exploring every part of him, but as his weight came over her willing body, and she thrust her hips up to meet his, she realized that she had always known him. It was meant to be, she thought, wrapping her arms around him and opening her mouth for his kiss; his weight was the sweetest burden she had ever known, and she could feel herself rushing out of control. She couldn't get enough of him. Quickly, propelled by the same swift rush of desire, they began to move in unison. He put his hands in her hair and pulled her head back so that he could drop hot kisses on her throat, her shoulders, her breasts. She kneaded the muscles in his buttocks, drawing him in even further. She moaned when he sucked first one nipple, then the other, and when one of his hands unwound itself from her tangled hair and reached down to caress her, she writhed under him and moved his hand even lower.

"Briar . . . !" he said hoarsely, his breath rasping in her ear. "I meant to . . . I don't think I can . . ."

"I can't, either!' she cried, and pulled him in even deeper. Her nails dug into his back as a glorious sensation began to rush through her, and with the muscles of her neck straining, she begged, "Come with me, Stefan! Come with me!"

He was there with her, swept along like two leaves in a gale, tumbling over and over. It was the most exquisite sensation she had ever known, and she clutched him tightly as the burst of pleasure grew and heightened and took them both even farther. She wanted him to meld with her, for their flesh to become one, to be united in passion and this spending of desire, but too soon the convulsions waned and then vanished. Both of them were drenched with perspiration; hearts pounding, breath coming in short gasps, they fell back to earth and were silent.

They didn't talk until much later that night, when they were both sitting up in bed, his arm around her bare shoulders, and her head on his chest. For the first time in a year, she felt almost at peace with herself, sure of what she wanted to do, positive of her course . . . and able to accept that her love for this man in no way diminished her memories of Hay. Stefan and Hayden Lord were completely different, and as she flattened her palm on Stefan's naked chest, she thought how fortunate she was to have known them both.

"I didn't expect for this to happen," Stefan murmured, his lips in her hair.

Playing with the golden hairs on his chest, she sighed. "Nor did I. But I'm glad it did. I haven't felt so . . . peaceful in a long, long time."

He laughed softly, shifting one long, muscled leg under the sheet. "Is that what you feel . . . peaceful?"

"What do you feel?" she asked, telling herself that no matter what he answered, she wouldn't be disappointed.

"Hungry."

She laughed. "You know, so am I." Turning her head, she glanced at the clock and saw disbelievingly that it was after ten. Throwing back the covers, she said, "How about an omelette?"

Watching from the bed as she padded, naked, to the closet, Stefan smiled. "You really want me to think about food when you're parading around like that?"

Pleased, she smiled to herself as she took a silk robe patterned with cabbage roses from a hook. Belting it around her waist, she said, "There. Better?"

"I preferred the other."

"Well, I'm not going to cook in the altogether," she said, and she tossed him a large white terry cloth robe she reserved for winter. "Here. I think this will fit you," she said, and added wickedly as she tugged off the sheet that covered him, "unless you prefer to come to the table like that."

"My granny never permitted any of her men to come bare chested to the table. I don't think she would have approved of bare assed, either."

She went downstairs, thinking that she was grateful to him on more than one level. The sexual release she had experienced had helped to calm her emotionally, and when she realized her panicked feeling had vanished, she felt even better. Things were bad, she knew, but the situation didn't seem as impossible as it had before, and she knew that now when she put her mind to the problem, she'd be able to think clearly.

She had just finished whisking the eggs and turning them into a pan on the stove when Stefan came into the kitchen, his hair still wet from a shower, but dressed in his clothes now, instead of the white robe. When he saw her expression, he shrugged and said, "I thought it might be better this way. We don't want Isabella to be scandalized when she comes in the morning."

"Isabella has been hinting for months now about what a wonderful husband *Señor* Stefan will make for some lucky woman," Briar said, reaching for the coffee she'd made. Then she thought about it and sighed. "But maybe you're right."

"For now, anyway," he said, coming up behind her. Putting his arms around her waist, he kissed the nape of her neck. "But don't think it was an easy decision."

Feeling a tingle inside her at his touch, she leaned back slightly into his body and closed her eyes. "It doesn't have to be this way, you know."

"Yes, it does. So you go take a shower yourself while I finish up," he said, and gave her a little push. "Get going before I change my mind."

"Are you sure you can manage?"

"I've been cooking eggs since before you were born."

"In that case," she said, deliberately glancing at the omelette pan. "Maybe you'd better turn them before they burn."

He looked down. "Damn it, you did that on purpose!" he said, and reached for the spatula as she turned and ran from the kitchen, her laughter floating back behind her.

Five minutes later, fresh from her own quick shower and dressed in a much less seductive outfit of peach-colored velour sweats, she came downstairs and saw that he had not only fixed the omelettes, but had sliced some fresh fruit, too, and set the table, including a flower from the arrangement in the living room.

"How did you do all this?' she asked admiringly, taking her place while he held her chair.

"I'm a whiz," he said with a grin.

"And a great cook, too," she added, after tasting the omelette. "I think I'll hire you."

They ate in silence for a few minutes, then Stefan finished

and pushed his plate away. Quietly, he said, "Do you want to talk about it?"

She did, especially now. But she didn't quite know how to begin, so she stalled by getting up to fetch more coffee. After refilling their cups, she put the carafe down on a tile and said, "It's not going to make sense unless I start at the beginning. . . ."

"I've got all the time in the world."

So she told him what she had learned since the last time she'd mentioned it: the story of Marguerite and Sloane and Heinrich and Mariel, and Kyle and Juliet and Andrew McKenna and Rupert—everything she had read, including the fire. He only stopped her once, with a question that surprised her.

"You said Heinrich disappeared for a few days just after Marguerite married Sloane. Did anyone ever find out where he went?"

She considered it, then shook her head. "I don't think so. Why?"

"I don't know. Just curious, I guess. From what you've said about him, it seems an uncharacteristic thing to do."

"Yes, Marguerite thought so, too. But she didn't mention it again—at least, I don't think she did. We could check if you like."

She thought he'd say it wasn't important, but he nodded. "Maybe we should. It might be a clue."

"To what?"

"I don't know. Maybe to Rupert's actions now."

"But Rupert wasn't born then," she pointed out. "What possible bearing could that have?"

Stefan shrugged. "I don't know. I just think it's wise to explore every avenue we can."

"Well, all right," she said uncertainly. She didn't understand why he was so interested in where Heinrich might have gone to those three days, but if he wanted to read through the journals, he was more than welcome. When she had collected them from upstairs so he could take them back to his house to read at his leisure, she told him what had happened at work that day, including her conversations with Spence and Fredrica and Rupert.

"So that's why you were so upset," Stefan said, nodding. "It's easy to see now."

Desperation returning, she said, "I can't lose the ranch, Stefan, I can't! But Hayden trusted me with the company, and now—"

"And now—nothing," he said firmly, grasping her hands. "You did what you thought was right—dividing the estate three ways. It's not your fault Hayden's daughter was too greedy to accept it. In my mind, you were more than generous."

"But—"

"She screwed you over, Briar," he said bluntly. "That's all there is to it. So did that brother of hers."

She glanced away. Even now, after what Jaz had done, she couldn't renege on her promise not to say why. It didn't matter anyway. What was done was done, and she had to deal with it.

Stefan misread her expression. Taking her hand, he said, "You're not responsible for what Hayden Lord's children do, Briar, only for yourself."

"But Hay loved that company!"

"And he loved you. Do you think he would really want you to be tearing yourself inside out to keep it intact? If he were here, he probably would be the first to sell."

"But not to Rupert Jaeger! Stefan, I told you the only reason Rupert wanted those shares was to force me to agree to the match race."

"Which is a moot point, since at this time, no one is sure your filly is ever going to run again."

"But there's a good possibility—"

"And there's an even better possibility that if she does try, she'll destroy herself completely. You don't want that."

She could feel herself getting agitated again, despite her efforts to stay calm. "No, I don't want that," she said. "But I might not have a choice."

"We always have a choice."

"Oh, yes," she said, unable to hide her bitterness. "And my choice might be to race Touch the Fire—or watch Rupert Jaeger destroy Lord Industries."

"All right, then," Stefan said patiently. "What other options do you have? How would you save Lord Industries if Rupert Jaeger was hell-bent on destroying it?"

She glanced away. She had thought about it ceaselessly, it seemed, and there was only one solution she could see. "If I have to, I'll sell my company to raise capital and buy him out," she said finally.

He looked shocked. "You'd sell McKenna TimeSave? But you said you'd never sell your company!"

"I know. But that was another day," she said, and her voice turned hard. "Before Rupert Jaeger came into my life."

"Briar, listen to me," he said, suddenly urgent. "Before you do anything . . . rash . . . like selling your company, please talk to me. Will you promise?"

"Well, sure, but—"

His fingers tightened almost painfully on hers. "Promise!"

She didn't know why he was so intent, but she agreed. "I promise," she said. "But why—"

"Never mind, I'll tell you one day. For now, just don't do anything without telling me first, all right?"

She was touched by his concern, warmed by his obvious care for her welfare. "I will, Stefan, I will," she said, smiling. Then she kissed him good night.

She didn't notice her briefcase on the hall table until after he had reluctantly gone down the drive toward his own house and disappeared inside. She exclaimed impatiently, remembering she had forgotten to give Stefan the last journal. She was just putting it on the coffee table so she wouldn't forget when it fell to the floor.

"For heaven's sake," she muttered, annoyed by her clumsiness. She bent down to retrieve the book, then stopped in surprise. It had fallen open to a section all the way to the back that she hadn't noticed before, and she saw immediately that the closely written page was not in Marguerite's penmanship, but in the second hand that had written about the fire. Wondering how she could have missed this, she carried the book over to the light.

She had been so sure she had read the last entry this afternoon. To discover another buried in the back pages of the book was a find, and she eagerly sat down to read it. The date at the top of the page was 1945, and she realized with a start that was the year she was born. Fifteen years had passed since the fire and during that time, her own mother, Ariana, had grown from an eleven-year-old child to a young woman in love with Duncan McKenna. Ariana was twenty-six at the time of this entry, and the world was at war. But it wasn't Briar's mother who had written this excerpt; as Briar had already realized, it was Juliet.

So much has happened since the night of that terrible fire, that I hardly know where to begin. I couldn't bear to continue writing after I added those details of the fire, so I put the books away and never thought about them until now. After all, they were Mama's private things, and I felt I had no right. But then I realized that the journals were a family history, and now that Ariana is gone and I am alone to fight, I knew I had to finish the last chapter at least. It was what Mama would have wanted, I know. So I will add my part, and then I will hide the journals where no one but family will ever see. I've made a space under the kitchen floor where they will be safe until . . . well, until the day when the last Caulfield heir comes home. I know it will come to pass, even though I've exhausted all my resources trying to find Ariana and Duncan's child. Everyone tells me—my lawyer and the banker and all the embassy and administration people I've written to, asking for help, that there's no hope, but in my heart I know it's not true. There *is* a child. There *is*, I know.

I used to pray daily for their safety—Ariana and Duncan, and all the people who were put in such peril, Juliet went on. But now my faith has dried up and I've no more words to pray. War is a terrible thing; it claims many more lives than those who die in battle. When Angus died a few years' back, dear Andrew never recovered. Duncan's going to war was the final blow; I had to bury our old friend soon after.

The place was so quiet with all the men gone; although Papa left us well fixed with his investments, I didn't have Mama's talent with horses, and I had no heart to rebuild the barn. I had spent all those years since that day I left for the library in a . . . kind of fog, a cloud. I knew how worried Mama and Papa were for me, and I wanted to reach out to them, but I just didn't have the means or the will. It was so much safer living in the gauzy world where nothing touched me, but then came the night of the fire, and without warning, the veil was lifted. Not completely, of course; I suppose I'll never know why that twilight world descended. But I know why I had to come back to the real world here, and that was to take care of Ariana. The darling child was only eleven when Mama perished in the fire. If I hadn't returned from my blank state, who would have cared for her?

But even now those lost years haunt me, and I wonder what happened and try to remember. But it all eludes me still, and I've come to think that perhaps it doesn't matter. What purpose would it serve now?

So instead I worried about Ariana, who I know is gone now—at peace with her beloved Duncan, who died at Normandy in 1944. I only heard once from her after that; with all the confusion caused by the war, the post wasn't as reliable as it could have been, but the letter was so full of hope and love. Duncan was gone, but she was carrying his child. She wrote to tell me she was in England, waiting for transport back. Refugees were everywhere, she said; things were . . . difficult. But, heavy with child, she managed to get on board a ship bound for New York. She had a fever, she said, nothing serious. I wasn't to worry, and when she came back to Caulfield Farm . . .

But her darling girl had never returned, Juliet wrote with a breaking heart. She had taken her courage in both hands and traveled to New York herself when there had been no further word. The ship had limped to port, and refugees had poured off. There had been so many pregnant women, so many who died of fever and childbirth and exhaustion. Everybody was sorry, but that was war.

I was frantic, Juliet wrote in a shaky hand; I scoured the docks—I, who had been terrified of strangers for years, plucking the sleeves of sailors, knocking on doors, begging people I'd never met for help. In the end, even I had to accept that it was hopeless. No one knew; no one could tell. No one was interested. It was war, they said, and told me to go home and wait.

For what? I wonder, sitting here now. Even though I encouraged her to go, I do miss her so much; she was like a daughter to me instead of just my niece; we were so close. Everyone seems to have gone away, and I am left alone to live out my days in worry and wonder.

But how could it have been any other way? Ariana had to live her life, and I would never have allowed her to stay and take care of me—not when I knew how desperate she was to be with Duncan. And her staying wouldn't have served any purpose, anyway; Ariana can't protect me, any more than I could her. And in the end, what does it matter, anyway?

So I encouraged her to follow her heart; in my mind, there

was no other way. Two people who loved each other as much as Duncan and Ariana weren't meant to be apart, whatever the peril. I would have done the same, if ever I'd had a love to follow. It was just not meant to be, for me.

There is a man named Rupert Jaeger, who lives over the hill at a splendid place called Mondragon Stud. I used to see the house from the road, before I became too frightened to go into town. Rupert Jaeger frightens me as well, for he is so cold, so cruel looking. He arrives periodically to threaten me, to insist that I give up my home, which he says belongs to him. I know it's not true, for I have the deed in my possession. But why does he want the farm?

I have no memory of so many things. One thing I do know, and that is where my home is. He will never take this land from me, nor from anyone living named Caulfield. And even though I failed in my search I have never given up hope. One day, a Caulfield will come again, to carry on in my place. My faith is absolute.

But it is a strange thing, I think, for while I fear this man, Rupert, it seems he is even more wary of me. I doubt he is afraid because I'm known now as "Crazy Juliet." It doesn't bother me. Who knows? It's probably true. But as for this Rupert, I don't know why he fears me. Sometimes, when I look at him, something hovers at the edge of my mind . . . a face . . . a look . . . and then it is gone, like so many things. I do not know why he is frightened, but if it keeps him at bay, I am grateful. I will do anything—*anything*—to keep Caulfield Farm in trust. I have nothing else to give, for I have wasted my life. Oh, the dreams I dreamed when I was a young girl; sometimes it makes me want to weep still. . . .

The entry ended at the bottom of the page, and when Briar hurriedly turned to the next and saw it was blank, she exclaimed in dismay. There had to be more! she thought, but when she rifled through the remaining pages, they were all blank, and she closed the book, feeling tears sting her eyes.

So that was Juliet, she thought. Poor, tortured, brave woman standing up to Rupert Jaeger without any real weapons at her command—except her fierce determination to keep Caulfield Farm from him at any cost. And here was her mother, Ariana, and her father, Duncan, war-torn lovers, who had been together until almost the last. Her father was a hero, and her mother had followed her heart.

Wiping her tears away with the back of her hand, Briar traced the gold lettering on the front of the journal, thinking of what she had read. She knew how brave her parents had been, but could she do less than Juliet had done? she asked herself, and carefully she put the book aside. Then she got up and went outside.

It was so late that the moon was setting through the trees to the west. Moonlight cast a faint silver glow making the pastures, the paddocks, the fences, look almost ethereal. As she gazed out, she saw a silhouette of a horse on one of the hills. She smiled as it lifted its head, almost as if it had sensed someone watching, before it went back to grazing again. The aroma of eucalyptus filled the air, and as Briar breathed deeply of the astringent scent, she heard the deep-throated call of a horned owl. The sound drifted out across the hills. . . . *Who-who . . . who . . . who . . .* and was answered by another from a different copse of trees. *Who-who . . . who . . . who . . .* Then all was quiet again.

She made her decision in that moment—or perhaps the choice had always been at the back of her mind. Caulfield Farm gave her peace, contentment, more of a sense of identity than she had ever known, and, like Marguerite and her great-aunt Juliet, she couldn't give it up. Everyone in her family had sacrificed in one way or another to keep this land. She could do no less now that she owned it herself. Rupert had made his move; now it was her turn. She loved McKenna TimeSave— the company was so dear to her she felt an almost physical pain at the thought of giving it up. But she had to follow in the steps of Sloane and Marguerite and Juliet. Tomorrow, she would put the company up for sale. The proceeds would keep her going for a while here even if Rupert did his best to destroy Lord Industries.

And after the money ran out?

She turned and gazed at the lone horse on the hill again. She would sell them all, she thought; she would sell all the mares— even her brave, beautiful Incandessence if she had to. All except Touch the Fire. No matter what, she would never give her black filly up, for she and the horse shared a bond that went as deep as the one Marguerite had shared with her beloved stallion, Fane. She hadn't forgotten her great-grandmother's

ringing assertion to Rupert the day he had come to gloat.
Through the years, she could hear the confidence in her great-
grandmother's voice.

*Fane may be gone, but one day one of his get will bring
glory back to Caulfield Farm!*

Marguerite had made her challenge to him, and more than
fifty years later that promise was being fulfilled by a spectacular daughter of Fane's called Touch the Fire. No, she would
*never* surrender her gallant filly, not even in defeat, Briar
thought. She would beat Rupert Jaeger somehow, just as her
great-grandmother and her great-aunt and everyone else in her
family had done. The blood of the Caulfields flowed as fiercely
through her veins as it had through Marguerite.

"Well, what do you think, Hay?" she whispered, thinking
of his company that she might have to sacrifice to keep the
ranch. "Do you approve?"

And it seemed to her, right then, the wind carried his answer. As he had told her once, long ago, Hayden spoke to her
heart now. "You are one of those who are special, Briar, who
have been . . . touched by fire. Without even knowing why,
perhaps, you have been singled out for a purpose. I don't know
why it's so, but I know it, I can feel it. So when the time
comes, my darling, don't hold back. Whatever it is, wherever
I am, I'll be there for you."

Well, Briar thought shakily, she knew what her purpose was
now. And as Hayden had told her, she wouldn't hold back.

------- ✿ -------

# CHAPTER THIRTY-ONE

Rupert Jaeger had planted the seed in his interview to *The
Morning Line*, but to Charlotte's dismay, the racing world
helped it grow. By March, after some enterprising sports reporter hid in the bushes outside the gates to Caulfield Farm and
snapped a telling picture of Touch the Fire being worked cautiously on the half-mile training track around the ranch, spec-

ulation about a possible match race between Briar's black filly and the big chestnut colt from Mondragon Farms coalesced into certainty. In the pundits' minds, the question was suddenly not "if," but "when," and as Rupert had intended, his sly suggestion seemed about to become a fait accompli.

But not to Charlotte Jaeger, who read the excited articles and viewed the increasingly demanding headlines in the sports pages with horror. Galland had recovered from the sore shins and the tendon sheath injury in time to start training for the first big stakes race of the season, which he had easily won. Now he was being prepped for the Santa Anita Derby in early April, and then on to the Wood Memorial later that month. Laine had called to tell her that one of the colt's knees had blown up after a workout the other day, and even though it had gone down on icing, she was on tenterhooks. Galland *had* to be ready for the two upcoming big races; after that, it was on to Kentucky. As Charlotte read the latest lurid headlines, her lips tightened. Nowhere in any of her plans for him, she thought grimly, was there time for a match race with Briar's filly.

On that thought, she grabbed the newspaper and went downstairs to confront her father in the study. He was sitting at his desk when she entered without knocking, and he looked up impatiently.

"Charlotte, can't you see I'm busy?"

She threw the paper at him. "Oh, yes, I can see you've been *very* busy, Father. You're responsible for these headlines today, aren't you?"

Rupert glanced down at the section of paper she had flung on the desk. "As a matter of fact, I'm not. But they are good, aren't they?"

" 'The Queen of the Track to meet the '*Bolt* of the Decade'?" she snapped. "If it weren't so nauseatingly sensational, it would be ludicrous."

"I don't know," he mused. "I think it has rather a nice ring to it. One of those catch phrases that so delights those 'spin' people."

She snatched back the paper. "Spin or not, the race is not going to happen, and I want you to stop feeding these sports reporters your little tidbits. You're only stirring things up to no avail."

"I wouldn't be so certain if I were you, Charlotte," Rupert said, calmly returning to his paperwork.

"Oh, but I *am* certain, Father. I told you, Galland is *not* going to race the filly, and that's final. Even if Briar McKenna *does* accept your ridiculous challenge, I w—"

With exaggerated patience, Rupert abandoned his paperwork again. "You still don't understand, do you, Charlotte? Briar McKenna will agree to this race, whether she likes it or not."

"And why is that?" she sneered. "I've heard she's got her company up for sale, so even if you utterly destroyed Lord Industries—which I'm *sure* you intend to do just for the fun of it—you won't be able to force her into anything by threatening her income. With the sale of her company, she'll have enough revenue to keep Caulfield Farm going until it starts to pay for itself. Which I'm certain, given the talent she's demonstrated so far for picking out good bloodstock, won't take long at all. So you see, all your plans will come to naught anyway. You might as well give in as gracefully as you're able at this stage and just leave her—and me—the hell alone!"

It was a long speech for Charlotte; when she finished, she was breathing hard. Rupert merely seemed amused. Toying with a Cross pen, he sat back in his chair and smiled his cold little smile.

"You're forgetting one thing," he observed.

"And what's that?"

"We have already established that, as much as you would like to deny it, you have no choice about this race. As for Ms. McKenna . . ." He shrugged. "She'll either agree, or I'll start proceedings to claim her horse."

Charlotte was sure she hadn't heard right. Her tone acid, she said, "Oh, really? And just how do you plan to do that?"

Impatiently, he threw down the pen. "Charlotte, you are so irritating when you are deliberately obtuse."

"Well, forgive me, Father," she said sarcastically, "but I do seem to have missed some essential point here. Obviously, I was laboring under the mistaken impression that Briar McKenna legally owns Touch the Fire."

"She thinks she does."

"She *thinks* she does," Charlotte repeated derisively. "Well, excuse me, Father, but so does all of the racing world." She paused heavily. "It's obvious you know something the rest of us don't."

"I do."

"Would you mind sharing it with me?"

"Not at all. Have you ever taken a look at the filly's pedigree?"

"Of course I have. She traces directly back to Fane, through a mare Grandfather once owned called Flame. So what?"

Rupert smiled. "I still hold the registration on those horses."

"That's impossible," she said flatly. "Grandfather Heinrich gave both animals to the war effort."

"True. But he held the papers. Technically, the horses were never sold. Therefore, they—and all their get—belong to us."

She looked at him as if he'd lost his mind. "That's absurd! No one would *ever* believe it! Much less could you ever prove such a ridiculous thing in court!"

Unconcerned, Rupert shrugged. "Perhaps not," he agreed calmly. "But with a good attorney, which we happen to have at our disposal, sorting it all out could tie up Touch the Fire in litigation for years, and by that time—"

Charlotte grasped the implications at once. "By that time, even if you lose, the filly's racing career would be over, and so would any productive breeding years," she said. She was so appalled she reached for a chair and sank down into it. She was a horsewoman to the core, and she was shocked at the thought the talent of the filly would be wasted. "You can't mean it," she choked. "If you do this, Touch the Fire would effectively be . . . finished."

Rupert's smile held supreme satisfaction. "Yes, indeed," he said. "She would be, wouldn't she?"

She sprang up from the chair again. "You can't do this, Father!"

"Oh, but I can. And I will, if our Ms. McKenna won't agree to the match race."

Charlotte looked at him as if he'd turned into a poisonous snake right before her eyes. But she knew attacking him wouldn't get her anywhere, and so she said pleadingly, "Think of what you're doing, please. I know how obsessed you are with ruining Briar, but . . . but this goes beyond that. Touch the Fire is one in a million. If you hamper her racing career or her chances as a broodmare, the sport will lose something that can't be replaced!"

He looked at her impatiently. "What sentimental rot! We both know I'm doing both the McKenna woman and her horse a favor by forcing this issue."

"A favor! Just how do you figure?"

"That filly could race until her legs drop off; she could have a foal every year until she was thirty, and still she wouldn't be worth what she can get out of this one match in publicity alone."

Feeling as if she'd stepped into another dimension, Charlotte stared at him in loathing. "Assuming that's true, what makes you think the filly is fit to race? Just because she was seen on Briar's training track—"

"She'll be fit, trust me."

Trusting him about as far as she could throw him with one hand, she tried again. "But even if you can arrange all this, what will you get out of it? As I said before, suppose Galland loses?"

Rupert looked at her sharply. "Will he?"

Thinking of his knee, she forced herself to say it. "It's possible."

"Anything is possible, Charlotte. Where are your gambling instincts?"

"Not as misplaced as yours!" she said, losing her composure at last. "This is insane! You can't think you'll beat Briar just by forcing her to this match race."

"Oh, but I don't think it at all," Rupert said, enjoying himself. "The stakes are much higher, my dear. I thought you realized that."

"What stakes? If you're talking about a big purse—"

"I don't care a jot about the purse. As far as I'm concerned, those two horses can run for free. No, as I said, I'm after something much more valuable. Once and for all, I want Caulfield Farm."

Wildly, Charlotte shook her head. "You'll never get her to agree! She won't give up so much even for that horse."

"Oh, I think she will," Rupert said complacently. "She'll have to. It's either that or take the chance of losing everything."

She felt she was going in circles. "But the way you have it figured, she's going to lose everything anyway!"

"Yes, yes," he said slowly, obviously savoring the thought. Then he gave her a considering glance. "Why are you defending this woman, Charlotte? Wasn't she just a tool to you before? Weren't you going to use her to get back at me?"

Shocked into the admission, she started to say, "Yes, but I—" Then she caught herself.

"Well?" he prodded.

She didn't know what to say. What she had originally intended no longer seemed important. All along, the conviction had been growing in her that she had made a terrible mistake about Briar, but she couldn't do much about that now. Her confused feelings aside, she still had racing in her blood herself, and she knew she had to do something to prevent this madness. If her father did somehow manage to force this race, Charlotte knew what a terrible chance Briar would be taking with Touch the Fire. Workouts were one thing, and racing was another. With the injury the filly had sustained, there was every chance it could happen again—but much worse this time. The horse might have to be destroyed. And for what? To satisfy her father's vendetta against the Caulfields? She couldn't let that happen.

*I would no more wish one of your horses ill than I suspect you would wish it of mine.*

Briar had said that to her the night of the Christmas party, Charlotte remembered. It had been true then, and it was true now. Neither horse was ready for this proposed match race, but of the two, she knew Galland had the better chance to win.

*But that didn't make it right*, she thought fiercely, and said, "You know what a terrible chance Briar would be taking with Touch the Fire if she accepts such an outrageous bet. Even if the filly looks fit to race, she could destroy herself trying!"

"Yes," Rupert said, obviously relishing the thought. "I know."

Charlotte couldn't believe they were having this conversation. "Then how can you ask her to do it?" she cried.

"Oh, really, Charlotte, where's your spirit?" he said impatiently. "Isn't racing the sport of taking chances? That's what separates the champions from the also-rans. Aren't you interested to see just how much Briar will gamble to keep what she thinks is hers?"

"No!"

He shrugged as if it didn't matter. "Well, then . . ."

But Charlotte had just thought of something. "If Briar does accept, she's more courageous than you, Father," she said, striking where she knew it would sting. "You've got her so boxed in, you've got everything to gain and nothing to lose. *You're* not risking anything!''

Rupert smiled. She had never seen such a malignant expression on anyone's face. "I know," he said.

She looked at him incredulously. "You don't really care if Galland wins the race at all, do you? You only care that Briar loses!''

"Yes, that's right," he said agreeably. "Horses are only tools, after all.''

"As are people, to you!''

"But of course. Only a sentimental fool would believe otherwise.''

"You're a monster!''

"That depends on how you look at it, my dear.''

She felt as if she were truly in the presence of evil. "How . . . how did you get so twisted?'' she choked.

He smiled. "That's a matter of opinion, too.''

She wanted to rush from the room in horrified revulsion, but some morbid fascination made her play out the scene to the end. "You . . ." she started to say, and then had to try again. "You keep talking about what Briar is going to sacrifice," she managed finally. "But what if Galland doesn't win? What then? Are you willing to give up all claim to the filly? To Caulfield Farm? Just what do you intend to offer to show your good faith?''

Rupert sat back thoughtfully, tenting his hands and resting his sharp chin on his fingers. "I haven't decided yet," he said.

She didn't believe that for a minute. "Well, perhaps you'd better before this goes any further. Otherwise, those reporters you're so fond of whispering things to will crucify you. They'll say you're not being fair—''

"Fair?" he repeated, turning to look at her. "*Fair?*" he said again, his expression so fierce that she actually shrank back a little. His voice rose. "Was Sloane Caulfield *fair* when he backed out of his agreement to sell Caulfield Farm to me? Was Marguerite *fair* when she returned to usurp the land that should have been mine, to start the breeding farm again?''

"For God's sake, Father! That was *years* in the past! Why can't you let it go?''

He turned on her so suddenly that she jumped. "I'll never let it go, not until I have crushed every last Caulfield to get what I want!''

"Even at the expense of your own family, or the best colt Mondragon has ever produced?"

The look he gave her seemed to shrivel her soul. "Even at that."

She knew he meant it, and when she thought of Galland, perhaps being ruined, certainly forced to pass up his chance—her chance after all these years!—at the Triple Crown, and of poor Touch the Fire forced to run when it might destroy her, she put her head in her hands in despair. "Oh, I'm sorry I ever hired the investigator to find Briar!" she cried. "If I hadn't done that—"

"Oh, but I knew where Briar was all the time," Rupert said.

Her head shot up. Sure she hadn't heard right, she said, "What?"

"Didn't I tell you?" he said, as she stared at him in sheer disbelief. "No, no, I remember now; I decided to let you play your little game without me. You thought you were being so clever that I just couldn't bear to spoil your pleasure, thinking you could best me."

Charlotte was very still. "You . . . knew about Briar?" she said.

He laughed, genuinely amused. "Did you really think I wouldn't keep track of the last surviving Caulfield heir? Really, Charlotte, I'm surprised at you. I thought you knew me better than that."

Her lips felt dry and cracked. "But you . . . you said never . . ."

"Why would I say? If you hadn't brought her back, I would have. It was just a matter of time, you see."

She couldn't believe they were having this conversation. She felt as if she was riding a roller coaster without end. "But why?" she asked. "Why would you want her found?"

"Oh, really, Charlotte, and here we were having such an intelligent discussion. The answer's obvious, of course. According to the terms of Juliet's will, if no heir stepped forward, the land would revert to the state for a national park. I couldn't allow that to happen, not when it should have been ours in the first place."

Charlotte was going to ask how he could have known what Juliet intended, but she realized how stupid the question would be. She had always known her father had ways of ferreting out the most private of information, so she wouldn't have put it past him to have somehow gained access even to Juliet Caulfield's will.

"And so, you . . . allowed me to hire Mr. Weitz to find Briar," she managed, over the growing stricture in her throat.

"Indeed, I did," Rupert said, pleased with himself. "It made things so much more challenging, after all."

"What do you mean?" she asked faintly.

"Well, Juliet was no challenge; she was just a crazy old woman. But Briar . . ." He paused, his eyes far away for a moment before he glanced at her again. "Briar was a different story."

She had to pursue this to the ugly end. "How did you know?"

"Because I've followed her since she was a child," Rupert said patiently. "Why? Did you not think I wouldn't track that silly Ariana, who was even more besotted with Duncan McKenna than you were? Oh, don't look so surprised, Charlotte. I knew you were in love with that irresponsible ne'er-do-well; you couldn't hide it from me. Why do you think I arranged to have him inducted?"

Charlotte felt dizzy and sick. They had never talked about Duncan; she had thought until now that her girlish infatuation with Angus's son—Briar's father—had been a secret safe with her. To think that her father—her father, who had never paid the slightest attention to her—had known about her feelings for the handsome Duncan McKenna made her feel dirty and guilty and ashamed and exposed.

But what had he said? Holding on to the last of her control, Charlotte looked at Rupert. "You were responsible for his going away? But he had a deferment . . . I remember. He was needed at the ranch. Juliet—"

"Oh, spare no pity for Juliet," Rupert said scornfully. "She managed quite well with her limited resources, didn't she? And so did Briar, who came in her place. Oh, yes, Briar has performed admirably. Beyond my expectations, in fact. But I always knew that if I couldn't break her spirit by blocking her adoption from the orphanage, she would be a worthy opponent when the time came, and I was right. So you see? Everything worked out perfectly."

Charlotte looked at her father in horror. She had always believed him capable of anything, but she had never imagined these depraved depths. What kind of man, she asked herself, could condemn a child to life as an orphan when that child had relatives anxiously searching for her? Oh, she remembered how Juliet had tried to find out what had become of Ariana and Duncan, who everyone thought had been lost in the war. Juliet's search had occupied her feverishly for years, all to no avail. She had spent all her money, squandered all her resources, only to die alone and lonely, without ever discovering what had become of Ariana—or knowing that she had a great-niece living as close as San Francisco.

Charlotte had liked Juliet, who, despite being slightly muddled and vacant, had always been kind to her whenever they met. As she stared at her father now, she couldn't believe that even Rupert could have done such a thing to anyone, especially not to a harmless, not-quite-right woman who couldn't possibly have been considered an enemy.

Rupert saw her expression, and his own hardened. "You're shocked, I see. Well, you shouldn't be. If you knew what Juliet had caused me—"

Somehow, Charlotte gathered herself together one last time. "It doesn't matter what she did!" she cried. "Oh, how could you be so . . . so unconscionable! This is too much, even for you!"

"Why, how can you say that, Charlotte?" he asked. "Didn't I give you a helping hand?"

"What helping hand? What are you talking about?"

Rupert got up and went to the study door, "Have you ever wondered why that investigator you hired was able to trace Briar so quickly? Who do you think gave him the first push in the right direction?"

Charlotte was still sitting; she turned jerkily in her chair. "You?"

"Of course it was I. You don't think that stupid man would have been able to find her on his own after all these years do you? Really, Charlotte, sometimes you amaze me."

He reached for the doorknob, but Charlotte somehow managed to get to her feet. She couldn't let him leave without trying to shake his smug complacency, even a little. "What about Stefan Yager?" she asked.

He turned back with an expression of distaste. "What about him?"

Her knees still felt weak; she put her hand on the back of the chair for balance. "He says he has a document that proves—"

"I've been assured by our lawyers that even if he does, it's of no importance. If worst comes to worst, we'll just . . ." He shrugged. "Pay him off."

She looked at him in disbelief. "Even you don't have enough money to do that, Father. You might not recognize it in someone else, but Stefan Yager isn't a man to be bought."

"Every man has his price."

"Even you, Father?"

"Even Duncan McKenna," he answered.

She went rigid. "What . . . do you mean?"

He looked at her pityingly. "Why, Ariana Caulfield was Duncan's price, of course. I told him that if he'd leave like a good boy, I'd look after the women he'd left behind."

"But you hounded Juliet until the day she died!"

"Hounded," Rupert repeated, pursuing his lips. "That's rather a harsh word, don't you think? Besides, I left Ariana alone, didn't I?"

"You didn't have any choice. She was so miserable when Duncan left she followed him to England!"

"But that wasn't my fault," he pointed out.

"And I suppose it wasn't your fault that she didn't come back, nor did Duncan, nor, as it turns out, did their daughter . . . until now!"

"Well, I can't be in control of *every* detail, Charlotte," he said reproachfully. "You can't possibly blame me for everything."

She wanted to fly across the room and scratch his eyes out. She hated him more in that moment than she had ever hated him in her life. "Yes, I can! I do! I blame you for it all!' she cried.

"Well, of course you do," he said, unimpressed. "I never expected anything else. I know we have never been close, but I did have my obligations. You were my daughter, after all, and you certainly didn't think I would ever have permitted you to become involved with someone like Duncan McKenna, did you?"

"Duncan McKenna was a fine man!"

Rupert's expression hardened. "He was a nobody!"

"That's not true. He was a better man than you ever hoped to be."

With an effort, Rupert collected himself. "Well!" he said

sharply, exhaling the word while he tugged at his tie. "I don't intend to stand here arguing about it. That's all in the past; I can't imagine why we're discussing it now."

"We're discussing it because of what you did to Briar!"

"Because of Briar," he repeated derisively. "Oh, yes. You thought finding Briar and having her installed at Caulfield Farm would be your revenge against me. Oh, don't bother to deny it, my dear; you are so transparent. But you failed in that, as you have in so many other things, didn't you? Don't you know by now that you'll never beat me? But I have to say, it's amusing to watch you try." Smiling, he opened the door. "Don't be late for dinner, Charlotte," he said before he went out. "To celebrate, I've had Elsa prepare a crown roast."

Feeling as if she would never have an appetite again, Charlotte watched him leave the room. Filled with loathing, she sank back down on the chair again and put her head in her hands. How had this happened? she wondered. *What are you going to do?*

She nearly laughed hysterically. As Rupert had pointed out so cruelly just now, she had never been able to fight her father successfully; no one had.

Except, she thought suddenly, Sloane Caulfield.

She had never known all the details about the day her grandfather Heinrich had been shot. The official version her father had given out was that Heinrich had been killed during a robbery at the summerhouse, where he had kept an office. But everyone in the family knew that wasn't true, or so they'd been told. Rupert had always insisted that Juliet was responsible for Heinrich's death, that there had been a struggle . . . and she had shot him. But Charlotte didn't know what to believe. If Juliet had been there that day, she couldn't imagine why. Considering the enmity that had existed between their two families, she doubted Juliet would ever have voluntarily gone anywhere near Heinrich, and she certainly wouldn't have visited him in a remote place.

Rupert had never been any help with the details. He insisted that Sloane had defaulted on the deal he'd made, but even when pressed, he would never relate how he'd been bested. All he would say was that Sloane had cheated him, and as the years passed, it gradually became accepted in the family that the Caulfield land was rightfully theirs.

Slumping in the chair, Charlotte felt defeated. She couldn't care about what had really happened so long ago, not when her entire future was at stake. She had always known her father to be cruel and merciless, but after what he had revealed to her tonight, she didn't doubt that he would crush her as he had crushed so many others who had gotten in his way. Still, she had to try. Her plan to avenge herself on him by finding Briar had failed, and unless she found some other way to stymie him about this match, her colt's future was in the balance. She couldn't stand by while he pitted the best horse she'd ever had against that filly in a vengeful high-stakes race. She had put too much of herself into her breeding program to take the chance that Galland would be destroyed along with everything else. Just the thought made her panic, and she gripped the chair to control herself.

She had to do something, but what? With despair threatening to overwhelm her, she tried to think. Her father had already made it very clear that he wouldn't tolerate interference, and she knew that legally he couldn't be stopped from doing whatever he wanted with any of the horses in the Stud. When he had threatened last time to take her control away, she had consulted a lawyer and found to her fury and dismay that he could do it. But she still had one weapon at her disposal, she thought grimly, and she left the study to find it.

Her bedroom suite was at the end of the second-floor hallway, but she passed the door on her way to the attic. The house was old—almost as old as the one at Caulfield Farm, and the short flight of three stairs at the end of the corridor led to a door that opened on another flight of stairs to the attic. As she reached for the key that always hung on a hook beside the door, she paused for an instant, her mind flooded with memories.

When she had been a child, lonesome and forbidden to play with anyone but her despised brother, she had spent many an hour up here by herself. The room under the eaves spanned the entire length of the house and was filled to bursting with cast-offs and trivia, old furniture and whatnots. No one had cleaned it since her grandmother had died, and just to enter was exciting because she wasn't supposed to be up there. But there were so many things to play with and so much to make up stories about that time flew. All during her childhood, the attic was the only place in the world where she'd never been lonely.

One of her favorite things to do was go through the big wardrobes that were filled with her grandmother Mariel's clothes. There were five armoires lined up against one wall, and they were stuffed full of everything from day dresses to ball gowns. Charlotte couldn't count the times she'd played dress up, parading back and forth in front of a cracked and cobwebbed cheval glass, enveloped in one of Mariel's voluminous gowns. She had never known her grandmother, who had died in the great San Francisco earthquake; Rupert never spoke of his mother at all. But she had always thought that Mariel must have been even more beautiful than the portrait in the library. All the dresses were so lovely, and her gloves were so small they might have fit a doll.

But it wasn't to the wardrobes that Charlotte went tonight when she came up the steps and emerged into the attic. By the light of the single bulb hanging from a cord in the ceiling, she went straight to a series of dressers stacked haphazardly together at one end of the big shadowy room. Unhesitatingly she shoved one big mahogany bureau aside so she could get to the oakwood vanity behind it.

The vanity had belonged to Mariel, of course, and as she paused before it, Charlotte could still remember the day long ago, when she had sat here pretending to be her grandmother. She was primping and making faces in the spotted mirror, and that was when she found the letter.

At first she had thought it was just an old piece of paper that had gotten stuck to the back of the top drawer, and she had been about to toss it back in when she realized it had writing inside. Curiosity got the best of her, and she had opened up the paper to read what was there. It hadn't made much sense to her at the time; the best she could make out was that the letter was addressed to her grandmother and was signed by someone named Flossie. At least, that's what she thought. The handwriting was so poor, and the pencil so faded, it was difficult to tell. Impatient and eager to get on with her game, she hadn't paid much attention to the document with it. Folding them together again, she had tossed the envelope back into the drawer, where it had lain, undisturbed, until she learned Ariana had run away to be with Duncan McKenna.

Even now, Charlotte could recall the terrible hurt she'd felt the day she found out that Ariana had found the courage she herself had lacked. Tonight her hand actually trembled as she reached for the drawer. Flooded with those painful memories, she sat down in a creaky chair nearby until she could get her feelings under control.

*Why did it still hurt so?* She felt silly and ashamed and foolish, all these years later. Was it because Duncan had been her first—and only—love? But it had been so long ago. He had been eight years older than she, she remembered—twenty-four to her sixteen—and to her girlish, inexperienced eyes, *so* romantic. With deep auburn hair and dark blue eyes, he had been the most handsome young man she had ever seen. She used to spend hours dreaming of him, only to become completely tongue-tied if they happened to meet by chance in town, as they did sometimes. But invariably, Ariana would be there too—Ariana, with her thick chestnut hair and flashing green eyes and brilliant smiles. . . .

Smiling sadly now as Charlotte thought of it, she knew why everyone at the time had said Duncan and Ariana were a beautiful couple. Even in her darkest moments of jealousy, she'd had to agree. Duncan had been handsome, all right, but there had been something special about Ariana, some . . . aura . . . that set her apart. It wasn't only that she was so lovely; it was something inside her—a restlessness, a fire.

Ariana never walked into a room, Charlotte remembered: she *swept* in, dominating with one smile all who were there, effortlessly entertaining, instantly becoming surrounded by admirers. Her quick intelligence and sparkling wit had drawn laughter even from strangers, but no matter where she went, she always made friends. She had been besieged by admirers from as far away as San Francisco, who often came out to Caulfield Farm just to visit for a day . . . an hour . . . a minute. She greeted them all; she entertained. But she gracefully refused everyone. She only had eyes for Duncan McKenna, her childhood chum.

And Duncan only had eyes for Ariana, Charlotte thought with a sigh. And who could blame him? With Ariana in his sight, how could he possibly notice anyone else—especially an awkward, painfully shy, horse-mad sixteen-year-old girl?

But even more difficult to bear than Ariana's natural, effortless beauty and her ability to charm everyone she met was her absolute loyalty to her aunt Juliet. By the time Duncan left—or was transcripted, Charlotte thought bitterly, remembering what her father had told her tonight—Caulfield Farm had gone to seed. Andrew had been an old man, and after he followed his son Angus to the grave, only Duncan had been there to try to manage the great sprawling place by himself.

To her credit, Ariana had tried to salvage what she could. The fire that had claimed Marguerite's life had destroyed not only the barn but a good many of Caulfield Farm's best horses, and because Juliet had no heart for the horses, or talent, no one could save what was left. By the time Ariana was old enough to manage, Caulfield Farm's reputation as a breeding stable was long gone, but because Juliet wouldn't—or couldn't—sell and go somewhere else, Ariana stubbornly refused to leave, too. The two women stayed on, barely managing, but squeaking by somehow, holding on to the land that had been in their family for over fifty years.

Then came the war, and everything changed. Duncan enlisted, and soon after Ariana began to lose her bloom. The once vibrant smile rarely appeared; the sparkling eyes looked shadowed and bruised. Charlotte knew, because she, who was so desperately eager for any news of Duncan herself, took to dropping by the ranch—without her father's knowledge or consent, of course. She thought she'd been so clever, sneaking over the hills by horseback, but she wondered if Rupert had known about those visits, too, as he seemed to know about everything else.

Except this letter, she thought somberly, looking down at the envelope she held in her hands. It was so old the paper was brittle, and she handled it carefully. She didn't want anything to happen to it at this late stage. Her face turned grim. This was her last chance at revenge.

With the letter in her hands, she briefly shut her eyes tight. Now that the shock at her father's actions had passed, she felt enraged all over again. It had taken her a long time, and a lot of the money she had inherited from her mother, to locate Briar. To think that Rupert had known all along where to find her . . . The thought was galling.

Without warning, the words he'd said to her tonight flashed into her mind again. You thought Briar would be your revenge, he had told her with a supercilious look. But you failed in that, as you have in so many other things. Don't you know you'll never beat me, Charlotte?

Charlotte opened her eyes again. Staring down at the precious letter she held, she muttered, ''Don't be too sure, Father. Don't be too sure.''

She had kept this letter secret for years, as had her grandmother. Maybe they had both somehow known that one day they might need it. Well, for her, the time had come. She wasn't as helpless as her father obviously thought, was she? Her smile turned cold when she pictured it.

None of them had believed Stefan Yager when he had arrived last year with his claim that he was Heinrich's great-grandson; they had all regarded the idea as preposterous. Rupert had been derisive, Carl incredulous, and she herself might have dismissed it as easily as they had—if she hadn't remembered the letter.

Her expression crafty, Charlotte looked down again at the envelope she held. It was time, she thought, to give Stefan Yager a ring. She hadn't put her entire life into Mondragon Stud only to lose everything now, and she was not going to allow her father's obsession to ruin her beautiful colt's chances for the Triple Crown. One way or another, Rupert Jaeger was about to learn a valuable lesson.

---

# CHAPTER THIRTY-TWO

Although he had passed by the place many times on his way to and from Caulfield Farm, Stefan had never been inside the Green Onion bar. He hadn't much use for bars to begin with, and he was surprised that Charlotte Jaeger had suggested meeting at a place where the pocket-sized parking lot was crammed with trucks and dualies, and where honkey-tonk music could be heard through the battered front door. Cowboys—or at least, men wearing cowboy hats—went in and out, some swaggering, some staggering, but all looking a little green around the gills due to the bilious lime-colored, onion-shaped neon sign at the edge of the parking lot. What an onion had to do with a bar, Stefan didn't know, but as he parked his own truck out in the street just to be safe from the cowboys in their mechanical horses, he was sure the night was going to be filled with surprises.

The first of the night had been Charlotte Jaeger's call. Thinking how glad he was that Briar didn't know, he got out of the truck and looked around. He wasn't sure what kind of car Charlotte drove, but there was no sense waiting for her in the parking lot, so he decided to go in.

The interior of the bar was dim and smoky, and some country-western tune was playing on the jukebox. A few people were dancing, but most were bellied up to the counter drinking beer. Two men down at the end were rolling dice for rounds, shouting and carrying on. Competing with all the other noise was a basketball game on the television set that hung from the ceiling behind the pool table at one end. He was just wondering if he had heard her right when he saw Charlotte rise from one of the booths at the back and beckon to him. Thinking how out of place she looked in her silk blouse and fancy slacks when everyone else was wearing jeans and boots, he headed toward her and sat down.

Charlotte didn't say anything for a moment; she was busy lighting a cigarette. As her lighter flared, he saw how tense she looked and decided to sit back and let her take the initiative. After all, she was the one who had called.

Through the smoke curling up, she looked across the table and met his eyes. Glancing down at the pack of cigarettes she had put on the table, she gestured. "Help yourself."

"No, thanks. I gave it up years ago."

"So did I," she said, and smiled tightly as she took a deep drag and let it out again, her eyes half-closed. "Amazing, isn't it, how it comes back, just like that?"

He shrugged. "They say it's just like riding a bicycle."

She took another drag, playing for time by toying with the square lighter, turning it up on one corner, down to the other, letting it fall to the long side, then lifting it up to the fourth corner, and starting all over. As he watched, he realized the lighter was gold, and that, despite the elegant outfit, Charlotte's nails were unpolished and cut short. When she saw him looking at her hands, she grabbed the lighter with a decisive snap and opened her mouth to say something. But just then a pert barmaid sashayed up, her flounced skirt bouncing. "What can I get y'all?" the girl asked.

Stefan looked across at Charlotte so she could order first. "I don't suppose you have any white wine?"

"Oh, yes, indeed," the girl said cheerily. "What kind would

you like?'' She proceeded to reel off a list that made Stefan's eyes glaze. She saw his expression and grinned as Charlotte ordered some kind of Chardonnay. ''We're in the heart of wine country, mister. We gotta compete. What would you like?''

''Would you have any beer?''

Grinning again at the mild sarcasm, she took his order and disappeared. When Stefan looked at Charlotte once more, he saw that she was ready to get down to business. Taking another drag off the cigarette, she said tersely, ''You're wondering why I asked you to come here. Well, before I tell you, we've got to get something straight between us.''

''What's that?''

''I need to know how serious you are about pursuing this claim of yours. Are you willing to go the distance, or are you just going to be a nuisance?''

''That depends on your father. If he'll leave Briar alone, I'll do the same for—''

Viciously, she stubbed out her nearly spent cigarette. ''He'll never leave her alone,' she said flatly. ''Not until he gets what he wants.''

''Caulfield Farm?''

Charlotte lit another cigarette. ''It's not as simple as that.''

''How complicated is it?''

She took another deep drag, considering. Then she said, ''He's going to destroy her, Mr. Yager. One way or another, he's going to drive her into the ground and take everything she has—everything, *including* Caulfield Farm.''

Hiding the chill he felt at the calm way she said those words, he replied, ''It isn't going to happen.''

''Oh, and how are you going to prevent it? Go to court with your claim that you're a member of the family?''

He sat back. ''I'll go to court with something more serious than that. If I have to, I'll produce evidence that your grandfather was a bigamist, and that he was married first to my great-grandmother, which makes me the rightful descendent to Mondragon Enterprises.''

''My father's attorneys will laugh you out of court.''

''Not with proof.''

''Which is?''

''The marriage certificate I found among my great-grandmother's things. The right names, the right date . . .''

''It could be a fake.''

''It isn't,'' he said flatly.

"My father will say it is," she said. "You need something else."

"And that is?'

"A birth certificate."

He was about to reply when the perky waitress returned with their drinks.

"Go on," Stefan said, ignoring his beer. "I'm all ears."

Toying with the thick stem of her glass, Charlotte was silent a moment. Then she leaned forward. "First things first," she said.

"Ah, now we come to the *real* purpose of this meeting," Stefan said, taking a swig of beer. He didn't trust her; in the final analysis, she was a Jaeger, too. "I should have known you'd have a price for whatever information it is you think you have. Well, go ahead. It can't hurt to name it."

Surprisingly, she didn't seem offended by his sarcasm. Her mind was obviously on more important things. Leaning over the table, she said, "If I help you, and you do succeed in pressing your claim, I want you to sign over all the Mondragon horses to me, without reservation."

"Done," he said, wondering what she was really up to. "But I'm sure there's something else. What about the Stud itself?"

She waved an impatient hand. "I don't care about the ranch; it has too many . . . memories. I can always start up somewhere else. But I won't give up what I've spent my entire life building, and I've earned the right to the Mondragon name as well. Agreed?"

He shrugged. It didn't matter to him. He wasn't after the name, just everything else. "Agreed."

She looked surprised—and relieved—at his quick acceptance. "You didn't need much time to think about it."

"What is there to think about? The horses are yours. I just want Briar left alone."

"Well, she's not going to be, unless we stop him," she said. She took a sip of wine, grimaced, and put the glass back on the table.

He sat back, studying her. "Why are you doing this?"

"Because of the match race, of course," she answered. "I'm not going to stand by and allow my colt to be ruined just to satisfy my father's vendetta against anyone named Caulfield."

He still watched her face. "No," he said slowly, "it's more than that."

"No, it isn't," she insisted, but she avoided his eyes. "Or maybe it is," she added suddenly. "Maybe I think you *should* be part of the family."

He laughed. "That's why you greeted me so warmly the first time I showed up, right?"

She finally met his glance. "That was then. This is now."

"Before the match race."

"That, and . . . other things," she said, and then added impatiently, "Look, what does it matter? The point is we're going to stop him."

He still wasn't convinced. He had the marriage license, but the birth certificate had been lost—destroyed along with many other items during the war. He squinted at Charlotte. "And you think we can do it together."

"Oh, yes," she said, and reached down to take something from her purse. It was an envelope, and she handed it across.

"What's this?" Stefan asked.

Charlotte sat back. "Read it yourself. This is a copy, but I have the original."

Holding her eyes for a moment, he finally looked down at what she had given him. Lifting the flap of the envelope, he took out the two sheets of paper inside. When he saw what one was, his heart lurched; then, when he read the other, he wanted to stand up and cheer.

The ink was faded; even the excellent copy machine Charlotte had used was only able to lift it to legibility. But as soon as he deciphered the heading, he glanced up sharply at Charlotte.

Her head was wreathed in smoke from yet another cigarette, she gave him a catlike smile. "Well? Do you believe me now? Go on, read the whole thing."

He looked down again.

The penmanship was poor at best, and there were numerous misspellings. But after the salutation, Stefan didn't even notice. Completely forgetting everything else, even his table companion, he read the letter twice, and then again. He was almost afraid to believe his eyes.

To Mister Heinrich Jaeger of Mondragon Farm.

I am in receet of the money you sent to cover the expenses of our sons birth. But Im afraid I cant in conshunse return the marriage certificat like you asked. To make up for it, I am sending a copy of the birth registry—but only a copy, as my aunt advised. If I sent along the orijinal, too, what would I tell the boy when he grows up? As I know alreddy, its diffikult enuf in this world without being calld a bastard, specialy when your not. But I am staying in England, with my aunt in Kent, so that shuld make you happy at least. Im sorry things didn't work out. We did have a fine few days, dint we? By the way, I namd the boy Rudy.

As ever,

Your wife, Flossie.

PS. I promise Ill never tell, just like you asked.

Stefan looked up, blinking back tears in his eyes. *Flossie,* he thought. His great-grandmother, who had come to America to make her fortune, and who had ended up being a maid in a San Francisco hotel at the same time Heinrich Jaeger, his pride in tatters because Marguerite Kendall had married Sloane Caulfield instead of him, arrived for a three-day drunk. He'd heard the story so many times that he could have repeated it word for word. Glancing up at Charlotte now, he said, "Where did you get this?"

She waved the cigarette. "It doesn't matter. If you've meant what you said about Briar, and you do what you've said you'll do, it's yours."

He couldn't believe his good fortune. The birth certificate, notarized and authenticated, proving that Heinrich Jaeger had been the father of Flossie's first born—of *Heinrich's* first born, and only legitimate issue—was the missing piece of the puzzle. Without it, he'd only been able to threaten. With it . . .

"Why are you doing this, Charlotte?" he asked suddenly.

"Because I knew the marriage certificate you said you had might not be enough. My father has *very* good lawyers, Mr. Jaeger," she said, and looked down at the copies he still held. "But not *that* good," she said with a cold smile.

Carefully, he folded the papers and put them back in the envelope. "That's not what I meant. Why are you really doing this?"

"My father is not the only Jaeger with thoughts of vengeance," she said, and suddenly seemed to look back into the past. Her tone took on a musing quality, and Stefan could have sworn that for a moment, she forgot him. "For years, I've blamed Ariana for being the cause of my unhappiness," she said. "And when I found Briar, she seemed the perfect tool—through her, I would avenge myself on all those who had hurt me. But then I met her and got to know her a little, and suddenly she wasn't just a tool anymore, but—"

She seemed abruptly to realize what she was saying and broke off. With a guilty glance in Stefan's direction, she finished with a mutter, "Well, it doesn't matter. And I see things differently now."

Stefan wasn't sure what to say, but he watched curiously as she straightened, and before his eyes became the hardened Charlotte Jaeger again. "It was a long time ago," she said, shrugging to show it was of no importance. "A long time ago. It doesn't matter anymore."

She left before he did, promising to deliver the originals of the copies he held when she had a signed statement of their agreement about the horses. Because he had seen something in her eyes before she departed, he sat where he was for a few minutes, to give her time to get safely out of the parking lot. When he finally did get up to leave, he caught the waitress's eye and she gave him a broad wink. He smiled, but shook his head, and when she looked disappointed, he waved on his way out.

The parking lot was emptying now, and his truck stood alone under the street lamp out in the street. As he walked toward it, he shivered. He thought it was the cool Northern California night air, but then he realized he was keyed up about what had happened tonight. Charlotte's offer had been an unexpected bonus, and the thought that he might actually be able to pull it off elated him—not for his sake, but for Briar's.

As he unlocked the truck and got in, he sat back. "Who're you kidding, buddy?" he muttered, and sat there, fiddling with the keys while he forced himself to be honest. In the beginning, when he'd found the marriage certificate in his grandmother's attic and realized the stories he'd heard all his life about his great-grandmother having been married to a rich man in California were true, he'd decided to come here to meet the family and introduce himself. After all, he *was* a member of the clan—in fact, if he wanted to be pushy about it—he was the only *legitimate* member left. Heinrich had never gotten a divorce from Flossie, so that meant his second marriage was bigamous, and all the children from that union were illegitimate. But he hadn't wanted to play the upstart rightful heir. At that point, he didn't think anything of theirs belonged to him; he'd just wanted to extend a hand, so to speak.

But then Rupert had started to play rough with Briar, and because he'd been half in love with her by that time himself, he had realized he had a lever to force the old man back into line. Even then, he hadn't intended to press his claim of rightful inheritance; he'd just wanted to get Rupert to back off.

But then things changed again, with Rupert's insistence on this match race between Mondragon's Galland and Briar's black filly. To force Briar's hand, the crafty old bastard had somehow gotten together with Fredrica and her brother and bought up two-thirds of the company that Briar had so generously handed to them on a silver platter in the first place. Now he and Briar had developed a relationship.

But what a relationship, he thought, diverted for an instant. Ever since that night a month ago when they had first gone to bed together, he'd felt like he was walking about in a dream. He had always suspected that underneath the cool exterior of hers beat the heart of a passionate woman, and he'd subsequently been delighted to discover he'd been right. Even now when he thought of her warm, pliant body writhing under his hands, of her small waist, her round breasts with the deep-rose nipples, her long legs winding around him, he could feel his response. He never tired of her; he could be content just lying there naked in the same bed, watching the play of light and shadow on that glorious body of hers, touching her soft skin, smelling her hair, or even just looking into her eyes. He loved the way her faced changed with her moods. Sometimes he thought that they could be together a hundred years or more and he'd never be bored. Being with Briar was like living inside a kaleidoscope, where, by a twist of the cylinder, all those beautiful jewels inside instantly changed shape.

Not that she couldn't be frustrating, too, he thought with a frown, remembering how irate he'd been when he found she'd put her company up for sale without talking to him first, as she had promised. His frown deepened as he recalled the argument that followed. He'd come close to telling her just why he was so angry, but even then something had held him back.

*You should have told her*, a little voice whispered. But he hadn't wanted to tell her because—because why? Because he sensed it would be the end of their relationship, that's why. How could he take the chance of losing her completely when they'd just found each other at last? Oh, damn it, it was all so complicated. Now, despite his elation about what had happened tonight, it was even worse. He had to go back to Caulfield Farm and . . . confess. Confronting Rupert Jaeger at his absolute worst seemed infinitely preferable to telling Briar the truth.

"Bloody hell," he muttered, and sat back against the truck seat, trying to think of the best approach. It was too late now to castigate himself for not being honest with Briar from the beginning. He closed his eyes briefly, feeling a sudden, sharp pain. He couldn't lose her, not after all this, he thought. He couldn't speak for her feelings, but he knew about his. The old cliche about never having met anyone like her was true in this case. He never *had* met anyone like Briar—so proud and independent and self-sufficient on the one hand, and so vulnerable and sensitive and touchy on the other. She was a contradiction in terms, all right; perfectly capable of running a big business single-handedly, but moved to tears over a horse that had just died. The contrasts fascinated him—and exasperated him at times—he couldn't deny it. How could Briar make tough, instant decisions involving hundreds of people and thousands of dollars but dither over whether to get rid of a few barn cats or not? She could be single-minded, nearly ruthless, he knew, when she decided what she wanted. He would never forget the Keeneland sale when, surprising everyone, including himself, she had finessed that old bastard Jaeger and forced him to pay far too much for Heat of Night, when the horse she'd really wanted all the time was Touch the Fire.

She had been right about that filly, he couldn't deny it. And about Incandessence, he conceded, too, who had returned, just as Briar said she would, for another successful racing season before being retired. But where, he wondered dismally, was that same steely-eyed determination of hers the day she bought the injured Mi Flor Amor off the track?

Her only mistake had been Gillie, Stefan thought, his face tightening for an instant as he pictured the old man. He had never seen better hands or a more healing touch with horses than Gillie had, but he'd never forgive him for running out on Briar.

But what was he doing sitting here thinking of Gillie in the first place? Instead of dwelling on a drunk who had vanished, he should be trying to think of how to tell Briar he had lied to her all this time.

"It wasn't exactly a *lie*," he muttered, and knew he was begging the case. The point was he hadn't told her the truth, either, and if he had it in mind to confront Rupert, he had to do it tonight.

He was still trying to think of the best approach when he arrived back at the ranch. He was so preoccupied with his increasingly gloomy thoughts that he didn't see the black Bentley coming down the drive toward him until it was almost past. Just when the vehicle drew near him, he recognized the driver's face, and he was so startled, he nearly put on the brakes. The driver saw him, too, but the car whipped past him without even slowing down, and as it headed toward the front gates, Stefan watched it with a scowl. What in the hell, he wondered, where Carl and Rupert Jaeger doing here at this late hour?

Suddenly deciding he'd better find out, he put on the gas and drove in a cloud of dust up toward the big house.

---

# CHAPTER THIRTY-THREE

Rupert Jaeger hadn't called at Caulfield Farm by the time Briar got home that night. It had been a terrible day, and as she wearily stopped down by the barn to look in on the horses before she went up to the house, she just sat in the car for a few minutes, too tired to get out. Even though she had tried to anticipate this day ever since she decided to sell her company, she realized now she hadn't really been prepared to sign over the ownership of McKenna TimeSave to anyone, not even Galt Core Management, who had paid her handsomely.

Sighing, she put her head back against the seat and thought about the wrenching experience of giving up the company she felt had *defined* her identity for so long. When she had met with Galt's executives in her office that afternoon, she'd been holding herself together by sheer force of will. Patsy had made things even more difficult by sniffling at her desk, and with Spence tight-lipped and not saying much, and Gabe looking like the walking wounded, she had felt even worse. The only saving grace of the depressing business was that she had gotten a good price. Now at least she could keep the ranch going for months until Spence straightened out this business with Rupert Jaeger and Lord Industries—as he had promised her he would try.

"It'll take some time, that's all," Spence had told her painfully when they discussed her lack of options before she informed him of her decision to sell the company. Dear friend that he was, he hadn't even whispered an I told you so; all he'd said was, "I'm sorry, Briar. I'll do what I can."

She knew he would, but she wasn't holding out much hope. Managing a smile so he wouldn't feel responsible, she said, "It's all right—really, Spence. I've been saying for a year now that I can't manage both the ranch and the business, and this has forced me into making a choice. Maybe it's a blessing in disguise."

"You don't believe that any more than I do," he'd said sourly. "Damn, I hate this!"

"Spence, please, it's not your fault."

"*I know.* I keep *telling* myself that. But I don't believe it. Briar," he said, reaching impulsively for one of her hands. "Please let me help. You know whatever I have is yours."

She was more grateful for his offer than he knew. But she had to refuse all the same. "I appreciate it, Spence, I do. But I can't accept."

"Why not? Damn it, Briar, it wouldn't kill you to accept my help, would it? No strings attached, I promise. You don't even have to say thanks, just let me *do* something!"

"But you are. You're going to find out how to block this man from running Lord Industries any further into the ground than he already has."

That's when he told her it would take time—time she didn't have. As she had already figured, her options had narrowed down to just two: either sell Caulfield Farm and keep the business, or sell McKenna TimeSave to keep the ranch running. There really wasn't any choice. Selling the company she had worked hard to build had been more painful than she had anticipated, but at least she had negotiated with the new owners to keep Patsy and Gabe on, at better salaries than they'd had before. Tearfully, Patsy made her promise not to lose touch, and when Gabe surprised her by giving her a big hug before she left, she nearly started sobbing herself. She maintained her self-control until she reached her car, but as she drove across the bridge, she had to wipe away tears with a tissue she'd found in the glove box.

Now, as she sat in her car outside the barn at twilight, she felt so exhausted she closed her eyes. "There really wasn't much choice at all, was there, grandmother?" she murmured, and thought—or maybe she just imagined—she heard an affirmative sigh from somewhere close.

Startled, she lifted her head and looked around. The ranch this time of day seemed deserted. Jaime and Isabella and all the other hands had already gone to their quarters to have dinner and spend the night as they wished. She was alone—or thought she was. Then she saw the tree branches swaying gently high above her and realized with relief that it must have been some trick of the wind. Of course it was, she thought with a shaky laugh. Surely she wasn't hearing voices on top of everything else!

Thinking that she must be more tired than she realized, she decided to give the horses a quick check and then go on up to the house. She wasn't hungry at all, but after what she'd gone through today, she did need a long, comforting, hot bath.

She was just getting out of the car when she thought she saw something move in the deepening inky shadows around the barn. Her nerves were so on edge that she nearly cried out, then almost did scream when she saw the shadow become a man. When the man stepped into the fading light, she gasped.

"Gillie!" She hadn't seen him in months, not since the awful Christmas party when Rupert Jaeger had first issued his challenge about the match race. She remembered how desperate she had been when she had discovered he was gone—and how angry she'd been at Stefan for saying she couldn't trust an old drunk.

"I . . . I came back," he said, stating the obvious.

He wouldn't look at her, but she knew the courage it had taken for him to return, and she said gently, "I can see that, Gillie. I'm glad. Are you all right? I was worried about you."

"You was?"

"Of course I was. When you disappeared, I didn't know where you'd gone . . . or why."

"I'm sorry, Miz Briar. I know how . . . how disappointed you mus' be in me."

Very quietly, she closed the car door all the way. She wanted to suggest that they go up to the house, or at least to his old room above the barn. However, she sensed that communication between them was a fragile thing at this point, and she didn't want to frighten him into disappearing again.

"I'm not disappointed," she said. "You came back."

"I did, I did. I had to, Miz Briar. I owed it to you. The filly is goin' to need me if she's to run aginst that colt."

She tensed. "I haven't agreed to any race, Gillie."

"I know, I know. But if you do . . . Well, I couldn't stay away, not even because of—" he shuddered "—him."

"Him?"

"Mr. Rupert," he said, and raised his sad eyes to her again. "I'm tired of runnin', Mis Briar. I want to tell you what I know."

She could barely hide her elation. "In that case," she said as calmly as she could, "I think we'd better go inside, don't you?"

They went up to his old room, which had only been cleaned and straightened, his pitifully few poor possessions left as they were. He'd gone in such a hurry he hadn't taken anything, and when Briar turned the light on and he saw that everything was as he'd left it, tears formed in his eyes. Rubbing at his face with the back of his hand, he looked around, at the threadbare brushes on the bureau, at the cracked silver hand mirror beside them. With reverence, he touched the tattered satin-backed stable jacket hanging on the peg behind the door. The letters on the back were so faded they were no longer legible, but Briar hadn't allowed Isabella to throw it out; she knew despite its disreputable appearance, it had sentimental value.

Gillie turned to her, his veined, reddened eyes shining. "You're jus' like Miz Marguerite, God res' her lovely soul," he said hoarsely. "She would have done somethin' like this for me, too."

Touched by the compliment, Briar smiled. "It wasn't a big deal, Gillie. Thanks aren't necessary."

Shakily, Gillie sat down on the edge of the bed while she took one of the hard-backed chairs. He looked at his hat for a moment before carefully setting it aside. Then he stared at the floor for so long that she wondered if he'd changed his mind. "Gillie?" she said softly.

"I was there, you know," he said finally, his voice so low she could hardly hear him.

"There?"

"At the summerhouse."

Her heart skipped a beat when she realized he was talking about the day of Juliet's disappearance. "Go on," she said calmly, so as not to frighten him.

He closed his eyes. "I was there that day, God help me," he said. "I wasn't s'posed to be, but I was. Miss Juliet tol' me she wanted to drive herself home, but I couldn't let her do that, not when she was going up to the summerhouse with him." Gillie opened his eyes, but Briar had the feeling he wasn't seeing her, he was seeing what had happened so long ago. Then he did look at her, and his eyes focused. "I didn't want her to go, you know. I didn't trust him. But he tol' her he had some books up there that he wanted to donate to the lib'ry sale, so she went up to get 'em." His seamed old face crumpled. "He didn't have no books, Miz Briar, jus' like I knew he didn't. No ma'am, all he wanted was to get her alone so he could . . . so he could . . ."

Shuddering violently, he shook his head and buried his face in his hands. Briar didn't know what to do; she wasn't sure whether to go to him and comfort him or to encourage him to go on. He made the decision for her. Visibly pulling himself together, he wiped his eyes with the backs of his hands and sat up. "I said I'd tell it, and I will," he mumbled. "I jus' . . . need a bit."

"Take all the time you need, Gillie," she said softly.

After a moment, he went on, his voice a cracked whisper. "Miz Juliet had let me off on the road to Caulfield Farm, so's I could walk the rest of the way home. An' I started to, I did. But then . . . I don't know . . . it was this feelin' I had. It wasn't right; I couldn't let her go up there by herself. So I turned and ran back, but I was too late. . . . When I did get there, and I heard her beggin' him to stop, and I looked through the window and I saw what was goin' on, I knew I had to do *somethin'*. He was hurtin' her, that man, and so I came through the door yellin' my head off. I pulled him offa her, I did, but then things happened so fas'. Poor Miss Juliet, she was sobbin' and cryin'—not loud, jus' quiet-like, like a little animal that's been terrible hurt. I was jus' goin' to help her, but afore I got there, I gets hit from behind. It knocked me down, it did, and I guess I must have blacked out for a minute, 'cause the nex' thing I knew, I hears all this shoutin' goin' on. When I look up, there's poor Miz Juliet huddled there by the sofa, and I'm jus' reachin' for her when the gun goes off. It all happen so fas', Miz Briar—not like I'm tellin' it here. It was over afore I knew it, and the nex' thing I know, Mr. Heinrich is dead and he's puttin' that gun in her hand. He sees me lookin' at him, and that's when he tells me if I ever say what happen there, he'll say I did it all—'tackin' Mis Juliet, and shootin' the gun. . . ."

Gillie shuddered again and looked at Briar, begging her to understand. "You don't know what it was like for a little black boy in those times, Miz Briar. My word agains' a white man, a rich man at that?" He shivered. "My mama said I didn't have a choice. After I brought poor Miz Juliet back to the ranch—oh, so cold she was, so still, like she was dead herself—I knew my mama was right. Miz Juliet was in no condition to talk—I couldn't even get the gun out of her hand, she was holdin' on to it so fierce. So I said good-bye to my mama and never came back."

With a deep, shuddering breath, Gillie stopped. It was as if the confession he'd held inside all these years had both lifted a terrible burden from his soul and allowed too many horrible memories to come flooding back at the same time. "Until now," he said, and closed his eyes. "Oh, God forgive me, I didn't know what else to do!"

Briar had been sitting glued to the chair during this story. But at the sight of Gillie in such misery, she quickly got up and went to sit beside him on the bed. Putting her arm around his thin, old shoulders, she soothed, "It's all right, Gillie. It wasn't your fault. There wasn't anything else you could do."

Tears shone in his eyes. "You mean it, Miz Briar?" he said hopefully. "You really think that's true?"

"Yes, I do. You tried to help, you tried to save her. It's just—"

"Jus' what?" He looked frightened again.

She frowned. "I've read all Marguerite's journals, and I know how . . . strained things were between the Caulfields and the Jaegers. I don't understand how Juliet could have gone to the summerhouse with Heinrich."

"Oh, but it wasn't Mr. Heinrich who asked her to come up," he said, shaking his head violently. "It was Mr. Rupert."

There was a moment of silence. Then Briar said, "I don't understand, Gillie. If Heinrich was the one who attacked Juliet—"

"No, no," the old man said, agitated. "It wasn't Mr. Heinrich; he was the one who came along after. It was Mr. Rupert all the time."

"But Juliet shot *Heinrich*—"

"No," Gillie insisted. "It was Mr. Rupert!"

Feeling confused, Briar said carefully, "All right. You're saying that Juliet went up to the summerhouse with Rupert."

"Yes, ma'am."

"And Rupert attacked her once they got there."

He cringed. "Yes."

"And you had followed . . ."

He seemed anxious for her to understand. "Yes, I did. She tol' me it was all right, that she was jus' goin' up there to get those books, and that I should go on home to get my chores done, and she'd follow when she was through."

"But someone followed *you*."

"I don't know if he *followed*. Maybe he was there all along. But when he hears the screamin' and the shoutin' and the carryin's on, he comes in, Mr. Heinrich, he does. Oh, and he was *angry*, I can tell you that. When I came to again, he and Mr. Rupert were shoutin' at each other, and he was sayin' that now he'd *never* get Caulfield Farm, and it was all his fault, and he was goin' to kill him for messin' up his plans. And *that's* when Mr. Rupert picked up the gun from the desk. It was in a fancy case, along with the other one—"

"What other one? I thought there was only one gun."

"No, ma'am. There were two. I distinctly remember. They was in a fancy case on the desk, two little guns, pretty as you please—until one of them killed Mr. Heinrich, that is."

Briar would think about the implications of the other gun later. Right now, she said, "Go on. Then what happened?"

"Well, I 'member I was tryin' to get up, thinkin' I had to stop it, I s'pose—I don't know what I was thinkin', it was all happenin' so fast. But afore I could move, Mr. Rupert points the gun right straight at his papa and tells him he don't need to worry nothin' no more 'bout Caulfield Farm, 'cause *he's* gonna take over. Then, just as calm as anything, he pulls the trigger."

Stunned, Briar sat back. "This is incredible," she murmured. "What you're saying is that Rupert *murdered* his own father!"

Gillie stared down at the floor. "I should have told," he said miserably. "I never should have run away."

Thinking he had carried a heavy enough burden of guilt all these years, Briar put her hand on his arm. "You were a boy, Gillie," she said softly. "You weren't responsible for the attitudes of the time. You did what you could. You tried to help."

Tears started streaming unchecked down his face. "But I loved Miss Juliet," he said mournfully. "She was so kind to me, so beautiful. Like an angel, she was, like a sweet, sweet angel. . . ."

Briar patted his hand and let him cry. When at last his tears finally dried and he looked exhausted enough to sleep, she gently pressed him back onto the bed and covered him with a blanket. "You sleep now," she said. "And Gillie—"

"Yes, ma'am?" he murmured. He was so tired he could hardly keep his eyes open.

Smiling down at him, she said softly, "I'm glad you came back."

His gnarled old hand came out from under the blanket and sought hers. Squeezing her fingers gratefully, he smiled in return, a shadow of the old Gillie come back.

"I had to," he said sleepily. "I had to see if that filly's ready to run."

Briar's own smile faded, and she wondered if he were aware of all the pressures come to bear on her about Touch the Fire. "And is she ready?" she heard herself ask.

He seemed almost ready to drift off. "Oh, yassum, she is," he murmured sleepily. "You can bet on it."

Briar knew her filly would run; racing was in her blood. Racing *was* her blood. But wanting to and being able were two different things. Everyone had told her that if Touch the Fire started to train again, everything might look fine until an actual race. Then, the strain and stress of running full out could cause a repeat of the same injury, only the next time it would be infinitely worse. They had been lucky the first go around; the filly hadn't had to be put down. But if it happened again, there was every chance that her valiant horse would hurt herself too badly to be fixed. Briar shuddered even at the idea. Could she ask Touch the Fire to do something that, even if she was more than willing, might destroy her?

She couldn't leave it alone. "I know she'll run if asked, Gillie," she said. "But what if she injures the leg again? I can't in good conscience—"

He smiled, half-asleep. "That leg is *strong*, Miz Briar," he said. "I *know*. Didn't I sleep with her when she first came home? Didn't I spend practically every minute with her, talkin' to her and fixin' her with my medicines and rubbin' her down?"

"Yes, yes, you did, Gillie. But you've been gone a long time, and the doctors say—"

"Doctors don't know everythin'. You trust old Gillie. I know when a horse is ready to run. . . ."

She wanted to believe him, but still she held back. She couldn't forget the warnings from Kara and Denise and those two other veterinarians from Davis—not to mention Stefan and Wayne. They all said the same thing: they advised resting the filly until next season. They they would try—cautiously—to bring her back. Beyond that, they couldn't promise anything. But in all their considered opinions, if Touch the Fire ran before then, the race could be her last.

"Don't you worry, Miz Briar," Gillie said sleepily, as if he had read her thoughts. "I'm here now, and if you need her to, she'll do what she has to for you."

She wasn't sure what to say. "Well, we'll see, Gillie. . . ."

He looked at her one last time before he fell into a heavy, blank sleep. "She's got it in her, Miz Briar," he said. "Jus' like you . . . like Miz Marguerite before you . . . she's a champion. If you ask, she'll race again. And she'll win."

She was beginning to feel exasperated. How could he be so sure? "Gillie—"

"I knows, Miz Briar," he said, beginning to drift off. "I knows."

As he fell asleep, Briar stood there a moment and watched him. Did he really know more than she and all her experts did—or was he just an old drunk, as Stefan had said so many times? Maybe he did sense something; maybe he had another instinct that none of them were aware of because he'd spent so many years around horses and seen so many things. As scornful as he'd been about this old man, even Stefan had admitted Gillie had a healing gift, and from what she had seen herself, she knew it was true. But how great a gift was it?

Hoping she wouldn't have to find out, she quietly switched off the light and tiptoed out. It was late, and after all the day's emotional swings—selling the company, saying good-bye to old friends, having Gillie come back—she was exhausted. But she couldn't leave without checking on the horses, and with Irish and Mi Flor Amor out at pasture, she went through the barn, stopping first to say hello to Night Fever, who *would* be racing this year after her long layoff, and then moving on to her beautiful Incandessence.

"Hello, girl," she murmured. The bay mare's ears pricked at the sound of her voice, and she came immediately to the stall bars and thrust her nose out. No longer the high-strung, nervous racehorse, impending motherhood had softened her tense edges, and she looked rounder and fuller and very content. Briar knew without a doubt that the foal she was carrying would be a champion, just like its mother, and its father, Aubergine, who two years ago had won the English version of the Triple Crown.

As always, the last horse she went to look in on was Touch the Fire. She kept the hot-tempered filly in a double-box stall at one end of the barn, and as she finished her inspection of the other horses and finally headed in that direction, she heard a soft nicker and smiled. Temperamental as this horse might be, she always recognized Briar's footsteps and greeted her.

"Hi, girl," Briar murmured, shoving open the stall door and going inside.

As was their custom, she waited until the filly came up to her and nuzzled her hand, then she smiled again as she stroked the soft muzzle. With no one else in the world was Touch the Fire so gentle. People who had seen the high-spirited horse fling grooms in one direction or another at the racetrack's saddling enclosure would have been stunned to see her stand quietly like this while Briar stood so close. Anyone who had felt the power underneath them as they exercised or raced her would have been equally amazed at the sight of Briar burying her face now in the filly's neck—and to see Touch the Fire bend down to snuffle the nape of her owner. Even Gillie, who could handle the hot-tempered horse better than anyone except Stefan, would have been transfixed at the sight of the woman and her horse standing quietly in the stall. Briar was unaware of what people might think. The past few weeks had been such a strain that she was trying to gather strength.

She hadn't been able to explain it, but she had never felt such a kinship with a horse—not even with Irish. It wasn't because her judgment about the filly had been vindicated, or that she owned a horse that had already made a mark for herself at the track. She would never have said so to anyone, even to Stefan, but she . . . loved . . . this horse. Touch the Fire symbolized everything that was wonderful and powerful and good in her life. She represented the struggle Briar herself had endured, growing up alone and unwanted in the orphanage, being on her own at such a young age, knowing that no one was going to help her, and that if she were ever going to succeed, she had to do it on her own. The horse made a tiny, cramped room with the cracked ceiling at the Y seem less significant, and the nights Briar had fallen asleep over her homework after working two shifts at the diner ceased to matter. Touch the Fire was the reward for all the sacrifice, all the sorrow, all her suffering; and as she hugged the warm, glossy black neck and the filly blew a breath on her cheek, Briar felt she *had* touched the fire. Because of what this gallant black horse had given her, nothing would ever be the same.

At last, spying a wisp of alfalfa she'd missed during dinner, the filly moved away, and Briar gave her a last pat and went outside to the car again. The moon had come up during the time she'd spent in the barn, and in the silvery light she could make out the silhouettes of Irish and Mi Flor Amor up on the hill of their pasture. Just to see if he still remembered that she had once trained him to come to her signal, she whistled softly and was rewarded when Irish's head snapped up from his grazing and he looked toward her.

So, she thought with a smile, he hasn't forgotten, the old rogue. It had been a game between them; when she came down the aisle at the riding club, she always whistled to let him know she was coming, and he would immediately go to the door and whicker impatiently and start to paw, demanding to be let out and saddled.

How simple it was then, she thought with a sigh, turning away from the gate. She didn't expect him to come now; lately, having found companionship with Mi Flor Amor, both geldings had become very independent. If she wanted to ride, she and Jaime had to spread out and sort of funnel the two horses down to the gate so she could get a halter on one, after which the other would follow.

But Irish needed no such encouragement tonight, it seemed. He whinnied softly as she turned away, and when she looked back, she saw he was trotting toward her, Mi Flor Amor not far behind. Irish was cantering by the time he reached the gate, pulling up melodramatically just before it looked like he might crash through.

"You old show-off," she scolded fondly, giving his forelock a tug when he put his head over the fence. Mi Flor Amor was right behind, butting in, wanting to be petted, too. She was just rubbing his face when headlights behind her swept the driveway. Because she hadn't seen Stefan's truck when she pulled in, she thought it was him, and she turned, intending to wave. Then she saw the black Bentley heading up the drive toward the house, and she froze. She recognized the car, of course, but as she stood there watching, she wondered why Rupert Jaeger had come, uninvited, at this late hour.

Forgetting the horses, she went to her own car and climbed in. But her hand started to shake when she tried to insert the key in the ignition, and she had to take a hard grip on herself. She knew Rupert hadn't come to be sociable, and she suspected that tonight was going to be some kind of showdown. Her heart beginning to beat fast, she looked in the direction of Stefan's house. The place was dark and deserted, and suddenly she felt angry. The one time she needed him! she thought unfairly, and she managed to start the car this time. Whipping the Mercedes around, she followed the Bentley up the drive to the house.

Rupert was waiting for her on the porch as she pulled to a stop. When she saw Carl standing there with him, she felt even more aggravated. Getting out of the car, she slammed the door and said rudely, "What do you want?"

Rupert didn't waste words. "We came to make you a proposition."

"You could have called first."

"We took the chance you would be home."

"You also took the chance I'd be willing to speak to you."

"Oh, I think you'll want to listen to what we have to say."

"Don't be too sure," she said, but she unlocked the front door and let them in. As she had learned very young, better the enemy you know than the one you don't. . . . It seemed especially appropriate in Rupert's case.

Switching on lights, she led them into the living room where she turned to face them without offering any hospitality. "All right. I'm listening."

"Do you mind if we sit down?" Carl asked.

She looked at him coldly. "Yes, I do. You won't be staying long."

"It doesn't matter," Rupert said, before Carl could get them more off track. Turning to Briar, he said, "I came because I recently discovered a discrepancy."

"If it involves what's left of Lord Industries," she said icily, "you should take it up with our attorneys."

"This has nothing to do with your husband's soon-to-be-defunct company," Rupert said calmly. "I'm talking about Touch the Fire."

Despite herself, Briar felt a cold stab of dread. She knew what Rupert was capable of, and she wouldn't put past him any malignancy. Her lips stiff, she said, "What about her?"

"What about her," Carl said, his expression ugly, "is she belongs to us."

Jerkily, Briar turned to him. Then she looked back at Rupert. This was too much, even for someone named Jaeger, she thought, and snapped, "That's ridiculous. Get out."

"I thought you might feel that way," Rupert said. "But if compelled, we can present proof."

She looked at him with contempt. "And just how do you intend to do that? I bought Touch the Fire at the Keeneland Sale. I have the papers to prove it."

"Do you?" Rupert asked calmly.

"Of course I do!" she said, exasperated. She didn't know what he was getting at, and she didn't care. She just wanted them to get out and leave her alone.

"Perhaps you'd better examine those papers more closely, then," Rupert suggested.

"I don't have to examine them. They're duly registered by the Jockey Club."

"Which, unfortunately, has always been under the impression that Touch the Fire's great-great granddam, Flame, was able to produce a registerable foal for anyone but Mondragon Stud." He shrugged, a malicious glint in his eye. "I'm so sorry, but after reviewing all the records we've kept over the years, I suddenly realized that my father made a ghastly mistake when he sent Flame off to war after Fane. I do believe there was some kind of mix-up at the time. You see, Flame was a bay mare with no markings, and it seems . . . well, we did have a similar bay mare at the time called Flamma. Wouldn't it be confusing if the mares and their papers got switched? You can see how . . . complicated it would make things.''

"It might, if that's what happened!" Briar said angrily. "You can't possibly hope to pull this off!"

"Probably not," Rupert said easily. "But we do have all that terrible confusion during the war in our favor, I remember. Things were so . . . feverish then. It would be an understandable mistake."

"It's not understandable at all!" Briar cried in a fury. Her heart was pounding so hard that she thought she might faint. She felt dizzy and sick, and she couldn't believe this was happening. Could he do it? she wondered, and wished she could get to the phone to call Spence. She didn't think it was possible, but with the way lawyers manipulated the court system these days. . . .

Her eyes blazing, she flung back her head. "What do you want, Rupert?" she demanded. "Do you want Touch the Fire? Well, you're not going to get her. I'll fight you; I'll fight you with everything I have. So, call your lawyers. Go to court. It's all the same to me!"

"Is it?" he asked, apparently unmoved by her outburst. "Remember, I can tie up ownership of this filly for years, if I like. After which time, her racing career will certainly be finished . . . as will the hope of her becoming a broodmare of any value at all." He shrugged, as if it didn't matter to him. "It's your choice, of course."

Briar thought for a moment that she would kill him. She'd been too angry before to think this through to its horrible logical conclusion, but now she realized what Rupert said was true. He could have them in court for years if he wished. Would he really do it? Without a qualm, she thought. This was child's play after what he had done in the past. What would stop a man who had cold-bloodedly murdered his own father after raping her own great-aunt?

"You're insane," she said. "You'll never get away with it."

He laughed. "You'd be surprised at what I can get away with, Ms. McKenna," he said smugly. Then his smile vanished. "Don't try me on this."

If she'd had any doubts left, they were gone now. She knew that she was truly in the presence of evil. Even Carl was silent, struck by something in his father's tone. Clenching her hands into fists, she said, "I won't let you have her, Rupert. No matter what it takes, I won't let you have her."

His pale eyes looked like bits of gray glass. "There is another way."

She knew he was talking about the match race, but even though she could feel the net closing inexorably around her, she wasn't ready to give up yet. Years of living on her own had given her the strength to face up to bullies, to beat them at their own game—or at least not flinch. After all, she had had the best lessons in how life really was lived, first in the orphanage, then later, on her own in the streets. The Y had been in a bad part of town, and even in those days, she'd had to step over drunks and addicts lying around when she came home from school or work. She'd had to protect her books and her purse and her body itself from thieves looking for money for their next fix.

She might be scared of Rupert—and rightfully so—and frightened of what he might do, but she wasn't going to show it. It would be a fatal mistake.

"Yes, there is another way," she said, her voice steely. "We *could* go to court. But not to prove whether Touch the Fire belongs to you or me. We could put you on trial. How would you like that?"

"I?" he said.

"You," she bore down. Looking him straight in the eye, she said, "As far as I know, there's no statute of limitations on murder, Rupert."

She had the satisfaction of seeing him flinch. But he was more a master than she at this game, and he recovered instantly. "I don't know what you're talking about."

"Oh, I think you do," she said. "Surely not even you can forget the day your father was shot at the summerhouse."

She was sure she'd seen a flash of fear in his eyes. "I remember it very well," he replied. "That was when your great-aunt Juliet was—"

"Raped by you," she said, advancing on him.

"That's a lie!" he exclaimed angrily, as Carl gave him a strange look. He saw his son staring at him, and he gestured wildly. "Don't believe her; she doesn't know—"

She took another step. "I know you killed your father," she said, holding his cold eyes.

Carl looked stunned. "You killed grandfather?" he whispered.

"No!" Rupert shouted. "It was Juliet!"

"It wasn't Juliet," Briar said inexorably. "You forget. There was a witness, a boy named Gillie. A little black boy, terrified out of his wits. But Gillie is a man now, and he remembers everything that day. Everything, Rupert. So—"

He astonished her by uttering a genuine laugh. "*That's* your proof?" he said delightedly. "An old drunk who barely knows his name, much less what day it is? I understand he disappeared some time ago, but if you can find him, I'd love to hear what he has to say! If you can sober him up long enough, that is!"

"I'm sure the police will take a different view," she said coldly, but inside she was shaken. How could he laugh? Was he so sure of himself that even an eyewitness to his appalling crimes didn't upset him?

Apparently it didn't, for he looked at her delightedly again. "Do you really think anyone will take that crazy old man seriously?" he asked. "Or, better yet, if anyone were so foolishly inclined, would he be able to get his story straight, or hold up under cross-examination? Even if he could stumble through, who do you think a jury would believe—me or him? No, Ms. McKenna, if you're going to threaten me, you should have better ammunition."

Briar refused to be beaten. She felt a rage building inside her, a terrible anger for all the pain and suffering and hurt this man had caused her family, all the members of it, until their deaths. He'd gotten away with everything so far; all these years he'd been on air, sure of his power to win, to intimidate, to do as he pleased. But no more, she thought, no more. She was the last Caulfield, the only one left who could fight him as he deserved to be fought. She despised him for what he was and for what he had done, and in that moment she didn't want just to bring him down; she wanted to *destroy* him.

"All right," she said, her voice as cold as her heart, "let's stop playing games here, Rupert. You came for a reason tonight, and it wasn't to say you could take me to court over my horse. Why don't you tell me right now just what it is you do want."

His eyes narrowed, reminding her of a snake underwater. "You know what I want, Ms. McKenna," he said silkily. But with each word his voice suddenly rose, until he was shouting. "I want you off this ranch. I want you out of racing. I want every last Caulfield ever *born* out of my life forever!"

"I see," she said, unimpressed. With relief, she realized she was no longer afraid of him. And why? she wondered. Because some part of her had always known if she didn't accept his challenge, she'd never forgive herself. *It's all coming full circle now, great-grandmother, isn't it?* she thought, and she felt an answering surge of power within her. As she had told herself in the barn earlier tonight with her arms around her black horse, everything had been leading her toward this moment, and if she didn't seize it, she'd never know peace. Her great-grandmother had sacrificed everything for this ranch; so had her great-aunt, Juliet. Even her own mother had paid a high price. She couldn't do any less.

She thought of her gallant filly down in the barn, and then of Touch the Fire's great-great grandsire, Fane, who had courageously run his own race. *Are you willing to run for me, girl?* she wondered, and knew, with conviction, that, as Gillie had said tonight, the horse would do as she asked. *But would it be enough?* she wondered. And then, chillingly, *Would it be too much?* She didn't have the answer.

Oh, *God!*, she thought in angry despair, and then looked her enemy right in the face. The moment was now, and she had to take it.

With Carl still standing there silently, looking sick and shocked and stunned at what had been said, she lifted her head and spoke directly to Rupert, whom she hated at the moment with all her heart. "My great-grandmother didn't give in to you, nor did Juliet, and I've no intention of surrendering, either. I'll agree to the match race on one condition."

Rupert's eyes had begun to gleam at her acceptance; he immediately looked cautious. "What condition is that?"

"We both know if I race my filly, it could be her last race." Despite herself, her voice broke at the thought of how much she could lose. But she lifted her head and went on. "So the stakes here are very high."

"And you think I should match."

Contempt flared in her eyes, quickly disguised. "You say

you're a gambler, Mr. Jaeger," she said. "Well, let's see just how much of a gambler you are."

As she had anticipated, he couldn't resist the challenge. If he beat her at a higher stakes game than he'd planned, his victory would be that much sweeter, so she wasn't surprised when he said, "Go on. Name your price."

"Father . . ." Carl said nervously.

Neither paid any attention to him. Holding Rupert's cold gaze, Briar said, "Once before when a match race was held between our two ranches, the winner had his choice of the other's stock—"

Disdain gleamed in Rupert's eyes. He had expected more. "Ah, you want the same wager."

"No," she said evenly. "This time, I think it should be winner take all."

"Er . . . Father . . . Briar!" Carl said, sounding a little panicked. He turned to Briar. "Just what do you mean, winner take all? What does that mean, exactly?" He turned back to his father. "Don't you think we should talk about this?"

Briar barely glanced at him. She took a step toward Rupert, her hands clenched so tight her knuckles were white. Holding Rupert's pale eyes, she said, "If Touch the Fire wins, you'll back off—completely, without question. You'll sign over Lord Industries to me again; you'll drop this lawsuit about owning my filly; and you'll give up trying to take my land or my horses or anything I own. In other words, you'll *leave me the hell alone*. Those are my terms. Accept or not."

A cold little smile played on Rupert's face. They both knew the terrible chance Briar was taking with her filly. "And if she loses?" he asked.

Briar's chin came up. She looked imperious at that moment, gallant, undefeated. Without a quaver, she said, "If she loses, I'll give you Caulfield Farm."

Despite himself, Rupert's eyes widened slightly. "I salute you, Ms. McKenna. You have courage."

"So did my great-grandmother," she said. "So did Juliet, and Ariana. Does that mean you accept?"

"Father!" Carl wailed. "Do you know how much money we have tied up in that deal with Lord Industries? Not to mention—"

"Shut up, Carl," Rupert said. "And go start the car. We've got a match race to get ready for." He turned to Briar with a cold, evil smile. "Since you accepted the challenge, you may set the date."

"Two months from now, Mr. Jaeger," she said, knowing how Wayne would scream. But she couldn't think of him now, nor Stefan's reaction. "You name the time and the place."

"My trainer will be in touch," Rupert said, but Briar didn't miss the wild look of triumph that flashed across his pale, ascetic face as he bowed to her. She didn't show them the way out.

---

## CHAPTER THIRTY-FOUR

Briar managed to wait until she heard the sound of the Bentley pulling away before she sank onto the couch and put her head in her hands. But then, as she fought rising panic, she heard another car approaching, coming fast. Bolting upright again, she just had time to look out the window and see Stefan taking the steps two at a time before he burst in through the front door.

"I saw Jaeger's Bentley going out the gates," he said, gasping for breath. "Are you all right?"

At this point, now that she'd flung her gauntlet down, she wasn't sure she would ever be right again. She didn't want to tell him, but she couldn't put it off; he had to know sooner or later. She said, "I accepted the match race, Stefan. Just now. Tonight."

For a long moment, he just stared at her. Then, his voice strangled, he said, "No . . . you didn't."

"I did. I had no choice."

"Yes, you did!" he said, more agitated than she had ever seen him. "You did! Damn it, Briar! I thought we agreed to talk about this before—"

How could she explain? It was all tied up with her great-grandparents, and her great-aunt Juliet, and the mother and father she had never known, and the . . . the history of this place, the house she was standing in, the land it was built on. "I know," she said, feeling guilty and justified at the same time. "I know I promised I wouldn't do anything rash—"

"Rash! This is insane! Do you realize what you've done?"

She flinched. She knew all too well. "It gets worse."

"Worse! How much worse could it get?"

She made herself say it; she had to, so that she'd know it was real herself. "I bet it all, Stefan. I told him that if I won, he had to leave me alone—stop hounding me about this place, give me back Lord Industries . . . everything."

He couldn't have looked more stunned than if she'd said she had signed up her filly to be the first horse in space. "And . . . and if he wins?"

"He won't."

"But if he does?"

She thought she'd be able to say it without feeling panic set in. She'd been wrong. "If he does, he . . . he gets Caulfield Farm."

"*What?*"

"Well, I couldn't help it," she said. "He was threatening to take me to court over ownership, and I had to do *something.*"

"You didn't have to do *this!*"

"I did, I did," she cried, wanting him to understand when she wasn't sure she understood at the moment herself. "You don't know, Stefan! You weren't here!"

"No, I was—" he started to say, but then he stopped. "Never mind that. When is the race?"

"Two months from now."

He closed his eyes. "I don't believe it. All this, and you don't even know if she'll be ready to run. If she even can—"

"Gillie says she will be."

"*Gillie!* Gillie hasn't been here in months!"

"He came back tonight," she said, realizing it sounded weak. "We had a long talk."

"Oh, and I suppose *he* told you she was racing fit—he, who's probably been spending all this time passed out in some flophouse dead drunk!" He was so agitated he came forward and took her by the shoulders. "My God, Briar, what's the matter with you? Do you realize what you've done?"

She knew what she had done; she was much more agonizingly aware of it than he ever could be. But the accusation in his eyes, the pain, the hurt, were too much to bear right now.

She couldn't attend to his injured feelings when she felt so panicked and desperate herself. "Yes, I know. Now, let it go, all right? It's done!"

"I can't let it go!" he said, his fingers tightening on her arms. "Jesus Christ, woman! Couldn't you even discuss it with me? I thought we meant something to each other!"

"We do! But it . . . it wasn't your decision! Stefan, please try to understand—"

"No, no, I can't understand! You bet your entire ranch—your entire *future* on one single race, and you don't even think you have to *talk* about it with me? God, I don't believe it!"

"I'm sorry. There wasn't time. It all happened so fast—"

He dropped his hands from her arms. "No, that's not it," he said. "You didn't trust me. You don't trust anybody but yourself. But damn it!" He turned away from her, running both hands through his hair before he shoved them in his pockets for control. "If only you'd asked me, you wouldn't have to . . . you wouldn't have to . . ." He turned back toward her, his face a white mask. "If only you'd asked me! I could have helped!"

She felt almost at the end of her her endurance. She knew he'd be upset, but she couldn't understand exactly why he was talking like this. "How?" she demanded, her voice shrill. "How could you have helped?"

He looked furious and sick at the same time. "I had him right where I wanted him, that's how! After tonight, I could have forced his hand!"

"What are you talking about? You're not making sense!"

He took a deep breath. "Then does this? I would have been able to stop him because after tonight I could have proven that *I'm* the rightful heir to Mondragon. *That's* what I'm talking about!"

Briar's first thought was that with all the stress and strain and emotional storms she had endured today, she just hadn't heard him right. "What . . . did you say?"

"Oh, bloody hell, I can't believe this!" he muttered. "If only you'd waited—"

"Well, I didn't wait!" she cried in sudden fury. "I didn't wait! How did I know I should have? How do I know now? You haven't told me a goddamned thing!"

So, finally, now that it was too late, he told her about the marriage certificate he'd found in his grandmother's attic after she had died. He told her about the stories his great-grandmother had passed down about the fine rich man she had married so many years ago in far-away California, when she had been a maid in a San Francisco hotel and a drunken dandy named Heinrich Jaeger had cried on her breast about being jilted. He told her about how Flossie had married this fine man, who had sent her away after only three days when he finally regained his senses. He told her about how Heinrich had paid for Flossie's baby—Heinrich's firstborn son, whom she had named Rudy—Stefan's grandfather—with the stipulation that she never see or try to contact him again.

Briar didn't know what to say. "And she agreed to it all?"

"She was an ignorant girl, far from home. What did she know? What else could she have done?"

Chastened, she sat back. "Go on."

There wasn't much more. Rudy had been married to Nona, the grandmother who had raised Stefan. Long ago, he'd made a promise to her to try to meet the Jaeger branch of the family after she died. She'd had some foolish notion that once he was all alone, they would welcome him as a long-lost relative. And after he'd found the certificates that proved the stories he'd heard all his life *were* true, and not some figment of Nona's imagination, he had decided to honor his promise and come to America to meet them. He hadn't wanted anything at the time; he was just going to introduce himself.

But the Jaeger family hadn't welcomed him at all, and even though he'd assured them that he never intended to make any claims, Rupert especially had reacted with such hostility that Stefan had begun to suspect something more was at stake than the possible claims of some long-lost relative. The more he learned about Rupert, the more he realized he'd stumbled onto something. He'd taken another look at the marriage certificate he'd found, and after some digging through the local archives, had discovered the most interesting thing of all. Heinrich had not only legally married Stefan's great-grandmother after a three-day binge at that San Francisco hotel, he had neglected to divorce her after sending her away. That meant his subsequent marriage to Mariel had been bigamous, and therefore, any issue from that union was illegitimate. In the eyes of the law, Stefan's grandfather Rudy had been the right heir to the Mondragon empire.

"My God," Briar said, when he had finished. "That means—"

"I'm next in line," Stefan finished, looking thoroughly miserable instead of ecstatic as he should have been. "But even then, I wouldn't have done anything about it if he hadn't started threatening you. And tonight when Charlotte called me and I went to meet her—"

"You met with Charlotte!"

"It wasn't what you think. She was so upset about her father taking control of Mondragon Stud away from her that when she couldn't fight him alone, she needed an ally. Naturally, she thought of me."

"Naturally," Briar said, her voice strange.

Stefan didn't notice her tone. "Yes, well, anyway, when we met tonight she gave me the last piece of proof I needed—an authorized copy of my grandfather's birth certificate. Flossie had sent it to Heinrich after their son Rudy was born—along with a letter thanking him for sending money for the child. That copy of the birth certificate is the only one in existence; I tried to track down the original after my grandmother died, but it was among some hospital records that were destroyed in the war."

"I see."

"She'd had the copy all this time, but when she gave it to me, I—" He stopped abruptly, finally alerted by her expression. She had been sitting on the arm of the couch during his recital, but when she got to her feet, he stood with her, sensing disaster. "Briar, what is it?"

He had never seen her so angry. "Now I see," she said, her eyes beginning to blaze with fury. "It was all a trick!"

He didn't know what she was talking about. "A trick? What do you mean, a trick?"

She stepped back from him as if he were something she had found under a rock. "Oh, how could I have been so stupid?" she muttered, more to herself than him. "How could I have let my feelings—" Abruptly she turned her back to him. "Get out," she said. "Just get out."

He felt totally confused. "What? Why?"

She whirled toward him again. "Why? *Why?* After what you did, you dare ask me *why*?" she cried angrily. "All this time I thought it was coincidence you came here, a happy accident that you were free when I needed a ranch manager. A miracle that you . . . that you cared for me! But it was all planned, wasn't it? It was all part of some stupid game you were involved in to—''

He was appalled. The thing he'd feared most was happening right before his eyes. He had to make her understand; he had to make her see that it hadn't turned out the way he'd planned at all. Reaching for her arm, he said, ''What are you saying? It wasn't like—''

She jerked her arm away. For an instant, he thought she might strike him. ''You didn't know when you came to work for me that you were related to Rupert Jaeger and his clan?''

He couldn't lie to her, not at this point. Wishing to hell he'd just told the truth when he'd had the chance, he said desperately, ''Well, sure, I did. But—''

''And you hadn't already gone to see him before we met?''

''Yes, yes, I had,'' he said, feeling as if he were sinking in quicksand. Even to him, it sounded weak. ''But that d—''

''Then why didn't you tell me?'' she cried. ''You knew what he was trying to do to me! Why weren't you honest? Why did you have to keep it a goddamned *secret*!''

''I don't know,'' he said miserably. ''I don't—''

Her voice started to shake with rage. ''That's not good enough, Stefan! It's bad enough I find out you're related to a man who declared himself my sworn enemy even before I met him, now I discover you—''

''It's not my fault I'm related to the man! For God's sake—''

She wouldn't listen. ''Rupert Jaeger has vowed to destroy me; he's done everything in his power to try. And now I find that all this time . . .'' She was so angry she could hardly speak. Closing her eyes briefly, she summoned every ounce of self-control. ''And all this time, you never told me what you knew, Stefan. You never told me who you really were!''

''Yes, I did, I did tell you,'' he said, knowing he was fighting a losing battle, wanting to reach out and take her in his arms, but not daring to move. ''I'm Stefan Yager; that hasn't changed. Rupert Jaeger is nothing to me. I never wanted anything that was his; I swear it. I never would have even pursued it if he hadn't started threatening you! Briar, please, you have to believe me!''

''I don't have to believe a thing you say! You lied to me, Stefan! But worst of all, you betrayed my trust! And to think

I actually thought I was in love with you! It's so pitiful, I could cry!''

"Briar, please listen. I never intended to—"

"It doesn't matter! It doesn't matter what you intended, only what happened!"

"No, no, that's not true. Briar, please listen—"

"I don't want to listen. I want you to get out. Get all your things and go!"

"You don't know what you're saying. I know you're upset, but if we could just talk ab—"

"We're done talking, Stefan! I never want to see you, or speak to you, or hear from you again! Is that clear? Now get your things and get off this ranch. Now. Tonight!"

He hesitated a moment, wondering if he should try once more. But one look at her blazing green eyes and her face white with anger, and he knew how futile it would be.

"All right," he said, not wanting to make things worse. Although, he wondered, how much worse could they be? "All right, I'll go. But I'd like to say one more thing before I do."

Her jaw was tight. "Not that it matters, but what?"

"Don't do this match race, Briar. You won't win. The filly isn't ready—"

"Oh, this is too much! You're advising *me* about what to do when you've lied and cheated and pretended to be someone you weren't! What gall!"

His eyes flashed at that, but he held on to his control. "It doesn't matter what you think of me," he said quietly. "What I'm telling you is for the horse's best interests."

"Well, it's too late now."

"It doesn't have to be."

"I told you, I've already accepted."

"Well, then *un*accept it! This isn't written in stone, Briar. You don't know what could happen!"

"I'm very aware of what could happen, Stefan. But unlike you, Touch the Fire will do her best for me."

"That's not fair!"

"That's too bad! And Gillie says she'll be ready to run when she's asked!"

"Gillie! Gillie! I think if I hear that name once more I'm going to go mad! You can't possibly be thinking of betting everything you have on the judgment of an old drunk!"

"That old drunk," she said between her teeth, "is more

loyal to me than *you* ever were. We've seen that, haven't we? Good-bye, Stefan. Close the door on your way out."

He hesitated a moment, loathe to leave it like this, but not knowing what else to do. "Good-bye, Briar," he said. "I wish . . . I wish this hadn't happened. Maybe when we've had some time—"

"There isn't time enough in the *world* for me to forgive you for this, Stefan Yager! Good-bye. And don't come back!"

Briar didn't even cry after he had gone; her pain was too deep for tears. Oh, how could he have done this to her? she wondered mournfully. How could he have betrayed her like this? If she hadn't heard him admit it, she would never have believed he could have done such a thing. As she stood alone in her living room, in a silence that still vibrated with echoes of all the angry, hurtful words that had been flung about tonight, she put her hands over her face. To think that she had thought herself in love with him. To think that she had given him her trust! She felt like a fool.

Wondering if she would ever recover from the wound he had dealt her, she went out onto the porch. She knew she wouldn't be able to sleep the rest of the night, and she sat down wearily in the swing she'd had put up at one end of the porch. So many thoughts were whirling without pattern in her brain that she had a fierce headache, and when she felt a tentative touch on her leg, she looked down with a start, and then nearly sobbed when she saw the little barn cat she had rescued sitting at her feet. The mama cat never came up to the house. She'd always been far too shy, and Briar didn't know why she had appeared tonight, but she was too grateful to question it. She was in need of the comfort the little animal could offer, and as she scooped the tiny brown cat up onto her lap and it began to purr, she felt tears in her eyes. Another of the orphans she had rescued, she thought, remembering what Stefan had once said. Suddenly Briar did start to weep.

"Oh, Cocoa," she said, burying her face in the thick brown fur. "Everything is such a mess!"

The little cat just purred even more mightily, and after a while wriggled around to settle herself in a tiny ball in Briar's lap. Briar sat there for hours, thinking of everything: Hay, Jaz, Fredrica, Spence . . . Stefan, her great-grandparents, Mondragon Enterprises, the present, the past. . . .

What the future might bring she wasn't sure, and as the sky

began to lighten and the birds began to rustle in the bushes, she realized with surprise that she had sat there all night. Cocoa left to find her breakfast, and Briar was just thinking about getting up herself when a horse neighed from one of the pastures, and another answered from one of the paddocks. Caulfield Farm was coming to life for another day, and as she looked soberly down at the showpiece of the ranch, the big main barn, she imagined Touch the Fire was pacing her stall, eager to get out. On that gallant heart rested her entire future, Briar thought, and closed her eyes.

"Well, great-grandmother," she said, "we're going for broke again. I hope to God it's for the last time."

She was just getting up, stiff from sitting for so long when she felt a sudden light early morning breeze. It blew a little dust devil right across the porch, and as Briar looked at it, she could have sworn she heard a ghost of a confident, merry laugh.

---

# CHAPTER THIRTY-FIVE

The day of the much-publicized and highly touted match race between Briar's black filly and Mondragon Stud's Galland—the "Queen of the Track and the Bolt of the Decade" as the pundits persisted in calling the two horses—dawned warm and relatively clear in Arcadia. As Briar walked with Wayne and Gillie and two other handlers up to the saddling enclosure before the sixth race, which had been designated for the match, she wondered how she was going to get through the next hour. Like her stable sister Incandessence, Touch the Fire had made a triumphant return, taking faultlessly to Wayne's careful training, responding better than even Briar could have wished. As soon as she set foot on Santa Anita Racetrack after her long absence, the black filly acted like she had come home again, and even Wayne had grudgingly said she might make it. But training was one thing; racing was another.

When Briar looked at her beautiful black horse, who was almost dancing up the path on the way to the receiving barn, she had faith. Touch the Fire had known since dawn from the change in her schedule that she was going to run. As the morning went on, she had become more difficult, baring her teeth at her grooms, laying back her ears at Kara, who had come to give her a final pre-race check, even aiming a mock kick at Wayne when he went in to take her temperature and run his hands prayerfully down her legs for the last time. Then, at one o'clock, when she heard the beginning notes from the bugler calling the horses onto the track for the first race, the filly's entire manner changed. She suddenly became calm, almost remote, her large, luminous eyes fixed on some distant point. Wayne had described the expression as the look of eagles, but to Briar, who knew her so well, she saw fire burning in her filly's blue-brown eyes, and she knew her horse was ready to do what she had been born to do, what she did best. She knew, too, that she had made the only decision she could have made. She had done what she had to; the rest was up to her horse.

"I hope to God we're doing the right thing," Wayne muttered beside her as they followed the filly and her entourage up to the track. Gillie was proudly leading the horse, and he turned just then to grin broadly at Briar, who smiled back.

"It's right," she said to Wayne. "Trust me."

He muttered something under his breath. He'd had Touch the Fire for the past two months, ever since Briar had called and asked if he'd train her for the match race. They'd had some words, but Briar had prevailed simply because she said she'd made up her mind. Since then, even at his gloomiest, Wayne admitted that she was now as ready to run as she ever would be, but he hadn't been happy bringing her back so soon after her injury. Like so many others, he had argued in vain to rest the filly until the following year, but Briar couldn't wait.

"It's not only foolish, it's downright stupid to bet this filly's entire future on a race she probably won't win," Wayne had claimed. "What does Stefan feel about it?"

"Stefan is no longer with Caulfield Farm," Briar had answered, in a tone that indicated the subject was closed. "Now, do you want to train her or not?"

Wayne had been around a long time; he had trained a lot of good horses, two Derby winners and three who had placed in the Preakness and the Belmont. He'd had more stakes winners in his barn than any other trainer of his age and experience, and he knew a good horse when he saw one. But Touch the Fire hadn't merely been good; she was that one horse in a lifetime—a true champion, a special creature who not only makes a mark but touches a heart. Like so many others, he was afraid that if this race didn't kill her, it would ruin her forever, and he couldn't understand why Briar was taking such a chance. But if she was hellbent on doing it, he was going to see that she was ready, and so he had accepted.

But Briar still saw the worry on his face as they walked up to the receiving barn the day of the race, and because he'd been more than a trainer to her—a friend as well—she wished she could tell him the real story. She could say that she felt the filly would not only win, but would race again.

Wayne wanted to believe her, but experience sadly told him otherwise. Wordlessly, she put her hand on his arm, and when he glanced at her, she tried to smile through her own increasing tension. She knew that if nothing went wrong, her horse would win. It was just that so much could go wrong.

"It'll be all right," she said. "I know it will."

Muttering something in response, he looked sourly ahead. They were just coming onto the path that led to the receiving barn, where both horses would be checked by the horse identifier against the official registration papers before they went on to be saddled. Usually the saddling took place in the building that also housed the jockey's room, but with so many racegoers eager to see the two great horses, today they'd be saddled in the walking ring.

The Mondragon people were already inside the ring that was encircled by a wrought-iron fence to keep eager spectators out of the way. Rupert and Carl barely glanced in Briar's direction when she and her entourage came in, and she certainly didn't intend to seek them out, either, but she noticed immediately that Charlotte wasn't present. She forgot to wonder why; she was too busy looking at Galland. She had seen the big Mondragon colt before, but not this closely. With her tightening nerves, it seemed that he'd grown even bigger since she had watched his lightning-fast morning work the other day. When she glanced at her own filly, she tried not to quiver. Despite her feminine appearance and dainty manner, Touch the Fire wasn't a small mare, but this year Galland had put on both weight and substance, and to Briar he looked so strong and powerful and *fit* she felt her spirits plummet. As if to underscore his readiness, the colt suddenly let out a shrill neighing challenge that seemed to reverberate throughout the entire racecourse, provoking an approving murmur from the people standing nearby.

But if Galland's challenge was meant to inspire fear in his equine opponent, he was a failure. Her small ears pricked, Touch the Fire merely glanced over at him. Then, like a queen dismissing a peon, she haughtily turned her glossy black hindquarters. Seeing the gesture, the spectators laughed, and Briar found herself smiling shakily. If the filly wasn't worried, why should she be?

But that was easier said than done, of course, especially when she realized that Galland's jockey, the highly regarded Roland Dermont, who was wearing Mondragon's red and black silks, had emerged from the jockey's room behind them.

"Where's Pat Shannon?" she murmured to Wayne, who was occupied with checking the filly's girth. The black horse was running as she always did, with the minimum of equipment, whereas for this race, Galland was fitted with blinkers. His hand on the girth buckle, Wayne glanced at her. He hadn't approved of her choice of jockey because Pat hadn't been racing well this season. The situation with Touch the Fire seemed to have shaken his confidence, and he hadn't been the same rider since. But Briar felt she owed it to Pat to put him up again, and she had argued and pleaded until Wayne had reluctantly given in.

"Might as well," he'd growled, "since this whole thing is going to be a circus anyway."

But when Wayne realized now that despite her outward calm, Briar wasn't as serene as she pretended, he relented. "He's got a few minutes yet," he told her. "If he doesn't come soon, I'll send Gillie after him."

She gave him a relieved look. Although they were surrounded by people looking, pointing, commenting, laughing, calculating, gesturing, conferring, arguing, she hardly heard the babble of sound. She was intent only on her trainer. She hadn't told him how indebted she was for all he had done, and she put her hand on his arm.

"Wayne, no matter how the race comes out, I want you to know how grateful I am you've gone along with me on this," she said quietly. She glanced toward the filly's head, where

Gillie, pleased at being included, was fussily adjusting the bridle. Then she looked into Wayne's eyes again. "And I appreciate your letting Gillie participate. It means a lot to him. And for Pat, too, allowing him to ride. I know you think he's lost his confidence."

Wayne wasn't a demonstrative man, but despite the crowd that surrounded them, watching their every move, he took her hand. "It's how I feel about you that counts" he said gruffly. "I respect you, Briar. I always have. You know what you're doing, and you know horses. I figure you got your reasons for today—reasons none of us knows about, and maybe shouldn't. But I know you wouldn't ask something like this of your filly unless it was damned important—damned important," he repeated. He paused for a moment. "I owe you, Briar. I wanted to do what I could to help."

"I appreciate it, Wayne," she said shakily. "I just want you to know that I couldn't have done it without you. You've brought her along just perfectly. I know she's ready to run. And maybe one day when we both have time, we'll go somewhere and I'll tell you why."

He started to say something, but just then they were interrupted by word that the horses were due out on the track. "I'd like that, I would," he said, summoning a grin. Then he turned back to give the girth a last check. "But for now, I've got to get this little girl ready to strut her stuff."

Smiling tensely herself, Briar was just turning around to look for Pat when she realized the diminutive jockey was right behind her. "There you are!" she exclaimed. "I was wondering what—"

She realized just then that he looked furious. "What's wrong?" she asked, and thought, Oh, not now! If he's lost his nerve, I don't know what I'll do!

Jamming his hard hat onto his head, Pat turned a murderous look in the other jockey's direction. Roland was just being given a leg up by Mondragon's trainer, and when he saw Pat looking his way, he gave a jaunty wave. Pat glowered.

"Bastard," he muttered.

Briar put a hand on his arm. "What happened?"

He looked even more indignant. "He tried to give me some stuff, can you believe that? Dutch courage, he said, as if I'd need it! Well, I told him what he could do with his stuff. That's why I was late coming out. I was going through his locker.

Boy, will he be surprised when he finds everything's gone!''

Briar broke through her growing tension long enough to laugh. "Good for you!"

Pat smiled with her, but as Wayne gestured it was time for a leg up, he sobered again. "I want you to know I appreciate this chance, Briar, I do," he said fervently. "You believed in me, and I swear to God, I won't let you down. We'll do you proud, this filly and me. And in a little while, I'll bring her right back to you, safe and sound, into the winner's circle."

For the second time that morning, Briar felt tears in her eyes. "Just run your race, Pat, and let her run hers," she said. "No matter what happens, I can't ask for any more."

"Pat!" Wayne said behind them.

"Yeah, coming!" Pat said, but he didn't take his eyes off Briar. "Thanks, I mean it," he said, and saluted her with his whip.

As Wayne took him aside for some last-minute instructions, Briar looked again at her horse. Touch the Fire had never been more beautiful, she thought. Her glossy coat shone like black diamonds in the sun, and she looked every inch the champion she was. She was acting like it, too. Half dragging her two handlers around with all that pent-up energy, she was flattening her ears, giving little bucks, and generally behaving like a spoiled princess, as she always did before a race. She was fit and eager to go, and she didn't want to be held back while petty humans discussed how she was going to run.

Aware of his charge's impatience, Wayne finished talking to Pat, then tossed him light as a feather up into the saddle, where he immediately picked up the reins and stuck his feet in the irons. He knew his horse. As soon as Touch the Fire felt the jockey settle over her back, she started to jig around and prance in place. She was ready to go; it was time to race.

Looking proud as punch, Gillie came just then on a pony horse. Wayne had given him the honor of leading the filly out, and as he reached over and clipped the lead line onto the bridle, he grinned down delightedly at Briar, who gave him a thumbs-up signal.

"She's fit, Miz Briar," he said, as the filly suddenly lurched forward, so eager to go that she was determined to take every-body with her. "She's ready, all right."

But suddenly Briar wasn't. With Galland already disappearing into the tunnel that led to the track, Briar suddenly couldn't let her beloved horse go without touching her a last time.

"Wait, Gillie," she said, and came around to the filly's head.

Being an outrider for Touch the Fire was always a trial; eager to get going, she nipped at the pony horse and tried to bite the handler and generally made a nuisance of herself until she was free to start warming up. But as soon as Briar touched her, the hot-tempered horse went quiet. So did the murmur of the crowd. Amazed at the transformation in the great horse, everyone stopped to watch.

Briar was oblivious to her audience; her entire attention was on her horse. There wasn't much time, but she had to let Touch the Fire know how much was depending on her. She had gambled everything on her courageous filly's great heart. Everything she owned.

A pain stabbed through her at the thought, and she bent her head. As they had so many times at home, horse and woman stood together, heads bowed, as if in silent communication. Touch the Fire nuzzled her, and without volition, Briar thought of a line from Shakespeare.

Through his mane and tail the high wind sings
Fanning the hairs like feather'd wings . . .

Placing her hand on the filly's neck, Briar whispered, "Everything we have depends on you, girl. Long, long ago, a horse named Fane gave you wings. So go out now and . . . *fly.*"

As if she understood, Touch the Fire snorted and jerked her head. Then Gillie took hold of her again and they were off, disappearing into the tunnel. Briar knew when they had emerged onto the track by the roar that rose from the grandstand, and she was just turning to tell Wayne where she would meet him when she saw Spence through the thinning crowd. Now that the walking ring was empty, the race-goers were disappearing to place their bets, but Spence came over to the fence. She joined him there.

"I didn't think you'd be here," she said. "You don't even like racing."

"I wouldn't have missed it for the world," he said, and took her hand. She had, of course, told him the terms of the bet on the match race, and now he squeezed her tightly. "I want you to know that no matter what happens, Briar, we've got the bastard. After this race, win or lose, Mondragon Enterprises won't exist.''

As much as she would have loved to have believed it, she shook her head. ''Nice try, Spence, but—''

''No, I mean it, Briar. I'm telling the truth.''

He was trying to be encouraging, but what he'd said wasn't possible, she was sure. If she won, she'd have back Lord Industries and the ranch and everything else, but if she lost, Rupert would take everything. Mondragon Enterprises didn't figure into it, and she didn't know what Spence was talking about.

He looked as if he wanted to say more, but for some reason, couldn't. ''We'll talk about it after the race, okay?'' he said, and gave her hand a last squeeze. ''Good luck.''

Frowning at the odd exchange, she watched him melt into the crowd before she could ask him to join her in her owner's box. Aware that time was passing too quickly, she started that way herself, only to run right into Fredrica and Jaz. Deep in thought, she hadn't noticed them standing there, but it was obvious Fredrica had been waiting for her. As always, even though it was a warm, amazingly smog-free Los Angeles day, Fredrica was swathed in black—black hose, black dress, black shoes, black hat. Amid the shorts and sandals and sundresses and visors, she stood out like a mourner at a wedding feast. When Briar saw them, she came to a stop.

''Fredrica! Jaz! What are you doing here?''

She hadn't seen Jaz since she'd explained her decision about dividing Hay's estate to him. She had always thought he looked young for his age; now he seemed to have aged ten years since that meeting. His famed tan had a yellowish hue, and there were lines around his once come-hither blue eyes. Feeling pity stir, Briar thought that he looked . . . dissolute.

Fredrica, on the other hand, was at the ditop of her form. Her eyes heavily made up, and her lipstick a garish red, she said with hauteur, ''What are we doing here? Why we wouldn't have missed it for the world, my dear. When darling Rupert told us what you had so foolishly bet him on the outcome today, we had to come to cheer Galland on.''

Briar gave her a cool look. ''I wouldn't have expected anything else, Fredrica. Now, if you'll excuse me, I've got to get to my box.''

She started to pass, but to her surprise, Fredrica reached out and grabbed her arm, forcing her to stop. "When you lose, you'll lose everything," Fredrica hissed into her face. "You'll end up the way you should be—a *nobody* with *nothing!*"

Calmly, Briar removed her arm from her former stepdaughter's grasp. "*When* my horse wins," she said evenly, "I'll have Lord Industries back, the way your father intended it."

Something flashed in Fredrica's eyes. "You slut!"

Alarmed by the look on his sister's face, if not by the curious glances of passersby, Jaz tried to pull Fredrica back. "For God's sake, Freddie!" he pleaded, embarrassed.

Leaving brother and sister struggling behind her, Briar walked quickly off. Her eyes on the track, and on Touch the Fire cantering evenly on the far side of the oval, the powerful Galland not far behind her as they headed around toward the starting gate, she didn't see the visitor in her owner's box until she was almost there.

"Charlotte!" she exclaimed, forgetting the horses for an instant in her shock. She was so startled to see the woman she didn't know what to say.

Charlotte had been watching the horses down below, too. Turning with her lightweight binoculars in her hand, she studied Briar for a long moment before she said, "Your filly looks fit."

Briar flicked a glance out at the track. Both horses were approaching the starting gate, and she was starting to feel a little strung out with nerves. "Thank you," she said tersely. "So is your colt."

Charlotte gazed at her for a long moment, then she looked down at the ground. "I never imagined when I had Mr. Weitz contact you things would turn out like this," she said, her voice low. "I'm so sorry, Briar—more than you know. You see, I'm paying, too. I never wanted Galland to run this race, but—" hatred flashed in her eyes, so palpable that Briar imagined she could almost feel the heat "—but it was taken out of my hands. If it's any help, I despise my father even more than you do. I've done what I can to see him destroyed."

Briar hardly heard the part about Rupert. "You . . . *you* contacted Albert Weitz? *You* were the one who found out I had inherited Caulfield Farm?"

"Oh, yes, I was the one."

"But . . . but I don't understand! Why?"

"It's a long story," Charlotte said, with a glance down at the tote board that showed it was almost post time. "And we don't have time to go into it now. But . . . but no matter what happens in the next few minutes, I wanted you to know that I don't regret having found you. You're the best of both parents, Briar. I loved them both, Ariana and Duncan, and perhaps one day, I'll tell you about them."

"But—"

Charlotte quickly shook her head. "Good luck, Briar," she said. "May the best horse win."

And with that, she left the box. Briar was still staring after her when she heard: *"It is now post time!"*

Instantly the babble of sound ebbing and flowing from the grandstand died away. A murmuring quiet descended as thousands of people gathered under the closed-circuit television screens, or pressed up against the rail along the course, or sat down in the clubhouse, or turned from their tables in the terrace. In her owner's box, Briar realized she was gripping the seat in front of her so tightly she was getting a cramp. With an effort, she loosened her tight fingers, but she didn't take her eyes off the track. With only two horses in, the gate loomed large and forbidding to her left, and for a panicked instant, she couldn't even see her filly's head. Touch the Fire had drawn the outside post position, which meant that she would have to break fast and swing inside before Galland could get there; otherwise she would have to expend much more energy trying to get around the big colt. Briar didn't believe in praying for what she wanted, but she closed her eyes now.

*I don't care if she wins, just don't let anything happen to her, please . . .* she thought, and then felt guilty and ashamed. She had vowed long ago not to bargain with fate.

"The flag is up!" the announcer shouted, and Briar's eyes flew open just as the gate did. The crowd roared, and for better or worse, the race was on.

Except for the one time when she had ripped a hoof coming out of the gate, Touch the Fire always broke well, and today was no exception. The instant the doors crashed open, she was out and onto the track, a flying streak of black going so fast that Briar wondered how Pat could stay on. With Galland right beside her, she sprinted toward the rail and managed to get there a fraction of a second before the colt could swing his bigger body in.

"Thank God," Briar murmured. She was so intent she didn't even hear the announcer calling the race. Her entire attention was on her horse. If she saw the slightest bobble, the merest break in stride . . .

But the filly was doing what she had been bred to do for generations. Running was in her blood, and her blood was running now. Both horses passed the stands for the first time neck and neck, and when it seemed that Galland was edging slightly out in front, Briar gripped the chair again. She had no need for binoculars. She was so attuned to what was going on that she could have been in the saddle herself. She could feel the stirrups pressing into her feet and the wind in her face as the filly's powerful hindquarters surged her forward.

But Galland was right beside her, running just as effortlessly, playing, it seemed to Briar's experienced eye, with the filly until he decided to head for home and leave her behind.

Neck and neck, the two horses flew around the clubhouse turn, and then it was onto the backstretch. Briar knew just when Touch the Fire changed leads after the second turn, suspending her left forefoot in midair until the right forefoot touched the track, then driving on. With no visible loss of speed or rhythm, she switched front and back and geared down again, into the blistering pace that had left so many other horses gasping behind.

But not Galland.

The colt switched leads a fraction of a second later than the filly, but as he drove in toward the rail, Briar gasped. She had seen Pat glance across at the other jockey and shake his whip; she saw, just for a split second, her horse hesitate. Then, to her horrified eyes, the big colt pulled out in front. With the crowd roaring, he drove forward inch by inch until he was ahead by a neck. The announcer was screaming something. Briar realized it was the pace. When she looked down and saw the postings on the tote board, she nearly fainted. The horses had run the first quarter mile in twenty-three and one-fifth seconds; the half mile in a flat forty-seven. *No!* she thought in a panic. *It's too fast!*

But the horses were already thundering around the far turn, and with Galland steadily pulling away, Briar felt as if her heart were going to burst right out of her throat. She knew Wayne had given instructions to Pat about not going to the whip too early because the filly didn't like it, and when she saw her jockey press his stick between his teeth and remove it with his left hand in order to slap the filly's left hip, she couldn't believe it. *He can't mean to go around the colt!* she thought in horror.

But that's what it seemed Pat was going to try to do. Galland had taken enough of a lead to tuck into the rail in front of the filly, and Pat, with less experience, but more determination, perhaps, had seen the trap. Instead of checking his horse and throwing her off again, he elected to pick her up and go around him.

It was a tough decision. By running outside of Galland around the turn, Touch the Fire had to travel at least fifteen feet, or two lengths, farther than Galland just to stay abreast of him. But she wasn't abreast. She was behind him, and to catch up, Pat had to lengthen her stride and ask for more speed at the same time. Briar put a hand to her mouth and bit hard on a knuckle when she saw Pat change whip hands again, slacken the reins, and give the filly's right hip a tap. As she had in all her other races past, the gallant horse responded immediately, almost effortlessly, it seemed, accelerating to a speed nearly forty miles an hour. Like the champion she was, she'd started to *fly*.

The crowd roared again when the filly began to gain on Galland; there was such a crush at the fence that it seemed the spectators would spill out onto the track. Briar could hardly hear the announcer for all the wild screaming and yelling going on around her. When she realized that her own voice was rising in the din, she just screamed louder as she heard the famous shout: "And down the stretch they come!"

And what a stretch run it was! After rounding the turn almost as one, Briar saw her filly momentarily suspend a foot in midair one last time in a lead switch so she could run the stretch leading with the rested muscles of her right foreleg. For Touch the Fire, it was like shifting into a higher gear. But Galland hadn't been called the bolt of the decade for nothing. He came on as if he'd been shot out of a cannon, and for the next heart-stopping few seconds, both straining horses seemed to match stride for stride. With the crowd going wild, they came down the track almost as one, muscles strained to the bursting point, neither horse giving quarter. Then, at the three-sixteenths pole, Galland, in the moment everyone had antici-pated, stuck his head out just a fraction of an inch farther than his rival's as they drove toward the wire. It seemed in an instant, that the battle had finally been won. The prolonged intensity of the pace, the assertive move by the bigger, stronger colt, would have caused most colts, let alone fillies, to back off and settle for second place.

But Touch the Fire wasn't most horses; she never had been. Even when it looked as if she would tire and slow, Briar knew she would never give in. With tears in her eyes and a burst of love for her indomitable filly, she saw Touch the Fire reach down inside her for that indefinable something, that inexpressible spark that made her the great horse she was. Call it heart or class or just sheer refusal to be defeated, by any name it defined a champion. In one bold move of excruciating courage, her black filly gathered every ounce of power that was in her and thrust her nose out two inches past Galland's just as they thundered under the wire.

Instantly, a PHOTO sign flashed, but Briar was beyond caring what the official result might claim. As far as she was concerned, her horse had won the race, and as she turned and headed down to the winner's circle, she barely heard the congratulations and applause. All she wanted to do was get down to the track and make sure the filly wasn't hurt. The press of the crowd prevented her from hurrying. She felt hemmed in by bodies and good wishes and people wanting to talk to her, to tell her what a great horse she had, and how wonderful it had all been, and how they had known all along that Touch the Fire would win.

"Yes, yes, yes . . ." she said over and over again, frantically trying to see above the crowd, to push her way through. The throng was so thick she couldn't see the tote board, but even worse, she couldn't see her horse. She felt frantic. She'd had nightmares about the filly coming back drenched in blood again, and her heart was in her throat.

"Briar!"

She whirled around, the noise and the confusion and the terror suddenly put on hold. She had known he was here; she had felt it. She hadn't seen Stefan since the last wrenching night they had quarreled, but when she watched him coming through the crowd toward her, she realized that no matter how she had convinced herself she could forget him, she was never going to get him out of her mind, her blood . . . her heart.

"Stefan," she said, as he came up to her. It was all she could say.

"I tried to call you. I left messages on your answering machine," he said. "You didn't answer. You never let me explain."

She didn't want to talk to him, not here, not now, not ever. Even though she knew he was part of her, she couldn't forgive him for what he had done.

"There's nothing to explain."

"Yes, there is. You think I betrayed you, but I didn't, Briar. I swear it. You've got to believe me. Events just overtook me like they did you. I never wanted to get involved, but I did, and by then it was too late. I didn't know how to explain. When Rupert started threatening you, I saw a way to make him back off, and I—"

"Why are you telling me all this?" she cried. She didn't want to hear it; she didn't want to feel vulnerable, to *depend* on anyone ever again. She had learned her lesson this time. She had spent these past two months shoring up her determination. Every time she heard his voice on the answering machine tape, it was like a knife had plunged right through her.

"Because I have to tell you," Stefan said, reaching for her. "Because I want to." He hesitated. "Because I love you."

She turned her head away. She didn't have time for this. She didn't want it! "Don't say that."

"Why not? I have to. It's true. Briar, please—look at me. I know now's not the time, but you know we had something going, something good between us. You can't just let it go!"

"I can!" she cried, struggling against his grasp. The crowd was swirling around them, but it was as if no one noticed. "I will!"

He held her with his deep blue gaze. "No, you won't. I won't let you. Not until you can look me in the eye and say you don't have any feelings for me."

She didn't know what she felt. Love was so complicated at times; it changed things, it changed people, it made them weak, like she had been. Like she had vowed never to be again.

"Briar," he said urgently, forcing her to look at him. "Gillie told me his story, and Charlotte filled me in on the rest. I know all about Rupert, what he did, what he tried to do to you. And I want you to know that no matter what happens between us, I'm pressing my claim to Mondragon Enterprises. I called

Spence a long time ago, and he thinks soon we'll be going to court. And we'll win, he's sure of it.''

His words stopped her. "You're going to court?"

"I had to. After you bet everything you had, how could I do any less? By the time we're finished with Rupert Jaeger, he'll have nothing, Briar—nothing at all! He'll finally be punished for all the harm he's done to you and your family . . . to my family, too.'' He hesitated. "I think Marguerite would like that, don't you?"

But before she could answer, another throaty roar went up from the crowd. The PHOTO sign went out and as the official results were announced, the throng went wild. Although it wasn't customarily done, a message appeared on the tote board, four words that jubilently flashed the glorious news: THE QUEEN STILL REIGNS!

As another wild cheer erupted all around, Stefan looked down at Briar. "Congratulations," he said, beginning to grin from ear to ear.

Briar looked from the flashing board up to his face. In a daze, she said, "She won, Stefan." And then, louder, "She won!"

Stefan had tears in his eyes as he grabbed her hand. "I think," he said joyfully, "that you're wanted in the winner's circle!"

Feeling as if she were treading on air, Briar followed him through the crowd. Touch the Fire was just coming in, prancing as if she knew what she had done. Briar had already seen that she was all right, and collapsed slightly against Stefan's broad chest. "Thank God," she murmured. She'd been so afraid.

Kara came rushing up just then, a broad grin on her face. "Congratulations, Briar! Some filly you've got! She broke a track record, did you realize that?"

"No, I didn't—" Briar started to say, but just then Fredrica appeared, hauling Jaz behind her.

"Rupert Jaeger just told me about the bet you made!" Fredrica screamed. "Well, it isn't fair! I want my inheritance back! Do you hear me? I want my inheritance back! He had no right to . . . to *bet* it all on one race! It's outrageous! One third of Daddy's company should be mine! That's what you said, isn't it, Briar? Isn't that what you said?"

Briar wanted to laugh with sheer happiness. She was just

beginning to realize what all this meant. "Too late, Fredrica!" she said, "You had your chance, and you gambled just like I did."

"I'll sue!" Fredrica shrieked.

Jaz had been embarrassed enough. Gripping his sister's arm so tightly she howled and whirled his way, he said, "If you say another word, I'll rip that stupid hat off your face and stuff it down your throat." Then he turned and grinned at Briar. "To the victor belongs all the spoils, you wench. Dad would have been proud of you, and so am I. Well done. I admire your grit."

"Thank you, Jaz," she said gratefully, but that's all she had time to say. Rupert Jaeger appeared, Carl in tow. She had never seen him look so menacing. But she didn't care, she thought giddily; no matter what he did, he couldn't hurt her now. Somehow, she knew he wouldn't go back on his agreement. Not now, not after all this.

"So," he said, oblivious of the people shouting at her, demanding she come into the winner's circle with her gallant black filly. "You won." He flicked a glance toward Stefan, and his eyes became even more murderous. "You both won." His wintry eyes returned to Briar's face. "Congratulations. *This* time. But I have weapons still, and I'll be back."

"Not to Caulfield Farm," Briar said, holding his gaze.

Something flashed across his face. Was it acceptance after all these years? Briar couldn't believe it. "No," he said. "Not to Caulfield Farm. We gambled, and I . . ." Even in defeat, he couldn't say it. Instead he said, "I will honor our agreement."

"For now," Briar said.

He bowed. "For now," he agreed, and disappeared into the crowd, a sick-looking Carl trailing behind him.

Briar was still staring after him when Stefan touched her arm. "Your admirers await," he said, nodding in the direction of the winner's circle. Then he turned and started to walk away.

"Wait!" Briar cried. She didn't know what was happening to her. She only knew she couldn't let him go. These past two months at the ranch had been miserable without him. It seemed that the place had lost an essential part when he had gone. That *she* had lost an essential part of herself without him. Now that they were face-to-face again, she realized they had both made mistakes. They had both kept secrets. They were both to blame.

The knowledge was painful and liberating at the same time, and she knew that whatever she did, she couldn't make the same mistake twice. She couldn't let him go, not now.

"Don't go," she said haltingly. "I've missed you so."

He searched her face. "You'd better be sure about this, Briar. Because if I come now, I'm not going away. I can't go through this a second time, I'll lose my mind."

She smiled shakily. "Neither can I."

The winner's circle was crowded with officials and dignitaries and heaven knew who else. But when Briar and Stefan entered, a great shout went up. Before he was lifted into the saddle again by Wayne for the official picture, Pat gave her a big hug.

"I told you we'd get there first," he whispered. "Thanks for giving me the chance to keep my promise."

Then Pat was legged up and the photographer was trying to arrange everyone for pictures. With a blanket of white roses over her neck, Touch the Fire looked every inch the queen the tote board proclaimed her to be, and as Briar stepped up to her at the photographer's orders, the horse turned and looked around as if to say, See?

Laughing with sheer joy, Briar was just about to throw her arms around the filly's neck when she thought she heard someone call her name. She looked around, but everyone, even Stefan, was busy paying attention to the photographer's assistant, and no one seemed to be looking at her. Again, she thought she heard someone call her.

Shading her eyes against the sun, she looked around. Then on impulse, she could not explain why, she glanced up toward the stands. A woman was looking down at her, a woman she thought she recognized. Then she started violently. Aside from the old-fashioned suit and cloche hat, the woman could have been she. It was like looking into a mirror, and Briar gasped.

"Marguerite . . . ?" she whispered disbelievingly. She knew it was crazy, but the woman looked so . . . real.

No, it couldn't be, she thought, as the woman laughed and waved. Sure she was seeing things, she blinked and then squinted. When she looked up again, the place in the stands was empty. Had it been? she wondered. Could it be?

No, no, it was impossible, she thought. It was all the excitement, the stress and strain of the past months, the elation of winning.

"Miss McKenna, we're waiting," someone said.

Feeling dazed, Briar looked around. Everyone was posed near Touch the Fire, who was becoming impatient at the delay. She had run her race, and now she deserved her rest.

Her heart beating fast, Briar took her place. *We did it, great-grandmother,* she thought fiercely. *We did it. After all these years, victory belongs to Caulfield Farm!*

Just as the flashbulbs started to go off, she heard it again—the joyous, merry laugh that Sloane Caulfield had always said made him fall in love. Briar had loved it, too. In her heart and in her mind, she had listened to it in the pages of Marguerite's journals. She had heard it echoing down through the years. Now she had no need to turn and look up at the vision in the grandstands. The circle was complete, and the tinkling notes of joy that rang out and then faded gently on the breeze were Marguerite's way of saying good-bye.

"One more, Miss McKenna!" the photographer called.

Through his mane and tail the high wind sings,
Fanning the hairs like feather'd wings . . .

With everything riding on her filly's courageous heart, Briar had asked Touch the Fire to win back the past, and the gallant filly had obliged. As Marguerite had promised, the great Fane had reached down through the years and blessed his valiant daughter with wings so she could fly.

The flashbulbs popped; the racing crowd cheered. The Caulfield Farm silks of amber and green and gold flashed in the sun—as they would through the following years.

And as for Stefan . . . Her eyes shining with love and a sudden new awareness, Briar moved to his side. She would always be grateful to Hayden Lord, who had been so much older and wiser than she and who had taught her to trust someone other than herself. Because he had been who he was, he had showed her how, and then stood by, allowing her to learn that without the hurt love could wield, she could never know the joy.

*Thank you, Hay,* she thought, at last saying good-bye. Then she looked up into Stefan's bright, strong gaze. Touch the Fire had done her part; now it was time for Briar to take wing and fly.

## ABOUT THE AUTHOR

Born in Montana and raised in Colorado and California, Janis Flores worked for ten years as a medical technologist before she turned to full-time writing. She lives on a small ranch in Sebastopol, California, with her husband, an array of house pets and four pampered horses in various stages of training. She is also the author of LOVING TIES, RUNNING IN PLACE, DIVIDED LOYALTIES, and ABOVE REPROACH.